HER SMOKE
ROSE UP
FOREVER

HER SMOKE ROSE UP FOREVER

JAMES TIPTREE, JR.

TACHYON PUBLICATIONS
SAN FRANCISCO, CALIFORNIA

HER SMOKE ROSE UP FOREVER

TACHYON PUBLICATIONS
1459 18TH STREET #139
SAN FRANCISCO, CA 94107
(415) 285-5615
www.tachyonpublications.com

EDITED BY JEFFREY D. SMITH
SERIES EDITOR: JACOB WEISMAN

ISBN: 1-892391-20-1

Printed in the United States of America
by Worzalla

0   9   8   7   6   5

If I could describe a "human being" I would be more than I am—and probably living in the future, because I think of human beings as something to be realized ahead.... But clearly "human beings" have something to do with the luminous image you see in a bright child's eyes—the exploring, wondering, eagerly grasping, undestructive quest for life. I see that undescribed spirit as central to us all.

—TIPTREE/SHELDON

Table of Contents

INTRODUCTION

By Michael Swanwick

A stream ran through the living room of the house in
McLean, Virginia, and there were pet tarantulas as well and
a tank of Siamese fighting fish atop the toilet. But strangest
of all were the three writing desks, each with its own distinct
typewriter, stationery, and color of ink. One belonged to James
Tiptree, Jr. A second was used exclusively by Raccoona Sheldon.
The third was for Alice Sheldon, a sometime scientist, artist,
newspaper critic, soldier, businesswoman, and retired CIA
officer, who on occasion moved to one of the other desks to
write science fiction in the persona of Tiptree or Raccoona.
Those stories established her firmly as one of the finest short
fiction writers the genre has ever produced.

But who *was* Alice Sheldon?

That question has hung over the science fiction community
since long before anybody in it knew her real name. In the late
1960s, during a period of considerable stress and for reasons
she could never adequately explain, Sheldon began writing
fiction as James Tiptree, Jr., a nom de plume plucked from a jar
of marmalade. Tiptree's first four stories, published in 1968,
attracted little or no attention, and deservedly so. But then
came "The Last Flight of Doctor Ain."

What a knockout! It's told backwards, in a flat documentary
voice, like the forensic recreation of a crime. But who's
compiled this information? To whom is it being reported?
Formally, this story is like Goya's *Los Caprichos* etchings, whose
figures exist in an uneasy grey zone that bears no identifiable

relationship to background and horizon as we know them. And it has a stinger in its tail, in the revelation that it is not Doctor C. Ain but his companion who is the true criminal, and that this is not her first offense.

"The Last Flight of Doctor Ain" placed on the Nebula Award ballot, a surefire attention-getter for a previously unknown writer. It was followed by other works, equally startling, equally original. Continuing in order of publication, "And I Awoke and Found Me Here on the Cold Hill's Side" introduced one of Tiptree's great themes, the destructive force of cultural contact when one culture is far richer and more technologically advanced than the other. It also made explicit another theme, already present in "Doctor Ain," that of individual human beings caught in the grip of biological imperatives they are helpless to resist. Moreover, it was a classic example of an artist biting the hand that feeds him. The very xenophilia and sense of wonder that fuel the science fiction enterprise are portrayed as negative forces leading to the destruction of human culture, and possibly the species as well. "And I Have Come Upon This Place by Lost Ways" is almost a zen koan, simple and clean but lending itself to several interpretations. I would argue that it's about responsibility and that callow young Evan (callow young men are recurrent in Tiptree's fiction) dies in a state of grace. But if you care to read it as a parable of scientific integrity, that's there too. "The Man Who Walked Home" is another koan-like tale, and one that became talismanic for Tiptree, after a critic pointed out that it was the distilled essence of his work: a lone protagonist desperately striving to reach home, whatever the consequences, however improbable his chances of success. By now the fact that the story begins with its conclusion and proceeds backwards into the future, relating the future history of humanity through furtive glimpses along the way, until understanding is achieved and the tale can end, was no more than we expected from this brilliant, brilliant writer.

"On the Last Afternoon" is about communication, of course. Communication between Mysha and the *noion*, between the old man and his wife and daughter, between the individual and the community at large. Most importantly, it's about communication with one's self. Tiptree thought that it was a miracle people were able to communicate at all. No surprise, then, that communication must so often fail.

Meanwhile, Tiptree had begun corresponding with fans and other writers, and contributing occasional pieces to the fanzines. From these letters and articles a portrait emerged of an elderly WASP, born into privilege and possessed of shadowy connections with the American intelligence community, who was a habitual globe-trotter and had spent much of his childhood in colonial India and Africa. More significantly, his writings established him as a man of rare sensitivity and possibly even wisdom. "When you're old enough," he wrote, "you're *free*. Your energy is not only less, it is different. It's in—if you've done it right—a different place. Your last, hottest organ." And elsewhere, "You know as well as I do we all go around in disguise. The halo stuffed in the pocket, the cloven hoof awkward in the shoe, the X-ray eye blinking behind thick lenses, the two midgets dressed as one tall man, the giant stooping in a pinstripe, the pirate in a housewife's smock, the wings shoved into sleeveholes, the wild racing, wandering, raping, burning, loving pulses of reality decorously disguised as a roomful of Human beings. I know goddam well what's out there, under all those masks. Beauty and Power and Terror and Love."

Here was a rara avis indeed and, understandably, everybody wanted to meet him. Yet meet people Tiptree would *not* do. He didn't give talks, show up at conventions, accept awards in person, or drop by a correspondent's house for coffee. Given his gregarious and confiding personality, his admirers could only conclude that he was hiding something. There were rumors that he was a government spook, a Native American, black, even (but most people scoffed at this one) a woman.

The stories kept coming. "The Girl Who Was Plugged In" is yet another tour de force, a rude, jeering narrative that leads with the chin, sets up a horrible and inevitable human tragedy, and as good as lays the blame at the reader's feet. Even with the tacked-on and perfectly unconvincing happy ending, it remains one of Tiptree's key works. In "Love Is the Plan the Plan Is Death," the loving, optimistic Moggadeet leads an emotionally rich and intellectually self-examined life, which all leads to . . . well, nothing more than our own lives do. Here is the distilled essence of Tiptree's darkest pessimism. "A Momentary Taste of Being" extends this sense of individual futility in the face of biological determinism to its logical extreme. A dispassionate reader might even conclude that there is nothing inherently tragic in this tale at all. Alas, we are human, and cannot afford to be that dispassionate.

"The Women Men Don't See" was the story that established Tiptree as a feminist. Had it been the only such in his career, it would have done the trick. From the concept embodied in its title to the final six words, it was the work of somebody who understood the predicament of women in our society in a clear-eyed and visceral way. Morever, it was written (we thought) by a man. There was hope!

Well, as it would later turn out, in a very Tiptree-esque way, perhaps there wasn't. But, whether taken as feminist SF or simply straight up, it was an instant classic.

Tiptree came perilously close to giving his secret away in the title of "Her Smoke Rose Up Forever." Many autobiographical elements, particularly the Fox CE shotgun that was his obsession for three teenage years, were familiar to his fans. But who else could the female pronoun refer to but Alice Sheldon? This story explores everything she feared most, inadequacy in particular. Sheldon had astonishing parents: an attorney, naturalist, and explorer for a Dad, an explorer and two-time O. Henry award finalist for a Mom. Prior to science fiction, her many accomplishments were, in her own eyes anyway, not equal to such a heritage.

"Houston, Houston, Do You Read?" was another feminist fable, this one positing a familiar thought-experiment, that possibly the only way to ensure the survival of humanity and the earth is to kill all the men. But Tiptree, never one to settle for a revenge fantasy when something deeper and more disquieting could be achieved, went on to demonstrate its wrongness. When Lady Blue says, "Why, we call ourselves . . . the human race," the note of complacency is horribly familiar. Humanity, despite all final solutions, remains what it has always been. Similarly, "She Waits for All Men Born" may well be the history of the battle between Life and Death that it sets itself up to be. But the outcome of that battle reflects Tiptree's antipathy for all ultimate resolutions, whether imposed by human beings or by something greater and more basic.

Because Alice had stories to tell that Tiptree could not, she created a second persona, Raccoona Sheldon—named after the raccoons which occasionally wandered into her house by the same entryway the stream did—to write them. One of these, "Your Faces, O My Sisters! Your Faces Filled of Light!"

(she had a particular genius for titles), is the story of the only free woman in the world and what inevitably becomes of her. Its dark beauty is enough to make you weep for a way of life that can only be imagined, never achieved. This belongs right up there with the best of Tiptree's works and yet, ironically enough, because it was published under a woman's name, it got nowhere near the attention it deserved.

But while Sheldon was industriously working away, the fans were closing in on Tiptree. More than one threatened to stake out his post office box. Another got as far as Sheldon's door, only to be turned away by a lie. Nevertheless (and in retrospect, one has to wonder if this were deliberate), little autobiographical hints kept popping up in Tiptree's letters and nonfiction. Until one day a woman died whose obituary perfectly described the career, books, and remarkable life of the mother that Tiptree had so often reminisced about. Her name was Mary Hastings Bradley and her sole surviving child was a woman named Alice B. Sheldon.

Sheldon professed to be delighted at being outed. "How great," she wrote. "At last it's out." But she got very little in exchange for the Tiptree glamour. She met only a handful of her fans and compeers, and a certain fraction of her male readers fell away. In the aftermath, she wrote, "After this only the feminists would remain delighted, but on a different basis, having nothing to do with the stories. Tiptree, by merely existing unchallenged for eleven years, had shot the stuffing out of male stereotypes of women writers. Even nonfeminist women were secretly gleeful." The problem with this being, as she later lamented, "No one talked about the *stories* anymore at all."

Perhaps they didn't talk about the stories to Sheldon herself. But everybody was talking about "The Screwfly Solution," when it came out the following year, as by Raccoona Sheldon. This one had everything—hard science, engaging characters, and a truly terrifying premise. The plot could only be read literally; but it had a symbolic weight as well. It forced the reader to think. It proved that the woman who was no longer Tiptree was still one of our best.

Being discovered, however, precipitated Sheldon into a crisis. In some way, she needed Tiptree—as a mask, as a buffer, as a liberating excuse, the reason doesn't matter. The sad truth was that after she became herself, the truly first-rate stories were much slower in the coming.

One strategy she employed to work around this was to write wide-screen, galaxy-spanning space opera. "We Who Stole the *Dream*" is an excellent example of its kind, the tale of a terrorist hijacking as seen from the viewpoint of some of the most engaging aliens Sheldon ever created. This was science fiction of a rather old-fashioned sort, with military hierarchies, captains whose power was absolute, and more than a whiff of the 1940s about it. Sheldon was perhaps the last major writer to work this territory with a straight face. But that doesn't mean she couldn't make magic with it. As witness "With Delicate Mad Hands," wherein a woman who has been horribly mutilated, both physically and spiritually, is called outward and in her brief freedom discovers both love and death. It's a sentimental story on the surface; but on reflection, the question inevitably arises: Was CP ever truly free?

Slowly, a new picture of the author was emerging. She was a handsome and impressive woman. Her beloved husband was retired intelligence officer Huntington Sheldon, an aristocratic man who had been her commanding officer in WWII and looked, one admirer said, like Commander Whitehead in the old Schweppes ads. She was paralyzingly afraid of meeting people. She was fiercely, blazingly feminist.

"Slow Music" is an elegiac tale of the rediscovery of death. Ignore the protagonists, the callow Jakko and the marvelously named Peachthief, and keep your eye and ear instead on the dying old, poetry-spouting man-woman who midwifes the attempt at a new beginning. It's hard not to read him/her as Sheldon/Tiptree making a cameo. It's hard not to read her/his words as prescient.

On May 19, 1987, at 3:30 A.M., Alice Sheldon took a shotgun and killed her husband, "Ting," and then herself. Huntington Sheldon was ill and almost blind at the time of his death. Police found their bodies in bed together.

Dear God.

An embarrassed silence fell over the field. Nobody could reconcile this act with sweet old Uncle Tip, who dispensed kindly advice from afar and wrote to editors urging them to buy more work from struggling young women writers. Nor was it the work of the flinty, tough-minded Alice Sheldon we were all coming to know. We thought we'd learned the lessons we were supposed to take from her life. And now this. What did it *mean?*

Which was, of course, nonsense. Sheldon had suffered for decades from clinical depression so bad that she once said it was like having a vulture perched on either shoulder. Depression is a literal illness. She died of it as surely as she might have of leukemia or a car crash.

In the aftermath, Tiptree's name has been kept alive chiefly by an award given annually in Sheldon's honor for science fiction or fantasy that expands or explores our understanding of gender. But, in part because of her death and in part because short fiction doesn't stay in print the way novels can, her stories sank into an undeserved obscurity.

You hold in your hands a partial corrective.

This collection was originally put together by the late, lamented, and intensely valuable Jim Turner—I picture him a little pleased, like a child, to be briefly the center of attention, while simultaneously scowling with embarrassment and disapproval because he believed an editor should, like a ninja, be both anonymous and invisible—and, with Sheldon's help he assembled the Tiptree volume we all wished for. It can never be the perfect collection, of course. We all have our favorites and blind spots, and if you want to stay up half the night arguing why Story X should have been left out in favor of Story Y . . . well, that sounds like good clean fun to me, and exactly the sort of tribute that Alice B. Sheldon would have most savored.

Read. Enjoy. These are the works that will remain long after the woman who was Tiptree, the mystery that was Sheldon, are forgotten.

They will endure.

THE LAST FLIGHT OF DOCTOR AIN

DOCTOR AIN WAS RECOGNIZED on the Omaha-Chicago flight. A biologist colleague from Pasadena came out of the toilet and saw Ain in an aisle seat. Five years before, this man had been jealous of Ain's huge grants. Now he nodded coldly and was surprised at the intensity of Ain's response. He almost turned back to speak, but he felt too tired; like nearly everyone, he was fighting the flu.

The stewardess handing out coats after they landed remembered Ain too: a tall thin nondescript man with rusty hair. He held up the line staring at her; since he already had his raincoat with him she decided it was some kooky kind of pass and waved him on.

She saw Ain shamble off into the airport smog, apparently alone. Despite the big Civil Defense signs, O'Hare was late getting underground. No one noticed the woman.

The wounded, dying woman.

Ain was not identified en route to New York, but a 2:40 jet carried an "Ames" on the checklist, which was thought to be a misspelling of Ain. It was. The plane had circled for an hour while Ain watched the smoky seaboard monotonously tilt, straighten, and tilt again.

The woman was weaker now. She coughed, picking weakly at the scabs on her face half-hidden behind her long hair. Her hair, Ain saw, that great mane which had been so splendid, was drabbed and thinning now. He looked to seaward, willing himself to think of cold, clean breakers. On the horizon he saw a vast black rug: somewhere a tanker had opened its vents. The woman coughed again. Ain closed his eyes. Smog shrouded the plane.

He was picked up next while checking in for the BOAC flight to Glasgow. Kennedy Underground was a boiling stew of people, the air system unequal to the hot September afternoon. The check-in line swayed and sweated, staring dully at the newscast. SAVE THE LAST GREEN MANSIONS—a conservation group was protesting the defoliation and drainage of the Amazon basin. Several people recalled the beautifully colored shots of the new clean bomb. The line squeezed together to let a band of uniformed men go by. They were wearing buttons inscribed: WHO'S AFRAID?

That was when a woman noticed Ain. He was holding a newssheet, and she heard it rattling in his hand. Her family hadn't caught the flu, so she looked at him sharply. Sure enough, his forehead was sweaty. She herded her kids to the side away from Ain.

He was using *Instac* throat spray, she remembered. She didn't think much of *Instac*; her family used *Kleer*. While she was looking at him, Ain suddenly turned his head and stared into her face, with the spray still floating down. Such inconsiderateness! She turned her back. She didn't recall his talking to any woman, but she perked up her ears when the clerk read off Ain's destination. Moscow!

The clerk recalled that too, with disapproval. Ain checked in alone, he reported. No woman had been ticketed for Moscow, but it would have been easy enough to split up her tickets. (By that time they were sure she was with him.)

Ain's flight went via Iceland with an hour's delay at Keflavik. Ain walked over to the airport park, gratefully breathing the sea-filled air. Every few breaths he shuddered. Under the whine of bulldozers the sea could be heard running its huge paws up and down the keyboard of the land. The little park had a grove of yellowed birches, and a flock of wheatears foraged by the path. Next month they would be in North Africa, Ain thought. Two thousand miles of tiny wing-beats. He threw them some crumbs from a packet in his pocket.

The woman seemed stronger here. She was panting in the sea wind, her large eyes fixed on Ain. Above her the birches were as gold as those where he had first seen her, the day his life began. ... Squatting under a stump to watch a shrewmouse he had been, when he caught a falling ripple of green and recognized the shocking girl-flesh, creamy, pink-tipped—coming toward him among the golden bracken! Young Ain held his breath, his nose in the sweet moss and his heart going *crash—crash*. And then he was staring at the outrageous fall of that hair down her narrow back, watching it dance around her heart-shaped buttocks, while the shrewmouse ran over his paralyzed hand. The lake was utterly still, dusty silver under the misty sky, and she made no more than a muskrat's ripple to rock the floating golden leaves. The silence closed back, the trees burning like torches where the naked girl had walked the wild wood, reflected in Ain's shining eyes. For a time he believed he had seen an oread.

Ain was last on board for the Glasgow leg. The stewardess recalled dimly that he seemed restless. She could not identify the woman. There were a lot of women on board, and babies. Her passenger list had had several errors.

At Glasgow airport a waiter remembered that a man like Ain had called for Scottish oatmeal, and eaten two bowls, although of course it wasn't really oatmeal. A young mother with a pram saw him tossing crumbs to the birds.

When he checked in at the BOAC desk, he was hailed by a Glasgow professor who was going to the same conference at Moscow. This man had been one of Ain's teachers. (It was now known that Ain had done his postgraduate work in Europe.) They chatted all the way across the North Sea.

"I wondered about that," the professor said later. "Why have you come round about? I asked him. He told me the direct flights were booked up." (This was found to be untrue: Ain had, apparently avoided the Moscow jet to escape attention.)

The professor spoke with relish of Ain's work.

"Brilliant? Oh, aye. And stubborn, too; very very stubborn. It was as though a concept—often the simplest relation, mind you—would stop him in his tracks, and fascinate him. He would hunt all round it instead of going on to the next thing as a more docile mind would. Truthfully, I wondered at first if he could be just a bit thick. But you recall who it was said that the capacity for wonder at matters of common acceptance occurs in the superior mind? And, of course, so it proved when he shook us all up over that enzyme conversion business. A pity your government took him away from his line, there. No, he said nothing of this, I say it to you, young man. We spoke in fact largely of my work. I was surprised to find he'd kept up. He asked me what my *sentiments* about it were, which surprised me again. Now, understand, I'd not seen the man for five years, but he seemed—well, perhaps just tired, as who is not? I'm sure he was glad to have a change; he jumped out for a legstretch wherever we came down. At Oslo, even Bonn. Oh, yes, he did feed the birds, but that was nothing new for Ain. His social life when I knew him? Radical causes? Young man, I've said what I've said because of who it was that introduced you, but I'll have you know it is an impertinence in you to think ill of Charles Ain, or that he could do a harmful deed. Good evening."

The professor said nothing of the woman in Ain's life.

Nor could he have, although Ain had been intimately with her in the university time. He had let no one see how he was obsessed with her, with the miracle, the wealth of her body, her inexhaustibility. They met at his every spare moment; sometimes in public pretending to be casual strangers under his friends' noses, pointing out a pleasing view to each other with grave formality. And later in their privacies—what doubled intensity of love! He reveled in her, possessed her, allowed her no secrets. His dreams were of her sweet springs and shadowed places and her white rounded glory in the moonlight, finding always more, always new dimensions of his joy.

The danger of her frailty was far off then in the rush of birdsong and the springing leverets of the meadow. On dark days she might cough a bit, but so did he.... In those years he had had no thought to the urgent study of disease.

At the Moscow conference nearly everyone noticed Ain at some point or another, which was to be expected in view of his professional stature. It was a small, high-caliber meeting. Ain was late in; a day's reports were over, and his was to be on the third and last.

Many people spoke with Ain, and several sat with him at meals. No one was surprised that he spoke little; he was a retiring man except on a few memorable occasions of argument. He did strike some of his friends as a bit tired and jerky.

An Indian molecular engineer who saw him with the throat spray kidded him about bringing over Asian flu. A Swedish colleague recalled that Ain had been called away to the transatlantic phone at lunch; and when he returned Ain volunteered the information that something had turned up missing in his home lab. There was another joke, and Ain said cheerfully, "Oh, yes, quite active."

At that point one of the Chicom biologists swung into his daily propaganda chores about bacteriological warfare and accused Ain of manufacturing biotic weapons. Ain took the wind out of his sails by saying: "You're perfectly right." By tacit consent, there was very little talk about military applications, industrial dusting, or subjects of that type. And nobody recalled seeing Ain with any woman other than old Madame Vialche, who could scarcely have subverted anyone from her wheelchair.

Ain's one speech was bad, even for him. He always had a poor public voice, but his ideas were usually expressed with the lucidity so typical of the first-rate mind. This time he seemed muddled, with little new to say. His audience excused this as the muffling effects of security. Ain then got into a tangled point about the course of evolution in which he seemed to be trying to show that something was very wrong indeed. When he wound up with a reference to Hudson's bellbird "singing for a later race," several listeners wondered if he could be drunk.

The big security break came right at the end, when he suddenly began to describe the methods he had used to mutate and redesign a leukemia virus. He explained the procedure with admirable clarity in four sentences and paused. Then gave a terse description of the effects of the mutated strain, which were maximal only in the higher primates. Recovery rate among the lower mammals and other orders was close to ninety percent. As to vectors, he went on, any warm-blooded animal served. In addition, the virus retained its viability in most environmental media and performed very well airborne. Contagion rate was extremely high. Almost offhand, Ain added that no test primate or accidentally exposed human had survived beyond the twenty-second day.

These words fell into a silence broken only by the running feet of the Egyptian delegate making for the door. Then a gilt chair went over as an American bolted after him.

Ain seemed unaware that his audience was in a state of unbelieving paralysis. It had all come so fast: a man who had been blowing his nose was staring pop-eyed around his handkerchief. Another who had been lighting a pipe grunted as his fingers singed. Two men chatting by the door missed his words entirely, and their laughter chimed into a dead silence in which echoed Ain's words: "—really no point in attempting."

Later they found he had been explaining that the virus utilized the body's own immunomechanisms, and so defense was by definition hopeless.

That was all. Ain looked around vaguely for questions and then started down the aisle. By the time he got to the door, people were swarming after him. He wheeled about and said rather crossly, "Yes, of course it is very wrong. I told you that. We are all wrong. Now it's over."

An hour later they found he had gone, having apparently reserved a Sinair flight to Karachi.

The security men caught up with him at Hong Kong. By then he seemed really very ill, and went with them peacefully. They started back to the States via Hawaii.

His captors were civilized types; they saw he was gentle and treated him accordingly. He had no weapons or drugs on him. They took him out handcuffed for a stroll at Osaka, let him feed his crumbs to the birds, and they listened with interest to his account of the migration routes of the common brown sandpiper. He was very hoarse. At that point, he was wanted only for the security thing. There was no question of a woman at all.

He dozed most of the way to the islands, but when they came in sight he pressed to the window and began to mutter. The security man behind him got the first inkling that there was a woman in it, and turned on his recorder.

". . . Blue, blue and green until you see the wounds. O my girl, O beautiful, you won't die. I won't let you die. I tell you girl, it's over. . . . Lustrous eyes, look at me, let me see you now alive! Great queen, my sweet body, my girl, have I saved you? . . . O terrible to know, and noble, Chaos's child green-robed in blue and golden light . . . the thrown and spinning ball of life alone in space. . . . Have I saved you?"

On the last leg, he was obviously feverish.

"She may have tricked me, you know," he said confidentially to the government man. "You have to be prepared for that, of course. I know her!" He chuckled confidentially. "She's no small thing. But wring your heart out—"

Coming over San Francisco he was merry. "Don't you know the otters will go back in there? I'm certain of it. That fill won't last; there'll be a bay there again."

They got him on a stretcher at Hamilton Air Base, and he

went unconscious shortly after takeoff. Before he collapsed, he'd insisted on throwing the last of his birdseed on the field.

"Birds are, you know, warm-blooded," he confided to the agent who was handcuffing him to the stretcher. Then Ain smiled gently and lapsed into inertness. He stayed that way almost all the remaining ten days of his life. By then, of course, no one really cared. Both the government men had died quite early, after they finished analyzing the birdseed and throat spray. The woman at Kennedy had just started feeling sick.

The tape recorder they put by his bed functioned right on through, but if anybody had been around to replay it they would have found little but babbling. "Gaea Gloriatrix," he crooned, "Gaea girl, queen . . ." At times he was grandiose and tormented. "Our life, your death!" he yelled. "Our death would have been your death too, no need for that, no need."

At other times he was accusing. "What did you do about the dinosaurs?" he demanded. "Did they annoy you? How did you fix *them?* Cold. Queen, you're too cold! You came close to it this time, my girl," he raved. And then he wept and caressed the bedclothes and was maudlin.

Only at the end, lying in his filth and thirst, still chained where they had forgotten him, he was suddenly coherent. In the light clear voice of a lover planning a summer picnic he asked the recorder happily:

"Have you ever thought about bears? They have so much . . . funny they never came along further. By any chance were you saving them, girl?" And he chuckled in his ruined throat, and later, died.

THE SCREWFLY SOLUTION

THE YOUNG MAN sitting at 2°N, 75°W, sent a casually venomous glance up at the nonfunctional shoofly *ventilador* and went on reading his letter. He was sweating heavily, stripped to his shorts in the hotbox of what passed for a hotel room in Cuyápan.

> How do other wives *do* it? I stay busy-busy with the Ann Arbor grant review-programs and the seminar, saying brightly "Oh yes, Alan is in Colombia setting up a biological pest-control program, isn't it wonderful?" But inside I imagine you surrounded by nineteen-year-old raven-haired cooing beauties, every one panting with social dedication and filthy rich. And forty inches of bosom busting out of her delicate lingerie. I even figured it in centimeters, that's 101.6 centimeters of busting. Oh, darling, darling, do what you want only *come home safe.*

Alan grinned fondly, briefly imagining the only body he longed for. His girl, his magic Anne. Then he got up to open the window another cautious notch. A long pale mournful face looked in—a goat. The room opened on the goat pen, the stench was vile. Air, anyway. He picked up the letter.

> Everything is just about as you left it, except that

the Peedsville horror seems to be getting worse. They're calling it the Sons of Adam cult now. Why can't they *do* something, even if it is a religion? The Red Cross has set up a refugee camp in Ashton, Georgia. Imagine, refugees in the U.S.A. I heard two little girls were carried out all slashed up. Oh, Alan.

Which reminds me, Barney came over with a wad of clippings he wants me to send you. I'm putting them in a separate envelope; I know what happens to very fat letters in foreign POs. He says, in case you don't get them, what do the following have in common? Peedsville, São Paulo, Phoenix, San Diego, Shanghai, New Delhi, Tripoli, Brisbane, Johannesburg, and Lubbock, Texas. He says the hint is, remember where the Intertropical Convergence Zone is now. That makes no sense to me, maybe it will to your superior ecological brain. All I could see about the clippings was that they were fairly horrible accounts of murders or massacres of women. The worst was the New Delhi one, about "rafts of female corpses" in the river. The funniest (!) was the Texas Army officer who shot his wife, three daughters, and his aunt, because God told him to clean the place up.

Barney's such an old dear, he's coming over Sunday to help me take off the downspout and see what's blocking it. He's dancing on air right now; since you left, his spruce budworm-moth antipheromone program finally paid off. You know he tested over 2,000 compounds? Well, it seems that good old 2,097 *really* works. When I asked him what it does he just giggles, you know how shy he is with women. Anyway, it seems that a one-shot spray program will save the forests, without harming a single other thing. Birds and people can eat it all day, he says.

Well, sweetheart, that's all the news except Amy goes back to Chicago to school Sunday. The place will be a tomb, I'll miss her frightfully in spite of her being at the stage where I'm her worst enemy. The sullen sexy subteens, Angie says. Amy sends love to her daddy. I send you my whole heart, all that words can't say.

Your Anne

Alan put the letter safely in his note file and glanced over the rest of the thin packet of mail, refusing to let himself dream of home and Anne. Barney's "fat envelope" wasn't there. He threw himself on the rumpled bed, yanking off the light cord a minute before the town generator went off for the night. In the darkness the list of places Barney had mentioned spread themselves around a misty globe that turned, troublingly, in his mind. Something . . .

But then the memory of the hideously parasitized children he had worked with at the clinic that day took possession of his thoughts. He set himself to considering the data he must collect.

Look for the vulnerable link in the behavioral chain—how often Barney—Dr. Barnhard Braithwaite—had pounded it into his skull. Where was it, where? In the morning he would start work on bigger canefly cages. . . .

At that moment, five thousand miles north, Anne was writing.

Oh, darling, darling, your first three letters are here, they all came together. I *knew* you were writing. Forget what I said about swarthy heiresses, that was all a joke. My darling, I know, I know . . . us. Those dreadful canefly larvae, those poor little kids. If you weren't my husband I'd think you were a saint or something. (I do anyway.)

I have your letters pinned up all over the house, makes it a lot less lonely. No real news here except things feel kind of quiet and spooky. Barney and I got the downspout out, it was full of a big rotted hoard of squirrel nuts. They must have been dropping them down the top, I'll put a wire over it. (Don't worry, I'll use a ladder this time.)

Barney's in an odd, grim mood. He's taking this Sons of Adam thing very seriously, it seems he's going to be on the investigation committee if that ever gets off the ground. The weird part is that nobody seems to be doing anything, as if it's just too big. Selina Peters has been printing some acid comments, like: When one man kills his wife you call it murder, but when enough do it we call it a life-style. I think it's spreading, but nobody knows because the media have been asked to downplay it. Barney says it's being viewed as a form of contagious hysteria. He insisted I send you this ghastly interview, printed on thin paper. It's *not* going to be published, of course. The quietness is worse, though, it's like something terrible was going on just out of sight. After reading Barney's thing I called up Pauline in San Diego to make sure she was all right. She sounded funny, as if she wasn't saying everything . . . my own sister. Just after she said things were great she suddenly asked if she could come and stay here awhile next month. I said come right away, but she wants to sell her house first. I wish she'd hurry.

The diesel car is okay now, it just needed its filter changed. I had to go out to Springfield to get one, but Eddie installed it for only $2.50. He's going to bankrupt his garage.

In case you didn't guess, those places of Barney's are all about latitude 30° N or S—the horse latitudes. When I said not exactly, he said remember the Equatorial Convergence Zone shifts in winter, and to add in Libya, Osaka, and a place I forget—wait, Alice Springs, Australia. What has this to do with anything, I asked. He said, "Nothing—I hope." I leave it to you, great brains like Barney can be weird.

Oh my dearest, here's all of me to all of you. Your letters make life possible. But don't feel you *have* to, I can tell how tired you must be. Just know we're together, always everywhere.

Your Anne

Oh PS I had to open this to put Barney's thing in, it wasn't the secret police. Here it is. All love again. A.

In the goat-infested room where Alan read this, rain was drumming on the roof. He put the letter to his nose to catch the faint perfume once more, and folded it away. Then he pulled out the yellow flimsy Barney had sent and began to read, frowning.

PEEDSVILLE CULT/SONS OF ADAM SPECIAL.
Statement by driver Sgt. Willard Mews, Globe Fork, Ark.

We hit the roadblock about 80 miles west of Jacksonville. Major John Heinz of Ashton was expecting us, he gave us an escort of two riot vehicles headed by Capt. T. Parr. Major Heinz appeared shocked to see that the N.I.H. medical team included two women doctors. He warned us in the strongest terms of the danger. So Dr. Patsy Putnam (Urbana, Ill.), the psychologist, decided to stay behind at the Army cordon. But Dr. Elaine Fay (Clinton, N.J.) insisted on going with us, saying she was the epi-something (?epidemiologist).

We drove behind one of the riot cars at 30 m.p.h. for about an hour without seeing anything unusual. There were two big signs Saying SONS OF ADAM—LIBERATED ZONE. We passed some small pecan-packing plants and a citrus-processing plant. The men there looked at us but did not do anything unusual. I didn't see any children or women, of course. Just outside Peedsville we stopped at a big barrier made of oil drums in front of a large citrus warehouse. This area is old, sort of a shantytown and trailer park. The new part of town with the shopping center and developments is about a mile farther on. A warehouse worker with a shotgun came out and told us to wait for the mayor. I don't think he saw Dr. Elaine Fay then, she was sitting sort of bent down in back.

Mayor Blount drove up in a police cruiser, and our chief, Dr. Premack, explained our mission from the Surgeon General. Dr. Premack was very careful not to make any remarks insulting to the mayor's religion. Mayor Blount agreed to let the party go on into Peedsville to take samples of the soil and water and so on and talk to the doctor who lives there.

The mayor was about 6'2", weight maybe 230 or 240, tanned, with grayish hair. He was smiling and chuckling in a friendly manner.

Then he looked inside the car and saw Dr. Elaine Fay and he blew up. He started yelling we had to all get the hell back. But Dr. Premack talked to him and cooled him down, and finally the mayor said Dr. Fay should go into the warehouse office and stay there with the door closed. I had to stay there too and see she didn't come out, and one of the mayor's men would drive the party.

So the medical people and the mayor and one of the riot vehicles went on into Peedsville, and I took Dr. Fay back into the warehouse office and sat down. It was real hot and stuffy. Dr. Fay opened a window, but then I heard her trying to talk to an old man outside and I told her she couldn't do that and closed the window. The old man went away. Then she wanted to talk to me, but I told her I did not feel like conversing. I felt it was real wrong, her being there.

So then she started looking through the office files and reading papers there. I told her that was a bad idea, she shouldn't do that. She said the government expected her to investigate. She showed me a booklet or magazine they had there, it was called *Man Listens to God* by Reverend McIllhenny. They had a carton full in the office. I started reading it, and Dr. Fay said she wanted to wash her hands. So I took her back along a kind of enclosed hallway beside the conveyor to where the toilet was. There were no doors or windows, so I went back. After a while she called out that there was a cot back there, she was going to lie down. I figured that was all right because of the no windows; also, I was glad to be rid of her company.

When I got to reading the book it was very intriguing. It was very deep thinking about how man is now on trial with God and if we fulfill our duty God will bless us with a real new life on Earth. The signs and portents show it. It wasn't like, you know, Sunday-school stuff. It was deep.

After a while I heard some music and saw the soldiers from the other riot car were across the street by the gas tanks, sitting in the shade of some trees and kidding with the workers from the plant. One of them was playing a guitar, not electric, just plain. It looked so peaceful.

Then Mayor Blount drove up alone in the cruiser and came in. When he saw I was reading the book he smiled at me sort of fatherly, but he looked tense. He asked me where Dr. Fay was, and I told him she was lying down in back. He said that was okay. Then he kind of sighed and went back down the hall, closing the door behind him. I sat and listened to the guitar man, trying to hear what he was singing. I felt really hungry, my lunch was in Dr. Premack's car.

After a while the door opened and Mayor Blount came back in. He looked terrible, his clothes were messed up, and he had bloody scrape marks on his face. He didn't say anything, he just looked at me hard and fierce, like he might have been disoriented. I saw his zipper was open and there was blood on his clothing and also on his (private parts).

I didn't feel frightened, I felt something important had happened. I tried to get him to sit down. But he motioned me to follow him back down the hall, to where Dr. Fay was. "You must see," he said. He went into the toilet and I went into a kind of little room there, where the cot was. The light was fairly good, reflected off the tin roof from where the walls stopped. I saw Dr. Fay lying on the cot in a peaceful appearance. She was lying straight, her clothing was to some extent different but her legs were together, I was glad to see that. Her blouse was pulled up, and I saw there was a cut or incision on her abdomen. The blood was coming out there, or it had been coming out there, like a mouth. It wasn't moving at this time. Also her throat was cut open.

I returned to the office. Mayor Blount was sitting down, looking very tired. He had cleaned himself off. He said, "I did it for you. Do you understand?"

He seemed like my father. I can't say it better than that. I realized he was under a terrible strain, he had taken a lot on himself for me. He went on to explain how Dr. Fay was very dangerous, she was what they call a cripto-female (crypto?), the most dangerous kind. He had exposed her and purified the situation. He was very straightforward, I didn't feel confused at all, I knew he, had done what was right.

We discussed the book, how man must purify himself and show God a clean world. He said some people raise the question of how can man reproduce without women, but such people miss the point. The point is that as long as man depends on the old filthy animal way, God won't help him. When man gets rid of his animal part which is woman, this is the signal God is awaiting. Then God will reveal the new true clean way, maybe angels will come bringing new souls, or maybe we will live forever, but it is not our place to speculate, only to obey. He said some men here had seen an Angel of the Lord. This was very deep, it seemed like it echoed inside me, I felt it was an inspiration.

Then the medical party drove up and I told Dr. Premack that Dr. Fay had been taken care of and sent away, and I got in the car to drive them out of the Liberated Zone. However, four of the six soldiers from the roadblock refused to leave. Capt. Parr tried to argue them out of it but finally agreed they could stay to guard the oil-drum barrier.

I would have liked to stay too, the place was so peaceful, but they needed me to drive the car. If I had known there would be all this hassle I never would have done them the favor. I am not crazy and I have not done anything wrong and my lawyer will get me out. That is all I have to say.

In Cuyapán the hot afternoon rain had temporarily ceased. As Alan's fingers let go of Sgt. Willard Mews's wretched document, he caught sight of pencil-scrawled words in the margin in Barney's spider hand. He squinted.

"Man's religion and metaphysics are the voices of his glands. Schönweiser, 1878."

Who the devil Schönweiser was Alan didn't know, but he knew what Barney was conveying. This murderous crackpot religion of McWhosis was a symptom, not a cause. Barney believed something was physically affecting the Peedsville men, generating psychosis, and a local religious demagogue had sprung up to "explain" it.

Well, maybe. But cause or effect, Alan thought only of one thing: eight hundred miles from Peedsville to Ann Arbor. Anne should be safe. She *had* to be.

He threw himself on the lumpy cot, his mind going back exultantly to his work. At the cost of a million bites and cane cuts he was pretty sure he'd found the weak link in the canefly cycle. The male mass-mating behavior, the comparative scarcity of ovulant females. It would be the screwfly solution all over again with the sexes reversed. Concentrate the pheromone, release sterilized females. Luckily the breeding populations were comparatively isolated. In a couple of seasons they ought to have it. Have to let them go on spraying poison meanwhile, of course; damn pity, it was slaughtering everything and getting in the water, and the caneflies had evolved to immunity anyway. But in a couple of seasons, maybe three, they could drop the canefly populations below reproductive viability. No more tormented human bodies with those stinking larvae in the nasal passages and brain. . . . He drifted off for a nap, grinning.

Up north, Anne was biting her lip in shame and pain.

> Sweetheart, I shouldn't admit it but your wife is ~~scared~~ a bit jittery. Just female nerves or something, nothing to worry about. Everything is normal up here. It's so eerily normal, nothing in the papers, nothing anywhere except what I hear through Barney and Lillian. But Pauline's phone won't answer out in San Diego; the fifth day some strange man yelled at me and banged the phone down. Maybe she's sold her house—but why wouldn't she call?
>
> Lillian's on some kind of Save-the-Women

committee, like we were an endangered species, ha-ha—you know Lillian. It seems the Red Cross has started setting up camps. But she says, after the first rush, only a trickle are coming out of what they call "the affected areas." Not many children, either, even little boys. And they have some air photos around Lubbock showing what look like mass graves. Oh, Alan . . . so far it seems to be mostly spreading west, but something's happening in St. Louis, they're cut off. So many places seem to have just vanished from the news, I had a nightmare that there isn't a woman left alive down there. And nobody's doing anything. They talked about spraying with tranquilizers for a while and then that died out. What could it do? Somebody at the UN has proposed a convention on—you won't believe this—*femicide*. It sounds like a deodorant spray.

Excuse me, honey, I seem to be a little hysterical. George Searles came back from Georgia talking about God's Will—Searles the lifelong atheist. Alan, something crazy is happening.

But there aren't any facts. Nothing. The Surgeon General issued a report on the bodies of the Rahway Rip-Breast Team—I guess I didn't tell you about that. Anyway, they could find no pathology. Milton Baines wrote a letter saying in the present state of the art we can't distinguish the brain of a saint from a psychopathic killer, so how could they expect to find what they don't know how to look for?

Well, enough of these jitters. It'll be all over by the time you get back, just history. Everything's fine here, I fixed the car's muffler again. And Amy's coming home for the vacations, *that'll* get my mind off faraway problems.

Oh, something amusing to end with—Angie told me what Barney's enzyme does to the spruce budworm. It seems it blocks the male from turning around after he connects with the female, so he mates with her *head* instead. Like clockwork with a cog missing. There're going to be some pretty puzzled female spruceworms. Now why couldn't Barney tell me that? He really is such a sweet shy old dear. He's given me some stuff to put in, as usual. I didn't read it.

Now don't worry, my darling, everything's fine.

I love you, I love you so.

Always, all ways your Anne

Two weeks later in Cuyápan when Barney's enclosures slid out of the envelope, Alan didn't read them, either. He stuffed them into the pocket of his bush jacket with a shaking hand and started bundling his notes together on the rickety table, with a scrawled note to Sister Dominique on top. The hell with the canefly, the hell with everything except that tremor in his fearless Anne's firm handwriting. The hell with being five thousand miles away from his woman, his child, while some deadly madness raged. He crammed his meager belongings into his duffel. If he hurried he could catch the bus through to Bogota and maybe make the Miami flight.

He made it to Miami, but the planes north were jammed. He failed a quick standby; six hours to wait. Time to call Anne. When the call got through some difficulty, he was unprepared for the rush of joy and relief that burst along the wires.

"Thank god—I can't believe it—Oh, Alan, my darling, are you really—I can't believe—"

He found he was repeating too, and all mixed up with the canefly data. They were both laughing hysterically when he finally hung up.

Six hours. He settled in a frayed plastic chair opposite *Aerolineas Argentinas*, his mind half back at the clinic, half on the throngs moving by him. Something was oddly different here, he perceived presently. Where was the decorative fauna he usually enjoyed in Miami, the parade of young girls in crotch-tight pastel jeans? The flounces, boots, wild hats and hairdos, and startling expanses of newly tanned skin, the brilliant fabrics barely confining the bob of breasts and buttocks? Not here—but wait; looking closely, he glimpsed two young faces hidden under unbecoming parkas, their bodies draped in bulky nondescript skirts. In fact, all down the long vista he could see the same thing: hooded ponchos, heaped-on clothes and baggy pants, dull colors. A new style? No, he thought not. It seemed to him their movements suggested furtiveness, timidity. And they moved in groups. He watched a lone girl struggle to catch up with the others ahead of her, apparently strangers. They accepted her wordlessly.

They're frightened, he thought. Afraid of attracting notice. Even that gray-haired matron in a pantsuit resolutely leading a flock of kids was glancing around nervously.

And at the Argentine desk opposite he saw another odd thing; two lines had a big sign over them: *MUJERES.* Women. They were crowded with the shapeless forms and very quiet.

The men seemed to be behaving normally; hurrying, lounging, griping, and joking in the lines as they kicked their luggage along. But Alan felt an undercurrent of tension, like an irritant in the air. Outside the line of storefronts behind him a few isolated men seemed to be handing out tracts. An airport attendant spoke to the nearest man; he merely shrugged and moved a few doors down.

To distract himself Alan picked up a *Miami Herald* from the next seat. It was surprisingly thin. The international news occupied him for a while; he had seen none for weeks. It too had a strange empty quality, even the bad news seemed to have dried up. The African war which had been going on seemed to be over, or went unreported. A trade summit meeting was haggling over grain and steel prices. He found himself at the obituary pages, columns of close-set type dominated by the photo of an unknown defunct ex-senator. Then his eye fell on two announcements at the bottom of the, page. One was too flowery for quick comprehension, but the other stated in bold plain type:

THE FORSETTE FUNERAL HOME
REGRETFULLY ANNOUNCES
IT WILL NO LONGER ACCEPT FEMALE CADAVERS

Slowly he folded the paper, staring at it numbly. On the back was an item headed *Navigational Hazard Warning,* in the shipping news. Without really taking it in, he read:

AP/Nassau: The excursion liner *Carib Swallow* reached port under tow today after striking an obstruction in the Gulf Stream off Cape Hatteras. The obstruction was identified as part of a commercial trawler's seine floated by female corpses. This confirms reports from Florida and the Gulf of the use of such seines, some of them over a mile in length. Similar reports coming from the Pacific coast and as far away as Japan indicate a growing hazard to coastwise shipping.

Alan flung the thing into the trash receptacle and sat rubbing his forehead and eyes. Thank god he had followed his impulse to come home. He felt totally disoriented, as though he had landed by error on another planet. Five hours more to wait . . . At length he recalled the stuff from Barney he had thrust in his pocket, and pulled it out and smoothed it.

The top item seemed to be from the *Ann Arbor News*. Dr. Lillian Dash, together with several hundred other members of her organization, had been arrested for demonstrating without a permit in front of the White House. They had started a fire in a garbage can, which was considered particularly heinous. A number of women's groups had participated; the total struck Alan as more like thousands than hundreds. Extraordinary security precautions were being taken, despite the fact that the President was out of town at the time.

The next item had to be Barney's acerbic humor.

UP/Vatican City 19 June. Pope John IV today intimated that he does not plan to comment officially on the so-called Pauline Purification cults advocating the elimination of women as a means of justifying man to God. A spokesman emphasized that the Church takes no position on these cults but repudiates any doctrine involving a "challenge" to or from God to reveal His further plans for man.

Cardinal Fazzoli, spokesman for the European Pauline movement, reaffirmed his view that the Scriptures define woman as merely a temporary companion and instrument of man. Women, he states, are nowhere defined as human, but merely as a transitional expedient or state. "The time of transition to full humanity is at hand," he concluded.

The next item appeared to be a thin-paper Xerox from a recent issue of *Science:*

SUMMARY REPORT OF THE AD HOC EMERGENCY COMMITTEE ON FEMICIDE

The recent worldwide though localized outbreaks of femicide appear to represent a recurrence of similar outbreaks by groups or sects which are not uncommon in world history in times of psychic stress. In this case the root cause is undoubtedly the speed of social and technological change, augmented by population pressure, and the spread and scope are aggravated by instantaneous world communications, thus exposing more susceptible persons. It is not viewed as a medical or epidemiological problem; no physical pathology has been found. Rather it is more akin to the various manias which swept Europe in the seventeenth century, e.g., the Dancing Manias, and like them, should run its course and disappear. The chiliastic cults which have sprung up around the affected areas appear to be unrelated, having in common only the idea that a new means of human reproduction will be revealed as a result of the "purifying" elimination of women.

We recommend that (1) inflammatory and sensational reporting be suspended; (2) refugee centers be set up and maintained for women escapees from the focal areas; (3) containment of affected areas by military cordon be continued and enforced; and (4) after a cooling-down period and the subsidence of the mania, qualified mental-health teams and appropriate professional personnel go in to undertake rehabilitation.

SUMMARY OF THE MINORITY REPORT OF THE AD HOC COMMITTEE

The nine members signing this report agree that there is no evidence for epidemiological contagion of femicide in the strict sense. *However,* the geographical relation of the focal areas of outbreak strongly suggests that they cannot be dismissed as purely psychosocial phenomena. The initial outbreaks have occurred around the globe near the 30th parallel, the area of principal atmospheric downflow of upper winds coming from the Intertropical Convergence Zone. An agent or condition in the upper equatorial atmosphere would thus be expected to reach ground level along the 30th parallel, with certain seasonal variations. One principal variation is that the downflow moves north over the East Asian continent during the late winter months, and those areas south of it (Arabia, Western India, parts of North Africa) have in fact been free of outbreaks until recently, when the downflow zone moved south. A similar downflow occurs in the Southern Hemisphere, and outbreaks have been reported along the 30th parallel running through Pretoria and Alice Springs, Australia. (Information from Argentina is currently unavailable.)

This geographical correlation cannot be dismissed, and it is therefore urged that an intensified search for a physical cause be instituted. It is also urgently recommended that the rate of spread from known focal points be correlated with wind conditions. A watch for similar outbreaks along the secondary down-welling zones at 60° north and south should be kept.

(signed for the minority)
BARNHARD BRAITHWAITE

Alan grinned reminiscently at his old friend's name, which seemed to restore normalcy and stability to the world. It looked as if Barney was on to something, too, despite the prevalence of horses' asses. He frowned, puzzling it out.

Then his face slowly changed as he thought how it would be, going home to Anne. In a few short hours his arms would be around her, the tall, secretly beautiful body that had come to obsess him. Theirs had been a late-blooming love. They'd married, he supposed now, out of friendship, even out of friends' pressure. Everyone said they were made for each other, he big and chunky and blond, she willowy brunette; both shy, highly controlled, cerebral types. For the first few years the friendship had held, but sex hadn't been all that much. Conventional necessity. Politely reassuring each other, privately—he could say it now—disappointing.

But then, when Amy was a toddler, something had happened. A miraculous inner portal of sensuality had slowly opened to them, a liberation into their own secret unsuspected heaven of fully physical bliss. . . . Jesus, but it had been a wrench when the Colombia thing had come up. Only their absolute sureness of each other had made him take it. And now, to be about to have her again, trebly desirable from the spice of separation—feeling-seeing-hearing-smelling-grasping. He shifted in his seat to conceal his body's excitement, half mesmerized by fantasy.

And Amy would be there, too; he grinned at the memory of that prepubescent little body plastered against him. She was going to be a handful, all right. His manhood understood Amy a lot better than her mother did; no cerebral phase for Amy. . . . But Anne, his exquisite shy one, with whom he'd found the way into the almost unendurable transports of the flesh. . . . First the conventional greeting, he thought; the news, the unspoken, savored, mounting excitement behind their eyes; the light touches; then the seeking of their own room, the falling clothes, the caresses, gentle at first—the flesh, the *nakedness*—the delicate teasing, the grasp, the first thrust—

A terrible alarm bell went off in his head. Exploded from his dream, he stared around, then finally down at his hands. *What was he doing with his open clasp knife in his fist?*

Stunned, he felt for the last shreds of his fantasy, and realized that the tactile images had not been of caresses, but of a frail neck strangling in his fist, the thrust had been the plunge of a blade seeking vitals. In his arms, legs, phantasms of striking and trampling bones cracking. And Amy—

Oh, god. Oh, god—

Not sex, blood lust.

That was what he had been dreaming. The sex was there, but it was driving some engine of death.

Numbly he put the knife away, thinking only over and over, it's got me. It's got me. Whatever it is, it's got me. *I can't go home.*

After an unknown time he got up and made his way to the United counter to turn in his ticket. The line was long. As he waited, his mind cleared a little. What could he do, here in

Miami? Wouldn't it be better to get back to Ann Arbor and turn himself in to Barney? Barney could help him, if anyone could. Yes, that was best. But first he had to warn Anne.

The connection took even longer this time. When Anne finally answered he found himself blurting unintelligibly, it took a while to make her understand he wasn't talking about a plane delay.

"I tell you, I've caught it. Listen, Anne, for god's sake. If I should come to the house don't let me come near you. I mean it. I mean it. I'm going to the lab, but I might lose control and try to get to you. Is Barney there?"

"Yes, but darling—"

"Listen. Maybe he can fix me, maybe this'll wear off. But I'm not safe. Anne, Anne, I'd kill you, can you understand? Get a—get a weapon. I'll try not to come to the house. But if I do, don't let me get near you. Or Amy. It's a sickness, it's real. Treat me—treat me like a fucking wild animal. Anne, say you understand, say you'll do it."

They were both crying when he hung up.

He went shaking back to sit and wait. After a time his head seemed to clear a little more. *Doctor, try to think.* The first thing he thought of was to take the loathsome knife and throw it down a trash slot. As he did so he realized there was one more piece of Barney's material in his pocket. He uncrumpled it; it seemed to be a clipping from *Nature*.

At the top was Barney's scrawl: "Only guy making sense. U.K. infected now, Oslo, Copenhagen out of communication. Damfools still won't listen. Stay put."

COMMUNICATION FROM PROFESSOR IAN MACINTYRE, GLASGOW UNIV.

A potential difficulty for our species has always been implicit in the close linkage between the behavioral expression of aggression/predation and sexual reproduction in the male. This close linkage is shown by (a) many of the same neuromuscular pathways which are utilized both in predatory and sexual pursuit, grasping, mounting, etc., and (b) similar states of adrenergic arousal which are activated in both. The same linkage is seen in the males of many other species; in some, the expression of aggression and copulation alternate or even coexist, an all-too-familiar example being the common house cat. Males of many species bite, claw, bruise, tread, or otherwise assault receptive females during the act of intercourse; indeed, in some species the male attack is necessary for female ovulation to occur.

In many if not all species it is the aggressive behavior which appears first, and then changes to copulatory behavior when the appropriate signal is presented (*e.g.*, the three-tined stickleback and the European robin). Lacking the inhibiting signal, the male's fighting response continues and the female is attacked or driven off.

It seems therefore appropriate to speculate that the present crisis might be caused by some substance, perhaps at the viral or enzymatic level, which effects a failure of the switching or triggering function in the higher primates. (Note: Zoo gorillas and chimpanzees have recently been observed to attack or destroy their mates; rhesus not.) Such a dysfunction could be expressed by the failure of mating behavior to modify or supervene over the aggressive/predatory response; i.e., sexual stimulation would produce attack only, the stimulation discharging itself through the destruction of the stimulating object.

In this connection it might be noted that exactly this condition is a commonplace of male functional pathology, in those cases where murder occurs as a response to, and apparent completion of, sexual desire.

It should be emphasized that the aggression/ copulation linkage discussed here is specific to the male; the female response (*e.g.*, lordotic reflex) being of a different nature.

Alan sat holding the crumpled sheet a long time; the dry, stilted Scottish phrases seemed to help clear his head, despite the sense of brooding tension all around him. Well, if pollution or whatever had produced some substance, it could presumably be countered, filtered, neutralized. Very very carefully, he let himself consider his life with Anne, his sexuality. Yes; much of their loveplay could be viewed as genitalized, sexually gentled savagery. Play-predation . . . He turned his mind quickly away. Some writer's phrase occurred to him: "The panic element in all sex." Who? Fritz Leiber? The violation of social distance, maybe; another threatening element.

Whatever, it's our weak link, he thought. Our vulnerability . . . The dreadful feeling of *rightness* he had experienced when he found himself knife in hand, fantasizing violence, came back to him. As though it was the right, the only, way. Was that what Barney's budworms felt when they mated with their females wrong-end-to?

At long length, he became aware of body need and sought a toilet. The place was empty, except for what he took to be a heap of clothes blocking the door of the far stall. Then he saw the red-brown pool in which it lay, and the bluish mounds of bare, thin buttocks. He backed out, not breathing, and fled into the nearest crowd, knowing he was not the first to have done so.

Of course. Any sexual drive. Boys, men, too.

At the next washroom he watched to see men enter and leave normally before he ventured in.

Afterward he returned to sit, waiting, repeating over and over to himself: *Go to the lab. Don't go home. Go straight to the lab.* Three more hours; he sat numbly at 26°N, 81°W, breathing, breathing. . . .

Dear diary. Big scene tonite, Daddy came home!!! Only he acted so funny, he had the taxi wait and just held on to the doorway, he wouldn't touch me or let us come near him. (I mean funny weird, not funny ha-ha.) He said, I have something to tell you, this is getting worse not better. I'm going to sleep in the lab but I want you to get out, Anne, Anne, I can't trust myself anymore. First thing in the morning you both get on the plane for Martha's and stay there. So I thought he had to be joking, I mean with the dance next week and Aunt Martha lives in Whitehorse where there's nothing nothing nothing. So I was yelling and Mother was yelling and Daddy was groaning, Go now! And then he started crying. Crying!!! So I realized, wow, this is serious, and I started to go over to him but Mother yanked me back and then I saw she had this big *knife!!!* And she shoved me in back of her and started crying too: Oh Alan, Oh Alan, like she was insane. So I said, Daddy, I'll never leave you, it felt like the perfect thing to say. And it was thrilling, he looked at me real sad and deep like I was a grown-up while Mother was treating me like I was a mere infant as usual. But Mother ruined it raving, Alan the child is mad, darling go. So he ran out of the door yelling, Be gone. Take the car. Get out before I come back.

Oh I forgot to say I was wearing what but my gooby *green* with my curl-tites still on, wouldn't you know of all the shitty luck, how could I have known such a beautiful scene was ahead we never know life's cruel whimsy. And Mother is dragging out suitcases yelling, Pack your things hurry! So she's going I guess but I am not repeat not going to spend the fall sitting in Aunt Martha's grain silo and lose the dance and all my summer credits. And Daddy was trying to *communicate* with us, right? I think their relationship is obsolete. So when she goes upstairs I am splitting. I am going to go over to the lab and see Daddy.

Oh PS Diane tore my yellow jeans she promised me I could use her pink ones ha-ha that'll be the day.

I ripped that page out of Amy's diary when I heard the squad car coming. I never opened her diary before, but when I found she'd gone I looked. . . . Oh, my darling little girl. She went to him, my little girl, my poor little fool child. Maybe if I'd taken time to explain, maybe—

Excuse me, Barney. The stuff is wearing off, the shots they gave me. I didn't feel anything. I mean, I knew somebody's daughter went to see her father and he killed her. And cut his throat. But it didn't mean anything.

Alan's note, they gave me that but then they took it away. Why did they have to do that? His last handwriting, the last words he wrote before his hand picked up the, before he—

I remember it. *"Sudden and light as that, the bonds gave. And we learned of finalities besides the grave. The bonds of our humanity have broken, we are finished. I love—"*

I'm all right, Barney, really. Who wrote that, Robert Frost? *The bonds gave. . . .* Oh, he said, tell Barney: *The terrible rightness.* What does that mean?

You can't answer that, Barney dear. I'm just writing this to stay sane, I'll put it in your hidey-hole. Thank you, thank you, Barney dear. Even as blurry as I was, I knew it was you. All the time you were cutting off my hair and rubbing dirt on my face, I knew it was right because it was you. Barney, I never thought of you as those horrible words you said. You were always Dear Barney.

By the time the stuff wore off I had done everything you said, the gas, the groceries. Now I'm here in your cabin. With those clothes you made me put on—I guess I do look like a boy, the gas man called me "Mister."

I still can't really realize, I have to stop myself from rushing back. But you saved my life, I know that. The first trip in I got a paper, I saw where they bombed the Apostle Islands refuge. And it had about those three women stealing the Air Force plane and bombing Dallas, too. Of course they shot them down, over the Gulf. Isn't it strange how we do nothing? Just get killed by ones and twos. Or more, now they've started on the refuges. . . . Like hypnotized rabbits. We're a toothless race.

Do you know I never said "we" meaning women before? "We" was always me and Alan, and Amy of course. Being killed selectively encourages group identification. . . . You see how sane-headed I am.

But I still can't really realize.

My first trip in was for salt and kerosene. I went to that little Red Deer store and got my stuff from the old man in the back, as you told me—you see, I remembered! He called me "Boy," but I think maybe he suspects. He knows I'm staying at your cabin.

Anyway, some men and boys came in the front. They were all so *normal*, laughing and kidding. I just couldn't believe, Barney. In fact I started to go out past them when I heard one of them say, "Heinz saw an angel." An *angel*. So I stopped and listened. They said it was big and sparkly. Coming to see if man is carrying out God's Will, one of them said. And he said, Moosenee is now a liberated zone, and all up by Hudson Bay. I turned and got out the back, fast. The old man had heard them, too. He said to me quietly, "I'll miss the kids."

Hudson Bay, Barney, that means it's coming from the north

too, doesn't it? That must be about 60°.

But I have to go back once again, to get some fishhooks. I can't live on bread. Last week I found a deer some poacher had killed, just the head and legs. I made a stew. It was a doe. Her eyes; I wonder if mine look like that now.

⊞

I went to get the fishhooks today. It was bad, I can't ever go back. There were some men in front again, but they were different. Mean and tense. No boys. And there was a new sign out in front, I couldn't see it; maybe it says Liberated Zone, too.

The old man gave me the hooks quick and whispered to me, "Boy, them woods'll be full of hunters next week." I almost ran out.

About a mile down the road a blue pickup started to chase me. I guess he wasn't from around there, I ran the VW into a logging draw and he roared on by. After a long while I drove out and came on back, but I left the car about a mile from here and hiked in. It's surprising how hard it is to pile enough brush to hide a yellow VW.

Barney, I can't stay here. I'm eating perch raw so nobody will see my smoke, but those hunters will be coming through. I'm going to move my sleeping bag out to the swamp by that big rock, I don't think many people go there.

Since my last lines I moved out. It feels safer. Oh, Barney, how did this *happen*?

Fast, that's how. Six months ago I was Dr. Anne Alstein. Now I'm a widow and bereaved mother, dirty and hungry, squatting in a swamp in mortal fear. Funny if I'm the last woman left alive on Earth. I guess the last one around here, anyway. Maybe some are holed up in the Himalayas, or sneaking through the wreck of New York City. How can we last?

We can't.

And I can't survive the winter here, Barney. It gets to 40° below. I'd have to have a fire, they'd see the smoke. Even if I worked my way south, the woods end in a couple hundred miles. I'd be potted like a duck. No. No use. Maybe somebody is trying something somewhere, but it won't reach here in time ... and what do I have to live for?

No. I'll just make a good end, say up on that rock where I can see the stars. After I go back and leave this for you. I'll wait

a few days to see the beautiful color in the trees one last time.
Good-bye, dearest dearest Barney.
I know what I'll scratch for an epitaph.

HERE LIES THE SECOND MEANEST
PRIMATE ON EARTH

I guess nobody will ever read this, unless I get the nerve and energy to take it back to Barney's. Probably I won't. Leave it in a Baggie, I have one here; maybe Barney will come and look. I'm up on the big rock now. The moon is going to rise soon, I'll do it then. Mosquitoes, be patient. You'll have all you want.

The thing I have to write down is that I saw an angel, too. This morning. It was big and sparkly, like the man said; like a Christmas tree without the tree. But I knew it was real because the frogs stopped croaking and two blue jays gave alarm calls. That's important; it was *really there*.

I watched it, sitting under my rock. It didn't move much. It sort of bent over and picked up something, leaves or twigs, I couldn't see. Then it did something with them around its middle, like putting them into an invisible sample pocket.

Let me repeat—it was *there*. Barney, if you're reading this, *there are things here*. And I think they've done whatever it is to us. Made us kill ourselves off.

Why?

Well, it's a nice place, if it wasn't for the people. How do you get rid of people? Bombs, death rays—all very primitive. Leave a big mess. Destroy everything, craters, radioactivity, ruin the place.

This way there's no muss, no fuss. just like what we did to the screwfly. Pinpoint the weak link, wait a bit while we do it for them. Then only a few bones around; make good fertilizer.

Barney dear, good-bye. I saw it. It was there.

But it wasn't an angel.

I think I saw a real estate agent.

AND I AWOKE AND FOUND ME HERE ON THE COLD HILL'S SIDE

HE WAS STANDING absolutely still by a service port, staring out at the belly of the *Orion* docking above us. He had on a gray uniform and his rusty hair was cut short. I took him for a station engineer.

That was bad for me. Newsmen strictly don't belong in the bowels of Big Junction. But in my first twenty hours I hadn't found any place to get a shot of an alien ship.

I turned my holocam to show its big World Media insigne and started my bit about What It Meant to the People Back Home who were paying for it all.

"—it may be routine work to you, sir, but we owe it to them to share—"

His face came around slow and tight, and his gaze passed over me from a peculiar distance.

"The wonders, the drama," he repeated dispassionately. His eyes focused on me. "You consummated fool."

"Could you tell me what races are coming in, sir? If I could even get a view—"

He waved me to the port. Greedily I angled my lenses up at the long blue hull blocking out the starfield. Beyond her I could see the bulge of a black and gold ship.

"That's a Foramen," he said. "There's a freighter from Belye on the other side, you'd call it Arcturus. Not much traffic right now."

"You're the first person who's said two sentences to me since I've been here, sir. What are those colorful little craft?"

"Procya," he shrugged. "They're always around. Like us."

I squashed my face on the vitrite, peering. The walls clanked. Somewhere overhead aliens were off-loading into their private sector of Big Junction. The man glanced at his wrist.

"Are you waiting to go out, sir?"

His grunt could have meant anything.

"Where are you from on Earth?" he asked me in his hard tone.

I started to tell him and suddenly saw that he had forgotten my existence. His eyes were on nowhere, and his head was slowly bowing forward onto the port frame.

"Go home," he said thickly. I caught a strong smell of tallow.

"Hey, sir!" I grabbed his arm; he was in rigid tremor. "Steady, man."

"I'm waiting . . . waiting for my wife. My loving wife." He gave a short ugly laugh. "Where are you from?"

I told him again.

"Go home," he mumbled. "Go home and make babies. While you still can."

One of the early GR casualties, I thought.

"Is that all you know?" His voice rose stridently. "Fools. Dressing in their styles. Gnivo suits, Aoleelee music. Oh, I see your newscasts," he sneered. "Nixi parties. A year's salary for a floater. Gamma radiation? Go home, read history. *Ballpoint pens and bicycles—*"

He started a slow slide downward in the half gee. My only informant. We struggled confusedly; he wouldn't take one of my sobertabs but I finally got him along the service corridor to a bench in an empty loading bay. He fumbled out a little vacuum cartridge. As I was helping him unscrew it, a figure in starched whites put his head in the bay.

"I can be of assistance, yes?" His eyes popped, his face was covered with brindled fur. An alien, a Procya! I started to thank him but the red-haired man cut me off.

"Get lost. Out."

The creature withdrew, its big eyes moist. The man stuck his pinky in the cartridge and then put it up his nose, gasping deep in his diaphragm. He looked toward his wrist.

"What time is it?"

I told him.

"News," he said. "A message for the eager, hopeful human

race. A word about those lovely, lovable aliens we all love so much." He looked at me. "Shocked, aren't you, newsboy?"

I had him figured now. A xenophobe. Aliens plot to take over Earth.

"Ah, Christ, they couldn't care less." He took another deep gasp, shuddered and straightened. "The hell with generalities. What time d'you say it was? All right, I'll tell you how I learned it. The hard way. While we wait for my loving wife. You can bring that little recorder out of your sleeve, too. Play it over to yourself some time . . . when it's too late." He chuckled. His tone had become chatty—an educated voice. "You ever hear of supernormal stimuli?"

"No," I said. "Wait a minute. White sugar?"

"Near enough. Y'know Little Junction Bar in D.C.? No, you're an Aussie, you said. Well, I'm from Burned Barn, Nebraska."

He took a breath, consulting some vast disarray of the soul.

"I accidentally drifted into Little Junction Bar when I was eighteen. No. Correct that. You don't go into Little Junction by accident, any more than you first shoot skag by accident.

"You go into Little Junction because you've been craving it, dreaming about it, feeding on every hint and clue about it, back there in Burned Barn, since before you had hair in your pants. Whether you know it or not. Once you're out of Burned Barn, you can no more help going into Little Junction than a sea-worm can help rising to the moon.

"I had a brand-new liquor I.D. in my pocket. It was early; there was an empty spot beside some humans at the bar. Little Junction isn't an embassy bar, y'know. I found out later where the high-caste aliens go—when they go out. The New Rive, the Curtain by the Georgetown Marina.

"And they go by themselves. Oh, once in a while they do the cultural exchange bit with a few frosty couples of other aliens and some stuffed humans. Galactic Amity with a ten-foot pole.

"Little Junction was the place where the lower orders went, the clerks and drivers out for kicks. Including, my friend, the perverts. The ones who can take humans. Into their beds, that is."

He chuckled and sniffed his finger again, not looking at me.

"Ah, yes. Little Junction is Galactic Amity night, every night. I ordered . . . what? A margarita. I didn't have the nerve to ask the snotty spade bartender for one of the alien liquors behind the bar. It was dim. I was trying to stare everywhere at once without showing it. I remember those white boneheads—Lyrans, that is. And a mess of green veiling I decided was a multiple being from some place. I caught a couple of human glances in the bar mirror. Hostile flicks. I didn't get the message, then.

"Suddenly an alien pushed right in beside me. Before I could get over my paralysis, I heard this blurry voice:

"'You air a futeball enthusiash?'

"An alien had spoken to me. An *alien*, a being from the stars. Had spoken. To me.

"Oh, god, I had no time for football, but I would have claimed a passion for paper-folding, for dumb crambo—anything to keep him talking. I asked him about his home-planet sports, I insisted on buying his drinks. I listened raptly while he spluttered out a play-by-play account of a game I wouldn't have turned a dial for. The 'Grain Bay Pashkers.' Yeah. And I was dimly aware of trouble among the humans on my other side.

"Suddenly this woman—I'd call her a girl now—this girl said something in a high nasty voice and swung her stool into the arm I was holding my drink with. We both turned around together.

"Christ, I can see her now. The first thing that hit me was *discrepancy*. She was a nothing—but terrific. Transfigured. Oozing it, radiating it.

"The next thing was I had a horrifying hard-on just looking at her.

"I scrooched over so my tunic hid it, and my spilled drink trickled down, making everything worse. She pawed vaguely at the spill, muttering.

"I just stared at her trying to figure out what had hit me. An ordinary figure, a soft avidness in the face. Eyes heavy, satiated-looking. She was totally sexualized. I remember her throat pulsed. She had one hand up touching her scarf, which had slipped off her shoulder. I saw angry bruises there. That really tore it, I understood at once those bruises had some sexual meaning.

"She was looking past my head with her face like a radar dish. Then she made an *ahhhh* sound that had nothing to do with me and grabbed my forearm as if it were a railing. One of the men behind her laughed. The woman said, 'Excuse me,' in a ridiculous voice and slipped out behind me. I wheeled around after her, nearly upsetting my football friend, and saw that some Sirians had come in.

"That was my first look at Sirians in the flesh, if that's the word. God knows I'd memorized every news shot, but I wasn't prepared. That tallness, that cruel thinness. That appalling alien arrogance. Ivory-blue, these were. Two males in immaculate metallic gear. Then I saw there was a female with them. An ivory-indigo exquisite with a permanent faint smile on those bone-hard lips.

"The girl who'd left me was ushering them to a table. She reminded me of a goddamn dog that wants you to follow it. Just as the crowd hid them, I saw a man join them too. A big man, expensively dressed, with something wrecked about his face.

"Then the music started and I had to apologize to my furry friend. And the Sellice dancer came out and my personal introduction to hell began."

The red-haired man fell silent for a minute enduring self-pity. Something wrecked about the face, I thought; it fit.

He pulled his face together.

"First I'll give you the only coherent observation of my entire evening. You can see it here at Big Junction, always the same. Outside of the Procya, it's humans with aliens, right? Very seldom aliens with other aliens. Never aliens with humans. It's the humans who want in."

I nodded, but he wasn't talking to me. His voice had a druggy fluency.

"Ah, yes, my Sellice. My first Sellice.

"They aren't really well-built, y'know, under those cloaks. No waist to speak of and short-legged. But they flow when they walk.

"This one flowed out into the spotlight, cloaked to the ground in violet silk. You could only see a fall of black hair and tassels over a narrow face like a vole. She was a mole-gray. They come in all colors. Their fur is like a flexible velvet all over; only the color changes startlingly around their eyes and lips and other places. Erogenous zones? Ah, man, with them it's not zones.

"She began to do what we'd call a dance, but it's no dance, it's their natural movement. Like smiling, say, with us. The music built up, and her arms undulated toward me, letting the cloak fall apart little by little. She was naked under it. The spotlight started to pick up her body markings moving in the slit of the cloak. Her arms floated apart and I saw more and more.

"She was fantastically marked and the markings were writhing. Not like body paint—alive. Smiling, that's a good word for it. As if her whole body was smiling sexually, beckoning, winking, urging, pouting, speaking to me. You've seen a classic Egyptian belly dance? Forget it—a sorry stiff thing compared to what any Sellice can do. This one was ripe, near term.

"Her arms went up and those blazing lemon-colored curves pulsed, waved, everted, contracted, throbbed, evolved unbelievably welcoming, inciting permutations. *Come do it to me, do it, do it here and here and here and now.* You couldn't see the rest of her, only a wicked flash of mouth. Every human male in the room was aching to ram himself into that incredible body. I mean it was *pain.* Even the other aliens were quiet, except one of the Sirians who was chewing out a waiter.

"I was a basket case before she was halfway through. . . . I won't bore you with what happened next; before it was over there were several fights and I got cut. My money ran out on the third night. She was gone next day.

"I didn't have time to find out about the Sellice cycle then, mercifully. That came after I went back to campus and discovered you had to have a degree in solid-state electronics to apply for off-planet work. I was a pre-med but I got that degree. It only took me as far as First Junction then.

"Oh, god, First Junction. I thought I was in heaven—the alien ships coming in and our freighters going out. I saw them all, all but the real exotics, the tankies. You only see a few of those a cycle, even here. And the Yyeire. You've never seen that.

"Go home, boy. Go home to your version of Burned Barn . . .

"The first Yyeir I saw, I dropped everything and started walking after it like a starving hound, just breathing. You've seen the pix of course. Like lost dreams. *Man is in love and loves what vanishes.* . . . It's the scent, you can't guess that. I followed until I ran into a slammed port. I spent half a cycles's credits sending the creature the wine they call stars' tears. . . . Later I found out it was a male. That made no difference at all.

"You can't have sex with them, y'know. No way. They breed by light or something, no one knows exactly. There's a story about a man who got hold of a Yyeir woman and tried. They had him skinned. Stories—"

He was starting to wander.

"What about that girl in the bar, did you see her again?"

He came back from somewhere.

"Oh, yes. I saw her. She'd been making it with the two Sirians, y'know. The males do it in pairs. Said to be the total sexual thing for a woman, if she can stand the damage from those beaks. I wouldn't know. She talked to me a couple of times after they finished with her. No use for men whatever. She drove off the P Street bridge. . . . The man, poor bastard, he was trying to keep that Sirian bitch happy single-handed. Money helps, for a while. I don't know where he ended."

He glanced at his wrist watch again. I saw the pale bare place where a watch had been and told him the time.

"Is that the message you want to give Earth? Never love an alien?"

"Never love an alien—" He shrugged. "Yeah. No. Ah, Jesus, don't you see? Everything going out, nothing coming back. Like the poor damned Polynesians. We're gutting Earth, to begin with. Swapping raw resources for junk. Alien status symbols. Tape decks, Coca-Cola, Mickey Mouse watches."

"Well, there is concern over the balance of trade. Is that your message?"

"The balance of trade." He rolled it sardonically. "Did the Polynesians have a word for it, I wonder? You don't see, do you? All right, why are you here? I mean *you*, personally. How many guys did you climb over—"

He went rigid, hearing footsteps outside. The Procya's hopeful face appeared around the corner. The red-haired man snarled at him and he backed out. I started to protest.

"Ah, the silly reamer loves it. It's the only pleasure we have left. . . . Can't you see, man? That's *us*. That's the way we look to them, to the real ones."

"But—"

"And now we're getting the cheap C-drive, we'll be all over just like the Procya. For the pleasure of serving as freight monkeys and junction crews. Oh, they appreciate our ingenious little service stations, the beautiful star folk. They don't *need* them, y'know. Just an amusing convenience. D'you know what I do here with my two degrees? What I did at First Junction. Tube cleaning. A swab. Sometimes I get to replace a fitting."

I muttered something; the self-pity was getting heavy.

"Bitter? Man, it's a *good* job. Sometimes I get to talk to one of them." His face twisted. "My wife works as a—oh, hell, you wouldn't know. I'd trade—correction, I have traded—everything Earth offered me for just that chance. To see them. To speak to them. Once in a while to touch one. Once in a great while to find one low enough, perverted enough to want to touch me. . ."

His voice trailed off and suddenly came back strong.

"And so will you!" He glared at me. "Go home! Go home and tell them to quit it. Close the ports. Burn every god-lost alien thing before it's too late! That's what the Polynesians didn't do."

"But surely—"

"But surely be damned! Balance of trade—balance of *life*, man. I don't know if our birth rate is going, that's not the point. Our soul is leaking out. We're bleeding to death!"

He took a breath and lowered his tone.

"What I'm trying to tell you, this is a trap. We've hit the supernormal stimulus. Man is exogamous—all our history is one long drive to find and impregnate the stranger. Or get impregnated by him; it works for women too. Anything different-colored, different nose, ass, anything, man *has* to fuck it or die trying. That's a drive, y'know, it's built in. Because it works fine as long as the stranger is human. For millions of years that kept the genes circulating. But now we've met aliens we can't screw, and we're about to die trying. . . . Do you think I can touch my wife?"

"But —"

"Look. Y'know, if you give a bird a fake egg like its own but bigger and brighter-marked, it'll roll its own egg out of the nest and sit on the fake? That's what we're doing."

"We've been talking about sex so far." I was trying to conceal my impatience. "Which is great, but the kind of story I'd hoped—"

"Sex? No, it's deeper." He rubbed his head, trying to clear the drug. "Sex is only part of it—there's more. I've seen Earth missionaries, teachers, sexless people. Teachers—they end cycling waste or pushing floaters, but they're hooked. They stay. I saw one fine-looking old woman, she was servant to a Cu'ushbar kid. A defective—his own people would have let him die. That wretch was swabbing up its vomit as if it was holy water. Man, it's deep . . . some cargo-cult of the soul. We're built to dream outwards. They laugh at us. They don't have it."

There were sounds of movement in the next corridor. The dinner crowd was starting. I had to get rid of him and get there; maybe I could find the Procya.

A side door opened and a figure started towards us. At first I thought it was an alien and then I saw it was a woman wearing an awkward body-shell. She seemed to be limping slightly. Behind her I could glimpse the dinner-bound throng passing the open door.

The man got up as she turned into the bay. They didn't greet each other.

"The station employs only happily wedded couples," he told me with that ugly laugh. "We give each other . . . comfort."

He took one of her hands. She flinched as he drew it over his arm and let him turn her passively, not looking at me. "Forgive me if I don't introduce you. My wife appears fatigued."

I saw that one of her shoulders was grotesquely scarred.

"Tell them," he said, turning to go. "Go home and tell them." Then his head snapped back toward me and he added quietly, "And stay away from the Syrtis desk or I'll kill you."

They went away up the corridor.

I changed tapes hurriedly with one eye on the figures passing that open door. Suddenly among the humans I caught a glimpse of two sleek scarlet shapes. My first real aliens! I snapped the recorder shut and ran to squeeze in behind them.

THE GIRL
WHO WAS
PLUGGED IN

LISTEN, ZOMBIE. BELIEVE me. What I could tell you—you with your silly hands leaking sweat on your growth-stocks portfolio. One-ten lousy hacks of AT&T on twenty-point margin and you think you're Evel Knievel. AT&T? You doubleknit dummy, how I'd love to show you something.

Look, dead daddy, I'd say. See for instance that rotten girl?

In the crowd over there, that one gaping at her gods. One rotten girl in the city of the future (That's what I said.) Watch.

She's jammed among bodies, craning and peering with her soul yearning out of her eyeballs. Love! Oo-ooh, love them! Her gods are coming out of a store called Body East. Three youngbloods, larking along loverly. Dressed like simple street-people but . . . smashing. See their great eyes swivel above their nosefilters, their hands lift shyly, their inhumanly tender lips melt? The crowd moans. Love! This whole boiling megacity, this whole fun future world loves its gods.

You don't believe gods, dad? Wait. Whatever turns you on, there's a god in the future for you, custom-made. Listen to this mob. "I touched his foot! Ow-oow, I TOUCHED Him!"

Even the people in the GTX tower up there love the gods—in their own way and for their own reasons.

The funky girl on the street, she just loves. Grooving on their beautiful lives, their mysterioso problems. No one ever told her about mortals who love a god and end up as a tree or a sighing sound. In a million years it'd never occur to her that her gods might love her back.

She's squashed against the wall now as the godlings come by. They move in a clear space. A holocam bobs above, but its shadow never falls on them. The store display-screens are magically clear of bodies as the gods glance in and a beggar underfoot is suddenly alone. They give him a token. "Aaaaah!" goes the crowd.

Now one of them flashes some wild new kind of timer and they all trot to catch a shuttle, just like people. The shuttle stops for them—more magic. The crowd sighs, closing back. The gods are gone.

(In a room far from—but not unconnected to—the GTX tower a molecular flipflop closes too, and three account tapes spin.)

Our girl is still stuck by the wall while guards and holocam equipment pull away. The adoration's fading from her face. That's good, because now you can see she's the ugly of the world. A tall monument to pituitary dystrophy. No surgeon would touch her. When she smiles, her jaw—it's half purple—almost bites her left eye out. She's also quite young, but who could care?

The crowd is pushing her along now, treating you to glimpses of her jumbled torso, her mismatched legs. At the corner she strains to send one last fond spasm after the godlings' shuttle. Then her face reverts to its usual expression of dim pain and she lurches onto the moving walkway, stumbling into people. The walkway junctions with another. She crosses, trips and collides with the casualty rail. Finally she comes out into a little bare place called a park. The sportshow is working, a basketball game in three-di is going on right overhead. But all she does is squeeze onto a bench and huddle there while a ghostly free-throw goes by her ear.

After that nothing at all happens except a few furtive hand-mouth gestures which don't even interest her bench mates. But you're curious about the city? So ordinary after all, in the FUTURE?

Ah, there's plenty to swing with here—and it's not all that *far* in the future, dad. But pass up the sci-fi stuff for now, like for instance the holovision technology that's put TV and radio in museums. Or the worldwide carrier field bouncing down from satellites, controlling communication and transport systems all over the globe. That was a spin-off from asteroid mining, pass it by. We're watching that girl.

I'll give you just one goodie. Maybe you noticed on the sportshow or the streets? No commercials. No ads.

That's right. NO ADS. An eyeballer for you.

Look around. Not a billboard, sign, slogan, jingle, sky-write, blurb, sublimflash, in this whole fun world. Brand names? Only in those ticky little peep-screens on the stores, and you could hardly call that advertising. How does that finger you?

Think about it. That girl is still sitting there.

She's parked right under the base of the GTX tower, as a matter of fact. Look way up and you can see the sparkles from the bubble on top, up there among the domes of godland. Inside that bubble is a boardroom. Neat bronze shield on the door: Global Transmissions Corporation—not that that means anything.

I happen to know there are six people in that room. Five of them technically male, and the sixth isn't easily thought of as a mother. They are absolutely unremarkable. Those faces were seen once at their nuptials and will show again in their obituaries and impress nobody either time. If you're looking for the secret Big Blue Meanies of the world, forget it. I know. Zen, do I know! Flesh? Power? Glory? You'd horrify them.

What they do like up there is to have things orderly, especially their communications. You could say they've dedicated their lives to that, to freeing the world from garble. Their nightmares are about hemorrhages of information; channels screwed up, plans misimplemented, garble creeping in. Their gigantic wealth only worries them, it keeps opening new vistas of disorder. Luxury? They wear what their tailors put on them, eat what their cooks serve them. See that old boy there—his name is Isham—he's sipping water and frowning as he listens to a databall. The water was prescribed by his medistaff. It tastes awful. The databall also contains a disquieting message about his son, Paul.

But it's time to go back down, far below to our girl. Look! She's toppled over sprawling on the ground.

A tepid commotion ensues among the bystanders. The consensus is she's dead, which she disproves by bubbling a little. And presently she's taken away by one of the superb ambulances of the future, which are a real improvement over ours when one happens to be around.

At the local bellevue the usual things are done by the usual team of clowns aided by a saintly mop-pusher. Our girl revives enough to answer the questionnaire without which you can't die, even in the future. Finally she's cast up, a pumped-out hulk on a cot in the long, dim ward.

Again nothing happens for a while except that her eyes leak a little from the understandable disappointment of finding herself still alive.

But somewhere one GTX computer has been tickling another, and toward midnight something does happen. First comes an attendant who pulls screens around her. Then a man in a business doublet comes daintily down the ward. He motions the attendant to strip off the sheet and go.

The groggy girl-brute heaves up, big hands clutching at bodyparts you'd pay not to see.

"Burke? P. Burke, is that your name?"

"Y-yes." Croak. "Are you . . . policeman?"

"No. They'll be along shortly, I expect. Public suicide's a felony."

". . . I'm sorry."

He has a 'corder in his hand. "No family, right?"

"No."

"You're seventeen. One year city college. What did you study?"

"La—languages."

"H'mm. Say something."

Unintelligible rasp.

He studies her. Seen close, he's not so elegant. Errand-boy type.

"Why did you try to kill yourself?"

She stares at him with dead-rat dignity, hauling up the gray sheet. Give him a point, he doesn't ask twice.

"Tell me, did you see Breath this afternoon?"

Dead as she nearly is, that ghastly love-look wells up. Breath is the three young gods, a loser's cult. Give the man another point, he interprets her expression.

"How would you like to meet them?"

The girl's eyes bug out grotesquely.

"I have a job for someone like you. It's hard work. If you did well you'd be meeting Breath and stars like that all the time."

Is he insane? She's deciding she really did die.

"But it means you never see anybody you know again. Never, *ever*. You will be legally dead. Even the police won't know. Do you want to try?"

It all has to be repeated while her great jaw slowly sets. *Show me the fire I walk through.* Finally P. Burke's prints are in his 'corder, the man holding up the big rancid girl-body without a sign of distaste. It makes you wonder what else he does.

And then—THE MAGIC. Sudden silent trot of litterbearers tucking P. Burke into something quite different from a bellevue stretcher, the oiled slide into the daddy of all luxury ambulances—real flowers in that holder!—and the long jarless rush to nowhere. Nowhere is warm and gleaming and kind with nurses. (Where did you hear that money can't buy genuine kindness?) And clean clouds folding P. Burke into bewildered sleep.

... Sleep which merges into feedings and washings and more sleeps, into drowsy moments of afternoon where midnight should be, and gentle businesslike voices and friendly (but very few) faces, and endless painless hyposprays and peculiar numbnesses. And later comes the steadying rhythm of days and nights, and a quickening which P. Burke doesn't identify as health, but only knows that the fungus place in her armpit is gone. And then she's up and following those few new faces with growing trust, first tottering, then walking strongly, all better now, clumping down the short hall to the tests, tests, tests, and the other things.

And here is our girl, looking—

If possible, worse than before. (You thought this was Cinderella transistorized?)

The disimprovement in her looks comes from the electrode jacks peeping out of her sparse hair, and there are other meldings of flesh and metal. On the other hand, that collar and spinal plate are really an asset; you won't miss seeing that neck.

P. Burke is ready for training in her new job.

The training takes place in her suite and is exactly what you'd call a charm course. How to walk, sit, eat, speak, blow her nose, how to stumble, to urinate, to hiccup—DELICIOUSLY. How to make each nose-blow or shrug delightfully, subtly, different from any ever spooled before. As the man said, it's hard work.

But P. Burke proves apt. Somewhere in that horrible body is a gazelle, a houri, who would have been buried forever without this crazy chance. See the ugly duckling go!

Only it isn't precisely P. Burke who's stepping, laughing, shaking out her shining hair. How could it be? P. Burke is doing it all right, but she's doing it through something. The something is to all appearances a live girl. (You were warned, this is the FUTURE.)

When they first open the big cryocase and show her her new body, she says just one word. Staring, gulping, "How?"

Simple, really. Watch P. Burke in her sack and scuffs stump down the hall beside Joe, the man who supervises the technical part of her training. Joe doesn't mind P. Burke's looks, he hasn't noticed them. To Joe, system matrices are beautiful.

They go into a dim room containing a huge cabinet like a one-man sauna and a console for Joe. The room has a glass wall that's all dark now. And just for your information, the whole shebang is five hundred feet underground near what used to be Carbondale, Pa.

Joe opens the sauna cabinet like a big clamshell standing on end with a lot of funny business inside. Our girl shucks her shift and walks into it bare, totally unembarrassed. *Eager.* She settles in face-forward, butting jacks into sockets. Joe closes it carefully onto her humpback. Clunk. She can't see in there or hear or move. She hates this minute. But how she loves what comes next!

Joe's at his console, and the lights on the other side of the glass wall come up. A room is on the other side, all fluff and kicky bits, a girly bedroom. In the bed is a small mound of silk with a rope of yellow hair hanging out.

The sheet stirs and gets whammed back flat.

Sitting up in the bed is the darlingest girl child you've EVER seen. She quivers—porno for angels. She sticks both her little arms straight up, flips her hair, looks around full of sleepy pazazz. Then she can't resist rubbing her hands down over her minibreasts and belly. Because, you see, it's the god-awful P. Burke who is sitting there hugging her perfect girl-body, looking at you out of delighted eyes.

Then the kitten hops out of bed and crashes flat on the floor.

From the sauna in the dim room comes a strangled noise. P. Burke, trying to rub her wired-up elbow, is suddenly smothered in *two* bodies, electrodes jerking in her flesh. Joe juggles inputs, crooning into his mike. The flurry passes; it's all right.

In the lighted room the elf gets up, casts a cute glare at the glass wall, and goes into a transparent cubicle. A bathroom, what else? She's a live girl, and live girls have to go to the bathroom after a night's sleep even if their brains are in a sauna cabinet in the next room. And P. Burke isn't in that cabinet, she's in the bathroom. Perfectly simple, if you have the glue for that closed training circuit that's letting her run her neural system by remote control.

Now let's get one thing clear. P. Burke does not *feel* her brain is in the sauna room, she feels she's in that sweet little body. When you wash your hands, do you feel the water is running on your brain? Of course not. You feel the water on your hand, although the "feeling" is actually a potential-pattern flickering over the electrochemical jelly between your ears. And it's delivered there via the long circuits from your hands. Just so, P. Burke's brain in the cabinet feels the water on her hands in the bathroom. The fact that the signals have jumped across space on the way in makes no difference at all. If you want the jargon, it's known as eccentric projection or sensory reference and you've done it all your life. Clear?

Time to leave the honeypot to her toilet training—she's made a booboo with the toothbrush, because P. Burke can't get used to what she sees in the mirror—

But wait, you say. Where did that girl-body come from?

P. Burke asks that too, dragging out the words.

"They grow 'em," Joe tells her. He couldn't care less about the flesh department. "PDs. Placental decanters. Modified embryos, see? Fit the control implants in later. Without a Remote Operator it's just a vegetable. Look at the feet—no callus at all." (He knows because they told him.)

"Oh . . . oh, she's incredible. . . ."

"Yeah, a neat job. Want to try walking-talking mode today? You're coming on fast."

And she is. Joe's reports and the reports from the nurse and the doctor and style man go to a bushy man upstairs who is some kind of medical cybertech but mostly a project administrator. His reports in turn go—to the GTX boardroom? Certainly not, did you think this is *a big* thing? His reports just go up. The point is, they're green, very green. P. Burke promises well.

So the bushy man—Dr. Tesla—has procedures to initiate. The little kitten's dossier in the Central Data Bank, for instance. Purely routine. And the phase-in schedule which will put her on the scene. This is simple: a small exposure in an off-network holoshow.

Next he has to line out the event which will fund and target her. That takes budget meetings, clearances, coordinations. The Burke project begins to recruit and grow. And there's the messy business of the name, which always gives Dr. Tesla an acute pain in the bush.

The name comes out weird, when it's suddenly discovered that Burke's "P." stands for "Philadelphia." Philadelphia? The astrologer grooves on it. Joe thinks it would help identification. The semantics girl references *brotherly love, Liberty Bell, main line, low teratogenesis,* blah-blah. Nicknames Philly? Pala? Pooty? Delphi? Is it good, bad? Finally "Delphi" is gingerly declared goodo. ("Burke" is replaced by something nobody remembers.)

Coming along now. We're at the official checkout down in the underground suite, which is as far as the training circuits reach. The bushy Dr. Tesla is there, braced by two budgetary types and a quiet fatherly man whom he handles like hot plasma.

Joe swings the door wide and she steps shyly in.

Their little Delphi, fifteen and flawless.

Tesla introduces her around. She's child-solemn, a beautiful baby to whom something so wonderful has happened you can feel the tingles. She doesn't smile, she . . . brims. That brimming joy is all that shows of P. Burke, the forgotten hulk in the sauna next door. But P. Burke doesn't know she's alive— it's Delphi who lives, every warm inch of her.

One of the budget types lets go a libidinous snuffle and freezes. The fatherly man, whose name is Mr. Cantle, clears his throat.

"Well, young lady, are you ready to go to work?"

"Yes, sir," gravely from the elf.

"We'll see. Has anybody told you what you're going to do for us?"

"No, sir." Joe and Tesla exhale quietly.

"Good." He eyes her, probing for the blind brain in the room next door.

"Do you know what *advertising* is?"

He's talking dirty, hitting to shock. Delphi's *eyes* widen and her little chin goes up. Joe is in ecstasy at the complex expressions P. Burke is getting through. Mr. Cantle waits.

"It's, well, it's when they used to tell people to buy things." She swallows. "It's not allowed."

"That's right." Mr. Cantle leans back, grave. "Advertising as it used to be is against the law. *A display other than the legitimate use of the product, intended to promote its sale.* In former times every manufacturer was free to tout his wares any way, place, or time he could afford. All the media and most of the landscape was taken up with extravagant competing displays. The thing became uneconomic. The public rebelled. Since the so-called Huckster Act sellers have been restrained to, I quote, displays in or on the product itself, visible during its legitimate use or in on-premise sales." Mr. Cantle leans forward. "Now tell me, Delphi, why do people buy one product rather than another?"

"Well . . ." Enchanting puzzlement from Delphi. "They, um, they see them and like them, or they hear about them from somebody?" (Touch of P. Burke there; she didn't say, from a friend.)

"Partly. Why did *you* buy your particular body-lift?"

"I never had a body-lift, sir."

Mr. Cantle frowns; what gutters do they drag for these Remotes?

"Well, what brand of water do you drink?"

"Just what was in the faucet, sir," says Delphi humbly. "I—I did try to boil it—"

"Good god." He scowls; Tesla stiffens. "Well, what did you boil it in? A cooker?"

The shining yellow head nods.

"What *brand* of cooker did you buy?"

"I didn't buy it, sir," says frightened P. Burke through Delphi's lips. "But—I know the best kind! Ananga has a Burnbabi. I saw the name when she—"

"Exactly!" Cantle's fatherly beam comes back strong; the Burnbabi account is a strong one, too. "You saw Ananga using one so you thought it must be good, eh? And it is good, or a great human being like Ananga wouldn't be using it. Absolutely right. And now, Delphi, you know what you're going to be doing for us. You're going to show some products. Doesn't sound very hard, does it?"

"Oh, no, sir . . ." Baffled child's stare; Joe gloats.

"And you must never, *never* tell anyone what you're doing." Cantle's eyes bore for the brain behind this seductive child.

"You're wondering why we ask you to do this, naturally. There's a very serious reason. All those products people use, foods and healthaids and cookers and cleaners and clothes and cars—they're all made by *people*. Somebody put in years of hard work designing and making them. A man comes up with a fine new idea for a better product. He has to get a factory and machinery, and hire workmen. Now. What happens if people have no way of hearing about his product? Word of mouth is far too slow and unreliable. Nobody might ever stumble onto his new product or find out how good it was, right? And then he and all the people who worked for him—they'd go bankrupt, right? So, Delphi, there has to be *some way* that large numbers of people can get a look at a good new product, right? How? By letting people see you using it. You're giving that man a chance."

Delphi's little head is nodding in happy relief.

"Yes, Sir, I do see now—but sir, it seems so sensible, why don't they let you—"

Cantle smiles sadly.

"It's an overreaction, my dear. History goes by swings. People overreact and pass harsh unrealistic laws which attempt to stamp out an essential social process. When this happens, the people who understand have to carry on as best they can until the pendulum swings back." He sighs. "The Huckster Laws are bad, inhuman laws, Delphi, despite their good intent. If they were strictly observed they would wreak havoc. Our economy, our society, would be cruelly destroyed. We'd be back in caves!" His inner fire is showing; if the Huckster Laws were strictly enforced he'd be back punching a databank.

"It's our duty, Delphi. Our solemn social duty. We are not breaking the law. You will be using the product. But people wouldn't understand, if they knew. They would become upset just as you did. So you must be very, very careful not to mention any of this to anybody."

(And somebody will be very, very carefully monitoring Delphi's speech circuits.)

"Now we're all straight, aren't we? Little Delphi here"—he is speaking to the invisible creature next door—"little Delphi is going to live a wonderful, exciting life. She's going to be a girl people watch. And she's going to be using fine products people will be glad to know about and helping the good people who make them. Yours will be a genuine social contribution." He keys up his pitch; the creature in there must be older.

Delphi digests this with ravishing gravity.

"But sir, how do I—?"

"Don't worry about a thing. You'll have people behind you whose job it is to select the most worthy products for you to use. Your job is just to do as they say. They'll show you what outfits to wear to parties, what suncars and viewers to buy, and so on. That's all you have to do."

Parties—clothes—suncars! Delphi's pink mouth opens. In P. Burke's starved seventeen-year-old head the ethics of product sponsorship float far away.

"Now tell me in your own words what your job is, Delphi."

"Yes, Sir. I—I'm to go to parties and buy things and use them as they tell me, to help the people who work in factories."

"And what did I say was so important?"

"Oh—I shouldn't let anybody know, about the things."

"Right." Mr. Cantle has another paragraph he uses when the subject shows, well, immaturity. But he can sense only eagerness here. Good. He doesn't really enjoy the other speech.

"It's a lucky girl who can have all the fun she wants while doing good for others, isn't it?" He beams around. There's a prompt shuffling of chairs. Clearly this one is go.

Joe leads her out, grinning. The poor fool thinks they're admiring her coordination.

It's out into the world for Delphi now, and at this point the up-channels get used. On the administrative side account schedules are opened, subprojects activated. On the technical side the reserved bandwidth is cleared. (That carrier field, remember?) A new name is waiting for Delphi, a name she'll never hear. It's a long string of binaries which have been quietly cycling in a GTX tank ever since a certain Beautiful Person didn't wake up.

The name winks out of cycle, dances from pulses into modulations of modulations, whizzes through phasing, and shoots into a giga-band beam racing up to a synchronous satellite poised over Guatemala. From there the beam pours twenty thousand miles back to Earth again, forming an all-pervasive field of structured energics supplying tuned demand-points all over the CanAm quadrant.

With that field, if you have the right credit rating, you can sit at a GTX console and operate an ore-extractor in Brazil. Or—if you have some simple credentials like being able to walk on water—you could shoot a spool into the network holocam shows running day and night in every home and dorm and rec site. Or you could create a continentwide traffic jam. Is it any wonder GTX guards those inputs like a sacred trust?

Delphi's "name" appears as a tiny analyzable nonredundancy in the flux, and she'd be very proud if she knew about it. It would strike P. Burke as magic; P. Burke never even understood robotcars. But Delphi is in no sense a robot. Call her a waldo if you must. The fact is she's just a girl, a real-live girl with her brain in an unusual place. A simple real-time on-line system with plenty of bit-rate—even as you and you.

The point of all this hardware, which isn't very much hardware in this society, is so Delphi can walk out of that underground suite, a mobile demand-point draining an omnipresent fieldform. And she does—eighty-nine pounds of tender girl flesh and blood with a few metallic components, stepping out into the sunlight to be taken to her new life. A girl, with everything going for her including a meditech escort. Walking lovely, stopping to widen her eyes at the big antennae system overhead.

The mere fact that something called P. Burke is left behind down underground has no bearing at all. P. Burke is totally unselfaware and happy as a clam in its shell. (Her bed has been moved into the waldo cabinet room now.) And P. Burke isn't in the cabinet; P. Burke is climbing out of an airvan in a fabulous Colorado beef preserve, and her name is Delphi. Delphi is looking at live Charolais steers and live cottonwoods and aspens gold against the blue smog and stepping over live grass to be welcomed by the reserve super's wife.

The super's wife is looking forward to a visit from Delphi and her friends, and by a happy coincidence there's a holocam outfit here doing a piece for the nature nuts.

You could write the script yourself now, while Delphi learns a few rules about structural interferences and how to handle the tiny time lag which results from the new forty-thousand-mile parenthesis in her nervous system. That's right—the people with the leased holocam rig naturally find the gold aspen shadows look a lot better on Delphi's flank than they do on a steer. And Delphi's face improves the mountains too, when you can see them. But the nature freaks aren't quite as joyful as you'd expect.

"See you in Barcelona, kitten," the headman says sourly as they pack up.

"Barcelona?" echoes Delphi with that charming little

subliminal lag. She sees where his hand is and steps back. "Cool, it's not her fault," another man says wearily. He knocks back his grizzled hair. "Maybe they'll leave in some of the gut."

Delphi watches them go off to load the spools on the GTX transport for processing. Her hand roves over the breast the man had touched. Back under Carbondale, P. Burke has discovered something new about her Delphi-body.

About the difference between Delphi and her own grim carcass.

She's always known Delphi has almost no sense of taste or smell. They explained about that: only so much bandwidth. You don't have to taste a suncar, do you? And the slight overall dimness of Delphi's sense of touch—she's familiar with that, too. Fabrics that would prickle P. Burke's own hide feel like a cool plastic film to Delphi.

But the blank spots. It took her a while to notice them. Delphi doesn't have much privacy; investments of her size don't. So she's slow about discovering there's certain definite places where her beastly P. Burke body *feels* things that Delphi's dainty flesh does not. H'mm! Channel space again, she thinks—and forgets it in the pure bliss of being Delphi.

You ask how a girl could forget a thing like that? Look. P. Burke is about as far as you can get from the concept *girl*. She's a female, yes—but for her, sex is a four-letter word spelled P-A-I-N. She isn't quite a virgin. You don't want the details; she'd been about twelve and the freak lovers were bombed blind. When they came down, they threw her out with a small hole in her anatomy and a mortal one elsewhere. She dragged off to buy her first and last shot, and she can still hear the clerk's incredulous guffaws.

Do you see why Delphi grins, stretching her delicious little numb body in the sun she faintly feels? Beams, saying, "Please, I'm ready now."

Ready for what? For Barcelona like the sour man said, where his nature-thing is now making it strong in the amateur section of the Festival. A winner! Like he also said, a lot of strip mines and dead fish have been scrubbed, but who cares with Delphi's darling face so visible?

So it's time for Delphi's face and her other delectabilities to show on Barcelona's Playa Nueva. Which means switching her channel to the EurAf synchsat.

They ship her at night so the nanosecond transfer isn't even noticed by that insignificant part of Delphi that lives five hundred feet under Carbondale, so excited the nurse has to make sure she eats. The circuit switches while Delphi "sleeps," that is, while P. Burke is out of the waldo cabinet. The next time she plugs in to open Delphi's eyes it's no different—do you notice which relay boards your phone calls go through?

And now for the event that turns the sugarcube from Colorado into the PRINCESS.

Literally true, he's a prince, or rather an Infante of an old Spanish line that got shined up in the Neomonarchy. He's also eighty-one, with a passion for birds—the kind you see in zoos. Now it suddenly turns out that he isn't poor at all. Quite the reverse; his old sister laughs in their tax lawyer's face and starts restoring the family hacienda while the Infante totters out to court Delphi. And little Delphi begins to live the life of the gods.

What do gods do? Well, everything beautiful. But (remember Mr. Cantle?) the main point is Things. Ever see a god empty-handed? You can't be a god without at least a magic girdle or an eight-legged horse. But in the old days some stone tablets or winged sandals or a chariot drawn by virgins would do a god for life. No more! Gods make it on novelty now. By Delphi's time the hunt for new god-gear is turning the earth and seas inside-out and sending frantic fingers to the stars. And what gods have, mortals desire.

So Delphi starts on a Euromarket shopping spree squired by her old Infante, thereby doing her bit to stave off social collapse.

Social what? Didn't you get it, when Mr. Cantle talked about a world where advertising is banned and fifteen billion consumers are glued to their holocam shows? One capricious self-powered god can wreck you.

Take the nose-filter massacre. Years, the industry sweated years to achieve an almost invisible enzymatic filter. So one day a couple of pop-gods show up wearing nose-filters like *big purple bats*. By the end of the week the world market is screaming for purple bats. Then it switched to bird-heads and skulls, but by the time the industry retooled the crazies had dropped bird-heads and gone to injection globes. Blood!

Multiply that by a million consumer industries, and you can see why it's economic to have a few controllable gods.

Especially with the beautiful hunk of space R & D the Peace Department laid out for and which the taxpayers are only too glad to have taken off their hands by an outfit like GTX, which everybody knows is almost a public trust.

And so you—or rather, GTX—find a creature like P. Burke and give her Delphi. And Delphi helps keep things *orderly*, she does what you tell her to. Why? That's right, Mr. Cantle never finished his speech.

But here come the tests of Delphi's button-nose twinkling in the torrent of news and entertainment. And she's noticed. The feedback shows a flock of viewers turning up the amps when this country baby gets tangled in her new colloidal body-jewels. She registers at a couple of major scenes, too, and when the Infante gives her a suncar, little Delphi trying out suncars is a tiger. There's a solid response in high-credit country. Mr. Cantle is humming his happy tune as he cancels a Benelux subnet option to guest her on a nude cook-show called Wok Venus.

And now for the superposh old-world wedding! The hacienda has Moorish baths and six-foot silver candelabra and real black horses, and the Spanish Vatican blesses them. The final event is a grand gaucho ball with the old prince and his little Infanta on a bowered balcony. She's a spectacular doll of silver lace, wildly launching toy doves at her new friends whirling by below.

The Infante beams, twitches his old nose to the scent of her sweet excitement. His doctor has been very helpful. Surely now, after he has been so patient with the suncars and all the nonsense—

The child looks up at him, saying something incomprehensible about "breath." He makes out that she's complaining about the three singers she had begged for.

"They've changed!" she marvels. "Haven't they changed? They're so dreary. I'm so happy now!"

And Delphi falls fainting against a gothic vargueno.

Her American duenna rushes up, calls help. Delphi's eyes are open, but Delphi isn't there. The duenna pokes among Delphi's hair, slaps her. The old prince grimaces. He has no idea what she is beyond an excellent solution to his tax problems, but he had been a falconer in his youth. There comes to his mind the small pinioned birds which were flung up to stimulate the hawks. He pockets the veined claw to which he had promised certain indulgences and departs to design his new aviary.

And Delphi also departs with her retinue to the Infante's newly discovered yacht. The trouble isn't serious. It's only that five thousand miles away and five hundred feet down P. Burke has been doing it too well.

They've always known she has terrific aptitude. Joe says he never saw a Remote take over so fast. No disorientations, no rejections. The psychomed talks about self-alienation. She's going into Delphi like a salmon to the sea.

She isn't eating or sleeping, they can't keep her out of the body-cabinet to get her blood moving, there are necroses under her grisly sit-down. Crisis!

So Delphi gets a long "sleep" on the yacht and P. Burke gets it pounded through her perforated head that she's endangering Delphi. (Nurse Fleming thinks of that, thus alienating the psychomed.)

They rig a pool down there (Nurse Fleming again) and chase P. Burke back and forth. And she loves it. So naturally when they let her plug in again Delphi loves it too. Every noon beside the yacht's hydrofoils darling Delphi clips along in the blue sea they've warned her not to drink. And every night around the shoulder of the world an ill-shaped thing in a dark burrow beats its way across a sterile pool.

So presently the yacht stands up on its foils and carries Delphi to the program Mr. Cantle has waiting. It's long-range; she's scheduled for at least two decades' product life. Phase One calls for her to connect with a flock of young ultrariches who are romping loose between Brioni and Djakarta where a competitor named PEV could pick them off.

A routine luxgear op, see; no politics, no policy angles, and the main budget items are the title and the yacht, which was idle anyway. The storyline is that Delphi goes to accept some rare birds for her prince—who cares? The *point* is that the Haiti area is no longer radioactive and look!—the gods are there. And so are several new Carib West Happy Isles which can afford GTX rates, in fact two of them are GTX subsids.

But you don't want to get the idea that all these newsworthy people are wired-up robbies, for pity's sake. You don't need many if they're placed right. Delphi asks Joe about that when he comes down to Barranquilla to check her over. (P. Burke's own mouth hasn't said much for a while.)

"Are there many like me?"

"Nobody's like you, buttons. Look, are you still getting Van Allen warble?"

"I mean, like Davy. Is he a Remote?"

(Davy is the lad who is helping her collect the birds. A sincere redhead who needs a little more exposure.)

"Davy? He's one of Matt's boys, some psychojob. They haven't any channel."

"What about the real ones? Djuma van O, or Ali, or Jim Ten?"

"Djuma was born with a pile of GTX basic where her brain should be, she's nothing but a pain. Jimsy does what his astrologer tells him. Look, peanut, where do you get the idea you aren't real? You're the realest. Aren't you having joy?"

"Oh, Joe!" Flinging her little arms around him and his analyzer grids. "Oh, *me gusto mucho, muchísimo!*"

"Hey, hey." He pets her yellow head, folding the analyzer.

Three thousand miles north and five hundred feet down a forgotten hulk in a body-waldo glows.

And is she having joy. To waken out of the nightmare of being P. Burke and find herself a peri, a star-girl? On a yacht in paradise with no more to do than adorn herself and play with toys and attend revels and greet her friends—her, P. Burke, having friends!—and turn the right way for the holocams? Joy!

And it shows. One look at Delphi and the viewers know: DREAMS CAN COME TRUE.

Look at her riding pillion on Davy's sea-bike, carrying an apoplectic macaw in a silver hoop. Oh, *Morton, let's go there this winter!* Or learning the Japanese chinchona from that Kobe group, in a dress that looks like a blowtorch rising from one knee, and which should sell big in Texas. *Morton, is that real fire?* Happy, happy little girl!

And Davy. He's her pet and her baby, and she loves to help him fix his red-gold hair. (P. Burke marveling, running Delphi's fingers through the curls.) Of course Davy is one of Matt's boys—not impotent exactly, but very *very* low drive. (Nobody knows exactly what Matt does with his bitty budget, but the boys are useful and one or two have made names.) He's perfect for Delphi; in fact the psychomed lets her take him to bed, two kittens in a basket. Davy doesn't mind the fact that Delphi "sleeps" like the dead. That's when P. Burke is out of the body-waldo up at Carbondale, attending to her own depressing needs.

A funny thing about that. Most of her sleepy-time Delphi's just a gently ticking lush little vegetable waiting for P. Burke to get back on the controls. But now and again Delphi all by herself smiles a bit or stirs in her "sleep." Once she breathed a sound: "Yes."

Under Carbondale P. Burke knows nothing. She's asleep too, dreaming of Delphi, what else? But if the bushy Dr. Tesla had heard that single syllable, his bush would have turned snow white. Because Delphi is TURNED OFF.

He doesn't. Davy is too dim to notice, and Delphi's staff boss, Hopkins, wasn't monitoring.

And they've all got something else to think about now, because the cold-fire dress sells half a million copies, and not only in Texas. The GTX computers already know it. When they correlate a minor demand for macaws in Alaska the problem comes to human attention: Delphi is something special.

It's a problem, see, because Delphi is targeted on a limited consumer bracket. Now it turns out she has mass-pop potential—those macaws in *Fairbanks,* man!—it's like trying to shoot mice with an ABM. A whole new ball game. Dr. Tesla and the fatherly Mr. Cantle start going around in headquarters circles and buddy-lunching together when they can get away from a seventh-level weasel boy who scares them both.

In the end it's decided to ship Delphi down to the GTX holocam enclave in Chile to try a spot on one of the mainstream shows. (Never mind why an Infanta takes up acting.) The holocam complex occupies a couple of mountains where an observatory once used the clean air. Holocam total-environment shells are very expensive and electronically superstable. Inside them actors can move freely without going off-register, and the whole scene or any selected part will show up in the viewer's home in complete three-di, so real you can look up their noses and much denser than you get from mobile rigs. You can blow a tit ten feet tall when there's no molecular skiffle around.

The enclave looks—well, take everything you know about Hollywood-Burbank and throw it away. What Delphi sees coming down is a neat giant mushroom-farm, domes of all sizes up to monsters for the big games and stuff. It's orderly. The idea that art thrives on creative flamboyance has long been torpedoed by proof that what art needs is computers. Because

this showbiz has something TV and Hollywood never had—
automated inbuilt viewer feedback. Samples, ratings, critics,
polls? Forget it. With that carrier field you can get real-time
response-sensor readouts from every receiver in the world,
served up at your console. That started as a thingie to give the
public more influence on content.

Yes.

Try it, man. You're at the console. Slice to the sex-age-educ-
econ-ethno-cetera audience of your choice and start. You can't
miss. Where the feedback warms up, give 'em more of that.
Warm—warmer—*hot!* You've hit it—the secret itch under
those hides, the dream in those hearts. You don't need to know
its name. With your hand controlling all the input and your
eye reading all the response, you can make them a god. . . and
somebody'll do the same for you.

But Delphi just sees rainbows, when she gets through the
degaussing ports and the field relay and takes her first look at
the insides of those shells. The next thing she sees is a team of
shapers and technicians descending on her, and millisecond
timers everywhere. The tropical leisure is finished. She's in
gigabuck mainstream now, at the funnel maw of the unceasing
hose that's pumping the sight and sound and flesh and blood
and sobs and laughs and dreams of *reality* into the world's
happy head. Little Delphi is going plonk into a zillion homes in
prime time and nothing is left to chance. Work!

And again Delphi proves apt. Of course it's really P. Burke
down under Carbondale who's doing it, but who remembers
that carcass? Certainly not P. Burke, she hasn't spoken
through her own mouth for months. Delphi doesn't even recall
dreaming of her when she wakes up.

As for the show itself, don't bother. It's gone on so long no
living soul could unscramble the plotline. Delphi's trial spot
has something to do with a widow and her dead husband's
brother's amnesia.

The flap comes after Delphi's spots begin to flash out along
the world-hose and the feedback appears. You've guessed it, of
course. Sensational! As you'd say, they IDENTIFY.

The report actually says something like InskinEmp with
a string of percentages, meaning that Delphi not only has it
for anybody with a Y chromosome, but also for women and
everything in between. It's the sweet supernatural jackpot, the
million-to-one.

Remember your Harlow? A sexpot, sure. But why did bitter hausfraus in Gary and Memphis know that the vanilla-ice-cream goddess with the white hair and crazy eyebrows was *their baby girl?* And write loving letters to Jean warning her that their husbands weren't good enough for her? Why? The GTX analysts don't know either, but they know what to do with it when it happens.

(Back in his bird sanctuary the old Infante spots it without benefit of computers and gazes thoughtfully at his bride in widow's weeds. It might, he feels, be well to accelerate the completion of his studies.)

The excitement reaches down to the burrow under Carbondale where P. Burke gets two medical exams in a week and a chronically inflamed electrode is replaced. Nurse Fleming also gets an assistant who doesn't do much nursing but is very interested in access doors and identity tabs.

And in Chile, little Delphi is promoted to a new home up among the stars' residential spreads and a private jitney to carry her to work. For Hopkins there's a new computer terminal and a full-time schedule man. What is the schedule crowded with? Things.

And here begins the trouble. You probably saw that coming too.

"What does she think she is, a goddamn *consumer rep?*" Mr. Cantle's fatherly face in Carbondale contorts.

"The girl's upset," Miss Fleming says stubbornly. "She *believes* that, what you told her about helping people and good new products."

"They are good products," Mr. Cantle snaps automatically, but his anger is under control. He hasn't got where he is by irrelevant reactions.

"She says the plastic gave her a rash and the glo-pills made her dizzy."

"Good god, she shouldn't swallow them," Dr. Tesla puts in agitatedly.

"You told her she'd use them," persists Miss Fleming.

Mr. Cantle is busy figuring how to ease this problem to the feral-faced young man. What, was it a goose that lays golden eggs?

Whatever he says to Level Seven, down in Chile the offending products vanish. And a symbol goes into Delphi's tank matrix, one that means roughly *Balance unit resistance against PR index.*

This means that Delphi's complaints will be endured as long as her Pop Response stays above a certain level. (What happens when it sinks need not concern us.) And to compensate, the price of her exposure-time rises again. She's a regular on the show now and response is still climbing.

See her under the sizzling lasers, in a holocam shell set up as a walkway accident. (The show is guesting an acupuncture school shill.)

"I don't think this new body-lift is safe," Delphi's saying. "It's made a funny blue spot on me—look, Mr. Vere."

She wiggles to show where the mini-gray pak that imparts a delicious sense of weightlessness is attached.

"So don't leave it *on*, Dee. With your meat—watch that deck-spot, it's starting to synch."

"But if I don't wear it it isn't honest. They should insulate it more or something, don't you see?"

The show's beloved old father, who is the casualty, gives a senile snigger.

"I'll tell them," Mr. Vere mutters. "Look now, as you step back bend like this so it just shows, see? And hold two beats."

Obediently Delphi turns, and through the dazzle her eyes connect with a pair of strange dark ones. She squints. A quite young man is lounging alone by the port, apparently waiting to use the chamber.

Delphi's used by now to young men looking at her with many peculiar expressions, but she isn't used to what she gets here. A jolt of something somber and knowing. *Secrets.*

"Eyes! Eyes, Dee!"

She moves through the routine, stealing peeks at the stranger. He stares back. He knows something.

When they let her go she comes shyly to him.

"Living wild, kitten." Cool voice, hot underneath.

"What do you mean?"

"Dumping on the product. You trying to get dead?"

"But it isn't right," she tells him. "They don't know, but I do, I've been wearing it."

His cool is jolted.

"You're out of your head."

"Oh, they'll see I'm right when they check it," she explains. "They're just so busy. When I tell them—"

He is staring down at little flower-face. His mouth opens,

closes. "What are you doing in this sewer anyway? Who are you?"

Bewilderedly she says, "I'm Delphi."

"Holy Zen."

"What's wrong? Who are you, please?"

Her people are moving her out now, nodding at him.

"Sorry we ran over, Mr. Uhunh," the script girl says.

He mutters something, but it's lost as her convoy bustles her toward the flower-decked jitney.

(Hear the click of an invisible ignition-train being armed?)

"Who was he?" Delphi asks her hairman.

The hairman is bending up and down from his knees as he works.

"Paul. Isham. Three," he says and puts a comb in his mouth.

"Who's that? I can't see."

He mumbles around the comb, meaning, "Are you jiving?" Because she has to be, in the middle of the GTX enclave.

Next day there's a darkly smoldering face under a turban-towel when Delphi and the show's paraplegic go to use the carbonated pool.

She looks.

He looks.

And the next day, too.

(Hear the automatic sequencer cutting in? The system couples, the fuels begin to travel.)

Poor old Isham senior. You have to feel sorry for a man who values order: when he begets young, genetic information is still transmitted in the old ape way. One minute it's a happy midget with a rubber duck—look around and here's this huge healthy stranger, opaquely emotional, running with god knows who. Questions are heard where there's nothing to question, and eruptions claiming to be moral outrage. When this is called to Papa's attention—it may take time, in that boardroom—Papa does what he can, but without immortality-juice the problem is worrisome.

And young Paul Isham is a bear. He's bright and articulate and tender-souled and incessantly active, and he and his friends are choking with appallment at the world their fathers made. And it hasn't taken Paul long to discover that *his* father's house has many mansions and even the GTX computers can't relate everything to everything else. He noses out a decaying project which adds up to something like, Sponsoring Marginal Creativity (the free-lance team that "discovered" Delphi was one such grantee). And from there it turns out that an agile lad named Isham can get his hands on a viable packet of GTX holocam facilities.

So here he is with his little band, way down the mushroom-farm mountain, busily spooling a show which has no relation to Delphi's. It's built on bizarre techniques and unsettling distortions pregnant with social protest. An *underground* expression to you.

All this isn't unknown to his father, of course, but so far it has done nothing more than deepen Isham senior's apprehensive frown.

Until Paul connects with Delphi.

And by the time Papa learns this, those invisible hypergolics have exploded, the energy-shells are rushing out. For Paul, you see, is the genuine article. He's serious. He dreams. He even reads—for example, *Green Mansions*—and he wept fiercely when those fiends burned Rima alive.

When he hears that some new GTX pussy is making it big, he sneers and forgets it. He's busy. He never connects the name with this little girl making her idiotic, doomed protest in the holocam chamber. This strangely simple little girl.

And she comes and looks up at him and he sees Rima, lost Rima the enchanted bird girl, and his unwired human heart goes twang.

And Rima turns out to be Delphi.

Do you need a map? The angry puzzlement. The rejection of the dissonance Rima-hustling-for-GTX-My-Father. Garbage, cannot be. The loitering around the pool to confirm the swindle . . . dark eyes hitting on blue wonder, jerky words exchanged in a peculiar stillness. . . the dreadful reorganization of the image into Rima-Delphi *in my Father's tentacles*—

You don't need a map.

Nor for Delphi either, the girl who loved her gods. She's seen their divine flesh close now, heard their unamplified voices call her name. She's played their god-games, worn their garlands. She's even become a goddess herself, though she doesn't believe it. She's not disenchanted, don't think that. She's still full of love. It's just that some crazy kind of *hope* hasn't—

Really you can skip all this, when the loving little girl on the yellow-brick road meets a Man. A real human male burning with angry compassion and grandly concerned with human justice, who reaches for her with real male arms and—boom! She loves him back with all her heart.

A happy trip, see?

Except.

Except that it's really P. Burke five thousand miles away who loves Paul. P. Burke the monster down in a dungeon smelling of electrode paste. A caricature of a woman burning, melting, obsessed with true love. Trying over twenty-double-thousand miles of hard vacuum to reach her beloved through girl-flesh numbed by an invisible film. Feeling his arms around the body he thinks is hers, fighting through shadows to give herself to him. Trying to taste and smell him through beautiful dead nostrils, to love him back with a body that goes dead in the heart of the fire.

Perhaps you get P. Burke's state of mind?

She has phases. The trying, first. And the shame. The SHAME. *I am not what thou lovest.* And the fiercer trying. And the realization that there is no, no way, none. Never. *Never . . .* A bit delayed, isn't it, her understanding that the bargain she made was forever? P. Burke should have noticed those stories about mortals who end up as grasshoppers.

You see the outcome—the funneling of all this agony into one dumb protoplasmic drive to fuse with Delphi. To leave, to close out the beast she is chained to. *To become Delphi.*

Of course it's impossible.

However, her torments have an effect on Paul. Delphi-as-Rima is a potent enough love object, and liberating Delphi's mind requires hours of deeply satisfying instruction in the rottenness of it all. Add in Delphi's body worshiping his flesh, burning in the fire of P. Burke's savage heart—do you wonder Paul is involved?

That's not all.

By now they're spending every spare moment together and some that aren't so spare.

"Mr. Isham, would you mind staying out of this sports sequence? The script calls for Davy here."

(Davy's still around, the exposure did him good.)

"What's the difference?" Paul yawns. "It's just an ad. I'm not blocking that thing."

Shocked silence at his two-letter word. The script girl swallows bravely.

"I'm sorry, sir, our directive is to do the *social sequence* exactly as scripted. We're having to respool the segments we did last week, Mr. Hopkins is very angry with me."

"Who the hell is Hopkins? Where is he?"

"Oh, please, Paul. *Please.*"

Paul unwraps himself, saunters back. The holocam crew nervously check their angles. The GTX boardroom has a foible about having things *pointed* at them and theirs. Cold shivers, when the image of an Isham nearly went onto the world beam beside that Dialadinner.

Worse yet, Paul has no respect for the sacred schedules which are now a full-time job for ferret boy up at headquarters. Paul keeps forgetting to bring her back on time, and poor Hopkins can't cope.

So pretty soon the boardroom data-ball has an urgent personal action-tab for Mr. Isham senior. They do it the gentle way, at first.

"I can't today, Paul."

"Why not?"

"They say I have to, it's *very* important."

He strokes the faint gold down on her narrow back. Under Carbondale, Pa., a blind mole-woman shivers.

"Important. Their importance. Making more gold. Can't you see? To them you're just a thing to get scratch with. *A huckster.* Are you going to let them screw you, Dee? Are you?"

"Oh, Paul—"

He doesn't know it, but he's seeing a weirdie; Remotes aren't hooked up to flow tears.

"Just say no, Dee. No. Integrity. You have to."

"But they say, it's my job—"

"Will you believe I can take care of you, Dee? Baby, baby, you're letting them rip us. You have to choose. Tell them, no."

"Paul . . . I w-will. . . ."

And she does. Brave little Delphi (insane P. Burke). Saying, "No, please, I promised, Paul."

They try some more, still gently.

"Paul, Mr. Hopkins told me the reason they don't want us to be together so much. It's because of who you are, your father."

She thinks his father is like Mr. Cantle, maybe.

"Oh, great. Hopkins. I'll fix him. Listen, I can't think about Hopkins now. Ken came back today, he found out something."

They are lying on the high Andes meadow watching his

friends dive their singing kites.

"Would you believe, on the coast the police have *electrodes in their heads?*"

She stiffens in his arms.

"Yeah, weird. I thought they only used PP on criminals and the army. Don't you see, Dee—something has to be going on. Some movement. Maybe somebody's organizing. How can we find out?" He pounds the ground behind her: "We should make *contact!* If we could only find out."

"The, the news?" she asks distractedly.

"The news." He laughs. "There's nothing in the news except what they want people to know. Half the country could burn up, and nobody would know it if they didn't want. Dee, can't you take what I'm explaining to you? They've got the whole world programmed! Total control of communication. They've got everybody's minds wired in to think what they show them and want what they give them and they give them what they're programmed to want—you can't break in or out of it, you can't get *hold* of it anywhere. I don't think they even have a plan except to keep things going round and round—and god knows what's happening to the people or the Earth or the other planets, maybe. One great big vortex of lies and garbage pouring round and round, getting bigger and bigger, and nothing can ever change. If people don't wake up soon we're through!"

He pounds her stomach softly.

"You have to break out, Dee."

"I'll try, Paul, I will—"

"You're mine. They can't have you."

And he goes to see Hopkins, who is indeed cowed.

But that night up under Carbondale the fatherly Mr. Cantle goes to see P. Burke.

P. Burke? On a cot in a utility robe like a dead camel in a tent, she cannot at first comprehend that he is telling *her* to break it off with Paul. P. Burke has never seen Paul. *Delphi* sees Paul. The fact is, P. Burke can no longer clearly recall that she exists apart from Delphi.

Mr. Cantle can scarcely believe it either, but he tries.

He points out the futility, the potential embarrassment, for Paul. That gets a dim stare from the bulk on the bed. Then he goes into her duty to GTX, her job, isn't she grateful for the opportunity, etcetera. He's very persuasive.

The cobwebby mouth of P. Burke opens and croaks.

"No."

Nothing more seems to be forthcoming.

Mr. Cantle isn't dense, he knows an immovable obstacle when he bumps one. He also knows an irresistible force: GTX. The simple solution is to lock the waldo-cabinet until Paul gets tired of waiting for Delphi to wake up. But the cost, the schedules! And there's something odd here . . . he eyes the corporate asset hulking on the bed and his hunch-sense prickles.

You see, Remotes don't love. They don't have real sex, the circuits designed that out from the start. So it's been assumed that it's *Paul* who is diverting himself or something with the pretty little body in Chile. P. Burke can only be doing what comes natural to any ambitious gutter-meat. It hasn't occurred to anyone that they're dealing with the real hairy thing whose shadow is blasting out of every holoshow on Earth.

Love?

Mr. Cantle frowns. The idea is grotesque. But his instinct for the fuzzy line is strong; he will recommend flexibility. And so, in Chile:

"Darling, I don't have to work tonight! And Friday too—isn't that right, Mr. Hopkins?"

"Oh, great. When does she come up for parole?"

"Mr. Isham, please be reasonable. Our schedule—surely your own production people must be needing you?"

This happens to be true. Paul goes away. Hopkins stares after him, wondering distastefully why an Isham wants to ball a waldo. How sound are those boardroom belly-fears—garble creeps, creeps in! It never occurs to Hopkins that an Isham might not know what Delphi is.

Especially with Davy crying because Paul has kicked him out of Delphi's bed.

Delphi's bed is under a real window.

"Stars," Paul says sleepily. He rolls over, pulling Delphi on top. "Are you aware that this is one of the last places on Earth where people can see the stars? Tibet, too, maybe."

"Paul . . . "

"Go to sleep. I want to see you sleep."

"Paul, I . . . I sleep so *hard,* I mean, it's a joke how hard I am to wake up. Do you mind?"

"Yes."

But finally, fearfully, she must let go. So that five thousand miles north a crazy spent creature can crawl out to gulp concentrates and fall on her cot. But not for long. It's pink dawn when Delphi's eyes open to find Paul's arms around her, his voice saying rude, tender things. He's been kept awake. The nerveless little statue that was her Delphi-body nuzzled him in the night.

Insane hope rises, is fed a couple of nights later when he tells her she called his name in her sleep.

And that day Paul's arms keep her from work and Hopkins's wails go up to headquarters where the weasel-faced lad is working his sharp tailbone off packing Delphi's program. Mr. Cantle defuses that one. But next week it happens again, to a major client. And ferret-face has connections on the technical side.

Now you can see that when you have a field of complexly heterodyned energy modulations tuned to a demand-point like Delphi, there are many problems of standwaves and lashback and skiffle of all sorts which are normally balanced out with ease by the technology of the future. By the same token they can be delicately unbalanced too, in ways that feed back into the waldo operator with striking results.

"Darling—what the hell! What's wrong? DELPHI!"

Helpless shrieks, writhings. Then the Rima-bird is lying wet and limp in his arms, her eyes enormous.

"I . . . I wasn't supposed to . . ." she gasps faintly. "They told me not to. . . ."

"Oh, my god—*Delphi*."

And his hard fingers are digging in her thick yellow hair. Electronically knowledgeable fingers. They freeze.

"You're a *doll!* You're one of those PP implants. They control you. I should have known. Oh, god, I should have known."

"No, Paul," she's sobbing. "No, no, no—"

"Damn them. Damn them, what they've done—you're not *you*—"

He's shaking her, crouching over her in the bed and jerking her back and forth, glaring at the pitiful beauty.

"No!" she pleads (it's not true, that dark bad dream back there). "I'm Delphi!"

"My father. Filth, pigs—damn them, damn them, damn them."

"No, no," she babbles. "They were good to me—" P. Burke underground mouthing, "They were good to me—AAH-

AAAAH!"

Another agony skewers her. Up north the sharp young man wants to make sure this so-tiny interference works. Paul can scarcely hang on to her, he's crying too. "I'll kill them."

His Delphi, a wired-up slave! Spikes in her brain, electronic shackles in his bird's heart. Remember when those savages burned Rima alive?

"I'll *kill* the man that's doing this to you."

He's still saying it afterward, but she doesn't hear. She's sure he hates her now, all she wants is to die. When she finally understands that the fierceness is tenderness, she thinks it's a miracle. *He knows—and he still loves!*

How can she guess that he's got it a little bit wrong?

You can't blame Paul. Give him credit that he's even heard about pleasure-pain implants and snoops, which by their nature aren't mentioned much by those who know them most intimately. That's what he thinks is being used on Delphi, something to *control* her. And to listen—he burns at the unknown ears in their bed.

Of waldo-bodies and objects like P. Burke he has heard nothing.

So it never crosses his mind as he looks down at his violated bird, sick with fury and love, that he isn't holding *all* of her. Do you need to be told the mad resolve jelling in him now?

To free Delphi.

How? Well, he is, after all, Paul Isham III. And he even has an idea where the GTX neurolab is. In Carbondale.

But first things have to be done for Delphi, and for his own stomach. So he gives her back to Hopkins and departs in a restrained and discreet way. And the Chile staff is grateful and do not understand that his teeth don't normally show so much.

And a week passes in which Delphi is a very good, docile little ghost. They let her have the load of wildflowers Paul sends and the bland loving notes. (He's playing it coony.) And up in headquarters weasel boy feels that *his* destiny has clicked a notch onward and floats the word up that he's handy with little problems.

And no one knows what P. Burke thinks in any way whatever, except that Miss Fleming catches her flushing her food down the can and next night she faints in the pool. They haul her out and stick her with IVs. Miss Fleming frets, she's seen expressions like that before. But she wasn't around when crazies who called themselves Followers of the Fish looked through flames to life everlasting. P. Burke is seeing Heaven on the far side of death, too. Heaven is spelled P-a-u-l, but the idea's the same. *I will die and be born again in Delphi.*

Garbage, electronically speaking. No way.

Another week and Paul's madness has become a plan. (Remember, he does have friends.) He smolders, watching his love paraded by her masters. He turns out a scorching sequence for his own show. And finally, politely, he requests from Hopkins a morsel of his bird's free time, which duly arrives.

"I thought you didn't *want* me anymore," she's repeating as they wing over mountain flanks in Paul's suncar. "Now you *know—*"

"Look at me!"

His hand covers her mouth, and he's showing her a lettered card.

DON'T TALK THEY CAN HEAR EVERYTHING WE SAY. I'M TAKING YOU AWAY NOW.

She kisses his hand. He nods urgently, flipping the card.

DON'T BE AFRAID. I CAN STOP THE PAIN IF THEY TRY TO HURT YOU.

With his free hand he shakes out a silvery scrambler-mesh on a power pack. She is dumbfounded.

THIS WILL CUT THE SIGNALS AND PROTECT YOU DARLING.

She's staring at him, her head going vaguely from side to side, No.

"Yes!" He grins triumphantly. "Yes!"

For a moment she wonders. That powered mesh will cut off the field, all right. It will also cut off Delphi. But he is *Paul*. Paul is kissing her, she can only seek him hungrily as he sweeps the suncar through a pass.

Ahead is an old jet ramp with a shiny bullet waiting to go. (Paul also has credits and a Name.) The little GTX patrol courier is built for nothing but speed. Paul and Delphi wedge in behind the pilot's extra fuel tank, and there's no more talking when the torches start to scream.

They're screaming high over Quito before Hopkins starts to worry. He wastes another hour tracking the beeper on Paul's suncar. The suncar is sailing a pattern out to sea. By the time they're sure it's empty and Hopkins gets on the hot flue to headquarters, the fugitives are a sourceless howl above Carib West.

Up at headquarters weasel boy gets the squeal. His first impulse is to repeat his previous play, but then his brain snaps to. This one is too hot. Because, see, although in the long run they can make P. Burke do anything at all except maybe *live*, instant emergencies can be tricky. And—Paul Isham III.

"Can't you order her back?"

They're all in the GTX tower monitor station, Mr. Cantle and ferret-face and Joe and a very neat man who is Mr. Isham senior's personal eyes and ears.

"No, sir," Joe says doggedly. "We can read channels, particularly speech, but we can't interpolate organized pattern. It takes the waldo op to send one-to-one—"

"What are they saying?"

"Nothing at the moment, sir." The console jockey's eyes are closed. "I believe they are, ah, embracing."

"They're not answering," a traffic monitor says. "Still heading zero zero three zero—due north, sir."

"You're certain Kennedy is alerted not to fire on them?" the neat man asks anxiously.

"Yes, sir."

"Can't you just turn her off?" The sharp-faced lad is angry. "Pull that pig out of the controls!"

"If you cut the transmission cold you'll kill the Remote," Joe explains for the third time. "Withdrawal has to be phased right, you have to fade over to the Remote's own autonomics. Heart, breathing, cerebellum, would go blooey. If you pull Burke out you'll probably finish her too. It's a fantastic cybersystem, you don't want to do that."

"The investment." Mr. Cantle shudders.

Weasel boy puts his hand on the console jock's shoulder, it's the contact who arranged the no-no effect for him.

"We can at least give them a warning signal, sir." He licks his lips, gives the neat man his sweet ferret smile. "We know that does no damage."

Joe frowns, Mr. Cantle sighs. The neat man is murmuring into his wrist. He looks up. "I am authorized," he says reverently, "I am authorized to, ah, direct a signal. If this is the only course. But minimal, minimal."

Sharp-face squeezes his man's shoulder.

In the silver bullet shrieking over Charleston Paul feels Delphi arch in his arms. He reaches for the mesh, hot for action. She thrashes, pushing at his hands, her eyes roll. She's afraid of that mesh despite the agony. (And she's right.) Frantically Paul fights her in the cramped space, gets it over her head. As he turns the power up she burrows free under his arm and the spasm fades.

"They're calling you again, Mr. Isham!" the pilot yells.

"Don't answer. Darling, keep this over your head damn it how can I—"

An AX90 barrels over their nose, there's a flash.

"Mr. Isham! Those are Air Force jets!"

"Forget it," Paul shouts back. "They won't fire. Darling, don't be afraid."

Another AX90 rocks them.

"Would you mind pointing your pistol at my head where they can see it, sir?" the pilot howls.

Paul does so. The AX90s take up escort formation around them. The pilot goes back to figuring how he can collect from GTX too, and after Goldsboro AB the escort peels away.

"Holding the same course." Traffic is reporting to the group around the monitor. "Apparently they've taken on enough fuel to bring them to towerport here."

"In that case it's just a question of waiting for them to dock." Mr. Cantle's fatherly manner revives a bit.

"Why can't they cut off that damn freak's life-support," the sharp young man fumes. "It's ridiculous."

"They're working on it," Cantle assures him.

What they're doing, down under Carbondale, is arguing. Miss Fleming's watchdog has summoned the bushy man to the waldo room.

"Miss Fleming, you will obey orders."

"You'll kill her if you try that, sir. I can't believe you meant it, that's why I didn't. We've already fed her enough sedative to affect heart action; if you cut any more oxygen she'll die in there."

The bushy man grimaces. "Get Dr. Quine here fast."

They wait, staring at the cabinet in which a drugged, ugly madwoman fights for consciousness, fights to hold Delphi's eyes open.

High over Richmond the silver pod starts a turn. Delphi is sagged into Paul's arm, her eyes swim up to him.

"Starting down now, baby. It'll be over soon, all you have to do is stay alive, Dee."

". . . stay alive . . ."

The traffic monitor has caught them. "Sir! They've turned off for Carbondale—Control has contact—"

"Let's go."

But the headquarters posse is too late to intercept the courier wailing into Carbondale. And Paul's friends have come through again. The fugitives are out through the freight dock and into the neurolab admin port before the guard gets organized. At the elevator Paul's face plus his handgun get them in.

"I want Doctor—what's his name, Dee? Dee!"

". . . Tesla . . ." She's reeling on her feet.

"Dr. Tesla. Take me down to Tesla, fast."

Intercoms are squalling around them as they whoosh down, Paul's pistol in the guard's back. When the door slides open the bushy man is there.

"I'm Tesla."

"I'm Paul Isham. *Isham*. You're going to take your flaming implants out of this girl—now. Move!"

"What?"

"You heard me. Where's your operating room? Go!"

"But—"

"Move! Do I have to burn somebody?"

Paul waves the weapon at Dr. Quine, who has just appeared.

"No, no," says Tesla hurriedly. "But I can't, you know. It's impossible, there'll be nothing left."

"You screaming well can, right now. You mess up and I'll kill you," says Paul murderously. "Where is it, there? And wipe the feke that's on her circuits now."

He's backing them down the hall, Delphi heavy on his arm.

"Is this the place, baby? Where they did it to you?"

"Yes," she whispers, blinking at a door. "Yes . . ."

Because it is, see. Behind that door is the very suite where she was born.

Paul herds them through it into a gleaming hall. An inner door opens, and a nurse and a gray man rush out. And freeze.

Paul sees there's something special about that inner door. He crowds them past it and pushes it open and looks in.

Inside is a big mean-looking cabinet with its front door panels ajar.

And inside that cabinet is a poisoned carcass to whom something wonderful, unspeakable, is happening. Inside is P. Burke, the real living woman who knows that HE is there, coming closer—Paul whom she had fought to reach through forty thousand miles of ice—PAUL is here!—is yanking at the waldo doors—

The doors tear open and a monster rises up.

"Paul darling!" croaks the voice of love, and the arms of love reach for him.

And he responds.

Wouldn't you, if a gaunt she-golem flab-naked and spouting wires and blood came at you clawing with metal-studded paws—

"Get away!" He knocks wires.

It doesn't much matter which wires. P. Burke has, so to speak, her nervous system hanging out. Imagine somebody jerking a handful of your medulla—

She crashes onto the floor at his feet, flopping and roaring *PAUL-PAUL-PAUL* in rictus.

It's doubtful he recognizes his name or sees her life coming out of her eyes at him. And at the last it doesn't go to him. The eyes find Delphi, fainting by the doorway, and die.

Now of course Delphi is dead, too.

There's a total silence as Paul steps away from the thing by his foot.

"You killed her," Tesla says. "That was her."

"Your control." Paul is furious, the thought of that monster fastened into little Delphi's brain nauseates him. He sees her crumpling and holds out his arms. Not knowing she is dead.

And Delphi comes to him.

One foot before the other, not moving very well—but moving. Her darling face turns up. Paul is distracted by the terrible quiet, and when he looks down he sees only her tender little neck.

"Now you get the implants out," he warns them. Nobody moves.

"But, but she's dead," Miss Fleming whispers wildly.

Paul feels Delphi's life under his hand, they're talking about their monster. He aims his pistol at the gray man.

"You. If we aren't in your surgery when I count three, I'm burning off this man's leg."

"Mr. Isham," Tesla says desperately, "you have just killed the person who animated the body you call Delphi. Delphi herself is dead. If you release your arm you'll see what I say is true."

The tone gets through. Slowly Paul opens his arm, looks down.

"Delphi?"

She totters, sways, stays upright. Her face comes slowly up. "Paul . . ." Tiny voice.

"Your crotty tricks," Paul snarls at them. "Move!"

"Look at her eyes," Dr. Quine croaks.

They look. One of Delphi's pupils fills the iris, her lips writhe weirdly.

"Shock." Paul grabs her to him. "*Fix* her!" He yells at them, aiming at Tesla.

"For god's sake . . . bring it in the lab." Tesla quavers.

"Good-bye-bye," says Delphi clearly. They lurch down the hall, Paul carrying her, and meet a wave of people.

Headquarters has arrived.

Joe takes one look and dives for the waldo room, running into Paul's gun.

"Oh, no, you don't."

Everybody is yelling. The little thing in his arm stirs, says plaintively, "I'm Delphi."

And all through the ensuing jabber and ranting she hangs on, keeping it up, the ghost of P. Burke or whatever whispering crazily, "Paul . . . Paul . . . Please, I'm Delphi . . . Paul?"

"I'm here, darling, I'm here." He's holding her in the nursing bed. Tesla talks, talks, talks unheard.

"Paul . . . don't sleep . . . ." The ghost-voice whispers. Paul is in agony, he will not accept, WILL NOT believe.

Tesla runs down.

And then near midnight Delphi says roughly, "Ag-ag-ag—" and slips onto the floor, making a rough noise like a seal.

Paul screams. There's more of the *ag-ag* business and more gruesome convulsive disintegrations, until by two in the morning Delphi is nothing but a warm little bundle of vegetative functions hitched to some expensive hardware—the same that sustained her before her life began. Joe has finally persuaded Paul to let him at the waldo-cabinet. Paul stays by her long enough to see her face change in a dreadfully alien and coldly convincing way, and then he stumbles out bleakly through the group in Tesla's office.

Behind him Joe is working wet-faced, sweating to reintegrate the fantastic complex of circulation, respiration, endocrines, midbrain homeostases, the patterned flux that was a human being—it's like saving an orchestra abandoned in midair. Joe is also crying a little; he alone had truly loved P. Burke. P. Burke, now a dead pile on a table, was the greatest cybersystem he has ever known, and he never forgets her.

The end, really.

You're curious?

Sure, Delphi lives again. Next year she's back on the yacht getting sympathy for her tragic breakdown. But there's a different chick in Chile, because while Delphi's new operator is competent, you don't get two P. Burkes in a row—for which GTX is duly grateful.

The real belly-bomb of course is Paul. He was *young*, see. Fighting abstract wrong. Now life has clawed into him and he goes through gut rage and grief and grows in human wisdom and resolve. So much so that you won't be surprised, sometime later, to find him—where?

In the GTX boardroom, dummy. Using the advantage of his birth to radicalize the system. You'd call it "boring from within."

That's how he put it, and his friends couldn't agree more. It gives them a warm, confident feeling to know that Paul is up there. Sometimes one of them who's still around runs into him and gets a big hello.

And the sharp-faced lad?

Oh, he matures too. He learns fast, believe it. For instance, he's the first to learn that an obscure GTX research unit is actually getting something with their loopy temporal anomalizer project. True, he doesn't have a physics background, and he's bugged quite a few people. But he doesn't really learn about that until the day he stands where somebody points him during a test run—

—and wakes up lying on a newspaper headlined NIXON UNVEILS PHASE TWO.

Lucky he's a fast learner.

Believe it, zombie. When I say growth, I mean *growth*. Capital appreciation. You can stop sweating. There's a great future there.

THE MAN
WHO WALKED
HOME

TRANSGRESSION! TERROR! AND *he thrust and lost there—*
punched into impossibility, abandoned never to be known how,
the wrong man in the most wrong of all wrong places in that
unimaginable collapse of never-to-be-reimagined mechanism—
he stranded, undone, his lifeline severed, he in that nanosecond
knowing his only tether parting, going away, the longest line
to life withdrawing, winking out, disappearing forever beyond
his grasp—telescoping away from him into the closing vortex
beyond which lay his home, his life, his only possibility of
being; seeing it sucked back into the deepest maw, melting,
leaving him orphaned on what never-to-be-known shore of
total wrongness—of beauty beyond joy, perhaps? Of horror? Of
nothingness? Of profound otherness only, certainly—whatever
it was, that place into which he transgressed, it could not
support his life there, his violent and violating aberrance; and
he, fierce, brave, crazy—clenched into total protest, one body-
fist of utter repudiation of himself there in that place, forsaken
there— what did he do? Rejected, exiled, hungering homeward
more desperate than any lost beast driving for its unreachable
home, his home, his HOME—and no way, no transport, no
vehicle, means, machinery, no force but his intolerable resolve
aimed homeward along that vanishing vector, that last and
only lifeline—he did, what?

He walked.

Home.

Precisely what hashed up in the work of the major industrial lessee of the Bonneville Particle Acceleration Facility in Idaho was never known. Or rather, all those who might have been able to diagnose the original malfunction were themselves obliterated almost at once in the greater catastrophe which followed.

The nature of this second cataclysm was not at first understood either. All that was ever certain was that at 1153.6 of May 2, 1989 Old Style, the Bonneville laboratories and all their personnel were transformed into an intimately disrupted form of matter resembling a high-energy plasma, which became rapidly airborne to the accompaniment of radiating seismic and atmospheric events.

The disturbed area unfortunately included an operational MIRV Watchdog womb.

In the confusion of the next hours the Earth's population was substantially reduced, the biosphere was altered, and the Earth itself was marked with numbers of more conventional craters. For some years thereafter, the survivors were existentially preoccupied and the peculiar dust bowl at Bonneville was left to weather by itself in the changing climatic cycles.

It was not a large crater; just over a kilometer in width and lacking the usual displacement lip. Its surface was covered with a finely divided substance which dried into dust. Before the rains began it was almost perfectly flat. Only in certain lights, had anyone been there to inspect it, a small surface-marking or abraded place could be detected almost exactly at the center.

Two decades after the disaster a party of short brown people appeared from the south, together with a flock of somewhat atypical sheep. The crater at this time appeared as a wide shallow basin in which the grass did not grow well, doubtless from the almost complete lack of soil microorganisms. Neither this nor the surrounding vigorous grass was found to harm the sheep. A few crude hogans went up at the southern edge and a faint path began to be traced across the crater itself, passing by the central bare spot.

One spring morning two children who had been driving sheep cross the crater came screaming back to camp. A monster had burst out of the ground before them, a huge flat animal making dreadful roar. It vanished in a flash and a shaking of the earth, leaving an evil smell. The sheep had run away.

Since this last was visibly true, some elders investigated. Finding no sign of the monster and no place in which it could hide, they settled for beating the children, who settled for making a detour around the monster-spot, and nothing more occurred for a while.

The following spring the episode was repeated. This time an older girl was present, but she could add only that the monster seemed to be rushing flat out along the ground without moving at all. And there was a scraped place in the dirt. Again nothing was found; an evil-ward in a cleft stick was placed at the spot.

When the same thing happened for the third time a year later, the detour was extended and other charm-wands were added. But since no harm seemed to come of it and the brown people had seen far worse, sheep-tending resumed as before. A few more instantaneous apparitions of the monster were noted, each time in the spring.

At the end of the third decade of the new era a tall old man limped down the hills from the south, pushing his pack upon a bicycle wheel. He camped on the far side of the crater, and soon found the monster-site. He attempted to question people about it, but no one understood him, so he traded a knife for some meat. Although he was obviously feeble, something about him dissuaded them from killing him, and this proved wise because he later assisted the women in treating several sick children.

He spent much time around the place of the apparition and was nearby when it made its next appearance. This excited him very much and he did several inexplicable but apparently harmless things, including moving his camp into the crater by the trail. He stayed on for a full year watching the site and was close by for its next manifestation. After this he spent a few days making a charm-stone for the spot and left northward, hobbling as he had come.

More decades passed. The crater eroded, and a rain-gully became an intermittent streamlet across the edge of the basin. The brown people and their sheep were attacked by a band of grizzled men, after which the survivors went away eastward. The winters of what had been Idaho were now frost-free; aspen and eucalyptus sprouted in the moist plain. Still the crater remained treeless, visible as a flat bowl of grass; and the bare place at the center remained. The skies cleared somewhat.

After another three decades a larger band of black people with ox-drawn carts appeared and stayed for a time, but left again when they too saw the thunderclap-monster. A few other vagrants straggled by.

Five decades later a small permanent settlement had grown up on the nearest range of hills, from which men riding on small ponies with dark stripes down their spines herded humped cattle near the crater. A herdsman's hut was built by the streamlet, which in time became the habitation of an olive-skinned, red-haired family. In due course one of this clan again observed the monster-flash, but these people did not depart. The stone the tall man had placed was noted and left undisturbed.

The homestead at the crater's edge grew into a group of three and was joined by others, and the trail across it became a cart road with a log bridge over the stream. At the center of the still faintly discernible crater the cart road made a bend, leaving a grassy place which bore in its center about a square meter of curiously impacted bare earth and a deeply etched sandstone rock.

The apparition of the monster was now known to occur regularly each spring on a certain morning in this place, and the children of the community dared each other to approach the spot. It was referred to in a phrase that could be translated as "the Old Dragon." The Old Dragon's appearance was always the same: a brief violent thunder-burst which began and cut off abruptly, in the midst of which a dragonlike creature was seen apparently in furious motion on the earth, although it never actually moved. Afterward there was a bad smell and the earth smoked. People who saw it from close by spoke of a shivering sensation.

Early in the second century two young men rode into town from the north. Their ponies were shaggier than the local breed, and the equipment they carried included two boxlike objects which the young men set up at the monster-site. They stayed in the area a full year, observing two materializations of the Old Dragon, and they provided much news and maps of roads and trading towns in the cooler regions to the north. They built a windmill which was accepted by the community and offered to build a lighting machine, which was refused. Then they departed with their boxes after unsuccessfully attempting to persuade a local boy to learn to operate one.

In the course of the next decades other travelers stopped by and marveled at the monster, and there was sporadic fighting over the mountains to the south. One of the armed bands made a cattle raid into the crater hamlet. It was repulsed, but the raiders left a spotted sickness which killed many. For all this time the bare place at the crater's center remained, and the monster made his regular appearances, observed or not.

The hill-town grew and changed, and the crater hamlet grew to be a town. Roads widened and linked into networks. There were gray-green conifers in the hills now, spreading down into the plain, and chirruping lizards lived in their branches.

At century's end a shabby band of skin-clad squatters with stunted milk-beasts erupted out of the west and were eventually killed or driven away, but not before the local herds had contracted a vicious parasite. Veterinaries were fetched from the market city up north, but little could be done. The families near the crater left, and for some decades the area was empty. Finally cattle of a new strain reappeared in the plain and the crater hamlet was reoccupied. Still the bare center continued annually to manifest the monster, and he became an accepted phenomenon of the area. On several occasions parties came from the distant Northwest Authority to observe it.

The crater hamlet flourished and grew into the fields where cattle had grazed, and part of the old crater became the town park. A small seasonal tourist industry based on the monster-site developed. The townspeople rented rooms for the appearances, and many more-or-less authentic monster-relics were on display in the local taverns.

Several cults now grew up around the monster. One persistent belief held that it was a devil or damned soul forced to appear on Earth in torment to expiate the catastrophe of three centuries back. Others believed that it, or he, was some kind of messenger whose roar portended either doom or hope according to the believer. One very vocal sect taught that the apparition registered the moral conduct of the townspeople over the past year, and scrutinized the annual apparition for changes which could be interpreted for good or ill. It was considered lucky, or dangerous, to be touched by some of the dust raised by the monster. In every generation at least one small boy would try to hit the monster with a stick, usually acquiring a broken arm and a lifelong tavern tale. Pelting the monster with stones or other objects was a popular sport, and for some years people systematically flung prayers and flowers at it. Once a party tried to net it and were left with strings and vapor. The area itself had long since been fenced off at the center of the park.

Through all this the monster made his violently enigmatic annual appearance, sprawled furiously motionless, unreachably roaring.

Only as the fourth century of the new era went by was it apparent that the monster had been changing slightly. He was now no longer on the earth but had an arm and a leg thrust upward in a kicking or flailing gesture. As the years passed he began to change more quickly until at the end of the century he had risen to a contorted crouching pose, arms outflung as if frozen in gyration. His roar, too, seemed somewhat differently pitched, and the earth after him smoked more and more.

It was then widely felt that the man-monster was about to do something, to make some definitive manifestation, and a series of natural disasters and marvels gave support to a vigorous cult teaching this doctrine. Several religious leaders journeyed to the town to observe the apparitions.

However, the decades passed and the man-monster did nothing more than turn slowly in place, so that he now appeared to be in the act of sliding or staggering while pushing himself backward like a creature blown before a gale. No wind, of course, could be felt, and presently the general climate quieted and nothing came of it all.

Early in the fifth century New Calendar three survey parties from the North Central Authority came through the area and stopped to observe the monster. A permanent recording device was set up at the site, after assurances to the townsfolk that no hardscience was involved. A local boy was trained to operate it; he quit when his girl left him but another volunteered. At this time nearly everyone believed that the apparition was a man, or the ghost of one. The record-machine boy and a few others including the school mechanics teacher referred to him as The Man John. In the next decades the roads were greatly improved; all forms of travel increased, and there was talk of building a canal to what had been the Snake River.

One May morning at the end of Century Five a young couple in a smart green mule-trap came jogging up the highroad from

the Sandreas Rift Range to the southwest. The girl was golden-
skinned and chatted with her young husband in a language
unlike that ever heard by The Man John either at the end or the
beginning of his life. What she said to him has, however, been
heard in every age and tongue.

"Oh, Serli, I'm so glad we're taking this trip now! Next
summer I'll be busy with baby."

To which Serli replied as young husbands often have, and so
they trotted up to the town's inn. Here they left trap and bags
and went in search of her uncle, who was expecting them there.
The morrow was the day of The Man John's annual appearance,
and her Uncle Laban had come from the MacKenzie History
Museum to observe it and to make certain arrangements.

They found him with the town school instructor of
mechanics, who was also the recorder at the monster-site.
Presently Uncle Laban took them all with him to the town
mayor's office to meet with various religious personages. The
mayor was not unaware of tourist values, but he took Uncle
Laban's part in securing the cultists' grudging assent to the
MacKenzie authorities' secular interpretation of the monster,
which was made easier by the fact that the cults disagreed
among themselves. Then, seeing how pretty the niece was, the
mayor took them all home to dinner.

When they returned to the inn for the night it was abrawl
with holidaymakers.

"Whew," said Uncle Laban. "I've talked myself dry, sister's
daughter. What a weight of holy nonsense is that Moksha
female! Serli, my lad, I know you have questions. Let me hand
you this to read, it's the guidebook we're giving them to sell.
Tomorrow I'll answer for it all." And he disappeared into the
crowded tavern.

So Serli and his bride took the pamphlet upstairs to bed with
them, but it was not until the next morning at breakfast that
they found time to read it.

"'All that is known of John Delgano,'" read Serli with his
mouth full, "'comes from two documents left by his brother
Carl Delgano in the archives of the MacKenzie Group in the
early years after the holocaust.' Put some honey on this cake,
Mira my dove. Verbatim transcript follows, this is Carl Delgano
speaking:

"'I'm not an engineer or an astronaut like John, I ran an
electronics repair shop in Salt Lake City. John was only trained

as a spaceman, he never got to space; the slump wiped all
that out. So he tied up with this commercial group who were
leasing part of Bonneville. They wanted a man for some kind
of hard vacuum tests, that's all I knew about it. John and his
wife moved to Bonneville, but we all got together several times
a year, our wives were like sisters. John had two kids, Clara and
Paul.

"'The tests were supposed to be secret, but John told me
confidentially they were trying for an antigravity chamber. I
don't know if it ever worked. That was the year before.

"'Then that winter they came down for Christmas and John
said they had something far out. He was excited. A temporal
displacement, he called it; some kind of time effect. He said
their chief honcho was like a real mad scientist. Big ideas. He
kept adding more angles every time some other project would
quit and leave equipment he could lease. No, I don't know who
the top company was—maybe an insurance conglomerate, they
had all the cash, didn't they? I guess they'd pay to catch a look at
the future, that figures. Anyway, John was go, go, go. Katharine
was scared, that's natural. She pictured him like, you know, H.
G. Wells—walking around in some future world. John told her
it wasn't like that at all. All they'd get would be this flicker, like
a second or two. All kinds of complications.' —Yes, yes, my
greedy piglet, some brew for me too. This is thirsty work!

"So. 'I remember I asked him, what about Earth moving?
I mean, you could come back in a different place, right? He
said they had that all figured. A spatial trajectory. Katharine
was so scared we dropped it. John told her, don't worry. I'll
come home. But he didn't. Not that it makes any difference,
of course, everything was wiped out. Salt Lake too. The only
reason I'm here is that I went up by Calgary to see Mom, April
twenty-ninth. May second it all blew. I didn't find you folks at
MacKenzie until July. I guess I may as well stay. That's all I
know about John, except that he was a solid guy. If that accident
started all this it wasn't his fault.

"'The second document'—in the name of love, little mother,
do I have to read all this? Oh, very well, but you will kiss
me first, madam. Must you look so delicious? 'The second
document. Dated in the year eighteen, New Style, written by
Carl'—see the old handwriting, my plump plump pigeon? Oh,
very well, very well.

"'Written at Bonneville Crater: I have seen my brother John

Delgano. When I knew I had the rad sickness I came down here to look around. Salt Lake's still hot. So I hiked up here by Bonneville. You can see the crater where the labs were, it's grassed over. It's different, not radioactive; my film's okay. There's a bare place in the middle. Some Indios here told me a monster shows up here every year in the spring. I saw it myself a couple of days after I got here, but I was too far away to see much, except I was sure it's a man. In a vacuum suit. There was a lot of noise and dust, took me by surprise. It was all over in a second. I figured it's pretty close to the day, I mean, May second, old.

"'So I hung around a year and he showed up again yesterday. I was on the face side, and I could see his face through the visor. It's John, all right. He's hurt. I saw blood on his mouth and his suit is frayed some. He's lying on the ground. He didn't move while I could see him but the dust boiled up, like a man sliding onto base without moving. His eyes are open like he was looking. I don't understand it anyway, but I know it's John, not a ghost. He was in exactly the same position each time and there's a loud crack like thunder and another sound like a siren, very fast. And an ozone smell, and smoke. I felt a kind of shudder.

"'I know it's John there and I think he's alive. I have to leave here now to take this back while I can still walk. I think somebody should come here and see. Maybe you can help John. Signed, Carl Delgano.

"'These records were kept by the MacKenzie Group, but it was not for several years'—etcetera, first light-print, etcetera, archives, analysts, etcetera—very good! Now it is time to meet your uncle, my edible one, after we go upstairs for just a moment.'"

"No, Serli, I will wait for you downstairs," said Mira prudently.

⌗

When they came into the town park Uncle Laban was directing the installation of a large durite slab in front of the enclosure around The Man John's appearance-spot. The slab was wrapped in a curtain to await the official unveiling. Townspeople and tourists and children thronged the walks, and a Ride-for-God choir was singing in the band shell. The morning was warming up fast. Vendors hawked ices and straw toys of the monster and flowers and good-luck confetti to throw at him. Another religious group stood by in dark robes; they belonged to the Repentance church beyond the park. Their pastor was directing somber glares at the crowd in general and Mira's uncle in particular.

Three official-looking strangers who had been at the inn came up and introduced themselves to Uncle Laban as observers from Alberta Central. They went on into the tent which had been erected over the closure, carrying with them several pieces of equipment which the townsfolk eyed suspiciously.

The mechanics teacher finished organizing a squad of students to protect the slab's curtain, and Mira and Serli and Laban went on into the tent. It was much hotter inside. Benches were set in rings around a railed enclosure about twenty feet in diameter. Inside the railing the earth was bare and scuffed. Several bunches of flowers and blooming poinciana branches leaned against the rail. The only thing inside the rail was a rough sandstone rock with markings etched on it.

Just as they came in, a small girl raced across the open center and was yelled at by everybody. The officials from Alberta were busy at one side of the rail, where the light-print box was mounted.

"Oh, no," muttered Mira's uncle, as one of the officials leaned over to set up a tripod stand inside the rails. He adjusted it, and a huge horsetail of fine feathery filaments blossomed out and eddied through the center of the space.

"Oh, *no*," Laban said again. "Why can't they let it be?"

"They're trying to pick up dust from his suit, is that right?" Serli asked.

"Yes, insane. Did you get time to read?"

"Oh, yes," said Serli.

"Sort of," added Mira.

"Then you know. He's falling. Trying to check his—well, call it velocity. Trying to slow down. He must have slipped or stumbled. We're getting pretty close to when he lost his footing and started to fall. What did it? Did somebody trip him?" Laban looked from Mira to Serli, dead serious now. "How would you like to be the one who made John Delgano fall?"

"Ooh," said Mira in quick sympathy. Then she said, "Oh."

"You mean," asked Serli, "whoever made him fall caused all the, caused—"

"Possible," said Laban.

"Wait a minute." Serli frowned. "He did fall. So somebody had to do it—I mean, he has to trip or whatever. If he doesn't fall the past would all be changed, wouldn't it? No war, no—"

"Possible," Laban repeated. "God knows. All *I* know is that John Delgano and the space around him is the most unstable, improbable, highly charged area ever known on Earth, and I'm damned if I think anybody should go poking sticks in it."

"Oh, come now, Laban!" One of the Alberta men joined them, smiling. "Our dust mop couldn't trip a gnat. It's just vitreous monofilaments."

"Dust from the future," grumbled Laban. "What's it going to tell you? That the future has dust in it?"

"If we could only get a trace from that thing in his hand."

"In his hand?" asked Mira. Serli started leafing hurriedly through the pamphlet.

"We've had a recording analyzer aimed at it," the Albertan lowered his voice, glancing around. "A spectroscope. We know there's something there, or was. Can't get a decent reading. It's severely deteriorated."

"People poking at him, grabbing at him," Laban muttered. "You—"

"TEN MINUTES!" shouted a man with a megaphone. "Take your places, friends and strangers."

The Repentance people were filing in at one side, intoning an ancient incantation, "Mi-seri-cordia, Ora pro nobis!"

The atmosphere suddenly became tense. It was now very dose and hot in the big tent. A boy from the mayor's office wiggled through the crowd, beckoning Laban's party to come and sit in the guest chairs on the second level on the "face" side. In front of them at the rail one of the Repentance ministers was arguing with an Albertan official over his right to occupy the space taken by a recorder, it being his special duty to look into The Man John's eyes.

"Can he really see us?" Mira asked her uncle.

"Blink your eyes," Laban told her. "A new scene every blink, that's what he sees. Phantasmagoria. Blink-blink-blink—for god knows how long."

"Mi-sere-re, pec-cavi," chanted the penitentials. A soprano neighed. "May the red of sin pa-aa-ass from us!"

"They believe his oxygen tab went red because of the state of their souls," Laban chuckled. "Their souls are going to have to stay damned awhile; John Delgano has been on oxygen reserve for five centuries—or rather, he *will be* low for five centuries more. At a half-second per year his time, that's fifteen minutes. We know from the audio trace he's still breathing more or less normally, and the reserve was good for twenty minutes. So they should have their salvation about the year seven hundred, if they last that long."

"FIVE MINUTES! Take your seats, folks. Please sit down so everyone can see. Sit down, folks."

"It says we'll hear his voice through his suit speaker," Serli whispered. "Do you know what he's saying?"

"You get mostly a twenty-cycle howl," Laban whispered back. "The recorders have spliced up something like *ayt*, part of an old word. Take centuries to get enough to translate."

"Is it a message?"

"Who knows? Could be his word for 'date' or 'hate.' 'Too late,' maybe. Anything."

The tent was quieting. A fat child by the railing started to cry and was pulled back onto a lap. There was a subdued mumble of praying. The Holy Joy faction on the far side rustled their flowers.

"Why don't we set our clocks by him?"

"It's changing. He's on sidereal time."

"ONE MINUTE."

In the hush the praying voices rose slightly. From outside a chicken cackled. The bare center space looked absolutely ordinary. Over it the recorder's silvery filaments eddied gently in the breath from a hundred lungs. Another recorder could be heard ticking faintly.

For long seconds nothing happened.

The air developed a tiny hum. At the same moment Mira caught a movement at the railing on her left.

The hum developed a beat and vanished into a peculiar silence and suddenly everything happened at once.

Sound burst on them, raced shockingly up the audible scale. The air cracked as something rolled and tumbled in the space. There was a grinding, wailing roar and—

He was there.

Solid, huge—a huge man in a monster-suit, his head was a dull bronze transparent globe, holding a human face, a dark smear of open mouth. His position was impossible, legs strained forward thrusting himself back, his arms frozen in a whirlwind swing. Although he seemed to be in frantic forward motion nothing moved, only one of his legs buckled or sagged slightly—

—And then he was gone, utterly and completely gone in a thunderclap, leaving only the incredible afterimage in their staring eyes. Air boomed, shuddering; dust rolled out mixed with smoke.

"Oh! Oh, my god," gasped Mira, unheard, clinging to Serli. Voices were crying out, choking. "He saw me, he saw me!" a woman shrieked. A few people dazedly threw their confetti into the empty dust-cloud, most had failed to throw at all. Children began to howl. "He *saw* me!" the woman screamed hysterically. "Red, oh, Lord have mercy!" a deep male voice intoned.

Mira heard Laban swearing furiously and looked again into the space. As the dust settled she could see that the recorder's tripod had tipped over into the center. There was a dusty mound lying against it—flowers. Most of the end of the stand seemed to have disappeared or been melted. Of the filaments nothing could be seen.

"Some damn fool pitched flowers into it. Come on, let's get out."

"Was it under, did it trip him?" asked Mira, squeezed in the crowd.

"It was still red, his oxygen thing," Serli said over her head. "No mercy this trip, eh, Laban?"

"Shsh!" Mira caught the Repentance pastor's dark glance. They jostled through the enclosure gate and were out in the sunlit park, voices exclaiming, chattering loudly in excitement and relief.

"It was terrible," Mira cried softly. "Oh, I never thought it was a real live man. There he is, he's *there*. Why can't we help him? Did we trip him?"

"I don't know, I don't think so," her uncle grunted. They sat down near the new monument, fanning themselves. The curtain was still in place.

"Did we change the past?" Serli laughed, looked lovingly at his little wife. For a moment he wondered why she was wearing such odd earrings; then he remembered he had given them to her at that Indian pueblo they'd passed.

"But it wasn't just those Alberta people," said Mira. She seemed obsessed with the idea. "It was the flowers really." She wiped at her forehead.

"Mechanics or superstition," chuckled Serli. "Which is the culprit, love or science?"

"Shsh." Mira looked about nervously. "The flowers were love, I guess. . . . I feel so strange. It's hot. Oh, thank you." Uncle Laban had succeeded in attracting the attention of the iced-drink vendor.

People were chatting normally now, and the choir struck into a cheerful song. At one side of the park a line of people were waiting to sign their names in the visitors' book. The mayor appeared at the park gate, leading a party up the bougainvillea alley for the unveiling of the monument.

"What did it say on that stone by his foot?" Mira asked. Serli showed her the guidebook picture of Carl's rock with the inscription translated below: WELCOME HOME JOHN.

"I wonder if he can see it."

The mayor was about to begin his speech.

Much later when the crowd had gone away the monument stood alone in the dark, displaying to the moon the inscription in the language of that time and place:

ON THIS SPOT THERE APPEARS ANNUALLY THE FORM OF MAJOR JOHN DELGANO, THE FIRST AND ONLY MAN TO TRAVEL IN TIME.

MAJOR DELGANO WAS SENT INTO THE FUTURE SOME HOURS BEFORE THE HOLOCAUST OF DAY ZERO. ALL KNOWLEDGE OF THE MEANS BY WHICH HE WAS SENT IS LOST, PERHAPS FOREVER. IT IS BELIEVED THAT AN ACCIDENT OCCURRED WHICH SENT HIM MUCH FARTHER THAN WAS INTENDED. SOME ANALYSTS SPECULATE THAT HE MAY HAVE GONE AS FAR AS FIFTY THOUSAND YEARS AHEAD. HAVING REACHED THIS UNKNOWN POINT MAJOR DELGANO APPARENTLY WAS RECALLED, OR ATTEMPTED TO RETURN, ALONG THE COURSE IN SPACE AND TIME THROUGH WHICH HE WAS SENT. HIS TRAJECTORY IS THOUGHT TO START AT THE POINT WHICH OUR SOLAR SYSTEM WILL OCCUPY AT A FUTURE TIME AND IS TANGENT TO THE COMPLEX HELIX WHICH OUR EARTH DESCRIBES AROUND THE SUN.

HE APPEARS ON THIS SPOT IN THE ANNUAL INSTANTS IN WHICH HIS COURSE INTERSECTS OUR PLANET'S ORBIT, AND HE IS APPARENTLY ABLE TO TOUCH THE GROUND IN THOSE INSTANTS. SINCE NO TRACE OF HIS PASSAGE INTO THE FUTURE HAS BEEN MANIFESTED, IT IS BELIEVED THAT HE IS RETURNING BY A DIFFERENT MEANS THAN HE WENT FORWARD. HE IS ALIVE IN

OUR PRESENT. OUR PAST IS HIS FUTURE AND OUR FUTURE IS HIS PAST. THE TIME OF HIS APPEARANCES IS SHIFTING GRADUALLY IN SOLAR TIME TO CONVERGE ON THE MOMENT OF 1153.6, ON MAY 2, 1989 OLD STYLE, OR DAY ZERO.

THE EXPLOSION WHICH ACCOMPANIED HIS RETURN TO HIS OWN TIME AND PLACE MAY HAVE OCCURRED WHEN SOME ELEMENTS OF THE PAST INSTANTS OF HIS COURSE WERE CARRIED WITH HIM INTO THEIR OWN PRIOR EXISTENCE. IT IS CERTAIN THAT THIS EXPLOSION PRECIPITATED THE WORLDWIDE HOLOCAUST WHICH ENDED FOREVER THE AGE OF HARDSCIENCE.

—He was falling, losing control, failing in his fight against the terrible momentum he had gained, fighting with his human legs shaking in the inhuman stiffness of his armor, his soles charred, not gripping well now, not enough traction to break, battling, thrusting as the flashes came, the punishing alternation of light, dark, light, dark, which he had borne so long, the claps of air thickening and thinning against his armor as he skidded through space which was time, desperately braking as the flickers of Earth hammered against his feet—only his feet mattered now, only to slow and stay on course—and the pull, the beacon was getting slacker; as he came near home it was fanning out, hard to stay centered; he was becoming, he supposed, more probable; the wound he had punched in time was healing itself. In the beginning it had been so tight—a single ray of light in a closing tunnel—he had hurled himself after it like an electron flying to the anode, aimed surely along that exquisitely complex single vector of possibility of life, shot and been shot like a squeezed pip into the last chink in that rejecting and rejected nowhere through which he, John Delgano, could conceivably continue to exist, the hole leading to home—had pounded down it across time, across space, pumping with desperate legs as the real Earth of that unreal time came under him, his course as certain as the twisting dash of an animal down its burrow, he a cosmic mouse on an interstellar, intertemporal race for his nest with the wrongness of everything closing round the rightness of that one course, the atoms of his heart, his blood, his every cell crying Home—HOME!—as he drove himself after that fading breath-hole, each step faster, surer, stronger, until he raced with invincible momentum upon the rolling flickers of Earth as a man might race a rolling log in a torrent. Only the stars stayed constant around him from flash to flash, he looking down past his feet at a million strobes

*of Crux, of Triangulum; once at the height of his stride he had risked
a century's glance upward and seen the Bears weirdly strung out from
Polaris—but a Polaris not the Pole Star now, he realized, jerking his
eyes back to his racing feet, thinking, I am walking home to Polaris,
home! to the strobing beat. He had ceased to remember where he
had been, the beings, people or aliens or things, he had glimpsed in
the impossible moment of being where he could not be; had ceased to
see the flashes of worlds around him, each flash different, the jumble
of bodies, shapes, walls, colors, landscapes—some lasting a breath,
some changing pell-mell—the faces, limbs, things poking at him; the
nights he had pounded through, dark or lit by strange lamps, roofed
or unroofed, the days flashing sunlight, gales, dust, snow, interiors
innumerable, strobe after strobe into night again; he was in daylight
now, a hall of some kind; I am getting closer at last, he thought,
the feel is changing—but he had to slow down, to check; and that
stone near his feet, it had stayed there some time now, he wanted to
risk a look but he did not dare, he was so tired, and he was sliding,
was going out of control, fighting to kill the merciless velocity that
would not let him slow down; he was hurt, too, something had hit
him back there, they had done something, he didn't know what,
back somewhere in the kaleidoscope of faces, arms, hooks, beams,
centuries of creatures grabbing at him—and his oxygen was going,
never mind, it would last—it had to last, he was going home, home!
And he had forgotten now the message he had tried to shout, hoping
it could be picked up somehow, the important thing he had repeated;
and the thing he had carried, it was gone now, his camera was gone
too, something had torn it away—but he was coming home! Home!
If only he could kill this momentum, could stay on the failing
course, could slip, scramble, slide, somehow ride this avalanche
down to home, to home—and his throat said Home!—called Kate,
Kate! And his heart shouted, his lungs almost gone now, as his legs
fought, fought and failed, as his feet gripped and skidded and held
and slid, as he pitched, flailed, pushed, strove in the gale of timerush
across space, across time, at the end of the longest path ever: the path
of John Delgano, coming home.*

AND I HAVE COME UPON THIS PLACE BY LOST WAYS

IT WAS so beautiful.

Evan's too-muscular stomach tightened as he came into the Senior Commons and saw them around the great viewport. Forgetting his mountain, forgetting even his ghastly vest, he stared like a layman at the white-clad Scientists in the high evening sanctum of their ship. He still could not believe.

A Star Research Ship, he marveled. A Star Science Mission, and I am on it. Saved from a Technician's mean life, privileged to be a Scientist and search the stars for knowledge—

"What'll it be, Evan?"

Young Dr. Sunny Isham was at the bevbar. Evan mumbled amenities, accepted a glass. Sunny was the other Junior Scientist and in theory Evan's equal. But Sunny's parents were famous Research Chiefs and the tissue of his plain white labcoat came from god knew where across the galaxy.

Evan pulled his own coarse whites across his horrible vest and wandered toward the group around the port. Why had he squandered his dress credit on Aldebaranian brocade when all these Star Scientists came from Aldebtech? Much better to have been simple Evan Dilwyn the general issue Galtech nobody—and an anthrosyke to boot.

To his relief the others ignored his approach. Evan skirted the silence around the lean tower of the Mission Chief and found a niche behind a starched ruff belonging to the Deputy, Dr. Pontreve. Pontreve was murmuring to the Astrophysics Chief. Beyond them was a blonde dazzle—little Cyberdoctor

Ava Ling. The girl was joking with the Sirian colleague. Evan listened to them giggle, wondering why the Sirian's scaly blue snout seemed more at home here than his own broad face. Then he looked out the port and his stomach knotted in a different way.

On the far side of the bay where the ship had landed a vast presence rose into the sunset clouds. The many-shouldered Clivorn, playing with its unending cloud-veils, oblivious of the alien ship at its feet. *An'druinn,* the Mountain of Leaving, the natives called it. Why "leaving," Evan wondered for the hundredth time, his eyes seeking for the thing he thought he had glimpsed. No use, the clouds streamed forward. And the routine survey scans could not—

The Deputy had said something important.

"The ship is always on status go," rumbled the Captain's voice from the bevbar. "What does the Chief say?"

Evan's gasp went unnoticed; their attention was on the Research Chief. For a moment the high Scientist was silent, smoke of his THC cheroot drifting from his ebony nostrils. Evan gazed up at the hooded eyes, willing him to say no. Then the smoke quivered faintly: *Affirmative.*

"Day after next, then." The Captain slapped the bar. They would leave without looking! And no ship would ever survey this sector again.

Evan's mouth opened, but before he could find courage Sunny Isham was smoothly reminding the Deputy of the enzyme his bioscan had found. "Oh, Sunny, may I touch you?" Ava Ling teased. And then a glance from the Chief started everyone moving toward the refectory, leaving Evan alone by the port.

They would process Sunny's enzyme. And they should, Evan told himself firmly. It was the only valid finding the computers had come up with on this planet. Whereas his mountain . . . he turned wistfully to The Clivorn now sinking behind its golden mists across the bay. If once he could see, could go and feel with his hands—

He choked back the Unscientism. *The computer has freed man's brain,* he repeated fiercely. Was he fit to be a Scientist? His neck hot, he wheeled from the port and hurried after his superiors.

Dinner was another magic scene. Evan's mood softened in the glittering ambience, the graceful small talk. The miracle of his being here. He knew what the miracle was: his old uncle at Galcentral fighting for an outworld nephew's chance. And the old man had won. When this ship's anthrosyke fell sick, Evan Dilwyn's name was topmost on the roster. And here he was among Star Scientists, adding his mite to man's noblest work. Where only merit counted, merit and honesty and devotion to the Aims of Research—

Ava Ling's glance jolted him out of his dream. The Captain was relating an anecdote of Evan's predecessor, the anthrosyke Foster.

"—hammering upon the lock with these wretched newt-women hanging all over him," the Captain chuckled. "Seems the mothers thought he was buying the girls as well as their boxes. When he wouldn't take them in they nearly tore him apart. Clothes all torn, covered with mud." His blue eyes flicked Evan. "What a decon job!"

Evan flushed. The Captain was bracing him for the numerous decontaminations he had required for field trips out of seal. Each decon was charged against his personal fund, of course, but it was a nuisance. And bad form. The others never went out of seal, they collected by probes and robots or—very rarely—a trip by sealed bubble-sled. But Evan couldn't seem to get his data on local cultures that way. Natives just wouldn't interact with his waldobot. He must develop the knack before he used up all his fund.

"Oh, they are beautiful!" Ava Ling was gazing at the three light-crystal caskets adorning the trophy wall. These were the "boxes" Foster had taken from the newt people. Evan frowned, trying to recall the passage in Foster's log.

"Soul boxes!" he heard himself blurt. "The boxes they kept their souls in. If they lost them the girls were dead, that's why they fought. But how could—" His voice trailed off.

"No souls in them now," said Dr. Pontreve lightly. "Well, what do we say? Does this wine have a point or does it not?"

When they finally adjourned to the gameroom it was Evan's duty to dim the lights and activate the servobots. He kept his eyes from the ports where The Clivorn brooded in its clouds, and went out to the laughter and flashes spilling from the gameroom. They were at the controls of a child's laser game called Sigma.

"Turning in?" Little Ava Ling panted brightly, momentarily out of the game. Evan caught her excited scent.

"I don't know," he smiled. But she had already turned away.

He stalked on, hating his own primitive olfactory reflexes, and pushed through the portal of the command wing of the Laboratories. Sound cut off as it closed behind him, the corridor gleamed in austere silence. He was among the high-status Labs, the temples of Hardscience. Beside him was the ever-lighted alcove holding the sacred tape of Mission Requirements in its helium seal.

He started down the hall, his nape as always prickling faintly. Into these Laboratories flowed all the data from the sensors, the probes, the sampling robots and bioanalyzers and cyberscans, to be shaped by the Scientists' skills into forms appropriate to the Mission Requirements and fit to be fed finally into the holy of holies, the Main Computer of the ship, which he was now approaching. From here the precious Data beamed automatically back across the galaxy into the Computer of Mankind at Galcentral.

By the entrance to the Master Console a sentry stood, guarding against Unauthorized Use. Evan tensed as he crossed the man's impassive gaze, tried to hold himself more like a Scientist. In his bones he felt himself an impostor here; he belonged back in Technician's gray, drudging out an anonymous life. Did the sentry know it too? With relief he turned into the staff wing and found his own little cubby.

His console was bare. His assistant had dutifully cleaned up his unprofessional mess of tapes and—embarrassing weakness—handwritten notes. Evan tried to feel grateful. It was not Scientific to mull over raw findings, they should be fed at once into the proper program. *The computer has freed man's brain,* he told himself, tugging at a spool rack.

From behind the rack fell a bulging file. That stupid business he had tried of correlating a culture's social rigidity with their interest in new information, as represented by himself and his waldobot. The results had seemed significant, but he had no suitable computer categories into which he could program. An anthrosyke had twenty-six program nouns . . . Sunny Isham had over five hundred for his molecular biology. But that was Hardscience, Evan reminded himself. He began to feed the worthless file into his disposer, idly flicking on his local note-tapes.

"—other mountains are called Oremal, Vosnuish, and so on," he heard himself say. "Only The Clivorn has the honorific *An* or *The.* Its native name *An'druinn* or The Mountain of Leaving may refer to the practice of ritual exile or death by climbing the mountain. But this does not appear to fit the rest of the culture. The Clivorn is not a taboo area. Herdsmen's paths run all over the slopes below the glaciation line. The tribe has a taboo area on the headland around their star-sighting stones and the fish-calling shrine. Moreover, the formal third-person case of the word *Leaving* suggests that it is not the natives who leave but some others who leave or have left. But who could that be? An invading tribe? Not likely; the inland ranges are uninhabited and all travel is by coracle along the coasts. And the terrain beyond *An'druinn* seems imp—"

These were his notes made before he began to search the survey scans of The Clivorn for something to explain its name—a cave or cairn or artifact or even a pass or trail. But the clouds had been too dense until that day when he had thought he'd seen that line. *Seen!* He winced. Did he hope to do Science with his feeble human senses?

"—transistorized tar pits of the galaxy!" said a hoarse voice.

Evan whirled. He was alone with the tape.

"Computer of Mankind!" sneered the voice. Evan realized it was the voice of his predecessor, the anthrosyke Foster, imperfectly erased from the old tape beyond his own notes. As he jumped to wipe it Foster's ghost-voice said loudly, "A planetary turd of redundant data on stellar processes on which no competent mind has looked for five hundred years."

Evan gasped. His hand missed the wiper, succeeded only in turning the volume down.

"Research!" Foster was cackling drunkenly. "Get their hands *dirty?*" A blur of static; Evan found himself crouching over the console. Horrified, he made out the words. "Shamans! Hereditary button-pushing imbeciles!" More blur, and Foster was mumbling something about DNA. "Call that *life?*" he croaked, "the behavior of living beings? . . . In all the galaxy, the most complex, the most difficult . . . our only hope . . ." The voice faded again.

Evan saw the spool was almost finished.

"Scientific utopia!" Foster guffawed. "The perfectly engineered society. No war. We no longer need study ourselves, because we're perfect." A gurgling noise blotted out the words. Foster had been drinking alcohol in his Laboratory, Evan realized. Out of his mind.

"And I'm their court clown." There was a long belch. "Learn a few native words, bring back some trinkets. . . good old Foster. Don't rock the boat." The voice made indistinct groaning noises and then cried dearly, "On your hands and knees! Down on the stones, alone. Simmelweiss. Galois. Dirty work. The hard lonely work of—"

The spool ran out.

Through the whirling in his head Evan heard brisk heel-taps. He stood up as his door opened. It was Deputy Pontreve. "Whatever are you up to, Evan? Did I hear voices?"

"Just my—local notes, sir."

Pontreve cocked his head.

"On that mountain, Evan?" His voice was dry.

Evan nodded. The thought of their leaving flooded back upon him.

"Dr. Pontreve, sir, it seems such a pity not to check it. This area won't be surveyed again."

"But what can we conceivably hope to find? And above all, what has this *mountain* to do with your specialty?"

"Sir, my cultural studies point to something anomalous there. Some—well, I don't exactly know what yet. But I'm sure I got a glimpse—"

"Of the mythical Time Gate, perhaps?" Pontreve's smile faded. "Evan. There is a time in every young Scientist's life which crucially tests his vocation. Is he a Scientist? Or is he merely an *overeducated Technician*? Science must not, will not, betray itself back into phenomenology and impressionistic speculation. . . . You may not know this, Evan," Pontreve went on in a different tone, "but your uncle and I were at PreSci together. He has done a great deal for you. He has faith in you. I would feel it deeply if you failed him."

Evan's heart shrank. Pontreve must have helped his uncle get him here. Appalled, he heard himself saying:

"But Dr. Pontreve, if Uncle has faith in me he'd want me to have faith in myself. Isn't it true that useful discoveries have been made by men who persisted in what seemed to be only a—hunch?"

Pontreve drew back.

"To speak of idle curiosity, which is all you really suffer from, Evan, in the same breath with the inspired intuition, the serendipity of the great Scientists of history? You shock me. I lose sympathy." He eyed Evan, licked his lips. "For your uncle's sake, lad," he said tightly, "I beg of you. Your position is shaky enough now. Do you want to lose everything?"

An acrid odor was in Evan's nostrils. Fear. Pontreve was really frightened. But why?

"Come out of this now, that's an order."

In silence Evan followed the Deputy down the corridors and back into the Commons. No one was in sight except three scared-looking Recreation youngsters waiting outside the gameroom for their nightly duty. As he passed, Evan could hear the grunting of the senior Scientists in final duel.

He slammed on into his quarters, for once leaving the view opaque, and tried to sort the nightmare. Pontreve's pinched face roiled with Foster's drunken heresy in his brain. Such fear. But of what? What if Evan did disgrace himself? Was there something that would be investigated, perhaps found out?

Was it possible that a Scientist could have been *bribed*?

That would account for the fear . . . and the "miracle."

Evan gritted his jaw. If so, Pontreve was a false Scientist! Even his warnings were suspect, Evan thought angrily, twisting on his airbed in vain search of something tangible to combat. The memory of Ava Ling's fragrance raked him. He slapped the port filters and was flooded with cold light.

The planet's twin moons were at zenith. Beneath them the mountain loomed unreal as foam in the perpetual racing mists. The Clivorn was not really a large mountain, perhaps a thousand meters to the old glaciation line, but it rose from sea level alone. Torch-glows winked from the village at its feet. A fish-calling dance in progress.

Suddenly Evan saw that the clouds were parting over The Clivorn's upper crags. As only once before, the turrets above the glacier's mark were coming clear. The last veils blew by.

Evan peered frantically. Nothing . . . No, wait! And there it was, a faintly flickering dead-level line around the whole top. Say two-hundred meters below the crest. What could it be?

The clouds closed back. Had he really seen anything?

Yes!

He leaned his forehead against the port. Pontreve had said, *there comes a time in every Scientist's life* . . . in a million barren planets he might never have another such chance. The knowledge of what he was about to do grew in his guts, and he was scared to death.

Before he could lose courage he flung himself back and

slammed his sleep-inducer to full theta.

Next morning he dressed formally, spent a few minutes with his Terms of Grant codex, and marched into Pontreve's office. The appointment ritual went smoothly.

"Doctor Deputy-Administrator," Evan's throat was dry. "As accredited anthrosyke of this Mission I hereby exercise my prerogative of ordering an all-band full sensor probe of the terrain above five hundred meters indicated by these coordinates."

Pontreve's pursed lips sagged. "An all-band probe? But the cost—"

"I certify that my autonomous funds are adequate," Evan told him. "Since this is our last on-planet day, I would like to have it done soonest, sir, if you would."

In the full daylight bustle of the Labs, before the ranked Technicians, Apprentices, and Mechs, Pontreve could say no more. Evan was within his rights. The older man's face grayed, and he was silent before ordering his aide to produce the authorization forms. When they were placed before Evan he stabbed his finger on the line where Evan must certify that the scan was relevant to his Requirements of Specialization.

Evan set his thumbprint down hard, feeling the eyes of the Tech-staff on him. This would take the last of his fund. But he had seen the Anomaly!

"Sir, you'll be interested to know I've had more evidence since—since our meeting."

Pontreve said nothing. Evan marched back to his lab, conscious of the whispers traveling through the wing. The probe would not take long once the sensor configuration was keyed in. He told his assistant to be ready to receive it and settled to wait.

Endless heartbeats later, his man came back holding the heavily sealed official canister before him in both hands. Evan realized he had never touched an original before; all-band scans were in practice ordered only by the Chief, and then rarely.

He took a deep breath and broke the seals. It would be a long decoding job.

At shiftover he was still sitting, stone-faced at his console. Noonbreak had sounded, the Labs had emptied and filled. A silence grew in the staff wing, broken finally by Pontreve's footsteps down the hall. Evan stood up slowly. Pontreve did not speak.

"Nothing, sir," Evan said into the Deputy's eyes. "I'm . . . sorry."

The eyes narrowed and a pulse twitched Pontreve's lip. He nodded in a preoccupied manner and went away. Evan continued to stand, mechanically reviewing his scan. According to every sensor and probe The Clivorn was an utterly ordinary mountain. It rose up in rounded folds to the glaciation limit and then topped off in strikingly weathered crags. The top was quite bare. There were no caves, no tunnels, no unusual minerals, no emissions, no artifacts nor traces of any sort. At the height where Evan had seen the strange line there was perhaps a faint regularity or tiny shelf, a chance coincidence of wind-eroded layers. The reflection of moonlight on this shelf must have been what he'd seen as a flickering line. Now he was finished as a Scientist.

For an anthrosyke to waste his whole fund on scanning a bare mountain was clear grounds for personality reassessment. At least. Surely he could also be indicted for misuse of ship's resources. And he had defied a Deputy-Administrator.

Evan felt quite calm, but his mind strayed oddly. What would have happened, he wondered, if he had found a genuine Anomaly? A big alien artifact, say; evidence of prior contact by an advanced race. Would it have been believed? Would anyone have looked? He had always believed that Data were Data. But what if the wrong person found them in the wrong, Unscientific way?

Well, he at any rate was no longer a Scientist.

He began to wonder if he was even alive, locked into this sealed ship. He seemed to have left his cubby; he was moving down the corridors leading to the lock.

Something was undoubtedly going to happen to him very soon. Perhaps they would begin by confining him to quarters. His was an unheard-of malfeasance, they might well be looking up precedents.

Meanwhile he was still free to move. To order the Tech-crew to open the personnel lock, to sign him out a bubble-sled.

Almost without willing it, he was out in the air of the planet.

Delphis Gamma Five, the charts called it. To the natives it was simply the World, *Ardhvenne*. He opened the bubble. The air of *Ardhvenne* was fresh. The planet was in fact not far from the set of abscissae Evan knew only as terranormal.

Beneath his sled the sea arm was running in long salty swells lit here and there by racing fingers of sunlight. Where the sun struck the rocks the spray was dazzling white. A flying creature plummeted past him from the low clouds into the swells below, followed by a tree of spray.

He drove on across the bay to the far shore by the village and grounded in a sandy clutter of fishnets. The sled's voder came alive.

"Dr. Dilwyn." It was Pontreve's voice. "You will return immediately."

"Acknowledged," said Evan absently. He got out of the sled and set the autopilot. The sled rose, wheeled over him, and fled away over the water to the gleaming ship.

Evan turned and started up the path toward the village, where he had come on his field trip the week before. He doubted that they would send after him. It would be too costly in time and decontamination.

It felt good to walk on natural earth with the free wind at his back. He hunched his shoulders, straining the formal labcoat. He had always been ashamed of his stocky, powerful body. Not bred to the Scientist life. He drew a lungful of air, turned the corner of a rock outcrop, and came face to face with a native.

The creature was his own height with a wrinkled olive head sticking out of a wool poncho. Its knobby shanks were bare, and one hand held a dub set with a soft-iron spike. Evan knew it for an elderly pseudofemale. She had just climbed out of a trench in which she had been hacking peat for fuel.

"Good day, Aunt," he greeted her.

"Good three-spans-past-high-sun," she corrected him tartly. Temporal exactitude was important here. She clacked her lips and turned to stack her peat sods. Evan went on toward the village. The natives of *Ardhvenne* were one of the usual hominid variants, distinguished by rather unstable sex morphology on a marsupial base.

Peat smoke wrinkled his nose as he came into the village street. It was lined by a double file of dry-rock huts, thatched with straw and set closer together for warmth. Under the summer sun it was bleak enough. In winter it must be desolate.

Signs of last night's ceremonials were visible in the form

of burnt-out resin brooms and native males torpid against the
sunnier walls. A number of empty gourds lay in the puddles.
On the shady side were mounds of dirty wool which raised
small baldheads to stare at him. The local sheep-creatures,
chewing cud. The native wives, Evan remembered, would now
be in the houses feeding the young. There was a desultory
clucking of fowl in the eaves. A young voice rose in song and
fell silent.

Evan moved down the street. The males' eyes followed him
in silence. They were a taciturn race, like many who lived by
rocks and sea.

It came to him that he had no idea at all what he was doing.
He must be in profound shock or fugue. Why had he come
here? In a moment he must turn back and submit himself
to whatever was in store. He thought about that. A trial,
undoubtedly. A long Reassessment mess. Then what? Prison?
No, they would not waste his training. It would be CNPTS,
Compulsory Non-Preferred Technicians Service. He thought
about the discipline, the rituals. The brawling Tech Commons.
The dorms. End of hope. And his uncle heartbroken.

He shivered. He could not grasp the reality.

What would happen if he didn't go back? What if the ship
had to leave tomorrow as programmed? It couldn't be worth
sterilizing this whole area just for him. He would be recorded
as escaped, lost perhaps after a mental breakdown.

He looked around the miserable village. The huts were dark
and reeked inside. Could he live here? Could he teach these
people anything?

Before him was the headman's house.

"Good, uh, four-spans-past-high-sun, Uncle."

The headman clicked noncommittally. He was a huge-
limbed creature, sprawled upon his lounging bench. Beside
him was the young male Parag from whom Evan had obtained
most of his local information.

Evan found a dry stone and sat down. Above the huts
streamed the unceasing mist-veils. The Clivorn was a shadow
in the sky; revealed, hidden, revealed again. A naked infant
wandered out, its mouth sticky with gruel. It came and stared
at Evan, one foot scratching the other leg. No one spoke. These
people were capable of convulsive activity, he knew. But when
there was nothing urgent to be done they simply sat, as they
had sat for centuries. Incurious.

With a start, Evan realized that he was comparing these scraggy hominids to the Scientists at ease in their ship. He must be mad. The ship—the very symbol of man's insatiable search for knowledge! How could he be so insane, just because they had rejected his data—or rather, his nondata? He shook his head to clear the heresy.

"Friend Parag," he said thickly.

Parag's eyes came 'round.

"Next sun-day is the time of going of the sky ship. It is possible that I-alone-without-co-family will remain here."

The chief's eyes came open and swiveled toward him too.

Parag clicked I-hear.

Evan looked up at the misty shoulders of The Clivorn. There was sunlight on one of the nearly vertical meadows cradled in its crags. It was just past *Ardhvenne*'s summer solstice, the days were very long now. In his pocket was the emergency ration from the sled.

Suddenly he knew why he was here. He stood up staring at The Clivorn. *An'druinn*, The Mountain of Leaving.

"An easy homeward path, Uncle." He had inadvertently used the formal farewell. He began to walk out of the village on the main Path. Other trails ran straight up the mountain flank behind the huts; the females used these to herd their flocks. But the main Path ran in long straight graded zigzags. On his previous trips he had gone along it as far as the cairn.

The cairn was nothing but a crumbled double-walled fire hearth, strewn with the remains of gourds and dyed fleeces. The natives did not treat it as a sacred place. It was simply the lower end of the Path of Leaving and a good place to boil dyes.

Beyond the cairn the Path narrowed to eroded gravel, a straight scratch winding over The Clivorn's shoulders to the clouds. The dead and dying were carried up this way, Evan knew, and abandoned when they died or when the bearers had had enough. Sometimes relatives returned to pile stones beside the corpse, and doubtless to retrieve the deceased's clothing. He had already passed a few small heaps of weathered rocks and bones.

Up this Path also were driven those criminals or witches of whom the tribe wished to be rid. None ever returned, Parag told him. Perhaps they made it to another village. More likely, they died in the mountains. The nearest settlement was ninety kilometers along the rugged coast.

He topped the first long grade over the lowest ridge, walking easily with the wind at his back. The gravel was almost dry at this season, though The Clivorn was alive with springs. Alongside ran a soppy sponge of peat moss and heather in which Evan could make out bones every few paces now.

When the Path turned back into the wind he found that the thin mists had already hidden the village below. A birdlike creature soared over him, keening and showing its hooked beak. One of the tenders of The Clivorn's dead. He watched it ride off on the gale, wondering if he were a puzzle to its small brain.

When he looked down, there were three olive figures ahead of him on the Path. The native Parag with two other males. They must have climbed the sheep-trails to meet him here. Now they waited stolidly as he plodded up.

Evan groped through the friends-met-on-a-journey greeting.

Parag responded. The other two merely clicked and stood waiting, blocking the Path. What did they want? Perhaps they had come after a strayed animal.

"An easy home-going," Evan offered in farewell. When they did not stir he started uphill around them. Parag confronted him.

"You go on the Path."

"I go on the Path," Evan confirmed. "I will return at sun-end."

"No," said Parag. "You go on the Path of Leaving."

"I will return," insisted Evan. "At sun-end we will have friendly speech."

"No." Parag's hand shot out and gripped Evan's jacket. He yanked.

Evan jumped back. The others surged forward. One of them was pointing at Evan's shoes. "Not needful."

Evan understood now. Those who went on this Path took nothing. They assumed he was going to his death, and they had come for his clothing.

"No!" he protested. "I will return! I go not to Leaving!" Scowls of olive anger closed in. Evan realized how very poor they were. He was stealing valuable garments, a hostile act. "I go to village now! I will return with you!"

But it was too late. They were pawing at him, jerking the strange fastenings with scarred olive claws. Dirty hair-smell in his nose. Evan pushed at them, and half his jacket ripped loose. He began running straight up the hillside. They started after him. To his surprise he saw that his civilized body was stronger and more agile than theirs. He was leaving them behind as he lunged up from sheep-track to track.

At the ridge he risked a look back and shouted. "Friends! I will return!" One of them was brandishing a sheep-goad.

He whirled and pounded on up the ridge. Next moment he felt a hard blow in his side and went reeling. The sheep-goad clattered by his legs. His side—they had speared him! He gulped air on a skewer of pain and made himself run on. Up. No track here but a smooth marsh tipped, skyward. He ran stumbling on the tussocks, on and up. Mist-wraiths flew by.

At a rock cornice he looked back. Below him three misty figures were turning away. Not following, up The Clivorn.

His breathing steadied. The pain in his side was localized now. He wedged his torn sleeve between arm and ribs and began to climb again. He was on the great sinew that was The Clivorn's lowest shoulder. As he climbed he found he was not quite alone in the streaming wraith-world; now and then a sheep bounded up with an absurd *kek-kek-kek* and froze to stare at him down its pointed nose.

He was, he realized, a dead man as far as the village was concerned. A dead man to the ship, a dead man here. Could he make the next village, wounded as he was? Without compass, without tools? And the pocket with his ration had been torn away. His best hope was to catch one of the sheep-creatures. That was not easily done by a single man. He would have to devise some sort of trap.

Curiously uncaring of his own despair, he climbed on. The first palisades were behind him now. Before him was a steep meadow moist with springs of clear peat water, sprigged with small flowers. Great boulders stood, or rather hung here, tumbled by the vanished batteries of ice. In the milky dazzle their cold black shadows were more solid than they. The sun was coming with the wind, lighting the underside of the cloud-wrack above him.

He clambered leaning sideways against the wind, his free hand clutching at wet rocks, tufts of fern. His heart was going too fast. Even when he rested, it did not slow but hammered in his chest. The wound must be deeper than he'd thought. It was burning now, and it hurt increasingly to lift his feet. Presently he found that he had made no progress at all but marched in place drunkenly for a dozen steps.

He ground his teeth, gasping through them. The task was to focus on a certain rock ahead—not too far—and push himself up into the sky. One rock at a time. Rest. Pick another, push on. Rest. Push on. Finally he had to stop between rocks. Breath was a searing ache. He wiped at the slaver on his jaw.

Make ten steps, then. Stop. Ten steps. Stop. Ten steps . . .

A vague track came underfoot. Not a sheep-track, he was above the sheep. Only the huge creatures of the clouds ranged here. The track helped, but he fell often to his knees. On ten steps. Fall. Struggle up. Ten steps. On your knees in the stones, someone had said. There was no more sunlight.

He did not at first understand why he was facing rocky walls. He looked up, stupid with pain, and saw he was against the high, the dreadful, cliffs. Somewhere above him was The Clivorn's head. It was nearly dark.

He sobbed, leaning on the stone flanks. When his body quieted, he heard water and staggered to it among the rocks. A spouting streamlet, very cold, acid-clear. The Water of Leaving. His teeth rattled.

While he was drinking, a drumming sound started up in the cliff beside him and a big round body caromed out, smelling of fat and fur. A giant rock-coney. He drank again, shivering violently, and pulled himself to the crevice out of which the creature had come. Inside was a dry heathery nest. With enormous effort he got himself inside and into the coney's form. It was safe here, surely. Safe as death. Almost at once he was unconscious.

⌘

Pain woke him in the night. Above the pain he watched the stars racing the mists. The moons rose, and cloud-shadows walked on the silver wrinkled sea below him. The Clivorn hung over him, held him fast. He was of The Clivorn now, living its life, seeing through its eyes.

Over the ridgeline, a hazy transcience. Moon-glints on a forest of antlers. The beasts of Clivorn were drifting in the night. Clouds streamed in, and they were gone. The wind moaned unceasing, wreathing the flying scud.

Moonlight faded to rose-whiteness. Cries of birds. Outside his den a musky thing lapped at the stream, chittered and fled. He moved. He was all pain now, he could not lie still. He crawled out into the pale rose dawn hoping for warmth, and drank again at Clivorn's water, leaning on the rock.

Slowly, with mindless caution he looked around. Above the thrumming of the wind he heard a wail. It rose louder.

An opening came in the loud stream below. He saw the headland beyond the bay. On it was a blinding rose-gold splinter. The ship. Thin vapor was forming at its feet.

While he watched, it began to slide gently upward, faster and faster. He made a sound as if to call out, but it was no use. Clouds came between. When they opened again the headland was empty. The wailing died, leaving only the winds of Clivorn. They had left him.

Cold came round his heart. He was utterly lost now. A dead man. Free as death.

His head seemed light and he felt a strange frail energy. Up on his right there seemed to be a ledge leading onto a slanting shield of rock. Could he conceivably go on? The thought that he should do something about killing a sheep troubled him briefly, died. He found he was moving upward. It was like his dreams of being able to soar. Up—easily—so long as he struck nothing, breathed without letting go of the thing in his side. The wind blew straight up here, helping him.

He had reached the slanting shield and was actually climbing now. Hand up and grasp, pull, foot up, push. A few steps sidling along a cleft. The Clivorn's gray lichened face was close to his. He patted it foolishly, caught himself from walking into space. Hand up, grasp. Pull. Foot up. How had he come so high? Handhold. Left hand would not grip hard. He forced it, felt warm wet start down his side. Pull.

The rocks had changed now. No longer smooth but wildly crystalloid. He had cut his cheek. Igneous extrusion weathered into fantastic shelves.

"I am above the great glaciation," he muttered to the carved chimney that rose beside him, resonating in the gale. Everything seemed acutely clear. His hand was caught overhead.

He frowned up at it, furious. Nothing there. He wrenched. Something. He was perched, he saw, on a small snug knob. Wind was a steady shrieking. Silver-gold floodlights wheeled across him; the sun was high now, somewhere above the cloud. One hand was still stuck in something above his head. Odd.

He strained at it, hauling himself upright.

As he rose, his head and shoulders jolted ringingly. Then it was gone and he was spread-eagled, hanging on The Clivorn, fighting agony. When it ebbed he saw that there was nothing there. What was it? What had happened?

He tried to think, decided painfully that it had been an hallucination. Then he saw that the rock beside his face was sterile. Lichenless. And curiously smooth, much less wind-eroded.

Something must have been shielding it slightly for a very long time. Something which had resisted him and then snapped away.

An energy barrier.

Bewildered, he turned his head into the wind-howl, peered along the cliffs. To either side of him a band of unweathered rock about a meter broad stretched away level around The Clivorn's crags. It was overhung in places by the rocks above. Invisible from a flyer, really.

This must be the faint shelf-line he had found on the scans. The effect of long shielding by an energy barrier. But why hadn't the detectors registered this energy? He puzzled, finally saw that the barrier could not be constant. It must only spring into existence when something came near, triggered it. And it had yielded when he pushed hard. Was it set to allow passage to larger animals which could climb these rocks?

He studied the surfaces. How long? How long had it been here, intermittently protecting this band of rock? Millennia of weathering, above and below. It was above the ice line. Placed when the ice was here? By whom?

This sourceless, passive energy was beyond all human technology and beyond that of the few advanced aliens that man had so far encountered.

There rose within him a tide of infinite joy, carrying on it like a cork his rational conviction that he was delirious. He began to climb again. Up. Up. The barrier was fifty meters below him now. He dislodged a stone, looked under his arm to see it fall. He thought he detected a tiny flash, but he could not see whether it had been deflected or not. Birds or falling stones would make such sparkles. That could have been the flickering he had glimpsed.

He climbed. Wetness ran down his side, made red ropes. The pain rode him, he carried it strongly up. Handhold. Wrench. Toehold. Push. Rest. Handhold. "I am pain's horse," he said aloud.

He had been in dense cloud for some time now, the wind-thrum loud in the rock against his body. But something was going wrong with his body and legs. They dragged, would not lift clear. After a bit he saw what it was. The rock face had leveled. He was crawling rather than climbing.

Was it possible he had reached The Clivorn's brow?

He rose to his knees, frightened in the whirling mists. Beside him was a smear of red. My blood with Clivorn's, he thought. On my knees in the stones. My hands are dirty. Sick hatred of The Clivorn washed through him, hatred of the slave for the iron, the stone that outwears his flesh. The hard lonely job. . . Who was Simmelweiss? "Clivorn, I hate you," he mumbled weakly. There was nothing here.

He swayed forward—and suddenly felt again the gluey resistance, the jolting crackle and release. Another energy barrier on Clivorn's top.

He fell through it into still air, scrabbled a length and collapsed, hearing the silence. The rocks were wonderfully cool to his torn cheek. But they were not unweathered here, he saw. It came to him slowly that this second barrier must have been activated by the first. It was only here when something pushed up through the one below.

Before his eyes as he lay was a very small veined flower. A strange cold pulse boomed under his ear. The Clivorn's heartbeat, harmonics of the gale outside his shield.

The changing light changed more as he lay there. Sometime later, he was looking at the stones scattered beyond the little plant. Water-clear gold pebbles, with here and there between them a singular white fragment shaped like a horn. The light was very odd. Too bright. After a while he managed to raise his head.

There was a glow in the mist ahead of him.

His body felt disconnected, and inexplicable agonies whose cause he could no longer remember bit into his breath. He began to crawl clumsily. His belly would not lift. But his mind was perfectly clear now and he was quite prepared.

Quite unstartled, as the mist passed, to see the shining corridor—or path, really, for it was made of a watery stonework from which the golden pebbles had crumbled—the glowing corridor-path where no path could be, stretching up from The Clivorn's summit among the rushing clouds.

The floor of the path was not long, perhaps a hundred meters if the perspective was true. A lilac-blue color showed at the upper end. Freshness flowed down, mingled with The Clivorn's spume.

He could not possibly get up it just now. . . . But he could look.

There was machinery, too, he saw. An apparatus of gelatinous complexity at the boundary where the path merged with Clivorn rock. He made out a dialed face pulsing with lissajous figures—the mechanism which must have been activated by his passage through the barriers, and which in turn had materialized this path.

He smiled and felt his smile nudge gravel. He seemed to be lying with his cheek on the tawny pebbles at the foot of the path. The alien air helped the furnace in his throat. He looked steadily up the path. Nothing moved. Nothing appeared. The lilac-blue, was it sky? It was flawlessly smooth. No cloud, no bird.

Up there at the end of the path—what? A field, perhaps? A great transspatial arena into which other such magical corridor-paths converged? He couldn't imagine.

No one looked down at him.

In his line of sight above the dialed face was a device like a translucent pair of helices. One coil was full of liquid coruscation. In the other were only a few sparks of light. While he watched, one of the sparks on the empty side winked out and the filled end flickered. Then another. He wondered, watched. It was regular.

A timing device. The readout of an energy bank, perhaps. And almost at an end. When the last one goes, he thought, the gate will be finished. It has waited here, how long?

Receiving maybe a few sheep, a half-dead native. The beasts of Clivorn.

There are only a few minutes left.

With infinite effort he made his right arm move. But his left arm and leg were deadweights. He dragged himself half his length forward, almost to where the path began. Another meter . . . but his arm had no more strength.

It was no use. He was done.

If I had climbed yesterday, he thought. Instead of the scan. The scan was by flyer, of course, circling The Clivorn. But the thing here couldn't be seen by a flyer because it wasn't here then. It was only in existence when something triggered the first barrier down below, pushed up through them both. Something large, warm-blooded maybe. Willing to climb.

The computer has freed man's brain.

But computers did not go hand by bloody hand across The Clivorn's crags. Only a living man, stupid enough to wonder, to drudge for knowledge on his knees. To risk. To experience. To be lonely.

No cheap way.

The shining ship, the sealed Star Scientists, had gone. They would not be back.

He had finished struggling now. He lay quiet and watched the brilliance at the end of the alien timer wink out. Presently there was no more left. With a faint no-sound the path and all its apparatus that had waited on Clivorn since before the glaciers fell, went away.

As it went the winds raged back, but he did not hear them. He was lying quite comfortably where the bones of his face and body would mingle one day with the golden pebbles on The Clivorn's empty rock.

THE WOMEN
MEN DON'T SEE

I SEE HER FIRST while the Mexicana 727 is barreling down to Cozumel Island. I come out of the can and lurch into her seat, saying "Sorry," at a double female blur. The near blur nods quietly. The younger blur in the window seat goes on looking out. I continue down the aisle, registering nothing. Zero. I never would have looked at them or thought of them again.

Cozumel airport is the usual mix of panicky Yanks dressed for the sand pile and calm Mexicans dressed for lunch at the Presidente. I am a gray used-up Yank dressed for serious fishing; I extract my rods and duffel from the riot and hike across the field to find my charter pilot. One Captain Estéban has contracted to deliver me to the bonefish flats of Belize three hundred kilometers down the coast.

Captain Estéban turns out to be four feet nine of mahogany *Maya puro*. He is also in a somber Maya snit. He tells me my Cessna is grounded somewhere and his Bonanza is booked to take a party to Chetumal.

Well, Chetumal is south; can he take me along and go on to Belize after he drops them? Gloomily he concedes the possibility—*if* the other party permits, and *if* there are not too many *equipajes*.

The Chetumal party approaches. It's the woman and her young companion—daughter?—neatly picking their way across the gravel and yucca apron. Their Ventura two-suiters, like themselves, are small, plain, and neutral-colored. No problem. When the captain asks if I may ride along, the mother says mildly, "Of course," without looking at me.

I think that's when my inner tilt-detector sends up its first faint click. How come this woman has already looked me over carefully enough to accept on her plane? I disregard it. Paranoia hasn't been useful in my business for years, but the habit is hard to break.

As we clamber into the Bonanza, I see the girl has what could be an attractive body if there was any spark at all. There isn't. Captain Estéban folds a serape to sit on so he can see over the cowling and runs a meticulous check-down. And then we're up and trundling over the turquoise Jell-O of the Caribbean into a stiff south wind.

The coast on our right is the territory of Quintana Roo. If you haven't seen Yucatán, imagine the world's biggest absolutely flat green-gray rug. An empty-looking land. We pass the white ruin of Tulum and the gash of the road to Chichén Itzá, a half-dozen coconut plantations, and then nothing but reef and low scrub jungle all the way to the horizon, just about the way the conquistadors saw it four centuries back.

Long strings of cumulus are racing at us, shadowing the coast. I have gathered that part of our pilot's gloom concerns the weather. A cold front is dying on the henequen fields of Mérida to the west, and the south wind has piled up a string of coastal storms: what they call *lloviznas*. Estéban detours methodically around a couple of small thunderheads. The Bonanza jinks, and I look back with a vague notion of reassuring the women. They are calmly intent on what can be seen of Yucatán. Well, they were offered the copilot's view, but they turned it down. Too shy?

Another *llovizna* puffs up ahead. Estéban takes the Bonanza upstairs, rising in his seat to sight his course. I relax for the first time in too long, savoring the latitudes between me and my desk, the week of fishing ahead. Our captain's classic Maya profile attracts my gaze: forehead sloping back from his predatory nose, lips and jaw stepping back below it. If his slant eyes had been any more crossed, he couldn't have made his license. That's a handsome combination, believe it or not. On the little Maya chicks in their minishifts with iridescent gloop on those cockeyes, it's also highly erotic. Nothing like the oriental doll thing; these people have stone bones. Captain Estéban's old grandmother could probably tow the Bonanza. . . .

I'm snapped awake by the cabin hitting my ear. Estéban is

barking into his headset over a drumming racket of hail; the windows are dark gray.

One important noise is missing—the motor. I realize Estéban is fighting a dead plane. Thirty-six hundred; we've lost two thousand feet!

He slaps tank switches as the storm throws us around; I catch something about *gasolina* in a snarl that shows his big teeth. The Bonanza reels down. As he reaches for an overhead toggle, I see the fuel gauges are high. Maybe a clogged gravity feed line; I've heard of dirty gas down here. He drops the set; it's a million to one nobody can read us through the storm at this range anyway. Twenty-five hundred—going down.

His electric feed pump seems to have cut in: the motor explodes—quits—explodes—and quits again for good. We are suddenly out of the bottom of the clouds. Below us is a long white line almost hidden by rain: the reef. But there isn't any beach behind it, only a big meandering bay with a few mangrove flats—and it's coming up at us fast.

This is going to be bad, I tell myself with great unoriginality. The women behind me haven't made a sound. I look back and see they've braced down with their coats by their heads. With a stalling speed around eighty, all this isn't much use, but I wedge myself in.

Estéban yells some more into his set, flying a falling plane. He is doing one jesus job, too—as the water rushes up at us he dives into a hair-raising turn and hangs us into the wind—with a long pale ridge of sandbar in front of our nose.

Where in hell he found it I never know. The Bonanza mushes down, and we belly-hit with a tremendous tearing crash—bounce—hit again—and everything slews wildly as we flat-spin into the mangroves at the end of the bar. Crash! Clang! The plane is wrapping itself into a mound of strangler fig with one wing up. The crashing quits with us all in one piece. And no fire. Fantastic.

Captain Estéban pries open his door, which is now in the roof. Behind me a woman is repeating quietly, "Mother. Mother." I climb up the floor and find the girl trying to free herself from her mother's embrace. The woman's eyes are closed. Then she opens them and suddenly lets go, sane as soap. Estéban starts hauling them out. I grab the Bonanza's aid kit and scramble out after them into brilliant sun and wind. The storm that hit us is already vanishing up the coast.

"Great landing, Captain."

"Oh, *yes!* It was beautiful." The women are shaky, but no hysteria. Estéban is surveying the scenery with the expression his ancestors used on the Spaniards.

If you've been in one of these things, you know the slow-motion inanity that goes on. Euphoria, first. We straggle down the fig tree and out onto the sandbar in the roaring hot wind, noting without alarm that there's nothing but miles of crystalline water on all sides. It's only a foot or so deep, and the bottom is the olive color of silt. The distant shore around us is all flat mangrove swamp, totally uninhabitable.

"Bahía Espíritu Santo." Estéban confirms my guess that we're down in that huge water wilderness. I always wanted to fish it.

"What's all that smoke?" The girl is pointing at the plumes blowing around the horizon.

"Alligator hunters," says Estéban. Maya poachers have left burn-offs in the swamps. It occurs to me that any signal fires we make aren't going to be too conspicuous. And I now note that our plane is well-buried in the mound of fig. Hard to see it from the air.

Just as the question of how the hell we get out of here surfaces in my mind, the older woman asks composedly, "If they didn't hear you, Captain, when will they start looking for us? Tomorrow?"

"Correct," Estéban agrees dourly. I recall that air-sea rescue is fairly informal here. Like, keep an eye open for Mario, his mother says he hasn't been home all week.

It dawns on me we may be here quite some while.

Furthermore, the diesel-truck noise on our left is the Caribbean piling back into the mouth of the bay. The wind is pushing it at us, and the bare bottoms on the mangroves show that our bar is covered at high tide. I recall seeing a full moon this morning in—believe it, St. Louis—which means maximal tides. Well, we can climb up in the plane. But what about drinking water?

There's a small splat! behind me. The older woman has sampled the bay. She shakes her head, smiling ruefully. It's the first real expression on either of them; I take it as the signal for introductions. When I say I'm Don Fenton from St. Louis, she tells me their name is Parsons, from Bethesda, Maryland. She says it so nicely I don't at first notice we aren't being given first names. We all compliment Captain Estéban again.

His left eye is swelled shut, an inconvenience beneath his attention as a Maya, but Mrs. Parsons spots the way he's bracing his elbow in his ribs.

"You're hurt, Captain."

"*Roto*—I think is broken." He's embarrassed at being in pain. We get him to peel off his Jaime shirt, revealing a nasty bruise in his superb dark-bay torso.

"Is there tape in that kit, Mr. Fenton? I've had a little first-aid training."

She begins to deal competently and very impersonally with the tape. Miss Parsons and I wander to the end of the bar and have a conversation which I am later to recall acutely.

"Roseate spoonbills," I tell her as three pink birds flap away.

"They're beautiful," she says in her tiny voice. They both have tiny voices. "He's a Mayan Indian, isn't he? The pilot, I mean."

"Right. The real thing, straight out of the Bonampak murals. Have you seen Chichén and Uxmal?"

"Yes. We were in Mérida. We're going to Tikal in Guatemala. . . . I mean, we were."

"You'll get there." It occurs to me the girl needs cheering up. "Have they told you that Maya mothers used to tie a board on the infant's forehead to get that slant? They also hung a ball of tallow over its nose to make the eyes cross. It was considered aristocratic."

She smiles and takes another peek at Estéban. "People seem different in Yucatán," she says thoughtfully. "Not like the Indians around Mexico City. More, I don't know, independent."

"Comes from never having been conquered. Mayas got massacred and chased a lot, but nobody ever really flattened them. I bet you didn't know that the last Mexican-Maya war ended with a negotiated truce in nineteen thirty-five?"

"No!" Then she says seriously, "I like that."

"So do I."

"The water is really rising very fast," says Mrs. Parsons gently from behind us.

It is, and so is another *llovizna*. We climb back into the Bonanza. I try to rig my parka for a rain catcher, which blows loose as the storm hits fast and furious. We sort a couple of malt bars and my bottle of Jack Daniel's out of the jumble in the cabin and make ourselves reasonably comfortable. The Parsons take a sip of whiskey each, Estéban and I considerably more. The Bonanza begins to bump soggily. Estéban makes an ancient one-eyed Mayan face at the water seeping into his cabin and goes to sleep. We all nap.

When the water goes down, the euphoria has gone with it, and we're very, very thirsty. It's also damn near sunset. I get to work with a bait-casting rod and some treble hooks and manage to foul-hook four small mullets. Estéban and the women tie the Bonanza's midget life raft out in the mangroves to catch rain. The wind is parching hot. No planes go by.

Finally another shower comes over and yields us six ounces of water apiece. When the sunset envelops the world in golden smoke, we squat on the sandbar to eat wet raw mullet and Instant Breakfast crumbs. The women are now in shorts, neat but definitely not sexy.

"I never realized how refreshing raw fish is," Mrs. Parsons says pleasantly. Her daughter chuckles, also pleasantly. She's on Mamma's far side away from Estéban and me. I have Mrs. Parsons figured now; Mother Hen protecting only chick from male predators. That's all right with me. I came here to fish.

But something is irritating me. The damn women haven't complained once, you understand. Not a peep, not a quaver, no personal manifestations whatever. They're like something out of a manual.

"You really seem at home in the wilderness, Mrs. Parsons. You do much camping?"

"Oh, goodness no." Diffident laugh. "Not since my girl scout days. Oh, look—are those man-of-war birds?"

Answer a question with a question. I wait while the frigate birds sail nobly into the sunset.

"Bethesda . . . Would I be wrong in guessing you work for Uncle Sam?"

"Why, yes. You must be very familiar with Washington, Mr. Fenton. Does your work bring you there often?"

Anywhere but on our sandbar the little ploy would have worked. My hunter's gene twitches.

"Which agency are you with?"

She gives up gracefully. "Oh, just GSA records. I'm a librarian."

Of course. I know her now, all the Mrs. Parsonses in records divisions, accounting sections, research branches, personnel and administration offices. Tell Mrs. Parsons we need a recap on the external service contracts for fiscal '73. So Yucatán is on the tours now? Pity . . . I offer her the tired little joke. "You know where the bodies are buried."

She smiles deprecatingly and stands up. "It does get dark quickly, doesn't it?"

Time to get back into the plane.

A flock of ibis are circling us, evidently accustomed to roosting in our fig tree. Estéban produces a machete and a Mayan string hammock. He proceeds to sling it between tree and plane, refusing help. His machete stroke is noticeably tentative.

The Parsons are taking a pee behind the tail vane. I hear one of them slip and squeal faintly. When they come back over the hull, Mrs. Parsons asks, "Might we sleep in the hammock, Captain?"

Estéban splits an unbelieving grin. I protest about rain and mosquitoes.

"Oh, we have insect repellent and we do enjoy fresh air."

The air is rushing by about force five and colder by the minute.

"We have our raincoats," the girl adds cheerfully.

Well, okay, ladies. We dangerous males retire inside the damp cabin. Through the wind I hear the women laugh softly now and then, apparently cozy in their chilly ibis roost. A private insanity, I decide. I know myself for the least threatening of men; my noncharisma has been in fact an asset jobwise, over the years. Are they having fantasies about Estéban? Or maybe they really are fresh-air nuts. . . . Sleep comes for me in invisible diesels roaring by on the reef outside.

We emerge dry-mouthed into a vast windy salmon sunrise. A diamond chip of sun breaks out of the sea and promptly submerges in cloud. I go to work with the rod and some mullet bait while two showers detour around us. Breakfast is a strip of wet barracuda apiece.

The Parsons continue stoic and helpful. Under Estéban's direction they set up a section of cowling for a gasoline flare in case we hear a plane, but nothing goes over except one unseen jet droning toward Panama. The wind howls, hot and dry and full of coral dust. So are we.

"They look first in sea," Estéban remarks. His aristocratic

frontal slope is beaded with sweat; Mrs. Parsons watches him concernedly. I watch the cloud blanket tearing by above, getting higher and dryer and thicker. While that lasts nobody is going to find us, and the water business is now unfunny.

Finally I borrow Estéban's machete and hack a long light pole. "There's a stream coming in back there, I saw it from the plane. Can't be more than two, three miles."

"I'm afraid the raft's torn." Mrs. Parsons shows me the cracks in the orange plastic; irritatingly, it's a Delaware label.

"All right," I hear myself announce. "The tide's going down. If we cut the good end off that air tube, I can haul water back in it. I've waded flats before."

Even to me it sounds crazy.

"Stay by plane," Estéban says. He's right, of course. He's also clearly running a fever. I look at the overcast and taste grit and old barracuda. The hell with the manual.

When I start cutting up the raft, Estéban tells me to take the serape. "You stay one night." He's right about that, too; I'll have to wait out the tide.

"I'll come with you," says Mrs. Parsons calmly.

I simply stare at her. What new madness has got into Mother Hen? Does she imagine Estéban is too battered to be functional? While I'm being astounded, my eyes take in the fact that Mrs. Parsons is now quite rosy around the knees, with her hair loose and a sunburn starting on her nose. A trim, in fact a very neat, shading-forty.

"Look, that stuff is horrible going. Mud up to your ears and water over your head."

"I'm really quite fit and I swim a great deal. I'll try to keep up. Two would be much safer, Mr. Fenton, and we can bring more water."

She's serious. Well, I'm about as fit as a marshmallow at this time of winter, and I can't pretend I'm depressed by the idea of company. So be it.

"Let me show Miss Parsons how to work this rod."

Miss Parsons is even rosier and more windblown, and she's not clumsy with my tackle. A good girl, Miss Parsons, in her nothing way. We cut another staff and get some gear together. At the last minute Estéban shows how sick he feels: he offers me the machete. I thank him, but no; I'm used to my Wirkkala knife. We tie some air into the plastic tube for a float and set out along the sandiest-looking line.

Estéban raises one dark palm. *"Buen viaje."* Miss Parsons has hugged her mother and gone to cast from the mangrove. She waves. We wave.

An hour later we're barely out of waving distance. The going is purely god-awful. The sand keeps dissolving into silt you can't walk on or swim through, and the bottom is spiked with dead mangrove spears. We flounder from one pothole to the next, scaring up rays and turtles and hoping to god we don't kick a moray eel. Where we're not soaked in slime, we're desiccated, and we smell like the Old Cretaceous.

Mrs. Parsons keeps up doggedly. I only have to pull her out once. When I do so, I notice the sandbar is now out of sight.

Finally we reach the gap in the mangrove line I thought was the creek. It turns out to open into another arm of the bay, with more mangroves ahead. And the tide is coming in.

"I've had the world's lousiest idea."

Mrs. Parsons only says mildly, "It's so different from the view from the plane."

I revise my opinion of the girl scouts, and we plow on past the mangroves toward the smoky haze that has to be shore. The sun is setting in our faces, making it hard to see. Ibis and herons fly up around us, and once a big hermit spooks ahead, his fin cutting a rooster tail. We fall into more potholes. The flashlights get soaked. I am having fantasies of the mangrove as universal obstacle; it's hard to recall I ever walked down a street, for instance, without stumbling over or under or through mangrove roots. And the sun is dropping down, down.

Suddenly we hit a ledge and fall over it into a cold flow.

"The stream! It's fresh water!"

We guzzle and garble and douse our heads; it's the best drink I remember. "Oh my, oh my—!" Mrs. Parsons is laughing right out loud.

"That dark place over to the right looks like real land."

We flounder across the flow and follow a hard shelf, which turns into solid bank and rises over our heads. Shortly there's a break beside a clump of spiny bromels, and we scramble up and flop down at the top, dripping and stinking. Out of sheer reflex my arm goes around my companion's shoulder—but Mrs. Parsons isn't there; she's up on her knees peering at the burnt-over plain around us.

"It's so good to see land one can walk on!" The tone is too innocent. *Noli me tangere.*

"Don't try it." I'm exasperated; the muddy little woman, what does she think? "That ground out there is a crush of ashes over muck, and it's full of stubs. You can go in over your knees."

"It seems firm here."

"We're in an alligator nursery. That was the slide we came up. Don't worry, by now the old lady's doubtless on her way to be made into handbags."

"What a shame."

"I better set a line down in the stream while I can still see."

I slide back down and rig a string of hooks that may get us breakfast. When I get back Mrs. Parsons is wringing muck out of the serape.

"I'm glad you warned me, Mr. Fenton. It is treacherous."

"Yeah." I'm over my irritation; god knows I don't want to *tangere* Mrs. Parsons, even if I weren't beat down to mush. "In its quiet way, Yucatán is a tough place to get around in. You can see why the Mayas built roads. Speaking of which—look!"

The last of the sunset is silhouetting a small square shape a couple of kilometers inland; a Maya *ruina* with a fig tree growing out of it.

"Lot of those around. People think they were guard towers."

"What a deserted-feeling land."

"Let's hope it's deserted by mosquitoes."

We slump down in the 'gator nursery and share the last malt bar, watching the stars slide in and out of the blowing clouds. The bugs aren't too bad; maybe the burn did them in. And it isn't hot anymore, either—in fact, it's not even warm, wet as we are. Mrs. Parsons continues tranquilly interested in Yucatán and unmistakably uninterested in togetherness.

Just as I'm beginning to get aggressive notions about how we're going to spend the night if she expects me to give her the serape, she stands up, scuffs at a couple of hummocks, and says, "I expect this is as good a place as any, isn't it, Mr. Fenton?"

With which she spreads out the raft bag for a pillow and lies down on her side in the dirt with exactly half the serape over her and the other corner folded neatly open. Her small back is toward me.

The demonstration is so convincing that I'm halfway under my share of serape before the preposterousness of it stops me.

"By the way. My name is Don."

"Oh, of course." Her voice is graciousness itself. "I'm Ruth."

I get in not quite touching her, and we lie there like two fish on a plate, exposed to the stars and smelling the smoke in the wind and feeling things underneath us. It is absolutely the most intimately awkward moment I've had in years.

The woman doesn't mean one thing to me, but the obtrusive recessiveness of her, the defiance of her little rump eight inches from my fly—for two pesos I'd have those shorts down and introduce myself. If I were twenty years younger. If I wasn't so bushed . . . But the twenty years and the exhaustion are there, and it comes to me wryly that Mrs. Ruth Parsons has judged things to a nicety. If I *were* twenty years younger, she wouldn't be here. Like the butterfish that float around a sated barracuda, only to vanish away the instant his intent changes, Mrs. Parsons knows her little shorts are safe. Those firmly filled little shorts, so close . . .

A warm nerve stirs in my groin—and just as it does I become aware of a silent emptiness beside me. Mrs. Parsons is imperceptibly inching away. Did my breathing change? Whatever, I'm perfectly sure that if my hand reached, she'd be elsewhere—probably announcing her intention to take a dip. The twenty years bring a chuckle to my throat, and I relax.

"Good night, Ruth."

"Good night, Don."

And believe it or not, we sleep, while the armadas of the wind roar overhead.

Light wakes me—a cold white glare.

My first thought is 'gator hunters. Best to manifest ourselves as *turistas* as fast as possible. I scramble up, noting that Ruth has dived under the bromel dump.

"Quién estás? Al socorro! Help, *señores!"*

No answer except the light goes out, leaving me blind.

I yell some more in a couple of languages. It stays dark. There's a vague scrabbling, whistling sound somewhere in the burn-off. Liking everything less by the minute, I try a speech about our plane having crashed and we need help.

A very narrow pencil of light flicks over us and snaps off.

"Eh-ep," says a blurry voice, and something metallic twitters. They for sure aren't locals. I'm getting unpleasant ideas.

"Yes, help!"

Something goes *crackle-crackle whish-whish,* and all sounds fade away.

"What the holy hell!" I stumble toward where they were.

"Look." Ruth whispers behind me. "Over by the ruin."

I look and catch a multiple flicker which winks out fast.

"A camp?"

And I take two more blind strides. My leg goes down through the crust, and a spike spears me just where you stick the knife in to unjoint a drumstick. By the pain that goes through my bladder I recognize that my trick kneecap has caught it.

For instant basket-case you can't beat kneecaps. First you discover your knee doesn't bend anymore, so you try putting some weight on it, and a bayonet goes up your spine and unhinges your jaw. Little grains of gristle have got into the sensitive bearing surface. The knee tries to buckle and can't, and mercifully you fall down.

Ruth helps me back to the serape.

"What a fool, what a god-forgotten imbecile—"

"Not at all, Don. It was perfectly natural." We strike matches; her fingers push mine aside, exploring. "I think it's in place, but it's swelling fast. I'll lay a wet handkerchief on it. We'll have to wait for morning to check the cut. Were they poachers, do you think?"

"Probably," I lie. What I think they were is smugglers.

She comes back with a soaked bandanna and drapes it on. "We must have frightened them. That light . . . it seemed so bright."

"Some hunting party. People do crazy things around here."

"Perhaps they'll come back in the morning."

"Could be."

Ruth pulls up the wet serape, and we say good-night again. Neither of us is mentioning how we're going to get back to the plane without help.

I lie staring south where Alpha Centauri is blinking in and out of the overcast and cursing myself for the sweet mess I've made. My first idea is giving way to an even less pleasing one.

Smuggling, around here, is a couple of guys in an outboard meeting a shrimp boat by the reef. They don't light up the sky or have some kind of swamp buggy that goes whoosh. Plus a big camp . . . paramilitary-type equipment?

I've seen a report of Guévarista infiltrators operating on the British Honduran border, which is about a hundred kilometers—sixty miles—south of here. Right under those clouds. If that's what looked us over, I'll be more than happy if they don't come back. . . .

I wake up in pelting rain, alone. My first move confirms that my leg is as expected—a giant misplaced erection bulging out of my shorts. I raise up painfully to see Ruth standing by the bromels, looking over the bay. Solid wet nimbus is pouring out of the south.

"No planes today."

"Oh, good morning, Don. Should we look at that cut now?"

"It's minimal." In fact the skin is hardly broken, and no deep puncture. Totally out of proportion to the havoc inside.

"Well, they have water to drink," Ruth says tranquilly. "Maybe those hunters will come back. I'll go see if we have a fish—that is, can I help you in any way, Don?"

Very tactful. I emit an ungracious negative, and she goes off about her private concerns.

They certainly are private, too; when I recover from my own sanitary efforts, she's still away. Finally I hear splashing.

"It's a big fish!" More splashing. Then she climbs up the bank with a three-pound mangrove snapper—and something else.

It isn't until after the messy work of filleting the fish that I begin to notice.

She's making a smudge of chaff and twigs to singe the fillets, small hands very quick, tension in that female upper lip. The rain has eased off for the moment; we're sluicing wet but warm enough. Ruth brings me my fish on a mangrove skewer and sits back on her heels with an odd breathy sigh.

"Aren't you joining me?"

"Oh, of course." She gets a strip and picks at it, saying quickly, "We either have too much salt or too little, don't we? I should fetch some brine." Her eyes are roving from nothing to noplace.

"Good thought." I hear another sigh and decide the girl scouts need an assist. "Your daughter mentioned you've come from Mérida. Have you seen much of Mexico?"

"Not really. Last year we went to Mazatlán and Cuernavaca. . . ." She puts the fish down, frowning.

"And you're going to see Tikal. Going to Bonampak too?"

"No." Suddenly she jumps up brushing rain off her face. "I'll bring you some water, Don."

She ducks down the slide, and after a fair while comes back

with a full bromel stalk.

"Thanks." She's standing above me, staring restlessly round the horizon.

"Ruth, I hate to say it, but those guys are not coming back and it's probably just as well. Whatever they were up to, we looked like trouble. The most they'll do is tell someone we're here. That'll take a day or two to get around, we'll be back at the plane by then."

"I'm sure you're right, Don." She wanders over to the smudge fire.

"And quit fretting about your daughter. She's a big girl."

"Oh, I'm sure Althea's all right. . . . They have plenty of water now." Her fingers drum on her thigh. It's raining again.

"Come on, Ruth. Sit down. Tell me about Althea. Is she still in college?"

She gives that sighing little laugh and sits. "Althea got her degree last year. She's in computer programming."

"Good for her. And what about you, what do you do in GSA records?"

"I'm in Foreign Procurement Archives." She smiles mechanically, but her breathing is shallow. "It's very interesting."

"I know a Jack Wittig in Contracts, maybe you know him?"

It sounds pretty absurd, there in the 'gator slide.

"Oh, I've met Mr. Wittig. I'm sure he wouldn't remember me."

"Why not?"

"I'm not very memorable."

Her voice is factual. She's perfectly right, of course. Who was that woman, Mrs. Jannings, Janny, who coped with my per diem for years? Competent, agreeable, impersonal. She had a sick father or something. But dammit, Ruth is a lot younger and better-looking. Comparatively speaking.

"Maybe Mrs. Parsons doesn't want to be memorable."

She makes a vague sound, and I suddenly realize Ruth isn't listening to me at all. Her hands are clenched around her knees, she's staring inland at the ruin.

"Ruth, I tell you our friends with the light are in the next county by now. Forget it, we don't need them."

Her eyes come back to me as if she'd forgotten I was there, and she nods slowly. It seems to be too much effort to speak. Suddenly she cocks her head and jumps up again.

"I'll go look at the line, Don. I thought I heard something—"
She's gone like a rabbit.

While she's away I try getting up onto my good leg and the
staff. The pain is sickening; knees seem to have some kind of
hot line to the stomach. I take a couple of hops to test whether
the Demerol I have in my belt would get me walking. As I do
so, Ruth comes up the bank with a fish flapping in her hands.

"Oh, no, Don! *No!*" She actually clasps the snapper to her
breast.

"The water will take some of my weight. I'd like to give it a
try."

"You mustn't!" Ruth says quite violently and instantly
modulates down. "Look at the bay, Don. One can't see a
thing."

I teeter there, tasting bile and looking at the mingled
curtains of sun and rain driving across the water. She's right,
thank god. Even with two good legs we could get into trouble
out there.

"I guess one more night won't kill us."

I let her collapse me back onto the gritty plastic, and she
positively bustles around, finding me a chunk to lean on,
stretching the serape on both staffs to keep rain off me,
bringing another drink, grubbing for dry tinder.

"I'll make us a real bonfire as soon as it lets up, Don. They'll
see our smoke, they'll know we're all right. We just have to
wait." Cheery smile. "Is there any way we can make you more
comfortable?"

Holy Saint Sterculius: playing house in a mud puddle. For a
fatuous moment I wonder if Mrs. Parsons has designs on me.
And then she lets out another sigh and sinks back onto her
heels with that listening look. Unconsciously her rump wiggles
a little. My ear picks up the operative word: *wait.*

Ruth Parsons is waiting. In fact, she acts as if she's waiting
so hard it's killing her. For what? For someone to get us out of
here, what else? . . . But why was she so horrified when I got up
to try to leave? Why all this tension?

My paranoia stirs. I grab it by the collar and start idly
checking back. Up to when whoever it was showed up last
night, Mrs. Parsons was, I guess, normal. Calm and sensible,
anyway. Now she's humming like a high wire. And she seems
to want to stay here and wait. Just as an intellectual pastime,
why?

Could she have intended to come here? No way. Where she planned to be was Chetumal, which is on the border. Come to think, Chetumal is an odd way round to Tikal. Let's say the scenario was that she's meeting somebody in Chetumal. Somebody who's part of an organization. So now her contact in Chetumal knows she's overdue. And when those types appeared last night, something suggests to her that they're part of the same organization. And she hopes they'll put one and one together and come back for her?

"May I have the knife, Don? I'll clean the fish."

Rather slowly I pass the knife, kicking my subconscious. Such a decent ordinary little woman, a good girl scout. My trouble is that I've bumped into too many professional agilities under the careful stereotypes. *I'm not very memorable. . . .*

What's in Foreign Procurement Archives? Wittig handles classified contracts. Lots of money stuff; foreign currency negotiations, commodity price schedules, some industrial technology. Or—just as a hypothesis—it could be as simple as a wad of bills back in that modest beige Ventura, to be exchanged for a packet from, say, Costa Rica. If she were a courier, they'd want to get at the plane. And then what about me and maybe Estéban? Even hypothetically, not good.

I watch her hacking at the fish, forehead knotted with effort, teeth in her lip. Mrs. Ruth Parsons of Bethesda, this thrumming, private woman. How crazy can I get? *They'll see our smoke. . . .*

"Here's your knife, Don. I washed it. Does the leg hurt very badly?"

I blink away the fantasies and see a scared little woman in a mangrove swamp.

"Sit down, rest. You've been going all out."

She sits obediently, like a kid in a dentist chair.

"You're stewing about Althea. And she's probably worried about you. We'll get back tomorrow under our own steam, Ruth."

"Honestly I'm not worried at all, Don." The smile fades; she nibbles her lip, frowning out at the bay.

"You know, Ruth, you surprised me when you offered to come along. Not that I don't appreciate it. But I rather thought you'd be concerned about leaving Althea alone with our good pilot. Or was it only me?"

This gets her attention at last.

"I believe Captain Estéban is a very fine type of man."

The words surprise me a little. Isn't the correct line more like "I trust Althea," or even, indignantly, "Althea is a good girl"?

"He's a man. Althea seemed to think he was interesting."

She goes on staring at the bay. And then I notice her tongue flick out and lick that prehensile upper lip. There's a flush that isn't sunburn around her ears and throat too, and one hand is gently rubbing her thigh. What's she seeing, out there in the flats?

Oho.

Captain Estéban's mahogany arms clasping Miss Althea Parsons's pearly body. Captain Estéban's archaic nostrils snuffling in Miss Parsons's tender neck. Captain Estéban's copper buttocks pumping into Althea's creamy upturned bottom. . . . The hammock, very bouncy. Mayas know all about it.

Well, well. So Mother Hen has her little quirks.

I feel fairly silly and more than a little irritated. *Now* I find out. . . . But even vicarious lust has much to recommend it, here in the mud and rain. I settle back, recalling that Miss Althea the computer programmer had waved good-bye very composedly. Was she sending her mother to flounder across the bay with me so she can get programmed in Maya? The memory of Honduran mahogany logs drifting in and out of the opalescent sand comes to me. Just as I am about to suggest that Mrs. Parsons might care to share my rain shelter, she remarks serenely, "The Mayas seem to be a very fine type of people. I believe you said so to Althea."

The implications fall on me with the rain. *Type.* As in breeding, bloodline, sire. Am I supposed to have certified Estéban not only as a stud but as a genetic donor?

"Ruth, are you telling me you're prepared to accept a half-Indian grandchild?"

"Why, Don, that's up to Althea, you know."

Looking at the mother, I guess it is. Oh, for mahogany gonads.

Ruth has gone back to listening to the wind, but I'm not about to let her off that easy. Not after all that *noli me tangere* jazz.

"What will Althea's father think?"

Her face snaps around at me, genuinely startled.

"Althea's father?" Complicated semismile. "He won't mind."

"He'll accept it too, eh?" I see her shake her head as if a fly were bothering her, and add with a cripple's malice: "Your husband must be a very fine type of a man."

Ruth looks at me, pushing her wet hair back abruptly. I have the impression that mousy Mrs. Parsons is roaring out of control, but her voice is quiet.

"There isn't any Mr. Parsons, Don. There never was. Althea's father was a Danish medical student. . . . I believe he has gained considerable prominence."

"Oh." Something warns me not to say I'm sorry. "You mean he doesn't know about Althea?"

"No." She smiles, her eyes bright and cuckoo.

"Seems like rather a rough deal for her."

"I grew up quite happily under the same circumstances." Bang, I'm dead. Well, well, well. A mad image blooms in my mind: generations of solitary Parsons women selecting sires, making impregnation trips. Well, I hear the world is moving their way.

"I better look at the fish line."

She leaves. The glow fades. *No*. Just no, no contact. Goodbye, Captain Estéban. My leg is very uncomfortable. The hell with Mrs. Parsons's long-distance orgasm.

We don't talk much after that, which seems to suit Ruth. The odd day drags by. Squall after squall blows over us. Ruth singes up some more fillets, but the rain drowns her smudge; it seems to pour hardest just as the sun's about to show.

Finally she comes to sit under my sagging serape, but there's no warmth there. I doze, aware of her getting up now and then to look around. My subconscious notes that she's still twitchy. I tell my subconscious to knock it off.

Presently I wake up to find her penciling on the water-soaked pages of a little notepad.

"What's that, a shopping list for alligators?"

Automatic polite laugh. "Oh, just an address. In case we— I'm being silly, Don."

"Hey," I sit up, wincing. "Ruth, quit fretting. I mean it. We'll all be out of this soon. You'll have a great story to tell."

She doesn't look up. "Yes . . . I guess we will."

"Come on, we're doing fine. There isn't any real danger here, you know. Unless you're allergic to fish?"

Another good-little-girl laugh, but there's a shiver in it.

"Sometimes I think I'd like to go . . . really far away."

To keep her talking I say the first thing in my head.

"Tell me, Ruth. I'm curious why you would settle for that kind of lonely life, there in Washington? I mean, a woman like you—"

"Should get married?" She gives a shaky sigh, pushing the notebook back in her wet pocket.

"Why not? It's the normal source of companionship. Don't tell me you're trying to be some kind of professional man-hater."

"Lesbian, you mean?" Her laugh sounds better. "With my security rating? No, I'm not."

"Well, then. Whatever trauma you went through, these things don't last forever. You can't hate all men."

The smile is back. "Oh, there wasn't any trauma, Don, and I *don't* hate men. That would be as silly as—as hating the weather." She glances wryly at the blowing rain.

"I think you have a grudge. You're even spooky of me."

Smooth as a mouse bite she says, "I'd love to hear about your family, Don?"

Touché. I give her the edited version of how I don't have one anymore, and she says she's sorry, how sad. And we chat about what a good life a single person really has, and how she and her friends enjoy plays and concerts and travel, and one of them is head cashier for Ringling Brothers, how about that?

But it's coming out jerkier and jerkier like a bad tape, with her eyes going round the horizon in the pauses and her face listening for something that isn't my voice. What's wrong with her? Well, what's wrong with any furtively unconventional middle-aged woman with an empty bed? And a security clearance. An old habit of mind remarks unkindly that Mrs. Parsons represents what is known as the classic penetration target.

"—so much more opportunity now." Her voice trails off.

"Hurrah for women's lib, eh?"

"The lib?" Impatiently she leans forward and tugs the serape straight. "Oh, that's doomed."

The apocalyptic word jars my attention.

"What do you mean, doomed?"

She glances at me as if I weren't hanging straight either and says vaguely, "Oh . . ."

"Come on, why doomed? Didn't they get that equal rights bill?"

Long hesitation. When she speaks again her voice is different.

"Women have no rights, Don, except what men allow us. Men are more aggressive and powerful, and they run the world. When the next real crisis upsets them, our so-called rights will vanish like—like that smoke. We'll be back where we always were: property. And whatever has gone wrong will be blamed on our freedom, like the fall of Rome was. You'll see."

Now all this is delivered in a gray tone of total conviction. The last time I heard that tone, the speaker was explaining why he had to keep his file drawers full of dead pigeons.

"Oh, come on. You and your friends are the backbone of the system; if you quit, the country would come to a screeching halt before lunch."

No answering smile.

"That's fantasy." Her voice is still quiet. "Women don't work that way. We're a—a toothless world." She looks around as if she wanted to stop talking. "What women do is survive. We live by ones and twos in the chinks of your world-machine."

"Sounds like a guerrilla operation." I'm not really joking, here in the 'gator den. In fact, I'm wondering if I spent too much thought on mahogany logs.

"Guerrillas have something to hope for." Suddenly she switches on a jolly smile. "Think of us as opossums, Don. Did you know there are opossums living all over? Even in New York City."

I smile back with my neck prickling. I thought I was the paranoid one.

"Men and women aren't different species, Ruth. Women do everything men do."

"Do they?" Our eyes meet, but she seems to be seeing ghosts between us in the rain. She mutters something that could be "My Lai" and looks away. "All the endless wars . . ." Her voice is a whisper. "All the huge authoritarian organizations for doing unreal things. Men live to struggle against each other; we're just part of the battlefield. It'll never change unless you change the whole world. I dream sometimes of—of going away—" She checks and abruptly changes voice. "Forgive me, Don, it's so stupid saying all this."

"Men hate wars too, Ruth," I say as gently as I can.

"I know." She shrugs and climbs to her feet. "But that's your problem, isn't it?"

End of communication. Mrs. Ruth Parsons isn't even living in the same world with me.

I watch her move around restlessly, head turning toward the ruins. Alienation like that can add up to dead pigeons, which would be GSA's problem. It could also lead to believing some joker who's promising to change the whole world. Which could just probably be my problem if one of them was over in that camp last night, where she keeps looking. *Guerrillas have something to hope for. . . ?*

Nonsense. I try another position and see that the sky seems to be clearing as the sun sets. The wind is quieting down at last too. Insane to think this little woman is acting out some fantasy in this swamp. But that equipment last night was no fantasy; if those lads have some connection with her, I'll be in the way. You couldn't find a handier spot to dispose of the body. . . . Maybe some Guévarista is a fine type of man?

Absurd. Sure . . . The only thing more absurd would be to come through the wars and get myself terminated by a mad librarian's boyfriend on a fishing trip.

A fish flops in the stream below us. Ruth spins around so fast she hits the serape. "I better start the fire," she says, her eyes still on the plain and her head cocked, listening.

All right, let's test.

"Expecting company?"

It rocks her. She freezes, and her eyes come swiveling around to me like a film take captioned FRIGHT. I can see her decide to smile.

"Oh, one never can tell!" She laughs weirdly, the eyes not changed. "I'll get the—the kindling." She fairly scuttles into the brush.

Nobody, paranoid or not, could call *that* a normal reaction.

Ruth Parsons is either psycho or she's expecting something to happen—and it has nothing to do with me: I scared her pissless.

Well, she could be nuts. And I could be wrong, but there are some mistakes you only make once.

Reluctantly I unzip my body belt, telling myself that if I think what I think, my only course is to take something for my leg and get as far as possible from Mrs. Ruth Parsons before whoever she's waiting for arrives.

In my belt also is a .32-caliber asset Ruth doesn't know about—and it's going to stay there. My longevity program leaves the shoot-outs to TV and stresses being somewhere else when the roof falls in. I can spend a perfectly safe and also perfectly horrible night out in one of those mangrove flats. . . . Am I insane?

At this moment Ruth stands up and stares blatantly inland with her hand shading her eyes. Then she tucks something into her pocket, buttons up, and tightens her belt.

That does it.

I dry-swallow two 100-mg tabs, which should get me ambulatory and still leave me wits to hide. Give it a few minutes. I make sure my compass and some hooks are in my own pocket and sit waiting while Ruth fusses with her smudge fire, sneaking looks away when she thinks I'm not watching.

The flat world around us is turning into an unearthly amber and violet light show as the first numbness sweeps into my leg. Ruth has crawled under the bromels for more dry stuff; I can see her foot. Okay. I reach for my staff.

Suddenly the foot jerks, and Ruth yells—or rather, her throat makes that *Uh-uh-hhh* that means pure horror. The foot disappears in a rattle of bromel stalks.

I lunge upright on the crutch and look over the bank at a frozen scene.

Ruth is crouching sideways on the ledge, clutching her stomach. They are about a yard below, floating on the river in a skiff. While I was making up my stupid mind, her friends have glided right under my ass. There are three of them.

They are tall and white. I try to see them as men in some kind of white jumpsuits. The one nearest the bank is stretching out a long white arm toward Ruth. She jerks and scuttles farther away.

The arm stretches after her. It stretches and stretches. It stretches two yards and stays hanging in the air. Small black things are wiggling from its tip.

I look where their faces should be and see black hollow dishes with vertical stripes. The stripes move slowly. . . .

There is no more possibility of their being human—or anything else I've ever seen. What has Ruth conjured up?

The scene is totally silent. I blink, blink—this cannot be real. The two in the far end of the skiff are writhing those arms around an apparatus on a tripod. A weapon? Suddenly I hear the same blurry voice I heard in the night.

"Guh-give," it groans. "G-give . . ."

Dear god, it's real, whatever it is. I'm terrified. My mind is trying not to form a word.

And Ruth—Jesus, of course—Ruth is terrified too; she's edging along the bank away from them, gaping at the monsters in the skiff, who are obviously nobody's friends. She's hugging something to her body. Why doesn't she get over the bank and circle back behind me?

"G-g-give." That wheeze is coming from the tripod. "Pee-eeze give." The skiff is moving upstream below Ruth, following her. The arm undulates out at her again, its black digits looping. Ruth scrambles to the top of the bank.

"Ruth!" My voice cracks. "Ruth, get over here behind me!"

She doesn't look at me, only keeps sidling farther away. My terror detonates into anger.

"Come back here!" With my free hand I'm working the .32 out of my belt. The sun has gone down.

She doesn't turn but straightens up warily, still hugging the thing. I see her mouth working. Is she actually trying to *talk* to hem?

"Please . . ." She swallows. "Please speak to me. I need your help."

"RUTH!!"

At this moment the nearest white monster whips into a great S-curve and sails right onto the bank at her, eight feet of snowy rippling horror.

And I shoot Ruth.

I don't know that for a minute—I've yanked the gun up so fast that my staff slips and dumps me as I fire. I stagger up, hearing Ruth scream, "No! No! No!"

The creature is back down by his boat, and Ruth is still farther away, clutching herself. Blood is running down her elbow.

"Stop it, Don! They aren't attacking you!"

"For god's sake! Don't be a fool, I can't help you if you won't get away from them!"

No reply. Nobody moves. No sound except the drone of a jet passing far above. In the darkening stream below me the three white figures shift uneasily; I get the impression of radar dishes focusing. The word spells itself in my head: *Aliens.*

Extraterrestrials.

What do I do, call the President? Capture them single-handed with my peashooter? . . . I'm alone in the arse end of nowhere with one leg and my brain cuddled in meperidine hydrochloride.

"Prrr-eese," their machine blurs again. "Wa-wat hep . . ."

"Our plane fell down," Ruth says in a very distinct, eerie voice. She points up at the jet, out toward the bay. "My—my child is there. Please take us *there* in your boat."

Dear god. While she's gesturing, I get a look at the thing she's hugging in her wounded arm. It's metallic, like a big glimmering distributor head. What—?

Wait a minute. This morning: when she was gone so long, she could have found that thing. Something they left behind. Or dropped. And she hid it, not telling me. That's why she kept going under that bromel clump—she was peeking at it. Waiting. And the owners came back and caught her. They want it. She's trying to bargain, by god.

"—Water," Ruth is pointing again. "Take us. Me. And him."

The black faces turn toward me, blind and horrible. Later on I may be grateful for that "us." Not now.

"Throw your gun away, Don. They'll take us back." Her voice is weak.

"Like hell I will. You—who are you? What are you doing here?"

"Oh, god, does it matter? He's frightened," she cries to them. "Can you understand?"

She's as alien as they, there in the twilight. The beings in the skiff are twittering among themselves. Their box starts to moan.

"Ss-stu-dens," I make out. "S-stu-ding . . . not—huh-arming . . . w-we . . . buh . . ." It fades into garble and then says, "G-give . . . we . . . g-go. . . ."

Peace-loving cultural-exchange students—on the interstellar level now. Oh, no.

"Bring that thing here, Ruth—right now!"

But she's starting down the bank toward them saying, "Take me."

"Wait! You need a tourniquet on that arm."

"I know. Please put the gun down, Don."

She's actually at the skiff, right by them. They aren't moving. "Jesus Christ." Slowly, reluctantly, I drop the .32. When I start down the slide, I find I'm floating; adrenaline and Demerol are a bad mix.

The skiff comes gliding toward me, Ruth in the bow clutching the thing and her arm. The aliens stay in the stern behind their tripod, away from me. I note the skiff is camouflaged tan and green. The world around us is deep shadowy blue.

"Don, bring the water bag!"

As I'm dragging down the plastic bag, it occurs to me that Ruth really is cracking up, the water isn't needed now. But my own brain seems to have gone into overload. All I can focus on is a long white rubbery arm with black worms clutching the far end of the orange tube, helping me fill it. This isn't happening.

"Can you get in, Don?" As I hoist my numb legs up, two long white pipes reach for me. *No, you don't.* I kick and tumble in beside Ruth. She moves away.

A creaky hum starts up, it's coming from a wedge in the center of the skiff. And we're in motion, sliding toward dark mangrove files.

I stare mindlessly at the wedge. Alien technological secrets? I can't see any, the power source is under that triangular cover, about two feet long. The gadgets on the tripod are equally cryptic, except that one has a big lens. Their light?

As we hit the open bay, the hum rises and we start planing faster and faster still. Thirty knots? Hard to judge in the dark. Their hull seems to be a modified trihedral much like ours, with a remarkable absence of slap. Say twenty-two feet. Schemes of capturing it swirl in my mind. I'll need Estéban.

Suddenly a huge flood of white light fans out over us from the tripod, blotting out the aliens in the stern. I see Ruth pulling at a belt around her arm, still hugging the gizmo.

"I'll tie that for you."

"It's all right."

The alien device is twinkling or phosphorescing slightly. I lean over to look, whispering, "Give that to me, I'll pass it to Estéban."

"No!" She scoots away, almost over the side. "It's theirs, they need it!"

"What? Are you crazy?" I'm so taken aback by this idiocy I literally stammer. "We have to, we—"

"They haven't hurt us. I'm sure they could." Her eyes are watching me with feral intensity; in the light her face has a lunatic look. Numb as I am, I realize that the wretched woman is poised to throw herself over the side if I move. With the alien thing.

"I think they're gentle," she mutters.

"For Christ's sake, Ruth, they're *aliens!*"

"I'm used to it," she says absently. "There's the island! Stop! Stop here!"

The skiff slows, turning. A mound of foliage is tiny in the light. Metal glints—the plane.

"Althea! Althea! Are you all right?"

Yells, movement on the plane. The water is high, we're floating over the bar. The aliens are keeping us in the lead with the light hiding them. I see one pale figure splashing toward us and a dark one behind, coming more slowly. Estéban must be puzzled by that light.

"Mr. Fenton is hurt, Althea. These people brought us back with the water. Are you all right?"

"A-okay." Althea flounders up, peering excitedly. "You all right? Whew, that light!" Automatically I start handing her the idiotic water bag.

"Leave that for the captain," Ruth says sharply. "Althea, can you climb in the boat? Quickly, it's important."

"Coming."

"No, no!" I protest, but the skiff tilts as Althea swarms in. The aliens twitter, and their voice box starts groaning. "Gu-give . . . now . . . give . . . "

"*Qué llega?*" Estéban's face appears beside me, squinting fiercely into the light.

"Grab it, get it from her—that thing she has—" but Ruth's voice rides over mine. "Captain, lift Mr. Fenton out of the boat. He's hurt his leg. Hurry, please."

"Goddamn it, wait!" I shout, but an arm has grabbed my middle. When a Maya boosts you, you go. I hear Althea saying, "Mother, your arm!" and fall onto Estéban. We stagger around in water up to my waist; I can't feel my feet at all.

When I get steady, the boat is yards away. The two women are head-to-head, murmuring.

"Get them!" I tug loose from Estéban and flounder forward. Ruth stands up in the boat facing the invisible aliens.

"Take us with you. Please. We want to go with you, away from here."

"Ruth! Estéban, get that boat!" I lunge and lose my feet again. The aliens are chirruping madly behind their light.

"Please take us. We don't mind what your planet is like; we'll learn—we'll do anything! We won't cause any trouble. Please. Oh, *please.*" The skiff is drifting farther away.

"Ruth! Althea! Are you crazy? Wait—" But I can only shuffle nightmarelike in the ooze, hearing that damn voice box wheeze, "N-not come . . . more . . . not come . . . " Althea's face turns to it, openmouthed grin.

"Yes, we understand," Ruth cries. "We don't want to come back. Please take us with you!"

I shout and Estéban splashes past me shouting too, something about radio.

"Yes-s-s," groans the voice.

Ruth sits down suddenly, clutching Althea. At that moment Estéban grabs the edge of the skiff beside her.

"Hold them, Estéban! Don't let her go."

He gives me one slit-eyed glance over his shoulder, and I recognize his total uninvolvement. He's had a good look at that camouflage paint and the absence of fishing gear. I make a desperate rush and slip again. When I come up Ruth is saying, "We're going with these people, Captain. Please take your money out of my purse, it's in the plane. And give this to Mr. Fenton."

She passes him something small; the notebook. He takes it slowly.

"Estéban! No!"

He has released the skiff.

"Thank you so much," Ruth says as they float apart. Her voice is shaky; she raises it. "There won't be any trouble, Don. Please send this cable. It's to a friend of mine, she'll take care of everything." Then she adds the craziest touch of the entire night. "She's a grand person; she's director of nursing training at N.I.H."

As the skiff drifts out, I hear Althea add something that sounds like "Right on."

Sweet Jesus . . . Next minute the humming has started; the light is receding fast. The last I see of Mrs. Ruth Parsons and Miss Althea Parsons is two small shadows against that light, like two opossums. The light snaps off, the hum deepens—and they're going, going, gone away.

In the dark water beside me Estéban is instructing everybody in general to *chingarse* themselves.

"Friends, or something," I tell him lamely. "She seemed to

want to go with them."

He is pointedly silent, hauling me back to the plane. He knows what could be around here better than I do, and Mayas have their own longevity program. His condition seems improved. As we get in I notice the hammock has been repositioned.

In the night—of which I remember little—the wind changes. And at seven-thirty next morning a Cessna buzzes the sandbar under cloudless skies.

By noon we're back in Cozumel. Captain Estéban accepts his fees and departs laconically for his insurance wars. I leave the Parsons' bags with the Caribe agent, who couldn't care less. The cable goes to a Mrs. Priscilla Hayes Smith, also of Bethesda. I take myself to a medico and by three P.M. I'm sitting on the Cabanas terrace with a fat leg and a double margarita, trying to believe the whole thing.

The cable said, *Althea and I taking extraordinary opportunity for travel. Gone several years. Please take charge our affairs. Love, Ruth.*

She'd written it that afternoon, you understand.

I order another double, wishing to hell I'd gotten a good look at that gizmo. Did it have a label, Made by Betelgeusians? No matter how weird it was, *how* could a person be crazy enough to imagine—?

Not only that but to hope, to plan? *If I could only go away. . . .* That's what she was doing, all day. Waiting, hoping, figuring how to get Althea. To go sight unseen to an alien world. . .

With the third margarita I try a joke about alienated women, but my heart's not in it. And I'm certain there won't be any bother, any trouble at all. Two human women, one of them possibly pregnant, have departed for, I guess, the stars; and the fabric of society will never show a ripple. I brood: do all Mrs. Parsons's friends hold themselves in readiness for any eventuality, including leaving Earth? And will Mrs. Parsons somehow one day contrive to send for Mrs. Priscilla Hayes Smith, that grand person?

I can only send for another cold one, musing on Althea. What suns will Captain Estéban's sloe-eyed offspring, if any, look upon? "Get in, Althea, we're taking off for Orion." "A-okay, Mother." Is that some system of upbringing? *We survive by ones and twos in the chinks of your world-machine. . . . I'm used to aliens. . . .* She'd meant every word. Insane. How could a woman choose to live among unknown monsters, to say good-bye to her home, her world?

As the margaritas take hold, the whole mad scenario melts down to the image of those two small shapes sitting side by side in the receding alien glare.

Two of our opossums are missing.

YOUR FACES, O MY SISTERS! YOUR FACES FILLED OF LIGHT!

HOT SUMMER NIGHT, big raindrops falling faster now as she swings along the concrete expressway, high over the old dead city. Lightning is sizzling and cracking over the lake behind her. Beautiful! The flashes jump the roofs of the city to life below her, miles of cube buildings gray and sharp-edged in the glare. People lived here once, all the way to the horizons. Smiling, she thinks of all those walls and windows full of people, living in turbulence and terror. Incredible.

She's passing a great billboard-thing dangling and banging in the wind. Part of a big grinning face: O-N-D-E-R-B-R-E-A, whatever that was, bright as day. She strides along enjoying the cool rain on her bare head. No need to pull up her parka for a few minutes yet, the freshness is so great. All headaches completely gone. The sisters were wrong, she's perfectly fine. There was no reason to wait any longer, with the messages in her pack and Des Moines out there ahead. They didn't realize how walking rests you.

Sandals just getting wet, she notes. It feels good, but she mustn't let them get wet through, they'll chafe and start a blister. Couriers have to think of things like that. In a few minutes she'll climb down one of the ramps and take shelter.

There's ramps along here every half-mile or so, all over the old city. Chi-cago or She-cago, which was it. She should find out, she's been this way several times now. Courier to the West. The lake behind her is Michigam, Michi-gami, the shining Big-Sea-Water. Satisfied, she figures she has come nearly seventy miles already since she left the hostel yesterday, and only one hitch. I'm not even tired. That beautiful old sister, she thinks. I'd have liked to talk with her more. Like the wise old Nokomis. That's the trouble, I always want to stop and explore the beautiful places and people, and I always want to get on too, get to the next. Couriers see so much. Someday she'll come back here and have a good swim in the lake, loaf and ramble around the old city. So much to see, no danger except from falling walls, she's expert at watching that. Some sisters say there are dog packs here, she doesn't believe it. And even if there are, they wouldn't be dangerous. Animals aren't dangerous if you know what to do. No dangers left at all, in the whole free wide world!

She shakes the rain out of her face, smiling up at the blowing night. To be a courier, what a great life! Rambling woman, on the road. Heyo, sister! Any mail, any messages for Des Moines and points west? Travel, travel on. But she is traveling in really heavy downpour now, she sees. She squeezes past a heap of old wrecked "cars" and splash! one foot goes in ankle-deep. The rain is drumming little fountains all over the old roadway. Time to get under; she reaches back and pulls the parka hood up from under her pack, thinking how alive the highway looks in the flashing lightning and rain. This road must have been full of the "cars" once, all of them shiny new, roaring along probably quite close together, belching gases, shining their lights, using all this space. She can almost hear them, poor crazy creatures. *Rrrr-oom!* A blazing bolt slaps down near her, strobes on and off. Whew! That was close. She chuckles, feeling briefly dizzy in the ozone. Ah, here's a ramp right by her, it looks okay.

Followed by a strange whirling light shaft, some trick of the storm, she ducks aside and runs lightly down from the Stevenson Expressway into the Thirty-fifth Street underpass.

"Gone." Patrolman Lugioni cuts the flasher, lets the siren growl diminuendo. The cruiser accelerates in the curb lane, broadcasting its need of a ring job. "Shitass kids out hitching on a night like this." He shakes his head.

Al, the driver, feels under his leg for the pack of smokes. "I thought it was a girl."

"Who can tell," Lugioni grunts. Lightning is cracking everywhere, it's a cloudburst. All around them the Saturday night madhouse tears on, every car towing a big bustle of dirty water in the lights of the car behind.

⊞

—Dry under the overpass, but it's really dark in here between the lightning flashes. She pushes back her parka, walks on carefully avoiding wrecks and debris. With all that flashing, her night vision won't develop. Too bad, she has keen night vision. Takes forty-five minutes to come up fully, she knows a lot of stuff like that.

She's under a long elevated roadway down the center of an old street, it seems to go on for miles straight ahead. Almost straight west, good. Outside on both sides the open street is jumping with rain, splashing up white like plaster grass as the lightning cracks. *Boom! Barooomm-m-m!* The Midwest has great storms. She loves the wild uproar, loves footing through a storm. All for her! How she'd like to strip and run out into it! Get a good bath, clean off all the dust and sweat. Her stuff would keep dry in here. Hey, shall I? . . . Almost she does, but she isn't really that dirty yet and she should get on, she lost so much time at that hostel. Couriers have to act responsible. She makes herself pad soberly along dodging junk in the dark, thinking, now here's the kind of place a horse would be no good.

She has always this perennial debate with herself about getting a horse. Some of the couriers like to ride. It probably is faster, she thinks. But not much, not much. Most people have no idea how fast walking goes, I'm up and moving while they're still fussing with the horse. And so much trouble, feeding them, worrying about their feet. You can carry more, of course. But the real point is how isolated it makes you. No more hitching, no more fun of getting to know all kinds of sisters. Like that wise motherly sister back there who picked her up coming into the city. Sort of a strange dialect, but I could understand her and the love showed through. A mother . . . Maybe I'll be a mother someday, she thinks. But not yet. Or I'll be the good old Nokomis. *The wrinkled old Nokomis, many things Nokomis taught her.* . . . And those horses she had, I never saw horses go like that. Must be some tremendous farms around here. Tomorrow when she's out of the city she'll get up on a high place where she can really look over the country. If I see a good horse-farm I'll remember. A horse would be useful if I take the next route, the route going all the way west, across the Rockies. But Des Moines is far enough now. Des Moines is just right, on my own good legs.

⊕

"She was one of *them,* one of those bra-burners," Mrs. Olmsted says pursily, sliding gingerly out of her plastic raincoat. She undoes her plastic Rainflower bonnet. "Oh, god, my set."

"You don't usually pick up hitchers, Mom." Bee is sitting in the dinette, doing her nails with Plum Love.

"It was starting to storm," the mother says defensively, hustling into the genuine Birds Eye kitchen area. "She had a big knapsack on her back. Oh, to tell you the truth, I thought it was a boy scout. That's why I stopped."

"Ha ha ha."

"I dropped her right at Stony Island. That's as far as we go, I said. She kept talking crazy about my face."

"Probably stoned. She'll get murdered out there."

"Bee, I told you, I wish you wouldn't use that word. I don't want to know about it, I have no sympathy at all. She's made her bed, I say. Now, where's the Fricolator lid?"

"In the bathroom. What about your face?"

"What's it doing in the bathroom?"

"I used it to soak my fluffbrush, it's the only thing the right shape. What'd she say about your face?"

"Oh, Bee, your father would murder you. That's no way to do, we eat out of that." Her voice fades and rises, still protesting, as she comes back with the lid.

"My hair isn't poison, Mom. Besides, the heat will fix it. You know my hair is pure hell when it rains, I have to look good at the office."

"I wish you wouldn't swear, either."

"What did she say about your face, Mom?"

"Oh, my face. Well! 'Your face has wisdom,' she says in this crazy way. 'Mother-lines full of wisdom and light.' *Lines.* Talk about rude! She called me the wrinkled old somebody. I told her what I thought about girls hitchhiking, believe me I told her. Here, help me clear this off, your father will be home any minute. You know what she said?"

"What did she say? Here, hand me that."

"She asked, did I mean dogs? *Dogs!* 'There is no fear,' she says, 'there is no fear on the whole wide Earth.' And she kept asking me where did I get the horses. I guess that's some word they have, she meant the Buick."

"Stoned, I told you. Poor kid."

"Bee, *please*. What I say is, a girl like that is asking for it. Just asking for whatever she gets. I don't care what you say, there are certain rules. I have no sympathy, no sympathy at all."

"You can say that again."

—Her sandals are damp but okay. Good leather, she sewed and oiled them herself. When she's real old she'll have a little cabin by the road somewhere, make sandals and stuff for the sisters going by. How would I get the leather, she thinks. She could probably deal with one of the peddler sisters. Or can she tan it herself? It isn't so hard. Have to look that up sometime.

The rain is still coming down hard, it's nice and cool now. She notices she has been scuffling through drifts of old paper, making it sail away into the gusty wind. All kinds of trash, here and everywhere. How they must have lived. The flashing outside is lighting up a solid wall of ruined buildings. Big black empty windows, some kind of factory. A piece of paper blows up and sticks on her neck. She peels it off, looks at it as she walks. In the lightning she can see it's a picture. Two sisters hugging. Neat. They're dressed in funny old clothes. And the small sister has such a weird look, all painted up and strange. Like she was pretending to smile. A picture from the troubles, obviously.

As she tucks it in her pocket she sees there's a light, right ahead between the pillars of the overpass. A hand-lantern, it moves. Somebody in here too, taking shelter. How great! Maybe they even live here, will have tales to tell! She hastens toward the light, calling the courier's cry:

"Heyo, sister! Any mail, any messages? Des Moines and going west!"

Yes—she sees there are two of them, wrapped up in rain gear, leaning on one of the old "cars." Probably travelers too. She calls again.

"Hello?" One of them replies hesitantly. They must be worried by the storm, some sisters are. She'll reassure them, nothing to be afraid of, nothing at all. How she loves to meet new sisters, that's the beautiest part of a courier's life. Eagerly she strides through papers and puddles and comes into the circle of their light.

⊞

"But who can we report it *to*, Don? You aren't even known here, city police wouldn't pay any attention."

He shrugs regretfully, knowing his wife is right.

"One more unfortunate, weary of breath, rashly importunate, gone to her death."

"What's that from?"

"Oh, Hood. Thomas Hood. When the Thames used to be full of ruined women."

"Wandering around in this district at night, it's suicide. We're not so safe here ourselves, you know. Do you think that AAA tow truck will really come?"

"They said they would. They have quite a few calls ahead of us. Nobody's moving out there, she'll probably be safe as long as this downpour lasts, anyway. We'll get inside when it eases up."

"Yes . . . I wish we could have done something, Don. She seemed so, I don't know, not just a tramp."

"We couldn't very well hit her over the head and take her in, you know. Besides, she was a fairly strong-looking little piece, if you noticed."

"Yes . . . Don, she *was* crazy, wasn't she? She didn't hear one thing you said. Calling you 'sister.' And that ad she showed us, she said it was two women. That's sick, isn't it—I mean, seriously disturbed? Not just drugs?"

He laughs ruefully. "Questions I'd love to be able to answer. These things interact, it's tough to unscramble. But yes, for what it's worth, my intuition says it was functional. Of course my intuition got some help, you heard her say she'd been in a hospital or hostel somewhere. . . . If I had to bet, Pam, I'd say post-ECS. That placid waxy cast to the face. Capillary patches. A lot of rapid eye movement. Typical."

"You mean, she's had electric shock."

"My guess."

"And we just let her walk away. . . . You know, I don't think that truck is coming at all. I think they just say yes and forget it. I've heard the Triple-A is a terrible fraud."

"Got to give them time on a night like this."

"Ummm . . . I wonder where she is now."

"Hey, look, the rain's letting up. We better hop inside and lock the doors."

"Right, sister."

"Don't you start that, I warn you. Lock that back window, too."

"Don . . ."

"Yeah, what?"

"Don, she seemed so, I don't know. Happy and free. She—she was *fun*."

"That's the sick part, honey."

⊞

—The rain is letting up now, she sees. How convenient, because the sheltering ramp is now veering away to the north. She follows the median strip of the old avenue out into the open, not bothering to put the parka up. It's a wrecked part of the city, everything knocked down flat for a few blocks, but the street is okay. In the new quiet she can hear the lake waves smacking the shore, miles behind. Really have to stop and camp here awhile some trip, she thinks, skirting a wreck or two on the center strip. By the shining Big-Sea-Waters.

Was it Michi-Gami or Gitche-Gumee? No matter; she loves the whole idea of Hiawatha. In fact she always felt she *was* the sister Hiawatha somehow; it's one of the few pieces from the old days that makes any sense to her. Growing up learning all the ways of the beautiful things, the names of the wild creatures, learning lovingly all the richness, learning how. There are words for it, some of the sisters talk so beautifully. But that's not her way, words; she just knows what's the way that feels right. The good way, and herself rambling through the wonderful world. Maybe she's a little superficial, but it takes all kinds. I'm the *working* kind, she thinks proudly. Responsible, too, a courier. Speaking of which, she's at a Y; better make sure she's still headed west, these old streets can twist you.

She stops and opens her belt compass, watches the dim green needle steady. There! Right that way. And what luck, in the last flickers of lightning she can see trees a couple of blocks ahead. Maybe a park!

How fast these storms go; she dodges across a wreck-filled intersection, and starts trotting for the sheer joy of strength and health down the open median toward the park. Yes, it looks like a long strip of greenery, heading due west for quite a ways.

She'll have nice walking. Somewhere ahead she'll hit another of the old freeways, the Kennedy or the Dan Ryan, that'll take her out of the city. Bound to be traffic on them too, in the morning. She'll get a hitch from a grain cart, maybe, or maybe a peddlar. Or maybe something she's never seen before, one more of the surprises of the happy world.

Jogging, feeling her feet fall fast and free, she thinks with respect of the two sisters she met back there under the ramp. The big one was some kind of healer, from down South. So loving together, making jokes. But I'm not going to get sick anymore, I'm really well. Proud of the vitality in her, she strides swiftly across the last intersection and spots a path meandering into the overgrown strip of park. Maybe I can go barefoot in there, no glass, she thinks. The last lightning flash helps her as she heads in under the dripping trees.

The biker cuts off his spotlight fast, accelerates past the park entrance. She looked okay, little and running. Scared. But something about her bothers him. Not quite right. Maybe she's meeting somebody in there?

He's running alone tonight, the rain freaked them all out. Alone isn't so good. But maybe she's alone, too? Small and alone . . .

Gunning up Archer Avenue, he decides to cut back once through the park crossover, check it out. The main thing is not to get the bike scratched up.

—Beautiful cool clean breeze on her face, and clouds are breaking up. Old moon is trying to shine out! The path is deep in leaves here, okay to get the sandals off and dry them awhile.

She balances one-legged, unbuckling. The left one is soaked, all right. She hangs them over her pack and steps out barefoot. Great.

Out beyond the trees the buildings are reared up high on both sides now, old cubes and towers sticking up at the racing clouds, glints of moonlight where the glass windows are still in. Fantastic. She casts a loving thought back toward the long-dead ones who had built all this. The Men, the city-builders. So complex and weird, so different from the good natural way. Too bad they never lived to know the beautiful peaceful free world.

But they wouldn't have liked it, probably. They were sick, poor things. But maybe they could have been different; they were people too, she muses.

Suddenly she is startled by the passage of something crashing across the path ahead, and without thinking springs nimbly into a big bush. Lightning, growling noises—in a minute it fades away. A deer, maybe, she wonders, rubbing her head. But what was the noise? One of those dogs, maybe? Could it be a dog pack?

H'mm. She rubs harder, frowning because the headache seems to have come back. Like a knife blade in her temple. Ouch! It's really bad again, it's making her dizzy. She blinks, sees the buildings beyond the park blaze up brightly—squares of yellow light everywhere like a million windows. Oh, no, not the bad hallucinations again. No, she's well now!

But yes, it is—and great lights seem to be suddenly everywhere, a roar of noise breaks out all around her in the dead streets, things are rushing and clanging. Maybe she isn't quite as well as she thought.

Grunting softly with pain, she strips a bunch of cool wet leaves, presses it against her forehead, the veins in her neck. Pressure. That's what it is, the air pressure must have changed fast in the storm. She'll be all right in a few minutes. . . . Even the memory of the deer seems strange, as if she'd glimpsed some kind of crazy machine with a sister riding on it. Crazy! The uproar around her has voices in it too, a ghostly whistle blows. . . . Go away, dreams. . . .

She stands quietly, pressing the coolness to her temples, willing the noisy hallucination to leave. Slowly it does; subsides, fades, vanishes. Leaving her in peace back in the normal, happy world. She's okay, that was nothing at all!

She tosses the leaves down and strikes out on the path, remembering—whew!—how bad it had been when she was back there at the hostel. All because of that funny flu or whatever that made her gut swell up so. Bad dreams all the time, real horrible hallucinations. Admit it; couriers do catch things. But it's worth it.

The sisters had been so scared. How they kept questioning her. Are you dreaming now? Do you see it now, dear? Making her describe it, like she was a historical play. They must read too much history, she thinks, splashing through a puddle, scaring up some little night-thing. A frog, probably, out in the rain like me. And all that talk about babies. Babies . . . Well, a baby might be nice, someday. Not till after a lot more trips, though. Right now she's a walking sister, traveling on, heading for Des Moines and points west!

Left-right, left-right, her slim strong legs carry her Indian style, every bit of her feeling good now in the rain-fresh night. Not a scrap weary; she loves her tough enduring wiry body. To be a courier, surely that's the best life of all. To be young and night-walking in the great free moonlit world. Heyo, sisters! She grins to herself, padding light-foot. Any messages, any mail?

⌗

"Of course she's not dangerous, Officer," the doctor says authoritatively. The doctor is a heavy, jolly-looking woman with a big Vuitton carryall parked on the desk. The haggard young man slumped in a lounger over at the side stares tiredly, says nothing.

"Jeans, green parka, knapsack, sandals. May have credit cards," the detective repeats, writing in his notebook. "Hair?"

"Short. Just growing out, in fact; it was shaved during treatment. I realize that isn't much to go on."

The policeman juts his lip out noncommittally, writing. Why can't they keep track of their patients, a big place like this? One medium-height, medium-looking girl in jeans and a parka . . .

"You see, she is quite, quite helpless," the heavy woman says seriously, fingering her desk calendar. "The delusional system has expanded."

"You were supposed to break that up," the young man says suddenly, not looking up. "My wife was, I mean, when I brought her here. . . ."

His voice is stale with exhausted anger, this has all been said before. The psychiatrist sighs briefly, says nothing.

"The delusion, is it dangerous? Is she hostile?" the detective asks hopefully.

"No. I told you. It takes the form of a belief that she's living in another world where everybody is her friend. She's completely trusting, you'll have no difficulty."

"Oh." He puts the notebook away with finality, getting up. The psychiatrist goes with him to the door. Out of earshot of the husband she says quietly, "I'll be at my office number when you've checked the morgue."

"Yeah."

He leaves, and she walks back to the desk, where the young man is now staring unseeingly at a drift of Polaroid snaps. The one on top shows a young brown-haired woman in a yellow dress in a garden somewhere.

—Moon riding high now in the summer night, cutting through a race of little silver clouds, making shafts of light wheel over the still city. She can see where the park is ending up ahead, there's a wreck-strewn traffic circle. She swings along strongly, feeling now just the first satisfying edge of tiredness, just enough to make her enjoy her own nimble endurance. Right-and-a-left-and-a right-and-a-left, toes-in Indian style, that trains the tendons. She can go on forever.

Now here's the traffic circle, better watch out for metal and glass underfoot. She waits for a bright patch of moonlight and trots across to the center, hearing one faint hallucinatory screech or roar somewhere. No, no more of *that.* She grins at herself firmly, making her way around the pieces of an old statue toppled here. *That is but the owl and owlet, talking in their native language,* something *Hiawatha's Sisters.* I'd like to talk with them in their native language, she thinks—and speaking of which, she sees to her delight there's a human figure on the far side of the circle. What, another sister out night-walking too!

"Heyo, sister!"

"Hi," the other replies. It's a Midwest person, she can tell. She must live here, can tell about the old city!

Eagerly she darts between the heaps in the roadway, joyfully comes to the beautiful sister, her face so filled in light.

"Where heading? Out to ramble? I'm a courier," she explains, taking the sister's arm. So much joy, a world of friends. "Any messages, any mail?" she laughs.

And they stride on together, free-swinging down the median strip of the old avenue to keep away from falling stuff in the peaceful old ruins. Over to one side is a bent sign saying To Dan Ryan Expressway, O'hare Airport. On the heading for Des Moines and points west!

"I don't remember," the girl, or woman, repeats hoarsely,

frowning. "I really don't remember, it was all strange. My head was really fucked up, I mean, all I wanted was to get back and sack out, the last john was a bummer. I mean, I didn't know the area. You know? I asked her could she give me some change."

"What did she say? Did she have money with her?" the older man asks with deadly patience. His wife is sitting on the leather sofa, her mouth trembling a little.

"I don't remember, really. I mean, she was talking but she wasn't listening, I could see she was behind the heavy stuff. She offered me some chocolate. Oh, shit, she was gone. Excuse me. She was really gone. I thought she was—well, she kept saying, y'know. Then she gave me all her cards."

The man looks down at them silently, lying on the coffee table. His daughter's married name embossed on the brown Saks plastic.

"So when I saw the paper I thought I should, well, you know." She gets up, smoothing her white Levi's. "It wasn't just the reward. She . . . Thanks anyway."

"Yes," he says automatically. "We do thank you, Miss Jackson, was it."

"Yes," his wife echoes shakily.

Miss Jackson, or whatever, looks around at the woman, the man, the elegantly lived-in library; hitches her white shoulder bag.

"I tried to tell her," she says vaguely. "She said, about going west. She wouldn't . . . I'm sorry."

"Yes, thank you." He's ushering her to the door. "I'm afraid there wasn't anything anyone could do."

"She wasn't in this world."

"No."

When the door closes behind her, the older woman makes an uncertain noise and then says heavily, "Why?"

Her husband shakes his head, performs a non-act of straightening the credit cards, putting them on another table.

"We'll have to call Henry, when he gets back from—"

"Why?" the wife repeats as if angry. "Why did she? What did she want? Always running away. Freedom. Doesn't she know you can't have freedom? Why isn't this world good enough for her? She had everything. If I can take it why can't she?"

He has nothing to say, only moves near her and briefly touches her shoulder.

"Why didn't Dr. Albers *do* something? All those drugs, those shocks, it just made her worse. Henry never should have taken her there, it's all his fault—"

"I guess Henry was desperate," her husband says in a gray tone.

"She was all right when she was with us."

"Maria. Maria, please. She was out of her head. He had to do something. She wouldn't even recognize her own baby."

His wife nods, trembling harder. "My little girl, my little girl . . ."

⊞

—Glorious how bright it is now, she pads along still barefoot on the concrete median, tipping her head back to watch the moon racing above the flying clouds, imparting life and motion to the silent street, almost as if it was alive again. Now watch it, she cautions herself cheerfully—and watch the footing too, no telling what kind of sharp stuff is lying out here. No more dreaming about the old days, that was what gave her the fever-nightmares. Dreaming she was stuck back in history like a caged-up animal. An "affluent young suburban matron," whatever that was. All those weird people, telling her. Don't go outside, don't do this, don't do that, don't open the door, don't breathe. Danger everywhere.

How did they *live*, she wonders, seeing the concrete good and clean underfoot. Those poor old sisters, never being free, never even being able to go walking! Well, those dreams really made history live and breathe for her, that was sure. So vivid— whew! Maybe some poor old sister's soul has touched hers, maybe something mystical like that. She frowns faintly, feeling a stab of pressure in her forehead.

Now really, watch it! She scolds herself, hoisting up the pack straps, flapping the dry parka. All secure. She breaks into a slow light-footed jog, just because she feels so good. Cities are so full of history. Time to forget all that, just appreciate being alive. Hello, moon! Hello, sky! She trots on carefully, tickled by it all, seeing a moon's-eye view of herself: one small purposeful dot resolutely moving west. Courier to Des Moines. All alone in the big. friendly night world, greeting the occasional night-bird sisters. One traveling woman, going on through.

She notes a bad scatter of debris ahead and slows to pick her way with care through the "cars," not wanting to put her sandals back on yet. It's so bright—and hello! The sky really is brightening in the east behind her. Sunrise in another hour or so.

She's been on the road about twenty hours but she isn't really weary at all, she could go on all day if it didn't get so hot. She peers ahead, looking for signs of the Ryan Freeway that'll carry her west. What she'll do is stop and have a snack in the sunrise, maybe boil up some tea. And then go on awhile until it heats up, time to find a nice cool ruin and hole up for the day. Hey, maybe she can make O'Hare! She stayed there once before, it's neat.

She has enough rations in her pack to go at least two days easy, she figures. But she's short on chocolate now; have to get some at the next settlement if they have it. Sweet stuff is good for calories when you're exercising. She pads on, musing about the sister she shared her chocolate with while they walked together after the park. Such a free sweet face, all the sisters are so great but this one was especially interesting, living here studying the old days. She knew so much, all those stories, whew! Imagine when people had to sell their sex organs to the Men just to eat!

It's too much for her, she thinks, grinning. Leave that to the students. I'm an action person, yes. A courier, a traveler, moving along looking at it all, the wonder-filled world. Sampling, enjoying, footing it over the miles. Right-and-a-left-and-a-right-and-a-left on the old roadways. A courier's feet are tough and brown as oak. *Of all beasts she learned the language, learned their names and all their secrets. Talked with them whene'er she met them*—a great rhythm for hiking, with a fresh breeze behind her and the moon setting ahead!

The breeze is making the old buildings on both sides creak and clank too, she notices. Better stay out here in the middle, even if it's getting narrow. The houses are really crowded in along here, all sagging and trashy. "Slums," probably. Where the crazy people lived on top of each other. What a mess it must have been; interesting to her but rotten for them. Well, they're gone now, she thinks, dodging around a heap of broken junk in the intersection, starting down the center strip of the next long block.

But something isn't gone, she notices; footsteps that have been pad-padding along after her for a while are still there. An animal, one of the poor dogs, she thinks. Following her. Oh, well, they must do all right in here, with rats and such.

She whirls around a couple of times, but sees nothing. It must be scared. What's its native language, she wonders, and forgets about it as she sees ahead, unmistakable, the misty silhouette of a freeway overpass. Hey, is that the Ryan already?

She casts a glance up at the floating-down moon, sees the sky is paling fast. And the left side of the street is passing an empty cleared place, the going looks all right there. She decides to cross over.

Yes, it's good walking, and she settles into her easy barefoot swing, letting one last loving thought go back to the poor maddened people who once strove here, who somehow out of their anguish managed to send their genes down to her, to give her happy life: courier going west! With the dawn wind in her hair and the sun coming up to light the whole free world!

"A routine surveillance assignment," the young policewoman, O'Hara, says carefully.

"A stakeout." The bald reporter nods.

"Well, yes. We were assigned to surveil the subject building entrance. Officer Alioto and myself were seated in the parked car."

"So you saw the assault."

"No," she says stiffly. "We did not observe anything unusual. Naturally we observed the pedestrians, I mean the female subject and the alleged—alleged assailants, they were moving west at the time."

"You saw four punks following her."

"Well, it could look that way."

"You saw them going after her and you just sat there."

"We carried out our *orders,*" she tells him. "We were assigned to surveil the building. We did not observe any alleged attack, nobody was running."

"You see the four of them jump this girl and you don't call that an attack?"

"We did not observe it. We were two blocks away."

"You could have seen if you wanted to," he says tiredly. "You could have cruised one block, you could have tapped the horn."

"I told you we were on a covert detail. You can't expect an officer to destroy his cover every time some little tramp runs down the street."

"You're a woman," he says wonderingly. "You'd sit there and let a girl get it."

"I'm not a nursemaid," she protests angrily. "I don't care if she was crazy. A spoiled brat if you ask me, all those women's-lib freaks. I work. Who does she think she is, running on the street at night? She thinks the police have nothing more important to do than that?"

⊞

—Sunrise coming on sure enough, though it's still dark down here. The magic hour. And that stupid dog or dogs are still coming on too, she notes. Pad-pad-pad, they've crossed over to the sidewalk behind her. Well, dogs don't attack people, it's just like those false wolf scares. *Learn of every beast its nature, learn their names and all their secrets.* They're just lonesome and curious, it's their nature to follow people. Tag along and veer off if I say boo.

She strides along, debating whether she should put her wet sandals on or whether it's going to stay this clean. If so, she can make it barefoot up to the expressway ramp—and it is the Ryan, she can see the big sign now. Great, that'll be the perfect place to make her breakfast, just about sunrise. Better remember to pick up a couple of dry sticks and some paper under the ramp, not much to burn on those skyways.

Ignoring the footfalls pattering behind, she lets her mind go back pleasurably to the great breakfasts she's had. All the sunrise views, how she loves that. Like the morning on the old Ohio Turnpike, when all the owls hooted at once, and the mists turned pink and rose up and there was the shining river all spread out below her. Beautiful. Even with the mosquitoes. If you're going to appreciate life, you can't let little things like mosquitoes bother you. . . . That was before her peculiar sickness, when she was at the hostel. So many good hostels she's stopped at, all the interesting different settlements and farms, all the great sister-people. Someday she'll do the whole west route, know people everywhere. . . . Pad-pad-pad, she hears them again momentarily, rubs away a tiny ache in her temple. *Boo*, she chuckles to herself, feeling her bare feet falling sturdy and swift, left-and-a-right-and-a-left, carrying her over the miles, across the free beautiful friendly Earth. O my sisters, living in light!

Pictures flit through her head, all the places she wants to

visit. The Western mountains, the real big ones. And the great real Sea. Maybe she'll visit the grave of the Last Man when she's out there, too. That would be interesting. See the park where he lived, hear the tapes of his voice and all. Of course he probably wasn't the actually last Man, just the one they knew about. It would be really something to hear such a different person's voice.

Pad-pad-pad-louder, closer than before. They're going to be a nuisance if they follow her up the ramp and hang around her breakfast.

"Boo!" she shouts, laughing, swinging around at them. They scatter so fast she can barely glimpse dark shapes vanishing into the old walls. Good. "Boo!" she shouts again, sorry to have to drive them away, and swings back on course, satisfied.

The buildings are beside her now, but they're pretty intact, no glass she can see underfoot. In fact, the glass is still in the old store windows here. She glances in curiously as she passes, heaps of moldy stuff and faded pictures and printing. "Ads." Lots of sisters' faces, all looking so weird and fake-grinning. One window has nothing but dummy heads in it, all with strange-looking imitation hair or something on them. Fantastic.

—But here they come again behind her, pad-pad-pad, and she really ought to discourage them before they decide to stick with her up the freeway.

"Boo, boo! No—" Just as she's turning on them, something fast and dark springs and strikes or snaps at her arm! And before she can react she sees they are suddenly all around her, ahead of her—rearing up weirdly, just like people!

"Get *out!*" she shouts, feeling a rush of something unknown—anger?—sending heat through her, this is almost like one of the dreams! But hardness strikes her neck, staggers her, with roaring in her ears.

She hits out awkwardly, feels herself slammed down on concrete—pain—her head is hurt. And she is striking, trying to fend them off, realizing unbelieving that the brutes are tugging at her, terribly strong, pulling her legs and arms apart, spread-eagling her.

"Sisters!" she shouts, really being hurt now, struggling strongly. "*Sisters!* Help!" But something gags her so that she can only choke, while she feels them tearing at her clothes, her belly. *No, no*—she understands with horror that they really are going to bite her, to eat her flesh, and remembers from somewhere that wild dogs tear out the victim's guts first.

A great wave of anger convulses her against their fangs, she knows this is a stupid accident, a mistake—but her blood is fountaining everywhere, and the pain, the *pain!* All in a moment she is being killed, she knows now she is going to die here.

—But as a truly terrible agony cuts into her crotch and entrails, she sees or thinks she sees—yes!—in the light, in the patches of sky between the terrible bodies of her attackers, she can see them coming—see far off but clear the beautiful faces of her sisters speeding to save her, to avenge her! O my sisters, yes—it will be all right now, she knows, choking in her blood. They will finish these animals. And my knapsack, my messages—somewhere inside the pain and the dying she knows it is all right, it will be all fixed when they get here; the beloved sisters will save her, this is just an accident—and soon she, or someone like her, will be going on again, will be footing over the wide free Earth, courier to Des Moines and points west—

HOUSTON, HOUSTON, DO YOU READ?

LORIMER GAZES AROUND the big crowded cabin, trying to listen to the voices, trying also to ignore the twitch in his insides that means he is about to remember something bad. No help; he lives it again, that long-ago moment. Himself running blindly— or was he pushed?—into the strange toilet at Evanston Junior High. His fly open, his dick in his hand, he can still see the gray zipper edge of his jeans around his pale exposed pecker. The hush. The sickening wrongness of shapes, faces turning. The first blaring giggle. *Girls.* He was in the *girls' can.*

He flinches wryly now, so many years later, not looking at the women's faces. The cabin curves around over his head, surrounding him with their alien things: the beading rack, the twins' loom, Andy's leatherwork, the damned kudzu vine wriggling everywhere, the chickens. So cozy . . . Trapped, he is. Irretrievably trapped for life in everything he does not enjoy. Structurelessness. Personal trivia, unmeaning intimacies. The claims he can somehow never meet. Ginny: *You never talk to me.* . . . Ginny, love, he thinks involuntarily. The hurt doesn't come.

Bud Geirr's loud chuckle breaks in on him. Bud is joking with some of them, out of sight around a bulkhead. Dave is visible, though. Major Norman Davis on the far side of the cabin, his bearded profile bent toward a small dark woman Lorimer can't quite focus on. But Dave's head seems oddly tiny and sharp, in fact the whole cabin looks unreal. A cackle bursts out from the "ceiling"—the bantam hen in her basket.

At this moment Lorimer becomes sure he has been drugged.

Curiously, the idea does not anger him. He leans or rather tips back, perching cross-legged in the zero gee, letting his gaze go to the face of the woman he has been talking with. Connie. Constantia Morelos. A tall moonfaced woman in capacious green pajamas. He has never really cared for talking to women. Ironic.

"I suppose," he says aloud, "it's possible that in some sense we are not here."

That doesn't sound too clear, but she nods interestedly. She's watching my reactions, Lorimer tells himself. Women are natural poisoners. Has he said that aloud too? Her expression doesn't change. His vision is taking on a pleasing local clarity. Connie's skin strikes him as quite fine, healthy-looking. Olive tan even after two years in space. She was a farmer, he recalls. Big pores, but without the caked look he associates with women her age.

"You probably never wore makeup," he says. She looks puzzled. "Face paint, powder. None of you have."

"Oh!" Her smile shows a chipped front tooth. "Oh, yes, I think Andy has."

"Andy?"

"For plays. Historical plays, Andy's good at that."

"Of course. Historical plays."

Lorimer's brain seems to be expanding, letting in light. He is understanding actively now, the myriad bits and pieces linking into patterns. Deadly patterns, he perceives; but the drug is shielding him in some way. Like an amphetamine high without the pressure. Maybe it's something they use socially? No, they're watching, too.

"Space bunnies, I still don't dig it," Bud Geirr laughs infectiously. He has a friendly buoyant voice people like; Lorimer still likes it after two years.

"You chicks have kids back home, what do your folks think about you flying around out here with old Andy, h'mm?" Bud floats into view, his arm draped around a twin's shoulders. The one called Judy Paris, Lorimer decides; the twins are hard to tell. She drifts passively at an angle to Bud's big body: a jut-breasted plain girl in flowing yellow pajamas, her black hair raying out. Andy's red head swims up to them. He is holding a big green spaceball, looking about sixteen.

"Old Andy." Bud shakes his head, his grin flashing under his thick dark mustache. "When I was your age, folks didn't let their women fly around with me."

Connie's lips quirk faintly. In Lorimer's head the pieces slide toward pattern. I know, he thinks. Do you know I know? His head is vast and crystalline, very nice really. Easier to think. Women . . . No compact generalization forms in his mind, only a few speaking faces on a matrix of pervasive irrelevance. Human, of course. Biological necessity. Only so, so . . . diffuse? Pointless? . . . His sister Amy, *soprano con tremulo: Of course women could contribute as much as men if you'd treat us as equals. You'll see!* And then marrying that idiot the second time. Well, now he can see.

"Kudzu vines," he says aloud. Connie smiles. How they all smile.

"How 'boot that?" Bud says happily. "Ever think we'd see chicks in zero gee, hey, Dave? Artits-stico. Woo-ee!" Across the cabin Dave's bearded head turns to him, not smiling.

"And ol' Andy's had it all to his self. Stunt your growth, lad." He punches Andy genially on the arm, Andy catches himself on the bulkhead. Bud can't be drunk, Lorimer thinks; not on that fruit cider. But he doesn't usually sound so much like a stage Texan either. A drug.

"Hey, no offense," Bud is saying earnestly to the boy, "I mean that. You have to forgive one underprilly, underprivileged brother. These chicks are good people. Know what?" he tells the girl. "You could look stu-pendous if you fix yourself up a speck. Hey, I can show you, old Buddy's a expert. I hope you don't-mind my saying that. As a matter of fact, you look real stupendous to me right now."

He hugs her shoulders, flings out his arm and hugs Andy too. They float upward in his grasp, Judy grinning excitedly, almost pretty.

"Let's get some more of that good stuff." Bud propels them both toward the serving rack, which is decorated for the occasion with sprays of greens and small real daisies.

"Happy New Year! Hey, Happy New Year, y'all!"

Faces turn, more smiles. Genuine smiles, Lorimer thinks, maybe they really like their new years. He feels he has infinite time to examine every event, the implications evolving in crystal facets. I'm an echo chamber. Enjoyable, to be the observer. But others are observing too. They've started something here. Do they realize? So vulnerable, three of us, five of them, in this fragile ship. They don't know. A dread unconnected to action lurks behind his mind.

"By god, we made it," Bud laughs. "You space chickies, I have to give it to you. I commend you, by god, I say it. We wouldn't be here, wherever we are. Know what, I jus' might decide to stay in the service after all. Think they have room for old Bud in your space program, sweetie?"

"Knock that off, Bud," Dave says quietly from the far wall. "I don't want to hear us use the name of the Creator like that." The full chestnut beard gives him a patriarchal gravity. Dave is forty-six, a decade older than Bud and Lorimer. Veteran of six successful missions.

"Oh, my apologies, Major Dave old buddy." Bud chuckles intimately to the girl. "Our commanding ossifer. Stupendous guy. Hey, Doc!" he calls. "How's your attitude? You making out dinko?"

"Cheers," Lorimer hears his voice reply, the complex stratum of his feelings about Bud rising like a kraken in the moonlight of his mind. The submerged silent thing he has about them all, all the Buds and Daves and big, indomitable, cheerful, able, disciplined, slow-minded mesomorphs he has cast his life with. Meso-ectos, he corrected himself; astronauts aren't muscleheads. They like him, he has been careful about that. Liked him well enough to get him on *Sunbird*, to make him the official scientist on the first circumsolar mission. That little Doc Lorimer, he's cool, he's on the team. No shit from Lorimer, not like those other scientific assholes. He does the bit well with his small neat build and his deadpan remarks. And the years of turning out for the bowling, the volleyball, the tennis, the skeet, the skiing that broke his ankle, the touch football that broke his collarbone. Watch that Doc, he's a sneaky one. And the big men banging him on the back, accepting him. Their token scientist . . . The trouble is, he isn't any kind of scientist anymore. Living off his postdoctoral plasma work, a lucky hit. He hasn't really been into the math for years, he isn't up to it now. Too many other interests, too much time spent explaining elementary stuff. I'm a half-jock, he thinks. A foot taller and a hundred pounds heavier, and I'd be just like them. One of them. An alpha. They probably sense it underneath, the beta bile. Had the jokes worn a shade thin in *Sunbird*, all that year going out? A year of Bud and Dave playing gin. That damn exercycle, gearing it up too tough for me. They didn't mean it, though. We were a team.

The memory of gaping jeans flicks at him, the painful end part—the grinning faces waiting for him when he stumbled out. The howls, the dribble down his leg. Being cool, pretending to laugh too. You shitheads, I'll show you. *I am not a girl.*

Bud's voice rings out, chanting, "And a hap-pee New Year to you-all down there!" Parody of the oily NASA tone. "Hey, why don't we shoot 'em a signal? Greetings to all you Earthlings, I mean, all you little Lunies. Happy New Year in the good year whatsis." He snuffles comically. "There is a Santy Claus, Houston, ye-ew nevah saw nothin' like this! Houston, wherever you are," he sings out. "Hey, Houston! Do you read?"

In the silence Lorimer sees Dave's face set into Major Norman Davis, commanding.

And without warning he is suddenly back there, back a year ago in the cramped, shook-up command module of *Sunbird*, coming out from behind the sun. It's the drug doing this, he thinks, as memory closes around him, it's so real. Stop. He tries to hang on to reality, to the sense of trouble building underneath.

—But he can't, he is *there*, hovering behind Dave and Bud in the triple couches, as usual avoiding his official station in the middle, seeing beside them their reflections against blackness in the useless port window. The outer layer has been annealed, he can just make out a bright smear that has to be Spica floating through the image of Dave's head, making the bandage look like a kid's crown.

"Houston, Houston, *Sunbird*," Dave repeats; "*Sunbird* calling Houston. Houston, do you read? Come in, Houston."

The minutes start by. They are giving it seven out, seven back; seventy-eight million miles, ample margin.

"The high gain's shot, that's what it is," Bud says cheerfully. He says it almost every day.

"No way." Dave's voice is patient, also as usual. "It checks out. Still too much crap from the sun, isn't that right, Doc?"

"The residual radiation from the flare is just about in line with us," Lorimer says. "They could have a hard time sorting us out." For the thousandth time he registers his own faint, ridiculous gratification at being consulted.

"Shit, we're outside Mercury." Bud shakes his head. "How we gonna find out who won the Series?"

He often says that, too. A ritual, out here in eternal night. Lorimer watches the sparkle of Spica drift by the reflection of Bud's curly face-bush. His own whiskers are scant and scraggly, like a blond Fu Manchu. In the aft corner of the window is a striped glare that must be the remains of their port energy accumulators, fried off in the solar explosion that hit them a month ago and fused the outer layers of their windows. That was when Dave cut his head open on the sexlogic panel. Lorimer had been banged in among the gravity-wave experiment, he still doesn't trust the readings. Luckily the particle stream has missed one piece of the front window; they still have about twenty degrees of clear vision straight ahead. The brilliant web of the Pleiades shows there, running off into a blur of light.

Twelve minutes . . . thirteen. The speaker sighs and clicks emptily. Fourteen. Nothing.

"*Sunbird* to Houston, *Sunbird* to Houston. Come in, Houston. *Sunbird* out." Dave puts the mike back in its holder. "Give it another twenty-four."

They wait ritually. Tomorrow Packard will reply. Maybe.

"Be good to see old Earth again," Bud remarks.

"We're not using any more fuel on attitude," Dave reminds him. "I trust Doc's figures."

It's not my figures, it's the elementary facts of celestial mechanics, Lorimer thinks; in October there's only one place for Earth to be. He never says it. Not to a man who can fly two-body solutions by intuition once he knows where the bodies are. Bud is a good pilot and a better engineer; Dave is the best there is. He takes no pride in it. "The Lord helps us, Doc, if we let Him."

"Going to be a bitch docking if the radar's screwed up," Bud says idly. They all think about that for the hundredth time. It will be a bitch. Dave will do it. That was why he is hoarding fuel.

The minutes tick off.

"That's it," Dave says—and a voice fills the cabin, shockingly.

"Judy?" It is high and clear. A girl's voice.

"Judy, I'm so glad we got you. What are you doing on this band?"

Bud blows out his breath; there is a frozen instant before Dave snatches up the mike.

"*Sunbird*, we read you. This is Mission *Sunbird* calling Houston, ah, *Sunbird One* calling Houston Ground Control. Identify, who are you? Can you relay our signal? Over."

"Some skip," Bud says. "Some incredible ham."

"Are you in trouble, Judy?" the girl's voice asks. "I can't hear, you sound terrible. Wait a minute."

"This is United States Space Mission *Sunbird One*," Dave repeats. "Mission *Sunbird* calling Houston Space Center. You are dee-exxing our channel. Identify, repeat, identify yourself and say if you can relay to Houston. Over."

"Dinko, Judy, try it again," the girl says.

Lorimer abruptly pushes himself up to the Lurp, the Long-Range Particle Density Cumulator experiment, and activates its shaft motor. The shaft whines, jars; lucky it was retracted during the flare, lucky it hasn't fused shut. He sets the probe pulse on max and begins a rough manual scan.

"You are intercepting official traffic from the United States Space Mission to Houston Control," Dave is saying forcefully. "If you cannot relay to Houston get off the air, you are committing a federal offense. Say again, can you relay our signal to Houston Space Center? Over."

"You still sound terrible," the girl says. "What's Houston? Who's talking, anyway? You know we don't have much time." Her voice is sweet but very nasal.

"Jesus, that's close," Bud says. "That is close."

"Hold it." Dave twists around to Lorimer's improvised radarscope.

"There." Lorimer points out a tiny stable peak at the extreme edge of the readout slot, in the transcoronal scatter. Bud cranes too.

"A bogey!"

"Somebody else out here."

"Hello, hello? We have you now," the girl says. "Why are you so far out? Are you dinko, did you catch the flare?"

"Hold it," warns Dave. "What's the status, Doc?"

"Over three hundred thousand kilometers, guesstimated. Possibly headed away from us, going around the sun. Could be cosmonauts, a Soviet mission?"

"Out to beat us. They missed."

"With a *girl*?" Bud objects.

"They've done that. You taping this, Bud?"

"Roger-r-r." He grins. "That sure didn't sound like a Russky chick. Who the hell's Judy?"

Dave thinks for a second, clicks on the mike. "This is Major Norman Davis commanding United States spacecraft *Sunbird One*. We have you on scope. Request you identify yourself. Repeat, who are you? Over."

"Judy, stop joking," the voice complains. "We'll lose you in a minute, don't you realize we worried about you?"

"*Sunbird* to unidentified craft. This is not Judy. I say again, this is not Judy. Who are you? Over."

"What—" the girl says, and is cut off by someone saying, "Wait a minute, Ann." The speaker squeals. Then a different woman says, "This is Lorna Bethune in *Escondita*. What is going on here?"

"This is Major Davis commanding United States Mission *Sunbird* on course for Earth. We do not recognize any spacecraft *Escondita*. Will you identify yourself? Over."

"I just did." She sounds older with the same nasal drawl. "There is no spaceship *Sunbird*, and you're not on course for Earth. If this is an andy joke it isn't any good."

"This is no joke, madam!" Dave explodes. "This is the American circumsolar mission, and we are American astronauts. We do not appreciate your interference. Out."

The woman starts to speak and is drowned in a jibber of static. Two voices come through briefly. Lorimer thinks he hears the words "*Sunbird* program" and something else. Bud works the squelcher; the interference subsides to a drone.

"Ah, Major Davis?" The voice is fainter. "Did I hear you say you are on course for Earth?"

Dave frowns at the speaker and then says curtly, "Affirmative."

"Well, we don't understand your orbit. You must have very unusual flight characteristics, our readings show you won't node with anything on your present course. We'll lose the signal in a minute or two. Ah, would you tell us where you see Earth now? Never mind the coordinates, just tell us the constellation."

Dave hesitates and then holds up the mike. "Doc."

"Earth's apparent position is in Pisces," Lorimer says to the voice. "Approximately three degrees from P. Gamma."

"It is not," the woman says. "Can't you see it's in Virgo? Can't you see out at all?"

Lorimer's eyes go to the bright smear in the port window.

"We sustained some damage—"

"Hold it," snaps Dave.

"—to one window during a disturbance we ran into at perihelion. Naturally we know the relative direction of Earth on this date, October nineteen."

"October? It's March, March fifteen. You must—" Her voice is lost in a shriek.

"E-M front," Bud says, tuning. They are all leaning at the speaker from different angles, Lorimer is head-down. Space-noise wails and crashes like surf, the strange ship is too close to the coronal horizon. "—Behind you," they hear. More howls. "Band, try . . . ship . . . if you can, your signal—" Nothing more comes through.

Lorimer pushes back, staring at the spark in the window. It has to be Spica. But is it elongated, as if a second point-source is beside it? Impossible. An excitement is trying to flare out inside him, the women's voices resonate in his head.

"Playback," Dave says. "Houston will really like to hear this."

They listen again to the girl calling Judy, the woman saying she is Lorna Bethune. Bud holds up a finger. "Man's voice in there." Lorimer listens hard for the words he thought he heard. The tape ends.

"Wait till Packard gets this one." Dave rubs his arms. "Remember what they pulled on Howie? Claiming they rescued him."

"Seems like they want us on their frequency." Bud grins. "They must think we're fa-a-ar gone. Hey, looks like this other capsule's going to show up, getting crowded out here."

"If it shows up," Dave says. "Leave it on voice-alert, Bud. The batteries will do that."

Lorimer watches the spark of Spica, or Spica-plus-something, wondering if he will ever understand. The casual acceptance of some trick or ploy out here in this incredible loneliness. Well, if these strangers are from the same mold, maybe that is it. Aloud he says, "*Escondita* is an odd name for a Soviet mission. I believe it means 'hidden' in Spanish."

"Yeah," says Bud. "Hey, I know what that accent is, it's Australian. We had some Aussie bunnies at Hickam. Or-stryle-ya, woo-ee! You s'pose Woomara is sending up some kind of com-bined do?"

Dave shakes his head. "They have no capability

whatsoever."

"We ran into some fairly strange phenomena back there, Dave," Lorimer says thoughtfully. "I'm beginning to wish we could take a visual check."

"Did you goof, Doc?"

"No. Earth is where I said, if it's October. Virgo is where it would appear in March."

"Then that's it," Dave grins, pushing out of the couch. "You been asleep five months, Rip Van Winkle? Time for a hand before we do the roadwork."

"What I'd like to know is what that chick looks like," says Bud, closing down the transceiver. "Can I help you into your space suit, miss? Hey, miss, pull that in, psst-psst-psst! You going to listen, Doc?"

"Right." Lorimer is getting out his charts. The others go aft through the tunnel to the small dayroom, making no further comment on the presence of the strange ship or ships out here. Lorimer himself is more shaken than he likes; it was that damn phrase.

The tedious exercise period comes and goes. Lunchtime: they give the containers a minimum warm to conserve the batteries. Chicken à la king again; Bud puts ketchup on his and breaks their usual silence with a funny anecdote about an Australian girl, laboriously censoring himself to conform to *Sunbird*'s unwritten code on talk. After lunch Dave goes forward to the command module. Bud and Lorimer continue their current task of checking out the suits and packs for a damage-assessment EVA to take place as soon as the radiation count drops.

They are just clearing away when Dave calls them. Lorimer comes through the tunnel to hear a girl's voice blare, "—dinko trip. What did Lorna say? *Gloria* over!"

He starts up the Lurp and begins scanning. No results this time. "They're either in line behind us or in the sunward quadrant," he reports finally. "I can't isolate them."

Presently the speaker holds another thin thread of sound.

"That could be their ground control," says Dave. "How's the horizon, Doc?"

"Five hours; northwest Siberia, Japan, Australia."

"I told you the high gain is fucked up." Bud gingerly feeds power to his antenna motor. "Easy, eas-ee. The frame is twisted, that's what it is."

"Don't snap it," Dave says, knowing Bud will not.

The squeaking fades, pulses back. "Hey, we can really use this," Bud says. "We can calibrate on them."

A hard soprano says suddenly, "—should be outside your orbit. Try around Beta Aries."

"Another chick. We have a fix," Bud says happily. "We have a fix now. I do believe our troubles are over. That monkey was torqued one hundred forty-nine degrees. Woo-ee!"

The first girl comes back. "We see them, Margo! But they're so small, how can they live in there? Maybe they're tiny aliens! Over."

"That's Judy," Bud chuckles. "Dave, this is screwy, it's all in English. It has to be some UN thingie."

Dave massages his elbows, flexes his fists; thinking. They wait. Lorimer considers a hundred and forty-nine degrees from Gamma Piscium.

In thirteen minutes the voice from Earth says, "Judy, call the others, will you? We're going to play you the conversation, we think you should all hear. Two minutes. Oh, while we're waiting, Zebra wants to tell Connie the baby is fine. And we have a new cow."

"Code," says Dave.

The recording comes on. The three men listen once more to Dave calling Houston in a rattle of solar noise. The transmission clears up rapidly and cuts off with the woman saying that another ship, the *Gloria*, is behind them, closer to the sun.

"We looked up history," the Earth voice resumes. "There was a Major Norman Davis on the first *Sunbird* flight. Major was a military title. Did you hear them say 'Doc'? There was a scientific doctor on board, Dr. Orren Lorimer. The third member was Captain—that's another title—Bernhard Geirr. Just the three of them, all males of course. We think they had an early reaction engine and not too much fuel. The point is, the first *Sunbird* mission was lost in space. They never came out from behind the sun. That was about when the big flares started. Jan thinks they must have been close to one, you heard them say they were damaged."

Dave grunts. Lorimer is fighting excitement like a brush discharge sparking in his gut.

"Either they are who they say they are or they're ghosts; or they're aliens pretending to be people. Jan says maybe the disruption in those superflares could collapse the local time dimension. Pluggo. What did you observe there, I mean the highlights?"

Time dimension . . . never came back . . . Lorimer's mind narrows onto the reality of the two unmoving bearded heads before him, refuses to admit the words he thought he heard: *Before the year two thousand.* The language, he thinks. The language would have to have changed. He feels better.

A deep baritone voice says, "Margo?" In *Sunbird* eyes come alert.

"—like the big one fifty years ago." The man has the accent too. "We were really lucky being right there when it popped. The most interesting part is that we confirmed the gravity turbulence. Periodic but not waves. It's violent, we got pushed around some. Space is under monster stress in those things. We think France's theory that our system is passing through a micro-black-hole cluster looks right. So long as one doesn't plonk us."

"France?" Bud mutters. Dave looks at him speculatively.

"It's hard to imagine anything being kicked out in time. But they're here, whatever they are, they're over eight hundred kays outside us scooting out toward Aldebaran. As Lorna said, if they're trying to reach Earth they're in trouble unless they have a lot of spare gees. Should we try to talk to them? Over. Oh, great about the cow. Over again."

"Black holes," Bud whistles softly. "That's one for you, Doc. Was we in a black hole?"

"Not in one or we wouldn't be here." If we are here, Lorimer adds to himself. A micro-black-hole cluster . . . what happens when fragments of totally collapsed matter approach each other, or collide, say in the photosphere of a star? Time disruption? Stop it. Aloud he says, "They could be telling us something, Dave."

Dave says nothing. The minutes pass.

Finally the Earth voice comes back, saying that it will try to contact the strangers on their original frequency. Bud glances at Dave, tunes the selector.

"Calling *Sunbird One?*" the girl says slowly through her nose. "This is Luna Central calling Major Norman Davis of *Sunbird One.* We have picked up your conversation with our ship *Escondita.* We are very puzzled as to who you are and how you got here. If you really are *Sunbird One* we think you must have been jumped forward in time when you passed the solar flare." She pronounces it Cockney-style, "toime."

"Our ship *Gloria* is near you, they see you on their radar. We think you may have a serious course problem because you told Lorna you were headed for Earth and you think it is now October with Earth in Pisces. It is not October, it is March fifteen. I repeat, the Earth date"—she says "dyte"—"is March fifteen, time twenty hundred hours. You should be able to see Earth very close to Spica in Virgo. You said your window is damaged. Can't you go out and look? We think you have to make a big course correction. Do you have enough fuel? Do you have a computer? Do you have enough air and water and food? Can we help you? We're listening on this frequency. Luna to *Sunbird One*, come in."

On *Sunbird* nobody stirs. Lorimer struggles against internal eruptions. *Never came back. Jumped forward in time.* The cyst of memories he has schooled himself to suppress bulges up in the lengthening silence. "Aren't you going to answer?"

"Don't be stupid," Dave says.

"Dave. A hundred and forty-nine degrees is the difference between Gamma Piscium and Spica. That transmission is coming from where they say Earth is."

"You goofed."

"I did not goof. It has to be March."

Dave blinks as if a fly is bothering him.

In fifteen minutes the Luna voice runs through the whole thing again, ending, "Please, come in."

"Not a tape." Bud unwraps a stick of gum, adding the plastic to the neat wad back of the gyro leads. Lorimer's skin crawls, watching the ambiguous dazzle of Spica. Spica-plus-Earth? Unbelief grips him, rocks him with a complex pang compounded of faces, voices, the sizzle of bacon frying, the creak of his father's wheelchair, chalk on a sunlit blackboard, Ginny's bare legs on the flowered couch, Jenny and Penny running dangerously close to the lawnmower. The girls will be taller now, Jenny is already as tall as her mother. His father is living with Amy in Denver, determined to last till his son gets home. *When I get home.* This has to be insanity, Dave's right; it's a trick, some crazy trick. The language.

Fifteen minutes more; the flat, earnest female voice comes back and repeats it all, putting in more stresses. Dave wears a remote frown, like a man listening to a lousy sports program.

Lorimer has the notion he might switch off and propose a hand of gin; wills him to do so. The voice says it will now change frequencies.

Bud tunes back, chewing calmly. This time the voice stumbles on a couple of phrases. It sounds tired.

Another wait; an hour, now. Lorimer's mind holds only the bright point of Spica digging at him. Bud hums a bar of "Yellow Ribbons," falls silent again.

"Dave," Lorimer says finally, "our antenna is pointed straight at Spica. I don't care if you think I goofed, if Earth is over there we have to change course soon. Look, you can see it could be a double light source. We have to check this out."

Dave says nothing. Bud says nothing, but his eyes rove to the port window, back to his instrument panel, to the window again. In the corner of the panel is a Polaroid snap of his wife. Patty: a tall, giggling, rump-switching redhead; Lorimer has occasional fantasies about her. Little-girl voice, though. And so tall . . . Some short men chase tall women; it strikes Lorimer as undignified. Ginny is an inch shorter than he. Their girls will be taller. And Ginny insisted on starting a pregnancy before he left, even though he'll be out of commo. Maybe, maybe a boy, a son—*stop it*. Think about anything. Bud . . . Does Bud love Patty? Who knows? He loves Ginny. At seventy million miles . . .

"Judy?" Luna Central or whoever it is says. "They don't answer. You want to try? But listen, we've been thinking. If these people really are from the past, this must be very traumatic for them. They could be just realizing they'll never see their world again. Myda says these males had children and women they stayed with, they'll miss them terribly. This is exciting for us, but it may seem awful to them. They could be too shocked to answer. They could be frightened, maybe they think we're aliens or hallucinations even. See?"

Five seconds later the nearby girl says, "Da, Margo, we were into that too. Dinko. Ah, *Sunbird*? Major Davis of *Sunbird*, are you there? This is Judy Paris in the ship *Gloria*, we're only about a million kay from you, we see you on our screen." She sounds young and excited. "Luna Central has been trying to reach you, we think you're in trouble and we want to help. Please don't be frightened, we're people just like you. We think you're way off course if you want to reach Earth. Are you in trouble? Can we help? If your radio is out can you make any sort of signal? Do you know Old Morse? You'll be off our screen soon, we're truly worried about you. Please reply somehow if you possibly can, *Sunbird*, come in!"

Dave sits impassive. Bud glances at him, at the port window, gazes stolidly at the speaker, his face blank. Lorimer has exhausted surprise, he wants only to reply to the voices. He can manage a rough signal by heterodyning the probe beam. But what then, with them both against him?

The girl's voice tries again determinedly. Finally she says, "Margo, they won't peep. Maybe they're dead? I think they're aliens."

Are we not? Lorimer thinks. The Luna station comes back with a different, older voice.

"Judy, Myda here, I've had another thought. These people had a very rigid authority code. You remember your history, they peck-ordered everything. You notice Major Davis repeated about being commanding. That's called dominance-submission structure, one of them gave orders and the others did whatever they were told, we don't know quite why. Perhaps they were frightened. The point is that if the dominant one is in shock or panicked, maybe the others can't reply unless this Davis lets them."

Jesus Christ, Lorimer thinks. Jesus H. Christ in colors. It is his father's expression for the inexpressible. Dave and Bud sit unstirring.

"How weird," the Judy voice says. "But don't they know they're on a bad course? I mean, could the dominant one make the others fly right out of the system? Truly?"

It's happened, Lorimer thinks; it has happened. I have to stop this. I have to act now, before they lose us. Desperate visions of himself defying Dave and Bud loom before him. Try persuasion first.

Just as he opens his mouth he sees Bud stir slightly, and with immeasurable gratitude hears him say, "Dave-o, what say we take an eyeball look? One little old burp won't hurt us."

Dave's head turns a degree or two.

"Or should I go out and see, like the chick said?" Bud's voice is mild.

After a long minute Dave says neutrally, "All right . . . Attitude change." His arm moves up as though heavy; he starts methodically setting in the values for the vector that will bring Spica in line with their functional window.

Now why couldn't I have done that, Lorimer asks himself for the thousandth time, following the familiar check sequence. Don't answer. . . . And for the thousandth time he is obscurely moved by the rightness of them. The authentic ones, the alphas. Their bond. The awe he had felt first for the absurd jocks of his school ball team.

"That's go, Dave, assuming nothing got creamed."

Dave throws the ignition safety, puts the computer on real time. The hull shudders. Everything in the cabin drifts sidewise while the bright point of Spica swims the other way, appears on the front window as the retros cut in. When the star creeps out onto clear glass, Lorimer can clearly see its companion. The double light steadies there; a beautiful job. He hands Bud the telescope.

"The one on the left."

Bud looks. "There she is, all right. Hey, Dave, look at that!" He puts the scope in Dave's hand. Slowly, Dave raises it and looks. Lorimer can hear him breathe. Suddenly Dave pulls up the mike.

"Houston!" he shouts harshly. "*Sunbird* to Houston, *Sunbird* calling Houston. Houston, come in!"

Into the silence the speaker squeals, "They fired their engines—wait, she's calling!" And shuts up.

In *Sunbird*'s cabin nobody speaks. Lorimer stares at the twin stars ahead, impossible realities shifting around him as the minutes congeal. Bud's reflected face looks downward, grin gone. Dave's beard moves silently; praying, Lorimer realizes. Alone of the crew Dave is deeply religious; at Sunday meals he gives a short, dignified grace. A shocking pity for Dave rises in Lorimer; Dave is so deeply involved with his family, his four sons, always thinking about their training, taking them hunting, fishing, camping. And Doris his wife so incredibly active and sweet, going on their trips, cooking and doing things for the community. Driving Penny and Jenny to classes while Ginny was sick that time. Good people, the backbone . . . This can't be, he thinks; Packard's voice is going to come through in a minute, the antenna's beamed right now. Six minutes now. This will all go away. *Before the year two thousand*—stop it, the language would have changed. Think of Doris. . . . She has that glow, feeding her five men; women with sons are different. But Ginny, but his dear woman, his *wife*, his *daughters*—grandmothers now? All dead and dust? *Quit that.*

Dave is still praying. . . . Who knows what goes on inside those heads? Dave's cry . . . Twelve minutes, it has to be all right. The second sweep is stuck, no, it's moving. Thirteen. It's all insane, a dream. Thirteen plus . . . fourteen. The speaker hissing clicking vacantly. Fifteen now. A dream . . . Or are those women staying off, letting us see? Sixteen . . .

At twenty Dave's hand moves, stops again. The seconds jitter by, space crackles. Thirty minutes coming up.

"Calling Major Davis in *Sunbird*?" It is the older woman, a gentle voice. "This is Luna Central. We are the service and communication facility for space flight now. We're sorry to have tell you that there is no space center at Houston anymore. Houston itself was abandoned when the shuttle base moved to White Sands, over two centuries ago."

A cool dust-colored light enfolds Lorimer's brain, isolating it. It will remain so a long time.

The woman is explaining it all again, offering help, asking if they were hurt. A nice dignified speech. Dave still sits immobile, gazing at Earth. Bud puts the mike in his hand.

"Tell them, Dave-o."

Dave looks at it, takes a deep breath, presses the send button.

"*Sunbird* to Luna Control," he says quite normally. (It's "Central," Lorimer thinks.) "We copy. Ah, negative on life support, we have no problems. We copy the course change suggestion and are proceeding to recompute. Your offer of computer assistance is appreciated. We suggest you transmit position data so we can get squared away. Ah, we are economizing on transmission until we see how our accumulators have held up. *Sunbird* out."

And so it had begun.

Lorimer's mind floats back to himself now floating in *Gloria*, nearly a year, or three hundred years, later; watching and being watched by them. He still feels light, contented; the dread underneath has come no nearer. But it is so silent. He seems to have heard no voices for a long time. Or was it a long time? Maybe the drug is working on his time sense, maybe it was only a minute or two.

"I've been remembering," he says to the woman Connie, wanting her to speak.

She nods. "You have so much to remember. Oh, I'm sorry— that wasn't good to say." Her eyes speak sympathy.

"Never mind." It is all dreamlike now, his lost world and this other which he is just now seeing plain. "We must seem like very strange beasts to you."

"We're trying to understand," she says. "It's history, you learn the events but you don't really feel what the people were like, how it was for them. We hope you'll tell us."

The drug, Lorimer thinks, that's what they're trying. Tell them . . . how can he? Could a dinosaur tell how it was? A montage flows through his mind, dominated by random shots of Operations's north parking lot and Ginny's yellow kitchen telephone with the sickly ivy vines. . . . Women and vines . . .

A burst of laughter distracts him. It's coming from the chamber they call the gym, Bud and the others must be playing ball in there. Bright idea, really, he muses: using muscle power, sustained mild exercise. That's why they are all so fit. The gym is a glorified squirrel-wheel, when you climb or pedal up the walls it revolves and winds a gear train, which among other things rotates the sleeping drum. A real Woolagong... Bud and Dave usually take their shifts together, scrambling the spinning gym like big pale apes. Lorimer prefers the easy rhythm of the women, and the cycle here fits him nicely. He usually puts in his shift with Connie, who doesn't talk much, and one of the Judys, who do.

No one is talking now, though. Remotely uneasy, he looks around the big cylinder of the cabin, sees Dave and Lady Blue by the forward window. Judy Dakar is behind them, silent for once. They must be looking at Earth; it has been a beautiful expanding disk for some weeks now. Dave's beard is moving, he is praying again. He has taken to doing that, not ostentatiously, but so obviously sincere that Lorimer the atheist can only sympathize.

The Judys have asked Dave what he whispers, of course. When Dave understood that they had no concept of prayer and had never seen a Christian Bible, there had been a heavy silence.

"So you have lost all faith," he said finally.

"We have faith," Judy Paris protested.

"May I ask in what?"

"We have faith in ourselves, of course," she told him.

"Young lady, if you were my daughter I'd tan your britches," Dave said, not joking. The subject was not raised again.

But he came back so well after that first dreadful shock,

Lorimer thinks. A personal god, a father-model, man needs that. Dave draws strength from it, and we lean on him. Maybe leaders have to believe. Dave was so great; cheerful, unflappable, patiently working out alternatives, making his decisions on the inevitable discrepancies in the position readings in a way Lorimer couldn't do. A bitch . . .

Memory takes him again; he is once again back in *Sunbird*, gritty-eyed, listening to the women's chatter, Dave's terse replies. God, how they chattered. But their computer work checks out. Lorimer is suffering also from a quirk of Dave's, his reluctance to transmit their exact thrust and fuel reserve. He keeps holding out a margin and making Lorimer compute it back in.

But the margins don't help; it is soon clear that they are in big trouble. Earth will pass too far ahead of them on her next orbit, they don't have the acceleration to catch up with her before they cross her path. They can carry out an ullage maneuver, they can kill enough velocity to let Earth catch them on the second go-by; but that would take an extra year and their life support would be long gone. The grim question of whether they have enough to enable a single man to wait it out pushes into Lorimer's mind. He pushes it back; that one is for Dave.

There is a final possibility: Venus will approach their trajectory three months hence, and they may be able to gain velocity by swinging by it. They go to work on that.

Meanwhile Earth is steadily drawing away from them and so is *Gloria*, closer toward the sun. They pick her out of the solar interference and then lose her again. They know her crew now, five of them. The man is Andy Kay, the senior woman is Lady Blue Parks; they appear to do the navigating. Then there is a Connie Morelos and the two twins, Judy Paris and Judy Dakar, who run the communications. The chief Luna voices are women too, Margo and Azella. The men can hear them talking to the *Escondita*, which is now swinging in toward the far side of the sun. Dave insists on monitoring and taping everything that comes through. It proves to be largely replays of their exchanges with Luna and *Gloria*, mixed with a variety of highly personal messages. As references to cows, chickens, and other livestock multiply, Dave reluctantly gives up his idea that they are code. Bud counts a total of five male voices.

"Big deal," he says. "There were more chick drivers on the road when we left. Means space is safe now, the girlies have taken over. Let them sweat their little asses off." He chuckles. "When we get this bird down, the stars ain't gonna study old Buddy no more, no ma'am. A nice beach and about a zillion steaks and ale and all those sweet things. Hey, we'll be living history, we can charge admission."

Dave's face takes on the expression that means an inappropriate topic has been broached. Much to Lorimer's impatience, Dave discourages all speculation as to what may await them on this future Earth. He confines their transmissions strictly to the problem in hand; when Lorimer tries to get him at least to mention the unchanged-language puzzle, Dave only says firmly, "Later." Lorimer fumes; inconceivable that he is three centuries in the future, unable to learn a thing.

They do glean a few facts from the women's talk. There have been nine successful *Sunbird* missions after theirs and one other casualty. And the *Gloria* and her sister ship are on a long-planned flyby of the two inner planets.

"We always go along in pairs," Judy says. "But those planets are no good. Still, it was worth seeing."

"For Pete's sake, Dave, ask them how many planets have been visited," Lorimer pleads.

"Later."

But about the fifth meal-break Luna suddenly volunteers.

"Earth is making up a history for you, *Sunbird*," the Margo voice says. "We know you don't want to waste power asking, so we thought we'd send you a few main points right now." She laughs. "It's much harder than we thought, nobody here does history."

Lorimer nods to himself; he has been wondering what he could tell a man from 1690 who would want to know what happened to Cromwell—was Cromwell then?—and who had never heard of electricity, atoms, or the U.S.A.

"Let's see, probably the most important is that there aren't as many people as you had, we're just over two million. There was a world epidemic not long after your time. It didn't kill people, but it reduced the population. I mean, there weren't any babies in most of the world. Ah, sterility. The country called Australia was affected least." Bud holds up a finger.

"And North Canada wasn't too bad. So the survivors all got together in the south part of the American states where they could grow food and the best communications and factories were. Nobody lives in the rest of the world, but we travel there sometimes. Ah, we have five main activities, was *industries* the word? Food, that's farming and fishing. Communications, transport, and space—that's us. And the factories they need. We live a lot simpler than you did, I think. We see your things all over, we're very grateful to you. Oh, you'll be interested to know we use zeppelins just like you did, we have six big ones. And our fifth thing is the children. Babies. Does that help? I'm using a children's book we have here."

The men have frozen during this recital; Lorimer is holding a cooling bag of hash. Bud starts chewing again and chokes.

"Two million people and a space capability?" He coughs. "That's incredible."

Dave gazes reflectively at the speaker. "There's a lot they're not telling us."

"I gotta ask them," Bud says. "Okay?"

Dave nods. "Watch it."

"Thanks for the history, Luna," Bud says. "We really appreciate it. But we can't figure out how you maintain a space program with only a couple of million people. Can you tell us a little more on that?"

In the pause Lorimer tries to grasp the staggering figures. From eight billion to two million . . . Europe, Asia, Africa, South America, America itself—wiped out. *There weren't any more babies.* World sterility, from what? The Black Death, the famines of Asia—those had been decimations. This is magnitudes worse. No, it is all the same: beyond comprehension. An empty world, littered with junk.

"*Sunbird?*" says Margo. "Da, I should have thought you'd want to know about space. Well, we have only the four real spaceships and one building. You know the two here. Then there's *Indira* and *Pech*, they're on the Mars run now. Maybe the Mars dome was since your day. You had the satellite stations though, didn't you? And the old Luna dome, of course—I remember now, it was during the epidemic. They tried to set up colonies to, ah, breed children, but the epidemic got there too. They struggled terribly hard. We owe a lot to you really, you men I mean. The history has it all, how you worked out a minimal viable program and trained everybody and saved it from the crazies. It was a glorious achievement. Oh, the marker here has one of your names on it. Lorimer. We love to keep it all going and growing, we all love traveling. Man is a rover, that's one of our mottoes."

"Are you hearing what I'm hearing?" Bud asks, blinking comically.

Dave is still staring at the speaker. "Not one word about their government," he says slowly. "Not a word about economic conditions. We're talking to a bunch of monkeys."

"Should I ask them?"

"Wait a minute. . . . Roger, ask the name of their chief of state and the head of the space program. And—no, that's all."

"President?" Margo echoes Bud's query. "You mean like queens and kings? Wait, here's Myda. She's been talking about you with Earth."

The older woman they hear occasionally says, *"Sunbird?* Da, we realize you had a very complex activity, your governments. With so few people we don't have that type of formal structure at all. People from the different activities meet periodically and our communications are good, everyone is kept informed. The people in each activity are in charge of doing it while they're there. We rotate, you see. Mostly in five-year hitches, for example, Margo here was on the zeppelins and I've been on several factories and farms and of course the, well, the education, we all do that. I believe that's one big difference from you. And of course we all work. And things are basically far more stable now, I gather. We change slowly. Does that answer you? Of course you an always ask Registry, they keep track of us all. But we can't, ah, take you to our leader, if that's what you mean." She laughs, a genuine jolly sound. "That's one of our old jokes. I must say," she goes on seriously, "it's been a joy to us that we can understand you so well. We make a big effort not to let the language drift, it would be tragic to lose touch with the past."

Dave takes the mike. "Thank you, Luna. You've given us something to think about. *Sunbird* out."

"How much of that is for real, Doc?" Bud rubs his curly head. "They're giving us one of your science-fiction stories."

"The real story will come later," says Dave. "Our job is to get there."

"That's a point that doesn't look too good."

By the end of the session it looks worse. No Venus trajectory is any good. Lorimer reruns all the computations; same result.

"There doesn't seem to be any solution to this one, Dave," he says at last. "The parameters are just too tough. I think we've had it."

Dave massages his knuckles thoughtfully. Then he nods. "Roger. We'll fire the optimum sequence on the Earth heading."

"Tell them to wave if they see us go by," says Bud.

They are silent, contemplating the prospect of a slow death in space eighteen months hence. Lorimer wonders if he can raise the other question, the bad one. He is pretty sure what Dave will say. What will he himself decide, what will he have the guts to do?

"Hello, *Sunbird?*" the voice of *Gloria* breaks in. "Listen, we've been figuring. We think if you use all your fuel you could come back in close enough to our orbit so we could swing out and pick you up. You'd be using solar gravity that way. We have plenty of maneuver but much less acceleration than you do. You have suits and some kind of propellants, don't you? I mean, you could fly across a few kays?"

The three men look at each other; Lorimer guesses he had not been the only one to speculate on that.

"That's a good thought, *Gloria*," Dave says. "Let's hear what Luna says."

"Why?" asks Judy. "It's our business, we wouldn't endanger the ship. We'd only miss another look at Venus, who cares. We have plenty of water and food, and if the air gets a little smelly we can stand it."

"Hey, the chicks are all right," Bud says. They wait.

The voice of Luna comes on. "We've been looking at that too, Judy. We're not sure you understand the risk. Ah, *Sunbird,* excuse me. Judy, if you manage to pick them up you'll have to spend nearly a year in the ship with these three male persons from a *very different culture.* Myda says you should remember history, and it's a risk no matter what Connie says. *Sunbird.* I hate to be so rude. Over."

Bud is grinning broadly, they all are. "Cavemen," he chuckles. "All the chicks land preggers."

"Margo, they're human beings," the Judy voice protests. "This isn't just Connie, we're all agreed. Andy and Lady Blue say it would be very interesting. If it works, that is. We can't let them go without trying."

"We feel that way too, of course," Luna replies. "But there's another problem. They could be carrying diseases. *Sunbird,* I know you've been isolated for fourteen months, but Murti says people in your day were immune to organisms that aren't around now. Maybe some of ours could harm you, too. You could all get mortally sick and lose the ship."

"We thought of that, Margo," Judy says impatiently. "Look, if you have contact with them at all somebody has to test, true? So we're ideal. By the time we get home you'll know. And how could we all get sick so fast we couldn't put *Gloria* in a stable orbit where you could get her later on?"

They wait. "Hey, what about that epidemic?" Bud pats his hair elaborately. "I don't know if I want a career in gay lib."

"You rather stay out here?" Dave asks.

"Crazies," says a different voice from Luna. "*Sunbird*, I'm Murti, the health person here. I think what we have to fear most is the meningitis-influenza complex, they mutate so readily. Does your Dr. Lorimer have any suggestions?"

"Roger, I'll put him on," says Dave. "But as to your first point, madam, I want to inform you that at time of takeoff the incidence of rape in the United States space cadre was zero point zero. I guarantee the conduct of my crew, provided you can control yours. Here is Dr. Lorimer."

But Lorimer cannot of course tell them anything useful. They discuss the men's polio shots, which luckily have used killed virus, and various childhood diseases which still seem to be around. He does not mention their epidemic.

"Luna, we're going to try it," Judy declares. "We couldn't live with ourselves. Now let's get the course figured before they get any farther away."

From there on there is no rest on *Sunbird* while they set up and refigure and rerun the computations for the envelope of possible intersecting trajectories. The *Gloria*'s drive, they learn, is indeed low-thrust, although capable of sustained operation. *Sunbird* will have to get most of the way to the rendezvous on her own if they can cancel their outward velocity.

The tension breaks once during the long session, when Luna calls *Gloria* to warn Connie to be sure the female crew members wear concealing garments at all times if the men came aboard.

"Not suit-liners, Connie, they're much too tight." It is the older woman, Myda. Bud chuckles.

"Your light sleepers, I think. And when the men unsuit, your Andy is the only one who should help them. You others stay away. The same for all body functions and sleeping. This is very important, Connie, you'll have to watch it the whole way

home. There are a great many complicated taboos. I'm putting
an instruction list on the bleeper, is your receiver working?"

"Da, we used it for France's black-hole paper."

"Good. Tell Judy to stand by. Now listen, Connie, listen
carefully. Tell Andy he has to read it all. I repeat, *he* has to read
every word. Did you hear that?"

"Ah, dinko," Connie answers. "I understand, Myda. He
will."

"I think we just lost the ball game, fellas," Bud laments.
"Old mother Myda took it all away."

Even Dave laughs. But later when the modulated squeal that
is a whole text comes through the speaker, he frowns again.
"There goes the good stuff."

The last factors are cranked in; the revised program spins,
and Luna confirms them. "We have a payout, Dave," Lorimer
reports. "It's tight, but there are at least two viable options.
Provided the main jets are fully functional."

"We're going EVA to check."

That is exhausting; they find a warp in the deflector housing
of the port engines and spend four sweating hours trying to
wrestle it back. It is only Lorimer's third sight of open space,
but he is soon too tired to care.

"Best we can do," Dave pants finally. "We'll have to
compensate in the psychic mode."

"You can do it, Dave-o," says Bud. "Hey, I gotta change those
suit radios, don't let me forget."

In the psychic mode . . . Lorimer surfaces back to his real self,
cocooned in Gloria's big cluttered cabin, seeing Connie's living
face. "It must be hours, how long has he been dreaming?"

"About two minutes," Connie smiles.

"I was thinking of the first time I saw you."

"Oh, yes. We'll never forget that, ever."

Nor will he. . . . He lets it unroll again in his head. The
interminable hours after the first long burn, which has sent
Sunbird yawing so they all have to gulp nausea pills. Judy's
breathless voice reading down their approach: "Oh, very good,
four hundred thousand . . . Oh, great, *Sunbird*, you're almost
three, you're going to break a hundred for sure—" Dave has
done it, the big one.

Lorimer's probe is useless in the yaw, it isn't until they
stabilize enough for the final burst that they can see the strange
blip bloom and vanish in the slot. Converging, hopefully, on a

theoretical near-intersection point.

"Here goes everything."

The final burn changes the yaw into a sickening tumble with the star field looping past the glass. The pills are no more use, and the fuel feed to the attitude jets goes sour. They are all vomiting before they manage to hand-pump the last of the fuel and slow the tumble.

"That's it, *Gloria*. Come and get us. Lights on, Bud. Let's get those suits up."

Fighting nausea, they go through the laborious routine in the fouled cabin. Suddenly Judy's voice sings out, "We see you, *Sunbird!* We see your light! Can't you see us?"

"No time," Dave says. But Bud, half-suited, points at the window. "Fellas, oh, hey, look at that."

Lorimer stares, thinks he sees a faint spark between the whirling stars before he has to retch.

"Father, we thank you," says Dave quietly. "All right, move it on, Doc. Packs."

The effort of getting themselves plus the propulsion units and a couple of cargo nets out of the rolling ship drives everything else out of mind. It isn't until they are floating linked together and stabilized by Dave's hand jet that Lorimer has time to look.

The sun blanks out their left. A few meters below them *Sunbird* tumbles empty, looking absurdly small. Ahead of them, infinitely far away, is a point too blurred and yellow to be a star. It creeps: *Gloria*, on her approach tangent.

"Can you start, *Sunbird*?" says Judy in their helmets. "We don't want to brake anymore on account of our exhaust. We estimate fifty kay in an hour, we're coming out on a line."

"Roger. Give me your jet, Doc."

"Good-bye, *Sunbird*," says Bud. "Plenty of lead, Dave-o."

Lorimer finds it restful in a childish way, being towed across the abyss tied to the two big men. He has total confidence in Dave, he never considers the possibility that they will miss, sail by, and be lost. Does Dave feel contempt? Lorimer wonders; that banked-up silence, is it partly contempt for those who can manipulate only symbols, who have no mastery of matter? . . . He concentrates on mastering his stomach.

It is a long, dark trip. *Sunbird* shrinks to a twinkling light, slowly accelerating on the spiral course that will end her ultimately in the sun with their precious records that are three hundred years obsolete. With, also, the packet of photos and letters that Lorimer has twice put in his suit-pouch and twice taken out. Now and then he catches sight of *Gloria*, growing from a blur to an incomprehensible tangle of lighted crescents.

"Woo-ee, it's big," Bud says. "No wonder they can't accelerate, that thing is a flying trailer park. It'd break up."

"It's a spaceship. Got those nets tight, Doc?"

Judy's voice suddenly fills their helmets. "I see your lights! Can you see me? Will you have enough left to brake at all?"

"Affirmative to both, *Gloria*," says Dave.

At that moment Lorimer is turned slowly forward again and he sees—will see it forever: the alien ship in the star field and on its dark side the tiny lights that are women in the stars, waiting for them. Three—no, four; one suit-light is way out, moving. If that is a tether, it must be over a kilometer.

"Hello, I'm Judy Dakar!" The voice is close. "Oh, mother, you're big! Are you all right? How's your air?"

"No problem."

They are in fact stale and steaming wet; too much adrenaline. Dave uses the jets again and suddenly she is growing, is coming right at them, a silvery spider on a trailing thread. Her suit looks trim and flexible; it is mirror-bright, and the pack is quite small. Marvels of the future, Lorimer thinks; Paragraph One.

"You made it, you made it! Here, tie in. Brake!"

"There ought to be some historic words," Bud murmurs. "If she gives us a chance."

"Hello, Judy," says Dave calmly. "Thanks for coming."

"Contact!" She blasts their ears. "Haul us in, Andy! Brake, brake—the exhaust is back there!"

And they are grabbed hard, deflected into a great arc toward the ship. Dave uses up the last jet. The line loops.

"Don't jerk it," Judy cries. "Oh, I'm *sorry*." She is clinging on them like a gibbon, Lorimer can see her eyes, her excited mouth. Incredible. "Watch out, it's slack."

"Teach me, honey," says Andy's baritone. Lorimer twists and sees him far back at the end of a heavy tether, hauling them smoothly in. Bud offers to help, is refused. "Just hang loose, please," a matronly voice tells them. It is obvious Andy has done this before. They come in spinning slowly, like space fish. Lorimer finds he can no longer pick out the twinkle that is *Sunbird*. When he is swung back, *Gloria* has changed to a disorderly cluster of bulbs and spokes around a big central cylinder. He can see pods and miscellaneous equipment stowed all over her. Not like science fiction.

Andy is paying the line into a floating coil. Another figure floats beside him. They are both quite short, Lorimer realizes as they near.

"Catch the cable," Andy tells them. There is a busy moment of shifting inertial drag.

"Welcome to *Gloria*, Major Davis, Captain Geirr, Dr. Lorimer. I'm Lady Blue Parks. I think you'll like to get inside as soon as possible. If you feel like climbing go right ahead, we'll pull all this in later."

"We appreciate it, ma'am."

They start hand-over-hand along the catenary of the main tether. It has a good rough grip. Judy coasts up to peer at them, smiling broadly, towing the coil. A taller figure waits by the ship's open airlock.

"Hello, I'm Connie. I think we can cycle in two at a time. Will you come with me, Major Davis?"

It is like an emergency on a plane, Lorimer thinks, as Dave follows her in. Being ordered about by supernaturally polite little girls.

"Space-going stews," Bud nudges him. "How 'bout that?" His face is sprouting sweat. Lorimer tells him to go next, his own LSP has less load.

Bud goes in with Andy. The woman named Lady Blue waits beside Lorimer while Judy scrambles on the hull securing their cargo nets. She doesn't seem to have magnetic soles; perhaps ferrous metals aren't used in space now. When Judy begins hauling in the main tether on a simple hand winch, Lady Blue looks at it critically.

"I used to make those," she says to Lorimer. What he can see of her features looks compressed, her dark eyes twinkle. He has the impression she is part black.

"I ought to get over and clean that aft antenna." Judy floats up. "Later," says Lady Blue. They both smile at Lorimer. Then the hatch opens, and he and Lady Blue go in. When the toggles seat, there comes a rising scream of air and Lorimer's suit collapses.

"Can I help you?" She has opened her faceplate, the voice is rich and live. Eagerly Lorimer catches the latches in his clumsy gloves and lets her lift the helmet off. His first breath surprises him, it takes an instant to identify the gas as fresh air. Then the inner hatch opens, letting in greenish light. She waves him through. He swims into a short tunnel. Voices are coming from around the corner ahead. His hand finds a grip and he stops, feeling his heart shudder in his chest.

When he turns that corner the world he knows will be dead. Gone, rolled up, blown away forever with *Sunbird*. He will be irrevocably in the future. A man from the past, a time traveler. In the future . . .

He pulls himself around the bend.

The future is a vast bright cylinder, its whole inner surface festooned with unidentifiable objects, fronds of green. In front of him floats an odd tableau: Bud and Dave, helmets off, looking enormous in their bulky white suits and packs. A few meters away hang two bareheaded figures in shiny suits and a dark-haired girl in flowing pink pajamas.

They are all simply staring at the two men, their eyes and mouths open in identical expressions of pleased wonder. The face that has to be Andy's is grinning openmouthed like a kid at the zoo. He is a surprisingly young boy, Lorimer sees, in spite of his deep voice; blond, downy-cheeked, compactly muscular. Lorimer finds he can scarcely bear to look at the pink woman, can't tell if she really is surpassingly beautiful or plain. The taller suited woman has a shiny, ordinary face.

From overhead bursts an extraordinary sound which he finally recognizes as a chicken cackling. Lady Blue pushes past him.

"All right, Andy, Connie, stop staring and help them get their suits off. Judy, Luna is just as eager to hear about this as we are."

The tableau jumps to life. Afterward Lorimer can recall mostly eyes, bright curious eyes tugging his boots, smiling eyes upside down over his pack—and always that light, ready laughter. Andy is left alone to help them peel down, blinking at the fittings which Lorimer still finds embarrassing. He seems easy and nimble in his own half-open suit. Lorimer struggles out of the last lacings, thinking, a boy! A boy and four women orbiting the sun, flying their big junky ships to Mars. Should he feel humiliated? He only feels grateful, accepting a short robe and a bulb of tea somebody—Connie?—gives him.

The suited Judy comes in with their nets. The men follow

Andy along another passage, Bud and Dave clutching at the small robes. Andy stops by a hatch.

"This greenhouse is for you, it's your toilet. Three's a lot, but you have full sun."

Inside is a brilliant jungle, foliage everywhere, glittering water droplets, rustling leaves. Something whirs away—a grasshopper.

"You crank that handle." Andy points to a seat on a large cross-duct. "The piston rams the gravel and waste into a compost process, and it ends up in the soil core. That vetch is a heavy nitrogen user and a great oxidator. We pump CO_2 in and oxy out. It's a real Woolagong."

He watches critically while Bud tries out the facility.

"What's a Woolagong?" asks Lorimer dazedly.

"Oh, she's one of our inventors. Some of her stuff is weird. When we have a pluggy-looking thing that works, we call it a Woolagong." He grins. "The chickens eat the seeds and the hoppers, see, and the hoppers and iguanas eat the leaves. When a greenhouse is going darkside, we turn them in to harvest. With this much light I think we could keep a goat, don't you? You didn't have any life at all on your ship, true?"

"No," Lorimer says, "not a single iguana."

"They promised us a Shetland pony for Christmas," says Bud, rattling gravel. Andy joins perplexedly in the laugh.

Lorimer's head is foggy; it isn't only fatigue, the year in *Sunbird* has atrophied his ability to take in novelty. Numbly he uses the Woolagong, and they go back out and forward to *Gloria*'s big control room, where Dave makes a neat short speech to Luna and is answered graciously.

"We have to finish changing course now," Lady Blue says. Lorimer's impression has been right, she is a small light part-Negro in late middle age. Connie is part something exotic too, he sees; the others are European types.

"I'll get you something to eat," Connie smiles warmly. "Then you probably want to rest. We saved all the cubbies for you." She says "syved"; their accents are all identical.

As they leave the control room, Lorimer sees the withdrawn look in Dave's eyes and knows he must be feeling the reality of being a passenger in an alien ship; not in command, not deciding the course, the communications going on unheard.

That is Lorimer's last coherent observation, that and the taste of the strange, good food. And then being led aft through what he now knows is the gym, to the shaft of the sleeping drum. There are six irised ports like dog-doors; he pushes through his assigned port and finds himself facing a roomy mattress. Shelves and a desk are in the wall.

"For your excretions." Connie's arm comes through the iris, pointing at bags. "If you have a problem stick your head out and call. There's water."

Lorimer simply drifts toward the mattress, too sweated out to reply. His drifting ends in a curious heavy settling and his final astonishment: the drum is smoothly, silently starting to revolve. He sinks gratefully onto the pad, growing "heavier" as the minutes pass. About a tenth gee, maybe more, he thinks, it's still accelerating. And falls into the most restful sleep he has known in the long weary year.

It isn't till next day that he understands that Connie and two others have been on the rungs of the gym chamber, sending it around hour after hour without pause or effort and chatting as they went.

How they talk, he thinks again, floating back to real present time. The bubbling irritant pours through his memory, the voices of Ginny and Jenny and Penny on the kitchen telephone, before that his mother's voice, his sister Amy's. Interminable. What do they always have to talk, talk, talk of?

"Why, everything," says the real voice of Connie beside him now, "it's natural to share."

"Natural . . ." Like ants, he thinks. They twiddle their antennae together every time they meet. Where did you go, what did you do? Twiddle-twiddle. How to you *feel*? Oh, I feel this, I feel that, blah blah twiddle-twiddle. Total coordination of the hive. Women have no self-respect. Say anything, no sense of the strategy of words, the dark danger of naming. Can't hold in.

"Ants, beehives," Connie laughs, showing the bad tooth. "You truly see us as insects, don't you? Because they're females?"

"Was I talking aloud? I'm sorry." He blinks away dreams.

"Oh, please don't be. It's so sad to hear about your sister and your children and your, your wife. They must have been wonderful people. We think you're very brave."

But he has only thought of Ginny and them all for an instant—what has he been babbling? What is the drug doing to him?

"What are you doing to us?" he demands, lanced by real alarm now, almost angry.

"It's all right, truly." Her hand touches his, warm and somehow shy. "We all use it when we need to explore something. Usually it's pleasant. It's a laevonoramine compound, a disinhibitor, it doesn't dull you like alcohol. We'll be home so soon, you see. We have the responsibility to understand, and you're so locked in." Her eyes melt at him. "You don't feel sick, do you? We have the antidote."

"No . . ." His alarm has already flowed away somewhere. Her explanation strikes him as reasonable enough. "We're not locked in," he says or tries to say. "We talk. . . ." He gropes for a word to convey the judiciousness, the adult restraint. Objectivity, maybe? "We talk when we have something to say." Irrelevantly he thinks of a mission coordinator named Forrest, famous for his blue jokes. "Otherwise it would all break down," he tells her. "You'd fly right out of the system." That isn't quite what he means; let it pass.

The voices of Dave and Bud ring out suddenly from opposite ends of the cabin, awakening the foreboding of evil in his mind. They don't know us, he thinks. They should look out, stop this. But he is feeling too serene, he wants to think about his own new understanding, the pattern of them all he is seeing at last.

"I feel lucid," he manages to say, "I want to think."

She looks pleased. "We call that the ataraxia effect. It's so nice when it goes that way."

Ataraxia, philosophical calm. Yes. But there are monsters in the deep, he thinks or says. The night side. The night side of Orren Lorimer, a self hotly dark and complex, waiting in leash. They're so vulnerable. They don't know we can take them. Images rush up: a Judy spread-eagled on the gym rungs, pink pajamas gone, open to him. Flash sequence of the three of them taking over the ship, the women tied up, helpless, shrieking, raped, and used. The team—get the satellite station, get a shuttle down to Earth. Hostages. Make them do anything, no defense whatever. . . . Has Bud actually said that? But Bud doesn't know, he remembers. Dave knows they're hiding something, but he thinks it's socialism or sin. When they find out. . . .

How has he himself found out? Simply listening, really, all these months. He listens to their talk much more than the others; "fraternizing," Dave calls it. . . . They all listened at first, of course. Listened and looked and reacted helplessly to the female bodies, the tender bulges so close under the thin, tantalizing clothes, the magnetic mouths and eyes, the smell of them, their electric touch. Watching them touch each other, touch Andy, laughing, vanishing quietly into shared bunks. *What goes on? Can I? My need, my need—*

The power of them, the fierce resentment . . . Bud muttered and groaned meaningfully despite Dave's warnings. He kept needling Andy until Dave banned all questions. Dave himself was noticeably tense and read his Bible a great deal. Lorimer found his own body pointing after them like a famished hound, hoping to Christ the cubicles are as they appeared to be, unwired.

All they learn is that Myda's instructions must have been ferocious. The atmosphere has been implacably antiseptic, the discretion impenetrable. Andy politely ignored every probe. No word or act has told them what, if anything, goes on; Lorimer was irresistibly reminded of the weekend he spent at Jenny's scout camp. The men's training came presently to their rescue, and they resigned themselves to finishing their mission on a super-*Sunbird*, weirdly attended by a troop of boy and girl scouts.

In every other way their reception couldn't be more courteous. They have been given the run of the ship and their own dayroom in a cleaned-out gravel storage pod. They visit the control room as they wish. Lady Blue and Andy give them specs and manuals and show them every circuit and device of *Gloria*, inside and out. Luna has bleeped up a stream of science texts and the data on all their satellites and shuttles and the Mars and Luna dome colonies.

Dave and Bud plunged into an orgy of engineering. *Gloria* is, as they suspected, powered by a fission plant that uses a range of Lunar minerals. Her ion drive is only slightly advanced over the experimental models of their own day. The marvels of the future seem so far to consist mainly of ingenious modifications.

"It's primitive," Bud tells him. "What they've done is sacrifice everything to keep it simple and easy to maintain. Believe it, they can hand-feed fuel. And the backups, brother! They have redundant redundancy."

But Lorimer's technical interest soon flags. What he really wants is to be alone awhile. He makes a desultory attempt to survey the apparently few new developments in his field, and finds he can't concentrate. What the hell, he tells himself, I stopped being a physicist three hundred years ago. Such a relief to be out of the cell of *Sunbird*; he has given himself up to drifting solitary through the warren of the ship, using their excellent 400-mm telescope, noting the odd life of the crew.

When he finds that Lady Blue likes chess, they form a routine of biweekly games. Her personality intrigues him; she has reserve and an aura of authority. But she quickly stops Bud when he calls her "Captain."

"No one here commands in your sense. I'm just the oldest." Bud goes back to "ma'am."

She plays a solid positional game, somewhat more erratic than a man but with occasional elegant traps. Lorimer is astonished to find that there is only one new chess opening, an interesting queen-side gambit called the Dagmar. One new opening in three centuries? He mentions it to the others when they come back from helping Andy and Judy Paris overhaul a standby converter.

"They haven't done much anywhere," Dave says. "Most of your new stuff dates from the epidemic, Andy, if you'll pardon me. The program seems to be stagnating. You've been gearing up this Titan project for eighty years."

"We'll get there." Andy grins.

"C'mon, Dave," says Bud. "Judy and me are taking on you two for the next chicken dinner, we'll get a bridge team here yet. Woo-ee, I can taste that chicken! Losers get the iguana."

The food is so good. Lorimer finds himself lingering around the kitchen end, helping whoever is cooking, munching on their various seeds and chewy roots as he listens to them talk. He even likes the iguana. He begins to put on weight, in fact they all do. Dave decrees double exercise shifts.

"You going to make us *climb* home, Dave-o?" Bud groans. But Lorimer enjoys it, pedaling or swinging easily along the rungs while the women chat and listen to tapes. Familiar music: he identifies a strange spectrum from Handel, Brahms, Sibelius, through Strauss to ballad tunes and intricate light jazz-rock. No lyrics. But plenty of informative texts doubtless selected for his benefit.

From the promised short history he finds out more about the epidemic. It seems to have been an airborne quasi-virus escaped from Franco-Arab military labs, possibly potentiated by pollutants.

"It apparently damaged only the reproductive cells," he tells Dave and Bud. "There was little actual mortality, but almost universal sterility. Probably a molecular substitution in the gene code in the gametes. And the main effect seems to have been on the men. They mention a shortage of male births afterward, which suggests that the damage was on the Y chromosome where it would be selectively lethal to the male fetus."

"Is it still dangerous, Doc?" Dave asks. "What happens to us when we get back home?"

"They can't say. The birthrate is normal now, about two percent and rising. But the present population may be resistant. They never achieved a vaccine."

"Only one way to tell," Bud says gravely. "I volunteer."

Dave merely glances at him. Extraordinary how he still commands, Lorimer thinks. Not submission, for Pete's sake. A team.

The history also mentions the riots and fighting which swept the world when humanity found itself sterile. Cities bombed, and burned, massacres, panics, mass rapes and kidnapping of women, marauding armies of biologically desperate men, bloody cults. The crazies. But it is all so briefly told, so long ago. Lists of honored names. "We must always be grateful to the brave people who held the Denver Medical Laboratories—" And then on to the drama of building up the helium supply for the dirigibles.

In three centuries it's all dust, he thinks. What do I know of the hideous Thirty Years' War that was three centuries back for me? *Fighting devastated Europe for two generations.* Not even names.

The description of their political and economic structure is even briefer. They seem to be, as Myda had said, almost ungoverned.

"It's a form of loose social credit-system run by consensus," he says to Dave. "Somewhat like a permanent frontier period. They're building up slowly. Of course they don't need an army or air force. I'm not sure if they even use cash money or recognize private ownership of land. I did notice one favorable reference to early Chinese communalism," he adds, to see Dave's mouth set. "But they aren't tied to a community. They travel about. When I asked Lady Blue about their police and legal system, she told me to wait and talk with real historians.

This Registry seems to be just that, it's not a policy organ."

"We've run into a situation here, Lorimer," Dave says soberly. "Stay away from it. They're not telling the story."

"You notice they never talk about their husbands?" Bud laughs. "I asked a couple of them what their husbands did, and I swear they had to think. And they all have kids. Believe me, it's a swinging scene down there, even if old Andy acts like he hasn't found out what it's for."

"I don't want any prying into their personal family lives while we're on this ship, Geirr. None whatsoever. That's an order."

"Maybe they don't have families. You ever hear 'em mention anybody getting married? That has to be the one thing on a chick's mind. Mark my words, there's been some changes made."

"The social mores are bound to have changed to some extent," Lorimer says. "Obviously you have women doing more work outside the home, for one thing. But they have family bonds; for instance, Lady Blue has a sister in an aluminum mill and another in health. Andy's mother is on Mars and his sister works in Registry. Connie has a brother or brothers on the fishing fleet near Biloxi, and her sister is coming out to replace her here next trip, she's making yeast now."

"That's the top of the iceberg."

"I doubt the rest of the iceberg is very sinister, Dave."

But somewhere along the line the blandness begins to bother Lorimer too. So much is missing. Marriage, love affairs, children's troubles, jealousy squabbles, status, possessions, money problems, sicknesses, funerals even—all the daily minutiae that occupied Ginny and her friends seems to have been edited out of these women's talk. *Edited?* Can Dave be right, is some big, significant aspect being deliberately kept from them?

"I'm still surprised your language hasn't changed more," he says one day to Connie during their exertions in the gym.

"Oh, we're very careful about that." She climbs at an angle beside him, not using her hands. "It would be a dreadful loss if we couldn't understand the books. All the children are taught from the same original tapes, you see. Oh, there's faddy words we use for a while, but our communicators have to learn the old texts by heart, that keeps us together."

Judy Paris grunts from the pedicycle. "You, my dear

children, will never know the oppression we suffered," she declaims mockingly.

"Judys talk too much," says Connie.

"We do, for a fact." They both laugh.

"So you still read our so-called great books, our fiction and poetry?" asks Lorimer. "Who do you read, H. G. Wells? Shakespeare? Dickens, ah, Balzac, Kipling, Brian?" He gropes; Brian had been a best-seller Ginny liked. When had he last looked at Shakespeare or the others?

"Oh, the historicals," Judy says. "It's interesting, I guess. Grim. They're not very realistic. I'm sure it was to you," she adds generously.

And they turn to discussing whether the laying hens are getting too much light, leaving Lorimer to wonder how what he supposes are the eternal verities of human nature can have faded from a world's reality. Love, conflict, heroism, tragedy—all "unrealistic"? Well, flight crews are never great readers; still, women read more. . . . Something *has* changed, he can sense it. Something basic enough to affect human nature. A physical development perhaps; a mutation? What is really under those floating clothes?

It is the Judys who give him part of it.

He is exercising alone with both of them, listening to them gossip about some legendary figure named Dagmar.

"The Dagmar who invented the chess opening?" he asks.

"Yes. She does anything, when she's good she's great."

"Was she bad sometimes?"

A Judy laughs. "The Dagmar problem, you can say. She has this tendency to organize everything. It's fine when it works, but every so often it runs wild, she thinks she's queen or what. Then they have to get out the butterfly nets."

All in present tense—but Lady Blue has told him the Dagmar gambit is over a century old.

Longevity, he thinks; by god,, that's what they're hiding. Say they've achieved a doubled or tripled life span, that would certainly change human psychology, affect their outlook on everything. Delayed maturity, perhaps? We were working on endocrine cell juvenescence when I left. How old are these girls, for instance?

He is framing a question when Judy Dakar says, "I was in the crèche when she went pluggo. But she's good, I loved her later on."

Lorimer thinks she has said "crash" and then realizes she means a communal nursery. "Is that the same Dagmar?" he asks. "She must be very old."

"Oh, no, her sister."

"A sister a hundred years apart?"

"I mean, her daughter. Her, her *grand*daughter." She starts pedaling fast.

"Judys," says her twin, behind them.

Sister again. Everybody he learns of seems to have an extraordinary number of sisters, Lorimer reflects. He hears Judy Paris saying to her twin, "I think I remember Dagmar at the crèche. She started uniforms for everybody. Colors and numbers."

"You couldn't have, you weren't born," Judy Dakar retorts.

There is a silence in the drum.

Lorimer turns on the rungs to look at them. Two flushed cheerful faces stare back warily, make identical head-dipping gestures to swing the black hair out of their eyes. Identical . . . But isn't the Dakar girl on the cycle a shade more mature, her face more weathered?

"I thought you were supposed to be twins."

"Ah, Judys talk a lot," they say together—and grin guiltily.

"You aren't sisters," he tells them. "You're what we called clones."

Another silence.

"Well, yes," says Judy Dakar. "We call it sisters. Oh, mother! We weren't supposed to tell you, Myda said you would be frightfully upset. It was illegal in your day, true?"

"Yes. We considered it immoral and unethical, experimenting with human life. But it doesn't upset me personally."

"Oh, that's beautiful, that's great," they say together. "We think of you as different," Judy Paris blurts, "you're more hu—more like us. Please, you don't have to tell the others, do you? Oh, *please* don't."

"It was an accident there were two of us here," says Judy Dakar. "Myda *warned* us. Can't you wait a little while?" Two identical pairs of dark eyes beg him.

"Very well," he says slowly. "I won't tell my friends for the time being. But if I keep your secret you have to answer some questions. For instance, how many of your people are created artificially this way?"

He begins to realize he *is* somewhat upset. Dave is right,

damn it, they are hiding things. Is this brave new world populated by subhuman slaves, run by master brains? Decorticate zombies, workers without stomachs or sex, human cortexes wired into machines? Monstrous experiments rush through his mind. He has been naive again. These normal-looking women could be fronting for a hideous world.

"How many?"

"There's only about eleven thousand of us," Judy Dakar says. The two Judys look at each other, transparently confirming something. They're unschooled in deception, Lorimer thinks; is that good? And is diverted by Judy Paris exclaiming, "What we can't figure out is, why did you think it was wrong?"

Lorimer tries to tell them, to convey the horror of manipulating human identity, creating abnormal life. The threat to individuality, the fearful power it would put in a dictator's hand.

"Dictator?" one of them echoes blankly. He looks at their faces and can only say, "Doing things to people without their consent. I think it's sad."

"But that's just what we think about you," the younger Judy bursts out. "How do you know who you *are*? Or who anybody is? All alone, no sisters to share with! You don't know what you can do, or what would be interesting to try. All you poor singletons, you—why, you just have to blunder along and die, all for nothing!"

Her voice trembles. Amazed, Lorimer sees both of them are misty-eyed.

"We better get this m-moving," the other Judy says.

They swing back into the rhythm, and in bits and pieces Lorimer finds out how it is. Not bottled embryos, they tell him indignantly. Human mothers like everybody else, young mothers, the best kind. A somatic cell nucleus is inserted in an enucleated ovum and reimplanted in the womb. They have each borne two "sister" babies in their late teens and nursed them awhile before moving on. The crèches always have plenty of mothers.

His longevity notion is laughed at; nothing but some rules of healthy living has as yet been achieved. "We should make ninety in good shape," they assure him. "A hundred and eight, that was Judy Eagle, she's our record. But she was pretty blah at the end."

The clone-strains themselves are old, they date from the

epidemic. They were part of the first effort to save the race when the babies stopped, and they've continued ever since.

"It's so perfect," they tell him. "We each have a book, it's really a library. All the recorded messages. The Book of Judy Shapiro, that's us. Dakar and Paris are our personal names, we're doing cities now." They laugh, trying not to talk at once about how each Judy adds her individual memoir, her adventures and problems and discoveries, in the genotype they all share.

"If you make a mistake it's useful for the others. Of course you try not to—or at least make a *new* one."

"Some of the old ones aren't so realistic," her other self puts in. "Things were so different, I guess. We make excerpts of the parts we like best. And practical things, like Judys should watch out for skin cancer."

"But we have to read the whole thing every ten years," says the Judy called Dakar. "It's inspiring. As you get older you understand some of the ones you didn't before."

Bemused, Lorimer tries to think how it would be, hearing the voices of three hundred years of Orren Lorimers. Lorimers who were mathematicians or plumbers or artists or bums or criminals, maybe. The continuing exploration and completion of self. And a dozen living doubles; aged Lorimers, infant Lorimers. And other Lorimers' women and children . . . would he enjoy it or resent it? He doesn't know.

"Have you made your records yet?"

"Oh, we're too young. Just notes in case of accident."

"Will we be in them?"

"You can say!" They laugh merrily, then sober. "Truly you won't tell?" Judy Paris asks. "Lady Blue, we have to let her know what we did. Oof. But *truly* you won't tell your friends?"

He hadn't told on them, he thinks now, emerging back into his living self. Connie beside him is drinking cider from a bulb. He has a drink in his hand too, he finds. But he hasn't told.

"Judys will talk." Connie shakes her head, smiling. Lorimer realizes he must have gabbled out the whole thing.

"It doesn't matter," he tells her. "I would have guessed soon anyhow. There were too many clues . . . Woolagongs invent, Mydas worry, Jans are brains, Billy Dees work so hard. I picked up six different stories of hydroelectric stations that were built or improved or are being run by one Lala Singh. Your whole way of life. I'm more interested in this sort of thing than a respectable physicist should be," he says wryly. "You're all clones, aren't you? Every one of you. What do Connies do?"

"You really do know." She gazes at him like a mother whose child has done something troublesome and bright. "Whew! Oh, well, Connies farm like mad, we grow things. Most of our names are plants. I'm Veronica, by the way. And of course the crèches, that's our weakness. The runt mania. We tend to focus on anything smaller or weak."

Her warm eyes focus on Lorimer, who draws back involuntarily.

"We control it." She gives a hearty chuckle. "We aren't all that way. There's been engineering Connies, and we have two young sisters who love metallurgy. It's fascinating what the genotype can do if you try. The original Constantia Morelos was a chemist, she weighed ninety pounds and never saw a farm in her life." Connie looks down at her own muscular arms. "She was killed by the crazies, she fought with weapons. It's so hard to understand. . . . And I had a sister Timothy who made dynamite and dug two canals and she wasn't even an andy."

"*An* andy," he says.

"Oh, dear."

"I guessed that too. Early androgen treatments."

She nods hesitantly. "Yes. We need the muscle-power for some jobs. A few. Kays are quite strong anyway. Whew!" She suddenly stretches her back, wriggles as if she'd been cramped. "Oh, I'm glad you know. It's been such a strain. We couldn't even sing."

"Why not?"

"Myda was sure we'd make mistakes, all the words we'd have had to change. We sing a lot." She softly hums a bar or two.

"What kinds of songs do you sing?"

"Oh, every kind. Adventure songs, work songs, mothering songs, roaming songs, mood songs, trouble songs, joke songs—everything."

"What about love songs?" he ventures. "Do you still have, well, love?"

"Of course, how could people not love?" But she looks at him doubtfully. "The love stories I've heard from your time are so, I don't know, so weird. Grim and pluggy. It doesn't seem like love. . . . Oh, yes, we have famous love songs. Some of them are partly sad, too. Like Tamil and Alcmene O, they're fated together. Connies are fated too, a little." She grins bashfully. "We love to be with Ingrid Anders. It's more one-sided. I hope there'll be an Ingrid on my next hitch. She's so exciting, she's like a little diamond."

Implications are exploding all about him, sparkling with questions. But Lorimer wants to complete the darker pattern beyond.

"Eleven thousand genotypes, two million people: that averages two hundred of each of you alive now." She nods. "I suppose it varies? There's more of some?"

"Yes, some types aren't as viable. But we haven't lost any since early days. They tried to preserve all the genes they could. We have people from all the major races and a lot of small strains. Like me, I'm the Carib Blend. Of course we'll never know what was lost. But eleven thousand is a lot, really. We all try to know everyone, it's a life hobby."

A chill penetrates his ataraxia. Eleven thousand, period. That is the true population of Earth now. He thinks of two hundred tall olive-skinned women named after plants, excited by two hundred little bright Ingrids; two hundred talkative Judys, two hundred self-possessed Lady Blues, two hundred Margos and Mydas and the rest. He shivers. The heirs, the happy pallbearers of the human race.

"So evolution ends," he says somberly.

"No, why? It's just slowed down. We do everything much slower than you did, I think. We like to experience things *fully*. We have time." She stretches again, smiling. "There's all the time."

"But you have no new genotypes. It is the end."

"Oh, but there are, now. Last century they worked out the way to make haploid nuclei combine. We can make a stripped egg-cell function like pollen," she says proudly. "I mean sperm. It's tricky, some don't come out too well. But now we're finding both Xs viable we have over a hundred new types started. Of course it's hard for them, with no sisters. The donors try to help."

Over a hundred, he thinks. Well. Maybe . . . But, both Xs viable, what does that mean? She must be referring to the epidemic. But he had figured it primarily affected the men. His mind goes happily to work on the new puzzle, ignoring a sound from somewhere that is trying to pierce his calm.

"It was a gene or genes on the X chromosome that was

injured," he guesses aloud. "Not the Y. And the lethal trait had to be recessive, right? Thus there would have been no births at all for a time, until some men recovered or were isolated long enough to manufacture undamaged X-bearing gametes. But women carry their lifetime supply of ova, they could never regenerate reproductively. When they mated with the recovered males, only female babies would be produced, since the female carries two Xs and the mother's defective gene would be compensated by a normal X from the father. But the male is XY, he receives only the mother's defective X. Thus the lethal defect would be expressed, the male fetus would be finished. . . . A planet of girls and dying men. The few odd viables died off."

"You truly do understand," she says admiringly.

The sound is becoming urgent; he refuses to hear it, there is significance here.

"So we'll be perfectly all right on Earth. No problem. In theory we can marry again and have families, daughters anyway."

"Yes," she says. "In theory."

The sound suddenly broaches his defenses, becomes the loud voice of Bud Geirr raised in song. He sounds plain drunk now. It seems to be coming from the main garden pod, the one they use to grow vegetables, not sanitation. Lorimer feels the dread alive again, rising closer. Dave ought to keep an eye on him. But Dave seems to have vanished too, he recalls seeing him go toward Control with Lady Blue.

"OH, THE SUN SHINES BRIGHT ON PRETTY RED WI-I-ING," carols Bud.

Something should be done, Lorimer decides painfully. He stirs; it is an effort.

"Don't worry," Connie says. "Andy's with them."

"You don't know, you don't know what you've started." He pushes off toward the garden hatchway.

"—AS SHE LAY SLE-EEPING, A COWBOY CREE-E-EEPING—" General laughter from the hatchway. Lorimer coasts through into the green dazzle. Beyond the radial fence of snap beans he sees Bud sailing in an exaggerated crouch after Judy Paris. Andy hangs by the iguana cages, laughing.

Bud catches one of Judy's ankles and stops them both with a flourish, making her yellow pajamas swirl. She giggles at him upside down, making no effort to free herself.

"I don't like this," Lorimer whispers.

"Please don't interfere." Connie has hold of his arm, anchoring them both to the tool rack. Lorimer's alarm seems to have ebbed; he will watch, let serenity return. The others have not noticed them.

"Oh, there once was an Indian maid," Bud sings more restrainedly, "who never was a-fraid, that some buckaroo would slip it up her, ahem, ahem," he coughs ostentatiously, laughing. "Hey, Andy, I hear them calling you."

"What?" says Judy. "I don't hear anything."

"They're calling you, lad. Out there."

"Who?" asks Andy, listening.

"*They* are, for Crissake." He lets go of Judy and kicks over to Andy. "Listen, you're a great kid. Can't you see me and Judy have some business to discuss in private?" He turns Andy gently around and pushes him at the bean stakes. "It's New Year's Eve, dummy."

Andy floats passively away through the fence of vines, raising a hand at Lorimer and Connie. Bud is back with Judy.

"Happy New Year, kitten," he smiles.

"Happy New Year. Did you do special things on New Year?" she asks curiously.

"What we did on New Year's." He chuckles, taking her shoulders in his hands. "On New Year's Eve, yes we did. Why don't I show you some of our primitive Earth customs, h'mm?"

She nods, wide-eyed.

"Well, first we wish each other well, like this." He draws her to him and lightly kisses her cheek. "Kee-rist, what a dumb bitch," he says in a totally different voice. "You can tell you've been out too long when the geeks start looking good. Knockers, ahhh—" His hand plays with her blouse. The man is unaware, Lorimer realizes. He doesn't know he's drugged, he's speaking his thoughts. I must have done that. Oh, god . . . He takes shelter behind his crystal lens, an observer in the protective light of eternity.

"And then we smooch a little." The friendly voice is back. Bud holds the girl closer, caressing her back. "Fat ass." He puts his mouth on hers; she doesn't resist. Lorimer watches Bud's arms tighten, his hands working on her buttocks, going under her clothes. Safe in the lens, his own sex stirs. Judy's arms are waving aimlessly.

Bud breaks for breath, a hand at his zipper.

"Stop staring," he says hoarsely. "One fucking more word, you'll find out what that big mouth is for. Oh, man, a flagpole. Like steel . . . Bitch, this is your lucky day." He is baring her breasts now, big breasts. Fondling them. "Two fucking years in the ass end of noplace," he mutters, "shit on me, will you? Can't wait, watch it—titty-titty-titties—"

He kisses her again quickly and smiles down at her. "Good?" he asks in his tender voice, and sinks his mouth on her nipples, his hand seeking in her thighs. She jerks and says something muffled. Lorimer's arteries are pounding with delight, with dread.

"I, I think this should stop," he makes himself say falsely, hoping he isn't saying more. Through the pulsing tension he hears Connie whisper back, it sounds like "Don't worry, Judy's very athletic." Terror stabs him, they don't know. But he can't help.

"Cunt," Bud grunts, "you have to have a cunt in there, is it froze up? You dumb cunt—" Judy's face appears briefly in her floating hair, a remote part of Lorimer's mind notes that she looks amused and uncomfortable. His being is riveted to the sight of Bud expertly controlling her body in midair, peeling down the yellow slacks. Oh, god—her dark pubic mat, the thick white thighs—a perfectly normal woman, no mutation. Ohhh, god . . . But there is suddenly a drifting shadow in the way: Andy again floating over them with something in his hands.

"You dinko, Jude?" the boy asks.

Bud's face comes up red and glaring. "Bug out, you!"

"Oh, I won't bother."

"Jee-sus Christ." Bud lunges up and grabs Andy's arm, his legs still hooked around Judy. "This is man's business, boy, do I have to spell it out?" He shifts his grip. "Shoo!"

In one swift motion he has jerked Andy close and backhanded his face hard, sending him sailing into the vines.

Bud gives a bark of laughter, bends back to Judy. Lorimer can see his erection poking through his fly. He wants to utter some warning, tell them their peril, but he can only ride the hot pleasure surging through him, melting his crystal shell. Go on, more—avidly he sees Bud mouth her breasts again and then suddenly flip her whole body over, holding her wrists behind her in one fist, his legs pinning hers. Her bare buttocks bulge up helplessly, enormous moons. "Ass-s-s," Bud groans. "Up you bitch, ahhh-hh—" He pulls her butt onto him.

Judy gives a cry, begins to struggle futilely. Lorimer's shell boils and bursts. Amid the turmoil, ghosts outside are trying to rush in. And something is moving, a real ghost—to his dismay he sees it is Andy again, floating toward the joined bodies, holding a whirring thing. Oh, no—a camera. The fools.

"Get away!" he tries to call to the boy.

But Bud's head turns, he has seen. "You little pissass." His long arm shoots out and captures Andy's shirt, his legs still locked around Judy.

"I've had it with you." His fist slams into Andy's mouth, the camera goes spinning away. But this time Bud doesn't let him go, he is battering the boy, all of them rolling in a tangle in the air.

"Stop!" Lorimer hears himself shout, plunging at them through the beans. "Bud, stop it! You're hitting a woman."

The angry face comes around, squinting at him.

"Get lost, Doc, you little fart. Get your own ass."

"Andy is a *woman*, Bud. You're hitting a girl. She's not a man."

"Huh?" Bud glances at Andy's bloody face. He shakes the shirtfront. "Where's the boobs?"

"She doesn't have breasts, but she's a woman. Her real name is Kay. They're all women. Let her go, Bud."

Bud stares at the androgyne, his legs still pinioning Judy, his penis poking the air. Andy puts up his/her hands in a vaguely combative way.

"A dyke?" says Bud slowly. "A goddamn little bull dyke? This I gotta see."

He feints casually, thrusts a hand into Andy's crotch.

"No balls!" he roars. "No balls at all!" Convulsing with laughter, he lets himself tip over in the air, releasing Andy, his legs letting Judy slip free. "Na-ah," he interrupts himself to grab her hair and goes on guffawing. "A dyke! Hey, dykey!" He takes hold of his hard-on, waggles it at Andy. "Eat your heart out, little dyke." Then he pulls up Judy's head. She has been watching unresisting all along.

"Take a good look, girlie. See what old Buddy has for you? Tha-a-at's what you want, say it. How long since you saw a real man, hey, dogface?"

Maniacal laughter bubbles up in Lorimer's gut, farce too strong for fear. "She never saw a man in her life before, none of them has. You imbecile, don't you get it? There aren't any other men, they've all been dead three hundred years."

Bud slowly stops chuckling, twists around to peer at Lorimer.

"What'd I hear you say, Doc?"

"The men are all gone. They died off in the epidemic. There's nothing but women left alive on Earth."

"You mean there's, there's two million women down there and no men?" His jaw gapes. "Only little bull dykes like Andy . . . Wait a minute. Where do they get the kids?"

"They grow them artificially. They're all girls."

"Gawd . . ." Bud's hand clasps his drooping penis, jiggles it absently until it stiffens. "Two million hot little cunts down there, waiting for old Buddy. Gawd. The last man on Earth . . . You don't count, Doc. And old Dave, he's full of crap."

He begins to pump himself, still holding Judy by the hair. The motion sends them slowly backward. Lorimer sees that Andy—Kay—has the camera going again. There is a big star-shaped smear of blood on the boyish face; cut lip, probably. He himself feels globed in thick air, all action spent. Not lucid.

"Two million cunts," Bud repeats. "Nobody home, nothing but pussy everywhere. I can do anything I want, anytime. No more shit." He pumps faster. "They'll be spread out for miles begging for it. Clawing each other for it. All for me, King Buddy . . . I'll have strawberries and cunt for breakfast. Hot buttered boobies, man. 'N' head, there'll be a couple little twats licking whip cream off my cock all day long. . . . Hey, I'll have contests! Only the best for old Buddy now. Not you, cow." He jerks Judy's head. "Li'l teenies, tight li'l holes. I'll make the old broads hot 'em up while I watch." He frowns slightly, working on himself. In a clinical corner of his mind Lorimer guesses the drug is retarding ejaculation. He tells himself that he should be relieved by Bud's self-absorption, is instead obscurely terrified.

"King, I'll be their god," Bud is mumbling. "They'll make statues of me, my cock a mile high, all over. . . . His Majesty's sacred balls. They'll worship it. . . . Buddy Geirr, the last cock on Earth. Oh, man, if old George could see that. When the boys hear that they'll really shit themselves, woo-ee!"

He frowns harder. "They can't all be gone." His eyes rove, find Lorimer. "Hey, Doc, there's some men left someplace, aren't there? Two or three, anyway?"

"No." Effortfully Lorimer shakes his head. "They're all dead, all of them."

"Balls." Bud twists around, peering at them. "There has to be some left. Say it." He pulls Judy's head up. "*Say* it, cunt."

"No, it's true," she says.

"No men," Andy/Kay echoes.

"You're lying." Bud scowls, frigs himself faster, thrusting his pelvis. "There has to be some men, sure there are. . . . They're hiding out in the hills, that's what it is. Hunting, living wild . . . Old wild men, I knew it."

"Why do there have to be men?" Judy asks him, being jerked to and fro.

"Why, you stupid bitch." He doesn't look at her, thrusts furiously. "Because, dummy, otherwise nothing counts, that's why. . . . There's some men, some good old buckaroos—Buddy's a good old buckaroo—"

"Is he going to emit sperm now?" Connie whispers.

"Very likely," Lorimer says, or intends to say. The spectacle is of merely clinical interest, he tells himself, nothing to dread. One of Judy's hands clutches something: a small plastic bag. Her other hand is on her hair that Bud is yanking. It must be painful.

"Uhhh, ahh," Bud pants distressfully, "fuck away, fuck—" Suddenly he pushes Judy's head into his groin, Lorimer glimpses her nonplussed expression.

"You have a mouth, bitch, get working! . . . Take it, for shit's sake, *take it!* Uh, uh—" A small oyster jets limply from him. Judy's arm goes after it with the bag as they roll over in the air.

"*Geirr!*"

Bewildered by the roar, Lorimer turns and sees Dave—Major Norman Davis—looming in the hatchway. His arms are out, holding back Lady Blue and the other Judy.

"Geirr! I said there would be no misconduct on this ship, and I mean it. Get away from that woman!"

Bud's legs only move vaguely, he does not seem to have heard. Judy swims through them bagging the last drops.

"You, what the hell are you doing?"

In the silence Lorimer hears his own voice say, "Taking a sperm sample, I should think."

"Lorimer? Are you out of your perverted mind? Get Geirr to his quarters."

Bud slowly rotates upright. "Ah, the reverend Leroy," he says tonelessly.

"You're drunk, Geirr. Go to your quarters."

"I have news for you, Dave-o," Bud tells him in the same flat voice. "I bet you don't know we're the last men on Earth. Two million twats down there."

"I'm aware of that," Dave says furiously. "You're a drunken disgrace. Lorimer, get that man out of here."

But Lorimer feels no nerve of action stir. Dave's angry voice has pushed back the terror, created a strange hopeful stasis encapsulating them all.

"I don't have to take that anymore. . . ." Bud's head moves back and forth, silently saying no, no, as he drifts toward Lorimer. "Nothing counts anymore. All gone. What for, friends?" His forehead puckers. "Old Dave, he's a man. I'll let him have some. The dummies . . . Poor old Doc, you're a creep but you're better'n nothing, you can have some too. . . . We'll have places, see, big spreads. Hey, we can run drags, there has to be a million good old cars down there. We can go hunting. And then we find the wild men."

Andy, or Kay, is floating toward him, wiping off blood.

"Ah, no you don't!" Bud snarls and lunges for her. As his arm stretches out Judy claps him on the triceps.

Bud gives a yell that dopplers off, his limbs thrash—and then he is floating limply, his face suddenly serene. But he is breathing, Lorimer sees, releasing his own breath, watching them carefully straighten out the big body. Judy plucks her pants out of the vines, and they start towing him out through the fence. She has the camera and the specimen bag.

"I put this in the freezer, dinko?" she says to Connie as they come by. Lorimer has to look away.

Connie nods. "Kay, how's your face?"

"I felt it!" Andy/Kay says excitedly through puffed lips. "I felt physical anger, I wanted to hit him. Woo-ee!"

"Put that man in my wardroom," Dave orders as they pass. He has moved into the sunlight over the lettuce rows. Lady Blue and Judy Dakar are back by the wall, watching. Lorimer remembers what he wanted to ask.

"Dave, do you really know?"

Dave eyes him broodingly, floating erect with the sun on his chestnut beard and hair. The authentic features of man. Lorimer thinks of his own father, a small pale figure like himself. He feels better.

"I always knew they were trying to deceive us, Lorimer. Now that this woman has admitted the facts, I understand the full extent of the tragedy."

It is his deep, mild Sunday voice. The women look at him interestedly.

"They are lost children. They have forgotten He who made them. For generations they have lived in darkness."

"They seem to be doing all right," Lorimer hears himself say. It sounds rather foolish.

"Women are not capable of running anything. You should know that, Lorimer. Look what they've done here, it's pathetic. Marking time, that's all. Poor souls." Dave sighs gravely. "It is not their fault. I recognize that. Nobody has given them any guidance for three hundred years. Like a chicken with its head off."

Lorimer recognizes his own thought; the structureless chattering, trivial, two-million-celled protoplasmic lump.

"The head of the woman is the man," Dave says crisply. "Corinthians one eleven three. No discipline whatsoever." He stretches out his arm, holding up his crucifix as he drifts toward the wall of vines. "Mockery. Abominations." At the stakes he turns, framed in the green arbor.

"We were sent here, Lorimer. This is God's plan. I was sent here. Not you, you're as bad as they are. My middle name is Paul," he adds in a conversational tone. The sun gleams on the cross, on his uplifted face, a strong, pure, apostolic visage. Despite some intellectual reservations Lorimer feels a forgotten nerve respond.

"Oh, Father, send me strength," Dave prays quietly, his eyes closed. "You have spared us from the void to bring Your light to this suffering world. I shall lead Thine erring daughters out of the darkness. I shall be a stern but merciful father to them in Thy name. Help me to teach the children Thy holy law and train them in the fear of Thy righteous wrath. Let the women learn in silence and all subjection; Timothy two eleven. They shall have sons to rule over them and glorify Thy name."

He could do it, Lorimer thinks, a man like that really could get life going again. Maybe there is some mystery, some plan. I was too ready to give up. No guts . . . He becomes aware of women whispering.

"This tape is about through." It is Judy Dakar. "Isn't that enough? He's just repeating."

"Wait," murmurs Lady Blue.

"And she brought forth a man child to rule the nations with

a rod of iron, Revelations twelve five," Dave says, louder. His eyes are open now, staring intently at the crucifix. *"For God so loved the world that He sent His only begotten Son."*

Lady Blue nods; Judy pushes off toward Dave. Lorimer understands, protest rising in his throat. They mustn't do that to Dave, treating him like an animal, for Christ's sake, a man —

"Dave! Look out, don't let her get near you!" he shouts.

"May I look, Major? It's beautiful, what is it?" Judy is coasting close, her hand out toward the crucifix.

"She's got a hypo, watch it!"

But Dave has already wheeled around. "Do not profane, woman!"

He thrusts the cross at her like a weapon, so menacing that she recoils in midair and shows the glinting needle in her hand.

"Serpent!" He kicks her shoulder away, sending himself upward. "Blasphemer. All right," he snaps in his ordinary voice, "there's going to be some order around here, starting now. Get over by that wall, all of you."

Astounded, Lorimer sees that Dave actually has a weapon in his other hand, a small gray handgun. He must have had it since Houston. Hope and ataraxia shrivel away, he is shocked into desperate reality.

"Major Davis," Lady Blue is saying. She is floating right at him, they all are, right at the gun. Oh, god, do they know what it is?

"Stop!" he shouts at them. "Do what he says, for god's sake. That's a ballistic weapon, it can kill you. It shoots metal slugs." He begins edging toward Dave along the vines.

"Stand back." Dave gestures with the gun. "I am taking command of this ship in the name of the United States of America under God."

"Dave, put that gun away. You don't want to shoot people."

Dave sees him, swings the gun around. "I warn you, Lorimer, get over there with them. Geirr's a man, when he sobers up." He looks at the women still drifting puzzledly toward him and understands. "All right, lesson one. Watch this."

He takes deliberate aim at the iguana cages and fires. There is a pinging crack. A lizard explodes bloodily, voices cry out. A loud mechanical warble starts up and overrides everything.

"A leak!" Two bodies go streaking toward the far end,

everybody is moving. In the confusion Lorimer sees Dave calmly pulling himself back to the hatchway behind them, his gun ready. He pushes frantically across the tool rack to cut them off. A spray canister comes loose in his grip, leaving him kicking in the air. The alarm warble dies.

"You will stay here until I decide to send for you," Dave announces. He has reached the hatch, is pulling the massive lock door around. It will seal off the pod, Lorimer realizes.

"Don't do it, Dave! Listen to me, you're going to kill us all." Lorimer's own internal alarms are shaking him, he knows now what all that damned volleyball has been for and he is scared to death. "Dave, listen to me!"

"Shut up." The gun swings toward him. The door is moving. Lorimer gets a foot on solidity.

"Duck! It's a bomb!" With all his strength he hurls the massive canister at Dave's head and launches himself after it.

"Look out!" And he is sailing helplessly in slow motion, hearing the gun go off again, voices yelling. Dave must have missed him, overhead shots are tough—and then he is doubling downward, grabbing hair. A hard blow strikes his gut, it is Dave's leg kicking past him but he has his arm under the beard, the big man bucking like a bull, throwing him around.

"Get the gun, get it!" People are bumping him, getting hit. Just as his hold slips, a hand snakes by him onto Dave's shoulder and they are colliding into the hatch door in a tangle. Dave's body is suddenly no longer at war.

Lorimer pushes free, sees Dave's contorted face tip slowly backward looking at him.

"Judas—"

The eyes close. It is over.

Lorimer looks around. Lady Blue is holding the gun, sighting down the barrel.

"Put that down," he gasps, winded. She goes on examining it.

"Hey, thanks!" Andy—Kay—grins lopsidedly at him, rubbing her jaw. They are all smiling, speaking warmly to him, feeling themselves, their torn clothes. Judy Dakar has a black eye starting, Connie holds a shattered iguana by the tail.

Beside him Dave drifts, breathing stertorously, his blind face pointing at the sun. *Judas* . . . Lorimer feels the last shield break inside him, desolation flooding in. *On the deck my captain lies.*

Andy-who-is-not-a-man comes over and matter-of-factly

zips up Dave's jacket, takes hold of it, and begins to tow him out. Judy Dakar stops them long enough to wrap the crucifix chain around his hand. Somebody laughs, not unkindly, as they go by.

For an instant Lorimer is back in that Evanston toilet. But they are gone, all the little giggling girls. All gone forever, gone with the big boys waiting outside to jeer at him. Bud is right, he thinks. *Nothing counts anymore.* Grief and anger hammer at him. He knows now what he has been dreading: not their vulnerability, his.

"They were good men," he says bitterly. "They aren't bad men. You don't know what bad means. You did it to them, you broke them down. You made them do crazy things. Was it interesting? Did you learn enough?" His voice is trying to shake. "Everybody has aggressive fantasies. They didn't act on them. Never. Until you poisoned them."

They gaze at him in silence. "But nobody does," Connie says finally. "I mean, the fantasies."

"They were good men," Lorimer repeats elegiacally. He knows he is speaking for it all, for Dave's Father, for Bud's manhood, for himself, for Cro-Magnon, for the dinosaurs too, maybe. "I'm a man. By god, yes, I'm angry. I have a right. We gave you all this, we made it all. We built your precious civilization and your knowledge and comfort and medicines and your dreams. All of it. We protected you, we worked our balls off keeping you and your kids. It was hard. It was a fight, a bloody fight all the way. We're tough. We had to be, can't you understand? Can't you for Christ's sake understand that?"

Another silence.

"We're trying," Lady Blue sighs. "We are trying, Dr. Lorimer. Of course we enjoy your inventions and we do appreciate your evolutionary role. But you must see there's a problem. As I understand it, what you protected people from was largely other males, wasn't it? We've just had an extraordinary demonstration in that. You have brought history to life for us." Her wrinkled brown eyes smile at him; a small tea-colored matron holding an obsolete artifact.

"But the fighting is long over. It ended when you did, I believe. We can hardly turn you loose on Earth, and we simply have no facilities for people with your emotional problems."

"Besides, we don't think you'd be very happy," Judy Dakar adds earnestly.

"We could clone them," says Connie. "I know there's people who would volunteer to mother. The young ones might be all right, we could try."

"We've been *over* all that." Judy Paris is drinking from the water tank. She rinses and spits into the soil bed, looking worriedly at Lorimer. "We ought to take care of that leak now, we can talk tomorrow. And tomorrow and tomorrow." She smiles at him, unselfconsciously rubbing her crotch. "I'm sure a lot of people will want to meet you."

"Put us on an island," Lorimer says wearily. "On three islands." That look; he knows that look of preoccupied compassion. His mother and sister had looked just like that the time the diseased kitten came in the yard. They had comforted it and fed it and tenderly taken it to the vet to be gassed.

An acute, complex longing for the women he has known grips him. Women to whom men were not simply—*irrelevant*. Ginny . . . dear god. His sister Amy. Poor Amy, she was good to him when they were kids. His mouth twists.

"Your problem is," he says, "if you take the risk of giving us equal rights, what could we possibly contribute?"

"Precisely," says Lady Blue. They all smile at him relievedly, not understanding that he isn't.

"I think I'll have that antidote now," he says.

Connie floats toward him, a big, warmhearted, utterly alien woman. "I thought you'd like yours in a bulb." She smiles kindly.

"Thank you." He takes the small pink bulb. "Just tell me," he says to Lady Blue, who is looking at the bullet gashes, "what do you call yourselves? Women's World? Liberation? Amazonia?"

"Why, we call ourselves human beings." Her eyes twinkle absently at him, go back to the bullet marks. "Humanity, mankind." She shrugs. "The human race."

The drink tastes cool going down, something like peace and freedom, he thinks. Or death.

WITH DELICATE MAD HANDS

CAROL PAGE, OR CP as she was usually known, was an expert at being unloved.

She was a sweetly formed, smallish girl of the red-hair-green-eyes-and-freckles kind, but her face was entirely spoiled and dominated by a huge, fleshy, obscenely pugged nose.

A nurse at the State Orphans' Crèche told her that a student OB had crushed it, in the birthing that killed her mother. What resulted was a truly hideous snout, the nostrils gaping level with her squinted eyes, showing hair and mucus. The other children called her Snotface.

As she grew older she became CP, and later yet, when her natural fastidiousness was known, the spacers called her Cold Pig, sometimes to her face.

Had CP been officially born to one of the world's ruling Managers, a few passes with a scalpel would have returned that snout to its dainty pixie form; her eyes would have been as nature intended, provocatively tilted green stars, and her lips would have retained their delicious curves. Then, too, her skin would have remained cream-and-rose petals, instead of its dry angry workhouse red, and her slim fingers would have stayed delightful.

The lack of these amenities cost the world a girl of delicate, impish beauty—but this world was precariously recovering from many and much more terrible losses, and individual desolations counted for little.

CP was, in fact, lucky to be alive at all.

At fifteen her mother had been assigned to a visiting Manager who fancied virgins. She became pregnant through an unexpected delay in his schedules. He had become fond enough of the child so that when he saw how passionately she wanted her baby, and how she dreaded her destined future, he took the trouble to find a place for her in a State hospital. Here, of course, she died, but the baby, CP, retained her place-rights in the State Enclave.

This Enclave was one of a small number of city-form complexes on clean ground, where a shadowy form of old-style middle-class life was maintained. It served as a source of skilled labor and very occasional potential Managers. CP's basic health needs were attended to and she was placed in the Enclave's Orphans' School, where she became Snotface.

Here CP developed two traits, the first well-known and the second totally secret.

What was known to all was that she was a hard, smart worker—tireless, unstoppable. Whatever came her way, she drove herself into the first percentile at it, and looked for more. It presently became clear what she was aiming at—in a school where mere survival was a feat, CP was dreaming of an all but impossible achievement: Space Crew Training.

She was doing it by simple hard work, undistracted, of course, by anyone who wanted personal relations with a Snotface. Whatever could conceivably be of help, she learned, fast and well. She plowed from arithmetic through calculus into vector math, she tackled metallurgy, electronics, computers of any and all kinds. Astronomy she devoured. Being a realist, she neglected no menial art—metal-cleaning, nutrition, space cookery, nursing, massage, the twenty-seven basic sexual stimulations, how to fix any common appliance, space laundry. She took a minor in space medicine. And always she went at engines; engines, more engines, and whatever she could find on orbital flight and thrust maneuvers. Her meager State allowance she saved from childhood until she could actually afford simple flying lessons at the Enclave strip.

And she made it—the incredible quantum leap into Basic Space Crew Training. A mathematician who had never touched a woman pushed her name, a State test administrator who wanted to up his school averages was of use. A general shortage of support personnel for the vital asteroid mining program helped. But basically it was her own unquenchable drive for the stars that carried her up.

Lots of people longed to go to space, of course; among other things, the spacers' life was thought to be a privileged one. And people admired the stars, when they could be seen. CP's longing wasn't unusual; it was only of another order of intensity. She didn't talk about it much—in fact, she didn't talk much at all—because she learned her fellows thought it was comical: Snotface in the stars. But, as one of them put it, "Better there than here."

In Basic Crew Training the story repeated itself; she simply worked twice as hard. And her next small savings went for a medical operation—not on her nose, as any normal girl would, but on the sterilization required of female students, for which they had to pay, if they wanted to get to actual flight. (For space-station workers it was desirable too, but not compulsory.)

And she made it there too, relatively easily. At nineteen she certified for work in space. She was ready to be assigned offplanet. Here, oddly, her dreadful looks helped. In her interview she had asked particularly for the far-out exploratory flights.

"Holy Haig," the young interviewer said to his superiors on the Assignment Board. "Imagine being cooped up for a year with that face! Stick her in the far end of station sewage reclamation, I say."

"And you'd be a damn fool, sonny. What caused the abort on the last Titan trip? Why were there three fatal so-called accidents on the last six Trojan runs? Why do so many computers 'accidentally' dump parts of the log on a lot of the long missions? We lost the whole mineralogical analysis of that good-looking bunch of rocks on the far side of the Belt. If you recall, we still don't know where we'll get our cesium. Why, junior?"

The young Personnel man sobered quickly.

"Ah . . . personality tensions, sir. Stress, clashes, unavoidable over long periods to men in confined quarters. The capsule-design people are working on privacy provisions, I understand they have some new concepts –"

"And to these tinderboxes you want to add an even reasonably attractive woman, sonny? We know the men do better with a female along, not only for physiological needs but for a low-status noncompetitive servant and rudimentary mother figure. What we do *not* need is a female who could incite competition or any hint of tension for her services. We have plenty of exciting-looking women back at the stations and the R & R depots, the men can dream of them and work to get back to them. But on board a long flight, what we need sexually is a human waste can. This—who is it?—Carol Page fits the bill like a glove, and she has all these skills as a bonus, if her marks mean anything. Talk about imagining a year with 'that face'— can you imagine any crew who wasn't blind or absolutely crazy experiencing the faintest additional tension over *her?*"

"I certainly see what you mean, sir—I was dead wrong. Thank you, sir."

"Okay, skip it. Hell, if she works out at all she may actually be a fair asset."

And so it was that CP went out to space, with a clause in her Articles certifying her for trial on long-run work.

On her very first run, a check on a large new incoming asteroid apparently dislodged from cis-Plutonian orbit, she proved the senior Personnel man right. She cleaned and dumped garbage and kept the capsule orderly and in repair at all times, she managed to make the food tastier than the men believed possible, she helped everybody do anything disagreeable, she nursed two men through space dysentery and massaged the pain out of another's sprained back; she kept her mouth strictly shut at all times, and performed her sexual duties as a "human waste can" with competence, although she could not quite successfully simulate real desire. (It was after this trip that she began to be known as Cold Pig.) She provoked no personal tensions; in fact, two of the crew forgot even to say good-bye to her, although they gave her superior marks in their report forms.

After several repetitions of this performance she began to be regarded by the Planners as something of an asset, as the Personnel chief had predicted. The crews didn't exactly love her, and made a great exhibition of groaning when Cold Pig showed up on their trip rosters; but secretly they were not displeased. Cold Pig missions were known to go well and be as comfortable as possible. And she could fill in for half a dozen specialties in emergencies. Things never went totally wrong with Cold Pig aboard. The Pig began to be privately regarded as lucky. She achieved a shadowy kind of status in the growing space network.

But not with Captain Bob Meich, on whose ship, *Calgary,*

her story begins. Captain Bob Meich loathed her, and despised a certain fact about Cold Pig that was the most precious possession of her life.

Among the various Articles of Contract by which she was bound, there were two unusual clauses that were all she had worked for, and which she prized above life: Cold Pig, almost alone among thousands of women in space, was fully certified for solo flight.

She had insisted on a general flight clause at first signing, and she had the attested experience to back it up. Authority showed no particular resistance: space work includes thousands of hours of dull routine ferrying of stuff from here to there, which the men disliked, and quite a few station women were allowed to help out. Cold Pig's looks were helpful here too; clearly her goings and comings would never cause a ripple. But Cold Pig had her sights set higher than this.

Once in space, she set out to achieve a solo cert for every type of rocket going. She piled up flight time between all her assignments. She would fly anything anywhere, even if it meant three months done in foul air, herding a rock in an old torch with a broken-down air regenerator she could barely keep functional. Her eagerness to fly the lousiest trips slowly made her an asset here, too.

The payoff came when there was a bad rock-hit on a hot new short-run mission; Cold Pig not only saved a couple of lives, but flew the new model home alone and docked it like a pro. The wounded captain she had saved was grateful enough to help her get the second Article she coveted, the big one: it was formally stipulated that if a scout became disabled on a multiship mission, Carol Page would be assigned as replacement to take over his mission and ship, solo, until he recovered. This was extended to include flying the mother ship itself should all other crew be totally disabled.

Thus it was that one day Cold Pig came head to head with Captain Bob Meich of the *Calgary*, on the extreme-range mission on the far side of Uranus, with four of the ship's five scouts out on long exploratory flights. Don Lamb, the fifth and last, lay stranded helpless in his sleeper with a broken hip, and his scout ship idled in its berth.

"No cunt is going to fly off my ship while I'm breathing," Meich said levelly. "I don't give a flying fuck what your Articles say. If you want to make a point of it back at Station you can try.

Or you can have a little accident and go out the waste hole, too. I am the captain and what I say goes."

"But, sir, that data Don's ship was assigned to is supposed to be crucial—"

He glared coldly at her; not sane, she saw. Nor was she, but she didn't know that.

"I'll show you once and for all what's crucial. Follow me, Pig." He spat out the name.

She followed him to the scout access tunnel; all the ports but one were empty. He opened the port of Don's scouter and crawled into the small capsule. *Calgary*'s pseudogravity of rotation was heavy out here; she could hear him grunting.

"Watch." He jerked the keys from the console and pocketed them. Then he yanked free the heavy pry-bar, and deliberately smashed it again and again into the on-board computer. Cold Pig was gasping.

He crawled out.

"Take your pants off."

He used her there on the cold grids beside the wreckage of her hopes, used her hard and with pain, holding her pants across her ugly face so she nearly smothered.

At one point a bulge in her shirt pocket attracted his notice: her notebook. He jerked it out, kneeling his weight hurtfully on her shoulders, and flipped through it.

"What the hell's this? *Poetry?*" He read in ferocious falsetto scorn: "*With delicate mad hands against his sordid bars*—aagh!" He flung the little book savagely toward the waster. It went skittering heavily across the grids, tearing pages.

Cold Pig, supine and in pain, twisted to see it, could not suppress a cry.

Meich was not normally a sexual man; several times she had felt him failing, and each time he slapped her head or invented some new indignity; but now he grinned jubilantly, not knowing that he had sealed his own fate. He jerked her head forward and, finally, ejaculated.

"All right. That's as close as you get to flying, Pig. Just remember that. Now get my dinner."

He was tired and withdrawn; he hit her covered face once more and left her. Cold Pig was grateful for the cover; she hadn't cried before in space—not, in fact, for years. Before dressing she rescued the little notebook, put it in a different pocket.

"Pig!" He may have had a moment's worry that he'd killed her. "Get that food."

"Yes, sir."

Quite insane now, she smiled—a doubly horrible effect on her bloodied face—and went to do as he ordered, smoothly, efficiently as always. Don was awake too, by now, looking curiously at her. She offered no explanation, merely inquired what he'd like to eat.

The dinner she produced was particularly tasty; she used some of her carefully hoarded spices to disguise any possible taste from another carefully hoarded ingredient—though she knew from long-ago paramed school it was tasteless.

The fact that she was crazy was made clear by her choice. She had other capabilities; she could have served a meal from which neither Don nor the captain would ever have wakened. In fact, she did give one such to Don, who had always been minimally decent to her. But for the captain she had another, and as it turned out, more perilous plan. Cold Pig was human; she wanted him to *know*.

He ate heartily. Another type of person might have been made slightly suspicious by the niceness, comprising just the foods she knew he was fondest of. Or by her compliant, quietly agreeable manner. To Bob Meich it only confirmed what his father had taught him, that all women needed was a little knocking about, to be shown who was boss. He announced thickly something to this effect to Don, on his bunk in the next "room"; expecting no answer and getting none.

Don was young, the captain mused. Too soft. He still talked about his mother. When Don got better he would teach him a thing or two about handling women.

Presently he began to slump toward the special dessert CP served him. Feeling some irony, she put his "nightcap" bottle where he liked it, within easy reach. She was impatient now, there was much to do. Waiting, she had to admire his extraordinary physical vitality. A dose that ought to have brought quick oblivion took a few minutes to work fully on him. She began to worry that he might hear Don begin to hyperventilate, but he gave no sign of this. Finally Meich stared about, focused on her, shouted "Wha—?" and half rose before he went down for good. She should have been warned.

But he *was* completely unconscious—she snapped her fingers by his ear, sprinkled salt on his exposed eye to make sure. She could get to work.

First she wanted to check on Don. She had saved enough of the substance she had fed him to serve her own necessities, and she wanted to see how painful it might be.

Don was half off his bunk, the last spasms subsiding into occasional leg jerks. His face was not excessively distorted, only sweat-covered, and the mouth was bloody. He'd bitten almost through his tongue, she found. But it did seem to have been quick. There was no heartbeat now except for one last faint thud that came during the minute she listened. Despite herself, she wiped his face a little, closed his eyes, and laid a hand for an instant on his soft brown hair. He *had* been considerate once.

Then she went to work, hard and fast. She blunted one scalpel and another—those suits and air tubes were tough—and had to go to pliers and other tools before she had things to her satisfaction. Next she got all essentials tied or taped in place. She also disconnected a few alarms to keep bedlam from breaking out prematurely. Early in the process, Meich startled her by sliding out of his chair, ending head down under the table.

One of the air canisters she'd wrestled loose rolled under the table too, the cut end of its hose wagging. This she noticed only subliminally, it didn't seem to matter. She was busy undogging heavy seals.

The main air-pressure alarm in the pilot's chamber was very loud. It roused Bob Meich.

He rolled convulsively, and pushed himself half upright, overturning table and seats, opening, closing, opening his eyes wide with obvious effort.

What he saw would probably have stunned a lesser man to fatal hesitancy. The room was in a gale—papers, clothes, objects of all description were flying past him, snapping out of the half-open main port.

The port was opening farther. As he looked, the suited, helmeted figure of Cold Pig pulled the great circular port seal back to its widest extent and calmly latched it. Alarms were howling and warbling all over the ship as air left from everywhere at once and pressure dropped; total uproar. Then the sounds faded as the air to carry them went out. The last to remain audible was a far faint squeal from the interior of Don's scouter. Then near silence.

CP had wondered whether Meich would go first for his suit

or directly to the door and herself.

His reflexes carried him, already gasping in airlessness, to the suit that hung on the wall behind, standing straight out as it tugged to fly. One heavy boot had already rolled and shot out the port—no matter, the helmet was there. Emergency suits were emplaced throughout *Calgary*, which was partly what had taken her so long.

He was halfway into it, staggered against the wall, when he saw the cuts. He grunted—or perhaps shouted, the air was now too thin to carry sound—and fell to his knees clasping the helmet. But he couldn't or didn't put it on—his dying eyes were still sharp enough to catch the neatly sliced air hoses. The helmet couldn't help him, it was now connected to nothing.

His mouth opening and closing, perhaps yelling curses, he toppled to the floor, taking great strangled gulps of near-vacuum. Finally he rolled again beneath the table. His last gesture was to grab the bolted-down table leg with one strong pink hand, to fight the pull that would carry him out the port. He held there through the last spasm CP decided was death. She couldn't see him fully, she wanted neither to touch him nor to peer, but he was totally moveless. Man cannot live without air. Not even a Meich, she told herself.

In her savage heart she was a shade disappointed that he had not put on the useless helmet. Further, she would have been better pleased never to have to see that face.

The gale was subsiding, the pull from the port was almost gone. CP waited impatiently until the VACUUM light flashed on the console; it was time to get to work. Don should go first.

Outside the port was a rushing, flickering grayness—the star fields flashing by as *Calgary* rolled. Only ahead and astern was there relatively stable vision. Ahead lay steadier stars, she knew—she dared not, of course, lean out to look—while behind lay the great dim starlit disk of Uranus, flame-edged on one limb. They were orbiting in outward-facing attitude, to maximize the chance of observing any events on the planet. By chance—she hadn't had endurance enough to plan—*Calgary* was just coming into that arc of her orbit where the sun and the world of men were almost directly in line beyond the planet.

Good. She hooked a safety web across the open port, and walked, cautious of any remaining air pockets, into the chamber where Don lay.

She had prepared jato units to send the corpses as fast as

possible down out of orbit and falling into Uranus. There would of course be no science-fiction nonsense about macabre objects orbiting *Calgary*; certainly not after she was on her way out and away forever—how she longed to start!—but more practically, she wanted no accidental discovery of the corpses. It would be, of course, a million-to-one freak. But freaks happen. CP knew that. In *Calgary*'s attitude, the temptation to set the jets directly at Uranus was strong, but she must arrange them to decelerate instead; most efficient.

She was figuring out the settings as she bent over Don. The hypo she had prepared in case Meich went for her was still clenched, almost hidden, in one glove. She must put it down somewhere safe.

As she reached toward a locker her body was touched from behind.

Terror. *What*—

An arm clamped hard around her neck.

As it passed her faceplate she had a glimpse of muscles and unmistakably pink, hairless skin.

A dead man had come after her. Meich had come back from death to kill her—was killing her now.

It would indeed have been Meich's impulse and delight to maul and kill her with his bare hands. But he was impeded. One hand was pressing the cut end of an air-tank hose to his mouth. And it is not easy in vacuum to batter a body in a pressure suit, nor to choke a neck enclosed in a hard helmet base. So he was contenting himself with yanking out her air hoses first, intending to get at her when she weakened, and keep her alive long enough to fully feel his wrath.

His first great jerk almost sent her reeling, but he had a leg hard about hers, holding her close.

Cold Pig, aghast to the bones, didn't keep her head. Adrenaline rush almost stopped her heart.

All was gone from her save only reflexes. The hand holding the hypo came round in one drive of horror-heightened power and precision—the needle he hadn't seen was there went straight in, against all likelihood not bending, not breaking, not striking plastic or bone, right through the suit he had pulled up, through liner, skin, and visceral sheath, while CP's clumsy gloved fingers found the triggers and her terrified muscles exerted impossible strength. The discharge shot directly into liver and stomach and ran out lodged in the lining of his renal vein. The strike was so clean Meich may never have felt it. He didn't know he was now truly a dead man. Or would be in seconds.

And seconds counted.

He had torn her air tubes loose, she was without air save only for the tiny amount lodged in her helmet and suit. And he was clamped to her, arm and leg. She began to choke, partly from sheer panic, as she twisted in his dying grasp, not understanding at first what was happening. The force of her turning blow had carried her partway round; she contorted frantically, and finally saw the air tank he was holding and the hose end he breathed from.

It took precious instants for her to understand that she must open her faceplate and get that air hose to her mouth.

Somehow, in spite of his mad battering and wrenching, she opened up. Dying girl fought with dead man for the hose end. She could not possibly pry loose his fingers, though she broke one. But the lethal drug was telling on him—she finally butted his head aside with her helmeted one, and managed to gulp air hissing from the hose he held.

In one last spasm of hate he tried to fling the air tank away from them both. But the tank struck her body. She held on.

And then it was over, really over at last. Meich lay slumped grotesquely at her feet, against Don's bunk.

It took infinite time for her to stop shaking. She vomited twice, fouling herself, but since the hose end was free she didn't aspirate it. She watched, watched, for any motion or, breath from the twice-dead man. Only the fear that the wildly escaping air—so precious—would give out, finally got her moving rationally.

It was almost more than her fingers could do to reconnect her hoses, fit a spare for the damaged one, wipe out and close her faceplate. She would have to live and work for a time in her own vomit, which she found appropriate.

And there was much work to do, in vacuum, before she could reseal *Calgary*. It was now getting very cold.

She had a message to send, and she wanted to dump everything of the men's before repressurizing, to use the waste flush later as little as possible. The bodies she would send out first, right now.

This time there was no question of Don preceding; she laid shuddering hands on Meich's legs and dragged him to the port and the jato rig. She managed to stop herself from leaning out to make sure he had jetted clean away, not caught on some part of *Calgary* to clamber back at her. But she did permit herself to go to the stern port and watch his jet dwindle among the whirling stars.

Then Don. Then everything she could lay hands on or dump from lockers, even to letters, private caches, the pinups on walls, even the duty roster. All, all went out, and did orbit *Calgary*, but only for a time.

Finally she unlatched and wrestled shut the cold main port.

Then without waiting to repressurize, she was free to yield to heart's desire. She didn't even bother to sit down, she simply ran through the basic emergency ignition sequence—Calgary was already in perfect attitude—and slammed the main thrust over and on.

Softly, with slowly growing, inexorable power, *Calgary* departed orbit and headed at maximum acceleration away from Uranus, away from Sol behind it, away from humanity, outward toward empty space and the unreachable stars.

Now the message.

She activated the high-gain transmitter, and plugged her suit mike in. And then Cold Pig undertook the first and last literary-dramatic exercise of her life. She was, after all, as noted, human.

First she keyed in the call signals for *Calgary*'s four other scouts, plus a general alarm. Next, gasping realistically, "—All scouts, do not try to return to *Calgary*; repeat, do not ... try return to *Calgary* ... there's nothing ... there. ... Head for ... the .. . *Churchill*—-*Wait*, maybe *Calhoun* closer ... repeat, *Calgary* . . . is not on station ... do not try to return. ... Wounded, will try to return log ... so much blood. ... Cause: Captain Robert Meich dead, self-inflicted ... gunshot ... Lieutenant ... Donald Lamb also dead by gunshot ... inflicted by Captain Meich. ... Both bodies lost in space. ... Captain Meich shot Don and ... unsealed ... main port. ... He took Don's body, and ... shot himself in the abdomen before ... going out. ... Cause: Captain Meich said we were docked at invisible spy station, when Don tried to stop him ... open port he said." Here her words were coming in a soft fainting rush, but clearly, oh, clear: "He said Don might be an alien and shot him, he was carrying gun three days ... sleeping with it. ... Cold, blood ... he made me strip and tied me to galley post but Don threw me ... helmet and air tank but I-have . . . shot wounds in body . . . since yesterday . . . fear *Calgary* lost, Captain Meich fired escape course, broke computer . . . cold . . . trans . . . mission . . . ends . . . will try. . . ." And then very weakly, "Don't repeat don't return. . . ."

After a few more deathly sounds, she unplugged, leaving the transmitter on. It was voice-activated, it wouldn't waste power, but she must be careful about any sounds she made, especially when the air came back.

Then she went carefully around the ship, sealing off everything but necessary living space, to conserve air, and turned the main air valves to pressurize.

Finally she snapped out the log cassette in a realistically fumbling manner, carefully tearing the tape head off before where she knew her argument with Meich began. It would look as if she had simply torn, it clumsily loose. To add verisimilitude—they would test oh, yes—she reopened one of the cuts Meich's blows had left on her face and dabbed her fresh blood on cassette and canister. The canister went into a wall slot, which would, when activated, encase it in its own small jato device with homing signal to Base. She fired it off.

The data from *Calgary's* exploratory mission would arrive, some day or year, near Base, beeping for pickup. That much, she thought, she owed the world of men. That much and no more.

The air pressure was rising slowly. No leaks so far, but it was not yet safe to unsuit. She checked the scanners once, to make sure Uranus and Sol were dwindling straight astern, and set the burn to turn off in an hour. If the fuel lasted that long.

Then she simply sat down in the copilot's chair, leaned back in her filthy helmet in the comfortless suit, and let herself lose consciousness. When she awoke she would be far enough away to turn the transmitter off.

She was headed for the Empire. Whose name, she knew quite rationally, was Death.

⊞

When she came to, the main torch was off. Had it run out of fuel? No, turned off, she saw, checking the console; there was still some energy left. Her eyes, nose, and lips were crusted, almost closed. Air pressure was back to cabin-normal.

Gratefully she opened her faceplate, unlatched and lifted off the heavy helmet assembly that had saved her life from Meich.

Don't think of all that, she told herself. Never again. Never ever again to suffer anything of man. Think of the fact that you're dehydrated and ravenous and dirty.

Gulping juice and water alternately, she checked position. She must have been unconscious a long, long time, they had passed Neptune's orbit; still accelerating, slightly. She should have saved the main burn till she was freer of Sol's gravity; she was glad she hadn't.

She got herself unsuited and minimally washed. There was a big cleanup to do. But first she'd better make herself count up her supplies, which was to say, her life.

She had long ago made the rough calculation that it was somewhere in the range of a hundred to a hundred fifty Earth-days.

Food—no problem. The dehydrated supplies were ample to take six men and herself another year.

Water was more serious. But the reclamation unit was new and worked well, all tanks were full. She would be drinking H_2O that had passed through all their kidneys and bladders the rest of her life, she thought. But in the humans of her Earth such thoughts no longer could evoke revulsion. She had drunk unrecycled water only a few times in her whole life; it had been desalinated water from a far sea. The importation of water-ice asteroids to Earth had been one of Base's routine jobs.

Calgary even had a small potential supply of fresh water, if she could reach it without too much loss of air. They had encountered a clean ice-rock and lashed it to the substructure of the hull.

She was gazing about, checking around the main console, at which she had never been allowed to sit before, deferring calculation of oxygen, when an odd glint above caught her eye. She stood up in the seat to peer at the thing embedded in the ceiling. A camouflaged lens.

She had stumbled onto one of the secret spy-eyes and spy-ears placed in all ships. She put a screwdriver between its rim and her ear, and caught a faint whirring. Somewhere in the walls a tape deck reeled. It had of course recorded the true events on *Calgary,* and the fisheye lens was set so that her present course-and-position readings would be recorded.

It was not, she was sure from former tales and trials at Base, transmitting now. People had confided that the eyes and ears sent off their main data in supercompressed blips, at rather long, random intervals. The detailed reading would wait until *Calgary* was back in human hands.

For that, they would have to catch her first. She smiled grimly through cracked lips.

But had it already sent off a data blip while she was unconscious? Or in the time before, for that matter? No way to tell. If so, her story would be only an addition to the catalog of her crimes. If not, good.

How to deactivate it, without tearing out the walls, or causing it to transmit in terminal alarm? Others must have tried it before her. She would have to think hard, and discard her first impulses.

Meanwhile she contented herself with taping over the lens. Then she thought for a moment, and continued searching. Sure enough, now that she knew what to look for, she found the backup—or perhaps the main one; it was much more skillfully hidden. She taped it, thinking too late that perhaps the blanking-out itself was a trigger to it to blip. Well, no help for that now. At least she was free of the feeling of being watched. This was actually a strange new sensation. People took the fact of being covertly observed almost for granted. Brash souls made jokes about what must be mountains of unread spy-eye data stored who knew where and how, perhaps an asteroid full.

She sank back down in the comfortable pilot's couch. If there was a third backup on her now, good luck to it.

The oxygen.

Even before she had dumped a shipful of air, the oxygen situation had not been very healthy. The regeneration system was old-style, dependent on at least some outside sunlight. The weak light at Uranus's orbit hadn't been enough for it; some of the bionic compounds had gone bad, and the regenerator was near the end of its life.

This had been well understood before the . . . incident. It had been planned to cut short the time in total shadow by establishing a semipolar semiorbit—Uranus rotated almost "lying down" relative to the solar plane—so as to maximize light. And the *Calhoun* was headed to an emergency rendezvous with them as far out as possible, to pass over oxygen and regenerator equipment. The water ice-rock might have had to be used inefficiently for air; they were on the lookout for others. Not a crisis, as such things went, but a potentially uncomfortable prospect.

Now she dreaded to think what a period of cold vacuum might have done to the system, and made herself go check. Damage, all right—some trays that had been photosynthesizing showed brown edges. Not a total wipeout, though, as she had feared. It would take care of some of her CO_2, more if she rigged emergency lights. She counted and recounted the suit tanks, and checked the high-compression ship supply of oxygen.

The answer came out surprisingly near her rough guess— oxygen for 140 days max, ten weeks. Actually the CO_2 buildup would probably sicken her seriously before that, unless she could contrive some help.

First was to supply all possible light of the correct wavelengths to the regenerator trays. She sorted out filters, power cords, and robbed all the lights she could spare from the rest of the ship, until she had all trays as fully lit as possible. She even found a packet of presumably long-dead culture starter—"seeds"—and planted them in the hope of restarting two dead trays.

That took hours, perhaps days; she kept no track, only stopping to eat and drink when the need was strong. The trays were huge and heavy, and she was sore. But she felt nothing but joy—joy in her perfect freedom. For the first time in years she was alone and unsupervised. But more: for the first time in her life she was truly free for good, accountable to no one but herself. Alone and *free* among her beloved stars.

The job completed, too tired to clean up herself and *Calgary*, she staggered back to the pilot's couch with a cold meal, and alternately ate and gazed out at those star fields straight ahead that could be seen through the gyrostabilized scope.

It wasn't enough. She wanted it all. What did she have to fear from the physical deterioration of zero gee?

She sank into sleep in the big pilot's chair, planning.

Over the next two Earth-days she cleaned ship intermittently, between work on her main task: to stop the rotation that gave *Calgary* its "gravity." She was careful to use as little energy as possible, letting every tiny burst take fullest possible effect before thrusting more.

Outside, the stars changed from a rushing gray tapestry to a whirl of streaks, shorter and shorter, steadying and condensing to blazing stubs against perpetual night.

Her touch was very accurate. At the end she scarcely had to brake. The bright blurs and stubs shrank and brightened—

until, with a perceptible jolt, there they were! Stars of all colors and brilliances, clouds dark and light, galaxies—tier beyond tier, a universe of glory.

CP toured the ship, unscreening every viewport. *Calgary* had many; she was an old belly-lander built originally to shuttle from the Mars sling, in the days when seeing outside with the living eyes was still important to men. *Calgary* even had a retracted delta wing, unused for who knew how long.

There were more cleanup chores to do as all gravity faded out and objects began to float. But always CP would pause as she passed a port, and revel silently in the wonders and beauties on every side. Her own wretched reflection in the vitrex bothered her; soon she turned off even the last lights, so that *Calgary's* interior became a dark starlit pocket of space-night.

Ahead of *Calgary* lay, relatively, nothing. She was flying to Galactic North, toward a region where the stars were relatively few and very far, without even a dust drift or any object closer than many human lifetimes. This didn't trouble her. She turned off most of the forward scanners and sensors, wanting to spend her last days studying and dwelling mentally in the richer, wondrous star fields on all sides.

The condition of weightlessness didn't bother her at all. She was one of those rare ones who found sustained pleasure in the odd life of free-fall. The exasperations of toolboxes squirmily unpacking themselves when opened merely amused her. And *Calgary* had many ingenious old zero-gee life and work aids. While CP's body healed, she was happy to be free of anything pressing her.

She was indeed grateful for all the comforts of the big mother ship. She'd never intended to steal it. A scout, the scout Meich had denied her, would have sufficed. This trans-Uranus trip was the farthest out she could ever have expected to be allowed to go. When Don broke his hip it was simply luck: she had been debating how most humanely to incapacitate the last pilot, so that she could take his scout as her Articles promised. The small capsules weren't comfortable, little more than flying torches, but their ample power would have served to carry her out, and not been worth pursuit.

Out was all she craved. Out, outward forever, past Oort's cloud—would she be alive and lucky enough to detect a "sleeping comet"?—outward at greatest acceleration from Sol and all the world of men—out free, in freedom dying, all too soon dead—but her body still flying free. Never to be pursued, touched, known of, by man or humanity.

Out to end among the stars. It was all she had dreamed of, worked and endured for, rationally.

No, not quite.

CP was not always rational, or rather, never "rational" at the core. There was always the thing she called for short the Empire.

It was noted before that CP had one total secret. The fact that she planned to steal a ship and fly out to her death she of course kept secret. But it was not her Secret, and it wasn't even unique. Others before her had now and then gone berserk under the strains of man's world, and taken off on death-flights to nowhere. Such loss of valuable equipment was spoken of rarely but very disparagingly, and accounted for much of the Managers' endless stringent screening, testing, and rechecking practices in space. But this plan was not her Secret.

"The Empire" was. The Empire of the Pigs.

The Empire was everything and nothing. It was basically only a story, a voice unreeling endlessly in her head. It had started before she could remember, and gone on ever since. It accounted for the inhuman sanity of her behavior, for her unshakable endurance under intolerable stress. It was an insanity that kept her functioning with superior competence and rationality, and it was known or suspected by nobody at all.

Not even the prespace test psychologists with all their truth serums and hypnotic techniques and secret, ceaseless spy records over every private, drug-relaxed hour of her test month, not even their most artfully sympathetic human-to-human congratulatory wind-downs, which had in the end brought so many secrets to so many hard-guarded lips; none of it had unsealed CP's. Her Secret lived unsuspected, unhinted-at to any other human soul.

Somewhere in her early years she had seized a chance to study the disapproved findings of psychology. What she really wanted was to know if the voice in her head meant she was truly crazy, although she didn't admit that to herself. It probably did, she decided subliminally, and buried her Secret deeper. As usual, she also studied hard and efficiently in the brief time allowed, and this knowledge helped her later to fend off assaults on her mind and to gratify those who controlled her fate.

The story had started very early.

She'd always been told she looked like a pig. One day the honors children were given a great treat—a visit to the city zoo. Here she saw a real pig; in fact, a great boar and sow. She lingered to read every word on the cage card. It told her how intelligent pigs were—and by nature cleanly, too. And somehow there started in her small head the story of the Empire of the Pigs.

The Empire was very far away on Earth, perhaps beyond the Chicago Pits. At first everyone in the Empire looked just like her, and life was simply very good. Every night, no matter how exhausted she was, Snotface would live there for a few instants. It took months of such instants to develop each satisfying aspect or event.

In the tale she always referred to herself as the Pig Person. At some early point things changed a little: she had volunteered to be surgically altered for temporary exile among Yumans.

And then one day she was taught about the stars. Right in the classroom her world gave a sort of silent snap, and the Empire moved off Earth, forever. Perhaps the Voice started too, she never troubled to make sure. She couldn't think then; she feared being inattentive.

But that night excitement fought off fatigue as she thought of the Empire in the stars. It was relatively quiet in the dormitory; she remembered that a star or something said very, very faintly but clearly, "Yes."

She fell asleep.

This starward move gave whole new dimensions to the physical Empire. She busied herself with adjustments and composing new, delicious stories of life there and the joys she would later return to.

Another quiet night the Voice said, stronger, "Come."

Such events she accepted tranquilly but happily. She would certainly come. Although even then a tiny part of her mind knew too that her return would also mean her end. This didn't disturb her; dying wasn't uncommon in Snotface's world.

The story soon grew very complicated, developed and abandoned subbranches, and changed greatly over the years.

Quite early the Empire people changed from being literal pigs to a somewhat shadowy physical form—though always entirely real. In one phase they ceased to be of two sexes.

About that time her unexplained exile also changed, first to an exciting spy mission. Real, Earthly pigs were sometimes failed spies, or persons being punished by some power. In one episode the Pig Person rescued them and helped them resume their real forms. "Pig" also took on an acronymic meaning, which she didn't use much: "Persons in Greatness." One of the main branches of the story, which tended to take over as she grew older, also had a title: "The Adventures (or Reports) of the Pig Person on Terra."

All this complex activity kept the deep inside of CP's head very busy, without in the least interfering with all her learning and work.

By the time she went to space, a typical entry might transcribe thus (in this branch she wasn't primarily a spy but a stranded, shipwrecked traveler trying—successfully—to work out her way home):

> Today the Pig Person judged best to open her legs twice to accommodate the hard, fleshy protuberances characterizing two male Yumans. One Yuman requested her to conceal her face during the procedure, so she improvised a mask from her underwear (see note on male-female Yuman attire). The Yuman appeared gratified. This is important because on return from this flight he will be promoted to Personnel Assignment, where he could help the Pig Person acquire more skills on some of these Yuman-type spacecraft. The Pig Person also made a mental note to improve this technique by making a real mask—better, masks of several types—as soon as materials can be procured. How her friends in the Empire will enjoy the notion that some poor Yumans cannot look at her fine Pig face without losing the ability to erect their absurd organs! But however amusing this is, the Pig Person must positively bend all efforts to returning to the Empire before all her information becomes obsolete.

So spoke the true, silent Voice of Cold Pig nightly—sometimes, in bad periods, hourly—in the dark shell under her shining red hair.

Or was it her voice?

Mostly, yes. By it she changed almost unbearable humiliation and pain into "funny" stories.

But there was another real Voice, too. The main one.

It didn't always speak in words. At first, and much of the time since, it "spoke" like a feeling, a sense of being listened to encouragingly, and responded to, quietly and often volubly, just beyond her hearing range.

But more and more, in those early years, the Voice rose to blend exactly with her own, as she composed-recited to herself the life and events of the Empire of the Pigs. Sometimes the Voice came alone into a mental silence, though what it told her wasn't usually quite clear. Very occasionally it rose to complete clarity; for example, it had four times given her the answers during her myriad academic exams.

Since the answers the Voice provided were actually known to CP, only lost from tiredness, she was subconsciously reassured. This proved that the Voice wasn't a craziness, but merely what the book had called a "projection" of her own memories, seeming to come from outside.

Such projections, she learned, weren't uncommon, especially under stress. And in dreams.

As for the Voice giving her new ideas, elaborating details about the Empire, she read that creators, artists and writers— usually the mediocre ones—often projected their inspirations onto some outside source like their "Muse."

CP was wholly Noncreative in any normal way, a personality deficit considered valuable, even essential, among non-Managers. Her secret Empire-story and the Voice must be some rudimentary Creativeness leaking out, luckily in a private way.

She took care to memorize every possible Noncreative test response and attitude, and sealed her Secret tighter.

And the Voice only rarely gave her totally new information. On a few occasions it had seemed to pull her from the Empire to tell her about—she was not quite sure what, only that there was often an accompanying large visual impression of blue or lavender, and once, very clear, a gray hand. It was doing something with a complex of fabric. . . . All meaningless, afterward.

What wasn't meaningless was an indescribable personal-reference "transmission." The Voice *knew her.* And now and then it repeated, "Come."

Twice it said very clearly, "Waiting."

All this concerned space too, she was sure. Well, her one

wish in life was to go to space. Projection again, nothing to worry about.

"I will. I will. I will. I will. . . . The Pig Person shall go to the stars," she told the Voice. "The Pig Person will end among the stars. Soon. Soon."

Now as she settled to her last days, on *Calgary*, she—or the Voice—composed as usual a succinct account of all that had passed. But it was cast in quite new terms. Gone were the flat hard tones of unutterable sadness, the terse descriptions of the intolerable. She still spoke as the "Pig Person"—but this person had at last found freedom and joy, found her way to the stars. A way that would lead her back to the Empire, could her human life be long enough to reach it. It would not be. But she would at least end on her free way home.

Thinking this, she perceived that her chance-determined course might not be quite right. Perhaps this was even told her. Conscious with most of her mind that she was giving way to real insanity, she carefully scanned the forward field. Empty, of course, save for the faint far stars. And yes—the Voice was right—she was not quite on course. She must correct just a trifle. It was important.

On course for *where*?

For the first time she faced her madness abruptly, hard. What "right" course, en route to *what*? To nothing—nothing but icy vacuum and nothingness and dying. She proposed to waste fuel "correcting" to an insane delusion? A delusion she knew perfectly well was born of her human need for support amid ugliness, rejection, and pain?

But if nothing lay ahead, how could the spent fuel matter? Slowly, almost but not quite amused at herself, she gave in. Her fingers played delicately over the thrust-angle keys, her eyes went back to the scope. Where? Where shall I come, show me! She let her eyelids almost close, feeling for it. *Where, where?* And dreamily, but clear, it came to her: there. *Here* . . . Random nonsense, she told herself angrily, almost turning away.

But the shadowy vector persisted dearly in her mind. She peered through her strongest scope, scanned every band of EM radiation. Absolutely nothing lay *there*.

"Come," the Voice sighed in her head. "Come. I have waited so long."

"Death calling," she muttered harshly. But the fact was, she couldn't be truly comfortable until she turned *Calgary* to head precisely that way.

Carefully, deliberately, she set in the course correction for Nowhere. She punched to activate. The burn was very brief, she had been, as usual, accurate. *Calgary* shuddered imperceptibly, the star field crawled slowly slightly slantwise, then steadied to a rest with almost no braking necessary, pointing exactly *there*.

And as it did so, the Empire died.

For the first time she could remember, the story that had run ceaselessly in her brain, the Voice that was mostly a feeling, fell silent. What had hit her? What had silenced her? Startled, yet somehow accepting, she stared about. Nothing had changed; it was simply gone. There was no Empire, no one to "report" to, ever again. She was alone. Or . . . was she? It didn't matter. Everything was all right. Had not the Voice been commanding her too, in its way? Now she was truly free of the very last outside orders.

She went back to her quiet routine of gazing, observing, using the scope and other analyzers on interesting objects. Of them all, she preferred the eye. She found an old but serviceable computer-enhanceable high-power scope in a rear locker, left unused in recent years when no one had desire nor time to look at things too far to give promise of gain. To her joy, with a bit of work it proved functional. She pored over star charts, identifying and memorizing. In some peculiar way, this activity was all right too, beyond her own personal fascination.

By using all the ports, she had a 360-degree field of view in all directions—the universe—and she scanned at least briefly, but systematically, over it all. A feeling almost like the old voice-in-her-head encouraged her. Habit, she knew. I'm projecting my own pleasure back at myself.

As the early days stretched to weeks—she kept only the vaguest track of time—she experienced only comfort. Small events: one of the regenerator trays she had planted "took," the other stayed dead. She scraped together a last sprinkle of seeds and tried again. She also arranged a contraption, a double-inlet tube that would carry her breath from her habitual seat and bunk directly to the trays, which at this time were actually short of CO_2. The later buildup to saturation and ensuing degeneration would go fast; she installed a gas sampler and alarm to give ample warning of the rise.

Absurdly, she minded the prospect of dying from simple oxygen lack less than the notion of positive poisoning by her own wastes. This was nonsense, because what she knew of physiology told her that internal CO_2 would be an agent of her death anyhow.

Despite her comfort, she made every possible effort at conservation. The possibilities were pitifully few, consisting primarily of minimal use of the waste flusher, which lost air. Even when she had collected quite a pile of the men's overlooked leavings—including souvenirs of Meich—she denied herself the luxury of flushing them out.

Aside from the star work, and simply indulging in a rest she'd never known, she occupied herself with recalling and writing down such words as had once struck her as wise, witty, or beautiful: sayings, doggerel, poetry, a few short descriptions of old Earth phenomena no one she knew had ever seen—a clear sunrise, a waterfall—the names of a few people, mainly women, she'd respected. Effortfully, she even composed a short account of a striking memory—an eclipse she and other children had been allowed to see in the open.

She mulled unhurriedly over practical matters, such as whether the expenditure of oxygen necessary to bring in that ice-rock lashed to the hull would repay her in oxygen theoretically extractible from it. Quiet . . . a blissful life.

But one day came disturbance. The lone bow scanner chirped. Doubtless a malfunction; she moved to turn it off, then paused. This might signal an oncoming rock; she didn't want to die so. She activated another. To her surprise it lit in confirmation. For one horrifying instant fear seized her—could the human world have somehow pursued her here?

She turned on more pickups, was reassured—and then so amazed that she peered out visually to orient the scopes. Not a rock, or a rocket, not small but vast: ahead and slightly "above" her floated something world-sized—no, nearly sun-sized—very dimly lavender, glowing and ringed.

For another sickening instant she feared she had, incredibly, flown a circle and was coming back among Sol's outposts. But no; the scanners told her that the body occulting the forward field was nothing in Sol's family. Huge, her sensors told her, but relatively small-massed. The surface gravity, if she was seeing the surface, would be a little less than Earth-normal. It was definitely, though faintly, self-luminous—a beautiful blue-rosy shade she had no name for.

And very highly radioactive.

Was she looking at a dead or dying star? Possible; yet this body conformed to nothing she knew of in the processes of star-death. Perhaps a star not dead, but still below the threshold of interior ignition? A star coming slowly to be born? Or one destined to remain thus, never to ignite to birth at all?

Without even considering it, she had automatically activated thrust and set in a course correction that would fly her straight at the body. Equally automatically, she noted that *Calgary*'s pile was so used out that she hadn't possibly enough fuel to shed her now tremendous velocity and slow *Calgary* into any kind of close orbit. She ignited thrust.

What was she doing—unconsciously planning to die by crashing into this silent mystery? Or, if it had atmosphere, be roasted to death in the friction of her fall? It was not the quiet death she had intended, among the eternal stars.

Yet approach she must. Approach, see, and know it, orbit closely if only for a last fiery instant.

She lost track of all time, as the mystery grew in the ports, with her terrible speed, from dim point to far disk to closer, larger, port-filling nearness. She was retrofiring repeatedly, trying to get effect from every precious erg, willing *Calgary* to slow as if her naked desire could affect the laws of physics.

Finally the time came when she felt uncomfortably upside down to the great surface; she expended a precious minimum of energy slowly righting *Calgary*'s attitude. On crazy impulse, she suited up, leaving only the faceplate open, and strapped herself in the pilot's cocoon. It was all futile madness—despite everything she could do, her velocity was impossibly too great. Still she retrofired intermittently, trying to judge exactly optimum angles of thrust, fighting the temptation to torch everything once and for all, straining back in the cocoon, willing, commanding, imploring aloud to *Calgary* to slow—slow—slow—slow—

And luck, or something logically nonexistent, was with her. She was still moving lethally, hopelessly too fast, but *Calgary* seemed to have shed more velocity than the computer predicted possible. The thing must be faulty; she took over completely from it, and against all calculated chance, achieved a brief quasi-orbit in what seemed to be the equatorial plane.

She could see the "surface" now—a smooth, softly glowing, vast-dappled racing shield, which the sensors told her was cloud. Two hundred kilometers beneath that lay solid "ground," some of which registered as liquid. Expecting nothing but nitrogen-methane at best, CP glanced at the spectroscope—and lunged against her straps to slap on the backup comparators.

Same readings!

That cloud cover was oxygen-hydrogen: water vapor. And the basic atmosphere was twenty-five percent oxygen on a nitrogen base. She was looking at an atmosphere of Earth-normal quality.

Hastily she ran through the tests for various poisons; they, were not there. This was preindustrial, prewar air such as CP had never breathed on Earth!

Except, of course, for its appalling radioactivity, which apparently emanated from ground level. It would quickly destroy her or any Earth-born living thing. To walk on this world, to breath its sweet air, would be to die. In days, perhaps only hours.

Her orbit was decaying fast. The visible cloud was no more than a few thousand kilometers below her now. Soon she would hit the upper atmosphere—hit it like a skipped rock, and perhaps break open before *Calgary* burst to flame. The ship's old ablatives had been designed only for Mars, and deteriorated since. Slower; slow down, she pleaded, using the last full thrust of the pile. In her mind was a vivid picture of her oncoming doom at her present inexorable speed. Only moments of life remained to her—yet she was content, to have found, in freedom, this great wondrous world.

Belatedly recalling that Don's scout capsule was still on umbilical, she managed to reverse-drain its small fuel supply into two of Calgary's back boosters that weren't operated off the pile. Slow down—slow! she willed, firing.

The small backfire did seem to slow her a trifle. She had abandoned the instruments, which foretold only her death, and was watching the cloud tear by below. *Slow down, slow down!* She pushed herself back so hard she ached, sensing, dreaming that the death clouds were rushing imperceptibly slower. The atmosphere that would kill her extended, of course, far above them. She was all but in it, the molecule counter was going red.

Then, while she noticed they were over "land," *Calgary* seemed actually, undeniably, to slow further. The clouds below changed from a featureless stream to show perceptible dark-light gradients flashing by. Still far too fast, of course; but it was as if she was passing through the backward tug of some unknown field. Perhaps the effect of the denser molecules around her?

But *Calgary* wasn't heating up. Some utterly alien energy was at work. Whatever it was, she needed more. Slow, much more. Desperately she urged it.

And *Calgary* slowed.

What mystery was helping her kill velocity? It had to be physical, explicable. But CP, knowing with part of her mind that she had gone crazy, gave herself over to a deep conviction that this was no impersonal "field." She *knew* it was connected in some way with her need, and with her visualizing—"broadcasting" mentally—her plight. Mad, she was. But she was being helped to slow.

Perhaps I'm already dead, she thought. Or perhaps she would come to, drugged and manacled, in Base Detention. What matter? She had reached her Empire's power, it was saving her at last.

Over and over again she "showed" the unknown her needs, her vulnerability, the onrushing terrors of impact and heat, all the while draining every tiniest output from the dying pile, which seemed to have regenerated slightly while she'd rested it.

And *Calgary* slowed, slowed, slowed as if flying through invisible cold molasses—so that the first wisps of atmosphere came past her at little more than common supersonic speeds. A miracle. There were no smashing impacts, only a jostling of loose objects, and very little heat. And then she was down to where the first visible tendrils of cloud rushed by.

It was so beautiful she laughed out loud—the blue-lavender-pearl streamers against the star-blazed night. For an instant she looked for *Calgary*'s shadow, and then checked herself and laughed again; this world had no sun, it had never known a shadow from the sky—all its light came from below, within.

Then she was in it, blinded, dependent only on her instruments. *Calgary* was barreling down, its orbital direction curving to a fall. It occurred to her that the delta wings would help now. Would they extend, and if so, would they tear off? She had an instant's neutral memory of another life, in which a captain's potential madness had driven him to a compulsive predeparture checkout of *Calgary*, even to the old, never-used wing, even to insisting that it be serviced to function. Strange.

She activated the extensors, pulled with all her strength on the manual backup. Gratings, groans—and the delta lurched from its slots and extended in the alien air, slowing *Calgary* into a yawing roll. She thanked fate that she had strapped in where she could reach the old flight controls. Now her hard Earth-side flight training served her well; she soon had *Calgary* on a rough downward glide. The wings vibrated violently, but stayed on, even at this wild speed.

Down, down through two hundred kilometers of brightening cloud. Until she burst abruptly out of the lowest, lightest layer, and saw—yes—a world-ocean far below. This ocean glowed. She looked up and saw the cloud ceiling lit grape-blue, krypton-green, by its reflection.

Next moment she was over land, too high to see anything but swaths of new luminous colors. Glowing orange, smoky turquoise, brilliant creams and crimsons, with rich dark-purple curves and flowings here and there; a sublime downscape, with tantalizing illusions of pattern. Above her the solid sky was lit up varicolored reflecting it, as if an immense stained-glass window were shining from below.

The ocean under her again, this time much lower. She could see the lucent pale-green V where it broke on a small island. The surface seemed very calm, save for long, smooth swells. More V's of green-blue light came under her—an archipelago? Or—wait—was there *movement* down there? Impossible. She strained to see—and suddenly there could be no doubt. Twenty or thirty somethings were each trailing its brilliant V of wake, moving contrary to others.

Life.

Life! Whalelike mythical beasts? Or was this perhaps a warm, shallow puddle-ocean, in which great creatures, like the Earth's Cretaceous saurians, sported? Or—she dared not think it—ships? Whatever, minutes from her death, she had found, or been found by, the first alien life known to humanity; on a dark solitary unseeable almost-sun.

She prayed aloud to no god to let her slow enough to have one sight of this marvel. To the unknown power that had helped her, she sent desperate fear-lit images of her onrushing crash, explosion, death—unless *Calgary* could be slowed enough for her to belly-land it in one piece. She had the momentary sense that the power was reluctant, perhaps tired—but desire to know more of this wonder drove her shamelessly. She pled with all her soul to slow more.

And sluggishly, but in time, response came. Once the slowing was so abrupt that her glide fell below *Calgary's* high stall speed. She went tail down and began to drop like a stone, until she found one last unbelievable gulp of fuel to send the ship back into level flight. She tried to send in careful detail the image of her needs. They were almost unfillable—to glide *Calgary* to some sort of bare, level landing place, large enough to absorb what would be her ground momentum. If only she could, once, *see* these marvels! No matter how injured she was, she longed only to die with her eyes filled with them.

Nothing but death lay ahead, but CP was in ecstasy such as she'd never dreamed of.

Releasing the controls for an instant, she flung her arms wide. "I name thee Cold Pig's Planet!" she said to Auln. (Auln? Whence did that come to her?) But no, she was not falling to the satellite of any sun. "I name thee Cold Pig's Dark Star!"

Appropriate, she thought wryly, grabbing the controls, and strapping in tighter. All those weary hours of Earth-flight kept returning to her aid. Skillfully she nursed the awkward old ship over the pale fires of this shoreless sea; she was too low to see beyond the far, high horizon to where land might lie. She could only fly straight with the direction of revolution toward where she remembered the continent bulged seaward.

Unsteady breezes tossed her, sometimes bringing her so low that *Calgary* barely skimmed the crests—and once she all but nose-dived in, as she caught a flash of strange life, dark-bodied, playing in the waves. Too fast, too low, *Calgary* could not survive splashdown here. Resolutely she ignored all wonders, made herself concentrate on staying airborne, above what seemed a world on fire. The horizon was so weirdly high! This world was huge.

And then a line of brighter fire showed on the horizon ahead, seeming almost above her. Shore! But forested, she saw. Those lighted shapes were a solid wall of trees—she was hurtling toward a fatal crash. Frantically she pictured, pled for what she needed—and then saw that the forest wall was not solid, there was a great opening, an estuary slanting out. She swung *Calgary* to aim into it; she could see now that it wasn't a wide river, but a relatively small stream edged with swamp, almost treeless. Perfect. But coming at her fast, too fast—if only there could be head wind! She was prepared for anything now, had no wonder left but only gratitude as the sudden shore wind struck and slowed her.

Into the opening they tore, over the margin that appeared barest. Then *Calgary's* belly structures hit sticky marshland, crushed clangorously—the ship bounced and careened past flying trees—flat-spun twice, throwing CP about in her straps—and went wing up, the down wing breaking off as it plowed fountains. And finally, incredibly, all motion stopped.

CP slowly, dizzily, stared around her at the cabin. No broken walls or glass, air-pressure reading constant. The cabin seemed to be intact. Intact. She was down safe! And, apart from a bruises, herself uninjured.

Her hearing was deadened by pressure change. When her ears opened, she could hear only the clanks of cooling metal and the crackle of a small flame by the jets, which died as she watched. No hiss of escaping air. But the silence outside had the unmistakable sense of density and resonance that told her the *Calgary* was no longer in vacuum but in air.

Weak almost to fainting, CP wiped her breath from the vitrex to peer out. It was confusing—a world like a color negative, all light coming from below, with strange-hued shadows above. So beautiful. Only trees and shrubs were around her—a wilderness of trees; CP had never seen so many trees all in one place. And they stretched on and on, she knew, to the horizon. Beyond them she could just see the lighted sparkle of running river water, *free water*, presumably fresh.

A paradise—save only for the lethal radioactivity, which had her scanning dial stuck against its high edge. A paradise, but not for her.

Nevertheless, her prayers were granted. She was seeing a New World. She could touch it if she wished. A deep, extraordinary happiness she could scarcely recognize filled her. Her lips trembled with a constant smile she'd never felt before. But she could no longer keep her eyes open. She knew she had spent some hours fighting the *Calgary* down; she didn't realize it had taken her three Earth-days.

As she lost consciousness, hanging sidewise in the straps, from somewhere outside a living creature gave a single unearthly echoing hoot, loud enough to penetrate the sealed cabin.

Her last thought was that she would probably awaken, if she did, in the bonds and cuffs of Base prison.

⊞⊞

She woke up painfully stiff and thirsty, but with the same marvelous alien world outside the port. And the air-pressure reading had stayed constant! All essential seals were intact—a final miracle.

Calgary had come to rest nose down on its broken wing stub; the "floor" was at a forty-degree angle. As CP unstrapped and slid down, she saw how good this was: the big port at her chair gave her the view outside right down to ground level, and so did one end of the bow window. The opposite port gave her the treetops. She paused curiously to study their strange adaptations of form to utilize light coming primarily from below. There seemed to be two general types, a pad-leaved sort, and a big tree fern, but there was extraordinary intervariation.

How much sealed air-space was left her? Gone, of course, was the whole underbody, the scouter dock, and the trailing space equipment-including the ice-rock. But she had the pilotage and observation chambers, and the door to the galley had sprung askew without causing leaks. So had the wash-and-wastes roomlet, and even the door of her own bad-memoried little cubicle—no leaks in there.

Gratefully she pulled off her heavy helmet and shook out her flaming hair. Her last days would be not only sublimely interesting but actually comfortable!

Her water supply was intact too, she had checked that when first slaking her huge thirst. She would have to conserve, but she would have quite enough for the twenty days or so of oxygen left to her. That lack would be her end, as had been foretold from the start.

Just as she settled by the window to open a food pouch, movement outside drew her eyes. *Calgary* had plowed a long open avenue through the swamp brush, and was turned so she could look right back down it to the far, high green glimmer of the sea.

Now something she had taken for vegetation moved, moved again, and became a long willowy pale animal. It was clambering down from a low fork in a tree by the "avenue," where it had perhaps spent the night. Had it been watching *Calgary*, shocked by the crashing intrusion of the ship? Even at this distance she could see that its eyes were enormous. They were shining with reflected light, set very far apart on a thin whitish head. The head resembled that of a goat or sheep which CP had seen alive in the zoo. It was definitely watching her now. She held her breath.

As it swung down, she could see that its side-skin hung in folds, and a long-ago memory of her one picture book came back. Earth had once had "flying" squirrels and other gliding animals. Perhaps this creature was a giant form like that, and used its flaps for gliding between trees?

Down from the tree, it sat on its haunches for a moment, still watching her. *Please, don't be frightened,* she begged it mentally, not daring even to close her mouth, which was open for a first bite of breakfast bar. The creature didn't seem alarmed. It stretched, in a laughably human way, and dropped its short forelimbs to the ground. It had a short, stout upcurled tail.

Now CP remembered a picture that was closest of all—the kangaroo. Like the kangaroo, this animal's rear end was higher than its shoulders on all fours, because of its long, strong hind limbs; and its neck was curved up to carry its long head level. Only its tail was much smaller and shorter than the picture she recalled.

To her delight, it began calmly to amble, or walk-hop, right toward *Calgary.* As it came closer she could see its draped pelt clearly.

It wasn't fur.

It wasn't bare hide or leather.

It was—yes, unmistakably—and CP's mind seemed to explode with silent excitement—it was *fabric.*

As it came closer still, she could make out that around the neck and along the back-ridge ran a pattern of what could only be embroidery. It was set with knots and small shiny stones or shells.

She simply stared at the approaching form, unable to take in all the implications at once.

A world not only bearing life, but bearing intelligent life.

Too much, that she had stumbled on *this.*

And yet—was she really so surprised? The feeling that something . . . or someone . . . was "hearing" and helping her down had been so strong. . . . Was she looking at the one who—?

Impossible. She could think no further, only stare.

The creature—no, the *person*—calmly returned her gaze, and then sat down again, upright. With delicate spatulate fingers, it unfastened the throat of its cloak—CP could clearly see its thumbs—and removed it, revealing its actual pelt, which was cream-white and short. It folded the cloak deftly into a long strip and tied it round its body, then dropped back on all fours and resumed its amble toward her.

But it did not head to her window, it detoured around *Calgary* on higher ground. As it passed, twitching one of its tall "ears" toward her, CP had a confused, faint mental impression of others—very diverse others—somewhere nearby, whom this one was going to meet. The notion vanished so quickly she decided she had made it up. Her visitor was passing out of sight from that port, into the undisturbed forest ahead of *Calgary*'s stopping place.

She clambered quickly to the side post, but the stranger was already beyond sight among the trees. Perhaps someone or something else would come from that direction? She made herself comfortable by the vitrex, and at last began to eat her bar, studying all she could see. She was over the broken wing stub now. *Calgary* had come to rest against a dry hillock, this side made a natural approach. Slowly, so as not to alarm anything, she extended the auditory pickup and tested it. It worked! A world of varied rustlings, soft tweets, a croak or grunt, filled the cabin.

After a moment's thought, she tested the sound transmitter and extruded that too, so that her voice could be heard outside.

Presently she became aware of a periodic crackling or crashing sound coming from the woods beyond the hillock. She watched, and saw a far treetop sway violently and go down. Soon another followed, a little closer, and then yet another smaller tree jumped high and disappeared. A big herbivore, perhaps, feeding?

But as the sounds came closer, they seemed clearly deliberate. Perhaps a path or road to *Calgary* was being cleared. If so, what would appear? An alien bulldozer? A siege ram? A weapon carrier brought to blast her and *Calgary* out of existence?

Yet she waited unafraid, only glad and fascinated. This world did not feel hostile. And had they not already helped her, saved her life? *Calgary* had rudimentary defenses, mainly of a ballistic sort, which in recent decades had been occasionally used only to break up rocks, but it never occurred to her to deploy them. Life here had saved her life, and she had intruded a great shipwreck upon them. Even if they wished to be rid of her now, whatever came she would accept.

And suddenly it was there—so different from her expectations that she didn't at first take it in. One—no, two— tall-humped forms were pushing through the trees. Their sides and tops seemed hard, she could hear thuds as they brushed against stems. Why, they were great tortoises, or turtles! She had once seen a tiny live one, much flatter in outline. Or could these carapaces be, like the Watcher's cloak, artificial shells? No, she decided. Their limbs and necks were formed to them, she seemed to see attachment in the openings' depths. Could they be trained beasts, used here instead of inorganic machines?

As she watched mesmerized, one of them backed ponderously into a tangle of tree trunks, sending them down like paper trees. Then it turned, reared up, and began neatly to break up, sort, and pile the debris. Just behind it, the other was doing the same. Then it came past the first, selected an obstructive giant tree, and repeated the process. She realized how very big they were; the tops of their shells would be higher than her head, and their push-force must be in tons.

As she saw the results of their work, she realized these couldn't be animals, however trained. They weren't merely clearing a way, they were creating order. Behind them stretched a neat, attractive clearway, without the edging tangle of damage usual on Earth. It wound away quite far; she could see perhaps a kilometer.

As the creatures reared up, worked, dropped down to push, it was evident to CP that they had a generic resemblance to the first one, whom she thought of as the Watcher. The same heavier hind limbs, here ponderous and half-hidden by their carapaces; the same shorter forelimbs, here massively muscled. When they extended their necks, these too were long, though thickly muscular, coming from very large front openings in the shell. They walked with heads high and level. The heads, now retracted to their shells, were somewhat similar to the Watcher's. Not at all reptilian, with upstanding "ears," heavy frontals, and protectively lidded eyes.

As they came closer, working rapidly but always neatly, she could see that their carapaces carried decorations. Some self-luminous pebbles or seeds had been set among the designs; their undershells, seen brightly illumined, were beautifully scrolled, and seemed to have straps or tool pockets mounted on them. Logical, she thought; frees the front limbs to walk. And finally, as the closest one rose up to grapple a tree fern, came the most bizarre touch of all—she could clearly see that it was wearing cuffed, decorated work gloves.

This perception set off her overloaded nerves—she nearly

dropped the kaffy from her shaking hands as a gale of giggles swept her, turned into peals of laughter that rang through the speaker into the swamp. Abashed, she thought how inappropriate this was, that the first human voice heard on this world should be not a proper formal speech, but laughing. She couldn't help herself. She had laughed little in her life. No one had told her the sound was very sweet.

She had it under control in a moment. Wiping her eyes, she saw that the turtlelike workers had dropped their logs and come closer, for a look-in. She hoped the sound she had made wasn't displeasing or ugly to them.

"Excuse me," she said absurdly through the speaker.

A vague feeling of all-rightness suffused her; one of the "turtles" made what was clearly an attempt at imitating her laugh, and they went back to their labor, now almost at the ship.

And when her vision cleared, she could see, in the distance, six or seven new shapes approaching up the path the "turtles" had made.

She finally bethought herself the binoculars, and peered with all her might. The glasses were of course set for celestial use, with a very small field, and she had trouble at first in counting how many were in the group.

Four—no, three of them—closely resembled the Watcher, but she could pick him, or her, out by the paler fur, and the color of the tied-up cloak. This method of transporting stuff seemed to be common. The other two kangaroolike ones differed among themselves too—she had a glimpse of more strangely formed heads, possibly even an extra very small set of forelimbs—but she was too busy trying to see all the others to check.

Another of the turtle or tortoise types was with them, its carapace heavy with encrustments. She gained a quick impression that it was quite old. It was even larger, and differed from the tree movers in its eyes, which were enormous and very bright beneath the heavy lids. Indeed, her first sight of the group had featured eyes—huge eyes, so bright and reflective that some seemed almost self-luminous. She noticed that all of them, as they advanced, looked about continuously and carefully, but with their major attention on *Calgary*—almost like a group of advancing headlamps.

Touching, partly leaning upon the carapaced one, came a

short figure so swathed in red fabric veils that CP could make nothing of it, except for the great eyes in a face much shorter and more pugged than the Watcher's. The fur on its skin was pale, too. CP had the impression that this creature—no, this *person*—was somewhat ill or weak, perhaps old, too. She or he paced upright, much of the time leaning on the big "tortoise," only now and then dropping to a quadrupedal amble. Their slower movements seemed to be setting the pace for all.

Another veiled person of the same general type, but taller and blue-veiled, came behind, moving strongly, so that the limbs often thrust through its veils. CP could definitely make out two pairs of upper "arms"; the lower pair seemed to be used for walking. Its upper body was upright so that, walking, it resembled a creature CP had only once seen a child's picture of—a being half-horse and half-human. But its face was neither horse nor human—the features were so snarled that only the big eyes, and four tall feathery protrusions that might be ears, or other sensory organs, could be identified.

Two more figures with gray pelts brought up the rear. One of them attracted CP's attention by swerving off the path into a pool of water, and drinking deeply with webbed hands held to a kind of bill or beak. She guessed that it might be at least partly aquatic. Its companion waited for it. Behind this one's shoulders were two hard-looking humps that might be vestigial wings.

The party was close now; CP had discarded the binoculars. As they passed the tree-moving turtles, the personages she thought of as the Senior Tortoise and its veiled companion paused, and the others halted with them.

There was a brief interchange, consisting of some short, voiced phrases mingled with odd, meaningful silences. CP could not tell which voices belonged to whom; only one was melodious, but they were not unpleasing. Nor did they sound tense, agitated, or hostile. She gleaned the notion that this visit was in some weird way routine, and also that the road had been constructed voluntarily, by nearby residents, perhaps.

Could it be that people were *used* to spaceships landing here? But no; the party gave no sign of familiarity with anything like *Calgary*.

Their first act was to tour deliberately around the ship—CP saw that the ground had been cleared around her while she slept—looking gravely at every detail. CP followed them around from inside. On impulse, when they could see both her and the remaining wing, she raised her hand and moved an aileron control.

There was a general, surprised backward start.

By this time, CP was sure that some at least were telepathic. She sent them the strongest feeling of friendship she could project, and then pictures of herself moving controls. The "kangaroo" types seemed to respond with eagerness, as did the "Senior Tortoise." They moved closer, eyeing her keenly. So CP spent a happy time moving and wiggling everything that functioned, at the same time naming it and its function through the speaker. The small red-veiled alien seemed particularly interested in her voice, often attempting to repeat words after her.

They all had no hesitation in touching anything and everything; the agile web-footed ones clambered over the remains of *Calgary*'s top, and all came up and peered into the cabin ports by turn.

Several times CP stopped herself from trying to warn them not to approach the "hot" thrust vents, or the debris of the reactor chamber. It was hard to realize that any residual radioactivity from *Calgary* was as nothing compared to the normal blizzard of hard radiation just outside, in which these visitors had evolved and lived.

Presently the small red-veiled alien limped, or hobbled, to the extended speaker and laid a fragile, pale, apparently deformed hand on it. At the same time, a very clear image came to CP; she closed her eyes to concentrate on it, and "saw" herself with opening and moving mouth. The image flickered oddly. The alien had made the connection between her voice and the speaker. But how to transmit "yes" by mental imagery? She nodded her head vigorously—a meaningless gesture here, no doubt—and said verbally, "Yes! Yes. Uh . . . hello!" pointing to her mouth and the speaker.

The little alien made a peculiar sound; was that a laugh? Next moment its hand moved to the auditory pickup, and CP experienced something new—a strikingly sharp image of the microphone, followed by a literal blanking of the mind— indescribable. As if an invisible blindfold had descended. Next instant came the mike image again, and again the blank—and back to the image; faster and faster, these two impressions alternated in her mind, to a flicker sequence that made her dizzy.

But she grasped it—as clearly as a human voice, the alien was saying, "And this thing is—what?"

So that was how questions were asked!

How to answer? She tried everything she could think of, pointing to the alien, to her own ears (which were doubtless not ears to the alien), saying "Hello" repeatedly like a parrot, all the while trying to picture an alien's mouth speaking. She'd never seen the red-veiled mouth, so she imaged another's.

Something worked—with apparent eagerness, the small alien put its face to the mike, and nearly blasted CP from her chair with "ER-ROW! ER-ROW! ES!"

CP was childishly delighted. She and the alien exchanged several "Hellos" and "Errows" through speaker and mike.

But shortly a new question emerged. She began to receive a strengthening picture—as if from several minds joining in—of herself coming out of *Calgary* and moving among them. After a few moments of her nonresponse, this image began to alternate slowly with a scene of the aliens inside *Calgary* with her. Again, the two images alternated faster and faster, to confusing flashes. But the meaning was plain—"Will you come out, or shall we come in?"

It took her a long, laborious effort to try to transmit the possibility. She concentrated hard on forming images of the port opening and air coming in, herself falling down, pictures of radiation (she hoped) coming from the ground. Suddenly, at those last pictures the old tortoise seemed to understand. He advanced and laid one heavy paw on *Calgary*, and then made a sweeping gesture that CP read as negation. Of course: *Calgary*, alone of most of this world, was inert, nonradioactive.

At this point they seemed to have had enough, or were tired; in very human fashion they drew off to sit in a group at the edge of the clearing with the tree-fellers, and produced packets of edibles. CP stared eagerly, wishing she could see and taste. As far as she could make out, most of them ate with more or less Earth-like mouths, but the veiled persons inserted their food beneath their throat veils.

Then the small red-clad alien seemed to notice her staring and CP suddenly felt her mouth and nose filled with an extraordinary alien sensation—neither good nor bad, but quite unknown—which must be the taste of what they were eating. She laughed again, and daringly transmitted a faint replica of the cheese-and-peanut-butter packet she was eating.

Refreshments were soon over. Now the large blue-veiled alien and the kangaroo-types came forward to the window. Looking directly at CP, the veiled one stood up and made motions of turning. CP understood; it was her time to be inspected. Obediently she turned, extended an arm, opened her mouth to show her teeth, wiggled her fingers.

Then the veiled one raised her top arm, unfastened something, and deliberately let drop a veil. The implication was plain: undress. For a moment CP was overcome with an ugly memory of Meich, the countless other humiliations she had undergone. She hesitated. But the alien eyes were insistent and seemed friendly. When CP didn't move, the big alien pulled off another veil, exposing this time its own bare and furless belly and haunches. A strong feeling of reassurance came to her—of course, to these people her body was as neutral as a mollusk or a map. She unzipped her suit and stepped out of it and her underclothes. At the same time, as if to encourage her, the alien removed its own upper-body covering. CP noticed that the others in its group had turned tactfully away.

CP was amazed—in the crotch where human sex and excretory organs would be, the alien had nothing but smooth muscle. But its chest region was as complex as a group of sea creatures; valves, lips, unidentifiable moist flaps and protrusions—clearly its intimate parts. CP could form no idea of its gender, if any.

Not to be outdone in scientific detachment, CP demonstrated her own nude self, and made an attempt at transmitting images of the human reproductive process. She got nothing in reply—or rather, nothing she could interpret. She and the alien apparently diverged so widely here that thought could not carry across the gulf. Only excretion seemed sufficiently similar to be at least referable to.

At length the alien gave it up, resuming its own veiling and indicating that CP should do likewise.

Then the whole group gathered round her windows and CP was astounded. Abruptly she was assailed by a thought-image that said, as plainly as a shout, "Go away!"

The image was of *Calgary* again taking to the air, and spiraling up and away. The feeling-tone wasn't hostile or threatening, merely practical. If she couldn't live here, she should go elsewhere.

"But I can't!"

Desperately she pointed to the wrecked wing, sent images of the empty fuel reserve.

A counterimage, of *Calgary* being literally lifted off and flung out of atmosphere, came back. Did they propose that the same presumably "mental" force that had slowed her should lift her back to orbit?

"No—no! It wouldn't work!" She sent images of *Calgary*, released in space, falling helplessly back upon them.

But the thought-send persisted. "You-go-away"—and the sequence repeated itself.

Then CP had an idea. But how to indicate time here in this never-changing world? Oh, for an hourglass! Finally she gathered up a handful of crumbs, broken glass, and other small debris of the wreck and let them trickle slowly and deliberately from one hand to the other. She held up her fingers, counting off a dozen or so—and acted out a scene of herself strangling in foul air, collapsing and dying. As an afterthought, she tried to express a feeling of contentment, even joy.

The Senior Tortoise got it first, and seemed to enlighten the others.

She would not be here long alive.

There ensued a brief colloquy among the aliens. Then one after the other came to her window, put up its "hands" to take a look around, and seemed to transmit something grave, and faint. She was not even sure she was receiving. The old tortoise-person came last, its great hands heavy on the glass as it shaded out reflections to look in. From it CP was sure something emanated to her. But she could not name it.

Then they all turned and walked, ambled, or hopped away as they had come, taking the "Watcher" with them. The tree-fellers brought up the rear. CP stared after them, surprised.

They had simply departed, leaving her alone to die.

Well, what more could she have expected?

But it was strange; no curiosity about the stars, for instance, nor whence she had come.

And what had they been trying to impart, there at the last? Of course: "Good-bye."

"Good-bye," CP said through the speaker softly, into the alien air.

Then began an unadmittedly lonely time, waiting to die there in the beauty of the swamp. CP began to wish it wasn't so viewless and closed in. She decided that soon, before the air was all gone, she would go out, and try to climb to some sort of view before she died.

On impulse, she set her Earth-day timer, which had ceased in the crash, to manual-battery operation. She who had fled the world of Earth forever yet had the whim to perish on Earth's time. Only so much of nostalgia persisted. That and her little copybook of poems.

She had long since smoothed out and repaired the captain's damage. Only one page was lost. She occupied herself in reconstructing it from memory:

> With delicate mad hands against the sordid bars,
> Surely he hath his posies, which they tear and twine—
> Those—*something*—wisps of straw that miserably line
> His strait caged universe, whereon the dull world stares.
> Pedant and pitiful. Oh—*something*—*something*—
> Know they what dreams divine
> *Something*—like enchanted wine—
> And make his melancholy germane to the stars?
> Oh, lamentable brother, if these pity thee,
> Am I not fain of all thy lost eyes promise me?
> Half a fool's kingdom, far from—*something*—
>   all their days vanity.
> Oh, better than mortal flowers
> Thy moon-kissed roses seem;
> Better than love or sleep,
> The star-crowned solitude of thine oblivious hours!

Much was muddled, but she had the essential lines. They had kept her company all those years behind her sordid bars. Well, she had had the stars, and now she had the moon-kissed roses, and the fool's kingdom. Presently she would open the port and go out to possess it. . . .

Ⴤ

It was late on Day Six, of the perhaps fifteen left to her, that someone else came. She had long ceased to watch the path, but now she felt a tug at her attention. At first there was nothing, and she almost turned away. And then, in the far distance, she made out a single, oddly-shaped figure. Quick, the binoculars. It became an alien something like the former Watcher, but ruddy and—yes—carrying or being ridden by a much smaller alien on its back. More—she saw the small alien was legless, with very tiny arms. She had the strong impression of fatigue, of a long-distant goal reached. They had, she thought, come a long, long way.

Then she understood: this world was huge, and she knew nothing of their means of transport, if any. Perhaps those who wished to see *Calgary* must walk so, even from the far side?

She watched, scarcely daring to blink, as these new aliens continued their weary way toward her into naked-eye view. The larger alien raised its head, and must have seen her waiting. She was quite unprepared for the jolt of feeling that shook her—like a shout of welcome and joy.

That she still lived! Had this alien been fearful it was too late, that she would have died before he or she could get here? That must be it.

As the alien came closer yet, she noticed an oddity about the big one's head—where others had had upstanding "ears" or antlerlike antennae, this one had large, triangular velvety flaps that drooped toward its eyes. Where had she seen these before? Oh, god—aching half with laughter, half pain, she recognized—the large, folded, triangular earflaps of a pig! And the alien's muzzle was pugged, like hers.

Dear stars, what cosmic joke was this?

The rest of the alien's body was not at all porcine, but seemed worn and gaunt from travel and bearing the weight of its companion. Built more ruggedly than the original Watcher, its pelt was dusty red and it was wearing a thin vest that covered the chest area and tied behind as a knot which its rider clung to. A cloak was also tied round it. Its eyes were not abnormally large, more like pale human eyes without visible whites. Walking quadrupedally, or walk-hopping as it was now, its shoulders were lower than its rump, and the stumpy tail stuck straight out behind, possibly from excitement.

As it approached *Calgary* its gaze shifted from her to the wrecked ship, and images of the starry night of space filled her head, alternating occasionally with a vision of the lavender cloud ceiling overhead, and the 200-kilometer thickness of cloud that had blanked her view coming down—and then back again to the stars—the stars as she had seen them in a hundred shifting views.

She began to receive a curious new impression.

When the creature, or person, came slowly right to *Calgary*, it sat up as far as it could without spilling its rider, and laid first one thin hand and then the other on *Calgary*'s broken wing. She became sure.

This was reverence. Here was a longing for the stars that filled its soul, the stars from which it was closed away forever by the implacable, never-ending cloud. As plainly as speech, its gesture said, "This—this came from the stars!"

When it raised its gaze to her, its face had changed to a strange openmouthed pursing, like a child trying to pronounce "th"; denoting she knew not what, until she received the image of what must be herself, weirdly exaggerated, among the stars; and understood, from her own experience.

"You—you, an intelligent alien—have come here *from the stars!* Life is out there, beyond our heavy sky!"

It was almost as if it were worshiping *Calgary* and herself— no, it was just that she and it were the most precious, exciting things in life to it. Perhaps, alone of its kind, it had insisted that there was life beyond the sky? And was now proved right? She had met a human astronomer who would have felt this way.

The alien had now clambered up onto the wing stub to peer in, pushing back its beautiful ears to see better. Close up, its muzzle was complex and pleasingly furred. As it alternately inspected the cabin and gazed at her, its small companion clambered off onto the wing, agilely pulling itself by its shrunken arms. She saw that it had a large, thick, apparently partly prehensile tail, which served to boost it along in place of the missing legs. Its bare skin was scurfy and wrinkled; CP understood that it was very old. It seemed to be interested in the length, the width, the sheer size, of *Calgary*.

But the larger alien's head kept sagging; it was spent with exhaustion, she saw its eyelids droop, pull open again, and reclose despite itself. It sank down into the uncomfortable corner between the wing stub and the window, not even untying its cloak, looking toward her as long as it could stay conscious. For a moment CP feared it was ill or dying, but received a faint image of it waking up animatedly.

She wished she could at least undo its cloak to cushion its head. A moment later the little old alien dragged itself over and did just that, as if "hearing" her.

Then it turned its bright eyes on her, far less tired than its friend. It seemed to have something to convey: images of herself, her hands as she fought *Calgary* down, came to her. What could this mean?

As if exasperated, the little being pulled itself to the remains of the booster rocket by the wing base; showing an odd combination of the activity of a child with great age. There it patted the booster, pointing first to her and then to itself. This was the first time she'd seen anyone here point manually.

Images of *Calgary* descending came again. She was baffled. Sensing this, the old creature seized a stout twig lying on the wing, raised it high, and dropped it.

The twig fell briskly—then slowed, slowed, halted before touching down—and as she stared, it reversed course and slowly rose upward, back to the alien's hand.

CP's eyes smarted with staring, she had consciously to blink. What had she seen if not movement-by-remote-will—telekinesis!

The act seemed to have tired the alien, but it looked at her intently, holding up one hand. In human gesture-language this would say, "Attend!"

CP "attended." The alien screwed up its small, wrinkled face, closed its eyes.

And *Calgary* rocked. A single startling lurch.

There was no question of some physical shift of weight doing it—the ship took a pull so strong she could hear mud sucking under the crushed hull.

She had to believe.

Incredible as it was, this tiny old being was, or exerted, the force that had slowed *Calgary* and brought her safely in. Somehow it had reached out all those thousands of kilometers, to the heavy, hurtling ship, and slowed it.

Saved her life.

She didn't know how to say thank you, even to show gratitude. She could only point to it and bow her head ignorantly, stammering, "Thank you, oh, thank you!" through the speaker. In the end she actually knelt on the tilted deck, but was not satisfied.

The little old being shied away from the speaker, but seemed to understand that she understood. It was panting with fatigue. But after a few moments' rest it did something new. Advancing to the speaker, it pointed to itself and said loudly, "Tadak."

Luckily it spoke loudly enough to reach the mike, too.

"Tadak," it said again with more self-pointing.

Its name, the first one she had known!

"Tadak. Hello, Tadak!" she said eagerly. But it seemed exasperated again. Of course: she pointed to herself. "Cee Pee."

It imitated her roughly, too faint to hear well. She was distracted, but her longing to show her gratitude had produced an idea. It would lose her several liters of air; she reproached herself for even the automatic thought. Too much—in return for her life?

Motioning to Tadak, she laid hold of her most precious human possession, the golden flight emblem pinned to her collar. Tadak watched intently as she demonstrated how to pin and secure it.

Then she crawled under the console, disconnected an old lubricant-intake valve, and rapped loudly on the inside cover to guide its attention. When she heard taps outside, she placed the pin in the opening and recapped it. A considerable struggle to communicate ensued; this world—or Tadak—did not seem familiar with toggles and screw threads. In the end she heard a fearful grinding sound, and guessed that it had used its TK to rip the cap straight off.

Tadak crawled weakly back into view, panting and clutching the shiny trinket with apparent reverence in its old gnarled fingers, first to its chest, then over its upturned face as though marveling. Then its bright eyes went sidewise to CP, carrying an impression of both joy and—yes—mischief. The old face puckered hard.

—And *Calgary* jumped again, higher than before. It came down with a jolt that made CP a trifle nervous.

A protesting grunt came from the sleeping alien by her window.

But Tadak was really tired now. It seemed to take all its remaining strength to hump up to where its friend lay and to bed down, too. One tiny hand twitched up at her and slumped. CP was left to watch over the sleep of her new acquaintances.

She felt herself drifting toward sleep, too. This must be a world without the dangers normal to hers; its inhabitants seemed to have no fear of lying vulnerable in the open. With Tadak quiescent she could see how very old and frail it was.

Her drowsy attention and wonder settled on the head and softly folded "ears" of the larger alien. In all her dream life in the Empire of the Pigs she had never imagined a pig head of such beauty and dignity. There was a shining metallic chain about its neck too, with a medallion of some sort. And its poncho was beautifully embroidered. Evidently her wondrous new visitors weren't paupers, if such things existed here. Still studying them, she fell asleep and dreamed of stars, mixed with her old story of safe arrival home in the Empire.

They were all awakened by more visitors.

By the time she was conscious, the newcomers had filtered into the clearing and quietly surrounded *Calgary*. It was a spoken utterance by the open microphone that awakened her to confront two strange yellow-colored rotund shapes right by the window, squinting in at her. Beyond them she glimpsed pale or dark alien forms on every side.

She reacted with automatic panic, diving under the console. Police? Army? Enemy of some kind?

But a cautious peek out reassured her.

Her two new "friends" were greeting the arrivals calmly, even joyfully. While the flap-eared alien raised its arms to touch palms with one group of newcomers, Tadak clambered onto the carapace of a large turtle-type, and was being carried around *Calgary*, to hand-greet other arrivals. She noticed there were different nuances of position and length of contact in the double-palm greeting, like different human handshakes for old friends or new, formal meetings. She saw, too, that most of the newcomers looked travel-worn; only a few seemed fresh. It was difficult to count, but she decided that about thirty strangers had arrived. Here she noticed a novelty—subdued voices were to be heard all around. Evidently many of those new aliens talked in verbal speech. Had she been meeting only mental-projection specialists?

As they saw she was awake, voices rose excitedly and they began to gather round her window and settle down. Clearly these weren't idle tourists. A meeting of some sort impended. Perhaps some ultimatum or scheme to urge her off-planet?

CP splashed her hands and face hurriedly, conserving the water for a second use, and retired to the wastes cubby. When she closed the door on herself, the wave of general disappointment was so strong it reached her. She grinned to herself; maybe, later, she would abandon all her Earth ways. Maybe.

Snatching up a breakfast bar and self-heating kaffy, she came back to the window. Her two new acquaintances had stationed themselves just outside, evidently as her official translators or keepers. All right. Now let's have it.

A truly strange-looking large alien advanced and held up its palms in formal greeting. It was dark ocher-orange and blue, wrinkled, and extravagantly horned, and it squinted. Its body was such a confusing combination of sluglike membranes and legs out behind that she never quite managed to separate it from its complex clothing and equipment. It was one of the road-worn—CP received a subliminal impression that others had waited for it as spokesman or leader.

Evidently it could mind-speak, perhaps assisted by one of the two on the wing. A misty image formed behind her eyes; she closed them to concentrate, and "saw" herself back in *Calgary*. She was—yes—going from port to port, scanning over the whole sky. This was the long Voiceless last period, after the Empire had faded out, when she was contentedly—but systematically—studying the visible universe. The image turned to her star charts.

On impulse she opened her eyes and pulled the real charts from their locker.

The impression of excited joy that came to her was unmistakable. Unmistakable too, now, was an odd "tone" to the communications, especially those from the antlered one. Familiar!

While Tadak and its large friend helped her explain why she couldn't pass the charts out now, but they'd have them soon, she searched her memory for that "tone," and found it.

Why, it was these aliens to whom she had been "transmitting" all those days after she was on course. They were too weak-voiced to reach her, but she had felt not alone, "all right." Who could they be?

Oh! While she'd been puzzling, a new, very strong phenomenon had emerged: above and around every new head in the clearing came a small halo of stars. Some were weak, barely floating pinpoints of light, others were a full-blown circlet of blackness lit with glory, before all faded.

The astronomers of this world had come to her.

But how could this sealed sunless world, surely without spaceflight, have "astronomers"? How could they ever have found out the stars at all, unless perhaps the clouds cleared once in a while, like an old story she'd read? Here she was wrong, but she only discovered it later, during one of the most exhausting yet pleasant twenty hours of her life.

They wanted to know everything.

Each had formed its one most vital question, each in turn would walk, hobble, crawl, hop forward, to "ask" it. But first the big antlered speaker "asked" a question so comprehensive that it obviated many other planned ones.

An image of a star field bloomed in her mind, stars of all the types she had unwittingly "shown" them from *Calgary*, each clear and specific before merging into the whole.

This great image was followed by a startlingly strong blankout. Then the stars came back, then the blank, faster to the now familiar flicker-meaning:

"The stars are—what?"

Whew.

She had to explain the universe wordlessly to a race whose concepts and measures—if any—of distance, motion, forces, matter, heat, she didn't know.

Afterward, she recalled mostly a mishmash, but she thought she must have given quite a performance. This was, after all, her own beloved study, at an amateur level.

She remembered first trying to convey some notion of energies and distances. She imaged this world's—Auln's—surface from above, then using old tape-teach effects, she "receded" down to a lavender point against the stars, then "pulled" one of the nearer small stars close for comparison, and showed the wild atomic fires of its surface compared with the colder weak processes of Auln. She "built" a star up out of a gas cloud, changed it through its life to red giant and nova, built another, richer one from the debris and condensed its planets. She "started life" on the planet, gave them a glimpse of her own Earth—typical astronomers, they cared little for this—then sent it receding again and built up the Milky Way, and galaxies beyond it, attempted the expanding universe.

It was there she had paused, exhausted.

While she rested and ate, someone sent her the answer to her question: how did they know of the stars?

She received an image of a new sort—framed! Multiply-framed, in fact, frame within frame. The image itself was oddly blurred in detail. Sharp, however, was a view of extraordinary metal wreckage, unidentifiable stuff strewn at a deep gash in the ground. Much was splashed with brilliant green, and there was a central ball or cylinder—no, wait, a *head*, not human.

Had these aliens actually attempted spaceflight?

No. The framed image jumped to show a fireball streaking down through the clouds, then back to the green-smeared head. Wrecked as it was, it did seem generically unlike anyone she had seen on Auln. As if to settle her problem, "her" ruddy flop-eared alien bent and pulled a wrap off its leg, showing a healing cut. Its blood was red, like hers.

So another, a *real* alien had crashed here! And long ago, too. The frames, the blur, suggested many transmissions of the scene. But this space alien was obviously dead. How, then—

Into the image came a head like the beaked "aquatics" among her first visitors. Huge-eyed, somehow rather special-seeming. It laid its head against the dead astronaut's. And the image dissolved to faint views of the starry sky from space, an incoming glimpse of Auln, strangeness.

Generations back, then, they had learned of outside space, the stars—by probing a dead brain!

She was so bemused by this that she barely attended to another, clearly contemporary, image sequence until a motion like wingbeats caught her. She reclosed her eyes in time to "see" a birdlike creature flapping desperately, up—up—it seemed to be driven, or lifted, higher than its wings could sustain it, higher than it could breathe. The image changed. On the ground, a far-"sighted" alien was looking through the dying bird's eyes, seeing weirdly focused images of thinning, darkening cloud. Just before the bird eyes died, a rift opened above it; blackness lit by two bright stars was briefly there.

A living telescope! But the "tone" in which these sequences came through suggested some sadness or disapproval. CP thought that perhaps they used this ruthless technique only rarely and reluctantly. It certainly wasn't sustained enough to be useful, but it sufficed to reassure them that the stars *were* there.

The ensuing hours and hours of sending, trying to understand queries, to invent visual ways to convey the barely communicable, not to omit too much of importance, to share in effect all she knew of the universe, condensed in memory into a great blur, of which she recalled only two things.

The first was rooting out the magnificent star and galaxy color photos poor Don Lamb had collected, and pasting them up inside the ports. This was a sensation; the crowding nearly did tip *Calgary*.

The other was her own graphic warning of all that could happen on Auln if Earthmen or another aggressive species found them.

This changed the mood to a great sobriety, in which she sensed that the thought was not entirely new to all. She sent all she could on human nuclear space bombardment, robot weapons, and air-to-ground attack, which seemed to be attentively received. The idea worried her, but she had done all she could. This telekinetic, mind-probing, perhaps mind-deceiving race might be able devise adequate defense. . . . How she hoped it!

And finally, after more than an Earth-day's wakefulness, they left as abruptly as they'd come, each giving her the two-handed gesture of farewell. Tadak left too, riding on the carapace of a strong young shelled one. But to her relief and pleasure, its larger flop-eared friend seemed prepared to stay. Indeed, she didn't acknowledge to herself how carefully she had watched for signs of its intentions. It was peculiarly, deeply important to her.

As she watched them straggle up the road, hearing the last of their rather high-pitched Asiatic converse, it seemed to her that one or two turned into a side path near the ship and disappeared behind a rise. Her attention was drawn to this by seeing the others pause and hand over cloaks, or packets of supplies. Perhaps these were headed another way, by a long route; she forgot it.

When they had all departed and the path was empty, the alien whom she was beginning timidly to think of as a friend came up onto the wing stub at her window. It looked at her, the same look she'd seen at the very first. But now it was looking solely into her eyes, long, deep, searchingly. Peculiar images, apparently just random memories, came to her; the dormitory of her old school-days, the streets of the Enclave. Her first real desk. And always in them was a figure she reluctantly recognized: herself.

She began to tremble.

These were not . . . memories.

More images of the past. And weaving through them, a gleaming red-gold cap—could that be her hair?

No one but herself knew of all these past scenes.

None but one other.

Could this be—was she at last looking at the one who—was

it this alien being who had "spoken" to her all her life? Was this her Voice?

She trembled harder, uncontrollably.

Then her "friend" reared up and placed both thin palms on the window by its head.

Cold struck her to her heart.

She tried to tell herself that this was just to see her better through the port. But that couldn't be, she realized dully; the light was not that bright, the vitrex wasn't that reflective.

This must be—oh, please, no, don't let it be like all the others, a final, formal good-bye. Not from the one who held her life, who had been with her lifelong, through all the dark nights, the pain. Who had said, Come.

The image of herself also holding her hands to the window came urgently to her. She was expected to respond.

Oh, please, she pleaded to no one, not good-bye from *you*, too. Not you, my Voice . . . Don't leave me alone. To die. Grief pushed huge tears past all her guards. To distract herself she thought how rude all the others must have thought her, when she failed to respond to them.

This one really wanted her to respond properly. Evidently it had enough personal feeling for her to make this important. Well, she would, in a moment, when she had herself under better control.

A thud shook the wing. Humanlike, but with far more strength, the alien stamped. Perhaps it was impatient to rejoin the others? It stamped again, harder, and slapped both hands on the window, sending a peremptory image of her holding her hands up against the vitrex, matching its own.

All right, then. Good-bye.

Blind with unshed tears, she stood up and spread her palms against the window opposite the red-and-cream blurs. The alien made an exasperated sound and moved its hands to cover hers as exactly as possible.

And something—began to flow. It was as if the vitrex grew hot, or not hot but charged. Almost alive. CP shook so hard her hands slid lower; feeling another stamp from outside, she tried to replace them. The "current" flowed again, carrying with it a bloom of feelings, images, wordless knowledge, she didn't know what, all bursting through her from their matched palms.

The alien's eyes caught and held hers, and slowly it brought its hands closer to its head. Hers followed jerkily.

Here the feelings strengthened, became overpowering. She sank to her knees, the alien followed, still holding her palm to palm, through five centimeters of hard vitrex. She couldn't remove her hands if she chose.

But she wouldn't have broken that contact for life itself. She was learning—she was understanding, oh, incredulously—that all her life—

Suddenly a strong, rich sound from the audio startled her: the alien's voice.

It had to be repeated before she understood.

"Ca-rol."

Her name. It was known to no one here.

"Ca-rol . . . ehy-ou . . . Iye . . ."

Unmistakable, though strange and jerky here, she recognized her Voice.

There was no need now for the alien to explain that his gesture was not a good-bye, but communion.

But there was more to it than that. Ludicrously, neither of them had her word for it, because it was a word CP had never had occasion to use. It seemed important, for a while, to find it. They went at it the long way round, through her feeling for the stars, and for a rat she had once briefly been allowed to make a pet of. The recognition, the realization, scared CP so badly that her teeth rattled. But the alien "held" her, insistently pressed the communication on her, out of its own need. In the end she had to know it fully.

Know that she—Carol-Page-Snotface-CP-Cold-Pig—had walked all her days and nights embraced by love. Alien love, at first for a little-alien-among-the-stars, but soon, soon for her alone.

She had never been alone.

She, Carol-Page-Snotface-etcetera was the Beloved . . . and always had been.

As this rosy fur-clad soft-eared glowing-eyed one was of course hers, though she had never used the word. Her lifelong love.

⊞

When two long-parted, unacknowledged lovers meet at last and reveal their love, it is always the same. Even though a wall of vitrex came between them.

Long intervals of speechless communion, absorbing the miracle of You Too Love . . . that You Are Here, that Me + You = One. In other intervals her lover showed her all this world of Auln, about the Viewers, about the early training to become a Star Caller. The alien was still young too, she gathered. It had been on its first Star Search when contact with her occurred. She wanted to be shown everything, she couldn't get enough of images, even trivia, of her lover's life. All hers was of course known in detail to her alien Voice.

As the current between them strengthened she took to thinking of the alien as "he," meaning no more by it than that "it" was insupportable and "she" or "sister" was not quite appropriate in a human sense. Like herself, she found the alien had never borne young. Besides, there were now no other "hes" in CP's universe.

Twice she touched on the violent acts that had brought her here, and each time the current jumped almost to real pain. Strongly, oh, how strongly he supported them and her!

Rather wildly, they both sought ways of closer contact, ending whole-body-plastered to the vitrex. Neither could bear to cease contact long enough to eat much. Vaguely she thought that accounted for a slight unnoticed ill feeling.

Then came the day when her timer blatted so insistently that she saw it was past the red mark. The illness she'd ignored was real.

Calgary's air had ended.

It was time to come out—to him. She explained what he already knew, and received grave assent.

When the huge port swung open, the air that rushed upon her was impossibly sweet and fresh—spring air such as CP'd never breathed before. *Calgary*'s foulness made a fog at the port. The first thing she saw through it was his hand, stretched to her. He led her out, to a different end.

Again, when two lovers win to real bodily contact, it is always the same. But these two were still separated, not by a mere wall, but by being prisoned in wholly different bodies with wholly different needs.

Unnecessary to follow all their efforts in those first hours. Sufficient that they learned two things. First, mutual laughter, and second, what all Earthbound lovers find, that *nothing* suffices.

They blamed this on their differences, but they suspected the truth. Where love has been intense and silent and all-consuming, only the impossible, the total merger into one, could slake its fires.

On this world, such a consummation was only a little less impossible than on Earth. In the end, they found the physical palm-to-palm contact deepest and most poignant, and they stayed so.

Outward events were few and slight, but the most important in the universe. While she was still feeling wonderfully well, he led her up a nearby hill to a small glade with a superb view. She saw in reality the glorious self-lit colors of great Auln's cultivated lands, its wildernesses and rivers, and in the distance, a small city or town, the sky overhead reflecting all. Behind them lay the luminous sea, from which blew a gentle breeze, and where she glimpsed strange sea creatures tumbling. Presently her lover lured a few of Auln's "birds" and other strange or charming creatures to them.

At one point she flinched about her nose, and he "told" her in pictures how his own flopped ears were viewed as deplorable. Even on this world where individuals mutated so wildly as scarcely to seem of the same species, by chance all but a few heads bore upright ears or other sensors. His own rounded head was almost the sole feature seen by all as ugly. This revelation caused much time to be occupied by caressing reassurances.

She was weakening fast, but pain seemed absent or muffled for a while. Her exposed pale skin burned and blistered shockingly by the second day, despite the gauzy cover he had made for her by tearing out the lining of his cloak. The burns did not hurt much either. Later, when she saw him wince, she began to suspect why. They had a battle of wills, in which hers was no match for his trained one.

On the third day her beautiful hair was falling out in sheaves. He collected it, strand by strand, smoothed and kept it.

That day she had the whim to cut their names on a stone, and could scarcely bear it when he left her to bring one. Amazed and delighted by the novelty, they realized she had never known his name—Cavaná. She said it, sang it, whispered it a thousand times, built it into all her memories. Finally she did, with help, scratch *Cavaná* and *Carol* onto the stone, and tried to make other lines, but was too weak. He never left her again.

By this time they were lying with their heads on a cushioned log, their hands as if grown together.

One of the last things she noticed was the amusingly fluffed, mossy little vine that made the log so comfortable. He told her its future.

⊕

The Fountain had flowed since the Viewers had been here last. Two farmers from Pyenro were now putting in part of their town duty clearing vine from the alien sky-box. They passed on news of two new young ones, and a possible animal-sickness the Viewers should keep track of.

Their task inside the now open sky-box busied the Viewers for some time. Old Andoul, of course, could not enter. While the others were occupied, she communed effortfully by sound with the three sky-obsessed ones who had remained here. They had stayed discreetly out of sight of Cavaná and the alien, but had caught nothing of consequence in that time. However, the open sky-box had given them much of overwhelming interest, including a sheaf of extraordinary flat, flexible, permanent images, which they called "stars." They asked Andoul and Askelon, a new young Viewer, to view them. This they did. The images were of nothing recognizable, being largely black-spangled, but oddly moving in addition to their fascinating new technique.

The farmers had widened the summit path for Andoul. When all was finished below, the Viewers started up. It was steep. The deformed child Mir-Mir, who was so young it hadn't yet chosen gender, had to clamber up on Andoul's back, tucking up its red veils and complaining aloud, "If you accept any more jewelry, *Saro* Andoul, I'll never find a place to sit. I believe you do it on purpose."

"Speak properly, child," Andoul told it. "And if you eat any more no one will be able to carry you. . . . Aah! I View." All halted, and Mir-Mir slid off.

They had arrived at a pretty little glade near the summit. An elongated mound, green-covered by vine, lay with one end on a green-clad log.

Looking more closely, all could see that the form was in fact two, closely apposed and entwined at the log end, where lateral mounding indicated arms.

Xerona and Ekstá advanced to it, squatted, and placed their webbed hands gently on what might be two vine-covered heads pressed tight together.

After a moment, both touched one body and Xerona sent them all an image.

"Cavaná," Mir-Mir said aloud. Andoul grunted in disapproval, both of Mir-Mir's vocalizing and what was in its mind. Ferdil, one of the three very silent, hardworking Viewers who resembled Cavaná, was actually Cavaná's cousin.

"See the bigger legs," Mir-Mir said defiantly. "Poor Cavaná, so ugly. But she lived in the sky!"

The two beaked Viewers were indicating the other form, transmitting a rather sketchy image of the orange-maned alien. They were all silent a moment, refining and supplementing the image. Finally Askelon sighed.

"I did ill," he mourned aloud. "It was my responsibility." He sent short images of himself inspecting the nude alien, and himself now, downcast with both hands drooped from the wrists. Shame.

Old Andoul gently corrected that image to raise the hands. "We all must begin," she said in words. "None of us considered it very important. Perhaps it isn't. Although—" She lapsed back to imagery, showed the alien in a framing of color that was short-speed for "Person of perhaps great soul," and then jumped to sketched-in multitudes of other redheaded aliens diving upon them with fantastic sky-boxes and explosions of flame.

The other Viewers sighed, too. Askelon revived slightly. Ferdil and her two friends went over by the feet of the dead ones, and gazed down at the hidden form of Cavaná, locked in death with her alien love. When Ferdil gave the sign of formal last farewell, the others, after a polite interval, did likewise.

Meanwhile Xerona and Ekstá were hard at work, their own heads against first one dead head and then the other. At length they arose, their expressions very sober.

"Nothing . . . of interest or use to others," Ekstá said. "Cavaná . . . took much of the alien's pain."

Xerona was trying to hide weeping, but missed an indigo tear at his throat gills.

"Ah, look!" Askelon, scanning hard to redeem himself, had come upon an odd corner of rock. When he lifted and cleared it, they saw a flat stone with chasings or scratches on it.

"Alien writing!" exclaimed Mir-Mir, hobbling to it. "Ferdil!"

Ferdil and her companions were already Viewing the stone. With a confirmatory transmission to old Andoul, she produced a small container from her belly pack, inserted a straw, and skillfully blew a mist of moss-inhibiting bacteria over the stone. Then she set it on edge beyond the lovers' heads.

Unexpectedly, Ferdil spoke in words.

"I knew Cavaná well, we were deep friends in the early days, before. . . . She had only just chosen gender when she made Contact. . . . Her love was very severe; changeless, unremitting. Almost a sickness. But she left us much. And one thing more—we know now her communication was real. Many doubted. But the one she Called really heard, answered, and with much effort came."

The others were silent, admitting her right to important verbal speech.

Around them Auln lay in beauty, under the eternal soft-colored cloud ceiling that was their sky. The plain in view here was vast, bioluminescent to the high horizon. Nothing had ever changed here, nothing would. No light of day, no dark of night, no summer, neither fall nor winter. Only their own works, like the *sumlac* fields, changed the tints reflected in the cloud. People came from great distances to watch the shifts at planting time and harvest, and for their enjoyment the farmers synchronized many crops. Now the sky carried pink bands that came from the simultaneous channeling of water into the *millin* lanes.

Characteristically it was the child Mir-Mir who broke the silence as they started to descend.

"I am going to change, and become a Star Caller!"

"Oh, child, you don't know what you're saying!" Askelon exclaimed involuntarily. "Look at the life Callers have, they must give up everything to Search and Search—and if they find and focus, they are—well—" He paused, gestured back at the mounds of the dead.

"Doomed!" finished Mir-Mir melodramatically.

Proper transmissions came from all sides now, from so many fellow Viewers at once that they blurred. But it understood that this was all discouragement, dismal images of a Star Caller's totally dedicated narrow prison plus Mir-Mir's own flightiness.

"No. I think I really mean this," Mir-Mir said soberly. "I'm not going to become a very good Viewer. And I have this different feeling"—Mir-Mir put its head up to look raptly skyward, stumbled, and almost fell—"not just since this. Before. I didn't say it. I think I . . . I think I'm capable of that love." It had halted them all and was rubbing the hurt, twisted little legs with its frail hands.

Old Andoul spoke, surprising them all.

"I too have felt. Long ago . . . a hint of love. The love of all that is alien. Of the stars. But I believe that with me it was too generalized. Those who Call must focus, and so lose everything to perhaps gain one. . . . More, in my youth we were not quite certain even that the stars were there, that it was not delusion. Think hard till you are sure, child. But more Callers are not unnecessary, now . . . and speaking of now we must move along."

"Yes," said Ekstá severely, pushing on at a determined waddle as he sent brisk images of the sessions now beginning at Amberamou, and the urgent matter of the flying herd. As he passed Mir-Mir he said, not unkindly, "Auln knows, child, you're loud enough!"

Presently the path was empty; summit and *Calgary*'s hollow lay silent again. Above, more salmon-colored rivers stream through the clouds, as the great farm channels filled. The pink light touched the stone, on which were scratched human letters trailing off unfinished:

CAVANÁ + CAROL

OF LOVE & OXYGE

Mir-Mir's intentions held. Sometime later, somewhere a man or alien would turn his gaze up to the stars with ardent longing, would begin to imagine he could hear. . . .

A MOMENTARY TASTE OF BEING

> *. . . A momentary taste*
> *Of Being from the Well amid the Waste—*
> —KHAYYÁM/FITZGERALD

IT FLOATS THERE *visibly engorged, blue-green against the blackness. He stares: it swells, pulsing to a terrifying dim beat, slowly extrudes a great ghostly bulge which extends, solidifies . . . it is a planet-testicle pushing a monster penis toward the stars. Its blood-beat reverberates through weeping immensities; cold, cold. The parsecs-long phallus throbs, probes blindly under intolerable pressure from within; its tip is a huge cloudy glans lit by a spark: Centaur. In grief it bulges, lengthens, seeking release—stars toll unbearable crescendo. . . .*

It is a minute or two before Dr. Aaron Kaye is sure that he is awake in his temporary bunk in *Centaur*'s quarantine ward. His own throat is sobbing reflexively, his eyes are weeping, not stars. Another of the damn dreams. Aaron lies still, blinking, willing the icy grief to let go of his mind.

It lets go. Aaron sits up still cold with meaningless bereavement. What the hell is it, what's tearing at him? "Great Pan is dead," he mutters stumbling to the narrow wash-stall. The lament that echoed round the world. . . . He sluices his head, wishing for his own quarters and Solange. He really should work on these anxiety symptoms. Later, no time now. "Physician, screw thyself," he jeers at the undistinguished, worried face in the mirror.

Oh, Jesus—the time! He has overslept while they are doing god knows what to Lory. Why hasn't Coby waked him? Because Lory is his sister, of course; Aaron should have foreseen that.

He hustles out into Isolation's tiny corridor. At one end is a vitrex wall; beyond it his assistant Coby looks up, takes off his headset. Was he listening to music, or what? No matter. Aaron glances into Tighe's cubicle. Tighe's face is still lax, sedated; he has been in sleep-therapy since his episode a week ago. Aaron goes to the speaker grille in the vitrex, draws a cup of hot brew: The liquid falls sluggishly; Isolation is at three-fourths gee in the rotating ship.

"Where's Dr. Kaye—my sister?"

"They've started the interrogation, boss. I thought you needed your sleep." Coby's doubtless meaning to be friendly, but his voice has too many sly habits.

"Oh, god." Aaron starts to cycle the cup out, forces himself to drink it. He has a persistent feeling that Lory's alien is now located down below his right heel.

"Doc."

"What?"

"Bruce and Åhlstrom came in while you were asleep. They complain they saw Tighe running around loose this morning."

Aaron frowns. "He hasn't been out, has he?"

"No way. They each saw him separately. I talked them into seeing you, later."

"Yeah. Right." Aaron cycles his cup and heads back up the hall, past a door marked *Interview*. The next is *Observation*. He goes in to a dim closet with viewscreens on two walls. The screen in front of him is already activated two-way. It shows four men seated in a small room outside Isolation's wall.

The gray-haired classic Anglo profile is Captain Yellaston, acknowledging Aaron's presence with a neutral nod. Beside him the two scout commanders go on watching their own screen. The fourth man is young Frank Foy, *Centaur*'s security officer. He is pursing his mouth over a wad of printout tape.

Reluctantly, Aaron activates his other screen one-way, knowing he will see something unpleasant. There she is—his sister Lory, a thin young red-haired woman wired to a sensor bank. Her eyes have turned to him, although Aaron knows she's seeing a blank screen. Hypersensitive as usual. Behind her is Solange in a decontamination suit.

"We will go over the questions once more, Miss Kaye," Frank Foy says in a preposterously impersonal tone.

"Dr. Kaye, please." Lory sounds tired.

"Dr. Kaye, of course." Why is young Frank so dislikable? Be fair, Aaron tells himself, it's the man's job. Necessary for the safety of the tribe. And he isn't "young" Frank anymore. Christ, none of us are, twenty-six trillion miles from home. Ten years.

"Dr. Kaye, you were primarily qualified as a biologist on the Gamma scout mission, is that right?"

"Yes, but I was also qualified in astrogation. We all were."

"Please answer yes or no."

"Yes."

Foy loops the printout, makes a mark. "And in your capacity as biologist you investigated the planetary surface both from orbit and on the ground from the landing site?"

"Yes."

"In your judgment, is the planet suitable for human colonization?"

"Yes."

"Did you observe anything harmful to human health or well-being?"

"No. No, it's ideal—I told you."

Foy coughs reprovingly. Aaron frowns too; Lory doesn't usually call things ideal.

"Nothing potentially capable of harming human beings?"

"No. Wait—even water is potentially capable of harming people, you know."

Foy's mouth tightens. "Very well, I rephrase. Did you observe any life-forms that attacked or harmed humans?"

"No."

"But"—Foy pounces—"when Lieutenant Tighe approached the specimen you brought back, he was harmed, was he not?"

"No, I don't believe it harmed him."

"As a biologist, you consider Lieutenant Tighe's condition unimpaired?"

"No—I mean yes. He was impaired to begin with, poor man."

"In view of the fact that Lieutenant Tighe has been hospitalized since his approach to this alien, do you still maintain it did not harm him?"

"Yes, it did not. Your grammar sort of confuses me. Please,

may we move the sensor cuff to my other arm? I'm getting a little capillary breakage." She looks up at the blank screen hiding the command staff.

Foy starts to object, but Captain Yellaston clears his throat warningly, nods. When Solange unhooks the big cuff Lory stands up and stretches her slim, almost breastless body; with that pleasant snub-nosed face she could pass for a boy.

Aaron watches her as he has all his life with a peculiar mixture of love and dread. That body, he knows, strikes most men as sexless, an impression confirmed by her task-oriented manner. *Centaur*'s selection board must have been composed of such men, one of the mission criteria was low sex-drive. Aaron sighs, watching Solange reattach the cuff. The board had been perfectly right, of course; as far as Lory herself was concerned she would have been happy in a nunnery. Aaron wishes she was in one. Not here.

Foy coughs primly into the microphone. "I will repeat, Dr. Kaye. Do you consider the effect of the alien specimen on Lieutenant Tighe was injurious to his health?"

"No," says Lory patiently. It's a disgusting scene, Aaron thinks; the helpless wired-up woman, the hidden probing men. Psychic rape. Do them justice, only Foy seems to be enjoying it.

"On the planet surface, did Commander Kuh have contact with these life-forms?"

"Yes."

"And was he affected similarly to Lieutenant Tighe?"

"No—I mean, yes, the contact wasn't injurious to him either."

"I repeat. Was Commander Kuh or his men harmed in any way by the life-forms on that planet?"

"No."

"I repeat. Were Commander Kuh or his men harmed in any way by the life-forms on that planet?"

"*No.*" Lory shakes her head at the blank screen.

"You state that the scout ship's computer ceased to record input from the sensors and cameras after the first day on the surface. Did you destroy those records?"

"No."

"Was the computer tampered with by you or anyone?"

"No. I told you, we thought it was recording, no one knew the dump cycle had cut in. We lost all that data."

"Dr. Kaye, I repeat: Did you dump those records?"

"No."

"Dr. Kaye, I will go back once more. When you returned alone, navigating Commander Kuh's scout ship, you stated that Commander Kuh and his crew had remained on the planet because they desired to begin colonization. You stated that the planet was, I quote, a paradise and that nothing on it was harmful to man. Despite the totally inadequate record of surface conditions you claim that Commander Kuh recommends that we immediately send the green signal to Earth to begin full-scale emigration. And yet when Lieutenant Tighe opened the port to the alien specimen in your ship he suffered a critical collapse. Dr. Kaye, I put it to you that what really happened on that planet was that Commander Kuh and his crew were injured or taken captive by beings on that planet and you are concealing this fact."

Lory has been shaking her short red hair vigorously during this speech. "No! They weren't injured or taken captive, that's silly! I tell you, they wanted to stay. I volunteered to take the message back. I was the logical choice, I mean I was non-Chinese, you know—"

"Please answer yes or no, Dr. Kaye. Did Commander Kuh or any of his people suffer a shock similar to Lieutenant Tighe?"

"No!"

Foy is frowning at his tapes, making tick-marks. Aaron's liver has been getting chilly; he doesn't need wiring to detect the extra sincerity in Lory's voice.

"I repeat, Dr. Kaye. Did—"

But Captain Yellaston stirs authoritatively behind him.

"Thank you, Lieutenant Foy."

Foy's mouth closes. On the blind side of the screen Lory says gamely, "I'm not really tired, sir."

"Nevertheless, I think we will complete this later," Yellaston says in his good gray voice. He catches Aaron's eye, and they all sit silent while Solange releases Lory from the cuff and body wires. Through Solange's visor Aaron can see her lovely French-Arab face projecting worried compassion. Empathy is Solange's specialty; a wire slips and Aaron sees her lips go "Ooh." He smiles, feels briefly better.

As the women leave, the two scout commanders in the other cubicle stand up and stretch. Both brown-haired, blue-eyed, muscular ectomesomorphs so much alike to Aaron's eye, although Timofaev Bron was born in Omsk and Don Purcell in Ohio. Ten years ago those faces had held only simple dedication to the goal of getting to a supremely difficult place in one piece. The failures of their respective scout missions have brought them back to *Centaur* lined and dulled. But in the last twenty days since Lory's return something has awakened in their eyes; Aaron isn't too eager to know its name.

"Report, please, Lieutenant Foy," says Yellaston, his glance making it clear that Aaron is to be included. The official recorder is still on.

Francis Xavier Foy sucks air through his teeth importantly; this is his second big interrogation on their entire ten-year voyage.

"Sir, I must regretfully report that the protocol shows persistent, ah, anomalous responses. First, the subject shows a markedly elevated and labile emotionality—" He glances irritatedly at Aaron, to whom this is no news.

"The level of affect is, ah, suggestive. More specifically, on the question of injury to Commander Kuh, Dr. Kaye—Dr. *Lory* Kaye, that is—the physiological reactions contraindicate her verbal responses, that is, they are not characteristic of her baseline truth-type—" He shuffles his printouts, not looking at Aaron.

"Lieutenant Foy, are you trying to tell us that in your professional judgment Dr. Kaye is lying about what happened to the Gamma scout crew?"

Frank Foy wriggles, reshuffling tapes. "Sir, I can only repeat that there are contraindications. Areas of unclarity. In particular these three responses, sir, if you would care to compare these peaks I have marked?"

Yellaston looks at him thoughtfully, not taking the tapes.

"Sir, if we could reconsider the decision not to employ, ah, chemical supplementation," Foy says desperately. He means, scop and EDC. Aaron knows Yellaston won't do this; he supposes he is grateful.

Yellaston doesn't bother answering. "Leaving aside the question of injury to Commander Kuh, Frank, what about Dr. Kaye's responses on the general habitability of the planet?"

"Again, there are anomalies in Dr. Kaye's responses." Foy visibly disapproves of any suspicions being left aside.

"What type of anomalies?"

"Abnormal arousal, sir. Surges of, ah, emotionality. Taken

together with terms like 'paradise,' 'ideal,' and so on in the verbal protocol, the indications are—"

"In your professional judgment, Lieutenant Foy, do you conclude that Dr. Kaye is or is not lying when she says the planet is habitable?"

"Sir, the problem is variability, in a pinpoint sense. What you have suggests the classic pattern of a covert *area.*"

Yellaston ponders; behind him the two scout commanders watch impassively.

"Lieutenant Foy. If Dr. Kaye does in fact believe the planet to be eminently suitable for colonization, can you say that her emotion could be accounted for by extreme elation and excitement at the successful outcome of our long and difficult mission?"

Foy stares at him, mouth slightly open.

"Elation, extreme—I see what you mean, sir. I hadn't—yes, sir, I suppose that could be one interpretation."

"Then do I correctly summarize your findings at this stage by saying that while Dr. Kaye's account of the events concerning Commander Kuh remains unclear, you see no specific counterindication of her statement that the planet is habitable?"

"Ah, yes, sir. Although—"

"Thank you, Lieutenant Foy. We will resume tomorrow."

The two scout commanders glance at each other. They are solidly united against Foy, Aaron sees. Like two combat captains waiting for an unruly pacifist to be disposed of so the contest can start. Aaron sympathizes, he can't make himself like Foy. But he didn't like that tone in Lory's voice, either.

"Man, the samples, the sensor records," Don Purcell says abruptly. "They don't lie. Even if they only got thirty hours on-planet, that place is perfect."

Tim Bron grins, nods at Aaron. Yellaston smiles remotely, his eyes reminding them of the official recorder. For the thousandth time Aaron is touched by the calm command presence of the man. Old Yellowstone. The solid whatever-it-is that has held them together, stuffed in this tin can all through the years. Where the hell did they find him? A New Zealander, educated at some extinct British school. Chief of the Jupiter mission, etcetera, etcetera. Last of the dinosaurs.

But now he notices an oddity: Yellaston, who has absolutely no nervous mannerisms, is massaging the knuckles of one hand. Is it indecision over Lory's answers? Or is it the spark that's sizzling behind the two scout commanders' eyes—the planet?

The planet . . .

A golden jackpot rushes uncontrollably up through some pipe in Aaron's midbrain. Is it really there at last? After all the grueling years, after Don and then Tim came back reporting nothing but gas and rocks around the first two Centaurus suns—is it possible our last chance has won? If Lory is to be believed, Kuh's people are at this moment walking in Earth's new Eden that we need so desperately. While we hang here in darkness, two long years away. If Lory is to be believed—

Aaron realizes Captain Yellaston is speaking to him.

"—You judge her to be medically fit, Dr. Kaye?"

"Yes, Sir. We've run the full program of tests designed for possible alien contact, plus the standard biomonitor spectrum. As of last night—I haven't checked the last six hours—and apart from weight loss and the ulcerative lesions in the duodenum which she suffered from when she got back to *Centaur*, Dr. Lory Kaye shows no significant change from her baseline norms when she departed two years ago."

"Those ulcers, Doctor; am I correct that you feel they can be fully accounted for by the strain of her solitary voyage back to this ship?"

"Yes, sir, I certainly do." Aaron has no reservations here. Almost a year alone, navigating for a moving point in space? My god, how did you do it, he thinks again. My little sister. She isn't human. And that alien thing on board, right behind her . . . For an instant Aaron can feel its location, down below the left wall. He glances at the recorder, suppressing the impulse to ask the others if they feel it too.

"Tomorrow is the final day of the twenty-one-day quarantine period," Yellaston is saying. "An arbitrary interval, to be sure. You will continue the medical watch on Dr. Lory Kaye until the final debriefing session at oh-nine-hundred tomorrow." Aaron nods. "If there are still no adverse indications, the quarantine will terminate at noon. As soon as feasible thereafter we should proceed to examine the specimen now sealed in scout ship Gamma. Say, the following day; will this give you sufficient time to coordinate your resources with the Xenobiology staff and be prepared to assist us, Dr. Kaye?"

"Yes, sir."

Yellaston voice-signs the log entry, clicks the recorder off.

"Are you going to wait to signal home until after we look at that specimen?" Don asks him.

"Certainly."

They go out then, four men moving carefully in cramped quarters. Roomier than they'd have on Earth now. Aaron sees Foy manage to get in Yellaston's way, feels a twinge of sympathy for the authority-cathected wretch. Anything to get Daddy's attention. He too has been moved by Yellaston's good-wise-father projection. Are his own responses more mature? The hell with it, he decides; after ten years self-analysis becomes ritual.

When he emerges into Isolation corridor, Lory has vanished into her cubicle and Solange is nowhere in sight. He nods at Coby through the vitrex and punches the food-dispenser chute. His server arrives on a puff of kitchen-scented air. Protein loaf, with an unexpected garnish; the commissary staff seems to be in good form.

He munches, absently eyeing the three-di shot of Earth mounted above his desk in the office beyond the wall. That photo hangs all over the ship, a beautifully clear image from the early clean-air days. What are they eating there now, each other? But the thought has lost its impact after a decade away; like everyone else on *Centaur*, Aaron has no close ties left behind. Twenty billion humans swarming on that globe when they went; doubtless thirty by now, even with the famines. Waiting to explode to the stars now that the technology is—precariously—here. Waiting for the green light from *Centaur*. Not literally green, of course, Aaron thinks; just one of the three simple codes they can send at this range. For ten long years they have been sending yellow—*Exploration continues*. And until twenty days ago they were facing the bleak red—*No planet found, returning to base*. But now, Lory's planet!

Aaron shakes his head, nibbling a slice of real egg, thinking of the green signal starting on its four-year trajectory back to Earth. *Planet found, launch emigration fleets, coordinates such-and-such*. Earth's teeming billions all pressing for the handful of places in those improbable transport cans.

Aaron frowns at himself; he rejects the "teeming billions" concept. Doggedly he thinks of them as people, no matter how many—individual human beings each with a face, a name, a unique personality, and a meaningful fate. He invokes now his personal ritual, his defense against mass-think, which is simply the recalling of people he has known. An invisible army streams through his mind as he chews. People . . . from each he has learned. What? Something, large or small. An existence . . . the face of Thomas Brown glances coldly from memory; Brown was the sad murderer who was his first psychosurgery patient a zillion years ago at Houston Enclave. Had he helped Brown? Probably not, but Aaron will be damned if he will forget the man. The living man, not a statistic. His thoughts veer to the reality of his present shipmates, the sixty chosen souls. Cream of Earth, he thinks, only half in sarcasm. He is proud of them. Their endurance, their resourcefulness, their effortful sanity. He thinks it is not impossible that Earth's sanest children are in this frail bubble of air and warmth twenty-six million million miles away.

He cycles his server, pulls himself together. He has eighteen hours of biomonitor tapes to check against the baseline medical norms of Tighe, Lory, and himself. And first he must talk to the two people who thought they saw Tighe. As he gets up, the image of Earth catches his eye again: their lonely, vulnerable jewel, hanging there in blackness. Suddenly last night's dream jumps back, he sees again the monster penis groping toward the stars with *Centaur* at its tip. Pulsing with pressure, barely able to wait for the trigger that will release the human deluge —

He swats his forehead; the hallucination snaps out. Angry with himself, he plods back to the Observation cubby.

The image of Bruce Jang is waiting on the screen; his compatriot, the young Chinese-American engineer on a ship where everyone is a token something. Only not "young" anymore, Aaron admonishes himself.

"They have me in the coop, Bruce. I'm told you saw Tighe. Where and when?"

Bruce considers. Two years ago Bruce had still looked like Supersquirrel, all fast reflexes, buckteeth, and mocking see-it-all eyes. Cal Tech's answer to the universe.

"He came by my quarters about oh-seven-hundred. I was cleaning up, the door was open, I saw him looking in at me. Sort of, you know, fon-nee." Bruce shrugs, a joyless parody of his old jive manner.

"Funny? You mean his expression? Or was there anything peculiar about him, I mean visually different?"

A complex pause.

"Now that you mention it, yes. His refraction index was a shade off."

Aaron puzzles, finally gets it. "Do you mean Tighe appeared somewhat blurred or translucent?"

"Yeah. Both," Bruce says tightly. "But it was him."

"Bruce, Tighe never left Isolation. We've checked his tapes."

Very complex pause; Aaron winces, remembering the shadow waiting to enshroud Bruce. The near-suicide had been horrible.

"I see," Bruce says too casually. "Where do I turn myself in?"

"You don't. Somebody else saw Tighe, too. I'm checking them out next."

"Somebody else?" The fast brain snaps, the shadow is gone. "Once is accident, twice is coincidence." Bruce grins, ghost of Supersquirrel. "Three times is enemy action."

"Check around for me, will you, Bruce? I'm stuck here." Aaron doesn't believe in enemy action, but he believes in helping Bruce Jang.

"Right. Not exactly my game of course, but—right."

He goes out. The Man Without a Country. Over the years Bruce had attached himself to the Chinese scout team and in particular to Mei-Lin, their ecologist. He had confidently expected to be one of the two nonnationals Commander Kuh would, by agreement, take on the planet-seeking mission. It had nearly been a mortal blow when Kuh, being more deeply Chinese, had chosen Lory and the Aussie mineralogist.

The second Tighe-seer is now coming on Aaron's screen: Åhlstrom, their tall, blonde, more-or-less human computer chief. Before Aaron can greet her she says resentfully, "It is not right you should let him out."

"Where did you see him, Chief Åhlstrom?"

"In my Number Five unit."

"Did you speak to him? Did he touch anything?"

"Nah. He went. But he was there. He should not be."

"Tell me, please, did he look different in any way?"

"Different, yah," the tall woman says scornfully. "He has half no head."

"I mean, outside of his injury," says Aaron carefully, recalling that Åhlstrom's humor had once struck him as hearty.

"Nah."

"Chief Åhlstrom, Lieutenant Tighe was never out of this Isolation ward. We've verified his heart rate and respiration record. He was here the entire time."

"You let him out."

"No, we did not. He was here."

"Nah."

Aaron argues, expecting Åhlstrom's customary punch line: "Okay, I am stubborn Swede. You show me." Her stubbornness is a *Centaur* legend; during acceleration she had saved the mission by refusing to believe her own computers' ranging data until the hull sensors were rechecked for crystallization. But now she suddenly stands up as if gazing into a cold wind and says bleakly, "I could wish to go home. I am tired of this machine."

This is so unusual that Aaron can find nothing useful to say before she strides out. He worries briefly; if Åhlstrom needs help, he is going to have a job reaching that closed crag of a mind. But he is all the same relieved; both the people who "saw" Tighe seem to have been under some personal stress.

Hallucinating Tighe, he thinks; that's logical. Tighe stands for disaster. Appropriate anxiety symbol, surprising more people haven't cathected on him. Again he feels pride in *Centaur*'s people, so steady after ten years' deprivation of Earth, ten years of cramped living with death lying a skin of metal away. And now something more, that spark of alien life, sealed in *China Flower*'s hold, tethered out there. Lory's alien. It is now hanging, he feels, directly under the rear of his chair.

"Two more people waiting to see you, boss," says Coby's voice on the intercom. This also is mildly unusual, *Centaur* is a healthy ship. The Peruvian oceanographer comes in, shamefacedly confessing to insomnia. He is religiously opposed to drugs, but Aaron persuades him to try an alpha regulator. Next is Kawabata, the hydroponics chief. He is bothered by leg spasms. Aaron prescribes quinine, and Kawabata pauses to chat enthusiastically about the state of the embryo cultures he has been testing.

"Ninety percent viability after ten-year cryostasis," he grins. "We are ready for that planet. By the way, Doctor, is Lieutenant Tighe recovering so well? I see you are allowing him freedom."

Aaron is too startled to do more than mumble. The farm

chief cuts him off with an encomium on chickens, an animal Aaron loathes, and departs.

Shaken, Aaron goes to look at Tighe. The sensor lights outside his door indicate all pickups functioning: pulse regular, EEG normal if a trifle flat. He watches the alpha-scope break into a weak REM, resume again. The printouts themselves are outside. Aaron opens the door.

Tighe is lying on his side, showing his poignant Nordic profile, deep in drugged sleep. He doesn't look over twenty: rose-petal flush on the high cheekbones, a pale gold cowlick falling over his closed eyes. The prototype Beautiful Boy who lives forever with his white aviator's silk blowing in the wind of morning. As Aaron watches, Tighe stirs, flings up an arm with the IV taped to it, and shows his whole face, the long blond lashes still on his cheek.

It is now visible that Tighe is a thirty-year-old boy with an obscene dent where his left parietal arch should be. Three years back, Tiger Tighe had been their first—and so far, only—serious casualty. A stupid accident; he had returned safely from a difficult EVA and nearly been beheaded by a loose oxy tank while unsuiting in the free-fall shaft.

As if sensing Aaron's presence Tighe smiles heartbreakingly, his long lips still promising joy. The undamaged Tighe had been the focus of several homosexual friendships, a development provided for in *Centaur*'s program. Like so much else that has brought us through sane, Aaron reflects ruefully. He had never been one of Tighe's lovers. Too conscious of his own graceless, utilitarian body. Safer for him, the impersonal receptivity of Solange. Which was undoubtedly also in the program, Aaron thinks. Everything but Lory.

Tighe's mouth is working, trying to say something in his sleep.

"Hoo, huh." The speech circuits hunt across the wastelands of his ruined lobe. "Huhhh . . . Huh-home." His lashes lift, the sky-blue eyes find Aaron.

"It's all right, Tiger," Aaron lies, touches him comfortingly. Tighe makes saliva noises and fades back into sleep, his elegant gymnast's body turning a slow arabesque in the low gee. Aaron checks the catheters and goes.

The closed door opposite is Lory's. Aaron gives it a brotherly thump and looks in, conscious of the ceiling scanner. Lory is on the bunk reading. A nice, normal scene.

"Tomorrow at oh-nine-hundred," he tells her. "The wrap-up. You okay?"

"You should know." She grimaces cheerfully at the biomonitor pickups.

Aaron squints at her, unable to imagine how he can voice some cosmic, lifelong suspicion with that scanner overhead. He goes out to talk to Coby.

"Is there any conceivable chance that Tiger could have got to where an intercom screen could have picked him up?"

"Absolute negative. See for yourself," Coby says, loading tape spools into the Isolation pass-through. His eyes flick up at Aaron. "I didn't bugger them."

"Did I say that?" Aaron snaps. But he's guilty, they both know it; because it was Coby who was Frank Foy's other important case, five years back. Aaron had caught his fellow doctor making and dealing dream-drugs. Aaron sighs. A miserable business. There had been no question of "punishing" Coby, or anyone else on *Centaur*, for that matter; no one could be spared. And Coby is their top pathologist. If and when they get back to Earth he will face—who knows what? Meanwhile he has simply gone on with his job; it was then he had started calling Aaron "boss."

Now Aaron sees a new animation flickering behind Coby's clever-ape face. Of course—the planet. Never to go back. Good, Aaron thinks. He likes Coby, he relishes the unquenchable primate ingenuity of the man.

Coby is telling him that the Drive chief Gomulka has come in with a broken knuckle, refusing to see Aaron. Coby pauses, waiting for Aaron to get the implication. Aaron gets it, unhappily; a physical fight, the first in years.

"Who did he hit?"

"One of the Russkies, if I had to guess."

Aaron nods wearily, pulling in the tapes he has to check. "Where's Solange?"

"Over with Xenobiology, checking out what you'll need to analyze that thing. Oh, by the way, boss"—Coby gestures at the service roster posted on their wall—"you missed your turn on the shit detail. Last night was Common Areas. I got Nan to swap you for a Kitchen shift next week, maybe you can talk Berryman into giving us some real coffee."

Aaron grunts and takes the tapes back to Interview to start the comparator runs. It is a struggle to keep awake while the spools speed through the discrepancy analyzer, eliciting no reaction. His own and Lory's are all nominal, nominal, nominal, nominal-all variation within normative limits. Aaron goes out to the food dispenser, hoping that Solange will show. She doesn't. Reluctantly he returns to run Tighe's.

Here, finally, the discrepancy indicator stirs. After two hours of input the analyzer has summed a deviation bordering on significance; it hovers there as Aaron continues the run. Aaron is not surprised; it's the same set of deviations Tighe has shown all week, since his problematical contact with the alien. A slight, progressive flattening of vital function, most marked in the EEG. Always a little less theta. Assuming theta correlates with memory, Tighe is losing capacity to learn.

Aren't we all, Aaron thinks, wondering again what actually happened in Gamma corridor. The scout ship *China Flower* had been berthed there with the ports sealed, attended by a single guard. Boring duty, after two weeks of nothing. The guard had been down by the stern end having a cup of brew. When he turned around, Tighe was lying on the deck up by the scout's cargo hatch and the port was open. Tighe must have come out of the access ramp right by the port; he had been EVA team-leader before his accident, it was a natural place for him to wander to. Had he been opening or closing the lock when he collapsed? Had he gone inside and looked at the alien, had the thing given him some sort of shock? Nobody can know.

Aaron tells himself that in all likelihood Tighe had simply suffered a spontaneous cerebral seizure as he approached the lock. He hopes so. Whatever happened, Yellaston ordered the scout ship to be undocked and detached from *Centaur* on a tether. And Tighe's level of vitality is on the downward trend, day after day. Unorthodox, unless there is unregistered midbrain deterioration. Aaron can think of nothing to do about it. Maybe better so.

Bone-weary now, he packs up and forces himself to go attend to Tighe's necessities. Better say good-night to Lory, too.

She is still curled on her bunk like a kid, deep in a book. *Centaur* has real books in addition to the standard microfiches; an amenity.

"Finding some good stuff?"

She looks up, brightly, fondly. The scanner will show that

wholesome sisterly grin.

"Listen to this, Arn." She starts reading something convoluted; Aaron's ears adjust only in time to catch the last of it.

". . . *Grow upward, working out the beast, and let the ape and tiger die.* . . . It's very old, Arn. Tennyson." Her smile is private.

Aaron nods warily, acknowledging the earnest Victorian. He has had enough tiger and ape and he will not get drawn into another dialogue with Lory, not with that scanner going.

"Don't stay up all night."

"Oh, this rests me," she tells him happily. "It's an escape into truth. I used to read and read on the way back."

Aaron flinches at the thought of that solitary trip. Dear Lory, little madwoman.

"Night."

"Good night, dear Arn."

He gets himself into his bunk, grumbling old curses at *Centaur*'s selection board. Pedestrian clots, no intuition. Lory the non-sex-object, sure. Barring the fact that Lory's prepubescent body is capable of unhinging the occasional male with the notion that she contains some kind of latent sexual lightning, some secret supersensuality lurking like hot lava in the marrow of her narrow bones. In their years on Earth, Aaron had watched a series of such idiots breaking their balls in the attempt to penetrate to Lory's mythical marrow. Luckily none on *Centaur*, so far.

But that wasn't the main item the selection board missed. Aaron sighs, lying in the dark. He knows the secret lightning in Lory's bones. Not sex, would that it were. Her implacable innocence—what was the old phrase, *a fanatic heart*. A too-clear vision of good, a too-sure hatred of evil. No love lost, in between. Not much use for living people. Aaron sighs again, hearing the frightening condemnation in her unguarded voice. Has she changed? Probably not. Probably doesn't matter, he tells himself; how could it matter that chance has put Lory's head between us and whatever's on that planet? It's all a technical problem, air and water and bugs and so on.
. . .

Effortfully he pushes the thoughts away. I've been cooped up here twenty days with her and Tighe, he tells himself; I'm getting deprivation fantasies. As sleep claims him his last thought is of Captain Yellaston. The old man must be getting low on his supplies.

II

. . . Immensely tall, eternally noble, the woman paces through gray streaming clouds. In rituals of grief she moves, her heavy hair bound with dark jewels; she gestures to her head, her heart, a mourning queen pacing beside a leaden sea. Chained beasts move slowly at her heels, the tiger stepping with sad majesty, the ape mimicking her despair. She plucks the bindings from her hair in agony, it streams on the icy wind. She bends to loose the tiger, urging it to freedom. But the beast form wavers and swells, thins out; the tiger floats to ghostly life among the stars. The ape is crouching at her feet; she lays her long fingers on its head. It has turned to stone. The woman begins a death chant, breaking her bracelets one by one beside the sea. . . .

Aaron is awake now, his eyes streaming with grief. He hears his own throat gasping, *Uh—uhh—uhh,* a sound he hasn't made since—since his parents died, he remembers sharply. The pillow is soaked. What is it? What the hell is doing it? That was Lory's goddamn ape and tiger, he thinks. Stop it! Quit.

He stumbles up, finds it's the middle of the night, not morning. As he douses his face he is acutely aware of a direction underfoot, an invisible line leading down through the hull to the sealed-up scouter, to the alien inside. Lory's alien in there.

All right. Face it.

He sits on his bunk in the dark. Do you believe in alien telepathic powers, Dr. Kaye? Is that vegetable in there broadcasting on a human wavelength, sending out despair?

Possible, I suppose, Doctor. Anything—almost anything—is *possible.*

But the tissue samples, the photos. They showed no differentiated structure, no neural organization. No brain. It's a sessile plant-thing. Like a cauliflower, like a big lichen; like a bunch of big grapes, she said. All it does is metabolize and put out a little bioluminescence. Discrete cellular potentials *cannot* generate anything complex enough to trigger human emotions. Or can they? No, he decides. We can't do it ourselves, for god's sake. And it's not anything physical like subsonics, not with the vacuum between. And besides, if it is doing this, Lory couldn't possibly have got back here sane. Nearly a year of living ten feet away from a thing sending out nightmares? Not even Lory. It has to be me. I'm projecting.

Okay; it's me.

He lies down again, reminding himself that it's time he ran another general checkup. He should expand the free-association session, too; other people may be getting stress phenomena. Those Tighe-sightings . . . Last time he caught two incipient depressions. And he'll do all that part himself, people won't take it from Coby, he thinks, and catches himself in the fatuity. The fact is that people talk a lot more to Coby than they do to him. Maybe I have some of Lory's holy-holies. He grins, drifting off.

. . . *Tighe drifts in through the walls, curled in a fôetal clasp, his genital sac enormous. But it's a different Tighe. He's green, for one thing, Aaron sees. And vastly puffy, like a huge cauliflower or a cumulus cloud. Not frightening. Not anything, really; Aaron watches neutrally as cumulus-cloud-green Tighe swells, thins out, floats to ghostly life among the stars. One bulbous baby hand waves slowly, Ta-ta. . . .*

With a jolt Aaron discovers it really is morning. He lurches up, feeling vile. When he comes out, Solange is sitting at the desk beyond the vitrex; Aaron feels instantly better.

"Soli! Where the hell were you?"

"There are so many problems, Aaron." She frowns, a severe flower. "When you come out you will see. I am giving you no more supplies."

"Maybe I'm not coming out." Aaron draws his hot cup.

"Oh?" The flower registers disbelief, dismay. "Captain Yellaston said three weeks, the period is over and you are perfectly healthy."

"I don't feel so healthy, Soli."

"Don't you want to come out, Aaron?" Her dark eyes twinkle, her bosom radiates the shapes of holding and being held, she warms him through the vitrex. Aaron tries to radiate back. They have been lovers for five years now, he loves her very much in his low-sex-drive way.

"You know I do, Soli." He watches Coby come in with Aaron's printouts. "How'm I doing, Bill? Any sign of alien plague?"

Solange's face empathizes again: tender alarm. She's like a

play Aaron thinks. If a brontosaurus stubbed its toe, Soli would go *Oooh* in sympathy. Probably do the same at the Crucifixion, but he doesn't hold that against her. Only so much bandwidth for anybody; Soli is set low.

"Don't pick up a thing on visual, boss, except you're not sleeping too good."

"I know. Bad dreams. Too much excitement, buried bogies stirring up. When I get out, we're going to run another general checkup."

"When the doc gets symptoms he checks everybody else," Coby says cheerfully, the leer almost unnoticeable. He's happy, all right. "By the way, Tiger's awake. He just took a pee."

"Good. I'll see if I can bring him out to eat."

When Aaron goes in, he finds Tighe trying to sit up.

"Want to come out and eat, Tiger?" Aaron releases him from the tubes and electrodes, assists him outside to the dispenser. As Tighe sees Solange, his hand whips up in his old jaunty greeting. Eerie to see the well-practiced movements so swift and deft; for minutes the deficit is hidden. Quite normally he takes the server, begins to eat. But after a few mouthfuls a harsh noise erupts from his throat and the server falls, he stares at it tragically as Aaron retrieves it.

"Let me, Aaron, I have to come in." Solange is getting into her decontamination suit.

She brings in the new batch of tapes. Aaron goes down the hall to run them. The Interview room is normally their data processing unit. *Centaur's* builders really did a job, he muses while the spools spin nominal-nominal, as before. Adequate provision for quarantine, provision for every damn thing. Imagine it, a starship. I sit here in a ship among the stars. *Centaur*, the second one ever . . . *Pioneer* was the first, Aaron had been in third grade when *Pioneer* headed out for Barnard's star. He was in high school when the signal came back red: Nothing.

What circles Barnard's star, a rock? A gasball? He will never know, because *Pioneer* didn't make it back to structured-signal range. Aaron was an intern when they declared her lost. Her regular identity code had quit, and there was a new faint radio source in her direction. What happened? No telling . . . She was a much smaller, slower ship. *Centaur's* builders had redesigned on the basis of the reports from *Pioneer* while she was still in talking distance.

Aaron pulls his attention back to the tapes, automatically suppressing the thought of what will happen if *Centaur* too finds nothing after all. They have all trained themselves not to think about that, about the fact that Earth is in no shape to mount another mission if *Centaur* fails. Even if they could, where next? Nine light-years to Sirius? Hopeless. The energy and resources to build *Centaur* almost weren't there ten years ago. Maybe by now they've cannibalized the emigration hulls, Aaron's submind mutters. Even if we've found a planet, maybe it's too late, maybe nobody is waiting for our signal.

He snaps his subconscious to order, confirms that the tapes show nothing, barring his own nightmare-generated peaks. Lory's resting rates are a little up too, that's within bounds. Tighe's another fraction down since yesterday. Failing; why?

It's time to pack up. Lory and Solange are waiting to come in and hook up for the final debriefing, as Yellaston courteously calls it. Aaron goes around into the Observation cubicle and prepares to observe.

Frank Foy bustles first onto his screen to run his response-standardizing questions. He's still at it when Yellaston and the two scout commanders come in. Aaron is hating the scene again; he makes himself admit that Don and Tim are wearing decently neutral expressions. Space training, they must know all about bodily humiliation.

Foy finishes. Captain Yellaston starts the sealed recorder and logs in the event-date.

"Dr. Kaye," Foy leads off, "referring to your voyage back to this ship. The cargo module in which you transported the alien life-form had a viewing system linked to the command module in which you lived. It was found welded closed. Did you weld it?"

"Yes. I did."

"Why did you weld it? Please answer concisely."

"The shutter wasn't light-tight. It would have allowed my daily light cycle to affect the alien: I thought this might harm it, it seems to be very photosensitive. This is the most important biological specimen we've ever had. I had to take every precaution. The module was equipped to give it a twenty-two-hour circadian cycle with rheostatic graded changes, just like the planet—it has beautiful long evenings, you know."

Foy coughs reprovingly.

"You went to the length of welding it shut. Were you afraid

of the alien?"

"No!"

"I repeat, were you afraid of the alien?"

"No. I was not—well, yes, I guess I was, a little, in a sense. You see I was going to be alone all that time. I was sure the life-form is harmless, but I thought it might, oh, grow toward the light, or even become motile. There's a common myxomycetes—a fungus that has a motile phase, *Lycogala epidendron,* called Coral Beads. I just didn't know. And I was afraid its luminescent activity might keep me awake. I have a little difficulty sleeping."

"Then you do believe the alien may be dangerous?"

"No! I know now it didn't do a thing, you can check the records."

"May I remind you to control your verbalization, Dr. Kaye. Referring again to the fact that the cover was welded; were you afraid to look at the alien?"

"Of course not. No."

Young Frank really is an oddy, Aaron thinks; more imagination than I figured.

"Dr. Kaye, you state that the welding instrument was left on the planet. Why?"

"Commander Kuh needed it."

"And the scout ship's normal tool complement is also missing. Why?"

"They needed everything. If something went wrong I couldn't make repairs; it was no use to me."

"Please, Dr. Kaye."

"Sorry."

"Were you afraid to have a means of unsealing the alien on board?"

"No!"

"I repeat. Dr. Kaye, were you afraid to keep with you a tool by which you could unseal the port to the alien?"

"No."

"I repeat. Were you afraid to have a means of unsealing the alien?"

"No. That's silly."

Foy makes checks on his tapes; Aaron's liver doesn't need tapes, it has already registered that hyped-up candor. Oh, god—what is she lying about?

"Dr. Kaye, I repeat—" Foy starts doggedly, but Yellaston has lifted one hand. Foy puffs out his cheeks, switches tack.

"Dr. Kaye, will you explain again why you collected no computerized data after the first day of your stay on the planet?"

"We did collect data. A great deal of data. It went to the computer, but it didn't get stored because the dump cycle had cut in. Nobody thought of checking it, I mean that's not a normal malfunction. The material we lost, it's sickening. Mei-Lin and Liu did a whole ecogeologic streambed profile, all the biota, everything—"

She bites her lips like a kid, a flush rising around her freckles. After ten years in outer space Lory still has freckles. "Did you dump that data, Dr. Kaye?"

"*No!*"

"Please, Dr. Kaye. Now, I want to refresh your memory of the voice recording allegedly made by Commander Kuh." He flips switches; a voice says thinly: "Very . . . well, Dr. Ka-yee. You . . . will go."

It's Kuh's voice, all right; Aaron knows the audiograms match. But the human ear doesn't like it.

"Do you claim that Commander Kuh was in good health when he spoke those words?"

"Yes. He was tired, of course. We all were."

"Please restrict your answers, Dr. Kaye. I repeat. Was Commander Kuh in normal physical health other than fatigue when he made that recording?"

"*Yes.*"

Aaron closes his eyes. Lory, what have you done?

"I repeat. Was Commander Kuh in normal physical and mental—"

"Oh, *all right!*" Lory is shaking her head desperately. "Stop it! Please, I didn't want to say this, sir." She gazes blindly at the screen behind which Yellaston must be, takes a breath. "It's really very minor. There was—there was a difference of opinion. On the second day."

Yellaston lifts a warning finger at Foy. The two scout commanders are statues.

"Two members of the crew felt it was safe to remove their space suits," Lory swallows. "Commander Kuh—did not agree. But they did so anyway. And they didn't—they were reluctant to return to the scouter. They wanted to camp outside." She stares up in appeal. "You see, the planet is so pleasant and we'd been living in that ship so long."

Foy scents a rat, pounces.

"You mean that Commander Kuh removed his suit and became ill?"

"Oh, no! There was a—an argument," Lory says painfully. "He was, he sustained a bruise in the laryngeal area. That's why—" She slumps down in the chair, almost crying.

Yellaston is up, brushing Foy away from the speaker.

"Very understandable, Doctor," he says calmly. "I realize what a strain this report has been for you after your heroic effort in returning to base alone. Now we have, I think, a very full account—"

Foy is staring bewilderedly. He has started a rat all right, but it is the wrong, wrong rat. Aaron understands now. The supersensitive Chinese, the undesirability of internal dissension on the official log. Implications, implications. There was a fracas among Kuh's crew, and somebody wiped *China Flower*'s memory.

So that is Lory's secret. Aaron breathes out hard, euphoric with relief. So that's all it was!

Captain Yellaston, an old hand at implications, is going on smoothly. "I take it, Doctor, that the situation was quickly resolved by Commander Kuh's decision to commence colonization, and his confidence that you would convey his report to us for transmission to Earth, as in fact you have done?"

"Yes, sir," says Lory gratefully. She is still trembling; everyone knows that violence of any sort upsets Lory. "You see, even if something serious happened to me, the scout ship was on automatic after midpoint. It would have come through. You picked it up."

She doesn't mention that she was unconscious from ulcerative hemorrhage when *China Flower*'s signal came through the electronic hash from Centaurus's suns; it had taken Don and Tim a day to grapple and bring her in. Aaron looks at her with love. My little sister, the superwoman. Could I have done it? Don't ask.

He listens happily while Yellaston winds it up with a few harmless questions about the planet's moons and throws the screen open two-way to record a formal commendation for Lory. Foy is still blinking; the two scout commanders look like tickled tigers. Oh, that planet! They nod benevolently at Lory, glance at Yellaston as if willing him to fire the green signal out of the top of his head.

Yellaston is asking Aaron to confirm the medical clearance. Aaron confirms no discrepancies, and the quarantine is officially terminated. Solange starts unwiring Lory. As the command party goes out, Yellaston's eye flicks over Aaron with the expressionlessness he recognizes; the old man will expect him in his quarters that evening with the usual.

Aaron draws himself a hot drink, takes it into his cubicle to savor his relief. Lory really did a job there, he thinks. Whatever kind of dustup the Chinese had, it must have shocked her sick. She used to get hives when I played hockey, he remembers. But she's really grown up, she didn't spill the bloody details all over the log. Don't mess up the mission. That idiot Foy . . . You did that nicely, little sister, Aaron tells the image at the back of his mind. You're not usually so considerate of our imperfect undertakings.

The image remains unmoving, smiling enigmatically. Not usually so considerate of official sensibilities? Aaron frowns.

Correction: Lory has *never* been considerate of man's imperfection. Lory has *never* been diplomatic. If I hadn't sat on her head, Lory would be in an Adjustment Center with a burn in her cortex instead of on this ship. And she's been as prickly as a bastard with poor old Jan. Has a year alone in that scouter worked a miracle?

Aaron ponders queasily; he doesn't believe in miracles. Lory conscientiously lying to preserve the fragile unity of man? He shakes his head. Very unlikely. A point occurs unwelcomely; that story did save something. It saved her own credibility. Say the Chinese wrangle happened. Was Lory using it, letting Foy pry it out of her to account for those blips on the tape? To get herself—and something—through Francis Xavier Foy's PKG readouts? She had time to figure it, ample time—

Aaron shudders from neck to bladder and strides out of his cubicle to collide with Lory coming out of hers.

"Hi!" She has a plain little bag in her hand. Aaron realizes the scanners are still on overhead.

"Glad to be getting out?" he asks lamely.

"Oh, I didn't mind." She wrinkles her nose. "It was a rational precaution for the ship."

"You seem to have become more, ah, tolerant."

"Yes." She looks at him with what the scanner will show as

sisterly humor. "Do you know when Captain Yellaston plans to examine the specimen I brought back?"

"No. Soon, I guess."

"Good." The smiley look in her eye infuriates him. "I really brought it back for you, Arn. I wanted us to look at it together. Remember how we used to share our treasures, that summer on the island?"

Aaron mumbles something, walks numbly back to his room. His eyes are squeezed like a man kicked in the guts. Lory, little devil—how could you? Her thirteen-year-old body shimmers in his mind, sends helpless heat into his penile arteries. He is imprinted forever, he fears; the rose-tipped nipples on her child's chest, the naked mons, the flushed-pearl labia. The incredible sweetness, lost forever. He had been fifteen, he had ended both their virginities on a spruce island in the Fort Ogilvy Officers' Recreational Reserve the year before their parents died. He groans, wondering if he has lost both their souls, too, though he doesn't believe in souls. Oh, Lory . . . is it really his own lost youth he aches for?

He groans again, his cortex knowing she is up to some damn thing while his medulla croons that he loves her only and forever, and she him. Damn the selection board who had dismissed such incidents as insignificant, even healthy!

"Coming out, boss?" Coby's head comes in. "I'm opening up, right? This place needs a shake-out."

Aaron shakes himself out and goes out to check over Coby's office log. Lots of catching up to do. Later on when he is more composed he will visit Lory and shake some truth out of her.

He walks through the now-open vitrex, finds freedom invigorating. The office log reveals three more insomnia complaints, that's four in all. Alice Berryman, the Canadian nutrition chief, is constipated; Jan Ing, his Xenobiology colleague, has the trots. Quartermaster Miriamne Stein had a migraine. Van Wal, the Belgian chemist, has back spasm again. The Nigerian photolab chief has sore eyes, his Russian assistant has cracked a toe-bone. And there's Gomulka's knuckle. No sign of whomever he hit, unless he broke Pavel's toe. Unlikely . . . For *Centaur*, it's a long list; understandable, with the excitement.

Solange bustles in carrying a mess of Isolation biomonitors. "We have much work to do on these, Aaron. Tighe will stay where he is, no? I have left his pickups on." She still pronounces it "peekups."

Warmed, Aaron watches her coiling input leads. Surprising, the forcefulness some small women show. Such a seductive little person. He knows he shouldn't find it mysterious and charming that she is so capable with any kind of faulty circuit.

"Tighe's not doing too well, Soli. Maybe you or Bill can lead him around a bit, stimulate him. But don't leave him alone at any time. Not even for a minute."

"I know, Aaron." Her face has been flashing through her tender repertory while her hands wham the sensor boxes around. "I know. People are saying he is out."

"Yeah . . . You aren't getting any, oh, anxiety symptoms yourself, are you? Bad dreams, maybe?"

"Only of you." She twinkles, closing a cabinet emphatically, and comes over to lay her hand on the faulty circuits in Aaron's head. His arms go gratefully around her hips.

"Oh, Soli, I missed you."

"Ah, poor Aaron. But now we have the big meeting downstairs. Fifteen hundred, that is twenty minutes. And you must help me with Tighe."

"Right." Reluctantly he lets sweet comfort go.

By fifteen hundred he is in a state of tentative stability, going down-ramp to the main Commons Ring where gravity is Earth-normal. Commons is *Centaur*'s chief amenity, as her designers put it. It really is an amenity, too, Aaron thinks as he comes around a tubbed sweet-olive tree and looks out into the huge toroid space stretching all the way round the hull, fragrant with greenery from the Farm. Kawabata's people must have moved in a fresh lot.

The unaccustomed sounds of voices and music intimidate him slightly; he peers into the varied lights and shadows, finding people everywhere. He can see only a chord of the great ring, with its rising perspective at each end showing only leaning legs and feet beyond the farthest banks of plants. He hasn't seen so many people all here at once since Freefall Day, their annual holiday when *Centaur*'s roll is stopped and the floor viewports opened. And even the last few viewing days people tended to slip in and look alone.

Now they are all here together, talking animatedly. Moving around some sort of display. Aaron follows Miriamne Stein and finds himself looking at a bank of magnificent backlighted photos.

Lory's planet.

He has been shown a few small frames from *China Flower*'s cameras, but these blowups are overpowering. The planet seen from orbit—it looks like a flower-painted textile. Its terrain seems old, eroded to gentleness. The mountains or hills are capped with enormous gaudy rosettes, multiringed labyrinths ruffled in lemon-yellow, coral, emerald, gold, turquoise, bile-green, orange, lavender, scarlet—more colors than he can name. The alien vegetables or whatever. Beautiful! Aaron gapes, oblivious of shoulders touching him. Those "plants" must cover miles!

The next shots are from atmosphere, they show horizon and sky. The sky of Lory's planet is violet-blue, spangled with pearl-edged cirrus wisps. Another view shows altostratus over a clear silver-green expanse of sea or lake, reflecting cobalt veins—an enchanting effect. Everything exhales mildness; there is a view of an immense smooth white beach lapped by quiet water. Farther on, a misty mountain of flowers.

"Isn't it wonderful?" Alice Berryman murmurs in his general direction. She's flushed, breathing strongly; the medical fraction of Aaron's mind surmises that her constipation problem has passed.

They move on together, following the display which goes on and on across the Commons's normal hobby bays and alcoves. Aaron cannot get his fill of looking at the great vegetable forms, their fantastic color and variety. It is hard to grasp their size; here and there Photolab has drawn in scales and arrows pointing out what appear to be fruits or huge seed-clusters. No wonder Akin's crew has sore eyes and stubbed toes, Aaron thinks; a tremendous job. He goes around an aviary cage and finds a spectacular array of night-shots showing the "plants'" bioluminescence. Weird auroral colors, apparently flickering or changing continuously. What the nights must be like! Aaron peers at the dark sky, identifies the two small moons of Lory's planet. He really must stop calling it Lory's planet, he tells himself. It's Kuh's now if it's anybody's. Doubtless it will be given some dismal official name.

The mynah bird squawks, drawing his attention to another panel in the chess alcove: close-ups of the detached fruit-clusters or whatever they are, with infrared and high-frequency collations. It was one of these detached clusters that Lory brought back, along with samples of soil and water and so on.

Aaron studies the display; the "fruits" are slightly warm and a trifle above background radiation level. They luminesce, too. Not dormant. A logical choice, Aaron decides, momentarily aware that the thing is out there on a line with his shoulder. Is it menacing? Are you giving me bad dreams, vegetable? He stares probingly at the pictures. They don't look menacing.

Beyond the aquariums he comes upon the ground pictures taken before the computer was dumped. The official first-landing photo, almost life-size, showing everybody in suits and helmets beside *China Flower's* port. Behind them is that enormous flat beach and a far-off sea. Faces are almost invisible; Aaron makes out Lory in her blue suit. Beside her is the Australian girl, her gloved hand very close to that of Kuh's navigator, whose name is also Kuh; "little" Kuh is identifiable by his two-meter height. In front of the group is a flagstaff flying the United Nations flag. Ridiculous. Aaron feels his throat tighten. Ludicrous, wondrous. And the flag, he sees, is blowing. The planet has winds. Moving air, imagine!

He has been too fascinated to read the texts by each display, but now the word "wind" catches his attention. "Ten to forty knots," he reads. "Continuous during the period. We speculate that the dominant life-forms, being sessile, obtain at least some nourishment from the air constantly moving through their fringed 'foliage.' (See atmospheric analyses.) A number of types of airborne cells resembling gametes or pollen have been examined. Although the dominant plantlike forms apparently reproduce by broadcast methods, they may represent the culmination of a long evolutionary history. Over two hundred less-differentiated forms ranging in size from meters to a single cell have been tentatively identified. No self-motile life of any kind has been found."

Looking more closely at the picture, Aaron sees that the foreground is covered with a tapestry of lichenlike small growths and soft-looking tufts. The smaller forms. He moves on through to a series of photos showing the crew deploying vehicles out of *China Flower's* cargo port, and bumps into a ring of people around the end of the display.

"Look at that," somebody sighs. "Would you look at that." The group makes way, and Aaron sees what it is. The last photo, showing three suited figures—with their helmets off.

Aaron's eyes open wide, he feels his guts stir. There is Mei-Lin, her short hair blowing in the wind. Liu En-Do, his bare head turned away to look at a range of hills encrusted with the great flower-castles. And "little" Kuh, smiling broadly at the camera. Immediately behind them is a ridge which seems to be covered with vermilion lace-fronds bending to the breeze.

Air, free air! Aaron can almost feel that sweet wind, he longs to hurl himself into the viewer, to stride out across the meadows, up to the hills. A paradise. Was it just after this that the crew ripped off their foul space suits and refused to go back to the ship?

Who could blame them, Aaron thinks. Not he. God, they look happy! It's hard to remember when we lived, really lived. A corner of his mind remembers Bruce Jang, hopes he will not linger too long by that picture.

The crowd has carried him half around the toroid now; he is entering a wide section full of individual console seats that is normally the library. With the privacy partitions down it is used for their rare general assemblies. The rostrum is at the middle, where the speaker's whole figure will be most visible. It's empty. Beyond it is a screen projecting the star field ahead; year by year Aaron and his shipmates have watched the suns of Centaurus growing on that screen, separating to doubles and double-doubles. Now it shows only a single sun. The great blazing component of Alpha around which Lory's planet circles.

Several people are using the scanners while they wait. Aaron sits down beside a feminine back he recognizes as Lieutenant Pauli, Tim Bron's navigator. Her head is buried in the scanner hood. The title-panel on the console reads: GAMMA CENTAURUS MISSION. V, VERBAL REPORT BY DR. LORY KAYE, EXCERPTS FROM. That would be Lory's original narrative session, Aaron decides. Nothing about the "argument" there.

Pauli clicks off and folds down the scanner hood. When Aaron catches her eye she smiles dreamily, looking through him. Åhlstrom is sitting down just beyond; unbelievably, she's smiling, too. Aaron looks around sharply at the rows of faces, thinking I've been shut away three weeks, I haven't realized what the planet is doing to them. Them? He finds his own risor muscle is tight.

Captain Yellaston is moving to the speaker's stand, being stopped by questions, Aaron hasn't heard so much chatter in years. The hall seems to be growing hot with so many bodies bouncing around. He isn't used to crowds anymore, none of them are. And this is only sixty people. Dear god—*what if we have to go back to Earth?* The thought is horrible. He remembers their first year when there was another viewscreen showing the view astern: yellow Sol, shrinking, dwindling. That had been a rotten idea, soon abolished. What if the planet is somehow no good, is toxic or whatever—what if they have to turn around and spend ten years watching Sol expand again? Unbearable. It would finish him. Finish them all. Others must be thinking this too, he realizes. Doctor, you could have a problem. A big, big problem. But that planet *has* to be all right. It looks all right, it looks beautiful.

The hall is falling silent, ready for Yellaston. Aaron catches sight of Soli on the far side, Coby is by her with Tighe between them. And there's Lory by the other wall, sitting with Don and Tim. She's holding herself in a tight huddle, like a rape victim in court; probably agonized by her tapes being on the scanners. Aaron curses himself routinely for his sensitivity to her, realizes he has missed Yellaston's opening words.

". . . the hope which we may now entertain." Yellaston's voice is reticent but warm; it is also a rare sound on *Centaur*—the captain is no speechmaker. "I have a thought to share with you. Doubtless it has occurred to others, too. One of my occupations in the abundant leisure of our recent years"—pause for the ritual smiles—"has been the reading of the history of human exploration and migrations on our own planet. Most of the story is unrecorded, of course. But in the history of new colonies one fact appears again and again. That is that people have suffered appalling casualties when they attempted to move to a new habitation in even the more favorable areas of our own home world.

"For example, the attempts by Europeans to settle on the Northeast coast of America. The early Scandinavian colonies may have lasted a few generations before they vanished. The first English colony in fertile, temperate Virginia met disaster, and the survivors were recalled. The Plymouth colony succeeded in the end, but only because they were continuously resupplied. from Europe and helped by the original Indian inhabitants. The catastrophe that struck them interested me greatly.

"They came from northern Europe, from above fifty degrees north. Winters there are mild because the coast is warmed by the Gulf Stream, but this ocean current was not understood at that time. They sailed south by west, to what should have been a warmer land. Massachusetts was then covered by wild forests, like a park if we can imagine such a thing, and it was indeed warm summer when they landed. But when winter came it brought a fierce cold like nothing they had ever experienced, because that coast has no warming sea-current. A simple problem to us. But their technical knowledge had not foreseen it and their resources could not meet it. The effect of the bitter cold was compounded by disease and malnutrition. They suffered a fearful toll of lives. Consider: there were seventeen married women in that colony; of these, fifteen died the first winter."

Yellaston pauses, looking over their heads.

"Similar misfortunes befell numberless other colonies from unforeseen conditions of heat or drought or disease or predators. I am thinking also of the European settlers in my own New Zealand and in Australia and of the peoples who colonized the islands of the Pacific. The archaeological records of Earth are filled with instance after instance of peoples who arrived in an area and seemingly vanished away. What impresses me here is that these disasters occurred in places that we now regard as eminently favorable to human life. The people were moving to an only slightly different terrain of our familiar Earth, the Earth on which we have evolved. They were under our familiar sun, in our atmosphere and gravity and other geophysical conditions. They met only very small differences. And yet these small differences killed them."

He was looking directly at them now, his fine light greenish eyes moving unhurriedly from face to face.

"I believe we should remind ourselves of this history as we look at the splendid photographs of this new planet which Commander Kuh has sent back to us. It is not another corner of Earth nor an airless desert like Mars. It is the first totally alien living world that man has touched. We may have no more concept of its true nature and conditions than the British migrants had of an American winter.

"Commander Kuh and his people have bravely volunteered themselves to test its viability. We see them in these photographs apparently at ease and unharmed. But I would remind you that a year has passed since these pictures were made, a year during which they have had only the meager resources of their camp.

We hope and trust that they are alive and well today. But we must remember that unforeseeable hazards may have assailed them. They may be wounded, ill, in dire straits. I believe it is appropriate to hold this in mind. We here are safe and well, able to proceed with caution to the next step. They may not be."

Very nice, Aaron thinks. He has been watching faces, seeing here and there a lip quirked at the captain's little homily, but mostly expressions like his own. Moved and sobered. He's our pacemaker, as usual. And he's taken the edge off our envy of the *China* crew. Dire straits—wonderful old phrase. Are they really in dire straits, maybe? Yellaston is concluding a congratulatory remark for Lory. With a start, Aaron recalls his own suspicion of her, his conviction that she is hiding something. And ten minutes ago I was ready to rush out onto that planet, he chides himself. I'm losing balance, I have to stop these mood swings. A thought has been percolating in him, something about Kuh. It surfaces. Yes. Bruised larynxes croak or wheeze. But Kuh's weak voice had been clear. Should check on that.

People are moving away. Aaron moves with them, sees Lory over by the ramp, surrounded by a group. She's come out of her huddle, she's answering their questions. No use trying to talk to her now. He wanders back through the displays. They still look tempting, but Yellaston has broken the spell, at least for him. Are those happy people now lying dead on the bright ground, perhaps devoured, skeletons left? Aaron jumps; a voice is speaking in his ear.

"Dr. Kaye?"

It's Frank Foy, of all people.

"Doctor, I wanted to say—I hope you understand? My role, the distressing aspects. One sometimes has to perform duties that are most repugnant, as a medical man you too must have had similar –"

"No problem." Aaron collects himself. Why is Frank so embarrassing? "It was your job."

Foy looks at him emotionally. "I'm so glad you feel that way. Your sister—I mean, Dr. Lory Kaye—such an admirable person. It seems incredible a woman could make that trip all alone."

"Yeah . . . By the way, speaking of incredible, Frank, I know Lory's voice pretty well. I believe I was able to spot the points that were bothering you, in fact I'm inclined to share your—"

"Oh, not at all, Aaron," Foy cuts him off. "You need say no

more, I'm entirely satisfied. *Entirely.* Her explanation clears up every point." He ticks them off on his fingers. "The fate of the recording system, the absence of the welder and other tools, Commander Kuh's words, the question of injury—he *was* injured—the emotion about living on the planet. Dr. Kaye's revelation of the, ah, conflict dovetails perfectly."

Aaron has to admit that it does. Frank goes in for chess problems, he remembers; a weakness for elegant solutions.

"What about welding that alien in and being afraid to look at it? Between us, that thing gives me willies, too."

"Yes," Foy says soberly. "Yes, I fear I was giving in to my natural, well, is *xenophobia* the word? But we mustn't let it blind us. Undoubtedly Commander Kuh's people stripped that ship, Aaron. A dreadful experience for your sister, I felt no need to make her relive all that must have gone on. Among all those Chinese, poor girl."

When xenophobias collide . . . Aaron sees Foy isn't going to be much help, but he tries again.

"The business of the planet being ideal, a paradise and so on, that bothered me, too."

"Oh, I feel that Captain Yellaston put his finger on the answer there, Aaron. The excitement, the elation. I hadn't appreciated it. Now that I've seen these, I confess I feel it myself."

"Yeah." Aaron sighs. In addition to the elegant solution, Frank has received the Word. Captain Yellaston (who art in Heaven) has explained.

"Aaron, I confess I *hate* these things!" Foy says unexpectedly.

Aaron mumbles, thinking, possible, maybe he does. On the surface, anyway. With a peculiar smiling-through-tears look Foy goes on, "Your sister is such a wonderful person. Her strength is as the strength of ten, because her heart is pure."

"Yeah, well . . ." Suddenly the evening chow-call chimes out, saving him. Aaron bolts into the nearest passageway. Oh, no. Not Frank Foy. No ball-breaking here, though. Abelard and Héloïse, so pure. A perfect match, really . . . What would Frank say if he told him about Lory and himself? Hey, Frank, when we were kids I humped my little sister all over the Sixth Army District, she screwed like a mink in those days. On second thought, forget it, Aaron tells himself. He knows how Frank would react. "Oh." Long grave pause. "I'm terribly sorry, Aaron. For you." Maybe even in priestly tones, "Would it help

you to talk about it?" Etsanctimoniouscetera. A tough case, will
the real Frank Foy ever stand up? No. Lucky it doesn't interfere
with his being a damn good mathematician. Maybe it helps, for
all I know. Humans! . . . A good food-smell is in his nose, lifting
his mood. Chemoreceptors have pathways to the primitive
brain. Ahead are voices, music, lights.

Maybe Foy's right, Aaron muses. How about that? Lory's
story does dovetail. Am I getting weird? Sex fantasies about
Sis, I haven't had that trouble for years. It's being locked up
with her, Tighe, that alien—a big armful of Soli, that's what I
need. Solace, Soul-ass . . . Resolutely ignoring a sensation that
the alien is now straight overhead outside the hull, Aaron fills
a server and takes it over to a seat by Coby and Jan Ing, the
Xenobiology chief with whom he will be working tomorrow.
He's Lory's boss; Lory herself isn't here.

"Quite a crowd tonight."

"Yeah." In recent years more and more of *Centaur's* people
have been eating alone at odd hours, taking their food to their
rooms. Now there's a hubbub here. Aaron sees the Peruvian
oceanographer has a chart propped by his server, he's talking
to a circle of people with his mouth full, pointing. Miriamne
Stein and her two girl friends—*women* friends, Aaron corrects
himself—who usually eat together are sitting with Bruce
Jang and two men from Don's crew. EVA Chief George
Brokeshoulder has shaved a black black war-crest on his copper
scalp, he hasn't bothered to do that in years. Åhlstrom is over
there with Akin the Photo chief, for heaven's sake. The whole
tranquillized ship is coming to life, tiger-eyes opening, ape-
brains reaching. Even the neat sign which for so long has read,
THE CENTRAL PROBLEM OF OUR LIVES IS GARBAGE.
PLEASE CLEAN YOUR SERVERS, has been changed:
someone has taped over GARBAGE and lettered BEAUTY.

"Notice the treat we're getting, boss," says Coby munching.
"How did Alice get Kawabata to let loose some chicken? Oh,
oh—look."

The room falls silent as Alice Berryman holds up dessert—a
plate of real, whole peaches.

"One half for each person," she says severely. She is wearing
a live flower over her ear.

"People are becoming excited," the XB chief observes. "How
will it sustain itself for nearly two years?"

"*If* we go to that planet," Aaron mutters.

"I could make an amoral suggestion," Coby grins. "Tranks in the water supply."

Nobody laughs. "We've made out so far without, uh, chemical supplementation, as Frank would say," says Aaron. "I think we'll hold out."

"Oh, I know, I know. But don't say I didn't warn you it may come to that."

"About tomorrow," Jan Ing says. "The first thing we will get will be the biomonitor records from the personnel section of the scout ship, right? Before we proceed to open the cargo space?"

"That's the way I hear it."

"Immediately after opening the alien's module I plan to secure biopsy sections. Very minimal, of course. Dr. Kaye says she doesn't believe that will harm the alien. We're working on extension probes that can be manipulated from outside the hatch."

"The longer the better," Aaron says, imagining tentacles.

"Assuming the alien life-form is still alive. . . . " The XB chief taps out a silent theme, probably from Sibelius. "We'll know when we get our hands on the record."

"It should be." Aaron has been feeling the thing lying out beyond the buffet wall. "Tell me, Jan, do you ever have an impression that the thing is, well, *present?*"

"Oh, we're all conscious of that." Ing laughs. "Biggest event in scientific history, isn't that so? If only it is alive."

"You getting bad vibrations, boss? The dreams?" Coby inquires.

"Yeah." But Aaron can't go on, not with Coby's expression. "Yeah, I am. A xenophobe at heart."

They go into a discussion of the tissue-analyzing program and the type of bioscanners that will be placed inside the alien's module.

"What if that thing comes charging out into the corridor?" Coby interjects. "What if it's had kittens or split into a million little wigglers?"

"Well, we have the standard decontaminant aerosols," Jan frowns. "Captain Yellaston has emphasized the precautionary aspect. He will, I believe, be personally standing by the emergency vent control, which could very quickly depressurize the corridor in case of real emergency. This means we will be wearing suits. Awkward working."

"Good." Aaron bites the delicious peach, delighted to hear that old Yellaston's hand will be on the button. "Jan, I want a clear understanding that no part of that thing is taken into the ship. Beyond the corridor, I mean."

"Oh, I entirely agree. We'll have a complete satellite system there. Including mice. It will be crowded." He swabs his server with cellulose granules from the dispenser, frowning harder. "It would be unthinkable to harm the specimen."

"Yeah." Lory has still not come in, Aaron sees. Probably eating in her room after that mob scene. He joins the recycle line, noticing that the usual glumness of the routine seems to have evaporated. Even Coby omits his scatological joke. What are Kuh's people eating now, Aaron wonders, telepathic vegetable steaks?

Lory is quartered—naturally—in the all-female dorm on the opposite side of the ship. Aaron hikes up a spiral cross-ship ramp, as usual not quite enjoying the sharp onset of weightlessness as he comes to *Centaur*'s core. Her central core is a wide free-fall service shaft from bow to stern, much patronized by the more athletic members of the crew. Aaron kicks awkwardly across it, savoring the rich air. It comes from a green-and-blue radiance far away at the stern end—the Hydroponics Farm and the Hull Pool, their other chief amenity. He shudders slightly, recalling the horrible months when the air even here was foul and the passageways dark. Five years ago an antibiotic from somebody's intestinal tract had mutated instead of being broken down by passage through the reactor coolant system. When it reached the plant beds it behaved as a chlorophyll-binding quasi-virus and Kawabata had had to destroy seventy-five percent of the oxygenating beds. A terrible time, waiting with all oxygen-consuming devices shut down for the new seedlings to grow and prove clean. Brr . . . He starts "down" the exit ramp to Lory's dorm, past the cargo stores and service areas. People aren't allowed to live in less than three-quarters gee. Corridors branch out every few meters leading to other dorms and living units. *Centaur* is a warren of corridors, that's part of the program, too.

He comes to the tiny foyer or commons room outside the dorm proper and sees red hair beyond a bank of ferns: Lory—chewing on her supper, as he'd guessed. What he hadn't expected is the large form of Don Purcell, hunched opposite her deep in conversation.

Well, well! Mildly astounded, Aaron right-flanks into another passage and takes himself off toward his office, blessing *Centaur's* design. The people of *Pioneer* had suffered severely from the stress of too much social contact in every waking moment; the answer found for *Centaur* was not larger spaces but an abundance of alternative routes that allow her people to enjoy privacy in their comings and goings about the ship, as they would in a village. Two persons in a two-meter corridor must confront each other, but in two one-meter corridors each is alone and free to be his private self. It has worked well, Aaron thinks; he has noticed that over the years people have developed private "trails" through the ship. Kawabata, for instance, makes his long way from Farm to Messhall by a weird route through the cold sensor blister. He himself has a few. He grins, aware that his mind is demonstrating his total lack of irritation at finding Lory with another man.

In the clinic office Bruce Jang is chatting up Solange. When Aaron comes in, Bruce holds up five spread fingers meaningfully. Aaron blinks, finally remembers.

"Five more people think they've seen Tighe?"

"Five and a half. I'm the half. I only heard him this time."

"You heard Tighe's voice? What did he say?"

"He said good-bye. That's all right with me, you know?" Bruce shows his teeth.

"Bruce, does your five include Åhlstrom or Kawabata?"

"Kawabata, yes. Åhlstrom, no. Six then."

Solange is registering discovery, puzzlement. "Do these people understand they have not really seen him?"

"Kidua and Morelli, definitely no. Legerski is suspicious, he said Tighe looked weird. Kawabata—who knows? The oriental physiognomy, very opaque." Supersquirrel lives.

"I think it is good I brought him to the meeting," Solange says. "I had the hunch, so people will see he is around and not worry."

"Yeah, good." Aaron takes a breath. "I've been having nightmares lately, if it's of any interest. The last one featured Tighe. He said good-bye to me, too."

Bruce's eyes snap. "Oh? You're in Beta section. That's bad."

"Bad?"

"My five sightings had a common factor before you blew it. Everyone was in Gamma section, fairly near the hull, too. That was nice."

"Nice." Aaron knows at once what Bruce means: *China Flower*'s official name is *Gamma,* and the Gamma section is above her berth. But of course she isn't docked, now.

"Bruce, does that tether extend straight out? I'm no engineer. I mean, we're rotating; is she trailing?"

"Not much. A shallow tractrix. She already had our rotation when they ran her out."

"Then that alien is right under all the people who hallucinated Tighe."

"Yeah. All but you. We're in Beta here. And of course Åhlstrom is pretty far forward."

"But Tighe himself is here," says Solange. "In Beta with you."

"Yeah, but look," Aaron leans back. "Aren't we getting into witch-doctoring? There are other common factors. First, we've all been under stress for a long time and we're in a damn spooky place. Then along come two big jolts—the news about the planet and a genuine alien from outer space no one can look at. You've seen the ship, Bruce, people are lighted up like Christmas. Hope is a terrible thing, it brings fear that the hope won't be realized. Suppress the fear and it surfaces as symbol— and poor Tiger is our official disaster symbol, isn't he? Talk about common factors, it's a wonder we aren't all seeing green space-boogies."

Aaron is pleased to find he believes his own argument; it sounds very convincing. "Moreover, Tighe is linked with the alien now."

"If you say so, Doc," says Bruce lightly.

"Well, I do say so. I say there's sufficient cause to account for the phenomena. Occam's razor, the best explanation is that requiring fewer unsupported postulates, or whatever."

Bruce chuckles. "You're citing the law of parsimony, actually." He jumps up, turns to examine a telescoping metal rod on Solange's desk. "Don't forget, Aaron, old William ended up proving god loves us. I shall continue to count."

"Do that," Aaron grins.

Bruce comes close, says softly to Aaron alone, "What would you say if I told you I also saw . . . Mei-Lin?"

Aaron looks up wordlessly. Bruce lays the rod diagonally across Aaron's console. "I thought so," he says dryly and goes out.

Solange comes over to take the rod, her face automatically

tuned to the pity on his. Bruce hallucinating Mei-Lin? That fits, too. It doesn't upset Aaron's theory. "What's this for, Soli?"

"The extension for the section cutter," she tells him, striking a fencing pose. "It needs many wires, it will be a mess."

"Oh, Soli —" Aaron finally gets his arms around her, where they begin to feel alive at last. "Smart and beautiful, beautiful and smart. You're such a healthy person. What would I do without you?" He buries his unhealthy nose in her fragrant flesh.

"You would do your house calls," she tells him tenderly, her hips delicious in his hands.

"Oh, god. Do I have to, now?"

"Yes, Aaron. Now. Think how it will be nice, afterward."

Ruefully Aaron extricates himself, confirming the board's estimate of his drives. Getting out his kit, he recalls another duty and stuffs two liter flasks into the kit while Solange checks her file.

"Bustamente number one," she tells him. "I think he is very tense."

"I wish to god we could get him in here for an EKG."

"He will not come. You must do your best." She ticks off two more people Aaron would have visited during his weeks in quarantine. "And your sister, h'mm?"

"Yeah." Closing the kit, he wonders for the thousandth time if Solange knows about the flasks inside. And Coby? Christ, Coby has to know, he'd have been checking that distillation apparatus from Day One. Probably saving it for some blackmail scheme, who knows, Aaron thinks. Could I ever explain that I'm not doing what I damned him for? Or am I?

"Make the records nicely, please, Aaron."

"I will, Soli, I will. For you."

"Ha ha."

He wants poignantly to turn back, forces himself to trot up a ramp at random and discovers he is heading again toward Lory's dorm. Don must be long gone now, but still he reconnoiters the lounge area before going in. Lory's head—and good god, Don is still there! Aaron retreats, but not before he has seen that the shoulders actually belong to Timofaev Bron.

Feeling almost ludicrously dismayed, like a character in a bedroom farce, Aaron strides through the mixed-dorm commons, vaguely aware of the number of couples among the shadows. What the hell is Lory becoming, Miss *Centaur*? They have no right to bother Lory this way, he fumes, not with that ulcer still unhealed. Don't they know she needs rest? *I am the doctor.* . . . The inner voice comments that more than Lory's ulcers are unhealed; he disregards it. If Tim is not out of there in thirty minutes he will break it up, and—what?

Sheepishly, he admits his intention to, well, question her, although he cannot for the moment recall the urgency of what he had to ask. Well, confession is good for ulcers, too.

The next turnoff leads to the quarters of his first patient, a member of Tim Bron's crew who came back to *Centaur* in full depressive retreat. Aaron has worked hard over him, prides himself on having involved the man in a set of correspondence chess games which he plays in solitary, never leaving his room. Now he finds the privacy-lock open, the room empty. Has Igor gone to Commons? His chess book is gone. Another point for the planet, Aaron decides, and goes cheerfully on to André Bachi's room.

Bachi is out of bed, his slender Latin face looking almost like its old self despite the ugly heaviness of glomerule dysfunction.

"To think I will live to see it," he tells Aaron. "Look, I have here the actual water, Jan sent it to me. Virgin water, Aaron. The water of a world, never passed through our bodies. Maybe it will cure me."

"Why not?" The man's intensity is heartbreaking; can he live two years, assuming they do go to Lory's world? Maybe . . . Bachi is the board's only failure so far. Merhan-Briggs syndrome, exceedingly rare, Coby's brilliant diagnosis.

"With this I can die happy, Aaron," Bachi says. "My god, for an organic chemist to experience this!"

"Is there life in it?" Aaron gestures at Bachi's scanning scope.

"Oh, yes. Fantastic. So like, so unlike. Ten lifetimes' work. I have only two mounts made yet; I am slow."

"I'll leave you to it." Aaron puts Bachi's urine and saliva vials in his kit.

When he comes out he will not turn back toward Lory; instead he takes a midship passage toward the bridge. *Centaur's* bridge is in her big, shielded nose-module, which is theoretically capable of sustaining them all in an emergency. Theoretically; Aaron does not believe that most of his fellow crewmen could bear to pack themselves into it now, merely to survive. Up here is most of their important hardware, Åhlstrom's computers, astrogation gear, backup generators, and the gyros and laser system, which are their only link with Earth. Yellaston, Don, and Tim have quarters just aft of the bridge command room. Aaron turns off before Computers at a complex of panels giving access to *Centaur's* circuitry and stops under the door-eye of *Centaur's* Communications chief. There is no visible call-plate.

Nothing happens—and then the wall beside his knee utters a grating cough. Aaron jumps.

"Enter, Doc, enter," says Bustamente's bass voice.

The door slides open. Aaron goes warily into a maze of low music and shifting light-forms in which six or seven big black men in various perspectives are watching him.

"I'm working on something in your field, Doc. Comparing startle stimuli. Nonlinear, low decibels give a bigger jump."

"Interesting." Aaron advances gingerly through unreal dimensions; visiting Ray Bustamente is always an experience. "Which one is you?"

"Over here." Aaron strikes some kind of mirrored surface and makes his way around it to comparative normality. Bustamente is on his lounger in a pose of slightly spurious relaxation.

"Roll up that sleeve, Ray. We have to do this, you know that."

Bustamente complies, grumbling. Aaron winds on the cuff, admiring the immense biceps. No fat on the triceps, either; maybe the big man really does pay some heed to his advice. Aaron watches his digital readout swing, relishing his feelings for Ray, what he thinks of as Ray's secret. The man is another rarity, a natural-born king. The real living original of which Yellaston is only the abstraction. Not a team-leader like Don or Tim. The archaic model, the Boss, Jefe, Honcho, whatever—the alpha human male who outfights you, outdrinks you, outroars you, outsmarts you, kills your enemies, begets his bastards on your woman, cares for you as his property, tells you what to do—and you do it. The primordial Big Man who organized the race and for whom the race has so little more use. Ten years ago it hadn't been visible; ten years ago there was a tall, quiet young Afro-American naval electronics officer with impeccable degrees and the ability to tune a Mannheim circuit in boxing gloves. That was before the shoulders thickened and the browridges grew heavy over the watchful eyes.

"I really wish you'd come by the clinic, Ray," Aaron tells him, unwinding the cuff. "This thing isn't a precision instrument."

"What the hell can you do if you don't like my sound? Give me a stupid-pill?"

"Maybe."

"I'm making that planet, you know, Doc. Dead or alive."

"You will." Aaron puts his instruments away, admiring Bustamente's solution to his problem. What does a king do, born into a termite world, barred even from the thrones of termites? Ray had seen the scene, spotted his one crazy chance. And his decision has brought him twenty trillion miles from the termite heap, headed for a virgin planet. A planet with room, maybe, for kings.

A girl-shape is wavering among the mirrors, suddenly materializes into Melanie, the little white-mouse air-plant tech. She has an odd utensil in her hand. Aaron identifies it as a food-cooking device.

"We're working on a few primitive arts," Bustamente grins. "What's it going to be tonight, Mela?"

"A tuber," she says seriously, pushing back her ash-pale hair. "It's sweet but not much protein, it would have to be combined with fish or meat. You'll get fat." She nods impersonally at Aaron, goes back behind the screens.

"She's mine, you know." Bustamente stretches, one eye on Aaron. "Is that air as good as it looks? Ask your sister if it *smells* good, will you?"

"I'll ask her when I drop by tonight."

"Lot of dropping by recently." Bustamente suddenly flicks a switch, and a screen Aaron hadn't noticed comes to life. It's an overhead shot of the Communications office. The gyro chamber beyond is empty. Bustamente grunts, rolls his switch; the view flips to the bridge corridor, flip-flip-flips to others he can't identify. No people in sight. Aaron goggles; the extent of Bustamente's electronic surveillance network is one of *Centaur*'s standing myths. Not so mythical, it seems; Ray really has been weaving in *Centaur*'s walls. Oddly, Aaron doesn't resent it.

"Tim dropped by the shop today. Just looking to talk, he said." Bustamente flips back to the gyro chamber, zooms in on the locked laser-console. There is a definitely menacing flavor to the show; Aaron recalls with pleasure the time Frank

Foy tried to set a scanner on Coby without clearing with the Commo chief.

As if reading his thought, Bustamente chuckles. "To quote the words of an ancient heavyweight boxing champion, George Foreman, *'Many a million has fall and stumble when he meet Big George in that ol' black jungle. . . .'* Plans to make, you know, Aaron? Melanie, that's one. She's tougher than she looks, but she's kind of puny. Need some muscle. That big old Daniela, she's my number two. Marine biology, she knows fish."

He flicks another image on the screen. Aaron gets a flash of a strong female back, apparently in the Commons game-bay.

"You're selecting your, your prospective family?" Aaron is charmed by the big man's grab at the guts of life. A king, all right.

"I don't plan to hang in too close, you know, Doc." His eye is on Aaron. "Should have medical capability. You'll be sticking with the others, right? So I figure number three is Solange."

"Soli?" Aaron stares, forces himself to hold his own grin. "But have you, I mean what does she—Ray, we're nearly two years away, we may not even—"

"Don't worry about that, Doc. Just thought I'd warn you. You can use the time to teach Soli what to do when the babies come."

"Babies." Aaron reels mentally; the word hasn't been heard on *Centaur* for years.

"Maybe time you did a little planning yourself. Never too soon, you know."

"Good thought, Ray." Aaron makes his way out through the light-show jungle, hoping his smile expresses professional cheer rather than the sickly grin of one whose mate has just been appropriated by The Man. Soli! Oh, Soli, my only joy . . . but there's years yet, nearly two years, he tells himself. Surely he can think of something. Or can he?

A ridiculous vision of himself fighting Bustamente in a field of giant cauliflowers floats through his mind. But the woman they're fighting for isn't Solange, Aaron realizes. It's Lory.

Shaking his head at his subconscious, Aaron goes on up to the command corridor, taps the viewplate at Captain Yellaston's door. He feels a renewed appreciation for the more abstract forms of leadership.

"Come in, Aaron." Yellaston is at his console, filing his nails. His eyes don't flicker; Aaron has never been able to catch him checking on his loaded kit. The old bastard knows.

"That speech was a good idea, sir," Aaron says formally.

"For the time being." Yellaston smiles—a surprisingly warm, almost maternal smile on the worn Caucasian face. He puts the file away. "There's a point or two we should discuss, Aaron, if you're not too pressed."

Aaron sits, noting that Yellaston's faint maxillary tic has surfaced again. The only indicator he has ever given of the solitary self-combat locked in there; Yellaston has an inhuman ability to function despite what must be extensive CNS toxicity. Aaron will never forget the day *Centaur* officially passed beyond Pluto's orbit; that night Yellaston had summoned him and announced without preamble, "Doctor, I am accustomed to taking an average of six ounces of alcohol nightly. I have done so all my life. For this trip I shall reduce it to four. You will provide them." Staggered, Aaron had asked him how he had come through the selection year? "Without." Yellaston's face had sagged then, his eyes had frightened Aaron. "If you care for the mission, Doctor, you will do as I say." Against every tenet of his training, Aaron had. Why? He has wondered that many times. He knows all the conventional names for the demons the old man must poison nightly. Hidden ragings and cravings and panics, all to be exorcised thusly. His business is those names—but the fact is that Aaron suspects the true name of Yellaston's demon is something different. Something inherent in life itself, time or evil maybe, for which he has no cure. He sees Yellaston as a complicated fortress surviving by strange rituals. Perhaps the demon is dead now, the fort empty. But he has never dared to risk inquiring.

"Your sister is a very brave girl." Yellaston's voice is extrawarm.

"Yes, incredible."

"I want to be sure you know that I appreciate the full extent of Dr. Kaye's heroism. The record will so show. I am recommending her for the Legion of Space."

"Thank you, sir." Glumly Aaron acknowledges Yellaston's membership in the Love Lory Club. Suddenly he wonders, Is this the start of one of Yellaston's breaks? It has only happened a few times, the giving-way of the iron man's defenses, but it has caused Aaron much grief. The first was when they were about two years out, Yellaston began chatting with young Alice Berryman. The chats became increasingly intense. Alice was star-eyed. So far nothing wrong, only puzzling. Alice told Miriamne that he spoke of strange strategic and philosophical principles that she found hard to grasp. The culmination came when Aaron found her weeping before breakfast and hauled her to his office to let the story out. He had been dismayed. Not sex—worse. A night of incoherent, unstoppable talk, ending in maudlin childhood. "How can he be so, so *silly*—?" All stars gone, traumatic disgust. Daddy is dead. Aaron had tried to explain to her the working of a very senior, idiosyncratic old primate; hopeless. He had given up and shamelessly narco-twisted her memory, made her believe it was she who had been drunk. For the good of the mission . . . After that he had kept watch. There were three more, periodicity about two years. The poor bastard, Aaron thinks; childhood must have been the last time he was free. Before the battle began. So far Yellaston has never used him for release. Perhaps he values his bootlegger; more likely, Aaron has decided, he is simply too old. Is that about to change?

"Her courage and her accomplishment will be an inspiration."

Aaron nods again, warily.

"I wanted to be sure you understand I have full confidence in your sister's report."

She snowed him, Aaron thinks dismally. Oh, Lory. Then he catches the tension in the pause and looks up. Is this leading somewhere?

"There is too much at stake here, Aaron."

"That's right, sir," says Aaron with infinite relief. "That's what I feel, too."

"Without in any way subtracting from your sister's achievement, it is simply too much to risk on anyone's unsupported word. Anyone's. We have no objective data on the fate of the Gamma crew. Therefore, I shall continue to send code yellow, not code green, until we arrive at the planet and confirm."

"Thank god," says Aaron the atheist.

Yellaston looks at him curiously. It's the moment for Aaron to speak about the Tighe-sightings, the dreams, to confess his fears of Lory and alien telepathic vegetables. But there's no need now, Yellaston wasn't snowed, it was just his weird courtesy.

"I mean, I do agree. . . . Does this mean we're going to

the planet, that is, you've decided before we check out that specimen?"

"Yes. Regardless of what we find, there is no alternative. Which brings up this point." Yellaston pauses. "My decision with respect to the signal may not be entirely popular. Although two years is a very short time."

"Two years is an eternity, sir." Aaron thinks of the flushed faces, the voices; he thinks of Bustamente.

"I realize it may seem so to some. I wish it could be shortened. *Centaur* does not have the acceleration of the scouters. More pertinently, Aaron, some crew members may also feel that we owe it to the home world to let them know as soon as possible. The situation there must be increasingly acute."

They are both silent for a moment, in deference to the acuteness of Earth's "situation."

"If *Centaur* were to have an accident before we verify the planet, this could deprive Earth of knowledge of the planet's existence, perhaps forever. The fear of such a catastrophe will weigh heavily with some. On the other hand, we have had no major malfunctions and no reason to think we shall. We are proceeding as planned. The most abysmal error we could make would be to send the green code now and then discover, after the ships have been irreversibly launched, that the planet is uninhabitable. Those ships cannot turn back."

Aaron perceives that Yellaston is using him to try out pieces of his formal announcement; a bootlegger has many uses. But why not his logical advisers, his execs, Don and Tim? Oh, oh. Aaron begins to suspect who "some" people may include.

"We would doom all the people in the pipeline. Worse, we would end forever any hope of a new emigration effort. Our hastiness would be criminal. Earth has trusted us. We must not risk betraying her."

"Amen."

Yellaston broods a moment, suddenly gets up and goes over to his cabinet wall. Aaron hears a gurgle. The old man must have saved his last one until relief arrived.

"Goddamn it." Yellaston suddenly sets a flask down hard. "We never should have had women on this mission."

Aaron grins involuntarily, thinking, there speaks the dead dick. Thinking also of Soli, of Åhlstrom, of all the female competences on *Centaur*, of the debates on female command that had yielded finally to the policy of minimal innovation on a mission where so much else would be new. But he knows exactly what Yellaston means.

Yellaston turns around, letting Aaron see his glass; an unusual intimacy. "Going to be a bitch, Doctor. These two will be the toughest we've had to face. Two years. The fact that we're going to the planet ourselves will suffice for most, I think." He massages his knuckles again. "It might not be a bad idea for you to keep your eyes and ears rather carefully open, Aaron, during the time ahead."

Implications, implications. Doctors, like bootleggers, have their uses, too.

"I believe I see what you mean, sir."

Yellaston nods. "On a continuing basis," he says authoritatively. He and Aaron exchange regards in which is implicit their mutual view of the relevance of Francis Xavier Foy.

"I'll do my best," Aaron promises; he has recalled his general checkup plan, maybe he can use that projective-recall session to spot trouble.

"Good. Now, tomorrow we examine that specimen. I'd like to hear your plans." Yellaston comes back, glassless, to his console, and Aaron gives him a rundown on his arrangements with the Xenobiology chief.

"All the initial work will take place in situ, right?" Aaron concludes, conscious that the alien's situ is now directly to his left. "Nothing goes into the ship?"

"Right."

"I'd like to have authority to enforce that. And guards on the corridor entrances, too."

"The authority is yours, Doctor. You'll have the guards."

"That's fine." Aaron rubs his neck. "There've been a couple of, oh, call them psychological reactions to the alien I'm looking into. Nothing serious, I think. For instance, have you experienced an impression of localization, about the alien, I mean? A sense of where the thing is, physically?"

Yellaston chuckles. "Why yes, as a matter of fact I do. Right north, over there." He points high toward Aaron's right. "Is that significant, Doctor?"

Aaron grins in relief. "Yeah, it is to me. It signifies that my personal orientation still isn't any good after ten years." He picks up his kit, moves over to Yellaston's cabinets. "I thought the thing was down under your bunk." Unobtrusively he substitutes the full flasks, noting that that drink had been indeed the old man's last.

"Give your sister my personal regards, Aaron. And don't forget."

"I'll remember, Captain."

Obscurely moved, Aaron goes out. He knows he must do some serious thinking; if Don or Tim decide to kick up, what the hell can Dr. Aaron Kaye do about it? But he is euphoric. The old man isn't buying Lory's story blind, he isn't going to rush it. Daddy will save us from the giant cauliflowers. I better get some exercise, he thinks, and trots down-ramp to one of the long outer corridors on the hull. There are six of these bow-stern blisters; they form the berths that hold the three big scout ships. Gravity is strong down here, slightly above Earth-normal, and people use the long tubes for games and exercise—another good program-element, Aaron thinks approvingly. He comes out into Corridor Beta, named for Don Purcell's scouter. *Beta* has long been known as the *Beast*, as in Beast-of-Fascist-Imperialism, a joke of *Centaur*'s early years when Tim's *Alpha* was likewise christened the *Atheist Bastard*. Kuh's *Gamma* became only *China Flower*—the flower which is now hanging on her stem with her cryptic freight.

This corridor is identical to Gamma where the alien will be examined tomorrow. Aaron strides along effortfully savoring the gee-loading, counting access portals which will need guards. There are fourteen, more than he had thought. Ramps lead down here from all over the ship—the scouters were designed as lifeboats, too. The corridor is so long the far end is hazy. He fancies he can feel a chill on his soles. Imagine, he is in a starship! A fly walking the wall of a rotating can in cosmic space: *There are suns beneath my feet.*

He remembers the scenes of ceremony that had taken place in these corridors three years back, when the scout ships were launched to reconnoiter the suns of Centaurus. And the sad returns four months ago when first Don and then Tim had come back bearing news of nothing but methane and rock. Will the *Beast* and the *Bastard* soon be ferrying us down to Lory's planet?—I mean in two years, and it's Kuh's planet, Aaron corrects himself, so preoccupied that he bumps blindly into the rear of Don Purcell, backing out of Beta's command lock.

"Getting ready to land us, Don?"

Don only grins, the all-purpose calm grin that Aaron

believes he would wear if he were going down in flames. Tough
to get behind a grin like that if Don really was, well, disaffected.
He doesn't look mutinous, Aaron thinks. Hard to imagine
him leading an assault on Ray's gyros. He looks like an order
man, a good jock. Like Tim. Kuh was the same breed, too,
transistorized. The genotype that got us here, the heavy-duty
transport of the race.

Aaron ducks into the ramp that leads to Lory's quarters,
imagining Don and the scout ships and them all superimposed
on that planet, that mellow flowery world. Pouring out to make
a new Earth. Will they find Kuh's colony, or silent bones? But
the freedom, the building . . . and then, then will come the fleet
from Earth. Fifteen years, that's what we'll have, Aaron thinks,
assuming we send the green signal when we land. Fifteen
years. And then the emigration ships will start coming in,
the—what was it Yellaston called it—the pipeline. Typical anal
imagery. The pipeline spewing Earth's crap across the light-
years. Technicians first, of course, basic machinery, agriculture.
Pioneer-type colonists. And then pretty soon people-type
people, administrators, families, politicians—whole industries
and nations all whirling down that pipeline onto the virgin
world. Covering it, spreading out. What of Bustamente, then?
What of himself and Lory?

He is by Lory's door now, the lounge is empty at last.

When she opens it Aaron is pleased to see she's doing
nothing more enigmatic than brushing her hair; the same old
hygienic black bristles pulling through the coppery curls which
are now just frosted gray, nice effect, really. She beckons him
in, brushing steadily; counting, he guesses.

"Captain sends you his personal regards." As he sits it
occurs to him that Foy may have bugged her room. No visuals,
though. Not Foy.

"Thank you, Arn . . . seventy . . . Your personal regards,
too?"

"Mine too. You must be tired, I notice you had company.
Tried to look in earlier."

"Seventy-five . . . Everybody wants to hear about it, it means
so much to them."

"Yeah. By the way, I admired your tactfulness about our
battling Chinese. I didn't know you had it in you, Sis."

She brushes harder. "I didn't want to *spoil* it. They—they
stopped all that, anyway. There." She lays the brush down,

smiles. "It's such a peaceful place, Arn. I think we could really live a new way there. Without violence and hatred and greed. Oh, I know how you—but that's the feeling it gave me, anyway."

The light tone doesn't fool him. Lory, lost child of paradise striving ever to return. That look in her eye, you could cast her as the young Jeanne, reminding the Dauphin of the Holy Cause. Aaron has always had a guilty sympathy for the Dauphin.

"There'll always be some bad stuff as long as you have people, Lor. People aren't all that rotten. Look at us here."

"Here? You look, Arn. Sixty handpicked indoctrinated specimens. Are we really good? Are we even gentle with each other? I can feel the—the savagery underneath, just waiting to break loose. Why, there was a *fight* yesterday. Here."

How does she hear these things?

"It's a hell of a strain, Lor. We're human beings."

"Human beings must change."

"Goddamn it, we don't have to change. Basically, I mean," he adds guiltily. Why does she do this to him? She makes me defend what I hate, too. She's right, really, but, but—"You might try caring a little for people as they are—it's been recommended," he says angrily and hates the unctuousness in his voice.

She sighs, straightens the few oddments on her stand. Her room looks like a cell. "Why do we use the word *human* for the animal part of us, Arn? Aggression—that's human. Cruelty, hatred, greed—that's human. That's just what *isn't* human, Arn. It's so sad. To be truly human we must leave all that behind. Why can't we try?"

"We do, Lor. We do."

"You'd make this new world into another hell like Earth."

He can only sigh, acknowledging her words, remembering too the horrible time after their parents died, when Lory was sixteen. . . . Their father had been Lieutenant-General Kaye, they had grown up sheltered, achievement-oriented in the Army enclaves' excellent schools. Lory had been into her biology program when the accident orphaned them. Suddenly she had looked up and seen the world outside—and the next thing Aaron knew he was hauling her out of a Cleveland detention center in the middle of the night. The ghetto command post had recognized her Army ID plate.

"Oh, Arn," she had wept to him in the copter going home.

"It isn't right! it isn't *right.*" Her face was blotched and raw where the gas had caught her, he couldn't bear to look.

"Lor, this is too big for you. I know it isn't right. But this is not like setting up a dog shelter on Ogilvy Island. Don't you understand you can get your brains cut?"

"That's what I mean, they're doing obscene things to people. It isn't *right.*"

"You can't fix it," he'd snapped at her in pain. "Politics is the art of the possible. This isn't possible, you'll only get killed."

"How do we know what's possible unless we try?"

Oh, god, that next year. Their father's name had helped some, luck had helped more. In the end what probably saved her was her own implacable innocence. He had finally tracked her down in the back shed of a mortuary in the old barrio section of Dallas; emaciated, trembling, barely able to speak.

"Arn, oh—they—" she whimpered while he wiped vomit off her chin, "Dave refused to help Vicky, he—he wants him to get caught. . . . So he can be leader. . . . He won't let us help him."

"I think that happens, Lor." He held her thin shoulders, trying to stop the shaking. "That does happen, people are human."

"No!" She jerked away fiercely. "It's terrible. It's terrible. They—*we* were fighting among ourselves, Arn. Fighting over *power.* Dave even wants his woman, I think—they hit each other. She, she was just property."

She heaved up the rest of the soup he'd brought her.

"When I said that they threw me out."

Aaron held her helplessly, thinking, her new friends can't live up to her any more than I can. Thank god.

"Arn," she whispered. "Vicky . . . *he took some money.* I know
. . . ."

"Lor, come on home now. I fixed it, you can still take your exams if you come back now."

". . . All right."

Aaron shakes his head, sitting in *Centaur* twenty trillion miles from Dallas, looking at that same fierce vision on the face of his little sister now going gray. His little sister whom chance has made their sole link with that planet, that thing out there.

"All right, Lor." He gets up, turns her around to face him. "I know you. What the hell happened on that planet? What are you covering?"

"Why, nothing, Arn. Except what I told you. What's the

matter with you?"

Is it too innocent? He distrusts everything, cannot tell.

"Please let go of me."

Conscious of Foy's problematical ears he lets go, steps back. This would sound crazy.

"Do you realize this isn't games, Lor? Our lives are depending on it. Real people's lives, much as you hate humanity. You better not be playing."

"I don't hate humanity, I just hate some of the things people do. I wouldn't *hurt* people, Arn."

"You'd liquidate ninety percent of the race to achieve your utopia."

"What a terrible thing to say!"

Her face is all soul, he aches for her. But Torquemada was trying to help people, too.

"Lor, give me your word that Kuh and his people are absolutely okay. Your faithful word."

"They *are*, Arn. I give you my word. They're beautiful."

"The hell with beauty. Are they physically okay?"

"Of course they are."

Her eyes still have that look, but he can't think of anything else to try. Praise be for Yellaston's caution.

She reaches out for him, thin electric hand burning his. "You'll see, Arn. Isn't it wonderful, we'll be together? That's what kept me going, all the way back. I'll be there tomorrow when we look at it."

"Oh, no!"

"Jan Ing wants me. You said I'm medically fit. I'm his chief botanist, remember?" She smiles mischievously.

"I don't think you should, Lor. Your ulcers."

"Waiting around would be much worse for them." She sobers, grips his arm. "Captain Yellaston—he's going to send the green, isn't he?"

"Ask him yourself. I'm only the doctor."

"How sad. Oh, well, he'll see. You'll all see." She pats his arm, turns away.

"*What'*ll we see?"

"How harmless it is, of course. . . . Listen, Arn. This is from some ancient work, the martyr Robert Kennedy quoted it before he was killed. 'To tame the savage heart of man, to make gentle the life of this world' . . . Isn't that fine?"

"Yeah, that's fine, Lor."

He goes away less than comforted, thinking, the life of this world is not gentle, Lory. It wasn't gentleness that got you out here. It was the drives of ungentle, desperate, glory-hunting human apes. The fallible humanity you somehow can't see. . . .

He finds he has taken a path through the main Commons. Under the displays the nightly bridge and poker games are in session as usual, but neither Don nor Tim is visible. As he goes out of earshot he hears the Israeli physicist ante what sounds like an island. An island? He climbs up toward the clinic, hoping he heard wrong.

Solange is waiting for him with the medical log. He recites Ray and Bachi's data with his head leaning against her warm front, remembering he has another problem. Forget it, he tells himself, I have two years to worry about Bustamente.

"Soli, tomorrow I want to rig up an array of decontaminant canisters over the examination area. With the release at my station. Say a good strong phytocide plus a fungicide with a mercury base. What should I get from Stores?"

"Decon Seven is the strongest, Aaron. But it cannot be mixed, we will have to place many tanks." Her face is mirroring pity for the hypothetically killed plants, concern for the crew.

"Okay, so we'll place many tanks. Everything the suits will take. I don't trust that thing."

Soli comes into his arms, holds him with her strong small hands. Peace, comfort. *To make gentle the life of mankind.* His body has missed her painfully, demonstrates it with a superior erection. Soli giggles. Fondly he caresses her, feeling like himself for the first time in weeks. Do I see you as property, Soli? Surely not . . . The thought of Bustamente's huge body covering her floats through his mind; his erection increases markedly. Maybe the big black brother will have to revise his planning, Aaron thinks genially, hobbling with her to his comfortable, comforting bunk. Two years is a long time. . . .

Drifting asleep with Soli's warm buttocks in his lap Aaron has a neutral, almost comic, hypnagogic vision: Tighe's face big as the wall, garlanded with fruits and flowers like an Italian bambino plaque. The pink-and-green flowers tinkle, chime elfland horns. *Tan tara!* Centripetal melodies. *Tan tara! Tara! TARA!*

—and fairy horns turn into his medical alarm signal, with Soli shaking him awake. The call is from the bridge.

He leaps out of bed, yanking shorts on, hits the doorway with one shoulder and runs "up" to the free-fall shaft. His kit is somehow in his hand. He has no idea what time it is. The thought that Yellaston has had a heart attack is scaring him to death. Oh, god, what will they do without Yellaston?

He kicks free, sails and grabs clumsily like a three-legged ape, clutching the kit, is so busy figuring alternative treatment spectrums that he almost misses the voices coming from the Commo corridor. He gets himself into the access, finds his feet and scurries "down," still so preoccupied that he does not at first identify the dark columns occupying the Communications step. They are Bustamente's legs.

Aaron pushes in past him and confronts a dreadful sight. Commander Timofaev Bron is sagging from Bustamente's grasp, bleeding briskly from his left eye.

"All right, all right," Tim mutters. Bustamente shakes him. "What the hell was that power drain?" Don Purcell comes in behind Aaron.

"This booger was sending," Bustamente growls. "Shit-eater, I was too slow. He was sending *on my beam.*" He shakes the Russian again.

"All right," Tim repeats unemotionally. "It is done."

The blood is coming from a supraorbital split. Aaron disengages Tim from Bustamente, sits him down with his head back to clamp the wound. As he opens his kit a figure comes slowly through the side door from Astrogation: Captain Yellaston.

"Sir—" Aaron is still confusedly thinking of that coronary. Then Yellaston's peculiar rigidity gets through to him. Oh, Jesus, no. The man is not sick but smashed to the gills.

Bustamente is yanking open the gyro housing. The room fills with a huge humming tone.

"I did not harm the beam," Tim says under Aaron's hands. "Certain equipment was installed when we built it; you did not look carefully enough."

"Son of a bitch," says Don Purcell.

"What do you mean, equipment?" Bustamente's voice rises, harmonic with the precessing gyros. "What have you done, flyboy?"

"I was not sent here to wait. The planet is there."

Aaron sees Captain Yellaston's lips moving effortfully, achieving a strange pursed look. "You indicated . . ." he says eerily. "You indicated . . . that is, you have preempted the green. . . ."

The others stare at him, look away one by one. Aaron is stabbed with unbearable pity, he is suspecting that what has happened is so terrible it isn't real yet.

"Son of a bitch," Don Purcell repeats neutrally.

The green signal has been sent, Aaron realizes. To the Russians, anyway, but everybody will find out, everybody will start. It's all over, he's committed us whether that planet's any good or not. Oh, god, Yellaston—he saw this coming, if he'd been younger, if he'd moved faster—if half his brains hadn't been scrambled in alcohol. I brought it to him.

Automatically his hands have completed their work. The Russian gets up. Don Purcell has left, Bustamente is probing the gyro chamber with a resonator, not looking at Tim. Yellaston is still rigid in the shadows.

"It was in the hull shielding," Tim says to Bustamente. "The contact is under the toggles. Don't worry, it was one-time."

Aaron follows him out, unable to believe in any of this. Lieutenant Pauli is waiting outside; she must be in it, too.

"Tim, how could you be so goddamn sure? You may have killed everybody."

The cosmonaut looks down at him calmly, one-eyed. "The records don't lie. They are enough, we will find nothing else. That old man would have waited forever." He chuckles, a dream-planet in his eye.

Aaron goes back in, leads Yellaston to his quarters. The captain's arm is trembling faintly. Aaron is trembling too with pity and disgust. That old man, Tim had called him. That old man . . . Suddenly he realizes the full dimensions of this night's disaster.

Two years. The hell with the planet, maybe they won't even get there. Two years in this metal can with a captain who has failed, an old man mocked at in his drunkenness? No one to hold us together, as Yellaston had done during those unbearable weeks when the oxygen ran low, when panic had hung over all their heads. He had been so good then, so right. Now he's let Tim take it all away from him, he's lost it. We aren't together anymore, not after this. It'll get worse. *Two years . . .*

"In the . . . fan," Yellaston whispers with tragic dignity, letting Aaron put him onto his bed. "In . . . the fan . . . my fault."

"In the morning," Aaron tells him gently, dreading the

thought. "Maybe Ray can figure some way."

" . . . ."

Aaron heads hopelessly for his bunk. He knows he won't sleep. *Two years . . .*

III

Silence . . . Bright clinical emptiness, no clouds, no weeping. Horizon, infinity. Somewhere words rise, speaking silence: I AM THE SPOUSE. Cancel sound. Aaron, invisible and microbe-sized, sees on the floor of infinity a very beautifully veined silver membrane which he now recognizes as an adolescent's prepuce, the disjecta of his first operation. . . .

Almost awake now, in foetal position; something terrible ahead if he wakes up. He tries to burrow back into dream, but a hand is preventing him, jostling him back to consciousness.

He opens his eyes and sees Coby handing him a hot cup; a very bad sign.

"You know about Tim." Aaron nods, sipping clumsily. "You haven't heard about Don Purcell, though. I didn't wake you. No medical aspects."

"What about Don Purcell? What happened?"

"Brace yourself, boss."

"For Christ's sake, don't piss around, Bill."

"Well, about oh-three-hundred we had this hull tremor. Blipped all Tighe's tapes. I called around, big flap, finally got the story. Seems Don fired his whole scouter off on automatic. It's loaded with a complete set of tapes, records, everything he could get his hands on. The planet, see? They say it can punch a signal through to Earth when it gets up speed."

"But Don, is Don in it?"

"Nobody's in it. It's set on autopilot. The *Beast* had some special goodies, too, our people must have a new ear up someplace. Mars, I heard."

"Jesus Christ . . ." So fast, it's happening, Aaron thinks. Where does Coby get his information, anything bad he knows it all. Then he sees the faint appeal under Coby's grin; this is what he can do, his wretched offering.

"Thanks, Bill." Aaron gets up effortfully. . . . First Tim and now Don—war games on *Centaur*. It's all wrecked, all gone.

"Things are moving too fast for the old man." Coby leans

back familiarly on Aaron's bunk. "Good thing, too. We have to get a more realistic political organization. This great leader stuff, he's finished. Oh, we can keep him on as a figurehead. . . . Don and Tim are out too, for now anyway. First thing to start with, we elect a working committee."

"You're crazy, Bill. You can't run a ship with a committee. We'll kill ourselves if we start politics."

"Want to bet?" Coby grins. "Going to see some changes, boss."

Aaron sluices water over his head to shut off the voice. Elections, two years from nowhere? That'll mean the Russian faction, the U.S. faction, the Third and Fourth Worlders; scientists versus humanists versus techs versus ecologists versus theists versus Smithites—all the factions of Earth in one fragile ship. What shape will we be in when we reach the planet, if we live that long? And any colony we start— Oh, damn Yellaston, damn me—

"General meeting at eleven hundred," Coby is saying. "And by the way, Tighe really did go wandering for about twenty minutes last night. My fault, I admit it, I forgot the isolation seal was off. No harm done. I got him right back in."

"Where was he?"

"Same place. By the port where *China* was."

"Take him with you to the meeting," Aaron says impulsively, punishing them all.

He goes out to get some breakfast, trying to shake out of the leaden feeling of oversleep, of doom impending. He dreads the meeting, dreads it. Poor old Yellaston trying futilely to cover his lapse, trying to save public face. A figurehead. He can't take that, he'll go into depression. Aaron makes himself set up Tighe's tapes to occupy his thoughts.

Tighe's tapes are worse than before, composite score down another five points, Aaron sees, even before the twenty-minute gap. His CNS functions are coming out of synch, too, an effect he hasn't seen in an ambulant patient, especially one as coordinated as Tighe. Curious . . . Have to study it, Aaron thinks apathetically. All our curves are coming out of synch, we're breaking up. Yellaston was our pacemaker. Can we make it without him? . . . Am I as dependent as Foy?

It is time for the meeting. He plods down to the Commons, sick with pity and dread; he is so reluctant to listen that he does not at first notice the miracle: there is nothing to pity. The

Yellaston before his eyes is firm-voiced, erect, radiating leaderly charisma; is announcing, in fact, that *Centaur's* official green code for the Alpha sun was beamed to Earth at oh-five-hundred this morning.

What?

"As some of you are aware," Yellaston says pleasantly, "our two scout commanders have also taken independent initiative to the same effect in messaging their respective Terrestrial governments. I want to emphasize that their actions were pursuant to specific orders from their superiors prior to embarkation. We all regret, we, here who are joined in this mission have always regretted—that the United Nations of Earth who sponsored our mission were not more perfectly united when we left. We may hope they are so now. But this is a past matter of no concern to us, arising from tensions on a world none of us may ever visit again. I want to say now that both Tim Bron and Don Purcell"—Yellaston makes a just-perceptible fatherly nod toward the two commanders, who are sitting quite normally on his left, despite Tim's taped eye—"faithfully carried out orders, however obsolete, just as I or any of us would have felt obligated to do in their places, had we been so burdened. Their duties have now been discharged. Their independent signals, if they arrive, will serve as confirmation to our official transmission to Earth as a whole.

"Now we must consider our immediate tasks."

Jesus god, Aaron thinks, the old bastard. The old fox, he's got it all back, he took the initiative right out from under them while I thought he was dead out. Fantastic. But how the hell? Running those lasers up is a job. Aaron looks around, catches a hooded gleam from Bustamente. Ol' Black George was cooking in his electronic jungle, he and Yellaston. Aaron grins to himself. He is happy, so happy that he ignores the inner murmur: *at a price.*

"The biologic examination of the planetary life-form returned to us by Commander Kuh will start at about sixteen hundred this afternoon. It will be conducted in Corridor Gamma One under decontaminant seal, but the entire operation will be displayed on your viewers." Yellaston smiles. "You will probably see it better than I will. Next, and concurrently, the Drive section will prepare to initiate change of course toward the Alpha planet. Each of you will secure your areas for acceleration and course-change as speedily as possible. The vector loadings will be posted tomorrow. Advise Don and Tim of any problems in their respective sections. First Engineer Singh will deal with Gamma section in the absence of Commander Kuh. And finally, we must commence the work of adapting and refining our general colonization plan to the planetary data now at hand. Our first objective is a planetary atlas incorporating every indicator that your specialties can extract from the *Gamma* tapes. On this we can build our plans. I remind you that this is a task requiring imagination and careful thought of every contingency and parameter. Gentlemen, ladies: the die is cast. We have only two years to prepare for the greatest adventure our race has known."

Aaron starts to smile at the archaism, finds he has a fullness in the throat. The hush around him holds for a minute; Yellaston nods to Don and Tim, and they get up and exit with him. Perfect, Aaron thinks. We'll make it, we're okay. Screw Coby. Daddy lives. Everyone is jabbering now, Aaron makes his way through them past the great flowering wonder of Lory's—of the Alpha planet. Our future home. Yellaston will get us there, he's pulled it out.

But at a price, the gloomy corner of his forebrain repeats. The big green light is on its way to Earth. Not only we but all the people of Earth are committed, committed to that world. That planet *has* to be all right now.

He goes to assemble his equipment, irrationally resolved to double his emergency decontaminant array.

log 124 586 sd 4100 x 1200 notice to all personnel
corridor gamma one will be under space hazard seal starting 1545 this day for the purpose of bioanalysis of alien life specimen/ /attendance will be limited to: [1] centaur command cadre alpha (2) designated xenobiosurvey/medical personnel [3] eva team charlie [4] safety/survival staff assigned to corridor access locks/ /the foregoing personnel will be suited at all times until the unsealing of the corridor/ /because of the unknown risk factor in this operation additional guards will also be stationed on the inboard side of all access ports: see special-duty roster attached/ /unauthorized personnel will not, repeat not, enter gamma one starting as of now/ /video cover of the entire operation from the closest feasible points will be available on all screens on ship channel one, starting approximately 1515 hours
    yellaston, cmdg

In Corridor Gamma One, the major risk-factor is wires. Aaron leans on a bulkhead amid his tangle of equipment, holding his bulky suit and watching Jan Ing wrangle with Electronics. The Xenobiology chief wants a complete computer capability in the corridor; there is no way of passing the cable through the lock seals. The EVA team is appealed to, but they refuse to give up any of their service terminals. Finally the issue is resolved by sacrificing an access-lock indicator panel. Engineer Gomulka, who will double as a guard, starts cutting it out to bring the computer leads in.

Wires are snaking all over the deck. XB has brought in half their laboratory, and he can see at least eight other waldo-type devices in addition to the biomonitor extension equipment. On top of it all the camera crew is setting up. One camera is opposite the small hatch that will open into *China Flower's* personnel section, two by the big cargo hatch behind which the alien thing will be, plus a couple of overhead views. They are also mounting some ceiling slave screens for the corridor, Aaron. is glad to find. He is too far back to see the hatches. The Safety team is trying to get the cables cleared into bundles along the wall, but the mess is bound to get worse when the suit umbilicals come into use. Mercifully, general suiting-up will not take place until the EVA team has winched *China Flower* up to her berth.

Aaron's station is the farthest one away at the stern end of the corridor. In front of him is an open space with the EVA floor lock, and then starts the long Xenobiology clutter. Beyond XB is the big cargo hatch and then the small hatch, and finally in the distance is the corridor command station. Command Cadre Alpha means Yellaston and Tim Bron. Aaron can just make out Tim's eye-patch, he's talking with Don Purcell who will go back to man *Centaur's* bridge. In case of trouble . . . Aaron peers at his racks of decontaminant aerosols mounted opposite the hatches. They have wires, too, running to a switch beside his hand. He had trouble with XB about those cans; Jan Ing would rather be eaten alive than risk damaging their precious specimen of alien life.

A hand falls on his shoulder—Captain Yellaston, coming in the long way round, his observant face giving no hint of what must be the chemical conditions in his bloodstream.

"The die is cast," Aaron observes.

Yellaston nods. "A gamble," he says quietly. "The mission . . .
I may have done a fearful thing, Aaron. They were bound to
come, on the strength of the other two."

"The only thing you could have done, sir."

"No." Aaron looks up. Yellaston isn't talking to him; his eyes
are on some cold cosmic scoreboard. "No. I should have sent
code yellow and announced I had sent the green. Ray would
have kept silent. That would have held back the UN ships at
least. It was the correct move. I failed to think it through in
time."

He moves on down the corridor, leaving Aaron stunned.
Sent the yellow and lied to us for two years? *Captain Yellaston?*
But yes, Aaron sees slowly, that would have saved something,
in case the planet is no good. It would have been better. What
he did was good, but it wasn't the best. Because he was drunk.
. . . My fault. My stupid susceptibilities, my—

People are jostling past him, it's the EVA team, suited and
ready to go out. Chief George Brokeshoulder's suit is a work of
art, painted with blazing Amerind symbols. The last man by
punches Aaron's arm—Bruce Jang, giving him a mean wink
through his gold-washed faceplate. Aaron watches them file
down into the EVA blister lock, remembering the same thing
three weeks ago when they had gone out to bring in *China
Flower* with Lory unconscious inside. This time all they have to
do is reel up the tether. Risky enough. The rotational mechanics
could send a man into space, Aaron thinks; he is always awed
by skills he doesn't have.

A videoscreen comes to life, showing spinning stars. A
space suit occults them; when it passes, three small yellow
lights are moving toward a blackness—the helmet lights of the
team going down to *China Flower* far below. Aaron's gut jumps;
an *alien* is out there, he is about to meet an *alien*. He blinks,
begins to sort and assemble the extensor mounts on which
his sensors will be intruded into the scouter's cargo hold. As
he does so, he notices faces peering at him through the vitrex
of the nearest access lock. He waves. The faces, perceiving
that the scenario has not yet started, go away. It will be, Aaron
realizes, a long afternoon.

By the time he and Ing have lined up their equipment,
all nonoperational people except the suit team have left the
corridor. The hull has been groaning softly; *China Flower* is
rising to them on her winch. Suddenly the wall beside him

clanks, grinds reverberatingly—the port probes engage, the grinding stops. Aaron shivers involuntarily: the alien is here.

As the EVA lock cycle begins flashing, Tim Bron's voice says on the audio, "All hands will now suit up."

The EVA team is coming back inside. The suit men work down the corridor, checking and paying out the umbilicals as neatly as they can. It's going to be cramped working. The suit team reach him last. As he seals in he sees more faces at the side lock. The videoscreens are all on now, giving a much better view, but still the faces remain. Aaron chuckles to himself; the old ape impulse to see with the living eye.

"All nonoperational personnel will now clear the area."

The EVA team is lined up along the wall opposite *China Flower's* personnel hatch. The plan is to open this first in order to retrieve the scout ship's automatic records of the alien's life-processes. Is it still alive in there? Aaron has no mystic intuitions now, only a great and growing tension in his gut. He makes himself breathe normally.

"Guards, secure the area."

The last corridor entrances are dogged tight. Aaron sees a faceplate turned toward him three stations up the XB line. The face belongs to Lory. He flinches slightly; he had forgotten she would be here. He lifts his gloved hand, wishing he was between her and that cargo port.

The area is secure, the guards stationed. George Brokeshoulder and two other EVA men move up to open the lock coupled to *China Flower's* personnel port. Aaron watches the close-up on the overhead screen. Metal clinks, the lock hatch slides sideways. The EVA men go in carrying vapor analyzers, the hatch rolls shut. Another wait. Aaron sees the XB people tuning their suit radios, realizes the EVA men are reporting. He gets the channel: "Nominal . . . Atmosphere nominal (crackle, crackle) . . ." The hatch is sliding back again, the men come out accompanied by a barely perceptible fogginess. Lory looks back at him again; he understands. This is the air she had breathed for nearly a year.

The ship's tapes are being handed out. The alien is, it appears, alive.

"Metabolic trace regular to preliminary inspection, envelope unchanged," Jan Ing's voice comes on the audio. "Intermittent bioluminescence, two to eighty candlepower." Eighty candlepower, that's *bright*. So Lory hadn't lied about that, anyway. "A strong peak coinciding with the original docking with *Centaur* . . . a second peak occurred, yes, about the time the scout ship was removed from its berth."

That would be about when Tighe did—or didn't—open the container, Aaron thinks. Or maybe it was stimulated by moving the ship.

"One of the fans which circulate its atmosphere is not operating," the XB chief goes on, "but the remaining fans seem to have provided sufficient movement for adequate gas exchange. Its surface atmosphere requires continuous renewal, since it is adapted to constant planetary wind. It also exhibits pulselike internal pressure changes—"

Aaron's mind is momentarily distracted by the vision of himself stepping out into planetary wind, a stream of wild unrecycled air. That creature in there dwells on wind. A podlike mass about four meters long, Lory had described it. Like a big bag of fruit. Squatting in there for a year, metabolizing, pulsing, luminescing—what else has it been doing? The functions of life: assimilation, excitation, reproduction. Has it been reproducing? Is the hold full of Coby's tiny monsters waiting to pounce out? Or ooze out, swallowing us all? Aaron notices he has drifted away from his decontaminant switches; he moves back.

"The mass is constant, activity vectors stable," Jan concludes.

So it hasn't been multiplying. Just squatting there. Thinking, maybe? Aaron wonders if those bioluminescence peaks would correlate with any phenomena on *Centaur*. What phenomena? Tighe-sightings, maybe, or nightmares? Don't be an idiot, he tells himself; the imp in his ear replies that those New England colonists didn't correlate ocean currents and winter temperatures, either. . . . Absently he has been following the EVA team's debate on whether to cut open the viewport to the alien that Lory welded shut. It is decided not to try this but to proceed directly to the main cargo lock.

The team comes out, and the men assigned to the extension probes pick up their equipment, cables writhing in a slow snake dance. Bruce and the EVA chief undog the heavy cargo hatch. This is the port through which the scout ship's groundside equipment, their vehicles and flier and generator, were loaded in. The hatch rolls silently aside, the two men go into the lock. Aaron can see them on the videoscreen, unsealing the scouter's port. It opens; no vapor comes out because the hold is unpressurized. Beyond the suited figures Aaron can see the shiny side of the cargo module in which the alien is confined. The sensor men advance, angling their probes into the lock like long-necked beasts. Aaron glances up at another screen which shows the corridor as a whole and experiences an odd oceanic awareness.

Here we are, he thinks, tiny blobs of life millions and millions of miles from the speck that spawned us, hanging out here in the dark wastes, preparing with such complex pains to encounter a different mode of life. All of us, peculiar, wretchedly imperfect-somehow we have done this thing. Incredible, really, the ludicrous tangle of equipment, the awkward suited men, the precautions, the labor, the solemnity—Jan, Bruce, Yellaston, Tim Bron, Bustamente, Alice Berryman, Coby, Kawabata, my saintly sister, poor Frank Foy, stupid Aaron Kaye—a stream of faces pours through his mind, hostile or smiling, suffering each in his separate flawed reality: all of us. Somehow we have brought ourselves to this amazement. Perhaps we really are saving our race, he thinks, perhaps there really is a new earth and heaven ahead. . . .

The moment passes; he watches the backs of the men inside *China*, still struggling with the module port. The sensor men have closed in, blocked the view. Aaron glances up at the bow end of the corridor where Yellaston and Tim Bron stand. Yellaston's arm is extended stiffly to the top of his console. That must be the evacuation control; if he pulls it the air ducts will open, the corridor will depressurize in a couple of minutes. So will the alien's module if it's open. Good; Aaron feels reassured. He checks his own canister-release switch, finds he has again strayed forward and moves back.

Confused exclamations, grunts are coming over the suit channel; apparently there is a difficulty with the module port. One of the sensor men drops his probe, moves in. Another follows. What's the trouble?

The screen shows nothing but suit backs, the whole EVA team is in there—Oh! Sudden light, cracks of radiance between the men silhouetting them blue against a weird pink light—Is it fire? Aaron's heart jumps, he clambers onto a stanchion to see over heads. Not fire, there's no smoke. Oh, of course, he realizes—that light is the alien's own luminescence! They have opened the module.

But why are they all in there, why aren't they falling back to push the sensors in? Wide rosy light flashes, hidden by bodies. They must have opened the whole damn port instead of just cracking it. Is that thing trying to come out?

"Close it, get out!" Aaron calls into his suit mike. But the channel is a bedlam of static. Everybody is crowding forward toward that hatch, too. That's dangerous. "Captain!" Aaron shouts futilely. He can see Yellaston's hand still on the panel, but Tim Bron seems to be holding on to his arm. The EVA men are all inside *China Flower*, inside the module even, it's impossible to tell. A pink flare lights up the corridor, winks out again.

"Move back! Get back to your stations!" Yellaston's voice cuts in on the command channel override and the intercom babble goes dead. Aaron is suddenly aware of pressure around him, discovers that he is all the way up at the XB stations, being crowded by someone behind. It's Akin's face inside the safety guard visor. They disengage clumsily, move back.

"Go back, to your stations! EVA team, report."

Aaron is finding movement oddly effortful. He wants very much to open his stifling helmet.

"George, can you hear me? Get your men out."

The screen is showing confused movement, more colored flashes. Is somebody hurt? There's a figure, coming slowly out of the hatch.

"What's going on in there, George? Why is your helmet open?"

Aaron stares incredulously as the EVA chief emerges into the corridor—his faceplate is open, tipped back showing his bronze ax-shaped face. What the hell is happening? Did the alien grab them? George's arm goes up, he is making the okay signal; the suit-to-suit channel is still out. The others are coming out behind him, the strange light shining on their backs, making a great peach-colored glow in the corridor. Their visors are open, too. But they seem to be all right, whatever happened in there.

The screen is showing the module port; all Aaron can make out is a big rectangle of warm-colored light. It seems to be softly bubbling or shifting, like a light show—globes of rose, yellow, lilac—it's beautiful, really. Hypnotic. They should close it, he thinks, hearing Yellaston ordering the men to seal their helmets. With an effort Aaron looks away, sees Yellaston still by his station, his arm rigid. Tim Bron seems to have moved away. It's all right, nothing has happened. It's all right.

"Get those suits closed before I depressurize!"

The EVA chief is slowly pulling his faceplate down, so are the others. Their movements seem vague, unfocused: One of them stumbles over the biopsy equipment. Why doesn't he pick it up? Something is wrong with them. Aaron frowns. His brain feels gassy. Why aren't they carrying out the program, doing something about the bioluminescence? It's probably all right, though, Yellaston is there. He's watching.

At this moment he is jostled hard. He blinks, recovers balance, looks around. Jesus—he's in the wrong place—everybody is in the wrong place. The whole corridor is jamming forward of where it's supposed to be, staring at that marvelous glow. The guards—they're not by the ports! Something is not all right at all, Aaron realizes. It's that light, it's doing something to us! *Close the port,* he wills, trying to get back to his station. It's like moving in water. The emergency switch—he has to reach it, how did he ever get so far away? And the ports, he sees, the vitrex is crowded with faces, people are in the access ramps staring into the corridor. They've come from all over the ship. What's wrong? What's happening to us?

Cold fear bursts up in his gut. He catches the EVA lock and clings to it, fighting an invisible slow tide. Part of him wants to push his helmet off and run forward to the radiance coming from that port. People ahead of him are opening their visors—he can see Jan Ing's sharp Danish nose.

"Stand away from that port!" Yellaston shouts. At that Jan Ing darts forward, pushing people aside. "Stop," Aaron yells into his useless mike, finds himself opening his own visor, moving after Jan. Voices, sounds, fill his ears. He grabs another stanchion, pulls himself up to look for Yellaston. The captain is still there; he seems to be struggling slowly with Tim Bron. The light is gone now, hidden by a press of bodies around the port. That thing in there is doing this, Aaron tells himself; he is terrified in a curious unreal way, his head is singing thickly. He is also angry with those people down there—they are going in, blocking it. Lost! But is it they who are lost or the wonderful light?

Someone bumps breast-to-breast with him, pulling at his arm. He looks down into Lory's blazing face. Her helmet is gone.

"Come on, Arn! We'll go together."

Primal distrust sends an icicle into his mind; he grabs her suit, anchors himself to a console with his other arm. Lory! She's in league with that thing, he knows it, this is her crazy plot. He has to stop it. Kill it! Where is his emergency release? It's too far, too far—

"Captain!" he shouts with all his strength, fighting Lory, thinking, two minutes, we can get out. "Depressurize! Dump the air!"

"No, Arn! It's beautiful—don't be afraid!"

"Dump the air, kill it!" he yells again, but his voice can't override the confusion. Lory is yanking on his arm, her exultant face fills him with sharp fright. "What is it?" He shakes her by the belt. "What are you trying to do?"

"It's time, Arn! It's *time*, come on—there're so many people—"

He tries to get a better grip on her, hearing metal clang behind him and realizes too late he has let go his hold on the console. But her words are now making a kind of sense to him—there *are* too many people, it is important, quite important to get there before something is all used up. Why is he letting them hide that light? Lory has his hand now, drawing him toward the press of people ahead.

"You'll see, it will all be gone, the pain. . . . Arn dear, we'll be together."

The beauty of it floods Aaron's soul, washes all fear away. Just beyond those bodies is the goal of man's desiring, the fountain—the Grail itself maybe, the living radiance! He sees an opening by the wall, pulls Lory through—and is suddenly squeezed by more bodies from the side, a wall of people flooding out of the access port. Aaron fights to hold his ground, hold Lory, only dimly aware that he is struggling against familiar faces—Åhlstrom is beside him, smiling orgasmically, he pushes past Kawabata, ducks under somebody's arm. As he does, a force slams their backs—he is clouted into something entangling and falls down under an XB analyzer still clutching Lory's wrist.

"Arn, Arn, come on!"

Legs are going by him. It was Bustamente who hit him, forging past followed by a forest of legs. They have all come here to claim the shining glory in the port! Wildly enraged, Aaron struggles up, falls again with his own leg deep in a web of cables.

"Arn, get up!" She jerks at him fiercely. But he is suddenly calmer, although he does not cease to wrench at his trapped leg. There is a small intercom screen by his head, he can see two tiny struggling figures—Yellaston and Tim Bron, their helmets gone. Dreamlike, tiny . . . Tim breaks away. Yellaston nods once, and fells Tim from behind with a blow of both locked fists. Then he slowly steps over the fallen man and goes offscreen. Pink light flares out.

They have all gone in there, Aaron realizes, heartbroken. It has called us and we have come—*I must go.* But he frowns, blinks; a part of him has doubts about the pull, the sweet longing. It feels fainter down here. Maybe that pile of stuff is shielding me, he thinks confusedly. Lory is yanking at the cables around his legs. He pulls her in to him.

"Lor, what's happening to them? What happened"—he cannot recall the Chinese commander's name—"what happened to your, your crew?"

"Changed," she is panting. Her face is incredibly beautiful. "Merged, healed. Made whole. Oh, you'll see, hurry—Can't you *feel* it, Arn?"

"But—" He can feel it all right, the pull, the promising urgency, but he feels something else too—the ghost of Dr. Aaron Kaye is screaming faintly in his head, threatening him. Lory is trying to lift him bodily. He resists, fearing to be drawn from his shielded nook. The corridor around them is empty now, but he can hear people in the distance, a thick babbling down by that hatch. No screams, nothing like panic. Disregarding Lory, he cranes to get a look at the big ceiling screen. They are all there, milling rather aimlessly, he has never seen so many people pressed so close. This is a medical emergency, he thinks. I am the doctor. He has a vision of Dr. Aaron Kaye getting to the levers that will seal that cargo hatch, standing firm against the crowd, saving them from whatever is in that hold. But he cannot; Dr. Aaron Kaye is only a thin froth of fear on a helpless, lunging desire to go there himself, to fling himself into that beautiful warm light. He is going to be very ashamed, he thinks vaguely, tied here like Ulysses against the siren call, huddling under an analyzer bench while the others—What? He studies the screen again, he can see no apparent trouble, no one has fallen. The EVA men came out all right, he tells himself. What I have to do is get out of here.

Lory laughs, pulling at his legs; she has freed him, he sees. He is sliding. Effortfully he reaches into his suit, finds the panic syringe.

"Arn dear—" Her slender neck muscles are exposed; he grabs her hair, seats the spray. She wails and struggles maniacally, but he holds on, waiting for the shot to work. His head feels clearer. The aching pull is less; maybe all those people are blocking it somehow. The thought hurts him. He tries to disregard it, thinking, if I can get across the corridor, into that access ramp, I can seal it behind me. Maybe.

Suddenly there is movement to his left—a pair of legs, slowly stepping by his refuge. Pale gold legs he recognizes.

"Soli! Soli, stop!"

The legs pause, a small hand settles on the overturned stand beyond him. Just within reach—he can spring and grab her, letting go of Lory—to reach her he must let Lory go. He lunges, feels Lory pull away and clutches her again. He falls short. The hand is gone.

"Soli! Soli! Come back!" Her footsteps move on down the corridor. Dr. Aaron Kaye will be ashamed, ashamed; he knows it. "The EVA men were okay," he mutters. Lory is weakening now, her eyes vague. "No, Arn," she sighs, sighs deeply again. Aaron rolls her, gets a firm grip on her suit-belt and crawls out into the corridor.

As his head clears the shelter, the sweet pull grabs him again. There—down there is the goal! "I'm a doctor," he groans, willing his limbs. A thick cable is under his hand. From miles away he recognizes it—the XB computer lead, running toward the inboard lock. If he can follow that across the corridor he will be at the ramp.

He clasps it, starts to shuffle on his knees, dragging Lory. The thing down there is pulling at the atoms of his soul, his head is filled with urgent radiance calling to him to drop the foolish cable and run to join his mates. "I'm a *doctor*," he mumbles; it requires all his strength to slide his gloved hand along his lifeline, he is turning away from bliss beyond his dreams. Only meters to go. It is impossible. Why is he refusing, going the wrong way? He will turn. But something has changed. . . . He is at the lock, he sees; he must let go the cable and drag Lory over the sill.

Sobbing, he does so; it is almost more than he can bear to nudge the heavy port with his heel and send it swinging closed behind them.

As it closes, the longing lessens perceptibly. Metal, he thinks vacantly, it has blocked it a little, maybe it is some kind of EM field. He looks up. A figure is standing by the lock.

"Tiger! What are you doing here?" Aaron pulls himself upright with Lory huddled by his feet. Tighe looks at them uncertainly, says nothing.

"What's in that boat, Tiger? The alien, did you see it? What is it?"

Tighe's face wavers, crumples. "Mu . . . muh," his mouth jerks. "Mother."

No help here. Just in time, Aaron notices his own hands opening the port-lever. He takes Lory under the arms and drags her farther away up the ramp to the emergency intercom panel. Her eyes are still open, her hands are fumbling weakly at her suit-fastenings.

Aaron breaks out the caller. It's an all-ship channel.

"Don! Commander Purcell, can you hear me? This is Dr. Kaye, I'm in ramp six, there's been trouble down here."

No answer. Aaron calls again, calls Coby, calls the Commo and Safety CQs, calls everybody he can think of, calls himself hoarse. No answer. Has everybody on *Centaur* gone into Corridor Gamma One, is the whole damned ship out there with that—

Except Tighe. Aaron frowns at the damaged man. He was in here, he didn't join the stampede.

"Tiger, did you go out there?"

Tighe mouths, emits what could be a negative. He seems uninterested in the port. What does it take to stay sane near that thing, Aaron wonders, cortical suppressants? Or did one contact immunize him? Can we prepare drugs, can I lobotomize myself and still function? He notices he has drifted closer to the port, that Lory is crawling toward it, half out of her suit. He pulls her out of it, gets them both back up the ramp.

When he looks up there is a shadow on the port view-panel.

For a terrified instant Aaron is sure it is the alien coming for him. Then he sees a human hand, slowly tapping. Somebody trying to get in—but he dare not go down there.

"Tiger! Open the port, let the man in." He gestures wildly at Tighe. "The port, look! You remember, hit the latch, Tiger. Open up!"

Tighe hesitates, turns in place. Then an old reflex fires; he sidesteps and slaps double-handed at the latch with perfect coordination—and as quickly sags again. The port swings open. Captain Yellaston stands there. Deliberately he steps through.

"Captain, Captain, are you all right?" Aaron starts to run forward, checks himself. "Tiger, close the port."

Yellaston is walking stiffly toward him, looking straight ahead. Face a little pale, Aaron thinks, no injuries visible. He's all right, whatever happened. It's all right.

"Captain, I—" But there are more figures at the port, Aaron sees, Tim Bron and Coby, coming in past Tighe. Others beyond. Aaron has never been so glad to see his assistant, he yells something at him and turns to catch up with Yellaston.

"Captain—" He wants to talk about sealing off the corridor, about examining them all. But Yellaston does not look around.

"The red," Yellaston says in a faint remote voice. "The red . . . is the correct . . . signal." He walks on, toward the bridge.

Some sort of shock, Aaron thinks, and sees movement by the wall ahead—it is Lory, up and staggering away from him. But she isn't going toward the corridor, she's going up a ramp into the ship. The clinic is where she belongs. Aaron starts after her, confident that the drug will slow her down. But his suit is awkward, he has not counted on that feral vitality. She stays ahead of him, she gains speed up the twisting tube as the gees let go. He pounds up after her, past the dormitory levels, past Stores; he is half-sailing now. Lory dives into the central free-fall shaft—but not going straight, he sees her twist left, toward the bridge.

Cursing, Aaron follows her in. His feet miss the guides, he ricochets, has trouble regaining speed. Lory is a receding minnow-shape ahead of him, going like a streak. She shoots through the command-section sphincter, checks. Damn, she's closing it against him.

By the time he gets it open and goes through, the core shaft is empty. Aaron kicks on into the Astrogation dome. Nobody there. He climbs out of the free-fall area and starts back around the computer corridor. Nobody here either. Åhlstrom's gleaming pets are untended. This has never happened before. It's like a ghost ship. Station after station is empty. The physics display-screen is running a calculation, unobserved.

A sound breaks the silence, coming from the next ring

aft. Oh, god, Bustamente's Commo room! Aaron can't find the inside door, he doubles back out into the corridor, races clumsily sternward, terror in his guts as the sound rises to a scream.

The Commo room is open. Aaron plunges in, checks in horror. Lory is standing in the sacred gyro chamber. The scream is coming from the open gyro housings. Her arm jerks out, sending a stream of objects—headsets, jacks, wrenches—into the flying wheels.

"Stop!" He lunges for her, but the sound has risen to a terrible yammering. A death cry—the great pure beings who have spun there faultlessly for a decade holding their lifeline to Earth are in mortal agony. They clash, collide horribly. A cam shoots past him, buries itself in the wall. She has killed them, his mad sister.

Gripping her he stands there stunned, scarcely able to take in other damage. The housing of the main laser crystals is wrecked; they have been hit with something. That hardly matters now, Aaron thinks numbly. Without the gyros to aim them, the beam is only an idiot's finger flailing across the stars.

"We, we'll go together, Arn," Lory hangs on him, weak now. "They can't—stop us anymore."

Aaron's substrate takes over; he utters a howl and starts to shake her by the neck, squeezing, crushing—but is startled into stasis by a voice behind him, saying, "Bustamente."

He wheels. It is Captain Yellaston.

"I will send . . . the red signal . . . now."

"You can't!" Aaron yells in rage. "You can't, it's broken! *She* broke it!" Preadolescent fury floods him, ebbs as he sees that remote, uncomprehending face.

"You will send . . . the red signal." The man is in shock, all right.

"Sir, we can't—we can't send anything right now." Aaron releases Lory, takes Yellaston's arm. Yellaston frowns down at him, purses his lips. A two-liter night. He lets himself be turned away, headed toward his quarters. Aaron is irrationally grateful: as long as Yellaston hasn't seen the enormity it isn't real. He pulls back the captain's glove, checks the pulse as they go. About sixty; slow but not arrhythmic.

"The technical capacity . . . " Yellaston mutters, going into his room. "If you have the efficiency . . . you'll wake up in the morning. . . ."

"Please lie down awhile, Captain." Aaron closes the door, sees Lory wandering behind him. He takes her arm and starts back toward his office, resisting the faint urge to turn toward Gamma One. If he can only get to his office he can begin to function, decide what to do. What has hit *Centaur*'s people, what did that alien do? A static discharge, maybe, like an electric eel? Better try his standard adrenergic stim-shot, if the heart rates are okay. That overwhelming attractant—he can feel it now, even here in Beta corridor on the far side of the ship. Like a pheromone, Aaron decides. That thing is a sessile life-form, maybe it attracts food, maybe it gets itself fertilized that way. Just happens that it works on man. A field, maybe, like gravity. Or some fantastically attenuated particle. The suits didn't stop it completely. I should seal it off, that's the first thing, he tells himself, leading Lory, docile now. They are passing Don's scout-ship berth. But the *Beast* isn't here, it's god knows how many thousand miles away now, blatting out its message.

Someone is here—Don Purcell is standing by an access ramp, staring at the deck. Aaron drags Lory faster.

"Don! Commander, are you okay?"

Don's head turns to him; the grin is there, the eyes have smile-wrinkles. But Aaron sees his pupils are unequally dilated, like a poleaxed steer. How severe was that shock? He takes the unresisting wrist.

"Can you recognize me, Don? It's Aaron. It's Doc. You've had a physical shock, you shouldn't be wandering around." Pulse slow, like Yellaston's; no irregularity Aaron can catch. "I want you to come with me to the clinic."

The strong body doesn't move. Aaron pulls at him, realizes he can't budge him alone. He needs his syringe kit, too.

"That's a medical order, Don. Report for treatment."

The smile slowly focuses on him, puzzled.

"The power," Don says in the voice he uses at chapel. "The hand of the Almighty on the deep . . ."

"See, Arn?" Lory reaches out toward Don, pats him. "He's changed. He's gentle." She smiles tremulously.

Aaron leads her on, wondering how seriously people have been hit. *Centaur* can sustain itself for days, that part's all right. He will not think of the more fearful hurt, the murdered gyros; Bustamente—Bustamente can do something, somehow. But how long are people going to remain in shock? How many of them got hit by that thing, who is functioning besides himself? Could it be permanent damage? Impossible, he tells himself firmly; a shock that severe would have finished poor Tighe. Impossible.

As he turns off to the clinic, Lory suddenly pulls back.

"No, Arn, this way!"

"We're going to the office, Lor. I have work to do."

"Oh, no, Arn. Don't you *understand*? We're going now, together." Her voice is plaintive, with a loose, slurred quality. Aaron's training wakes up. Chemical supplementation, as Foy said—this is the time to get some answers from the subject.

"Sis, talk to me a minute, then we'll go. What happened to them, what happened to Mei-Lin and the others on the planet?"

"Mei-Lin?" she frowns.

"Yes, what did you see them do? You can tell me now, Lor. Did you see them out there?"

"Oh, yes . . ." She gives a vague little laugh. "I saw them. They left me in the ship, Arn. They, they didn't want me." Her lips quiver.

"What did they do, Lor?"

"Oh, they walked. Little Kuh had the video, I could see where they went. Up the hills, toward the, toward the beauty . . . It was hours, hours and hours. And then Mei-Lin and Liu went on ahead, I could see them running—Oh, Arn, I wanted to run too, you can't imagine how they look—"

"What happened then, Lor?"

"They took off their helmets, and then the camera fell down, I guess the others were all running too. I could see their feet—it was like a mountain of jewels in the sun—" Tears are running down her face, she rubs her fist at them like a child.

"What did you see then? What did the jewel-thing do to them?"

"It didn't do anything." She smiles, sniffing. "They just touched it, you know, with their minds. You'll *see*, Arn. Please—let's go now."

"In a minute, Lor. Tell me, did they fight?"

"Oh, no!" Her eyes widen at him. "No! Oh, I made that up to protect it. No hurting anymore, never. They came back so gentle, so happy. They were all changed, they shed all that. It's waiting for us, Arn, see? It wants to deliver us. We'll be truly human at last." She sighs. "Oh, I wanted so much to go, too, it was terrible. I had to tie myself, even in the suit. I *had* to bring it back to you. And I did, didn't I?"

"You got that thing in the scouter all by yourself, Lor?"

She nods, dream-eyed. "I found a little one, I poked it with the front-end loader." The contrast between her words and her face is weird.

"What were Kuh and his men doing all this time? Didn't they try to stop you?"

"Oh, no, they watched. They were around. Please Arn, come *on*."

"How long did it take you?"

"Oh, days, Arn, it was so hard. I could only do a little at a time."

"You mean they didn't recover for days? What about that tape, Lor; you faked it, didn't you?"

"I, I edited it a little. He wasn't . . . interested." Her eyes shift evasively. Control returning. "Arn, don't be *afraid*. The bad things are over now. Can't you feel it, the goodness?"

He can—it's there, pulling at him faint and bliss-laden. He shudders awake, discovers he has let her lead him nearly to the core, toward Gamma One. Angrily he makes himself grab the handrail and start hauling her back toward the clinic. It is like moving through glue, his body doesn't want to.

"No, Arn, no!" She pulls back, sobbing. "You *have* to, I worked so hard—"

He concentrates grimly on his feet. The clinic door is ahead now, to his infinite relief he can see Coby inside at the desk.

"You aren't coming!" Lory wails and jerks violently out of his grasp. "You—oh—"

He jumps for her, but she is running away again, running like a goddamned deer. Aaron checks himself. He cannot chase after her now, he has evaded his duty too long as it is. Days, she said. This is appalling. And they were walking around. Brain damage . . . Don't think of it.

He goes into the office. Coby is looking at him.

"My sister is in psychotic fugue," Aaron tells him. "She damaged our communication equipment. Sedation ineffective—" He perceives he is acting irrationally, he should tackle the major medical situation first.

"How many people got shocked by that thing, Bill?" Coby's noncommittal gaze does not change. Finally he says dully,

"Shock. Oh, yes. Shock." His lip twists in a ghostly sneer. Oh, god, no . . . Coby was in that corridor, too.

"Jesus, Bill, did it get you? I'm going to give you a shot of AD-twelve. Unless you have other ideas?"

Coby's eyes are following him. Maybe he isn't as severely affected, Aaron thinks.

"Postcoitum tristum." Coby's voice is very low. "I am tristum."

"What did it do to you, Bill, can you tell me?"

The silent, sad stare continues. Just as Aaron opens the hypo kit Coby says clearly, "I know a ripe corpus luteum when I see one." He gives a faint, nasty chuckle.

"What?" Obscene visions leap to life in Aaron's head as he bares Coby's elbow and sends the epidermal jet into the vein. "Did you, you didn't have some sort of intercourse with that thing, Bill?"

"In-ter-course?" Coby echoes in a whisper. "No . . . not us, anyway. If somebody had . . . in-ter-course it was god, maybe. . . . Or a planet . . . Not us . . . It had us."

His pulse is slow, skin cold. "What do you mean, Bill?"

Coby's face quivers, he stares up into Aaron's eyes, fighting to hang on to consciousness. "Say we were carrying it . . . carrying a load of jizzum in our heads, I guess. . . . And the jizzum meets . . . the queen couzy, the queen couzy of all time . . . and it jumps . . . jumps across. It makes some kind of holy . . . zygote, out there . . . see? Only we're left . . . empty. . . . What happens to a sperm's tail . . . afterward?"

"Take it easy, Bill." Aaron will not listen, oh, no, not to delirium. His best diagnostician raving.

Coby emits another ghastly snicker. "Good old Aaron," he whispers. "You didn't. . . ." His eyes go blank.

"Bill, try to pull yourself together. Stay right there. People are in shock, they're wandering around disoriented. I have work to do, can you hear me? Stay here, I'll be back."

Visions of himself hustling through the ship, reviving people—more important, sealing off that corridor, too. He loads a kit of stim-hypos, adds cardiotropics, detoxicants. An hour too late, Dr. Aaron Kaye is on the job. He draws hot brew for them both. Coby doesn't look.

"Drink up, Bill. I'll be back."

He sets off to Stores, steering against the pull from Gamma One. It is weak here. He can make it quite easily. Is it in refractory phase, maybe? Shot its bolt. How long to recovery? Better attend to that first, can't let it get them all over again.

Miriamne Stein is at her desk, her face absolutely quiet.

"It's Doc, Miri. You've had a shock, this will help you." He hopes, administering it to her passive arm. Her empty eyes slowly turn. "I'm checking out some EVA rope, see? I'll leave you a receipt right here, Miri, look. You stay there until you feel better."

Outside, he lets himself start across the ship, going with the pull. Joy opens in him, it is like a delicious sliding, like letting go sexually in his head. . . . Am I acting rationally? He probes himself, scared. Yes—he can make himself turn, make himself go forward toward the first bow-ramp. His plan is to close all the ports the crowd left open on their way into the corridor. Fourteen. After that—after that he can, he knows, vent the air from the inboard side. Depressurizing will kill it, of course. The sensible thing to do. No, surely that isn't necessary? He will think about it later, something is hurting him right now.

At the bow-ramp his head still feels okay, the thing's . . . lure is weak. The port is open; Don probably came this way. Cautiously, Aaron risks going down to it without tying his rope. All right; he has it swinging shut. As it closes he peeks out down the corridor. A mess, no people he can see—but the rosy living radiance—his heart misses, jumps—and the port closes almost on his nose.

A near thing. He must take no chances on the next one—it will be nearer to that marvelous light, will be in fact behind the command console where Yellaston was. Aaron finds his feet hurrying, stops himself at the last turn in the ramp and ties one end of the tether to a wall-hold. The other end he knots around his waist. Multiple knottings, must not be able to untie these in a hurry.

It's well he did so, he finds; he is already stepping into the corridor itself, stumbling on helmets, gloves, cables. The great flare of warm light is about twenty meters ahead. He must go back, go back and close the port. He stops himself at the command console and looks up at the videoscreen, still focused on *China Flower*'s fiery heart. It *is* like jewels in there, he sees, awestruck—great softly glowing globes, dazzling, changing color as he looks . . . some are dark, like a heap of fiery embers burning out. *Dying?* Grief wells up in him, he puts his hand up to hide it, looks away. There are his useless,

evil canisters . . . and the corridor a shambles. Aftermath of a
stampede . . . What was Coby muttering about, sperm. They
went through here, tails thrashing—

"Arn—you came!"

From nowhere Lory is hugging his arm. "Oh, Arn dear, I
waited—"

"Get out of here, Lor!" But she is working at his waist,
trying to untie knots. Her face is ecstatic—a load of jizzum in
the head, all right. "Go away, Lor. I'm going to depressurize."

"We'll be *together*, don't be afraid."

Angrily he pushes her behind him. "I'm going to vent the
air, can't you hear me? The air is going out!"

He tries to head her back toward the ramp, but she twists
away from him, gasping, "Oh, Arn, please Arn, I can't—" And
she is running to the light, to *China*'s hatch.

"Come back here!" He runs at her, is brought up by the
rope. She wavers just beyond him outlined in pale fire,
turning, turning, her fists at her mouth, sobbing, "I—I'm
going — alone—"

"No! Lor, wait!"

His own hands are ripping at the knots, but she is going,
slipping away from him across the tangled floor. "No, no—"
The warm light enwraps her, she has turned, is walking into
it, is gone—

A harsh warble breaks into his ears, waking him. He
staggers back, finally makes out that the flashings on the
console are launch warnings. Somebody is in *China Flower*,
taking off!

"Who's in there? Stop!" He flips channels at random. "You
in the ship, answer me!"

"Good-bye . . . boy." Bustamente's voice echoes from the
speakers.

"Ray, are you in there? This is Aaron, Ray, come out, you
don't know what you're doing—"

"I know to . . . set course. Keep your shit . . . world." The
deep voice is flat, mechanical.

"Come out here! Ray, we need you. Please listen, Ray—the
gyros are broken. The *gyros*."

". . . Tough."

A heavy metal purring shivers the walls.

"Ray, wait!" Aaron screams. "My sister is in there, she'll be
killed—your hatch is open! I'll be killed too, please, Ray, let her

come out. I'll close it. Lory! Lory, get out!"

His eyes are seeking desperately for the hatch control, his hands tear at the knots.

"She can come, too." A deathlike chuckle—another lighter voice briefly there, too. Ray's women—is Soli in there? The knots are giving.

"I'm going to . . . that planet . . . boy."

"Ray, you'll wake up a million miles in space, for Christ's sake, wait!" He jerks, pulls loose—he has to get there, get Lory out—he has to save that living beauty, that promise—

Other lights are flashing, there is a shudder in the walls. *The ship, Lory,* his brain cries faintly. He pulls the rope free and sees her shadow, her body wavering out blue against the radiance waiting there, waiting for him. With his last sanity he strikes the hatch lever, shoves it home.

The big hatch starts to slide shut across the radiant port.

"No, wait! No!" Aaron starts to run to it, his hand still grasping the rope, he is running toward all he has ever longed for—but the walls clang, scrape thunderously, and a wind buffets him sideways. He grips the rope in reflex, sees Lory stagger and start to slide in the howling air, everything is sliding toward the closing hatch. *China Flower* is going, falling away—taking it from him. They will all be blown out after her—but as Lory nears it the hatch slides home, the last ray vanishes.

The wind stops, the corridor is totally silent.

He stands there, a foolish man holding a rope, knowing that all sweetness is fading. Life itself is falling out to the dark beneath him, going away forever. Come back, he whispers, aching. Oh, come back.

Lory stirs. He lets fall the idiotic rope, goes to her bowed under a loss beyond bearing. What have I saved, what have I lost? Going away, fainter, fainter yet.

She looks up. Her face is clear, empty. Very young. All gone now, the load in her head . . . A feeling of dumb weight comes over him. It is *Centaur,* the whole wonderful ship he had been so proud of, hanging over him mute and flaccid in the dark. The life-spark gone away. Voiceless, unfindable in the icy wastes . . . His gut knows it is forever now, nothing will ever be all right again.

Gently he helps Lory up and starts walking with her to noplace, she trustful to his hand; little sister as she had been long ago. As they move away from the corridor his eyes notice a body lying by the wall. It is Tighe.

IV

. . . Dr. Aaron Kaye recording. The ghosts, the new things I mean, they're starting to go. I see them quite well now awake. Yesterday—wait, was it yesterday? Yes, because Tim has only been here one night, I brought him in yesterday. His, his body, I mean. It was his ghost I saw—Christ, I keep calling them that—the *things*, the new things, I mean. The ghost is in Tim's bed. But I saw his go, it was still out in Beta corridor. Did I say they're fairly stationary? I forget what I said. Maybe I should go over it, I have the time. They're more or less transparent, of course, even at the end. They float. I think they're partly out of the ship. It's hard to tell their size, like a projection or afterimage. They seem big, say, six or eight meters in diameter, but once or twice I've thought they may be very small. They're alive, you can tell that. They don't respond or communicate. They're not . . . rational. Not at all. They change, too, they take on colors or something from your mind. Did I say that? I'm not sure they're really visible at all, maybe the mind senses them and constructs an appearance. But recognizable. You can see . . . traces. I can identify most of them. Tim's was by ramp seven. It was partly Tim and partly something else, very alien. It seemed to swell up and float away out through the hull, as if it was getting closer and farther at the same time. The first one to go, so far as I know. Except Tighe's, I dreamed that. They do *not* dissipate. It throbbed—no, that isn't quite right. It swelled and floated. Away.

They're not ghosts, I should repeat that.

What I think they are—my subjective impression, I mean, a possible explanatory hypothesis—Oh, hell, I don't have to talk that way anymore. What I think they are is some kind of energy-thing, some—

What I think they are is blastomeres.

Holy zygotes, Coby said. I don't think they're holy. They're just there, growing. Definitely not spirits or ghosts or higher essences, they're not the *person* at all. They're a, a combined product. They develop. They stay at the site awhile and then . . . move on out.

Maybe I should record the order they go in, maybe it will correlate with the person's condition. That would be of scientific interest. The whole thing is of deep scientific interest, of course. Who will it be of scientific interest to? That's a good question. Maybe somebody will stumble on this ship in about a thousand years. Hello, friend. Are you human? If you are you won't be long. Kindly listen to Dr. Aaron Kaye before you—Oh, god, wait—

This is Dr. Aaron Kaye recording a message of deep scientific interest. Where was I? It doesn't matter. Tim—I mean Commander Timofaev Bron died today. I mean Tim himself. That's the first actual death except Tighe. Oh, and Bachi—I reported him, didn't I? Yes. The others are still functioning more or less. In a vegetable way. They feed themselves now and then. Since the meals stopped, I carry rations around. We go over the ship every day or so. I'm pretty sure no one else has died. Some of them are still playing cards in Commons, they even say a word or two sometimes. Some cards have fallen down, the ten of spades has been by Don's foot for days. I made them drink water yesterday. I'm afraid they're badly dehydrated. . . . Kawabata's the worst off, I think, he's sleeping in a soil bed. Earth to earth . . . He'll probably go soon. I have to learn to run all that, I suppose. If I go on.

. . . I know now I'll never be able to fix that laser. Christ, I spent a week in Ray's spookhouse. Funny thing, they gave us a big nondirectional Mayday transmitter. That means, "Come here and rescue us." But how can I send, "Stay the hell away?" Flaw in the program. That's all too short-range, anyway. . . . I could blow up the ship, I guess I could work that out. What good would it do? It wouldn't stop them coming. They'd figure we had an accident. Too bad, hazards of space. Baby, you'll find out. . . .

Wonder where Ray is now, how long he lasted? His, his thing is here, of course. In Gamma One. The women too. I found Soli's, it's, no, I think we won't talk about that. They were with him, their bodies, I mean. *Them* . . . He was so strong, he did something, he acted, afterward. No use, of course. The dead saving the dead. Help me make it through the night—quit that.

. . . Functioning, we were discussing functioning. The most intact is Yellaston. I mean, he isn't intact at all, but we talk a little, sort of, when I go up there. Maybe a lifetime practice in carrying on with half of his cortex shot. I think he understands. It's not a highly technical concept, after all. He knows he's dying. He saw it as death, the whole thing. Intuition in his locked-up guts, the fear—Sex equals death. How right you are, old man. Funny, I used to treat patients for thinking that. Therapy—Of course it was a different, let's say order of sex. He's quit drinking. The thing he was holding in, the load, it's gone. . . . I think of what's left as him, damn it, it is him, the human part. I've seen his, his product, it's by the bow-port. It's very strange. I wonder, has he seen it? Does a spent sperm recognize the blastomere? I think he must have. I found him crying, once. Maybe it was joy, I don't think so. . . .

. . . Hello, friend. This is Dr. Aaron Kaye, your friendly scientific reporter. Dr. Aaron Kaye is also getting the tiniest bit ethanolized, maybe you'll forgive it. It has occurred to me as a matter of scientific justice that Coby deserves credit for the, the formulation of the hypothesis. Superb diagnostician, Coby, to the end. That's Dr. William F. Coby, late of Johns Hopkins/ M.I.T. Originator of Coby's final solution—hypothesis, I mean. Remember his name, friend. While you can. I tried to get him to record this, but he doesn't talk anymore. I think he's right; I know he's right. He still functions, though, in a dying way. Goes to the narcotics locker quite openly. I let him. Maybe he's trying something. Why is he so intact? Didn't he have much of whatever it is they lost, not much jizzum there? No—that's not fair. Not even true . . . Funny thing, I find myself liking him now, really liking him. Dangerous stuff all gone, I guess. Comment on me. Call me Lory—no, we aren't going to talk about Lory, either. We were talking about, I was talking about Coby. His hypothesis. Listen, friend. You on your way with a load in your head.

Coby's right, I know he's right. We're gametes.

Nothing but gametes. The dimorphic set—call it sperm. Two types, little boy sperms, little girl sperms—half of the germ-plasm of . . . something. Not complete beings at all. Half of the gametes of some . . . creatures, some race. Maybe they live in space, I think so. The, their zygotes do. Maybe they aren't even intelligent. Say they use planets to breed on, like amphibians going to the water. And they sowed their primordial seed-stuff around here, their milt and roe among the stars. On suitable planets. And the stuff germinated. And after the usual interval—say three billion years, that's what it took us, didn't it?—the milt, the sperm, evolved to *motility*, see? And we made it to the stars. To the roe-planet. To fertilize them. And that's all we are, the whole damn thing—the evolving, the achieving and fighting and hoping—all the pain and effort, just to get us there with the loads of jizzum in our heads. Nothing but sperms' tails. Human beings—does a sperm think it's somebody, too? Those beautiful egg-things, the creatures on that planet, evolving in their own way for millions of years . . . maybe they think and dream, too, maybe they think they're people. All the whole thing, just to make something else, all for nothing—

Excuse me. This is Dr. Aaron Kaye, recording two more deaths. They are Dr. James Kawabata and Quartermaster Miriamne Stein. I found her when I was taking Kawabata's body to cold Stores. They'll all be there, you'll find them, friend. Fifty-five icicles and one dust pile . . . maybe. Cause of death—have I been reporting cause of death? Cause of death, acute— Oh, hell, what does a sperm's tail die of? Acute loss of ability to live anymore. Acute postfunctional irrelevance . . . Symptoms; maybe you'd like to know the symptoms. You should be interested. The symptoms start after brief contact with a certain life-form from the Alpha planet—did I mention that there does seem to have been momentary physical contact, apparently through the forehead? The gross symptoms are disorientation, apathy, some aphasia, ataxia, anorexia. All responses depressed; aprosexia, speech echolalic. Reflexes weakly present, no typical catatonia. Cardiac functions subnormal, nonacute. Clinically—I've been able to test six of them—clinically the EEG shows generalized flattening, asynchrony. Early theta and alpha deficits. It is unlike, repeat totally unlike, post-ECS syndrome. Symptoms cannot be interpreted as due to a physical shock, electric or otherwise. Adrenergic systems most affected, cholinergic relatively less so. Adrenal insufficiency is not, repeat not, confirmed by hormonal bioassay. Oh, hell—they've been drained, that's what it is. Drained of something . . . something vital. Prognosis . . . yes.

The prognosis is death.

This is of great scientific interest, friend. But you won't believe it, of course. You're on your way there, aren't you? Nothing will stop you, you have reasons. All kinds of reasons— saving the race, building a new world, national honor, personal glory, scientific truth, dreams, hopes, plans—does every little sperm have its reasons, thrashing up the pipe?

It calls, you see. The roe calls us across the light-years, don't ask me how. It's even calling Dr. Aaron Kaye, the sperm who said no—Oh, Christ, I can feel it, the sweet pull. *Why did I let it go?* . . . Excuse me. Dr. Aaron Kaye is having another drink now. Quite a few, actually. Yellaston was right, it helps. . . . The infinite variety of us, all for nothing. Where was I? . . . We make our rounds, I check them all. They don't move much anymore. I look at the new things, too. . . . Lory comes with me, she helps me carry things. Like she used to, little sister— we're particularly not going to talk about Lory. The things, the zygotes—three more of them went away today, Kawabata's and the two Danes. Don's is still in Commons, I think it's going soon. Do they leave when the, the *person* dies? I think that's just coincidence. We're totally . . . *irrelevant*, afterward. The zygote remains near the site of impregnation for a variable period before moving on to implant. Where do they implant, in space, maybe? Where do they get born?—Oh, god, what are they like, the creatures that generated us, that we die to form? Can a gamete look at a king? Are they brutes or angels? Ah, Christ, is isn't fair, *it isn't fair!*

. . . Sorry, friend. I'm all right now. Don Purcell collapsed today, I left him in Commons. I visit my patients daily. Most of them are still sitting. Sitting at their stations, in their graves. We do what we can, Lory and I. *Making gentle the life of this world* . . . It may be of great scientific interest that they all saw it different the egg-things I mean. Don said it was god, Coby saw ova. Åhlstrom was whispering about the tree Yggdrasill. Bruce Jang saw Mei-Lin there. Yellaston saw death. Tighe saw Mother, I think. All Dr. Aaron Kaye saw was colored lights. Why didn't I go, too? Who knows. Statistical phenomenon. Defective tail. My foot got caught. . . . Lory saw utopia, heaven on earth, I guess. We will not talk about Lory. . . . She goes 'round with me, looking at the dying sperms, our friends. All the things in their rooms, the personal life, all this ship we were so proud of. *Mono no aware*, that's the pathos of things, Kawabata told me. The wristwatch after the wearer has died, the eyeglasses . . . the pathos of all our things now.

. . . Yes, Dr. Aaron Kaye is getting fairly well pissed, friend. Dr. Aaron Kaye, you see, is avoiding contemplating what he'll do, afterward . . . after they are all gone. Coby broke his leg today. I found him, I think he was pleased when I put him to bed. He didn't seem to be in much pain. His, the thing he made, it went away quite a while ago, I guess I haven't been recording too well. A lot of them have gone. Not Yellaston's last time I looked. He's up in Astrogation, I mean Yellaston himself. Gazing out the dome. I know he wants to end there. Ah, Christ, the poor old tiger, the poor ape, everything Lory hated—all gone now. Who cares about a sperm's personality? Answer: another sperm . . . Dr. Kaye grows maudlin. Dr. Kaye weeps, in fact. Remember that, friend. It has scientific interest. What will Dr. Kaye do, afterward? It will be quiet around here on the good ship *Centaur*, which will probably last forever, unless it falls into a star. . . . Will Dr. Kaye live out the rest of his life here, twenty-six trillion miles from his home testis? Reading, listening to music, tending his garden, writing notes of great scientific interest? Fifty-five frozen bodies and one skeleton. Keep your eye on the skeleton, friend . . . or check on that last scout ship, *Alpha*. Will Dr. Kaye one day take off in little old *Alpha*, trying to head for somewhere? Where? You guess . . . Tail-end Charlie, last man in the oviduct. Over the viaduct, via the oviduct. Excuse me.

. . . Not the last. Not at all, let's not forget all those fleets of ships, they'll start from Earth when the green signal gets there. And they'll keep on coming for a while, anyway. . . . The green got sent, didn't it, no matter how we tried? The goal of man's desiring. No way to stop it. No hope at all, really.

But of course it's only a handful, the ones that will ever make it to the planet, compared to the total population of Earth. About the proportion of one ejaculandum to total sperm production, wouldn't you say? Should compute sometime, great scientific interest there. So most of the egg-creatures will die unfertilized, too. Nature's notorious wastefulness. Fifty million eggs, a billion sperm—one salmon . . .

. . . What happens to the people who don't go, the ones who stay on Earth, all the rest of the race? Let us speculate, Dr. Kaye. What happens to unused sperm? Stuck in testes, die of overheating. Reabsorbed. Remind you of anything? Calcutta, say. Rio de Janeiro, Los Angeles . . . Previews. Born too soon or too late—too bad. Rot away unused. Function fulfilled, organs atrophy. . . . End of it all, just rot away. *Not even knowing*— thinking they were people, thinking they had a chance. . . .

Dr. Kaye is getting rather conclusively intoxicated, friend.

Dr. Kaye is also getting tired of talking to you. What good will it do you on your way up the pipe? Can you stop, man? Can you? Ha ha. As—someone used to say. . . . Goddamn it, why can't you try? Can't you stop, can't you stay human even if we're—Oh, lord, can a half of something, can a gamete build a culture? I don't think so. . . . You poor doomed bastard with a load in your head, you'll get there or die trying—

Excuse me. Lory stumbled a lot today. . . . Little sister, you were a good sperm, you swam hard. You made the connection. She wasn't crazy, you know. Ever, really. She knew something was wrong with us. . . . Healed, made whole? All those months . . . a wall away from heaven, the golden breasts of god. The end of pain, the queen couzy . . . fighting it all the way . . . Oh, Lory, stay with me, don't die—*Christ, the pull, the terrible sweet pull*—

. . . This is Dr. Aaron Kaye signing off. Maybe my condition is of deep scientific interest . . . I don't dream anymore.

WE WHO STOLE THE DREAM

THE CHILDREN *could survive only twelve minims in the sealed containers.*

Jilshat pushed the heavy cargo loader as fast as she dared through the darkness, praying that she would not attract the attention of the Terran guard under the floodlights ahead. The last time she passed he had roused and looked at her with his frightening pale alien eyes. Then, her truck had carried only fermenting-containers full of *amlat* fruit.

Now, curled in one of the containers, lay hidden her only-born, her son Jemnal. Four minims at least had already been used up in the loading and weighing sheds. It would take four more, maybe five, to push the load out to the ship, where her people would send it up on the cargo conveyor. And more time yet for her people in the ship to find Jemnal and rescue him. Jilshat pushed faster, her weak gray humanoid legs trembling.

As she came into the lighted gate the Terran turned his head and saw her.

Jilshat cringed away, trying to make herself even smaller, trying not to run. Oh, why had she not taken Jemnal out in an earlier load? The other mothers had taken theirs. But she had been afraid. At the last minute her faith had failed. It had not seemed possible that what had been planned so long and prepared for so painfully could actually be coming true, that her people, her poor feeble dwarf Joilani, could really overpower and subdue the mighty Terrans in that cargo ship. Yet there the big ship stood in its cone of lights, all apparently quiet. The impossible must have been done, or there would have been disturbance. The other young must be safe. Yes—now she could make out empty cargo trucks hidden in the shadows; their pushers must have already mounted into the ship. It was really and truly happening, their great escape to freedom—or to death. . . . And now she was almost past the guard, almost safe.

"Oy!"

She tried not to hear the harsh Terran bark, hurried faster. But in three giant strides he loomed up before her, so that she had to halt.

"You deaf?" he asked in the Terran of his time and place. Jilshat could barely understand; she had been a worker in the far *amlat* fields. All she could think of was the time draining inexorably away, while he tapped the containers with the butt of his weapon, never taking his eyes off her. Her huge dark-lashed Joilani gaze implored him mutely; in her terror, she forgot the warnings, and her small dove-gray face contorted in that rictus of anguish the Terrans called a "smile." Weirdly, he smiled back, as if in pain too.

"I wo'king, seh," she managed to bring out. A minim gone now, almost two. If he did not let her go at once her child was surely doomed. Almost she could hear a faint mew, as if the drugged baby was already struggling for breath.

"I go, seh! Men in ship ang'ee!" Her smile broadened, dimpled in agony to what she could not know was a mask of allure.

"Let 'em wait. You know, you're not bad-looking for a Juloo *moolie?*" He made a strange *hahnha* sound in his throat. "It's my duty to check the natives for arms. Take that off." He poked up her dingy *jelmah* with the snout of his weapon.

Three minims. She tore the *jelmah* off, exposing her wide-hipped, short-legged little gray form, with its double dugs and bulging pouch. A few heartbeats more and it would be too late, Jemnal would die. She could still save him—she could force the clamps and rip that smothering lid away. Her baby was still alive in there. But if she did so, all would be discovered; she would betray them all. *Jailasanatha*, she prayed. Let me have love's courage. O my Joilani, give me strength to let him die. I pay for my unbelief.

"Turn around."

Grinning in grief and horror, she obeyed.

"That's better, you look almost human. Ah, Lord, I've been out too long. C'mere." She felt his hand on her buttocks. "You think that's fun, hey? What's your name, *moolie?*"

The last possible minim had run out. Numb with despair, Jilshat murmured a phrase that meant *Mother of the Dead*.

"Joobly-woobly—" His voice changed. "Well, well! And where did *you* come from?"

Too late, too late: Lal, the damaged female, minced swiftly to them. Her face was shaved and painted pink and red; she swirled open a bright *jelmah* to reveal a body grotesquely tinted and bound to imitate the pictures the Terrans worshiped. Her face was wreathed in a studied smile.

"Me Lal." She flirted her fingers to release the flower essence the Terrans seemed to love. "You want I make fik-fik foh you?"

The instant Jilshat felt the guard's attention leave her, she flung her whole strength against the heavy truck and rushed naked with it out across the endless field, staggering beyond the limit of breath and heart, knowing it was too late, unable not to hope. Around her in the shadows the last burdened Joilani filtered toward the ship. Behind them the guard was being drawn by Lal into the shelter of the gatehouse.

At the last moment he glanced back and scowled.

"Hey, those Juloos shouldn't be going into the ship that way."

"Men say come. Say move cans." Lal reached up and caressed his throat, slid skillful Joilani fingers into his turgid alien crotch. "Fik-fik," she crooned, smiling irresistibly. The guard shrugged, and turned back to her with a chuckle.

The ship stood unwatched. It was an aging *amlat* freighter, a flying factory, carefully chosen because its huge cargo hold was heated and pressurized to make the fruit ferment en route, so that some enzyme the Terrans valued would be ready when it made port. That hold could be lived in, and the *amlat* fruit would multiply a thousandfold in the food-converter cycle. Also, the ship was the commonest type to visit here; over the decades the Joilani ship cleaners had been able to piece together, detail by painful detail, an almost complete image of the operating controls.

This one was old and shabby. Its Terran Star of Empire and identifying symbols were badly in need of paint. Of its name the first word had been eroded away, leaving only the alien letters: . . . N'S DREAM. Some Terran's dream once; it was now the Joilani's.

But it was not Lal's Dream. Ahead of Lal lay only pain and death. She was useless as a breeder; her short twin birth channels had been ruptured by huge hard Terran members, and the delicate spongy tissue that was the Joilani womb had been damaged beyond recovery. So Lal had chosen the greater love, to serve her people with one last torment. In her hair flower was the poison that would let her die when the *Dream* was safely away.

It was not safe yet. Over the guard's great bulk upon her Lal could glimpse the lights of the other ship on the field, the station's patrol cruiser. By the worst of luck, it was just readying for its periodic off-planet reconnaissance.

To our misfortune, when the Dream *was loaded, the Terran warship stood ready to lift off, so that it could intercept us before we could escape by entering what the Terrans called tau-space. Here we failed.*

Old Jalun hobbled as smartly as he could out across the Patrol's section of the spaceport, to the cruiser. He was wearing the white jacket and female *jelmah* in which the Terrans dressed their mess servants, and he carried a small napkin-wrapped object. Overhead three fast-moving moonlets were converging, sending triple shadows around his frail form. They faded as he came into the lights of the cruiser's lock.

A big Terran was doing something to the cruiser's lock tumblers. As Jalun struggled up the giant steps, he saw that the spacer wore a side arm. Good. Then he recognized the spacer, and an un-Joilani flood of hatred made his twin hearts pound. This was the Terran who had raped Jalun's granddaughter, and broken her brother's spine with a kick when the boy came to her rescue. Jalun fought down his feelings, grimacing in pain. *Jailasanatha; let me not offend Oneness.*

"Where you think you're going, Smiley? What you got there?" He did not recognize Jalun; to Terrans all Joilani looked alike. "Commandeh say foh you, seh. Say, celeb'ation. Say take to offiseh fi'st."

"Let's see."

Trembling with the effort to control himself, smiling painfully from ear to ear, Jalun unfolded a corner of the cloth.

The spacer peered, whistled. "If that's what I think it is, sweet stars of home. Lieutenant!" he shouted, hustling Jalun up and into the ship. "Look what the boss sent us!"

In the wardroom the lieutenant and another spacer were checking over the microsource charts. The lieutenant also was wearing a weapons belt—good again. Listening carefully, Jalun's keen Joilani hearing could detect no other Terrans on the ship. He bowed deeply, still smiling his hate, and unwrapped his packet before the lieutenant.

Nestled in snowy linen lay a small tear-shaped amethyst flask.

"Commandeh say, foh you. Say must d'ink now, is open."

The lieutenant whistled in his turn, and picked the flask up reverently.

"Do you know what this is, old Smiley?"

"No, seh," Jalun lied.

"What is it, sir?" the third spacer asked. Jalun could see that he was very young.

"This, sonny, is the most unbelievable, most precious, most delectable drink that will ever pass your dewy gullet. Haven't you ever heard of Stars Tears?"

The youngster stared at the flask, his face clouding.

"And Smiley's right," the lieutenant went on. "Once it's open, you have to drink it right away. Well, I guess we've done all we need to tonight. I must say, the old man left us a generous go. Why did he say he sent this, Juloo boy?"

"Celeb'ation, seh. Say his celeb'ation, his day."

"Some celebration. Well, let us not quibble over miracles. Jon, produce three liquor cups. *Clean* ones."

"Yes*sir!*" The big spacer rummaged in the lockers overhead.

Standing child-size among these huge Terrans, Jalun was overcome again by the contrast between their size and strength and perfection and his own weak-limbed, frail, slope-shouldered little form. Among his people he had been accounted a strong youth; even now he was among the ablest. But to these mighty Terrans, Joilani strength was a joke. Perhaps they were right; perhaps he was of an inferior race, fit only to be slaves. . . . But then Jalun remembered what he knew, and straightened his short spine. The younger spacer was saying something.

"Lieutenant, sir, if that's really Stars Tears I can't drink it."

"You can't *drink* it? Why not?"

"I promised. I, uh, swore."

"You'd promise such an insane thing?"

"My—my mother," the youngster said miserably.

The two others shouted with laughter.

"You're a long way from home now, son," the lieutenant said kindly. "What am I saying, Jon? We'd be delighted to take yours. But I just can't bear to see a man pass up the most beautiful thing in life, and I mean bar none. Forget Mommy and prepare your soul for bliss. That's an order. . . . All right, Smiley boy, equal shares. And if you spill one drop I'll *dicty* both your little *pnonks*, hear?"

"Yes, seh." Carefully Jalun poured the loathsome liquor into the small cups.

"You ever tasted this, Juloo?"

"No, seh."

"And never will. All right, now scat. Ah-h-h . . . Well, here's to our next station, may it have real live poogy on it."

Jalun went silently back down into the shadows of the gangway, paused where he could just see the spacers lift their cups and drink. Hate and disgust choked him, though he had seen it often: Terrans eagerly drinking Stars Tears. It was the very symbol of their oblivious cruelty, their fall from *Jailasanatha*. They could not be excused for ignorance; too many of them had told Jalun how Stars Tears was made. It was not tears precisely, but the body secretions of a race of beautiful, frail winged creatures on a very distant world. Under physical or mental pain their glands exuded this liquid which the Terrans found so deliciously intoxicating. To obtain it, a mated pair were captured and slowly tortured to death in each other's sight. Jalun had been told atrocious details which he could not bear to recall.

Now he watched, marveling that the hate burning in his eyes did not alert the Terrans. He was quite certain that the drug was tasteless and did no harm; careful trials over the long years had proved that. The problem was that it took from two to five minims to work. The last-affected Terran might have time to raise an alarm. Jalun would die to prevent that—if he could.

The three spacers' faces had changed; their eyes shone.

"You see, son?" the lieutenant asked huskily.

The boy nodded, his rapt gaze on nowhere.

Suddenly the big spacer Jon lunged up and said thickly, "What?" Then he slumped down with his head on one outstretched arm.

"Hey! Hey, Jon!" The lieutenant rose, reaching toward him. But then he too was falling heavily across the wardroom table. That left only the staring boy.

Would he act, would he seize the caller? Jalun gathered himself to spring, knowing he could do little but die in those strong hands.

But the boy only repeated, "What? . . . What?" Lost in a private dream, he leaned back, slid downward, and began to snore.

Jalun darted up to them and snatched the weapons from the two huge lax bodies. Then he scrambled up to the cruiser's control room, summoning all the memorized knowledge that had been gained over the slow years. Yes—that was the transmitter. He wrestled its hood off and began firing into its works. The blast of the weapon frightened him, but he kept on till all was charred and melted.

The flight computer next. Here he had trouble burning in, but soon achieved what seemed to be sufficient damage. A nearby metal case fastened to what was now the ceiling bothered him. It had not been included in his instructions— because the Joilani had not learned of the cruiser's new backup capability. Jalun gave it only a perfunctory blast, and turned to the weapons console.

Emotions he had never felt before were exploding in him, obscuring sight and reason. He fired at wild random across the board, concentrating on whatever would explode or melt, not realizing that he had left the heavy-weapons wiring essentially undamaged. Pinned-up pictures of the grotesque Terran females, which had done his people so much harm, he flamed to ashes.

Then he did the most foolish thing.

Instead of hurrying straight back down through the wardroom, he paused to stare at the slack face of the spacer who had savaged his young. His weapon was hot in his hand. Madness took Jalun: he burned through face and skull. The release of a lifetime's helpless hatred seemed to drive him on wings of flame. Beyond all reality, he killed the other two Terrans without pausing and hurried on down.

He was quite insane with rage and self-loathing when he reached the reactor chambers. Forgetting the hours of painful memorization of the use of the waldo arms, he went straight in through the shielding port to the pile itself. Here he began to tug with his bare hands at the damping rods, as if he were a suited Terran. But his Joilani strength was far too weak, and he could barely move them. He raged, fired at the pile, tugged again, his body bare to the full fury of radiation.

When presently the rest of the Terran crew poured into the ship they found a living corpse clawing madly at the pile. He had removed only four rods; instead of a meltdown he had achieved nothing at all.

The engineer took one look at Jalun through the vitrex and swung the heavy waldo arm over to smash him into the wall. Then he replaced the rods, checked his readouts, and signaled: Ready to lift.

There was also great danger that the Terrans would signal to one of their mighty warships, which alone can send a missile seeking through tau-space. An act of infamy was faced.

The Elder Jayakal entered the communications chamber just as the Terran operator completed his regular transmission for the period. That had been carefully planned. First, it would insure the longest possible interval before other stations became alarmed. Equally important, the Joilani had been unable to discover a way of entry to the chamber when the operator was not there.

"Hey, Pops, what do you think you're doing? You know you're not supposed to be in here. Scoot!"

Jayakal smiled broadly in the pain of his heart. This Terran She'gan had been kind to the Joilani in his rough way. Kind and respectful. He knew them by their proper names; he had never abused their females; he fed cleanly, and did not drink abomination. He had even inquired, with decorum, into the sacred concepts: *Jailasanatha*, the Living-with-in-honor, the Oneness-of-love. Old Jayakal's flexible cheekbones drew upward in a beaming rictus of shame.

"O gentle friend, I come to share with you," he said ritually.

"You know I don't really divvy your speech. Now you have to get out."

Jayakal knew no Terran word for *sharing;* perhaps there was none.

"F'iend, I b'ing you thing."

"Yeah, well bring it me *outside*." Seeing that the old Joilani did not move, the operator rose to usher him out. But memory stirred; his understanding of the true meaning of that smile penetrated. "What is it, Jayakal? What you got there?"

Jayakal brought the heavy load in his hands forward.

"Death."

"What-where did you get that? Oh, holy mother, get away from me! That thing is armed! *The pin is out —*"

The laboriously pilfered and hoarded excavating plastic had been well and truly assembled; the igniter had been properly attached. In the ensuing explosion, fragments of the whole transmitter complex, mingled with those of Jayakal and his Terran friend, rained down across the Terran compound and out among the *amlat* fields.

Spacers and station personnel erupted out of the post bars, at first uncertain in the darkness what to do. Then they saw torches flaring and bobbing around the transformer sheds. Small gray figures were running, leaping, howling, throwing missiles that flamed.

"The crotting Juloos are after the power plant! Come on!"

Other diversions were planned. The names of the Old Ones and damaged females who died thus for us are inscribed on the sacred rolls. We can only pray that they found quick and merciful deaths.

The station commander's weapons belt hung over the chair by his bed. All through the acts of shame and pain Sosalal had been watching it, waiting for her chance. If only Bislat, the commander's "boy," could come in to help her! But he could not—he was needed at the ship.

The commander's lust was still unsated. He gulped a drink from the vile little purple flask, and squinted his small Terran eyes meaningfully at her. Sosalal smiled, and offered her trembling, grotesquely disfigured body once more. But no: he wanted her to stimulate him. She set her emphatic Joilani fingers, her shuddering mouth, to do their work, hoping that the promised sound would come soon, praying that the commander's communicator would not buzz with the news of the attempt failed. Why, oh why, was it taking so long? She wished she could have one last sight of the Terran's great magical star projection, which showed at one far side those blessed, incredible symbols of her people. Somewhere out there, so very far away, was Joilani home space—maybe even, she thought wildly, while her body labored at its hurtful task, maybe a Joilani empire!

Now he wished to enter her. She was almost inured to the pain; her damaged body had healed in a form pleasing to this Terran. She was only the commander's fourth "girl." There had been other commanders, some better, some worse, and "girls" beyond counting, as far back as the Joilani records ran. It had been "girls" like herself and "boys" like Bislat who had first seen the great three-dimensional luminous star swarms in the commander's private room—and brought back to their people the unbelievable news: somewhere, a Joilani homeland still lived!

Greatly daring, a "girl" had once asked about those Joilani symbols. Her commander had shrugged. "That stuff! It's the hell and gone the other side of the system, take half your life to get there. I don't know a thing about 'em. Probably somebody just stuck 'em in. They aren't Juloos, that's for sure."

Yet there the symbols blazed, tiny replicas of the ancient Joilani Sun-in-splendor. It could mean only one thing, that the old myth was true: that they were not natives to this world, but descendants of a colony left by Joilani who traveled space as the Terrans did. And that those great Joilani yet lived!

If only they could reach them. But how, how?

Could they somehow send a message? All but impossible. And even if they did, how could their kind rescue them from the midst of Terran might?

No. Hopeless as it seemed, they must get themselves out and reach Joilani space by their own efforts.

And so the great plan had been born and grown, over years, over lifetimes. Painfully, furtively, bit by bit, Joilani servants and bar attendants and ship cleaners and *amlat* loaders had discovered and brought back the magic numbers, and their meaning: the tau-space coordinates that would take them to those stars. From discarded manuals, from spacers' talk, they had pieced together the fantastic concept of tau-space itself. Sometimes an almighty Terran would find a naive Joilani question amusing enough to answer. Those allowed inside the ships brought back tiny fragments of the workings of the Terran magic. Joilani, who were humble "boys" by day and "girls" by night, became clandestine students and teachers, fitting together the mysteries of their overlords, reducing them from magic to comprehension. Preparing, planning in minutest detail, sustained only by substanceless hope, they readied for their epic, incredible flight.

And now the lived-for moment had come.

Or had it? Why was it taking so long? Suffering as she had so often smilingly suffered before, Sosalal despaired. Surely nothing would, nothing could change. It was all a dream; all would go on as it always had, the degradation and the pain. . . . The commander indicated new desires; careless with grief, Sosalal complied.

"Watch it!" He slapped her head so that her vision spun. "Excuse, seh."

"You're getting a bit long in the tooth, Sosi." He meant that literally: mature Joilani teeth were large. "You better start training a younger *moolie*. Or have 'em pulled."

"Yes, seh."

"You scratch me again and I'll pull 'em myself—Holy Jebulibar, what's that?"

A flash from the window lit the room, followed by a rumbling that rattled the walls. The commander tossed her aside and ran to look out.

It had come! It was really true! *Hurry.* She scrambled to the chair.

"Good God Almighty, it looks like the transmitter blew. Wha—"

He had whirled toward his communicator, his clothes, and found himself facing the mouth of his own weapon held in Sosalal's trembling hands. He was too astounded to react. When she pressed the firing stud he dropped with his chest blown open, the blank frown still on his face.

Sosalal too was astounded, moving in a dream. She had killed. Really killed a Terran. A living being. "I come to share," she whispered ritually. Gazing at the fiery light in the window, she turned the weapon to her own head and pressed the firing stud.

Nothing happened.

What could be wrong? The dream broke, leaving her in dreadful reality. Frantically she poked and probed at the strange object. Was there some mechanism needed to reset it? She was unaware of the meaning of the red charge dot—the commander had grown too careless to recharge his weapon after his last game hunt. Now it was empty.

Sosalal was still struggling with the thing when the door burst open and she felt herself seized and struck all but senseless. Amid the boots and the shouting, her wrist glands leaked scarlet Joilani tears as she foresaw the slow and merciless death that would now be hers.

They had just started to question her when she heard it: the deep rolling rumble of a ship lifting off. The *Dream* was away— her people had done it, they were saved! Through her pain she heard a Terran voice say, "Juloo-town is empty! All the young ones are on that ship." Under the blows of her tormentors her twin hearts leaped with joy.

But a moment later all exultation died; she heard the louder fires of the Terran cruiser bursting into the sky. The *Dream* had failed, then: they would be pursued and killed. Desolate, she willed herself to die in the Terrans' hands. But her life resisted, and her broken body lived long enough to sense the thunderous concussion from the sky that must be the destruction of her race. She died believing all hope was dead. Still, she had told her questioners nothing.

Great dangers came to those who essayed to lift the Dream.

"If you monkeys are seriously planning to try to fly this ship, you better set that trim lever first or we'll all be killed."

It was the Terran pilot speaking—the third to be captured, so they had not needed to stop his mouth.

"Go on, push it! It's in landing attitude now, that red one. I don't want to be smashed up."

Young Jivadh, dwarfed in the huge pilot's chair, desperately reviewed his laboriously built-up memory engram of this ship's controls. Red lever, red lever . He was not quite sure. He twisted around to look at their captives. Incredible to see the three great bodies lying bound and helpless against the wall, which should soon become the floor. From the seat beside him Bislat held his weapon trained on them. It was one of the two stolen Terran weapons which they had long hoarded for this, their greatest task: the capture of the Terrans on the *Dream*. The first spacer had not believed they were serious until Jivadh had burned through his boots.

Now he lay groaning intermittently, muffled by the gag. When he caught Jivadh's gaze he nodded vehemently in confirmation of the pilot's warning.

"I left it in landing attitude," the pilot repeated. "If you try to lift that way we'll all die!" The third captive nodded, too.

Jivadh's mind raced over and over the remembered pattern. The *Dream* was an old unstandardized ship. Jivadh continued with the ignition procedure, not touching the red lever.

"Push it, you fool!" the pilot shouted. "Holy mother, do you want to die?"

Bislat was looking nervously from Jivadh to the Terrans. He too had learned the patterns of the *amlat* freighters, but not as well.

"Jivadh, are you *sure?*"

"I cannot be certain. I think on the old ships that is an emergency device which will change or empty the fuels so that they cannot fire. What they call *abort*. See the Terran symbol *a*."

The pilot had caught the words. '

"It's not abort, it's attitude! *A* for attitude, *attitude*, you monkey. Push it over or we'll crash!"

The other two nodded urgently.

Jivadh's whole body was flushed blue and trembling with tension. His memories seemed to recede, blur, spin. Never before had a Joilani disbelieved, disobeyed, a Terran order. Desperate, he clung to one fading fragment of a yellowed chart in his mind.

"I think not," he said slowly.

Taking his people's whole life in his delicate fingers, he punched the ignition-and-lift sequence into real time.

Clickings—a clank of metal below—a growling hiss that grew swiftly to an intolerable roar beneath them. The old freighter creaked, strained, gave a sickening lurch. Were they about to crash? Jivadh's soul died a thousand deaths.

But the horizon around them stayed level. The *Dream* was shuddering upward, straight up, moving faster and faster as she staggered and leaped toward space. All landmarks fell away—they were in flight! Jivadh, crushed against his supports, exulted. They had not crashed! He had been right: the Terran had been lying.

All outer sound fell away. The *Dream* had cleared atmosphere, and was driving for the stars!

But not alone.

Just as the pressure was easing, just as joy was echoing through the ship and the first of his comrades were struggling up to tell him all was well below, just as a Healer was moving to aid the Terran's burned foot—a loud Terran voice roared through the cabin.

"Halt, you in the *Dream!* Retrofire. Go into orbit for boarding or we'll shoot you down."

The Joilani shrank back. Jivadh saw that the voice was coming from the transceiver, which he had turned on as part of the lift-off procedures.

"That's the patrol," the Terran pilot told him. "They're coming up behind us. You have to quit now, monkey boy. They really will blow us out of space."

A sharp clucking started in an instrument to Jivadh's right. MASS PROXIMITY INDICATOR, he read. Involuntarily he turned to the Terran pilot.

"That's nothing, just one of those damn moons. Listen, you *have* to backfire. I'm not fooling this time. I'll tell you what to do."

"Go into orbit for boarding!" the great voice boomed.

But Jivadh had turned away, was busy doing something else. It was not right. Undoubtedly he would kill them all—but he knew what his people would wish.

"Last warning. We will now fire," the cruiser's voice said coldly.

"They mean it!" the Terran pilot screamed. "For god's sake let me talk to them, let me acknowledge!" The other Terrans were glaring, thrashing in their bonds. This fear was genuine, Jivadh saw, quite different from the lies before. What he had to do was not difficult, but it would take time. He fumbled the transceiver switch open and spoke into it, ignoring Bislat's horrified eyes.

"We will stop. Please wait. It is difficult."

"That's the boy!" The pilot was panting with relief. "All right now. See that delta-V estimator, under the thrust dial? Oh, it's too feking complicated. Let me at it, you might as well."

Jivadh ignored him, continuing with his doomed task. Reverently he fed in the coordinates, the sacred coordinates etched in his mind since childhood, the numbers that might possibly, if they could have done it right, have brought them out of tau-space among Joilani stars.

"We will give you three minims to comply," the voice said.

"Listen, they *mean* it!" the pilot cried. "What are you doing? Let me up!"

Jivadh went on. The mass-proximity gauge clucked louder; he ignored that, too. When he turned to the small tau-console the pilot suddenly understood.

"No! Oh, *no!*" he screamed. "Oh, for god's sake don't do that! You crotting idiot, if you go tau this close to the planet we'll be squashed right into its mass!" His voice had risen to a shriek; the other two were uttering wordless roars and writhing.

They were undoubtedly right, Jivadh thought bleakly. One moment's glory—and now the end.

"We fire in one more minim," came the cruiser's toneless roar.

"Stop! Don't! No!" the pilot yelled.

Jivadh looked at Bislat. The other had realized what he was doing; now he gave the true Joilani smile of pursed lips and made the ritual sign of Acceptance-of-ending. The Joilani in the passage understood that; a sighing silence rustled back through the ship.

"Fire one," the cruiser voice said briskly.

Jivadh slammed the tau-tumbler home.

An alarm shrieked and cut off, all colors vanished, the very structure of space throbbed wildly—as, by a million-to-one chance, the three most massive nearby moons occulted one another in line with the tiny extra energies of the cruiser and its detonating missile, in such a way that for one micromicrominim the *Dream* stood at a seminull point with the planetary mass. In that fleeting instant she flung out her tau-field, folded the normal dimensions around her, and shot like a squeezed pip into the discontinuity of being which was tau.

Nearby space-time was rocked by the explosion; concussion swept the moons and across the planet beneath. So narrow was the *Dream*'s moment of safe passage that a fin of bright metal from the cruiser and a rock with earth and herbs on it were later found intricately meshed into the substance of her stern cargo hold, to the great wonder of the Joilani.

Meanwhile the rejoicing was so great that it could be expressed in only one way: all over the ship, the Joilani lifted their voices in the sacred song.

They were free! The *Dream* had made it into tau-space, where no enemy could find them! They were safely on their way.

Safely on their way—to an unknown destination, over an unknown time, with pitifully limited supplies of water, food, and air.

Here begins the log of the passage of the Dream *through tau-space, which, although timeless, required finite time. . . .*

Jatkan let the precious old scroll roll up and laid it carefully aside, to touch the hand of a co-mate. He had been one of the babies in the *amlat* containers; sometimes he thought he remembered the great night of their escape. Certainly he remembered a sense of rejoicing, a feeling of dread nightmare blown away.

"The waiting is long," said his youngest co-mate, who was little more than a child. "Tell us again about the Terran monsters."

"They weren't monsters, only very alien," he corrected the child gently. His eyes met those of Salasvati, who was entertaining her young co-mates at the porthole of the tiny records chamber. It came to Jatkan that when he and Salas were old, they might be the last Joilani who had ever really seen a Terran. Certainly the last to have any sense of their terror and might, and the degradations of slavery burned into their parents' souls. Surely this is good, he thought, but is it not also a loss, in some strange way?

"—reddish, or sometimes yellow or brownish, almost hairless, with small bright eyes," he was telling the child. "And big, about the distance to that porthole there. And one day, when the three who were on the *Dream* were allowed out to exercise, they rushed into the control room and changed the— the *gyroscope* setting, so that the ship began to spin around faster and faster, and everybody fell down and was pressed flat into the walls. They were counting on their greater strength, you see."

"So that they could seize the *Dream* and break out of tau-space into Terran stars!" His two female co-mates recited in unison: "But old Jivadh saved us."

"Yes. But he was young Jivadh then. By great good luck he was at the central column, right where the old weapons were kept, that no one had touched for hundreds of days."

A co-mate smiled. "The luck of the Joilani."

"No," Jatkan told her. "We must not grow superstitious. It was simple chance."

"And he *killed them all!*" the child burst out excitedly. A hush fell.

"Never use that word so lightly," Jatkan said sternly. "Think what you are meaning, little one. *Jailasanatha*—"

As he admonished the child, his mind noted again the incongruity of his words: the "little one" was already as large as he, as he in turn was larger and stronger than his parents. This could only be due to the children's eating the Terran-mixed food from the ship's recycler, however scanty. When the older ones saw how the young grew, it confirmed another old myth: that their ancestors had once been giants, who had diminished through some lack in the planet's soil. Was every old myth-legend coming true at once?

Meanwhile he was trying once more to explain to the child, and to the others, the true horror of the decision Jivadh had faced, and Jivadh's frenzy of anguish when he was prevented from killing himself in atonement. Jatkan's memory was scarred by that day. First the smash against the walls, the confusion—the explosions—their release; and then the endless hours of ritual argument, persuading Jivadh that his knowledge of the ship was too precious to lose. The pain in Jivadh's voice as he confessed: "I thought also in selfishness, that we would have their water, their food, their air."

"That is why he doesn't take his fair share of food, and sleeps on the bare steel."

"And why he's always so sad," the child said, frowning with the effort to truly understand.

"Yes." But Jatkan knew that he could never really understand; nobody could who had not seen the horror of violently dead flesh that once was living, even though alien and hostile. The three corpses had been consigned with due ritual to the recycling bins, as they did with their own. By now all the Joilani must bear some particles in their flesh that once were Terran. Ironic.

A shadow passed his mind. A few days ago he had been certain that these young ones, and their children's children, would never need know what it was to kill. Now he was not quite so certain. . . . He brushed the thought away.

"Has the log been kept right up to now?" asked Salasvati from the port. Like Jatkan, she was having difficulty keeping her young co-mates quiet during this solemn wait.

"Oh, yes."

Jatkan's fingers delicately riffled through the motley pages of the current logbook on the stand. It had been sewn together from whatever last scraps and charts they could find. The clear

Joilani script flashed out at him on page after page: "Hunger . . . rations cut . . . broken, water low . . . repairs . . . adult rations cut again . . . oxygen low . . . the children . . . water reduced . . . the children need . . . how much more can we . . . end soon; not enough . . . when. . . ."

Yes, that had been his whole life, all their lives: dwindling life sustenance in the great rotating cylinder that was their world. The unrelenting uncertainty: would they ever break out? And if so, where? Or would it go on till they all died here in the timeless, lightless void?

And the rare weird events, things almost seen, like the strange light ghost ship that had suddenly bloomed beside them with ungraspably alien creatures peering from its parts—and as suddenly vanished again.

Somewhere in the *Dream*'s magical computers, circuits were clicking toward the predestined coordinates, but no one knew how to check on the program's progress, or even whether it still functioned. The merciless stress of waiting told upon them all in different ways, as the hundred-day cycles passed into thousands. Some grew totally silent; some whispered endless ritual; some busied themselves with the most minute tasks. Old Bislat had been their leader here; his courage and cheer were indomitable. But it was Jivadh, despite his dreadful deed, despite his self-imposed silence and reclusion, who was somehow still the symbol of their faith. It was not that he had lifted the *Dream*, had saved them not once but twice; it was the sensed trueness of his heart. . . . Jatkan, turning the old pages, reflected that perhaps it had all been easiest for the children, who had known no other life but only waiting for the Day.

And then—the changed writing on the last page spoke for itself—there had come the miracle, the first of the Days. All unexpectedly, as they were preparing for the three-thousandth-and-something sleep period, the ship had shuddered, and unfamiliar meshing sounds had rumbled around them. They had all sprung up wildly, reeling in disorientation. Great strainings of metal, frightening clanks—and the old ship disengaged her tau-field, to unfold her volume into normal space.

But what space! Stars—the suns of legend—blazed in every porthole, some against deep blackness, some shrouded in glorious clouds of light! Children and adults alike raced from port to port, crying out in wonder and delight.

It was only slowly that realization came: they were still alone in limitless, empty, unknown space, among unknown beings and forces, still perishingly short of all that was needful to life. The long-planned actions were taken. The transmitter was set to send out the Joilani distress call, at what old Jivadh believed was maximum reach. A brave party went outside, onto the hull, in crazily modified Terran space suits. They painted over the ugly Terran star, changing it to a huge Sun-in-splendor. Over the Terran words they wrote the Joilani word for *Dream*. If they were still in the Terran Empire, all was now doubly lost.

"My mother went outside," said Jatkan's oldest co-mate proudly. "It was dangerous and daring and very hard work."

"Yes." Jatkan touched her lovingly.

"I wish I could go outside now," said the youngest.

"You will. Wait."

"It's *always* 'wait.' We're waiting now."

"Yes."

Waiting—oh, yes, they had waited, with conditions growing ever worse and hope more faint. Knowing no other course, they set out at crawling pace for the nearest bright star. Few believed they were waiting for anything more than death.

Until that day—the greatest of Days—when a strange spark burst suddenly into being ahead, and grew into a great ship bearing down upon them.

And they had seen the Sun-in-splendor on her bow.

Even the youngest child would remember that forever.

How the stranger had almost magically closed and grappled them, and forced the long-corroded main lock. And they of the *Dream* had seen all dreams come true, as in a rush of sweet air the strange Joilani—the true, real Joilani—had come aboard. Joilani—but giants, as big as Terrans, strong and upright, glowing with health, their hands upraised in the ancient greeting. How they had narrowed their nostrils at the *Dream*'s foul air! How they had blinked in wonderment as the song of thanksgiving rose around them!

Through it all, their leader had patiently repeated in strange but understandable accents, "I am *Khanrid* Jemnal Visadh. Who *are* you people?" And when a tiny old Joilani female had rushed to him with leaves torn from the hydroponics bed and tried to wreathe him, crying, "Jemnal! Jemnal my lost son! Oh, my son, my son!" he had smiled embarrassedly, and stooped to embrace her, calling her "Mother," before he put her gently aside.

And then the explanations, the incredulity, as the great Joilani had spread out to examine the *Dream*, each with his train of awestruck admirers. They had scanned the old charts, and opened and traced the tau-program with casual skill. They too seemed excited; the *Dream*, it seemed, had performed an unparalleled deed. One of the giants had begun questioning them: arcane, incomprehensible questions as to types of Terran ships they had seen, the colors and insignia numbers on the Terrans' clothes. "Later, later," *Khanrid* Jemnal had said. And then had begun the practical measures of bringing in food and water, and recharging the air supply.

"We will plot your course to the sector base," he told them. "Three of our people will go with you when you are ready."

In all the excitement Jatkan found it hard to recall exactly when he had noticed that their Joilani saviors all were armed.

"They are patrol spacers," old Bislat said wonderingly. "*Khanrid* is a military title. That ship is a warship, a protector of the Joilani Federation of Worlds."

He had to explain to the young ones what that meant.

"It means we are no longer helpless!" His old eyes glowed. "It means that our faith, our Gentleness-in-honor, our *Jailasanatha* way, can never again be trodden to the dirt by brute might!"

Jatkan, whose feet could not remember treading dirt, yet understood. A marveling exultation grew in them all. Even old Jivadh's face softened briefly from its customary grim composure.

Female Joilani came aboard—new marvels. Beautiful giantesses, who did strange and sometimes uncomfortable things to them all. Jatkan learned new words: *inoculation, infestation, antisepsis.* His clothes and the others' were briefly taken away, and returned looking and smelling quite different. He overheard *Khanrid* Jemnal speaking to one of the goddesses.

"I know, *Khanlal*. You'd like to strip out this hull and blow everything but their bare bodies out to space. But you must understand that we are touching history here. These rags, this whole pathetic warren, is hot, living history. Evidence, too, if you like. No. Clean them up, depingee them, inoculate and dust and spray all you want. But leave it looking just the way it is."

"But, *Khanrid*—"

"That's it."

Jatkan had not long to puzzle over that; it was the day of their great visit to the wonderful warship. There they saw and touched marvels, all giant-size. And then were fed a splendid meal, and afterward all joined in singing, and they learned new words for some of the old Joilani songs. When they finally returned, the *Dream* seemed to be permeated with a most peculiar odor which made them all sneeze for days. Soon afterward they noticed that they were doing a lot less scratching; the fritlings that had been a part of their lives seemed to be gone.

"They sent them away," Jatkan's mother explained. "It seems they are not good on ships."

"They were killed," old Jivadh broke his silence to remark tonelessly.

The three giant Joilani spacers who were to get them safely to the sector base came aboard then. *Khanrid* Jemnal introduced them. "And now I must say good-bye. You will receive a warm welcome."

When they sang him and the others farewell, it was almost as emotional as on the first day.

Their three guardians had been busy at mysterious tasks in the *Dream*'s workings. Old Bislat and some of the other males watched them keenly, trying to understand, but Jivadh seemed no longer to care. Soon they were plunged back into tau-space, but how different this time, with ample air and water and food for all! In only ten sleep periods the now-familiar shudder ran through the *Dream* again, and they broke out into daylight with a blue sun blinding in the ports.

A planet loomed up beside them. The Joilani pilot took them down into the shadow-darkened limb, sinking toward a gigantic spaceport. Ships beyond count stood there, ablaze with lights, and beyond the field itself stretched a vast jeweled webwork, like myriad earthly stars.

Jatkan learned a new word: *city*. He could hardly wait to see it in the day.

Almost at once the *Dream*'s five Elders had been ceremoniously escorted out, to visit the High Elders of this wondrous place. They went in a strange kind of landship. Looking after them, the *Dream*'s people could see that a lighted barrier of some sort had been installed around the ship. Now they were awaiting their return.

"They're taking so long," Jatkan's youngest co-mate complained. He was getting drowsy.

"Let us look out again," Jatkan proposed. "May we exchange places, Salasvati?"

"With pleasure."

Jatkan led his little family to the port as Salasvati's moved back, awkward in the unfamiliar sternward weight.

"Look, out beyond—there are people!"

It was true. Jatkan saw what seemed to be an endless multitude of Joilani in the night, hundreds upon hundreds upon hundreds of pale gray faces beyond the barrier, all turned toward the *Dream*.

"We are history," he quoted *Khanrid* Jemnal.

"What's that?"

"An important event, I think. See—here come our Elders now!"

There was a commotion, a parting in the throng, and the landship which had taken the Elders away came slowly out into the free space around the *Dream*.

"Come look, Salasvati!"

Craning and crowding, they could just make out their Elders and their giant escorts emerging from the landship, and taking warm ritual leaving of each other.

"Hurry, they'll tell us all about it in the Center!"

It was difficult, with the ship in this new position and everything hanging wrong. Their parents were already sitting sideways in the doors of the center shaft. The youngsters scrambled to whatever perches or laps they could find. The party of Elders could be heard making their slow way up from below, climbing the long-unused central ladders to where they could speak to all.

As they came into view Jatkan could see how weary they were, and how their dark eyes radiated excitement, exultation. Yet with a queer tautness or tension stretching their cheekbones, too, he thought.

"We were indeed warmly received," old Bislat said when all had reached the central space. "We saw wonders it will take days to describe. All of you will see them, in due time. We were taken to meet the High Elders here, and ate the evening meal with them." He paused briefly. "We were also questioned, by one particular Elder, about the Terrans we have known. It seems that our knowledge is important, old as it is. All of you who remember our previous life must set yourselves to recalling every sort of small detail. The colors of their spacers' clothing, their ornaments of rank, the names and appearance of their ships that came and went." He smiled wonderingly. "It was . . . strange . . . to hear Terrans spoken of so lightly, even scornfully. We think now that their great Empire is not so mighty as we believed. Perhaps it has grown too old, or too big. Our people"—he spoke with his hands clasped in thanksgiving—"our people do not fear them."

A wordless, incredulous gasp of joy rose from the listeners around the shaft.

"Yes." Bislat stilled them. "Now, as to what is ahead for us. We are, you must understand, a great wonder to them. It seems our flight here from so far away was extraordinary, and has moved them very much. But we are also, well, so very different—like people from another age. It is not only our size. Their very children know more than we do of practical daily things. We could not quietly go out and dwell among the people of this city or the lands around it, even though they are our own Joilani, of the faith. We Elders have seen enough to understand that, and you will, too. Some of you may already have thought on this, have you not?"

A thoughtful murmur of assent echoed his words from door after door. Even Jatkan realized that he had been wondering about this, somewhere under his conscious mind.

"In time, of course, it will be different. Our young, or their young, will be as they are, and we all can learn."

He smiled deeply. But Jatkan found his gaze caught by old Jivadh's face. Jivadh was not smiling; his gaze was cast down, and his expression was tense and sad. Indeed, something of the same strain seemed to lie upon them all, even Bislat. What could be wrong?

Bislat was continuing, his voice strong and cheerful. "So they have found for us a fertile land, an empty land on a beautiful world. The *Dream* will stay here, as a permanent memorial of our great flight. They will take us there in another ship, with all that we need, and with people who will stay to help and teach us." His hands met again in thanksgiving; his voice rang out reverently. "So begins our new life of freedom, safe among Joilani stars, among our people of the faith."

Just as his listeners began quietly to hum the sacred song, old Jivadh raised his head.

"Of the faith, Bislat?" he asked harshly.

The singers hushed in puzzlement.

"You saw the Gardens of the Way." Bislat's tone was strangely brusque. "You saw the sacred texts emblazoned, you saw the Meditators—"

"I saw many splendid places," Jivadh cut him off. "With idle attendants richly gowned."

"It is nowhere written that the Way must be shabbily served," Bislat protested. "The richness is a proof of its honor here."

"And before one of those sacred places of devotion," Jivadh went on implacably, "I saw Joilani as old as I, in rags almost as poor as mine, toiling with heavy burdens. You did not mention that, Bislat. For that matter, you did not mention how strangely young these High Elders of our people here are. Think on it. It can only mean that the old wisdom is not enough, that new enterprises not of the Way are in movement here."

"But, Jivadh," another Elder put in, "there is so much here that we are not yet able to understand. Surely, when we know more—"

"There is much that Bislat refuses to understand," Jivadh said curtly. "He also has omitted to say what we were offered."

"No, Jivadh! Do not, we implore you." Bislat's voice trembled. "We agreed, for the good of all—"

"I did not agree." Jivadh turned to the tiers of listeners. His haggard gaze swept past them, seeming to look far beyond.

"O my people," he said somberly, "the *Dream* has not come home. It may be that it has no home. What we have come to is the Joilani Federation of Worlds, a mighty, growing power among the stars. We are safe here, yes. But Federation, Empire, perhaps it is all the same in the end. Bislat has told you what these so-called Elders kindly gave us to eat. But he has not told you what the High Elder offered us to drink."

"They said it was confiscated!" Bislat cried.

"Does that matter? Our high Joilani, our people of the faith—" Jivadh's eyelids closed in sadness; his voice broke to a hoarse rasp. "*Our Joilani* . . . were drinking Stars Tears."

HER SMOKE ROSE UP FOREVER

—DELIVERANCE QUICKENS, catapults him into his boots on mountain gravel, his mittened hand on the rusty 1935 International truck. Cold rushes into his young lungs, his eyelashes are knots of ice as he peers down at the lake below the pass. He is in a bare bleak bowl of mountains just showing rusty in the dawn; not one scrap of cover anywhere, not a tree, not a rock.

The lake below shines emptily, its wide rim of ice silvered by the setting moon. It looks small, everything looks small from up here. Is that scar on the edge his boat? Yes—it's there, it's all okay! The black path snaking out from the boat to the patch of tulegrass is the waterway he broke last night. Joy rises in him, hammers his heart. This is it. This—is—*it*.

He squints his lashes, can just make out the black threads of the tules. Black knots among them—sleeping ducks. Just you wait! His grin crackles the ice in his nose. The tules will be his cover—that perfect patch out there. About eighty yards, too far to hit from shore. That's where he'll be when the dawn flight comes over. Old Tom said he was loco. Loco Petey. Just you wait. Loco Tom.

The pickup's motor clanks, cooling, in the huge silence. No echo here, too dry. No wind. Petey listens intently: a thin wailing in the peaks overhead, a tiny croak from the lake below. Waking up. He scrapes back his frozen canvas cuff over the birthday watch, is oddly, fleetingly puzzled by his own knobby fourteen-year-old wrist. Twenty-five—no, twenty-four minutes to the duck season. Opening day! Excitement ripples down his stomach, jumps his dick against his scratchy longjohns. Gentlemen don't beat the gun. He reaches into the pickup, reverently lifts out the brand-new Fox CE double-barrel twelve-gauge.

The barrels strike cold right through his mitts. He'll have to take one off to shoot, too: it'll be fierce. Petey wipes his nose with his cuff, pokes three fingers through his cut mitten and breaks the gun. Ice in the sight. He checks his impulse to blow it out, dabs clumsily. Shouldn't have taken it in his sleeping bag. He fumbles two heavy sixes from his shell pocket, loads the sweet blue bores, is hardly able to breathe for joy. He is holding a zillion dumb bags of the *Albuquerque Herald*, a whole summer of laying adobe for Mr. Noff—all transmuted into this: his perfect, agonizingly chosen OWN GUN. No more borrowing old Tom's stinky over-and-under with the busted sight. His own gun with his *initials* on the silver stock-plate.

Exaltation floods him, rises perilously. Holding his gun, Petey takes one more look around at the enormous barren slopes. Empty, only himself and his boat and the ducks. The sky has gone cold gas-pink. He is standing on a cusp of the Great Divide at ten thousand feet, the main pass of the western flyway. At dawn on opening day . . . What if Apaches came around now? Mescalero Apaches own these mountains, but he's never seen one out here. His father says they all have TB or something. In the old days, did they come here on horses? They'd look tiny; the other side is ten miles at least.

Petey squints at a fuzzy place on the far shore, decides it's only sagebrush, but gets the keys and the ax out of the pickup just in case. Holding the ax away from his gun, he starts down to the lake. His chest is banging, his knees wobble, he can barely feel his feet skidding down the rocks. The whole world seems to be brimming up with tension.

He tells himself to calm down, blinking to get rid of a funny blackness behind his eyes. He stumbles, catches himself, has to stop to rub at his eyes. As he does so everything flashes black-white—the moon jumps out of a black sky like a locomotive headlight, he is sliding on darkness with a weird humming all around. Oh, Jeeze—mustn't get an altitude blackout, not now! And he makes himself breathe deeply, goes on down with his boots crunching hard like rhythmic ski turns, the heavy shell pockets banging his legs, down, going quicker now, down to the waiting boat.

As he gets closer he sees the open water-path has iced over a little during the night. Good job he has the ax. Some ducks are swimming slow circles right by the ice. One of them rears up and quack-flaps, showing the big raked head: canvasback!

"Ah, you beauty," Petey says aloud, starting to run now, skidding, his heart pumping love, on fire for that first boom and rush. "I wouldn't shoot a sitting duck." His nose-drip has frozen, he is seeing himself hidden in those tules when the flights come over the pass, thinking of old Tom squatting in the rocks back by camp. Knocking back his brandy with his old gums slobbering, dreaming of dawns on World War I airdromes, dreaming of shooting a goose, dying of TB. Crazy old fool. Just you wait. Petey sees his plywood boat heaped with the great pearly breasts and red-black Roman noses of the canvasbacks bloodied and stiff, the virgin twelve-gauge lying across them, fulfilled.

And suddenly he's beside the boat, still blinking away a curious unreal feeling. Mysterious to see his own footprints here. The midget boat and the four frosted decoys are okay, but there's ice in the waterway, all right. He lays the gun and ax inside and pushes the boat out from the shore. It sticks, bangs, rides up over the new ice.

Jeeze, it's really thick! Last night he'd kicked through it easily and poled free by gouging in the paddle. Now he stamps out a couple of yards, pulling the boat. The ice doesn't give. Darn! He takes a few more cautious steps—and suddenly hears the *whew-whew, whew-whew* of ducks coming in. Coming in—and he's out here in the open! He drops beside the boat, peers into the bright white sky over the pass.

Oh *Jeeze*—there they are! Ninety miles an hour, coming downwind, a big flight! And he hugs his gun to hide the glitter, seeing the hurtling birds set their wings, become bloodcurdling black crescent-shapes, webs dangling, dropping like dive-bombers—but they've seen him, they veer in a great circle out beyond the tules, all quacking now, away and down. He hears the far rip of water and stands up aching toward them. You wait. Just wait till I get this dumb boat out there!

He starts yanking the boat out over the creaking ice in the brightening light, cold biting at his face and neck. The ice snaps, shivers, is still hard. Better push the boat around ahead of him so he can fall in it when it goes. He does so, makes another two yards, three—and then the whole sheet tilts and slides under with him floundering, and grounds on gravel. Water slops over his boot tops, burns inside his three pair of socks.

But it's shallow. He stamps forward, bashing ice, slipping and staggering. A yard, a yard, a yard more—he can't feel his feet, he can't get purchase. Crap darn, this is too slow! He grabs the boat, squats, throws himself ahead and in with all his might. The boat rams forward like an icebreaker. Again! He'll be out of the ice soon now. Another lunge! And again!

But this time the boat recoils, doesn't ram. Darn *shit*, the crappy ice is so thick! How could it get this thick when it was open water last night?

'Cause the wind stopped, that's why, and it's ten above zero. Old Tom knew, darn him to hell. But there's only about thirty yards left to go to open water, only a few yards between him and the promised land. Get there. Get over it or under it or through it, go!

He grabs the ax, wades out ahead of the boat, and starts hitting ice, trying to make cracks. A piece breaks, he hits harder. But it doesn't want to crack, the axhead keeps going in, *thunk*. He has to work it out of the black holes. And it's getting deep, he's way over his boots now. So what? *Thunk!* Work it loose. *Thunk!*

But some remaining sanity reminds him he really will freeze out here if he gets his clothes soaked. Shee-it! He stops, stands panting, staring at the ducks, which are now tipping up, feeding peacefully well out of range, chuckling *paducah, paducah* at him and his rage.

Twenty more yards, shit darn, *God*-darn. He utters a caw of fury and hunger and at that moment hears a tiny distant crack. Old Tom, firing. Crack!

Petey jumps into the boat, jerking off his canvas coat, peeling off the two sweaters, pants, the gray longjohns. His fingers can barely open the icy knots of his bootlaces, but his body is radiant with heat, it sizzles the air, only his balls are trying to climb back inside as he stands up naked. Twenty yards!

He yanks the sodden boots back on and crashes out into the ice, whacking with the ax-handle, butting whole sheets aside. He's making it! Ten more feet, twenty! He rams with the boat, bangs it up and down like a sledgehammer. Another yard! Another! His teeth are clattering, his shins are bleeding, and it's cutting his thighs now, but he feels nothing, only joy, joy!—until suddenly he is slewing full-length under water with the incredible cold going up his ass and into his armpits like skewers and ice cutting his nose.

His hands find the edge, and he hauls himself up on the side of the boat. The bottom has gone completely. His ax—his ax is gone.

The ice is still there.

A black hand grabs him inside, he can't breathe. He kicks and flails, dragging himself up into the boat to kneel bleeding, trying to make his ribs work and his jaws stop banging. The first sunray slicks him with ice and incredible goose bumps; he gets a breath and can see ahead, see the gleaming ducks. So close!

The paddle. He seizes it and stabs at the ice in front of the boat. It clatters, rebounds, the boat goes backward. With all his force he flails the ice, but it's too thick, the paddle stem is cracking. No bottom to brace on. *Crack!* And the paddle blade skitters away across the ice. He has nothing left.

He can't make it.

Rage, helpless rage, vomits through him, his eyes are crying hot ice down his face. So close! *So close!* And sick with fury he sees them come—*whew-whew! whew-whew-whew-whew!*—a torrent of whistling wings in the bright air, the ducks are pouring over the pass. Ten thousand noble canvasbacks hurtling down the sky at him silver and black, the sky is wings beating above him, but too high, too high—they know the range, oh, yes!

He has never seen so many, he will never see it again—and he is standing up in the boat now, a naked bleeding loco ice-boy, raging, sweeping the virgin twelve-gauge, firing—BAM-BAM! both barrels at nothing, at the ice, at the sky, spilling out the shells, ramming them in with tearing frozen hands. A drake bullets toward him, nearer—it *has* to be near enough! BAM! BAM!

But it isn't, it isn't, and the air-riders, the magic bodies of his love beat over him yelling—canvasback, teal, widgeon, pintails, redheads, every duck in the world rising now, he is in a ten-mile swirl of birds, firing, firing, a weeping maniac under the flashing wings, white-black, black-white. And among the flashing he sees not only ducks but geese, cranes, every great bird that ever rode this wind: hawks, eagles, condors, pterodactyls—BAM! BAM! BAM-BAM!! in the crazy air, in the gale of rage and tears exploding in great black pulses—*black!*

light! black!—whirling unbearably, rushing him up—

⊕

—And he surfaces suddenly into total calm and dimness, another self with all fury shrunk to a tiny knot below his mind and his eyes feasting in the open throat of a girl's white shirt. He is in a room, a cool cave humming with secret promise. Behind the girl the windows are curtained with sheer white stuff against the glare outside.

"Your mother said you went to Santa Fe." He hears his throat threaten soprano and digs his fists into the pockets of his Levi's.

The girl Pilar—Pee-lar, crazy-name-Pilar—bends to pick at her tanned ankle, feathery brown bob swinging across her cheek and throat.

"Um-m." She is totally absorbed in a thin gold chain around her ankle, crouching on a big red leather thing her parents got in where, Morocco—Pilar of the urgently slender waist curving into her white Levi's, the shirt so softly holding swelling softness; everything so white against her golden tan, smelling of soap and flowers and girl. So *clean.* She has to be a virgin, his heart knows it; a marvelous slow-motion happiness is brimming up in the room. She likes me. She's so shy, even if she's a year older, nearly seventeen, she's like a baby. The pathos of her vulnerable body swells in him, he balls his fists to hide the bulge by his fly. Oh, Jeeze, I mean Jesus, let her not look, Pilar. But she does look up then, brushing her misty hair back, smiling dreamily up at him.

"I was at the La Fonda, I had a dinner date with René."

"Who's René?"

"I told you, Pe-ter." Not looking at him, she uncurls from the hassock, drifts like a child to the window, one hand rubbing her arm. "He's my cousin. He's old, he's twenty-five or thirty. He's a lieute*nant* now."

"Oh."

"An *older man.*" She makes a face, grins secretly, peeking out through the white curtains.

His heart fizzes with relief, with the exultance rising in the room. She's a virgin, all right. From the bright hot world outside comes the sound of a car starting. A horse whickers faintly down at the club stables, answered by the double wheeze of a donkey. They both giggle. Peter flexes his shoulders, opens and grips his hand around an imaginary mallet.

"Does your father know you were out with him?"

"Oh, yes." She's cuddling her cheek against her shoulder, pushing the immaculate collar, letting him see the creamy mounds. She wants me, Peter thinks. His guts jump. *She's going to let me do it to her.* And all at once he is calm, richly calm like that first morning at the corral, watching his mare come to him; knowing.

"Pa-*pa* doesn't care, it's nineteen forty-*four*. René is my cousin."

Her parents are so terribly sophisticated; he knows her father is some kind of secret war scientist: they are all here because of the war, something over at Los Alamos. And her mother talking French, talking about weird places like Dee-jon and Tan-jay. His own mother doesn't know French, his father teaches high school, he never would be going around with these sophisticated strangers except they need him for their sandlot polo. And he can play rings around them all, too, Peter thinks, grinning, all those smooth sweating old young men— even with his one mare for four chukkers and her tendons like big hot balloons, even with his spliced mallet he can cut it over their heads! If he could only get an official rating. Three goals, sure. Maybe four, he muses, seeing himself riding through that twerp Drexel with his four remounts, seeing Pilar smile, not looking at him. She's shy. That time he let her ride the mare she was really frightened, incredibly awkward; he could feel her thighs tremble when he boosted her up.

His own thighs tremble, remembering the weak tenderness of her in his hands. *Always before your voice my soul is as some smooth and awkward foal*—it doesn't sound so wet now, his mother's nutty line. His foal, his velvety vulnerable baby mare. Compared to her he's a gorilla, even if he's technically a virgin too, men are different. And he understands suddenly that weird Havelock Ellis book in her father's den. Gentle. He must be gentle. Not like—a what?—a baboon playing a violin.

"You shouldn't fool around with older men," he says and is gratified by the gruffness. "You don't know."

She's watching him now under the fall of her hair, coming close, still hugging herself with her hand going slowly up and down her arm, caressing it. A warm soap smell fills his nose, a sharp muskiness under it. She doesn't know what she's doing, he thinks choking, she doesn't know about men. And he grunts something like "Don't," or "Can it," trying to hold down the leaping heat between them, but is confused by her voice whispering.

"It *hurts*, Pe-ter."

"What, your arm?"

"Here, do-pee," and his hand is suddenly taken hold of by cool small fingers pulling it not to her arm but in wonder to her side, pressed in the rustling shirt under which he feels at first nothing and then shockingly too far in not his own wide ribs but the warm stem of her, and as his paralyzed hand fumbles, clasps, she half turns around so that his ignited hand rides onto a searing soft unnatural swelling—her *breast*—and the room blanks out, whirls up on a brimming, drumming tide as if all the dead buffalo were pounding back. And the window blinks once with lemon light shooting around their two bodies where her hip is butting into his thigh making it wholly impossible to continue standing there with his hands gentle on her tits.

"You don't know what you're doing, Pilar. Don't be a dope, your mother –"

"She's a-way now." And there is a confused interval of mouths and hands trying to be gentle, trying to hold her away from his fly, trying to stuff her into himself in total joy, if he had six hands he couldn't cope with electric all of her—until suddenly she pulls back, is asking inanely, "Pe-ter, don't you have a friend?"

The subtle difference in her voice makes him blink, answering stupidly, "Sure, Tom Ring," while her small nose wrinkles.

"Dopee Pe-ter, I mean a boyfriend. Somebody smooth."

He stands trying to pant dignifiedly, thinking Jeeze, I mean Christ, she knows I don't have any smooth friends; if it's for a picnic maybe Diego Martine? But before he can suggest this she has leaned into the window bay, cuddling the silky curtain around her, peeking at him so that his hands go pawing in the cloth.

"René has a friend."

"Uh."

"He's older too, he's twen-tee," she breathes teasingly. "Lieute*nant* Shar-lo. That's Charles to you, see?" And she turns around full into his arms, curtain and all, and from the press of silk and giggles comes a small voice saying forever, "And Re-*né* and Shar-*lo* and Pee-*lar* all went to bed together and they played with me, oh, for hours and hours, Pe-ter, it was too marvelous. I will ne-ver do it with just one boy again."

Everything drops then except her face before him horribly heavy and exalted and alien, and just as his heart knows it's dead and an evil so generalized he can hardly recognize it as fury starts tearing emptily at him inside, her hand comes up over her mouth and she is running doubled over past him.

"I'm going to be sick, Peter help me!"

And he stumbles after down the dim cool hall to find her crumpled down, her brown hair flowing into the toilet as she retches, retches, whimpering, convulses unbearably. The white shirt has ridden up to expose her pathetically narrow back, soft knobs of her spine curving down into her pants, her tender buttocks bumping his knees as he stands helplessly strangling a sopping towel instead of her neck, trying to swab at her hidden forehead. His own gullet is retching too, his face feels doughy, and water is running down into his open mouth while one of her hands grips his, shaking him with her spasms there in the dim hospital-like bathroom. The world is groaning, he is seeing not her father's bay rum bottle but the big tiled La Fonda bedroom, the three bodies writhing on the bed, performing unknown horrors. *Playing with her . . .*

His stomach heaves, only what it is, he is coming in his Levi's in a dreadful slow unrelieving ooze like a red-hot wire dragging through his crotch, while he stands by her uselessly as he will stand helplessly by in some near future he can't imagine or remember—and the tension keeps building, pounding, the light flickers—a storm is coming or maybe his eyes are going bad, but he can see below him her pure profile resting spent on the edge of the toilet, oblivious to his furious towel; in the flashing dimness sees the incomprehensible letters *S-E-P-T-I-C A-B-O-R-T-I-O-N* snaking shadowy down the spine of his virgin love, while the universe beats Black! Flash! Black! Drumming with hooves harsher than any storm—hurling him through lightning-claps of blinding darkness to a thrumming stasis in which what exists of him senses—something—but is instantly shot away on unimaginable energies—

—And achieves condensement, blooms into the green and open sunlight of another world, into a mellow springtime self—in which a quite different girl is jostling his hip.

"Molly," he hears his older voice say vaguely, seeing with joy how the willow fronds trail in the friendly, dirty Potomac. The bars and caduceus on his collar are pricking his neck.

"Yes, sir, Doctor sir." She spins around, kneels down in the scruffy grass to open Howard Johnson boxes. "Oh, god, the coffee." Handing him up a hot dog, swinging back her fair hair. Her arm is so female with its tender pale armpit, her whole body is edible, even her dress is like lemonade so fresh and clean—no, radiant, he corrects himself. That's the word, radiant. His radiant woman. He shrugs away a tiny darkness, thinking of her hair sliding on his body in the Roger Smith hotel bedroom.

"C'mon sit, Pete. It's only a little dirty."

"Nothing's dirty anymore." He flops down beside her, one arm finding its natural way around the opulence of her buttocks on the grass. She chuckles down at him, shaking her head.

"You're a hard case, Pete." She takes a big bite of hot dog with such lips that he considers flinging himself upon her then and there, barely remembers the cars tearing by above them. "I swear," she says, chewing, "I don't think you ever screwed anybody you were friends with before."

"Something like that." He puts his hot dog down to loosen his GI tie.

"Thirty days to civvies, you'll be in Baltimore." She licks her fingers happily. "Oh, wow, Pete, I'm so glad you got your fellowship. Try the coleslaw, it's all right. Will you remember us poor slaves when you're a big old pathologist?"

"I'll remember." To distract himself he pokes in the boxes, spills coleslaw on a book. "What you reading?"

"Oh, Whately Carington."

"Whatly what?"

"No, *Whate*-ly. Carington. A Limey. Psychical research man, they do that veddy seddiously, the Limies."

"Uh?" He beams at the river, blinks to get rid of a flicker back of his eyes. Amphetamine withdrawal, after six months?

"He has this theory, about K-objects. Whatever thing you feel most intense about, part of you lives on—Pete, what's wrong?"

"Nothing."

But the flicker won't quit, it is suddenly worse; through it he can just make out her face turned nurse-wary, coming

close, and he tries to hang on through a world flashing black—
green—BLACK!—is trapped for unbreathing timelessness
in dark nowhere, a phantom landscape of gray tumbled ash
under a hard black sky, seeing without eyes a distant tangle
of wreckage on the plain so menacing that his unbodied voice
screams at the shadow of a metal scrap beside him in the ashes,
2004 the ghostly unmeaning numbers—*STOP IT!*—And he
is back by the river under Molly's springtime eyes, his hands
gripping into the bones of her body.

"Hey-y-y, honey, the war's over." Sweet sensual pixie-smile
now watchful, her nurse's hand inside his shirt. "Korea's ten
thousand miles away, you're in good old D.C., Doctor."

"I know. I saw a license plate." He laughs unconvincingly,
makes his hands relax. Will the ghosts of Seoul never let him
go? And his body guiltily intact, no piece of him in the stained
waste cans into which he has—Stop it! Think of Molly. I like
Ike. Johns Hopkins research fellowship. Some men simply
aren't cut out for surgical practice.

"I'm a gutless wonder, Molly. Research."

"Oh, for Christ's sake, Pete," she says with total warmth,
nurse-hand satisfied, changing to lover's on his chest. "We've
been *over* all that."

And of course they have, he knows it and only mutters, "My
Dad wanted me to be an Indian doctor," which they have been
over too; and the brimming gladness is back now, buoyantly
he seizes the coleslaw, demands entertainment, demonstrating
reality-grasp.

"So what about Whatly?"

"It's serious-s-s," she protests, snickering, and is mercurially
almost serious too. "I mean, I'm an atheist, Pete, I don't believe
there's anything afterward, but this theory. . . ." And she rattles
on about K-objects and the pool of time, intense energic
structures of the mind undying—sweet beddable girl in the
springtime who has taught him unclaiming love. His friend.
Liberated him.

He stretches luxuriously, relishes a coleslaw belch. Free male
beside a willing woman. No problems. *What is it man in woman
doth require? The lineaments of gratified desire.* The radiance of
her. He has gratified her. Will gratify her again. . . .

"It's kind of spooky, though." She flings the box at the
river with tremendous effort, it flies twenty feet. "Damn! But
think of parts of yourself whirling around forever sticking to

whatever you loved!" She settles against the willow, watching the box float away. "I wonder if part of me is going to spend eternity hanging around a dumb cat. I loved that old cat. Henry. He died, though."

The ghost of a twelve-gauge fires soundlessly across his mind, a mare whickers. He sneezes and rolls over onto her lap with his nose in her warm scented thighs. She peers dreamily down at him over her breasts, is almost beautiful.

"Whatever you love, forever. Be careful what you love." She squints wickedly. "Only with you I think it'd be whatever you were maddest at—no, that's a horrible thought. Love *has* to be the most intense."

He doubts it but is willing to be convinced, rooting in her lap while she pretends to pound on him and then squirms, stretching up her arms, giving herself to the air, to him, to life.

"I want to spend eternity whirling around you." He heaves up to capture her, no longer giving a damn about the cars, and as the sweet familiar body comes pliantly under him he realizes it's true, he's known it for some time. Not friendship at all, or rather, the best of friendships. The real one. "I love you, Molly. We love."

"Ooh, Pete."

"You're coming to Baltimore with me. We'll get married," he tells her warm neck, feeling the flesh under her skirt heavy in his hand, feeling also an odd stillness that makes him draw back to where he can see her face, see her lips whispering, "I was afraid of that."

"Afraid?" His heart jumps with relief, jumps so hard that the flicker comes back in the air, through which he sees her lying too composed under his urgency. "Don't be afraid, Molly. I *love* you."

But she is saying softly, "Oh, damn, damn, Pete, I'm so sorry, it's a lousy thing women do. I was just so happy, because. . . ." She swallows, goes on in an absurd voice. "Because someone very dear to me is coming home. He called me this morning from Honolulu."

This he cannot, will not, understand among the flashing pulses, but repeats patiently, "You love me, Molly. I love you. We'll get married in Baltimore," while she fights gently away from him, saying, "Oh, I do, Pete, I *do*, but it's not the same."

"You'll be happy with me. You love me."

They are both up crouching now in the blinking, pounding

sunlight.

"No, Pete, I never *said*. I didn't—"Her hands are out seeking him, like knives.

"I *can't* marry you, honey. I'm going to marry a man called Charlie McMahon."

McMahon—Maaa—honn—aa—on-n-n the idiot sound flaps through the universe, his carotids are hammering, the air is drumming with his hurt and rage as he stands foolishly wounded, unable to believe the treachery of everything—which is now strobing in great blows of blackness as his voice shouts "Whore!" shouts "Bitch-bitch-bitch . . . " into a dwindling, flashing chaos—

—And explodes silently into a nonbeing which is almost familiar, is happening this time more slowly as if huge energy is tiding to its crest so slowly that some structure of himself endures to form in what is no longer a brain the fear that he is indeed dead and damned to live forever in furious fragments. And against this horror his essence strains to protest *But I did love!* at a horizon of desolation—a plain of endless, lifeless rubble under a cold black sky, in which he or some pattern of energies senses once more that distant presence: wreckage, machines, huge structures incomprehensibly operative, radiating dark force in the nightmare world, the force which now surges—

◰

—To incorporate him anew within familiar walls, with the words "But I did love" meaninglessly on his lips. He leans back in his familiarly unoiled swivel chair, savoring content. Somewhere within him weak darkness stirs, has power only to send his gaze to the three-di portraits behind the pile of printouts on his desk.

Molly smiles back at him over the computer sheets, her arm around their eldest daughter. For the first time in years the thought of poor Charlie McMahon crosses his mind, triggers the automatic incantation: Molly-never-would-have-been-happy-with-him. They had a bad time around there, but it worked out. Funny how vividly he recalls that day by the river, in spite of all the good years since. *But I did love,* his mind murmurs uneasily, as his eyes go lovingly to the computer printouts.

The lovely, elegant results. All confirmed eight ways now,

the variance all pinned down. Even better than he'd hoped. The journal paper can go in the mail tomorrow. Of course the pub-lag is nearly three years now; never mind: the AAAS panel comes next week. That's the important thing. Lucky timing, couldn't be neater. The press is bound to play it up. . . . Going to be hard not to watch Gilliam's face, Peter muses, his own face ten years younger, sparkling, all lines upturned.

"I do love it, that's what counts," he thinks, a jumble of the years of off-hours drudgery in his mind. . . . Coffee-ringed clipboards, the new centrifuge, the animal mess, a girl's open lab coat, arguments with Ferris in Analysis, arguments about space, about equipment, about costs—and arching over it like a laser-grid the luminous order of his hypothesis. His proven—no, mustn't say it—his meticulously *tested* hypothesis. The lucky lifetime break. The beauty one. Never do it again, he hasn't another one like this left in him; no matter! This is it, the peak. Just in time. Don't think of what Nathan said, don't think the word. (Nobel)—That's stupid. (Nobel) Think of the work itself, the explanatory power, the clarity.

His hand has been wandering toward the in-basket under the printouts where his mail has been growing moss (he'll get a secretary out of this, that's for sure!), but the idea of light turns him to the window. The room feels tense, brimming with a tide of energy. Too much coffee, he thinks, too much joy. I'm not used to it. Too much of a loner. From here in I share. Spread it around, encourage younger men. Herds of assistants now . . .

Across his view of tired Bethesda suburbs around the NIH Annex floats the train of multiple-author papers, his name as senior, a genial myth; sponsoring everybody's maiden publication. A fixture in the mainstream . . . Kids playing down there, he sees, shooting baskets by a garage, will some of them live to have a myeloma cured by the implications of his grubby years up here? If the crystallization can be made easier. Bound to come. But not by me, he thinks, trying to focus on the running figures through a faint stroboscopic blink which seems to arise from the streets below, although he knows it must be in his retinae.

Really too much caffeine, he warns himself. Let's not have a hypertensive episode, not *now*, for god's sake. Exultation is almost tangible in the room, it's not distracting but integrative; as if he were achieving some higher level of vitality, a norepinephrinelike effect. Maybe I really will live on a higher level, he muses, rubbing the bridge of his nose between two fingers to get rid of a black afterimage which seems almost like an Apollo moonscape behind his eyes, a trifle unpleasant.

Too much doom, he tells himself, vigorously polishing his glasses, too much bomb-scare, ecology-scare, fascism-scare, race-war-scare, death-of-everything scare. He jerks his jaw to stop the tinnitis thrumming in his inner ear, glancing at the big 1984 desk calendar with its scrawled joke: *If everything's okay why are we whispering?* Right. Let's get at it and get home. To Molly and Sue and little Pete, their late-born.

He grins, thinking of the kid running to him, and thrusts his hand under the printouts to his packet of stale mail—and as his hand touches it an icicle rams into his heart.

For an instant he thinks he really is having a coronary. But it isn't his real heart, it's a horrible cold current of knowledge striking from his fingers to his soul, from that hideous sleazy tan-covered foreign journal which he now pulls slowly out to see the penciled note clipped to the cover, the personally delivered damned journal which has been lying under there like a time bomb, for how long? Weeks?

Pete, you better look at this. Sorry as hell.

But he doesn't need to look, riffling through the wretchedly printed pages with fingers grown big and cold as clubs; he already knows what he'll find inside there published so neatly, so sweetly, and completely, with the confirmation even stronger and more elegant, the implication he hadn't thought of—and all so modest and terse. So young. Despair takes him as the page opens. *Djakarta University* for Jesus Christ's sake? And some Hindu's bloody paradigm—

Sick fury fulminates, bile and ashes rain through his soul as his hands fumble the pages, the gray unreal unreadable pages which are now strobing—Flash! Black! Flash! Black!— swallowing the world, roaring him in or up or out on a phantom whirlwind—

—Till unsensation crescendos past all limit, bursts finally into the silence of pure energy, where he—or what is left of him, or momentarily reconstituted of him—integrates to terrified insight, achieves actual deathly awareness of its extinct self immaterially spinning in the dust of an eons-gone NIH Annex on a destroyed planet. And comprehends with agonized lucidity the real death of everything that lived—excepting only that in himself which he would most desperately wish to be dead.

What happened? He does not know, can never know, which of the dooms or some other had finally overtaken them, nor when; only that he is registering eternity, not time, that all that lived here has been gone so long that even time is still. Gone, all gone; centuries or millennia gone, all gone to ashes under pulseless stars in the icy dark, gone forever. Saving him alone and his trivial pain.

He alone . . . But as the mercilessly reifying force floods higher there wakes in him a dim uncomforting sense of presence; a bodiless disquiet in the dust tells him he is companioned, is but a node in a ghostly film of dead life shrouding the cold rock-ball. Unreachable, isolate—he strains for contact and is incorporeally stricken by new dread. *Are they too in pain?* Was pain indeed the fiercest fire in our nerves, alone able to sustain its flame through death? What of love, of joy? . . . There are none here.

He wails voicelessly as conviction invades him, he who had believed in nothing before. All the agonies of Earth, uncanceled? Are broken ghosts limping forever from Stalingrad and Salamis, from Gettysburg and Thebes and Dunkirk and Khartoum? Do the butchers' blows still fall at Ravensbruck and Wounded Knee? Are the dead of Carthage and Hiroshima and Cuzco burning yet? Have ghostly women waked again only to resuffer violation, only to watch again their babies slain? Is every nameless slave still feeling the iron bite, is every bomb, every bullet and arrow and stone that ever flew, still finding its screaming mark—atrocity without end or comfort, forever?

Molly. The name forms in his canceled heart. She who was love. He tries to know that she or some fragment of her is warm among her children, but can summon only the image of her crawling forever through wreckage to Charlie McMahon's bloody head.

Let it not be! He would shriek defiance at the wastes, finding himself more real as the strange energy densens; he struggles bodilessly, flails perished nonlimbs to conjure love out of extinction to shield him against hell, calling with all his obliterated soul on the ultimate talisman: the sound of his little son's laugh, the child running to him, clasping his leg in welcome home.

For an instant he thinks he has it—he can see the small face turn up, the mouth open—but as he tries to grasp, the ghost-child fades, frays out, leaving in his destroyed heart only another echo of hurt—*I want Mommy, Mommy, my Mommy.* And he perceives that what he had taken for its head are forms. Presences intrusive, alien as the smooth, bleak regard of sharks met under water.

They move, precess obscurely—they *exist* here on this time-lost plain! And he understands with loathing that it is from *them* or *those*—machines or beings, he cannot tell—that the sustaining energy flows. It is *their* dark potency which has raised him from the patterns of the dust.

Hating them he hungers, would sway after them to suck his death-life, as a billion other remnants are yearning, dead sunflowers thirsting toward their black sun—but finds he cannot, can only crave helplessly as they recede.

They move, he perceives, toward those black distant cenotaphs, skeletal and alien, which alone break the dead horizon. What these can be, engines or edifices, is beyond his knowing. He strains sightlessly, sensing now a convergence, an inflowing as of departure like ants into no earthly nest. And at this he understands that the energy upbuoying him is sinking, is starting to ebb. The alien radiance that raised him is going, and he is guttering out. *Do you know?* he voicelessly cries after them, *Do you know? Do you move oblivious among our agonies?*

But he receives no answer, will never receive one; and as his tenuous structure fails he has consciousness only to wonder briefly what unimaginable errand brought such beings here to his dead cinder. Emissaries, he wonders, dwindling; explorers, engineers? Or is it possible that they are only sightseers? Idling among our ruins, perhaps even cognizant of the ghosts they raise to wail—turning us on, recreating our dead-show for their entertainment?

Shriveling, he watches them go in, taking with them his lacerating life, returning him to the void. Will they return? Or—his waning self forms one last desolation—have they returned already on their millennial tours? Has this recurred, to recur and recur again? Must he and all dead life be borne back each time helplessly to suffer, to jerk anew on the same knives and die again until another energy exhumes him for the next performance?

Let us die! But his decaying identity can no longer sustain protest, knows only that it is true, is unbearably all true, has all been done to him before and is all to do again and again and again without mercy forever.

And as he sinks back through the collapsing levels he can keep hold only of despair, touching again the deadly limp brown journal—*Djakarta University?* Flash—and he no longer knows the cause of the terror in his soul as he crumbles through lost springtime—*I don't love you that way, Pete*—and is betrayed to aching joy as his hand closes over the young breast within her white shirt—*Pe-ter, don't you have a friend?*—while his being shreds out, disperses among a myriad draining ghosts of anguish as the alien life deserts them, strands them lower and lower toward the final dark—until with uncomprehending grief he finds himself, or a configuration that was himself, for a last instant real—his boots on gravel in the dawn, his hand on a rusty pickup truck.

A joy he cannot bear rises in his fourteen-year-old heart as he peers down at the magic ducks, sees his boat safe by the path he's cut; not understanding why the wind shrieks pain through the peaks above as he starts leaping down the rocks holding his ax and his first own gun, down to the dark lake under the cold stars, forever.

LOVE IS THE PLAN THE PLAN IS DEATH

REMEMBERING—

Do you hear, my little red? Hold me softly. The cold grows.

I remember:

—I am hugely black and hopeful, I bounce on six legs along the mountains in the new warm! . . . *Sing the changer, Sing the stranger! Will the changes change forever?* . . . All my hums have words now. Another change!

Eagerly I bound on sunward following the tiny thrill in the air. The forests have been shrinking again. Then I see. It is me! Me-Myself, MOGGADEET—I have grown bigger more in the winter cold! I astonish myself, Moggadeet-the-small!

Excitement, enticement, shrilling from the sun-side of the world. I come! . . . The sun is changing again too. *Sun is walking in the night! Sun is walking back to Summer in the warming of the light!* . . . Warm is Me—Moggadeet Myself. Forget the bad-time winter.

Memory quakes me.

The Old One.

I stop, pluck up a tree. So much I wanted to ask the Old One. No time. Cold. Tree goes end over end down-cliff, I watch the fatclimbers tumble out. Not hungry.

The Old One warned me of the cold—I didn't believe him. I move on, grieving. . . . *Old One told you, The cold, the cold will hold you. Chill cold! Kill cold. In the cold I killed you.*

But it's warm now, all different. I'm Moggadeet again.

I bound over a hill and see my brother Frim.

At first I don't know him. A big black old one! I think. And in the warm, we can speak!

I surge toward him bashing trees. The big black is crouched over a ravine, peering down. Black back has shiny ripples like—It IS Frim! Frim-I-hunted-for, Frim-run-away! But he's so big now! Giant Frim! A *stranger, a changer*—

"Frim!"

He doesn't hear me; all his eye-turrets are under the trees. His end is sticking up oddlike, all atremble. What's he hunting?

"Frim! It's me, Moggadeet!"

But he only quivers his legs; I see his spurs pushing out. What a fool, Frim! I remind myself how timid he is, I try to move gently. When I get closer I'm astonished again. I'm bigger than he is now! Changes! I can see right over his shoulder into the ravine.

Hot yellow-green in there. A little glade all lit with sun. I bend my eyes to see what Frim is after, and all astonishments blow up the world.

I see you.

I saw you.

I will always see you. Dancing in the green fire, my tiny red star! So bright! So small! So perfect! So fierce! I knew you—Oh, yes, I knew you in that first instant, my dawnberry, my scarlet minikin. *Red!* A tiny baby red one, smaller than my smallest eye. And so brave!

The Old One said it. Red is the color of love.

I see you swat at a hopper twice your size, my eyes bulge as you leap after it and go rolling, shrilling *Lililee! Lilileee-ee!* in baby wrath. Oh, my mighty hunter, you don't know someone is looking right into your tender little love-fur! Oh, yes! Palest pink it is, just brushed with rose. My jaws spurt, the world flashes and reels.

And then Frim, poor fool, feels me behind him and rears up.

But what a Frim! His throat-sacs are ballooning purple-black, his plates are engorged like the Mother of the storm-clouds! Glittering, rattling his spurs! His tail booms! "It's mine!" he bellows—I can hardly understand him. He jumps straight at me!

"Stop, Frim, stop!" I cry, dodging away bewildered. It's warm—how can Frim be wild, kill-wild?

"Brother Frim!" I call gently, soothingly. But something is badly wrong! My voice is bellowing too! Yes, in the warm and I want only to calm him, I am full of love—but the kill-roar is rushing through me, I too am swelling, rattling, booming! Invincible! To crush—to rend—

Oh, I am shamed.

I came to myself in the wreckage of Frim, Frim-pieces everywhere, myself is sodden with Frim. But I did not eat him! I did not! Should I take joy in that? Did I defy the Plan? But my throat was closed. Not because it was Frim but because of darling you. *You!* Where are you? The glade is empty! Oh, fearful fear, I have frightened you, you are run away! I forget Frim. I forget everything but you my heartmeat, my precious tiny red.

I smash trees, I uproot rocks, I tear the ravine open! Oh, where are you hiding? Suddenly I have a new fear: has my wild search harmed you? I force myself calm. I begin questing, circling, ever wider over the trees, moving cloud-silent, thrusting my eyes and ears down into every glade. A new humming fills my throat. *Oooo, Oo-oo, Rum-a-looly-loo,* I moan. Hunting, hunting for you.

Once I glimpse a black bigness far away and I am suddenly up at my full height, roaring. Attack the black! Was it another brother? I would slay him, but the stranger is already vanishing. I roar again. No—*it roars me,* the new power of black. Yet deep inside, Myself-Moggadeet is watching, fearing. Attack the black—even in the warm? Is there no safety, are we truly like the fatclimbers? But at the same time it feels—Oh, right! Oh, good! Sweet is the Plan. I give myself up to seeking you, my new song longing *Oo-loo* and *Looly rum-a-loo-oo-loo.*

And you answered! You!

So tiny you, hidden under a leaf! Shrilling *Li! Li! Lililee!* Trilling, thrilling—half mocking, already imperious. Oh, how I whirl, crash, try to look under my feet, stop frozen in horror of squashing the *Lilili! Lee!* Rocking, longing, moaning Moggadeet.

And you came out, you did.

My adorable firemite, threatening ME!!

When I see your littlest hunting claws upraised my whole gut melts, it floods me. I am all tender jelly. Tender! Oh, tender-fierce like a Mother, I think! Isn't that how a Mother feels? My jaws are sluicing juice that isn't hunger-juice—I am choking with fear of frighting you or bruising your tininess—I ache to grip and knead you, to eat you in one gulp, in a thousand nibbles—

Oh, the power of *red*—the Old One said it! Now I feel my special hands, my tender hands I always carry hidden—now they come swelling out, come pushing toward my head! What? What?

My secret hands begin to knead and roll the stuff that's dripping from my jaws.

Ah, that arouses you too, my redling, doesn't it?

Yes, yes, I feel—torment—I feel your sly excitement! How your body remembers even now our love-dawn, our very first moments of Moggadeet-Leely. Before I knew You-Yourself, before you knew Me. It began then, my heartlet, our love-knowing began in that very first instant when your Moggadeet stared down at you like a monster bursting. I saw how new you were, how helpless!

Yes, even while I loomed over you marveling—even while my secret hands drew and spun your fate—even then it came to me in pity that long ago, last year when I was a child, I saw other little red ones among my brothers, before our Mother drove them away. I was only a foolish baby then; I didn't understand. I thought they'd grown strange and silly in their redness and Mother did well to turn them out. Oh, stupid Moggadeet!

But now I saw *you*, my flamelet—I understood! You were only that day cast out by your Mother. Never had you felt the terrors of a night alone in the world; you couldn't imagine that such a monster as Frim was hunting you. Oh, my ruby nestling, my baby red! Never, I vowed it, never would I leave you—and have I not kept that vow? Never! I, Moggadeet, *I would be your Mother.*

Great is the Plan, but I was greater!

All I learned of hunting in my lonely year, to drift like the air, to leap, to grip so delicately—all these learnings became for you! Not to bruise the smallest portion of your bright body. Oh, yes! I captured you whole in all your tiny perfection, though you sizzled and spat and fought me like the sunspark you are. And then—

And then—

I began to—Oh, terror! Delight-shame! How can I speak such a beautiful secret?—the Plan took me as a Mother guides

her child, and with my special hands I began to—
I began to bind you up!
Oh, yes! Oh, yes! My special hands that had no use, now all unfurled and engorged and alive, never stopping the working in the strong juice of my jaws—they began to *bind* you, passing over and around and beneath you, every moment piercing me with fear and joy. I wound among your darling little limbs, into your inmost delicate recesses, gently swathing and soothing you, winding and binding until you became a shining jewel. Mine!

—But you responded. I know that now. We know! Oh, yes, in your fierce struggles, shyly you helped me, always at the end each strand fell sweetly into place.... *Winding you, binding you, loving Leelyloo!* ... How our bodies moved in our first weaving song! I feel it even now, I melt with excitement! How I wove the silk about you, tying each tiny limb, making you perfectly helpless. How fearlessly you gazed up at me, your terrifying captor! You! You were never frightened, as I'm not frightened now. Isn't it strange, my loveling? This sweetness that floods our bodies when we yield to the Plan. Great is the Plan! Fear it, fight it—but hold the sweetness yet.

Sweetly began our lovetime, when first I became your new true Mother, never to cast you out. How I fed you and caressed and tended and fondled you! What a responsibility it is to be a Mother. Anxiously I carried you furled in my secret arms, savagely I drove off all intruders, even the harmless banlings in the grass, in fear every moment that you were stifled or crushed!

And all the warm nights long, how I cared for your helpless little body, carefully releasing each infant limb, flexing and stretching it, cleaning every scarlet morsel of you with my giant tongue, nibbling your baby claws with my terrible teeth, reveling in your baby hum, pretending to devour you while you shrieked with glee, *Li! Lillili! Love-lili, Leelylee!* But the greatest joy of all—
We spoke!
We spoke together, we two! We communed, we shared, we poured ourselves one into the other. Love, how we stammered and stumbled at the first, you in your strange Mother-tongue and I in mine! How we blended our singing wordlessly and then with words, until more and more we came to see with each other's eyes, to hear, to taste, to feel, the world of each

407

other, until I became Leelyloo and you became Moggadeet, until finally we became together a new thing, Moggadeet-Leely, Lilliloo-Mogga, Lili-Mogga-looly-deet!

Oh, love, are we the first? Have others loved with their whole selves? Oh, sad thinking, that lovers before us have left no trace. Remember us! Will you remember, my adored, though Moggadeet has spoiled everything and the cold grows? If only I could hear you speak once more, my red, my innocent one. You are remembering, your body tells me you remember even now. Softly, hold me softly yet. Hear your Moggadeet!

You told me how it was being you, yourself, tiny-redling-Lilliloo. Of your Mother, your dreams, your baby joys and fears. And I told you mine, and all my learnings in the world since the day when my own Mother—

Hear me, my heartmate! Time runs away.

—On the last day of my childhood my Mother called us all under her.

"Sons! S-son-n-nss!" Why did her dear voice creak so?

My brothers came in slowly, fearfully, from the summer green. But I, small Moggadeet, I climb eagerly up under the great arch of her body, seeking the golden Mother-fur. Right into her warm cave I come, where her Mother-eyes are glowing, the cave that sheltered us so strongly all our lives, as I shelter you, my dawnflower.

I long to touch her, to hear her speak and sing to us again. Her Mother-fur troubles me, it is tattered and drab. Shyly I press against one of her huge food-glands. It feels dry, but a glow sparks deep in her Mother-eye.

"Mother," I whisper. "It's me, Moggadeet!"

"SONNNNNS!" Her voice rumbles through her armor. My big brothers huddle by her legs, peering back at the sunlight. They look so funny, shedding, half gold, half black.

"I'm afraid!" whimpers my brother Frim nearby. Like me Frim still has his gold baby fur. Mother is speaking again, but her voice booms so I can hardly understand.

"WINNN-TER! WINTER, I SAY! AFTER THE WARM COMES THE COLD WINTER. THE COLD WINTER BEFORE THE WARM COMES AGAIN, COMES. . . ."

Frim whimpers louder, I cuff him. What's wrong, why is her loving voice so hoarse and strange now? She always hummed us so tenderly, we nestled in her warm Mother-fur sucking the lovely Mother-juices, rocking to her steady walking-song. *Ee mooly-mooly, Ee-mooly mooly,* while far below the earth rolled by. Oh, yes, and how we held our breaths and squealed when she began her mighty hunting hum! *Tann! Tann! Dir! Dir! Dir Hataan! HATONN!* How we clung in the thrilling climax when she plunged upon her prey and we heard the crunching, the tearing, the gurgling in her body that meant soon her food-glands would be richly full.

Suddenly I see a black streak down below—a big brother is running away! Mother's booming voice breaks off. Her great body tenses, her plates clash. Mother roars!

Running, screaming down below! I burrow up into her fur, am flung about as she leaps.

"OUT! GO OUT!" she bellows. Her terrible hunting-limbs crash down, she roars without words, shuddering, jolting. When I dare to peek out I see the others all have fled. All except one!

A black body is lying under Mother's claws. It's my brother Sesso—yes! But Mother is tearing him, is eating him! I watch in horror—Sesso she cared for so proudly, so tenderly! I sob, bury my head in her fur. But the beautiful fur is coming loose in my hands, her golden Mother-fur is dying! I cling desperately, trying not to hear the crunches, the gulps and gurgling. The world is ending, all is terrible, terrible.

And yet, my fireberry, even then I almost understood. Great is the Plan!

Presently Mother stops feeding and begins to move. The rocky ground jolts by far below. Her stride is not smooth but jerks me, even her deep hum is strange. *On! On! Alone! Ever alone. And on!* The rumbling ceases. Silence. Mother is resting.

"Mother!" I whisper. "Mother, it's Moggadeet. I'm here!"

Her stomach-plates contract, a belch reverberates in her vaults.

"Go," she groans. "Go. Too late. Mother no more."

"I don't want to leave you. Why must I go? Mother!" I wail, "Speak to me!" I keen my baby hum, *Deet! Deet! Tikki-takka! Deet!* hoping Mother will answer crooning deep, *Brum! Brrumm! Brumaloo-bruin!* Now I see one huge Mother-eye glow faintly, but she only makes a grating sound.

"Too late. No more . . . The winter, I say. I did speak. . . . Before the winter, go. Go."

"Tell me about Outside, Mother," I plead.

Another groan or cough nearly shakes me from my perch. But when she speaks again her voice sounds gentler.

"Talk?" she grumbles. "Talk, talk, talk. You are a strange son. Talk, like your Father."

"What's that, Mother? What's a Father?"

She belches again. "Always talk. The winters grow, he said. Oh, yes. Tell them the winters grow. So I did. Late. Winter, I spoke you. Cold!" Her voice booms. "No more! Too late." Outside I hear her armor rattle and clank.

"Mother, speak to me!"

"Go. Go-o-o!"

Her belly-plates clash around me. I jump for another nest of fur, but it comes loose in my grip. Wailing, I save myself by hanging to one of her great walking limbs. It is rigid, thrumming like rock.

"GO!" She roars.

Her Mother-eyes are shriveling, dead! I panic, scramble down, everything is vibrating, resonating around me. Mother is holding back a storm of rage!

I leap for the ground, I rush diving into a crevice, I wiggle and burrow under the fearful bellowing and clanging that rains on me from above. Into the rocks I go with the hunting claws of Mother crashing behind me.

Oh, my redling, my little tenderling! Never have you known such a night. Those dreadful hours hiding from the monster that had been my loving Mother!

I saw her once more, yes. When dawn came I clambered up a ledge and peered through the mist. It was warm then, the mists were warm. I knew what Mothers looked like. We had glimpses of huge horned dark shapes before our own Mother hooted us under her. Oh yes, and then would come Mother's earthshaking challenge and the strange Mother's answering roar, and we'd cling tight, feeling her surge of kill-fury, buffeted, deafened, battered, while our Mother charged and struck. And once while our Mother fed I peeped out and saw a strange baby squealing in the remnants on the ground below.

But now it was my own dear Mother I saw lurching away through the mists, that great rusty-gray hulk so horned and bossed that only her hunting-eyes showed above her armor, swiveling mindlessly, questing for anything that moved. She crashed her way across the mountains, and as she went she thrummed a new harsh song. *Cold! Cold! Ice and Lone. Ice! And cold! And end.* I never saw her again.

When the sun rose I saw that the gold fur was peeling from my shiny black. All by itself my hunting-limb flashed out and knocked a hopper right into my jaws.

You see, my berry, how much larger and stronger I was than you when Mother sent us away? That also is the Plan. For you were not yet born! I had to live on while the warm turned to cold and while the winter passed to warm again before you would be waiting. I had to grow and learn. To *learn*, my Lilliloo! That is important. Only we black ones have a time to learn—the Old One said it.

Such small learnings at first! To drink the flat water-stuff without choking, to catch the shiny flying things that bite, and to watch the storm-clouds and the moving of the sun. And the nights, and the soft things that moved on the trees. And the bushes that kept shrinking, shrinking—only it was me, Moggadeet, growing larger! Oh, yes! And the day when I could knock down a fatclimber from its vine!

But all these leanings were easy—the Plan in my body guided me. It guides me now, Lilliloo, even now it would give me peace and joy if I yielded to it. But I will not! I will remember to the end, I will speak to the end!

I will speak the big learnings. How I saw—though I was so busy catching and eating more, more, always more—I saw all things were changing, changing. *Changers!* The bushes changed their buds to berries, the fatclimbers changed their colors, even the sun changed, and the hills. And I saw all things were together with others of their kind but only me, Moggadeet. I was alone. Oh, so alone!

I went marching through the valleys in my shiny new black, humming my new song *Turra-tarra! Tarra Tan!* Once I glimpsed my brother Frim and I called him, but he ran like the wind. Away, alone! And when I went to the next valley I found the trees all mashed down. And in the distance I saw a black one like me—only many times as big! Huge! Almost as big as a Mother, sleek and glossy-new. I would have called, but he reared up and saw me and roared so terribly that I too fled like the wind to empty mountains. Alone.

And so I learned, my redling, how we are alone even though my heart was full of love. And I wandered, puzzling and eating ever more and more. I saw the Trails; they meant nothing to me then. But I began to learn the important thing.

The cold.

You know it, my little red. How in the warm days I am me, Myself-Moggadeet. Ever-growing, ever-learning. In the warm we think, we speak. We love! We make our own Plan. Oh, did we not, my lovemate?

But in the cold, in the night—for the nights were growing colder—in the cold night I was—what?—not Moggadeet. Not Moggadeet-thinking. Not Me-Myself. Only Something-that-lives, acts without thought. Helpless-Moggadeet. In the cold is only the Plan. I almost thought it.

And then one day the night chill lingered and lingered and the sun was hidden in the mists. And I found myself going up the Trails.

The Trails are a part of the Plan too, my redling.

The Trails are of winter. There we must go all of us, we blacks. When the cold grows stronger the Plan calls us upward, upward, we begin to drift up the Trails, up along the ridges to the cold, the night-side of the mountains. Up beyond the forests where the trees grow scant and turn to dead stonewood.

So the Plan drew me and I followed, only half-aware. Sometimes I came into warmer sunlight where I could stop and feed and try to think, but the cold fogs rose again and I went on, on and up. I began to catch sight of others like me far along the mountain-flank, moving steadily up. They didn't rear or roar when they saw me. I didn't call to them. Each one alone we climbed on toward the Caves, unthinking, blind. And so I would have gone too.

But then the great thing happened.

—Oh, no, my Lilliloo! Not the *greatest*. The greatest of all is you, will always be you. My precious sunmite, my red lovebaby! Don't be angry, no, no, my sharing one. Hold me softly. I must say our big learning. Hear your Moggadeet, hear and remember!

In the sun's last warm I found him, the Old One. A terrible sight! So maimed and damaged, parts rotting and gone. I stared, thinking him dead. Suddenly his head rolled feebly and a croak came out.

"Young . . . one?" An eye opened in his festering head, a flyer pecked at it. "Young one . . . wait!"

And I understood him! Oh, with love—

No, no, my redling! Gently! Gently hear your Moggadeet. We *spoke*—the Old One and I! Old to young, we shared. I think it cannot happen.

"No old ones," he creaked. "Never to speak . . . we blacks. Never. It is not . . . the Plan. Only me . . . I wait. . . ."

"Plan," I ask, half-knowing. "What is the Plan?"

"A beauty," he whispers. "In the warm, a beauty in the air . . . I followed . . . but another black one saw me and we fought . . . and I was damaged, but still the Plan made me follow until I was crushed and torn and dead. . . . But I lived! And the Plan let me go and I crawled here . . . to wait . . . to share . . . but—"

His head sags. Quickly I snatch a flyer from the air and push it to his torn jaws.

"Old One! What is the Plan?"

He swallows painfully, his one eye holding mine.

"In us," he says thickly, stronger now. "In us, moving us in all things necessary for the life. You have seen. When the baby is golden the Mother cherishes it all winter long. But when it turns red or black she drives it away. Was it not so?"

"Yes, but —"

"That's the Plan! Always the Plan. Gold is the color of Mother-care, but black is the color of rage. Attack the black! Black is to kill. Even a Mother, even her own baby, she cannot defy the Plan. Hear me, young one!"

"I hear. I have seen," I answer. "But what is red?"

"*Red!*" He groans. "Red is the color of love."

"No!" I say, stupid Moggadeet! "I know love. Love is gold."

The Old One's eye turns from me. "Love," he sighs. "When the beauty comes in the air, you will see . . . He falls silent. I fear he's dying. What can I do? We stay silent there together in the last misty sunwarm. Dimly on the slopes I can see other black ones like myself drifting steadily upward on their own Trails among the stone-tree heaps, into the icy mists.

"Old One! Where do we go?"

"You go to the Caves of Winter. That is the Plan."

"Winter, yes. The cold. Mother told us. And after the cold winter comes the warm. I remember. The winter will pass, won't it? Why did she say, the winters grow? Teach me, Old One. What is a Father?"

"Fa-ther? A word I don't know. But wait—" His mangled head turns to me. "*The winters grow?* Your mother said this? Oh, cold! Oh, lonely," he groans. "A big learning she gave you. This learning I fear to think."

His eye rolls, glaring. I am frightened inside.

"Look around, young one. These stony deadwoods. Dead
shells of trees that grow in the warm valleys. Why are they
here? The cold has killed them. No living tree grows here now.
Think, young one!"

I look, and true! It is a warm forest killed to stone.

"Once it, was warm here. Once it was like the valleys. But
the cold has grown stronger. The winter grows. Do you see?
And the warm grows less and less."

"But the warm is life! The warm is Me-Myself!"

"Yes. In the warm we think, we learn. In the cold is only
the Plan. In the cold we are blind. . . . Waiting here, I thought,
was there a time when it was warm here once? Did we come
here, we blacks, in the warm to speak, to share? Oh, young
one, a fearful thinking. Does our time of learning grow shorter,
shorter? Where will it end? Will the winters grow until we can
learn nothing but only live blindly in the Plan, like the silly
fatclimbers who sing but do not speak?"

His words fill me with cold fear. Such a terrible learning! I
feel anger.

"No! We will not! We must—we must hold the warm!"

"Hold the warm?" He twists painfully to stare at me. "Hold
the warm. . . . A great thinking. Yes. But how? How? Soon it
will be too cold to think, even here!"

"The warm will come again," I tell him. "Then we must
learn a way to hold it, you and I!"

His head lolls.

"No . . . When the warm comes I will not be here . . . and you
will be too busy for thinking, young one."

"I will help you! I will carry you to the Caves!"

"In the Caves," he gasps, "in each Cave there are two black
ones like yourself. One is living, waiting mindless for the
winter to pass. . . . And while he waits, he eats. He eats the
other, that is how he lives. That is the Plan. As you will eat me,
my youngling."

"No!" I cry in horror. "I will never harm you!"

"When the cold comes you will see," he whispers. "Great is
the Plan!"

"No! You are wrong! I will break the Plan," I shout. A cold
wind is blowing from the summit; the sun dies.

"Never will I harm you," I bellow. "You are wrong to say
so!"

My scaleplates are rising, my tail begins to pound. Through

the mists I hear his gasps.

I recall dragging a heavy black thing to my Cave.

Chill cold, kill cold . . . In the cold I killed you.

Leelyloo. He did not resist.

Great is the Plan. He accepted all, perhaps he even felt a strange joy, as I feel it now. In the Plan is joy. But if the Plan is wrong? *The winters grow.* Do the fatclimbers have their Plan too?

Oh, a hard thinking! How we tried, my redling, my joy. All the long warm days I explained it to you, over and over. How the winter would come and change us if we did not hold the warm. You understood! You share, you understand me now, my precious flame—though you can't speak I feel your sharing love. Softly . . .

Oh, yes, we made our preparations, our own Plan. Even in the highest heat we made our Plan against the cold. Have other lovers done so? How I searched, carrying you my cherry bud, I crossed whole mountain ranges, following the sun until we found this warmest of warm valleys on the sunward side. Surely the cold would be weak here, I thought. How could they reach us here, the cold fogs, the icy winds that froze my inner Me and drew me up the Trails into the dead Caves of Winter?

This time I would defy!

This time I have *you.*

"Don't take me there, my Moggadeet!" You begged, fearful of the strangeness. "Don't take me to the cold!"

"Never, my Leelyloo! Never, I vow it. Am I not your Mother, little redness?"

"But you will change! The cold will make you forget. Is it not the Plan?"

"We will break the Plan, Lilli. See, you are growing larger, heavier, my fireberry—and always more beautiful! Soon I will not be able to carry you so easily, I could never carry you to the cold Trails. And I will never leave you!"

"But you are so big, Moggadeet! When the change comes you will forget and drag me to the cold."

"Never! Your Moggadeet has a deeper Plan! When the mists start I will take you to the farthest, warmest cranny of this cave, and there I will spin a wall so you can never never be pulled out. And I will never never leave you. Even the Plan cannot draw Moggadeet from Leelyloo!"

"But you will have to go hunting for food and the cold will

take you then! You will forget me and follow the cold love of winter and leave me there to die! Perhaps that is the Plan!"

"Oh, no, my precious, my redling! Don't grieve, don't cry! Hear your Moggadeet's Plan! From now on I'll hunt twice as hard. I'll fill this cave to the top, my fat little blushbud, I will fill it with food now so I can stay by you all the winter through!"

And so I did, didn't I my Lilli? Silly Moggadeet, how I hunted, how I brought lizards, hoppers, fatclimbers, and banlings by the score. What a fool! For of course they rotted, there in the heat, and the heaps turned green and slimy—but still tasting good, eh, my berry?—so that we had to eat them then, gorging ourselves like babies. And how you grew!

Oh, beautiful you became, my jewel of redness! So bursting fat and shiny-full, but still my tiny one, my sun-spark. Each night after I fed you I would part the silk, fondling your head, your eyes, your tender ears, trembling with excitement for the delicious moment when I would release your first scarlet limb to caress and exercise it and press it to my pulsing throat-sacs. Sometimes I would unbind two together for the sheer joy of seeing you move. And each night it took longer, each morning I had to make more silk to bind you up. How proud I was, my Leely, Lilliloo!

That was when my greatest thinking came.

As I was weaving you so tenderly into your shining cocoon, my joyberry, I thought, why not bind up living fatclimbers? Pen them alive so their flesh will stay sweet and they will serve us through the winter!

That was a great thinking, Lilliloo, and I did this, and it was good. Fatclimbers in plenty I walled in a little tunnel, and many, many other things as well, while the sun walked back toward winter and the shadows grew and grew. Fatclimbers and banlings and all tasty creatures and even—oh, clever Moggadeet!—all manner of leaves and bark and stuffs for them to eat! Oh, we had broken the Plan for sure now!

"We have broken the Plan for sure, my Lilli-red. The fatclimbers are eating the twigs and bark, the banlings are eating juice from the wood, the great runners are munching grass, and we will eat them all!"

"Oh, Moggadeet, you are brave! Do you think we can really break the Plan? I am frightened! Give me a banling, I think it grows cold."

"You have eaten fifteen banlings, my minikin!" I teased you.

"How fat you grow! Let me look at you again, yes, you must let your Moggadeet caress you while you eat. Ah, how adorable you are!"

And of course—Oh, you remember how it began then, our deepest love. For when I uncovered you one night with the first hint of cold in the air, I saw that you had changed.

Shall I say it?

Your secret fur. Your *Mother-fur*.

Always I had cleaned you there tenderly, but without difficulty to restrain myself. But on this night when I parted the silk strands with my huge hunting claws, what new delights met my eyes! No longer pink and pale but fiery red! *Red!* Scarlet blaze like the reddest sunrise, gold-tipped! And swollen, curling, dewy—Oh! Commanding me to expose you, all of you. Oh, how your tender eyes melted me and your breath musky-sweet and your limbs warm and heavy in my grasp!

Wildly I ripped away the last strands, dazed with bliss as you slowly stretched your whole blazing redness before my eyes. I knew then—*we* knew!—that the love we felt before was only a beginning. My hunting-limbs fell at my sides and my special hands, my weaving hands grew, filled with new, almost painful life. I could not speak, my throat-sacs filling, filling! And my lovehands rose up by themselves, pressing ecstatically, while my eyes bent closer, closer to your glorious *red!*

But suddenly the Me-Myself, Moggadeet awoke! I jumped back!

"Lilli! What's happening to us?"

"Oh, Moggadeet, I love you! Don't go away!"

"What is it, Leelyloo? Is it the Plan?"

"I don't care! Moggadeet, don't you love me?"

"I fear! I fear to harm you! You are so tiny. I am your Mother."

"No, Moggadeet, look! I am as big as you are. Don't be afraid."

I drew back—oh, hard, hard!—and tried to look calmly.

"True, my redling, you have grown. But your limbs are so new, so tender. Oh, I can't look!"

Averting my eyes I began to spin a screen of silk, to shut away your maddening redness.

"We must wait, Lilliloo. We must go on as before. I don't know what this strange urging means; I fear it will bring you harm."

"Yes, Moggadeet. We will wait.

And so we waited. Oh, yes. Each night it grew more hard. We tried to be as before, to be happy. Leely-Moggadeet. Each night as I caressed your glowing limbs that seemed to offer themselves to me as I swathed and unswathed them in turn, the urge rose in me hotter, more strong. To unveil you wholly! To look again upon your whole body!

Oh, yes, my darling, I feel—unbearable—how you remember with me those last days of our simple love.

Colder . . . colder. Mornings when I went to harvest the fatclimbers there was a whiteness on their fur and the banlings ceased to move. The sun sank ever lower, paler, and the cold mists hung above us, reaching down. Soon I dared not leave the cave. I stayed all day by your silken wall, humming Motherlike, *Brum-a-loo, Mooly-mooly, Lilliloo, Love Leely*. Strong Moggadeet!

"We'll wait, fireling. We will not yield to the Plan! Aren't we happier than all others, here with our love in our warm cave?"

"Oh, yes, Moggadeet."

"I'm Myself now. I am strong. I'll make my own Plan. I will not look at you until . . . until the warm, until the Sun comes back."

"Yes, Moggadeet . . . Moggadeet? My limbs are cramped."

"Oh, my precious, wait—see, I am opening the silk very carefully, I will not look—I won't—"

"Moggadeet, don't you love me?"

"Leelyloo! Oh, my glorious one! I fear, I fear—"

"Look, Moggadeet! See how big I am, how strong!"

"Oh, redling, my hands—my hands—what are they doing to you?"

For with my special hands I was pressing, pressing the hot juices from my throat-sacs and tenderly, tenderly parting your sweet Mother-fur and *placing my gift within your secret places.* And as I did this our eyes entwined and our limbs made a wreath.

"My darling, do I hurt you?"

"Oh, no, Moggadeet! Oh, no!"

Oh, my adored one, those last days of our love!

Outside the world grew colder yet, and the fatclimbers ceased to eat and the banlings lay still and began to stink. But still we held the warmth deep in our cave and still I fed my beloved on the last of our food. And every night our new ritual of love became more free, richer, though I compelled myself to hide all but a portion of your sweet body. But each dawn it grew hard and harder for me to replace the silken bonds around your limbs.

"Moggadeet! Why do you not bind me! I am afraid!"

"A moment, Lilli, a moment. I must caress you just once more."

"I'm afraid, Moggadeet! Cease now and bind me!"

"But why, my lovekin? Why must I hide you? Is this not some foolish part of the Plan?"

"I don't know, I feel so strange. Moggadeet, I—I'm changing."

"You grow more glorious every moment, my Lilli, my own. Let me look at you! It is wrong to bind you away!"

"No, Moggadeet! No!"

But I would not listen, would I? Oh, foolish Moggadeet-who-thought-to-be-your-Mother. Great is the Plan!

I did not listen, I did not bind you up. No! I ripped them away, the strong silk strands. Mad with love, I slashed them all at once, rushing from each limb to the next until all your glorious body lay exposed. At last—I saw you whole!

Oh, Lilliloo, greatest of Mothers.

It was not I who was your Mother. You were mine.

Shining and bossed you lay, your armor newly grown, your mighty hunting limbs thicker than my head! What I had created. You! A Supermother, a Mother such as none have ever seen!

Stupefied with delight, I gazed.

And your huge hunting-limb came out and seized me.

Great is the Plan. I felt only joy as your jaws took me.

As I feel it now.

And so we end, my Lilliloo, my redling, for your babies are swelling through your Mother-fur and your Moggadeet can speak no longer. I am nearly devoured. The cold grows, it grows, and your Mother-eyes are growing, glowing. Soon you will be alone with our children and the warm will come again.

Will you remember, my heartmate? Will you remember and tell them?

Tell them of the cold, Leelyloo. Tell them of our love.

Tell them . . . *the winters grow.*

ON THE LAST
AFTERNOON

"YOU'LL HAVE TO help us," Mysha said painfully. "One last time.
You can do it, can't you?"

The *noion* said nothing. It hung on its stalk as it had hung
since he first found it here in the headland grove: a musty black
indescribably shabby object or entity, giving no more sign of
life than an abandoned termite nest. No one but he believed it
was alive. It had not changed in the thirty years of the colony's
life, but he had known for some time that it was dying.

So was he. That was not the point, now.

He pulled himself up from the case of tapes and frowned
out over the mild green sea, rubbing his wrecked thigh. The
noion's grove stood on a headland beside the long beach. To
the left lay the colony's main fields, jungle-rimmed. Below him
on his right were the thatch roofs, the holy nest itself. Granary,
kilns, cistern, tannery and workshops, the fish sheds. The
dormitories, and the four individual huts, one his and Beth's.
At the center was the double heart: the nursery and the library-
labs: their future and their past.

The man Mysha did not look there now, because he had
never stopped looking at it. Every brick and beam and pipe and
wire was mapped in his inner eye, every cunning device and
shaky improvisation, every mark of plan or accident down to
the last irreplaceable component from the ship whose skeleton
rusted at the jungle's edge behind him.

Instead he gazed out, beyond the people laboring and
splashing on the jetty in the bay, beyond the placid shoals that

stretched to a horizon calm as milk. Listening.

Faintly he heard it: a long sourceless whistle.

They were out there. Out beyond the horizon, where the world-ocean crashed forever on the continent's last reefs, the destroyers were gathering.

"You can do it one last time," he told the *noion*. "You must."

The *noion* was silent, as usual.

Mysha made himself stop listening, turned to study the sea-wall being built below him. A cribbed jetty stretched from the headland, slanting out across the shoals to meet a line of piling coming from the far side of the colony beach. They formed a broad arrowhead pointing at the sea. Shelter for the colony.

In the unfinished apex gap, brown bodies were straining and shouting among rafts piled with rock. Two pirogues wallowed, towing cribs. Another work-team splashed toward the pilings pulling a huge spliced beam.

"They can't finish in time," Mysha muttered. "It won't hold." His eyes roved the defense-works, reviewing for the thousandth time the placing of the piles, the weak points. It should have been in deeper water. But there was no time, it was all too late. They wouldn't believe him until the stuff had started washing ashore.

"They don't really believe yet," he said. "They aren't afraid."

He made a grimace of pride and agony, looking now at the near beach where boys and girls were binding logs with vineropes, assembling the cribs. Some of the girls were singing. One boy jostled another, who dropped his end of the log, tumbling them both. Hoots, laughter. "Get on with it, get on with it," he groaned, pounding his broken thighs, watching old Tomas fussing them back to work. Tomas would outlive him if they survived, if any of them survived what was coming. He groaned again softly. His beloved ones, seed of his race on this alien world. Tall, unfearing, unscarred, as he had never been.

"Man is an animal whose dreams come true and kill him," he told the *noion*. "Add that to your definitions. . . . You could have warned me. You were here before. You knew. You knew I didn't understand."

The *noion* continued silent. It was very alien. How could it grasp what this haven had meant to them, thirty years ago? This sudden great pale clearing at the last edge of the land, and they roaring down to death on the rocks and jungle in their crippled ship. At the last minute of their lives this place had opened under them and received them. He had led the survivors out to bleed thankfully into the churned sand.

A tornado, they decided, must have swept it bare, this devastated square mile stretching to the sea. It had been recent; green tips were poking up, fed with fresh water from an underground flow. And the sand was fertile with organic mulm, and their wheats and grasses grew and the warm lagoon teamed with fish. An Eden it had been, those first two years. Until the water—

"Are you not . . . mobile?" The *noion* had spoken in his head suddenly, interrupting his thought. As usual it had "spoken" when he was not looking at it. Also as usual, its speech had been a question.

From long habit he understood what it meant. He sighed.

"You don't understand," he told it. "Animals like me are nothing, in ourselves, without the accumulated work of other men. Our bodies can run away, yes. But if our colony here is destroyed, those who survive will be reduced to brutes using all their energy to eat and breed. The thing that makes us human will be lost. I speak with you as a rational being, knowing for example what the stars are, only because the work of dead men enables me to be a thinker."

In fact, he was not a thinker, his inmost mind commented sadly; he was a builder of drainage lines now.

The *noion* emanated blankness. How could it understand, a creature of solitary life? Hanging forever on its limb, it was more impressed with his ability to move his body than with anything in his mind.

"All right," he said. "Try this. Man is a creature that stores time, very slowly and painfully. Each individual stores a little and dies leaving it to his young. Our colony here is a store of past time." He tapped the box of tapes on which he rested.

"If that generator down there is destroyed, no one can use the time-store in these. If the labs and shops go, the kilns, the looms, the irrigation lines and the grain, the survivors will be forced back to hunting roots and fruits to live from day to day. Everything beyond that will be lost. Naked savages huddling in the jungle," he said bitterly. "A thousand generations to get back. You have to help us."

There was silence. Over the water the eerie whistling suddenly rose, faded again. Or did it fade?

"You do not . . . ripen?" The *noion*'s "words" probed stealthily in his mind, pricked a sealed-off layer.

"No!" He jerked around, glaring at it. "Never ask me that again! Never." He panted, clenching his mind against the memory. The thing the *noion* had shown him, the terrible thing. No. No.

"The only help I want from you is to protect them." He built intensity, flung it at the *noion*. "One last time."

"Mysha!"

He turned. A leathery little woman toiled up the rocks toward him, followed by a naked goddess. His wife and youngest daughter, bringing food.

"Mysha, are you all right up here?"

Bethel's sad bird-eyes boring into his. Not looking at the *noion*. He took the gourd, the leaf-wrapped fish.

"What I'm doing you can do anywhere," he grumbled, and repenting touched her sparrow wrists. The glorious girl watched, standing on one leg to scratch the other. How had these supernatural children come out of Bethel's little body?

It was time to say some kind of good-bye.

"Piet is coming to take you inland," Bethel was saying. "As soon as they get the laser mounted. Here's your medicine, you forgot it."

"No. I'm staying here. I'm going to try something."

He watched her freeze, her eyes at last flicking to the silent brown thing hanging from its branch, back again to him.

"Don't you remember? When we came here, this grove was the only untouched place. It saved itself, Bethel. I can make it help us again this time."

Her face was hard.

"Beth, Beth, listen." He shook her wrist. "Don't pretend now. You know you believe me, that's why you're afraid."

The girl was moving away.

"If you don't believe me, why wouldn't you let me love you here?" he whispered fiercely. "Melie!" he called. "Come here. You must hear this."

"We must go back, there isn't time." Bethel's wrist jerked. He held it.

"There's time. They're still whistling. Melie, this thing here, you've heard me call it the *noion*, it's alive. It isn't native to this planet. I don't know what it is—a spore from space, a bionic computer even, maybe—who knows. It was here when we came. What you must know, you must believe is that it saved us. Twice. The first time was before any of you were born, the year when the wells went dry and we almost died."

The girl Melie nodded, looking composedly from him to the *noion*.

"That was when you discovered the blackwater root," she smiled.

"I didn't discover it, Melie. No matter what they tell you. The *noion* did it. I came up here—"

He glanced away for an instant, seeing again the stinking mudflats where the lagoon was now, the dry wells, the jungle dying under the furnace that poured white fire on them week after parching week. That had been the year they decided it was safe to breed. Bethel's first child had been lost then along with all the others, desiccated in the womb.

"I came up here and it felt my need. It put an image in my mind, of the blackwater roots."

"It was your subconscious, Mysha! It was some memory!" Bethel said harshly. "Don't corrupt the girl."

He shook his head tiredly. "No. No. Lies corrupt, not the truth. The second time, Melie. You know about the still-death. Why we don't use the soap after the wheat has sprouted. When Piet was a baby. . . ."

The still-death . . . his memory shivered. It had hit the babies first. Stopped them breathing, with no sign of distress. Martine's baby started it, she'd seen the bubbles stop moving on its lips while it smiled at her. She got it breathing again, and again, and again, and then in the night Hugh's baby died.

After that they watched constantly, exhausted because it was harvest time and a smut had damaged the wheat, every grain had to be saved. And then the adults started to drop.

Everybody had to stay together then, in pairs, one always watching the other, and still it got worse. The victims didn't struggle, those who were brought back reported only a vague euphoria. There was no virus; the cultures were blank. They tried eliminating every food. They were living only on water and honey when Diera and her husband died together in the lab. After that they huddled in one room, still dying, and he had broken away and come up here—

"You were in a highly abnormal state," Bethel protested.

"Yes. I was in a highly abnormal state." On his knees here, cursing, his need raging at the *noion*. What is killing us? What can I do? *Tell me!* The broken gestalt of his ignorance clawing at the *noion*.

"It was the need, you see. The urgency. It—somehow, it let me *complete* myself through it. I can't describe it. But the fact remains I learned what to do."

Adrenaline, it had been, and febrifacients, and making them breathe their own carbon dioxide until they choked and choked again. He had come down from the hill and thrust his baby son's head in a plastic bag with Bethel fighting him.

"It was the enzyme in the soap," said Melie calmly. She cocked her head, reciting. "The-soap-traces-potentiate-the-ergotin-the-wheat-smut-resulting-in-a-stable—uh—choline-like-molecule-which-passes-the-blood-brain-barrier-and-is-accepted-by-the-homeostats-of-the-midbrain." She grinned. "I really don't understand that. But, I mean, I guess it's like jamming the regulator on our boiler. They didn't know when they had to breathe."

"Right." He held Bethel more gently, put his other arm around her thin rigidity. "Now, how could that have possibly come out of my mind?" The girl looked at him; he realized with despair that to her there were no limits on what he might know. Her father Mysha, the colony's great man.

"You must believe me, Melie. I didn't know it. I couldn't. The *noion* gave it to me. Your mother won't admit it, for reasons of her own. But it did, and you should know the truth."

The girl transferred her gaze to the *noion*.

"Does it speak to you, Father?"

Bethel made a sound.

"Yes. In a way. It took a long while. You have to want it to, to be very open. Your mother claims I'm talking to myself."

Bethel's mouth was trembling. He had made her come here and try once, leaving her alone. Afterward the *noion* had asked him, "Did anyone speak?"

"It's a projection," Bethel said stonily. "It's a part of your mind. You won't accept your own insights."

Suddenly the whole thing seemed unbearably trivial.

"Maybe, maybe," he sighed. "'Bethink ye, my lords, that ye may be mistaken. . . .' But know this. I intend to try to get its help once more, if the beasts break through. I believe it has the strength to do it just once more. It's dying, you see."

"The third wish." The girl said lightly. "Three wishes, it's like the stories."

"You see?" Bethel burst out. "You see? It's starting again. Magic! Oh, Mysha, after all we've been through—" Her voice broke with bitterness.

"Your mother is afraid you'll make a religion out of it. A fetish in a carved box." His lips quirked. "But you wouldn't believe a god in a box, would you, Melie?"

"Don't joke, Mysha, don't joke."

He held her, feeling nothing. "All right. Back to work. But don't bother trying to move me, tell Piet to use the time for another load. You have the lab packed, haven't you? If they get through there won't be any time."

She nodded dumbly. He tightened his arms, trying to summon feeling.

"Dying makes one cantankerous." It was not much of a good-bye.

He watched them going down the hill, the girl's peach-bloom buttocks gliding against each other. The ghost of lust stirred in him. How solemn they had been, the elaborate decisions about incest. . . . That would all go too, if the sea-wall failed.

Figures were swarming over the water tower now, mounting the old wrecking laser from the ship. That was Gregor's idea; he'd carried all the young men with him, even Piet. True, the laser was powerful enough to strike beyond the wall—but what would they aim at? Who knew where the things' vital centers were? Worst of all, it meant leaving the generator, all the precious energy-system in place.

"If we lose, we lose it all," he muttered. He sat down heavily on the tapes. The pain in his groin was much worse now. Bethel, he thought, I've left them a god in a box after all, if the generator's smashed that's all these tapes will be.

The box held the poetry, the music, that had once been his life, back in another world. The life he had closed out; his own private meanings. Abandoned it gladly for the work of fathering his race. But after his accident he had asked Piet to lug these up here, telling the *noion*, "Now you will hear the music of men." It had listened with him, often the whole night through, and sometimes there seemed to be a sharing. . . .

He smiled, thinking of alien communion in the echoes of music from a brain centuries dead and light-years away. Below him in the bay he saw the last rocks were being offloaded into the apex cribs. All the young ones were out there now, lashing a huge hawser in the outer piles.

Suddenly the sea-wall looked better to him. It was really very strong. The braces had gone in now, heavy trunks wedged slanting into the rock. Yes, it was a real fortress. Perhaps it would hold, perhaps everything would be all right.

I am projecting my own doom, he thought wryly. His eyes cleared, he let himself savor the beauty of the scene. Good, it was good; the strong young people, his children with unshadowed eyes. . . . He had made it, he had led them here out of tyranny and terror, he had planted them and built the complex living thing, the colony. They had come through. If there was one more danger, he had one last trick left to help them. Yes; even with his death he could help them one more time, make it all right. What more could a man ask, he wondered, smiling, all calm strength to the bottom of his being, now, all one. . . .

—And the sky fell in, the bottom of his being betrayed him with the memory that he would not remember. *What more could a man want?* He groaned, clenched his eyes.

⊞

. . . In the spring, it had begun. In the idle days after the planting was in. He and his eldest son, the young giant whose head he had once thrust into a bag, had made an exploration voyage.

A query had been in the back of his mind since Day One, the day the ship landed. In the last tumultuous minutes there had been a glimpse of another clearing, a white scar on the far south coast. A good site, perhaps, for a future settlement? And so he and Piet had taken the catamaran south to look.

They had found it. In use.

For a day and a night they had hidden, watching the appalling animals surge upon the devastated shore. And then they had cautiously threaded their way out through the fouled shoal waters toward the outer barrier reefs.

The shoals and keys extended far out of sight of land, and a south wind blew forever here. They shipped the sail and paddied outward under a bare mast, blinded by warm flying scud, the roar of the world-ocean ever louder. A huge hollow whistling began, like a gale in a pipe organ. They rounded the last rocky key and saw through the spume the towers and chimneys of the outmost reef.

"My god, it's alive!"

One of the towers was not gray but crimson. It swayed,

reared higher. Another loomed up beside it, fell upon it. There was a visceral wail. Under the two struggling pillars mountains thrashed, dwarfing the giant combers breaking over them.

The catamaran retreated, tried another channel. And another, and another, until there was only moonlight.

"They're all up and down the whole damned reef."

"The bulls, perhaps . . . hauled up, waiting for the cows."

"They look more like enormous arthropods."

"Does it matter?" he had asked bitterly. "What matters is that they're preparing to come ashore here too. To our clearing. They'll destroy it as they did the other. Get the sail up, Piet. There's enough light. We've got to warn them."

But there was not quite enough light to safely run before that wind. Piet had brought him home senseless and broken, lashed to half an outrigger.

When he awoke he demanded, "Have they started building the sea-wall yet?"

"The sea-wall?" Dr. Liu tossed a dressing into the waste can. "Oh, you mean your sea monsters. It's early harvest time, you know."

"*Harvest?* Liu, hasn't Piet told you? Don't they realize? Get Gregor in here right now. And Hugh and Tomas. Piet too. Bring them, Liu."

It was sometime after they came that he began to realize he was a ghost. He'd started calmly, aware that they might think his judgment was warped by his condition.

"The area was totally devastated," he told them. "Approximately a kilometer square. There was a decapitated body, still living, near us. It was at least twenty meters long and three or four meters thick. That was by no means the largest. They come ashore periodically, it seems, to the same locations to lay eggs. That's what created our clearing, not a tornado."

"But why should they come here, Mysha?" Gregor protested. "After thirty years?"

"This is one of their nest sites. The time doesn't matter, they apparently have a long cycle. Some Terran animals—turtles, eels, locusts—have long cycles. These things are gathering out there all along the reef. An early group came ashore in the south clearing; another will come here soon. We've got to build defenses."

"But maybe they've changed their habits. They may have been going to the south site every year, for all we know."

"No. The newly smashed trees were at least two decades old. They're coming, I tell you. Here!" He heard his voice go up, saw their closed faces. "I tell you we dare not wait for the harvest, Gregor! If you had seen—*Tell* them, Piet! Tell them, tell them—"

When his head cleared again, there was only Dr. Liu.

And shortly after that he discovered that he was a dead man indeed.

"It's in the lymph system, Mysha. I found it in the groin when I went in to ease the inguinal ligament." Liu sighed. "You'd have heard from it pretty soon."

"How long?"

"Back home we could stretch it out awhile. Largely unpleasantly. Here—" he glanced around the little surgery, dropped his hands.

"Outside limits. Tell me, Liu."

"Months. Maybe. I'm sorry, Mysha."

They had let him go out then. When he had found that they were still preoccupied with the harvest, he was too weak to plead. Instead he asked them to bring him up here to the *noion*'s grove, to silence.

"You ripen?" the *noion* had asked him.

He shrugged. "If that's what you call it."

The next day Piet had carried up his tapes and there had been the music and the poetry, and time passed . . . until the day when the stuff started to come ashore. Greasy man-sized wads it was, something like ambergris, or vomit, or sloughed-off hide. Nothing they had ever seen before.

Upon that Piet had been able to persuade Gregor to send a scouting party to the outer reefs, and then, having seen, they began calmly and gracefully to prepare the wall. Mysha found that his nagging did nothing to speed them and went back up to the grove.

A tape of poetry had been running when it happened. He had been half listening, half tracing with his eyes the roof poles of the new shed housing the fibers and minerals the exploration team had brought in. A waterwheel was clacking in the near field. There came to him the memory of his arms lifting the capstones of the cistern arch and he frowned, recalling for the thousandth time that they were not quite trued. Next season he would—

Next season he would be dead, leaving all this to the young

brown gods. He thought fondly of their occasional curious glances at the ship and then up, up at the sky. They would never know what he knew, but they thought as civilized men. That was what he had made. Not Ozymandias; Father. His immortality. I die but do not die.

"You do not ripen?" came the *noion's* thought.

The recorder was muttering Jeffers. *"Be in nothing so moderate as in love of man . . . ."*

"You can't understand," he told the *noion*. "You build nothing, leave nothing. Nothing beyond yourself."

"—This is the trap that catches noblest spirits, that caught, they say, God when he walked on earth."

He slapped the thing off.

"How could you understand?" he demanded. "A spore, a god-knows-what without species or posterity. Man is a mammal, we build nests, we cherish our young."

An enormous panorama of nests came to him—nests made of spittle or silk or down pulled from the breast, nests excavated, dug into rock, woven in the air, in icebergs; eggs encysted in deserts, in the deep sea mud, carried in pouches of flesh, in mouths, on backs, eggs held for frozen weeks on webbed feet, thrust into victims' bodies, guarded on the wind-torn crags.

"Even those monsters who are coming here," he said. "It's for their eggs, their young, although they die doing it. Yes, I die. But my species lives!"

"Why do you cease?" the *noion* asked.

That was when the fear started. With his mouth he said angrily, "Because I can't help it. Can you?"

Silence.

His "Can you?" hung in the air, took on unintended meaning. . . . Could it, this thing he called the *noion*, could it do . . . something?

An impalpable tension slighter than the pull of a star feathered his mind, the small cold seed of terror grew.

"Can you—" he started to say, *meaning* can you cure me? Can you fix my body? But as he framed it he knew it wasn't relevant. The pull was elsewhere, in a direction he did not want to look. He crouched, horrified. The *noion* meant, it meant—

"You . . . ripen?"

The tenderness opened in his mind, he felt a breach through which frightened tendrils of himself were leaking out, nakedly.

He felt himself start to slip, to float into dark lightness, a vast nonspace in which were—*voices?*—faint beyond galaxies, the ghosts of voices, untraceable filaments of drifting thoughts, a frail webwork of—something—in time-lost immensities, in—life? Death's-life? Immaterial energies on the winds of nonbeing, pulling, subtly pulling at him—pulling—

No! No!

Terrified, he clenched himself, broke, fought, gasped back to life on his hands and knees under the *noion*'s bough. Light, air. He gulped it, seized earth—and suddenly reached with his mind for the connection he had broken. It wasn't there.

"Dear mother of god, is that your immortality?"

The *noion* hung mute. He sensed that it was spent. It had somehow held open a dimension, to show him. . . .

To invite him.

He understood then; his third, his last wish could be . . . this.

He had lain unmoving while the sun ran down the sky, hearing no more sounds of the life around him. . . . To go out, naked, alone . . . To go out. Alone . . . Those voices . . . had there been meaning, some inconceivable *meaning* in that ultimate void? . . . To go out, forever out, to meet . . . strangeness . . . to go *alone,* his essence, his true self free forever from the blood and the begetting and the care. . . .

It sang to him, a sweet cold song. Out—alone—free . . . The other voice in the double heart of man. The deepest longing of that part of him that was most human. To be free of the tyranny of species. To be free of love. To live forever . . .

He had groaned, feeling the sky close, feeling the live blood pumping through his animal heart. He was an animal, a human animal, and his young were in danger. He could not do it.

Before the sun set he had sighed, and raised himself.

"No. Your way is not my way. I must stay here with my kind. We won't speak of it again. If you can help me one last time, help me save my young."

That had been weeks ago, before the sea-wall had been raised. He sat looking at it now, trying to seal off the memory, the deep traitorous pull. The laser was installed, he saw, and in the same. moments heard footsteps coming up the path.

"Father?"

Piet towered beside him, looking out to sea. Mysha realized the whistling had grown louder. On the beach they were running now, shouting more urgently.

"Bethel says you're going to stay here."

"That's right. I want to try, oh, something . . . where will you be?"

"On the laser. Pavel and I drew lots. He got the raft with the repair crew."

"See that your mother and the girls get out, will you? All the way back to the big trees."

Piet nodded. "Melie and Sara are with the nursery team."

They stood silent, listening. . . . Louder now.

"On my way," Piet said. "We're rigging an oil sprayer. We could get some carcasses burning beyond the wall."

He went, leaving a food parcel, and a flask. The afternoon was superbly beautiful, clear tourmaline sky melting to clear green opal sea. Only, where sea met sky, was there a stir of clouds, a faint mirage of low hills which shimmered and dissolved and formed again?

The horizon itself was coming closer.

Mysha peered, hearing the whistling strengthen. Under it now and then came a dim groaning, as though the reefs were in pain.

As he watched, a file of women carrying babies and bundles came out of the colony below him and began to walk hurriedly down the path toward the jungle. The groaning came again. Two of the women broke into a trot.

On his left the shadows of the horizon thickened, heaved. A mountain seemed to be detaching itself through the misty air. It became identifiable as five dune-sized creatures wallowing toward the shoals. Men shouted.

The forerunners were well south of the colony, heading at the flax-oil field. As they came closer they showed as huge soft-looking lobsters with upright heads and thoraxes, their front legs dragging their distended bellies. Mysha knew them as the "cows." They crashed and floundered across the low reefs, groaning hollowly.

Behind them from the haze appeared their five "bulls," staggering with heads thrown back and their enormous towerlike organs erect. It was from them that the whistling came, loud now as a rocket vent. An oddly sad mechanical bedlam . . . As they mounted the reefs Mysha saw that the males' bodies were haggard, wasted in upon longitudinal riblike flutes. All their substance and energy seemed concentrated in their great engorged heads, bulky as houses, and in the colossal members wagging up from their front plates.

The cows' groaning became bellowing. They were in the last shallows now. Their mountainous abdomens heaved fully into view, sleek and streaming. Brilliant spectral colors flared and faded on their flanks. The males pitched in their wakes, closing on them fast.

Two males lurched together, clashing. Both stopped, wailed, flung their heads completely over onto their backs so that their crimson organs reared into the sky. But the threat-response could not last, so close to their goal. Their cows plowed forward, the males' heads came up and they followed onto the land.

The lead cow was in the flax seedlings now, her belly gouging a canyon, her legs thrashing devastation. The two beyond her struck into jungle. Treetops flailed wildly, went down. The rending and crashing blended with the bellowing of the cows and the siren keening of the males. The last two cows were heading into the field. One struck the catamaran moorings a demolishing blow, ground on ashore.

The lead cow in the flax field slowed. Her abdomen was slashed by gouges and wounds, ichor streaming down. Her mate reached her. His forelegs flailed hugely. He grappled her head face-to-face and mounted clumsily onto her foreparts in a parody of human coupling. Under him she began to turn ponderously in place, throwing up a ring-wall down which tumbled tree-stumps, rocks. The male's spermatogonium battered blindly, arching. His mate continued her gargantuan churning, deeper and deeper, carrying him with her. Her head was straining back, exposing gaping frontal plates. The organ of the mounted male caught, penetrated into her thorax.

What followed was not the convulsive orgasm of mammals, but archaic insectile rigidity. The cow's legs continued their pistonlike churning, revolving the coupled monsters ever deeper into their crater, while the entire contents of the male's body appeared to drain into his mate. Presently he was only a deflated husk behind his gigantic head. Slowly they went round—and now Mysha saw that the male's forelegs were rasping, sawing at the cow's thorax.

In a few more revolutions he had severed it completely. Her

head came loose and was held aloft, spasming. There was no laying of eggs. Instead, the male now pushed, wrenched, so that his own head and forelimbs tore free from the genital section of his body. With his female's head held high, the bodiless head began lurching toward the sea, repeating in death the first act of his life.

Behind him the decorticate body of the cow churned on, burying itself deeper and deeper, a living incubator for the fertilized eggs within.

Mysha pulled his gaze with an effort from the two vast death's-heads reeling toward the sea in a trail of membranes and fluids. In the field two others were still coupled. Something had gone wrong with one. Her body had struck rock and canted, while her jerking legs toppled her onto the male and drummed on, grinding him under her.

Mysha shook his head, controlled his breathing. *The engines of delight . . .* He and Piet had seen this once before. He looked down at the colony, saw the watchers crowding the thatches, the water tower, on the pilings. "Now you know," he muttered and tried to shout until he heard Piet's roar, getting them moving. His pain was suddenly savage.

More horizon had thickened, was looming closer. It was deafening now, that ceaseless bone-deep whistle. The sun shone brilliantly on the ruined field where the three huge craters quaked. The walking heads had disappeared into the shoals, leaving only the diminishing drumming of the stranded pair.

A woman's voice pealed. Another line of burdened figures was hurrying from the colony on the jungle path. Mysha peered, fist pressed into his pain. Martine, Lila, Hallam, Chena—biologist, weaver, mineralogist, engineer. They looked like little monkeys. Naked primates fleeing with their young. That was how it would be, once the stored heritage was gone, the tools of culture ground to dust.

"If the wall goes, you must help me," he told the *noion.* "You know how to make them turn."

The *noion's* silence became emptiness. He understood the communication. *This is the last, I can do no more.* It was very weak.

That was enough, that was all he asked. All. To save his own.

Dead ahead of them a new mountain was rising from the

sea. The bellowing rose. Six ship-sized enormities, headed for the apex of the wall. Was this the test? They grew, loomed, floundering with surprising speed straight at the colony. Their males were following close, their phalli higher than the water tower.

Mysha held his breath, willing Piet to fire. The lead cow heaved, dwarfing the fragile wall. No beam came from Piet's laser. Mysha pounded helpless fists, not feeling his own pain. What was wrong with Piet?

Then at the last moment he saw he had misjudged the angle. The lead cow mounted the last reef and stuck, churning so that her followers plowed on past. They struck the pilings a glancing blow and turned along the reef line to the near fields. The stuck cow dragged free, swerved into their trail, and the males lurched after her.

Mysha breathed again. A new herd was coming ashore far to his right beyond the colony, their bellows almost inaudible below the rising bedlam from the field.

But these were only the forerunners. Behind them the horizon boiled with monster shapes.

He groaned, studying the repair crews as they dragged timbers to broken pilings; even that passing blow had done damage.

The oncoming mountains grew, birthed new herds to right and left. Their uproar was passing the quality of sound, becoming an environment of total stress. Numbly Mysha watched a huge mass detach itself from the line and start straight toward the wall. Ten of them.

They were larger, and the males behind them towered higher than any yet. The main herd-bulls were coming. The female in the lead crashed on, nearer and nearer. She was following the track of the first cow, which had stuck upon the reef before the wall.

But this was a stupendous animal. The reef only slowed her, so that the next cow struck her, rebounded upon the cribs of the side wall and slewed off, spilling rocks. Then the first cow was free, making straight for the apex of the walls. Her forebody reared. The head with its huge blind-looking eyes towered ten meters above the apex, a visitation from hell.

As it hung waiting for its limbs to churn it over, a line of light sliced out from the tower. The beam struck her thorax. Mysha saw the plates smoke. A charred crack cut across the monstrous body—it was the abscission line where the male would saw. He understood then what Piet was trying. If the abscission layer broke, the body might cease its forward motion, as they had in the fields.

The head wagged drunkenly, fell off backward. The huge decorticated body heaved, boosting itself onto the crumbling piles of the apex. It was still coming—no, it was not! The leg-action changed, began to oar with the revolving motion. The tons of belly canted sidewise, skewering itself on the pilings, ripping open to release cascades of boulder-sized eggs. Around it churned, becoming one with the ruins of the apex wall.

The male who had been following was mounting on her now, posturing mindlessly on the heaving mass. Piet's laser bored out again and sliced. The male's head tipped backward, and as it did the female's legs caught on one side and tipped them both. One set of legs came free of the water, still jerking like machines. They were thick as the pilings, a touch would break a man. But the monster-reinforced wall was still there.

Mysha had been so focused on the action at the apex that he had only vaguely seen the press of behemoths making shore along both bases of the wall. A chaos of craters was spreading far back in the fields as newcomers clambered bellowing over the encysted bodies of the earlier arrivals. Here and there among them the dying heads mowed and capered toward the sea, only to be crushed beneath the incoming cows.

The wall was damaged in several places now. Mysha could see men slipping in the ichor jellied over the cribs. They hauled, splashed, mouths working soundlessly. The din around them all was so great that it felt like a wall of agonizing silence. The pain in his groin fought with the pain in his ears; only his eyes lived.

For a long moment no animals came directly at the wall, and then a herd on the far side suddenly veered toward it. The lead cow hit the outer pilings midway and reared. As she did so Piet's weapon carved a line of fire into her thorax. But there was not enough time-another cow had reached the corpse-mound at the apex and was clambering up, crashing the dead cow's flailing limbs. Her mate was right beside her, Mysha saw the laser leave the first target half cut, strike at the pair mounting the corpse-pile.

Too late, too late—the incomers toppled forward, crashed into the bay behind the wall raising a thunderous wave. Rafts overturned, heads bobbed. The cow reared, bellowing, and smashed across the shoals to the fish-shed. There Piet's laser caught her thorax, but she made one more lunge before her forward motion stopped and she began to chum. The fish-shed had vanished. Debris of coracles, nets, sails spewed out, disappeared, flying rocks struck the kilns. Piet was working on the male behind her now.

Suddenly a flame shot from the sea-wall where the partially disabled cow had burst the pilings. The oil-spray crew had ignited her. He watched the male behind her posture and wail and then sheer off.

Mysha panted, clutched against a tree, his eyes going back and forth around the holy wall. Bodies were impaled on it, merged with it in several places now. They were working out to the apex now to fire the corpses there. That must be Gregor's son with the oil. Three huge cows were just ahead of them, coming in. The boys clambered, straining with a drum. The cows came on. Then the boys leaped for the water, and a rolling gout of flame blew out of the pile. Through the smoke Mysha saw the cows lurch, slew sidewise to miss the wall.

He pulled himself upright to look, around. The shoals directly ahead were momentarily clear. On either side of them was chaos and carnage as far as he could see. What had been their cropland was utterly unrecognizable, jumbled with the near jungle, heaving with nightmare shapes. Only the colony itself remained huddled behind its wall.

But the wall was still there, still holding! Defiance flamed from its oily pyres. Behind it their enclave, the heart of their life, was intact, still safe. Except where the dying cow weltered among the outbuildings, nothing had been lost. All held safe! The fires—and Piet up there, his marksman of light—were they really holding them off, stemming the onslaught?

He stared. The horizon seemed thinner. Yes! It was breaking up, there were gaps. The shoals were still thick with wallowing bodies, but no matter. The height of the attack was passing. Let the last ones come—they will be met with fire, be turned! The wall *will* hold, he thought, not feeling the water run from his eyes. The young gods have won through.

By nightfall it would be over. They would be safe.

Safe. They didn't need him.

In the numb heart of the unceasing din Mysha felt the faint stir in his mind, the silver hemorrhage of hope. They didn't need him. He was free! Free to let the *noion* take him forever to life among the stars. . . . He shut the thought fiercely away.

Time later—

—Suddenly a crack louder than all the rest struck him, coming from below the grove. A skein of cloud flew by.

He gave a cry and hobbled forward to look.

From the wreckage of the roof two gigantic eyes glared up at him, timbers collapsing around it. The thing was lying face up, it was the head of the male who had got ashore. Steam billowed out. A boy was lying on the ground. The head skewed into the open, pushed by scrabbling stumps of legs. Pavel and another boy ran into the steam. The steam lessened.

A man—it was Dr. Liu—ran up carrying a beaker. Pavel grabbed it, went after the colossal head which was grinding blind circles toward the generator house. Pavel danced aside from the legs, darted at the door-sized wound where the limb-stumps met. He flung the liquid, leaped back. There was a paroxysm that sprayed a brick-pile into the air. When the dust settled the head had stilled, its ganglia burned out.

But the broken roof had sheltered the main boiler that powered the generator.

The laser—the laser had only the batteries now.

Stunned, Mysha conjured frantic images of the auxiliary boiler that they used to charge the batteries, calculated amperage drains. Too little, too slow. Too slow.

He turned slowly to search the sea. The horizon humped closer, only scattered herds now, breaking apart as he watched. Gaps on both sides of them.

But in the far shoals, straight ahead, a solid phalanx was coming. Mysha stared, shaking his head as agonies stabbed at him. The moving mountains rocked, heaved, their course relentless toward the wall. He studied the cribs, the smoking pyres. Pavel had boys tearing at the thatch. For torches that would be.

When the laser gave out they were done for.

They needed him.

Die, hope . . . Loss tore his heart, his face contorted with the pain. I must die.

But that was not enough.

He must *want* it, he realized. He had to kill this traitorous hope, stamp out every trace of it and tune his whole being to the task, or it would not work.

Because he knew what moved the *noion*, what made it act. His need. Only when he hungered totally, intolerably, could the *noion* fulfill him. He must want this and this only in every living cell of his soul and body, as he had before.

But how can I, Mysha thought despairingly, not hearing the clamor, not seeing the flames and the wreckage. A man can make his body walk into flames for his children's sake, a man can make himself turn away even from life everlasting to save his own. But the deed is not enough, here. I must want with my whole soul. Sobs twisted his mouth. Too much—too much to ask of man, poor double-soul—that he desire his death with all his heart. To choose between his race and his life and *mean* it? If only the *noion* had never shown him—

"I can't," he whispered. "Can't—"

—And was suddenly aware of love returning, rising in him from some deepest, most secret reservoir. The world came back around him—his beloved ones came back. And he began to feel he could. He could! Fierceness rose, bringing the blood-need. What would the stars be worth, if he must live forever knowing he had abandoned them?

Through mists he saw that a new group of animals was heading for the wall.

"I will save you," he said thickly to the air. "The last wish is for you, Melie." And the need was there.

He turned back calmly to the tree from which the *noion* hung, biting his mouth with pain. A wave of repulsion rose against him, an almost physical push to right or left away from the tree. For an instant he faltered and then remembered what this was—the *noion*'s defense, the shield that had kept it safe even from the colony's boys.

"No, no," he told it, opening his mind. "You must let me."

The resistance around him shivered. He forced himself on, reached a hand painfully to the *noion*'s bough. This was not the place. The sea-wall. He felt they must be on the wall, closer.

"You must let me," he repeated, letting his need rise.

The thick air thinned, went to normalcy. He pulled awkwardly on the bough. It was long dead, but it would not give. Sick from the pain of pulling, he fumbled for his knife—and suddenly found himself involuntarily turning.

In silence the *noion* released its ancient hold, dropped against his chest.

He had touched it only once or twice before, carefully with

a finger feeling its peculiar musty, lifeless warmth. Now with the whole creature in his arms his body resonated with its currents, its field. It was hard to keep his arms around it, he enclosed more than held it. Were brush discharges coming out of his hair and elbows? He could see nothing.

He began to hobble with what speed he could down the rocky path to the base of the sea-wall below. The unceasing bellows battered at him, the pain of his body swamped his mind. He was in the smoke now, soot and flying spume rained on him.

When he could risk a glance from the rocks, he saw that the oncoming army was much closer. Still headed straight in. He stumbled, forced his legs to run. Outside the wall two monsters were grinding by toward, the field. The main group did not swerve after them. As he started to clamber out on the cribs he saw the defenders were bringing up more oil for the fire. Faces turned toward him. He could see mouths gape, but their voices were lost in the din.

The beslimed rocks were desperately slippery. He scrabbled, stumbled, not daring to free a hand from the core of silence in his arms. A patch of jelly sent him down on his ruined hip. He wrenched himself on sideways with knees and elbows, feeling a grating inside him, a skewering gush. One thigh was against the rocks now, his other foot kicking at the crib logs, somehow moving him on. Like the beasts, he thought, I go on.

A wave washed over him. When he could see again, there was a vast flank reeling by him along the wall, shifting the crib he lay on. He was quite near the apex now. A boy seemed to be scrambling back toward him. Over the boy's head nightmares were rising in the smoke.

He sagged, staring at monstrous masks, collecting himself. This was close enough, this would have to do. *"Noion, noion!"* he gasped. A cow reared up directly ahead of the flames, too closely flanked to be able to turn. *"Noion,* help me."

At that moment Mysha felt a connection open in his mind, a tiny struggling like the shadow of a fish on a gossamer line. It was—yes, he was sure it was—contact with the dim life of the cow. The faint spark writhed, as if torn between its driving forward and recoiling from the fire.

This was what the *noion* could do, had done before to save itself!

As he hung with his outer eyes on the cow and at the same

time . . . touching it, the pale streak of the laser came out overhead and scored her armor. She reared higher, her head slumped backward. The inner connection went out—and his eyes saw the cow's terrible bulk surge forward to smash down upon the flame in a blast of water and smoke. The pyre was extinguished.

Another cow was mounting the wall beside her. The laser cut, cut, swung to still another coming in. And now a monster of monsters heaved up upon the smoking carcass at the apex. Just as the laser touched her, its light paled, guttered, and went out.

The laser was done.

"*Noion, noion!*" Despair screamed out of him. "Make her turn! Turn, turn, turn—"

And it was there, the line, the channel—and his need, his need drove out, met, *completed* itself in potency. *Turn!* His outer eyes saw only chaos, it was the eye of his mind that sensed when impulse leaped ganglion, when energy became asymmetrical and the blind engines unbalanced the mighty belly—turning—veering it along the wall!

But as this web gave, he was aware of the others coming behind her, the dull energy-points of their beings blooming just ahead of his reaching mind. "Now, *noion!*" he prayed, trying to hurl himself, imploring, "Turn, turn. Oh, *noion,* help me—*MAKE THEM TURN!*"

Emptiness.

Vision came back to his eyes.

Beside him, beyond the wall, the behemoths were grinding ashore. They had turned. He had turned them!

Dazedly he saw others passing the far wall. The herd had split. As he watched, a last male tipped over the pilings, righted himself, and lurched away after the cows.

And the shoals ahead were clear as far as he could see through the choking smoke.

He felt unbodied, weightless with exaltation and relief. Pain gouted and wrenched at him from below, but he was remote from the pounding, crashing, bellowing all about. It came to him that he was quite probably dying.

As he thought it he felt also a wave of weakness from the entity in his arms. This was killing them both.

So be it.

Another herd of horrors showed now through the smoke

ahead. He reached for them from far, found the frail potency, fought, felt them shift, go slewwise. Wind blew the smoke flat.

He realized he was seeing the true horizon, almost empty now. The main herd was past.

Ahead of him on the wall, men wrestled torches toward the slippery crest. No one was near him. He found he was sobbing or screaming when he breathed, but he could not hear himself. Memory brushed him: a boy—had it been one of his sons?—had pawed at him, gone away.

He managed to twist agonizingly on his elbows so that he could look back at the colony.

Yes, there was more damage. The hideous bulk of a cow reared among the dormitories, shedding timbers. But it was still safe. Still safe! His last gift had saved them, his dying had given life to all he held dear. Cocooned in deafness he let his gaze go out to the beloved scene. Still so beautiful, despite the smoke! Golden figures ran as if playing a game. His nest, his life—

His life. Not the stars; this . . .

Why had the scene changed subtly, as if transparency had congealed around it, turning it into something curious and tiny like a toy in plastic? His lifework. The species lives, I die. The operative words, *I die*. Die, he thought, like a faithful ant whose nest lives on. Like those dying head-husks capering to the sea. Only that more may breed and die, to breed and die. The building, the breeding, the towers raised and fallen, without end. Disgust chilled him. For this I have forsaken—

Be in nothing so moderate as in love of man.

His traitor soul gasping, he fighting, fainting. Was it possible that a man could strive with his whole heart all his life for his kind, his young—and at the last turn away? It is my body's dying, only that, he told himself. In the end the brain goes.

He made himself turn back, peer.

They were still coming. One more assault. The last, the last ones. It was so dark here. Or was the day ending? All over by nightfall.

Here they come. This one will kill us.

Good, he thought, good! Faithful ant. Forget the soul's weak protest. Those who come after can perhaps—No time. He groped inwardly, eyes closed, for the channel, the focus . . . and felt nothing.

Noion!

Faint in his mind: "You need . . . this?"

"Yes, yes!" he shouted into the roaring. Oh, god, no time—the beasts were at the wall.

"Yes!" he screamed again, forcing himself to feel, to clench his need into the power, to touch, reach—ah! There! It came, it was there, the help, the opening—the *noion* was with him. He felt the beasts' lives now, touched. Turn, turn, turn! *Turn with my last strength, with my death that I give freely! TURN with my death that I did not need to die—*

The contact faded, was gone.

He opened his eyes.

A tower of armor was bulging through the murk above him, the rock he clung to tilted, slipped.

They had not turned.

They had breached the wall. An avalanche of piling was falling on his inshore side, the thunderous wake rocked his crib. And in the bay, on the beach, blotting out the colony from his horror-filled eyes—

"*Noion! Noion!*" He screamed, his death suspended over him, rushing in stasis—he knowing what had happened, what he had done. His need, his desire at the end, had not held true—he had betrayed them back to the jungle, to the running and the dust. His human heart, his soul, had betrayed them all—

"*Noion!*" his soul shouted. "Take me! Give me the other, give me back myself!"

But the life against his chest was draining, going away. Too late. Too late. All wasted. He felt the wraith-wind of its going in his brain, the alien immensities opening to the imago. Opening—for an instant it was as if the *noion* were still holding a way open, offering to share its dying with him if he could. The longing rose in him, the terrified love toward what he could not imagine—*O rich and sounding voices of the air—I come! I come!—*

—But he could not alone, no, and his useless death hung over him, the crashing was beating on his mortal ears. His lips moved, crying, "Man is the, is the, that—"

A vast impersonal tonnage fell upon him and the stars raveled away from his brain.

SHE WAITS FOR ALL MEN BORN

> Pale, beyond porch and portal,
>   Crowned with calm leaves, she stands
> Who gathers all things mortal
>   With cold immortal hands
>   —SWINBURNE

IN THE WASTES of nonbeing it is born, flickers out, is born again and holds together, swells and spreads. In lifelessness it lives, against the gray tide of entropy it strives, improbably persists, gathering itself into ever richer complexities until it grows as a swelling wave. As a wave grows it grows indeed, for while its crest surges triumphant in the sunlight its every particle is down falling forever into dark, is blown away into nothing in the moment of its leap. It triumphs perishing, for it was not born alone. Following it into being came its dark twin, its Adversary, the shadow which ceaselessly devours it from within. Pitilessly pursued, attacked in every vital, the living wave foams upward, its billion momentary crests blooming into the light above the pain and death that claims them. Over uncounted eons the mortal substance strives, outreaches. Death-driven, it flees ever more swiftly before its Enemy until it runs, leaps, soars, into flashing flight. But it cannot outrace the fire in its flesh, for the limbs that bear it are Death, and Death is the wing it flies on. In the agony of its myriad members, victorious and dying, Life drives upon the indifferent air. . . .

The burrow is dark. Pelicosaurus squats over her half-grown pups, her dim node of awareness holding only the sensation of their muzzles sucking the glandular skin of her belly among her not-quite hair. From outside comes a thunderous eructation, splashing. The burrow quakes. Pelicosaurus crouches, rigid; the huddled pups freeze. All but one—a large female pup has squirmed free, is nosing nervously toward the recesses of the burrow. She moves in a half-crawl, her body slung from the weak reptilian shoulder girdle.

More crashes outside. Earth showers down within the damp nest. The mother only crouches tighter, locked in reflexive stasis. The forgotten pup is now crawling away up a tunnel.

As she vanishes, the giant hadrosaur in the stream outside decides to clamber out. Twenty tons of reptile hit the soft bank. Earth, rocks, and roots slam together, crushing Pelicosaurus and her pups and all other bank-dwellers into an earthy gel, a trough of destruction behind the departing one. Leather wings clap; pterosaurs are gathering to stab in the wreckage.

Farther up the bank beside a gymnosperm root, the lone pup wriggles free. She cowers, hearing the hoarse grunts of the scavengers. Then an obscure tropism rises in her, an undefined urge toward space, toward up. Awkwardly she grips the bole of the gymnosperm with her forelimbs. A grub moves on the bark. Automatically she seizes and eats it, her eyes blinking as she strives to focus beyond. Presently she begins to clamber higher, carrying, in the intricacy of her genes, the tiny anomaly which has saved her. In the egg from which she grew, a molecule has imperceptibly shifted structure. From its aberrant program has unfolded a minute relaxation of the species-wide command to freeze, a small tendency to action under stress. The pup that is no longer wholly Pelicosaur feels her ill-adapted hind limb slip upon the branch, scrabbles for purchase, falls, and crawls weakly from the graveyard of her kind.

. . . So the wave of Life mounts under the lash of Death, grows, gathers force in unbounded diversity. Ever-perishing, ever-resurgent, it foams to higher, more complex victories upon the avalanche of its corpses. As a wave swells, it surges, swarming, striving ever more strongly, achieving ever more intricate strategies of evasion, flinging itself in wilder trajectories to escape its pain. But it bears its Enemy within it, for Death is the power of its uprush. Dying in every member, yet every moment renewed, the multiple-hearted wave of

Life crests into strangeness. . . .

Yelling, the hairless creature runs swiftly, knuckles to earth, and screams again as a rock strikes him. He swerves and scuttles, limping now; he is unable to avoid the hail of missiles flung by those stronger, more freely jointed arms. His head is struck. He goes down. The bipeds close around him. Shouting in still wordless joy, they fall upon their brother with thin jaws and sharpened stones.

. . . The living, dying tumult mounts, fountains into culminant light. Its billion tormented fragments take on intenser being; it leaps as a great beast above the ravenings of its Adversary. But it cannot shake free, for the force of its life is Death, and its strength is as the strength of the deaths that consume it, its every particle is propelled by the potency of the dark Assailant. In the measure of its dying, Life towers, triumphs, and rolls resistless across the planet that bore it. . . .

Two horsemen move slowly across the plain under the cold autumn rain. The first is a young boy on a spotted pony; he is leading a black-eared roan on which his father is riding slumped, breathing open-mouthed above the rifle-ball in his chest. The man's hand holds a bow, but there are no arrows. The Kiowas' stores and supplies were lost at Palo Duro Canyon, and the last arrows were fired in the slaughter at the Staked Plains three days back, where his wife and oldest son were killed.

As they pass a copse of willows the rain eases for a moment. Now they can see the white man's buildings ahead: Fort Sill with its gray stone corral. Into that corral their friends and relatives have vanished, family by family, surrendering to their merciless enemy. The boy halts his pony. He can see a column of soldiers riding out of the fort. Beside him his father makes a sound, tries to raise his bow. The boy licks his lips; he has not eaten for three days. Slowly he urges his pony forward again.

As they ride on, faint sounds of firing come to them on the wet wind, from a field west of the fort. The white men are shooting the Kiowas' horses, destroying the life of their life. For the Kiowas, this is the end. They were among the finest horsemen the world has ever known, and war was their sacred occupation. Three centuries before, they had come down out of the dark mountains, had acquired horses and a god and burst out in glory to rule a thousand miles of range. But they never understood the grim, unrelenting advance of the U.S. Cavalry. Now they are finished.

The Kiowas have been toughened by natural hardship, by millennia of death in the wilderness. But their death-strength is not enough. The pale soldiers before them are the survivors of more deadly centuries in the caldrons of Europe; they drive upon the Indians with the might derived from uncountable generations of close-quarter murder in battle, deaths under merciless tyrannies, by famines and plagues. As has happened before and before and before, the gray-faced children of the greater death roll forward, conquer and spread out across the land.

. . . So the great Beast storms among the flames that devour it, the myriad lives of its being a crucible of always fiercer deaths and more ascendant life. And now its agonized onrush changes. What had been flight becomes battle. The Beast turns on the enemy that savages it and strives to cast Death from its heart. Desperately it struggles; streaming from the wounds that are its life, it fights to save some fragment while Death slays whole members. For Death is the twin of its essence, growing as Life grows, and the fury of its attack mounts with the power that attacks it. Locked into intimate battle, the Beast and its Enemy are now nearing a consummating phase of pain. The struggle rages, breaches the norms of matter. Time accelerates. . . .

As night comes over the Mediterranean the battered freighter limps warily past the enemy ears on Cyprus. Rain and darkness hide it; it creeps with all lights extinguished, every human sound quenched. Only the throbbing of its engines and the thrashing of its rusty screw remain to betray it to the blockaders. In its body is the precious cargo, the huddled silent sparks of life. The children. The living ones, the handfuls saved from the six million corpses of the death camps, saved from the twenty million killed by the Reich. In darkness and desperation it crawls on, leaking, the crew not daring to work the creaking pumps. Hidden by the night it steams mile by daring mile through the gauntlet of the blockade, carrying the children to Palestine.

While on the other side of the world, in the morning of that same night, a single bomber leaves its escort and bores steadily westward through the high cold air. The *Enola Gay* is on course to Hiroshima.

   . . . *Pain-driven, death-sinewed, the convulsed Beast strives against its Enemy. In ever-new torment it grows, rears itself to new brilliancy, achieves ever-greater victories over Death, and is in turn more fearfully attacked. The struggle flames unseen across the planet, intensifying until it breaks from the bounds of Earth and flings portions of itself to space. But the Beast cannot escape, for it carries Death with it and fuels Death with its fire. The battle heightens, fills earth, sea, and air. In supreme agony it fountains into a crest of living fire that is a darkness upon the world. . . .*

"Doctor, that was beautiful." The senior surgical nurse's whisper barely carries beyond her mask.

The surgeon's eyes are on the mirror where the hands of the suturist can be seen delicately manipulating the clamped-back layers. *Lub-dub, lub-dub;* the surgeon's eyes go briefly to the biofeedback display, check the plasma exchange levels, note the intent faces of the anesthesiology team under their headsets, go back vigilantly to the mirror. Vigilant—but it is over, really. A success, a massive success. The child's organs will function perfectly now, the dying one will live. Another impossibility achieved.

The senior nurse sighs again appreciatively, brushing away a thought that comes. The thought of the millions of children elsewhere now dying of famine and disease. Healthy children too, not birth-doomed like this one but perfectly functional; inexorably dying in their millions from lack of food and care. Don't think of it. Here we save lives. We do our utmost.

The operating room is sealed against the sounds of the city outside, which yet comes through as a faint, all-pervading drone. Absently, the nurse notices a new sound in the drone: an odd high warbling. Then she hears the interns behind her stirring. Someone whispers urgently. The surgeon's eyes do not waver, but his face above the mask turns rigid. She must protect him from distraction. Careful that her clothing does not rustle, she wheels on the offenders. There is a far burst of voices from the corridor.

"Be quiet!" She hisses with voiceless intensity, raking the interns with her gray gaze. As she does so, she recalls what that continuous warbling tone is. Air-attack warning. The twenty minute alert, meaning that missiles are supposed to be on their way around the world from the alien land. But this cannot be serious. It must be some drill—very laudable, no doubt, but not to be allowed to disturb the operating room. The drill can be held another time; it will take more than twenty minutes to finish here.

"Quiet," she breathes again sternly. The interns are still. Satisfied, she turns back, holding herself proudly, ignoring fatigue, ignoring the shrill faint whining, ignoring at the end even the terrible flash that penetrates the seams of the ceiling far above.

. . . And the riven Beast crashes, bursts together with its Enemy into a billion boiling, dwindling fragments that form and reform under the fires of a billion radiant deaths. Yet it is still one, still joined in torment and unending vitality. With its inmost plasm laid bare to the lethal energies Life struggles more intensely still, more fiercely attacks the Death that quenches its reborn momentary lives. The battle grows to total fury, until it invades the very substrata of being. Culminant paroxysm is reached; in ultimate agony the ultimate response is found. The Beast penetrates at last into its Adversary's essence and takes it to itself. In final transcendence. Life swallows Death, and forges the heart of its ancient Enemy to its own. . . .

The infant between the dead thighs of its mother is very pale. Dismayed, the Healer frees it from the birth slime, holds it up. It is a female, and perfectly formed, he sees, despite the whiteness of its skin. It takes breath with a tiny choke, does not cry. He hands it to the midwife, who is covering the mother's corpse. Perhaps the pallor is natural, he thinks; all his tribe of Whites have heavy pale skins, though none so white as this.

"A beautiful baby girl," the midwife says, swabbing it. "Open your eyes, baby."

The baby squirms gently, but its eyes remain closed. The Healer turns back one delicate eyelid. Beneath is a large fully-formed eye. But the iris is snow-white around the black pupil. He passes his hand over it; the eye does not respond to light. Feeling an odd disquiet, he examines the other. It is the same.

"Blind."

"Oh, no. Such a sweet baby."

The Healer broods. The Whites are a civilized tribe, for all that they have lived near two great craters before they came here to the sea. He knows that his people's albinism is all too frequently coupled with optical defect. But the child seems healthy.

"I'll take her," says Marn, the midwife. "I still have milk, look."

They watch as the baby girl nuzzles Marn's breast and happily, normally, finds her food.

Weeks pass into months. The baby grows, smiles early, though her eyes remain closed. She is a peaceful baby; she babbles, chortles, produces a sound that is surely "Marn, Marn." Marn loves her fiercely and guiltily; her own children are all boys. She calls the pale baby "Snow."

When Snow begins to creep Marn watches anxiously, but the blind child moves with quiet skill, seeming to sense where things are. A happy child, she sings small songs to herself and soon pulls herself upright by Marn's leather trousers. She begins to totter alone, and Marn's heart fears again. But Snow is cautious and adroit, she strikes few obstacles. It is hard to believe that she is blind. She laughs often, acquires only a few small bumps and abrasions, which heal with amazing speed.

Though small and slight, she is a very healthy baby, welcoming new experience, new smells, sounds, tastes, touches, new words. She speaks in an unchildishly gentle voice. Her dark world does not seem to trouble her. Nor does she show the stigmata of blindness; her face is mobile, and when she smiles, the long white lashes tremble on her cheeks as if she is holding them closed in fun.

The Healer examines her yearly, finding himself ever more reluctant to confront that blank silver gaze. He knows he will have to decide if she should be allowed to breed, and he is dismayed to find her otherwise so thriving. It will be difficult. But in her third year the decision is taken from him. He feels very unwell at the time of her examination and shortly realizes that he has contracted the new wasting sickness which has been beyond his power to cure.

The daily life of the Whites goes on. They are a well-fed Ingles-speaking littoral people. Their year revolves around the massive catches of fish coming up from the sea-arm to spawn. Most of the fish are still recognizable as forms of trout and salmon. But each year the Whites check the first runs with their precious artifact, an ancient Geiger counter which is carefully recharged from their water-driven generator.

When the warm days come, Snow goes with Marn and her sons to the beach where the first-caught will be ritually tested. The nets are downstream from the village, set in the canyon's mouth. The beaches open out to the sea-arm, surrounded by tall ice-capped crags. Fires burn merrily on the sands, there is music, and children are playing while the adults watch the fishermen haul in the leaping, glittering nets. Snow runs and laughs, paddling in the icy stream edge.

"Fliers up there," the Netmaster says to Marn. She looks up at the cliffs where he points, searching for a flitting red shape. The Fliers have been getting bolder, perhaps from hunger. During the last winter they have sneaked into an outlying hut and stolen a child. No one knows exactly what they are. Some say they are big monkeys, some believe they are degenerated men. They are man-shaped, small but strong, with loose angry-looking folds of skin between their limbs on which they can make short glides. They utter cries which are not speech, and they are always hungry. At fish-drying times the Whites keep guards patrolling the fires day and night.

Suddenly there is shouting from the canyon.

"Fliers! They're heading to the town!"

Fishermen paddle swiftly back to shore, and a party of men go pounding upstream toward the village. But no sooner have they gone than a ring of reddish heads pops into sight on the near cliffs, and more Fliers are suddenly diving on the shore.

Marn snatches up a brand from a fire and runs to the attack, shouting at the children to stay back. Under the women's onslaught the Fliers scramble away. But they are desperate, returning again and again until many are killed. As the last attackers scramble away up the rocks Marn realizes that the blind baby is not among the other children by the fires.

"Snow! Snow, where are you?"

Have the Fliers snatched her? Marn runs frantically along the beach, searching behind boulders, crying Snow's name. Beyond a rocky outcrop she sees a Flier's crumpled legs and runs to look.

Two Fliers lie there unmoving. And just beyond them is what she feared to find—a silver-pale small body in a spread of blood.

"Snow, my baby, oh, no—"

She runs, bends over Snow. One of the little girl's arms is hideously mangled, bitten nearly off. A Flier must have started to eat her before another attacked him. Marn crouches above the body, refusing to know that the child must be dead. She makes herself look at the horrible wound, suddenly stares closer. She is seeing something that makes her distraught eyes widen more wildly. A new scream begins to rise in her throat. Her gaze turns from the wound to the white, still face.

Her last sight is of the baby's long pale lashes lifting, opening to reveal the shining silver eyes.

Marn's oldest son finds them so; the two dead Fliers, the dead woman, and the miraculously living, scarless child. It is generally agreed that Marn has perished saving Snow. The child cannot explain.

From that time, little Snow the twice-orphaned is cared for among the children of the Netmaster.

She grows, though very slowly, into a graceful, beloved little girl. Despite her blindness she makes herself skilled and useful at many tasks; she is clever and patient with the endless work of mending nets and fish-drying and pressing oil. She can even pick berries, her small quick hands running through the thickets almost as expert as eyes. She patrols Marn's old gathering paths, bringing back roots, mushrooms, birds' eggs, and the choicest camass bulbs.

The new Healer watches her troubledly, knowing he will have to make the decision his predecessor dreaded. How serious is her defect? The old Healer had thought that she must be interdicted, not allowed to breed lest the blindness spread. But he is troubled, looking at the bright, healthy child. There has been so much sickness in the tribe, this wasting which he cannot combat. Babies do not thrive. How can he interdict this little potential breeder, who is so active and vigorous? And yet—and yet the blindness must be heritable. And the child is not growing normally; year by year she does not mature. He becomes almost reassured, seeing that Snow is still a child while the Netmaker's baby son is attaining manhood and his own canoe. Perhaps she will never develop at all, he thinks. Perhaps there will be no need to decide.

But slowly, imperceptibly, Snow's little body lengthens and rounds out, until when the ice melts one year he sees that small breasts have budded on her narrow ribs. The day before she had been still a child; today she is unmistakably a baby woman.

The Healer sighs, studying her tender animated face. It is hard to see her as defective; the lightly closed eyes seem so normal. But two of the dead-born infants have been very pale and white-eyed. Is this a lethal mutation? His problem is upon him. He cannot resolve it; he determines to call a council of the tribe.

But his plan is never to be put to action. Someone else has been studying Snow too. It is the Weatherwoman's youngest son, who follows her to the fern-root grove.

"This is the kind you eat," Snow tells him, holding up the yellow fiddleheads. He stares down at her delicious little body. Impossible to remember or care that she is thrice his age.

"I want—I want to talk to you, Snow."

"Umm?" She smiles up at his voice. His heart pounds.

"Snow . . ."

"What, Byorg?" Listening so intently, the silvery lashes quivering as if they will lift and open to him. Yet they do not, and pity for her blindness chokes him. He touches her arm, she comes against him naturally. She is smiling, her breathing quickened. He holds her, thinking how she must feel his touch in her dark world, her helplessness. He must be gentle.

"Byorg?" she breathes. "Oh, Byorg—"

Trying to restrain himself he holds her more tightly to him, touching her, feeling her trembling. He is trembling too, caressing her beneath her light tunic, feeling her yielding, half trying to pull away, her breath hot on his neck.

"Oh, Snow—" Above the pounding of his blood he is vaguely conscious of a sound overhead, but he can think only of the body in his arms.

A harsh yowl breaks out behind him.

"Fliers!"

He whirls around too late—the red flapping figure has launched something at him, a spear—and he is staggering, grasping a bony shaft sunk in his own neck.

"Run, Snow!" he tries to shout. But she is there still, above him, trying to hold him as he falls. More Fliers pound past. As the world dims, he sees in last wonderment her huge eyes opening wide and white.

Silence.

Snow raises herself slowly, still open-eyed. She lets the dead boy's head down to the moss. Three dead Fliers sprawl around them. She listens, hears faintly the sound of screaming from the village. It is a major attack, she realizes. And Fliers have never used weapons before. Shivering, she strokes Byorg's hair. Her face is crumpled in grief, but the eyes remain open, silver reflectors focused at infinity.

"No," she says brokenly. "No!" She jumps up, begins running toward the village, stumbling as she races open-eyed, as a blind person runs. Three Fliers swoop behind her. She screams and turns to face them. They drop in red, ragged heaps and she runs on, hearing the clamor of battle at the village walls.

The frantic villagers do not see her coming, they are struggling in a horde of Fliers who have infiltrated the side gate and broken loose among the huts. At the main gate the torches have started thatch fires; Fliers and Whites alike have fallen back. Suddenly there is redoubled shouting from the huts. Six Fliers are seen clumsily hopping and gliding from roof to roof. They carry stolen infants.

Men and women clamber fiercely after them, shouting imprecations. A Flier pauses to bite savagely into his victim's neck, leaps onward. The evil band outrace their pursuers and launch themselves onto the outer wall.

"Stop them!" a woman shrieks, but there is no one there.

But as the Fliers poise to leap, something does halt them. Instead of sailing they are tumbling limply with their captives, falling on the ground below the walls. And other Fliers have stopped yowling and striking, they are falling too.

The villagers pause uncertainly and become aware of a stillness spreading from a point beside the gates.

Then they see her, the girl Snow, in the blue evening light. A slender white shape with her back to them, surrounded by a red ruin of dead Fliers. She is leaning bent over, dragged down by a shaft sticking in her side. Blood is flooding down her thighs.

Painfully she tries to turn toward them. They see her pull feebly at the spear in her belly. As they watch aghast she pulls the weapon out and drops it. And still stands upright, blood pouring down.

The Healer is nearest. He knows it is too late, but he runs toward her across the rank bodies of the Fliers on the ground. In the dimness he can see a shining loop of intestine torn and hanging from her mortal wound. He slows, staring. Then he sees the blood-flow staunch and cease. She is dead—but she stands there still.

"Snow—"

She lifts her head blindly, smiles with a strange, timid composure.

"You're hurt," he says stupidly, puzzled because the gaping flesh of her wound seems somehow radiant in the fading light. Is it—moving? He stops, staring fearfully, not daring to go closer. As he stares, the rent in which he has seen viscera seems to be filming over, is drawing itself closed. The white body before him is bloodstained but becoming whole before his unbelieving gaze. His eyes start from their sockets, he trembles violently. She smiles more warmly and stands straighter, pushing back her hair.

Behind them a last Flier yowls as it is run down.

Has he had an hallucination? Surely so, he tells himself. He must say nothing.

But as he thinks this he hears an indrawn gasp behind him. Another, others have seen this too. Someone mutters sibilantly. He senses panic.

Those Fliers, he thinks confusedly, how did they die? They show no wounds. What killed them? When they came near her, did she—what did she—

A word is being hissed behind him now, a word the Whites have not heard for two hundred years. The muttered hissing is rising. And then it is broken with wails. Mothers have found that the saved children are lying too still among the Fliers who had captured them, are in fact not saved but dead.

"Witch! Witch! Witch!"

The crowd has become a menacing ring behind him, they are closing warily but with growing rage upon the white, still girl. Her blind face turns questioningly, still half smiling, not understanding what threatens. A stone whizzes past her, another strikes her shoulder.

"Witch! Killer witch!"

The Healer turns on them, holding up his arms.

"No! Don't! She's not—" But his voice is lost in the shouting. His voice will not obey him, he too is terrified. More stones fly by from the shadows. Behind him the girl Snow cries out in pain. Women trample forward, shoving him aside. A man jumps past him with uplifted spear.

"No!" the Healer shouts.

In full leap the man is suddenly slumping, is falling bonelessly upon the dead Fliers. And women beyond him are falling too. Screams mingle with the shouts. Hardly knowing what he does, the Healer bends to the downed man, encounters lifelessness. No breath, no wound; only death. And the woman beside him the same, and the next, and all around.

The Healer becomes aware of unnatural quiet spreading through the twilight. He lifts his head. All about him the people of his village have fallen like scythed grain. Not one is standing. As he stares, a small boy runs from behind a hut, and is instantly struck down. Unable to grasp the enormity, the Healer sees his whole village lying dead.

Behind him where the girl Snow stands alone there is silence too, terror-filled. He knows she has not fallen; it is she who has done this thing. The Healer is a deeply brave man. Slowly he forces himself to turn and look.

She is there upright among the dead, a slight childish form turned away from him, one hand pitifully clutching her shoulder. Her face in profile is contorted, whether from pain or anger he cannot tell. *Her eyes are open.* He sees one huge silver orb glinting wide, roving the silent village. As he stares, her head turns slowly around to where he stands. Her gaze reaches him.

He falls.

When the dawn fills the valley with gray light, a small, pale figure comes quietly from the huts. She is alone. In all the valley no breath sighs, no live thing stirs. The dawn gleams on her open silver eyes.

Moving composedly, she fills her canteen from the well and places food in her simple backpack. Then she gazes for a last time on the tumbled bodies of her people, reaches out her hand and draws back again, her face without expression, her eyes blank and wide. She hoists her pack to her shoulders. Walking lightly, resiliently—for she is unwounded—she sets out on the path up the valley, toward where she knows another village lies.

The morning brightens around her. Her slight figure is tender with the promise of love, her face lifted to the morning breeze is sweet with life. In her heart is loneliness; she is of mankind and she goes in search of human companionship.

Her first journey will not be long. But it will be soon resumed, and resumed again, and again resumed and again, for she carries wasting in her aura, and Death in her open eyes. She will find and lose, and seek and find and lose again, and again seek. But she has time. She has all the time of forever, time to search the whole world over and over again, for she is immortal.

Of her own kind she will discover none. Whether any like her have been born elsewhere she will never know. None but she have survived.

Where she goes Death goes too, inexorably. She will wander forever, until she is the last human, is indeed Humanity itself. In her flesh the eternal promise, in her gaze the eternal doom, she will absorb all. In the end she will wander and wait alone through the slow centuries for whatever may come from the skies.

. . . And thus the Beast and its Death are at last at one, as when the fires of a world conflagration die away to leave at their heart one imperishable crystal shape. Forged of Life-in-Death, the final figure of humanity waits in perpetual stasis upon the spent, uncaring Earth. Until, after unimaginable eons, strangers driven by their own agonies come from the stars to provide her unknown end. Perhaps she will call to them.

The material on the Kiowa Indians here is due, with thanks, to N. Scott Momaday's beautiful elegy, *The Way to Rainy Mountain*, University of New Mexico Press, 1969, and Ballantine Books.

SLOW MUSIC

Caoilte tossing his burning hair,
And Niamh calling Away, come away;
Empty your heart of its mortal dream. . . .
We come between man and the deed of his hand,
We come between him and the hope of his heart.
                    —W. B. YEATS

LIGHTS CAME ON as Jakko walked down the lawn past the house; elegantly concealed spots and floods which made the night into a great intimate room. Overhead the big conifers formed a furry nave drooping toward the black lake below the bluff ahead. This had been a beloved home, he saw; every luxurious device was subdued to preserve the beauty of the forested shore. He walked on a carpet of violets and mosses, in his hand the map that had guided him here from the city.

It was the stillness before dawn. A long-winged night bird swirled in to catch a last moth in the dome of light. Before him shone a bright spearpoint. Jakko saw it was the phosphorescent tip of a mast against the stars. He went down velvety steps to find a small sailboat floating at the dock like a silver leaf reflected on a dark mirror.

In silence he stepped on board, touched the mast.

A gossamer sail spread its fan, the mooring parted

soundlessly. The dawn breeze barely filled the sail, but the craft moved smoothly out, leaving a glassy line of wake. Jakko half-poised to jump. He knew nothing of such playtoys, he should go back and find another boat. As he did so, the shore lights went out, leaving him in darkness. He turned and saw Regulus rising ahead where the channel must be. Still, this was not the craft for him. He tugged at the tiller and sail, meaning to turn it back.

But the little boat ran smoothly on, and then he noticed the lights of a small computer glowing by the mast. He relaxed; this was no toy, the boat was fully programmed and he could guess what the course must be. He stood examining the sky, a statue-man gliding across reflected night.

The eastern horizon changed, veiled its stars as he neared it. He could see the channel now, a silvery cut straight ahead between dark banks. The boat ran over glittering shallows where something splashed hugely, and headed into the shining lane. As it did so, all silver changed to lead and the stars were gone. Day was coming. A great pearl-colored blush spread upward before him, developed bands of lavender and rays of coral-gold fire melting to green iridescence overhead. The boat was now gliding on a ribbon of fiery light between black-silhouetted banks. Jakko looked back and saw dazzling cloud-cities heaped behind him in the west. The vast imminence of sunrise. He sighed aloud.

He understood that all this demonstration of glory was nothing but the effects of dust and vapor in the thin skin of air around a small planet, whereon he crawled wingless. No vastness brooded; the planet was merely turning with him into the rays of its mediocre primary. His family, everyone, knew that on the River he would encounter the Galaxy itself in glory. Suns beyond count, magnificence to which this was nothing. And yet—and yet to him this was not nothing. It was intimately his, man-sized. He made an ambiguous sound in his throat. He resented the trivialization of this beauty, and he resented being moved by it. So he passed along, idly holding the sail rope like a man leashing the living wind, his face troubled and very young.

The little craft ran on unerringly, threading the winding sheen of the canal. As the sun rose, Jakko began to hear a faint drone ahead. The sea surf. He thought of the persons who must have made this voyage before him: the ship's family, savoring their final days of mortality. A happy voyage, a picnic. The thought reminded him that he was hungry; the last groundcar's synthesizer had been faulty.

He tied the rope and searched. The boat had replenished its water, but there was only one foodbar. Jakko lay down in the cushioned well and ate and drank comfortably, while the sky turned turquoise and then cobalt. Presently they emerged into an enormous lagoon and began to run south between low islands. Jakko trailed his hand and tasted brackish salt. When the boat turned east again and made for a seaward opening, he became doubly certain. The craft was programmed for the River, like almost everything else on the world he knew.

Sure enough, the tiny bark ran through an inlet and straight out into the chop beyond a long beach, extruded outriggers, and passed like a cork over the reef foam on to the deep green swells beyond. Here it pitched once and steadied; Jakko guessed it had thrust down a keel. Then it turned south and began to run along outside the reef, steady as a knife cut with the wind on its quarter. Going Riverward for sure. The nearest River place was here called Vidalita or Beata, or sometimes Falaz, meaning "illusion." It was far south and inland. Jakko guessed they were making for a landing where a moveway met the sea. He had still time to think, to struggle with the trouble under his mind.

But as the sun turned the boat into a trim white-gold bird flying over green transparency, Jakko's eyes closed and he slept, protected by invisible deflectors from the bow-spray. Once he opened his eyes and saw a painted fish tearing along magically in the standing wave below his head. He smiled and slept again, dreaming of a great wave dying, a wave that was a many-headed beast. His face became sad and his lips moved soundlessly, as if repeating, "No . . . no . . ."

When he woke they were sailing quite close by a long bluff on his right. In the cliff ahead was a big white building or tower, only a little ruined. Suddenly he caught sight of a figure moving on the beach before it. A living human? He jumped up to look. He had not seen a strange human person in many years.

Yes—it was a live person, strangely colored gold and black. He waved wildly.

The person on the beach slowly raised an arm.

Alight with excitement, Jakko switched off the computer and

grabbed the rudder and sail. The line of reef surf seemed open here. He turned the boat shoreward, riding on a big swell. But the wave left him. He veered erratically, and the surf behind broached into the boat, overturning it and throwing him out. He knew how to swim; he surfaced and struck out strongly for the shore, spluttering brine. Presently he was wading out onto the white beach, a short, strongly built, reddened young male person with pale hair and water-blue eyes.

The stranger was walking hesitantly toward him. Jakko saw it was a thin dark-skinned girl wearing a curious netted hat. Her body was wrapped in orange silk, and she carried heavy gloves in one hand. Three nervous moondogs followed her. He began turning water out of his shorts pockets as she came up.

"Your . . . boat," she said in the language of that time. Her voice was low and uncertain.

They both turned to look at the confused place by the reef where the sailboat floated half-submerged.

"I turned it off. The computer." His words came jerkily too, they were both unused to speech.

"It will come ashore down there." She pointed, still studying him in a wary, preoccupied way. She was much smaller than he. "Why did you turn? Aren't you going to the River?"

"No." He coughed. "Well, yes, in a way. My father wants me to say good-bye. They left while I was traveling."

"You're not . . . ready?"

"No. I don't—" He broke off. "Are you staying alone here?"

"Yes. I'm not going, either."

They stood awkwardly in the sea wind. Jakko noticed that the three moondogs were lined up single file, tiptoeing upwind toward him with their eyes closed, sniffing. They were not, of course, from the moon, but they looked it, being white and oddly shaped.

"It's a treat for them," the girl said. "Something different." Her voice was stronger now. After a pause she added, "You can stay here for a while if you want. I'll show you, but I have to finish my work first."

"Thank you," he remembered to say.

As they climbed steps cut in the bluff Jakko asked, "What are you working at?"

"Oh, everything. Right now it's bees."

"Bees!" he marveled. "They made what—honey? I thought they were all gone."

"I have a lot of old things." She kept glancing at him intently as they climbed. "Are you quite healthy?"

"Oh, yes. Why not? I'm all alpha so far as I know. Everybody is."

"Was," she corrected. "Here are my bee skeps."

They came around a low wall and stopped by five small wicker huts. A buzzing insect whizzed by Jakko's face, coming from some feathery shrubs. He saw that the bloom-tipped foliage was alive with the golden humming things. Recalling that they could sting, he stepped back.

"You better go around the other way." She pointed. "They might hurt a stranger." She pulled her veil down, hiding her face. Just as he turned away, she added, "I thought you might impregnate me."

He wheeled back, not really able to react because of the distracting bees. "But isn't that terribly complicated?"

"I don't think so. I have the pills." She pulled on her gloves.

"Yes, the pills. I know." He frowned. "But you'd have to stay, I mean one just can't—"

"I know that. I have to do my bees now. We can talk later."

"Of course." He started away and suddenly turned back.

"Look!" He didn't know her name. "You, look!"

"What?" She was a strange little figure, black and orange with huge hands and a big veil-muffled head. "What?"

"I felt it. Just then, desire. Can't you see?"

They both gazed at his wet shorts.

"I guess not," he said finally. "But I felt it, I swear. Sexual desire."

She pushed back her veil, frowning. "It will stay, won't it? Or come back? This isn't a very good place. I mean, the bees. And it's no use without the pills."

"That's so."

He went away then, walking carefully because of the tension around his pubic bone. Like a keel, snug and tight. His whole body felt reorganized. It had been years since he'd felt flashes like that, not since he was fifteen at least. Most people never did. That was variously thought to be because of the River, or from their parents' surviving the Poison Centuries, or because the general alpha strain was so forebrain-dominant. It gave him an archaic, secret pride. Maybe he was a throwback.

He passed under cool archways, and found himself in a green protected place behind the seaward wall. A garden, he saw, looking round surprised at clumps of large tied-up fruiting plants, peculiar trees with green balls at their tops, disorderly rows of rather unaesthetic greenery. Tentatively he identified tomatoes, peppers, a feathery leaf which he thought had an edible root. A utilitarian planting. His uncle had once amused the family by doing something of the sort, but not on this scale. Jakko shook his head.

In the center of the garden stood a round stone coping with a primitive apparatus on top. He walked over and looked down. Water, a bucket on a rope. Then he saw that there was also an ordinary tap. He opened it and drank, looking at the odd implements leaning on the coping. Earth tools. He did not really want to think about what the strange woman had said.

A shadow moved by his foot. The largest moondog had come quite close, inhaling dreamily. "Hello," he said to it. Some of these dogs could talk a little. This one opened its eyes wide but said nothing.

He stared about, wiping his mouth, feeling his clothes almost dry now in the hot sun. On three sides the garden was surrounded by arcades; above him on the ruined side was a square cracked masonry tower with no roof. A large place, whatever it was. He walked into the shade of the nearest arcade, which turned out to be littered with myriad disassembled or partly assembled objects: tools, containers, who knew what. Her "work"? The place felt strange, vibrant and busy. He realized he had entered only empty houses on his yearlong journey. This one was alive, lived-in. Messy. It hummed like the bee skeps. He turned down a cool corridor, looking into rooms piled with more stuff. In one, three white animals he couldn't identify were asleep in a heap of cloth on a bed. They moved their ears at him like big pale shells but did not awaken.

He heard staccato noises and came out into another courtyard where plump white birds walked with jerking heads. "Chickens!" he decided, delighted by the irrational variety of this place. He went from there into a large room with windows on the sea, and heard a door close.

It was the woman, or girl, coming to him, holding her hat and gloves. Her hair was a dark curly cap, her head elegantly small; an effect he had always admired. He remembered something to say.

"I'm called Jakko. What's your name?"

"Jakko." She tasted the sound. "Hello, Jakko. I'm Peachthief."

She smiled very briefly, entirely changing her face.

"Peachthief." On impulse he moved toward her, holding out his hands. She tucked her bundle under her arm and took both of his. They stood like that a moment, not quite looking at each other. Jakko felt excited. Not sexually, but more as if the air was electrically charged.

"Well." She took her hands away and began unwrapping a leafy wad. "I brought a honeycomb even if it isn't quite ready." She showed him a sticky-looking frame with two dead bees on it. "Come on."

She walked rapidly out into another corridor and entered a shiny room he thought might be a laboratory.

"My food room," she told him. Again Jakko was amazed. There stood a synthesizer, to be sure, but beside it were shelves full of pots and bags and jars and containers of all descriptions. Unknown implements lay about, and there was a fireplace which had been partly sealed up. Bunches of plant parts hung from racks overhead. He identified some brownish ovoids in a bowl as eggs. From the chickens?

Peachthief was cleaning the honeycomb with a manually operated knife. "I use the wax for my loom, and for candles. Light."

"What's wrong with the lights?"

"Nothing." She turned around, gesturing emphatically with the knife. "Don't you understand? All these machines, they'll go. They won't run forever. They'll break or wear out or run down. There won't *be* any, anymore. Then we'll have to use natural things."

"But that won't be for centuries!" he protested. "Decades, anyhow. They're all still going, they'll last for us."

"For you," she said scornfully. "Not for me. I intend to stay. With my children." She turned her back on him and added in a friendlier voice, "Besides, the old things are aesthetic. I'll show you, when it gets dark."

"But you haven't any children! Have you?" He was purely astonished.

"Not yet." Her back was still turned.

"I'm hungry," he said, and went to work the synthesizer. He made it give him a bar with a hard filler; for some reason he wanted to crunch it in his teeth.

She finished with the honey and turned around. "Have you ever had a natural meal?"

"Oh, yes," he said, chewing. "One of my uncles tried that. It was very nice," he added politely.

She looked at him sharply and smiled again, on—off. They went out of the food room. The afternoon was fading into great gold-and-orange streamers above the courtyard, colored like Peachthief's garment.

"You can sleep here." She opened a slatted door. The room was small and bare, with a window on the sea.

"There isn't any bed," he objected.

She opened a chest and took out a big wad of string. "Hang this end on that hook over there."

When she hung up the other end he saw it was a large mesh hammock.

"That's what I sleep in. They're comfortable. Try it."

He climbed in awkwardly. The thing came up around him like a bag. She gave a short sweet laugh as brief as her smile.

"No, you lie on the diagonal. Like this." She tugged his legs, sending a peculiar shudder through him. "That straightens it, see?"

It would probably be all right, he decided, struggling out. Peachthief was pointing to a covered pail.

"That's for your wastes. It goes on the garden, in the end."

He was appalled, but said nothing, letting her lead him out through a room with glass tanks in the walls to a big screened-in porch fronting the ocean. It was badly in need of cleaners. The sky was glorious with opalescent domes and spires, reflections of the sunset behind them, painting amazing colors on the sea.

"This is where I eat."

"What is this place?"

"It was a sea station last, I think. Station Juliet. They monitored the fish and the ocean traffic, and rescued people and so on."

He was distracted by noticing long convergent dove-blue rays like mysterious paths into the horizon; cloud shadows cast across the world. Beauty of the dust. Why must it move him so?

"—even a medical section," she was saying. "I really could have babies, I mean in case of trouble."

"You don't mean it." He felt only irritation now. "I don't feel any more desire," he told her.

She shrugged. "I don't either. We'll talk about it later on."

"Have you always lived here?"

"Oh, no." She began taking pots and dishes out of an insulated case. The three moondogs had joined them silently; she set bowls before them. They lapped, stealing glances at Jakko. They were, he knew, very strong despite their sticklike appearance.

"Let's sit here." She plumped down on one end of the lounge and began biting forcefully into a crusty thing like a slab of drybar. He noticed she had magnificent teeth. Her dark skin set them off beautifully, as it enhanced her eyes. He had never met anyone so different in every way from himself and his family. He vacillated between interest and a vague alarm.

"Try some of the honey." She handed him a container and spoon. It looked quite clean. He tasted it eagerly; honey was much spoken of in antique writings. At first he sensed nothing but a waxy sliding, but then an overpowering sweetness enveloped his tongue, quite unlike the sweets he was used to. It did not die away but seemed to run up his nose and almost into his ears, in a peculiar physical way. An *animal* food. He took some more, gingerly.

"I didn't offer you my bread. It needs some chemical, I don't know what. To make it lighter."

"Don't you have an access terminal?"

"Something's wrong with part of it," she said with her mouth full. "Maybe I don't work it right. We never had a big one like this, my tribe were travelers. They believed in sensory experiences." She nodded, licking her fingers. "They went to the River when I was fourteen."

"That's very young to be alone. My people waited till this year, my eighteenth birthday."

"I wasn't alone. I had two older cousins. But they wanted to take an aircar up north, to the part of the River called Rideout. I stayed here. I mean, we never stopped traveling, we never *lived* anywhere. I wanted to do like the plants, make roots."

"I could look at your program," he offered. "I've seen a lot of different models, I spent nearly a year in cities."

"What I need is a cow. Or a goat."

"Why?"

"For the milk. I need a pair, I guess."

Another animal thing; he winced a little. But it was pleasant, sitting here in the deep blue light beside her, hearing the surf plash quietly below.

"I saw quite a number of horses," he told her. "Don't they use milk?"

"I don't think horses are much good for milk." She sighed in an alert, busy way. He had the impression that her head was tremendously energic, humming with plans and intentions. Suddenly she looked up and began making a high squeaky noise between her front teeth, "Sssswwt! Sssswwwt!"

Startled, he saw a white flying thing swooping above them, and then two more. They whirled so wildly he ducked.

"That's right," she said to them. "Get busy."

"What are they?"

"My bats. They eat mosquitoes and insects." She squeaked again, and the biggest bat was suddenly clinging to her hand, licking honey. It had a small, fiercely complicated face.

Jakko relaxed again. This place and its strange inhabitant were giving him remarkable memories for the River, anyway. He noticed a faint glow moving where the dark sky joined the darker sea.

"What's that?"

"Oh, the seatrain. It goes to the River landing."

"Are there people on it?"

"Not anymore. Look, I'll show you." She jumped up and was opening a console in the corner, when a sweet computer voice spoke into the air.

"Seatrain Foxtrot Niner calling Station Juliet! Come in, Station Juliet!"

"It hasn't done that for years," Peachthief said. She tripped tumblers. "Seatrain, this is Station Juliet, I hear you. Do you have a problem?"

"Affirmative. Passenger is engaging in nonstandard activities. He-slash-she does not conform to parameters. Request instructions."

Peachthief thought a minute. Then she grinned. "Is your passenger moving on four legs?"

"Affirmative! Affirmative!" Seatrain Foxtrot sounded relieved.

"Supply it with bowls of meat food and water on the floor and do not interfere with it. Juliet out."

She clicked off, and they watched the far web of lights go by on the horizon, carrying an animal.

"Probably a dog following the smell of people," Peachthief said. "I hope it gets off all right. . . . We're quite a wide genetic spread," she went on in a different voice. "I mean, you're so light, in body type and all."

"I noticed that."

"It would give good heterosis. Vigor."

She was talking about being impregnated, about the fantasy child. He felt angry.

"Look, you don't know what you're saying. Don't you realize you'd have to stay and raise it for years? You'd be ethically and morally bound. And the River places are shrinking fast, you must know that. Maybe you'd be too late."

"Yes," she said somberly. "Now it's sucked everybody out it's going. But I still mean to stay."

"But you'd hate it, even if there's still time. My mother hated it, toward the end. She felt she had begun to deteriorate energically, that her life would be lessened. And me—what about me? I mean, I should stay, too."

"You'd only have to stay a month. For my ovulation. The male parent isn't ethically bound."

"Yes, but I think that's wrong. My father stayed. He never said he minded it, but he must have."

"You only have to do a month," she said sullenly. "I thought you weren't going on the River right now."

"I'm not. I just don't want to feel bound, I want to travel. To see more of the world, first. After I say good-bye."

She made an angry sound. "You have no insight. You're going, all right. You just don't want to admit it. You're going just like Mungo and Ferrocil."

"Who are they?"

"People who came by. Males, like you. Mungo was last year, I guess. He had an aircar. He said he was going to stay, he talked and talked. But two days later he went right on again. To the River. Ferrocil was earlier, he was walking through. Until he stole my bicycle."

A sudden note of fury in her voice startled him; she seemed to have some peculiar primitive relation to her bicycle, to her *things*.

"Did you want them to impregnate you, too?" Jakko noticed an odd intensity in his own voice as well.

"Oh, I was thinking about it, with Mungo." Suddenly she turned on him, her eyes wide open in the dimness like white-ringed jewels. "Look! Once and for all, I'm not going! I'm alive, I'm a human woman. I am going to stay on this Earth and do human things. I'm going to make young ones to carry on the race, even if I have to die here. You can go on out, you—you pitiful shadows!"

Her voice rang in the dark room, jarring him down to his sleeping marrow. He sat silent as though some deep buried bell had tolled.

She was breathing hard. Then she moved, and to his surprise a small live flame sprang up between her cupped hands, making the room a cave.

"That's a candle. That's me. Now go ahead, make fun like Mungo did."

"I'm not making fun," he said, shocked. "It's just that I don't know what to think. Maybe you're right. I really . . . I really don't want to go, in one way," he said haltingly. "I love this Earth, too. But it's all so fast. Let me. . . ."

His voice trailed off.

"Tell me about your family," she said, quietly now.

"Oh, they studied. They tried every access you can imagine. Ancient languages, history, lore. My aunt made poems in English. . . . The layers of the Earth, the names of body cells and tissues, jewels, everything. Especially stars. They made us memorize star maps. So we'll know where we are, you know, for a while. At least the Earth-names. My father kept saying, when you go on the River you can't come back and look anything up. All you have is what you remember. Of course you could ask others, but there'll be so much more, so much new. . . ."

He fell silent, wondering for the millionth time: is it possible that I shall go out forever between the stars, in the great streaming company of strange sentiences?

"How many children were in your tribe?" Peachthief was asking.

"Six. I was the youngest."

"The others all went on the River?"

"I don't know. When I came back from the cities the whole family had gone on, but maybe they'll wait awhile, too. My father left a letter asking me to come and say good-bye, and to bring him anything new I learned. They say you go slowly, you know. If I hurry there'll still be enough of his mind left there to tell him what I saw."

"What did you see? We were at a city once," Peachthief said dreamily. "But I was too young, I don't remember anything but people."

"The people are all gone now. Empty, every one. But everything works, the lights change, the moveways run. I didn't believe everybody was gone until I checked the central control offices. Oh, there were so many wonderful devices." He sighed. "The beauty, the complexity. Fantastic what people made." He sighed again, thinking of the wonderful technology, the creations abandoned, running down. "One strange thing. In the biggest city I saw, old Chio, almost every entertainment screen had the same tape running."

"What was it?"

"A girl, a young girl with long hair. Almost to her feet, I've never seen such hair. She was laying it out on a sort of table, with her head down. But no sound, I think the audio was broken. Then she poured a liquid all over very slowly. And then she lit it, she set fire to herself. It flamed and exploded and burned her all up. I think it was real." He shuddered. "I could see inside her mouth, her tongue going all black and twisted. It was horrible. Running over and over, everywhere. Stuck."

She made a revolted sound. "So you want to tell that to your father, to his ghost or whatever?"

"Yes. It's all new data, it could be important."

"Oh, yes," she said scornfully. Then she grinned at him. "What about me? Am I new data, too? A woman who isn't going to the River? A woman who is going to stay here and make babies? Maybe I'm the last."

"That's very important," he said slowly, feeling a deep confusion in his gut. "But I can't believe, I mean, you—"

"*I mean it.*" She spoke with infinite conviction. "I'm going to live here and have babies by you or some other man if you won't stay, and teach them to live on the Earth naturally."

Suddenly he believed her. A totally new emotion was rising up in him, carrying with it sunrises and nameless bonds with Earth that hurt in a painless way; as though a rusted door was opening within him. Maybe this was what he had been groping for.

"I think—I think maybe I'll help you. Maybe I'll stay with you, for a while at least. Our—our children."

"You'll stay a month?" she asked wonderingly. "Really?"

"No, I mean I could stay longer. To make more and see them and help raise them, like Father did. After I come back from saying good-bye I'll really stay."

Her face changed. She bent to him and took his face between

471

her slim dark hands.

"Jakko, listen. If you go to the River you'll never come back. No one ever does. I'll never see you again. We have to do it now, before you go."

"But a month is too long!" he protested. "My father's mind won't be there, I'm already terribly late."

She glared into his eyes a minute and then released him, stepping back with her brief sweet laugh. "Yes, and it's already late for bed. Come on."

She led him back to the room, carrying the candles, and he marveled anew at the clutter of strange activities she had assembled. "What's that?"

"My weaving room." Yawning, she reached in and held up a small, rough-looking cloth. "I made this."

It was ugly, he thought; ugly and pathetic. Why make such useless things? But he was too tired to argue.

She left him to cleanse himself perfunctorily by the well in the moonlit courtyard, after showing him another waste-place right in the garden. Other people's wastes smelled bad, he noticed sleepily. Maybe that was the cause of all the ancient wars.

In his room he tumbled into his hammock and fell asleep instantly. His dreams that night were chaotic; crowds, storms, jostling, and echoing through strange dimensions. His last image was of a great whirlwind that bore in its forehead a jewel that was a sleeping woman, curled like an embryo.

He waked in the pink light of dawn to find her brown face bending over him, smiling impishly. He had the impression she had been watching him, and jumped quickly out of the hammock.

"Lazy," she said. "I've found the sailboat. Hurry up and eat."

She handed him a wooden plate of bright natural fruits and led him out into the sunrise garden.

When they got down to the beach she led him south, and there was the little craft sliding to and fro, overturned in the shallows amid its tangle of sail. The keel was still protruding. They furled the sail in clumsily, and towed it out to deeper water to right it.

"I want this for the children," Peachthief kept repeating excitedly. "They can get fish, too. Oh, how they'll love it!"

"Stand your weight on the keel and grab the side rail," Jakko told her, doing the same. He noticed that her silks had come loose from her breasts, which were high and wide-pointed, quite unlike those of his tribe. The sight distracted him, his thighs felt unwieldy, and he missed his handhold as the craft righted itself and ducked him. When he came up he saw Peachthief scrambling aboard like a cat, clinging tight to the mast.

"The sail! Pull the sail up," he shouted, and got another faceful of water. But she had heard him, the sail was trembling open like a great wing, silhouetting her shining dark body. For the first time Jakko noticed the boat's name, on the stern: *Gojack*. He smiled. An omen.

Gojack was starting to move smoothly away, toward the reef.

"The rudder!" he bellowed. "Turn the rudder and come back."

Peachthief moved to the tiller and pulled at it; he could see her strain. But *Gojack* continued to move away from him into the wind, faster and faster toward the surf. He remembered she had been handling the mast where the computer was.

"Stop the computer! Turn it off, turn it off!"

She couldn't possibly hear him. Jakko saw her in frantic activity, wrenching at the tiller, grabbing ropes, trying physically to push down the sail. Then she seemed to notice the computer, but evidently could not decipher it. Meanwhile *Gojack* fled steadily on and out, resuming its interrupted journey to the River. Jakko realized with horror that she would soon be in dangerous water; the surf was thundering on coral heads.

"Jump! Come back, jump off!" He was swimming after them as fast as he could, his progress agonizingly slow. He glimpsed her still wrestling with the boat, screaming something he couldn't hear.

"JUMP!"

And finally she did, but only to try jerking *Gojack* around by its mooring lines. The boat faltered and jibbed, but then went strongly on, towing the threshing girl.

"Let go! Let go!" A wave broke over his head.

When he could see again he found she had at last let go and was swimming aimlessly, watching *Gojack* crest the surf and wing away. At last she turned back toward shore, and Jakko swam to intercept her. He was gripped by an unknown emotion so strong it discoordinated him. As his feet touched bottom he realized it was rage.

She waded to him, her face contorted by weeping. "The children's boat," she wailed. "I lost the children's boat—"

"You're crazy," he shouted. "There aren't any children."

"I lost it—" She flung herself on his chest, crying. He thumped her back, her sides, repeating furiously, "Crazy! You're insane!"

She wailed louder, squirming against him, small and naked and frail. Suddenly he found himself flinging her down onto the wet sand, falling on top of her with his swollen sex crushed between their bellies. For a moment all was confusion, and then the shock of it sobered him. He raised to look under himself, and Peachthief stared too, round-eyed.

"Do you w-want to, now?"

In that instant he wanted nothing more than to thrust himself into her, but a sandy wavelet splashed over them and he was suddenly aware of chafing wet cloth and Peachthief gagging brine. The magic waned. He got awkwardly to his knees.

"I thought you were going to be drowned," he told her, angry again.

"I wanted it so, for—for them. . . ." She was still crying softly, looking up desolately at him. He understood she wasn't really meaning just the sailboat. A feeling of inexorable involvement spread through him. This mad little being had created some kind of energy vortex around her, into which he was being sucked along with animals, vegetables, chickens, crowds of unknown things; only *Gojack* had escaped her.

"I'll find it," she was muttering, wringing out her silks, staring beyond the reef at the tiny dwindling gleam. He looked down at her, so fanatic and so vulnerable, and his inner landscape tilted frighteningly, revealing some ancient-new dimension.

"I'll stay with you," he said hoarsely. He cleared his throat, hearing his voice shake. "I mean I'll really stay, I won't go to the River at all. We'll make them, our babies now."

She stared up at him openmouthed. "But your father! You promised!"

"My father stayed," he said painfully. "It's—it's right, I think."

She came close and grabbed his arms in her small hands. "Oh, Jakko! But no, listen—*I'll go with you*. We can start a baby as we go, I'm sure of that. Then you can talk to your father and keep your promise and I'll be there to make sure you come back!"

"But you'd be—you'd be pregnant!" he cried in alarm. "You'd be in danger of taking an embryo on the River!"

She laughed proudly. "Can't you get it through your head that I will *not* go on the River? I'll just watch you and pull you out. I'll see you get back here. For a while, anyway," she added soberly. Then she brightened. "Hey, we'll see all kinds of things. Maybe I can find a cow or some goats on the way! Yes, yes! It's a perfect idea."

She faced him, glowing. Tentatively she brought her lips up to his, and they kissed inexpertly, tasting salt. He felt no desire, but only some deep resonance, like a confirmation in the earth. The three moondogs were watching mournfully.

"Now let's eat!" She began towing him toward the cliff steps. "We can start the pills right now. Oh, I have so much to do! But I'll fix everything, we'll leave tomorrow."

She was like a whirlwind. In the food room she pounced on a small gold-colored pillbox and opened it to show a mound of glowing green-and-red capsules.

"The red ones with the male symbol are for you."

She took a green one, and they swallowed solemnly, sharing a water mug. He noticed that the seal on the box had been broken, and thought of that stranger, Mungo, she had mentioned. How far had her plans gone with him? An unpleasant emotion he had never felt before rose in Jakko's stomach. He sensed that he was heading into more dubious realms of experience than he had quite contemplated. He took his foodbar and walked away through the arcades to cool down.

When he came upon her again she seemed to be incredibly busy, folding and filling and wrapping things, closing windows and tying doors open. Her intense relations with things again . . . He felt obscurely irritated and was pleased to have had a superior idea.

"We need a map," he told her. "Mine was in the boat."

"Oh, great idea. Look in the old control room, it's down those stairs. It's kind of scary." She began putting oil on her loom.

He went down a white ramp that became a tunnel stairway, and came finally through a heavily armored portal to a circular room deep inside the rock, dimly illumined by portholes sunk in long shafts. From here he could hear the hum of the station energy source. As his eyes adjusted he made out a bank of sensor screens and one big console standing alone. It seemed to have been smashed open; some kind of sealant had been poured over the works.

He had seen a place like this before; he understood at once that from here had been controlled terrible ancient weapons that flew. Probably they still stood waiting in their hidden holes behind the station. But the master control was long dead. As he approached the console he saw that someone had scratched in the cooling sealant. He could make out only the words: —WAR NO MORE. Undoubtedly this was a shrine of the very old days.

He found a light switch that filled the place with cool glare, and began exploring side alleys. Antique gear, suits, cupboards full of masks and crumbling packets he couldn't identify. Among them was something useful—two cloth containers to carry stuff on one's back, only a little mildewed. But where were the maps?

Finally he found one on the control-room wall, right where he had come in. Someone had updated it with scrawled notations. With a tremor he realized how very old this must be; it dated from before the Rivers had touched Earth. He could hardly grasp it.

Studying it, he saw that there was indeed a big landing dock not far south, and from there a moveway ran inland about a hundred kilometers to an airpark. If Peachthief could walk twenty-five kilometers they could make the landing by evening, and if the cars were still running the rest would be quick. All the moveways he'd seen had live cars on them. From the airpark a dotted line ran southwest across mountains to a big red circle with a cross in it, marked VIDA! That would be the River. They would just have to hope something on the airpark would fly, otherwise it would be a long climb.

His compass was still on his belt. He memorized the directions and went back upstairs. The courtyard was already saffron under great sunset flags.

Peachthief was squatting by the well, apparently having a conference with her animals. Jakko noticed some more white creatures he hadn't *seen* before, who seemed to live in an open hutch. They had long pinkish ears and mobile noses. Rabbits, or hares perhaps?

Two of the strange white animals he had seen sleeping were now under a bench, chirruping irritably at Peachthief.

"My raccoons," she told Jakko. "They're mad because I woke them up too soon." She said something in a high voice Jakko couldn't understand, and the biggest raccoon shook his head up and down in a supercilious way.

"The chickens will be all right," Peachthief said. "Lotor knows how to feed them, to get the eggs. And they can all work the water lever." The other raccoon nodded crossly, too.

"The rabbits are a terrible problem." Peachthief frowned. "You just haven't much sense, Eusebia," she said fondly, stroking the doe. "I'll have to fix something."

The big raccoon was warbling at her; Jakko thought he caught the word "dog-g-g."

"He wants to know who will settle their disputes with the dogs," Peachthief reported. At this, one of the moondogs came forward and said thickly, "We go-o." It was the first word Jakko had heard him speak.

"Oh, good!" Peachthief cried. "Well, that's that!" She bounced up and began pouring something from a bucket on a line of plants. The white raccoons ran off silently with a humping gait.

"I'm so glad you're coming, Tycho," she told the dog. "Especially if I have to come back alone with a baby inside. But they say you're very vigorous—at first, anyway."

"You aren't coming back alone," Jakko told her. She smiled a brilliant noncommittal flash. He noticed she was dressed differently; her body didn't show so much, and she kept her gaze away from him in an almost timid way. But she became very excited when he showed her the backpacks.

"Oh, good. Now we won't have to roll the blankets around our waists. It gets cool at night, you know."

"Does it ever rain?"

"Not this time of year. What we mainly need is lighters and food and water. And a good knife each. Did you find the map?"

He showed it. "Can you walk, I mean really hike if we have to? Do you have shoes?"

"Oh, yes. I walk a lot. Especially since Ferrocil stole my bike."

The venom in her tone amused him. The ferocity with which she provisioned her small habitat!

"Men build monuments, women build nests," he quoted from somewhere.

"I don't know what kind of monument Ferrocil built with my bicycle," she said tartly.

"You're a savage," he said, feeling a peculiar ache that came out as a chuckle.

"The race can use some savages. We better eat now and go to sleep so we can start early."

At supper in the sunset-filled porch they scarcely talked. Dreamily Jakko watched the white bats embroidering flight on the air. When he looked down at Peachthief he caught her gazing at him before she quickly lowered her eyes. It came to him that they might eat hundreds, thousands of meals here; maybe all his life. And there could be a child—children— running about. He had never seen small humans younger than himself. It was all too much to take in, unreal. He went back to watching the bats.

That night she accompanied him to his hammock and stood by, shy but stubborn, while he got settled. Then he suddenly felt her hands sliding on his body, toward his groin. At first he thought it was something clinical, but then he realized she meant sex. His blood began to pound.

"May I come in beside you? The hammock is quite strong."

"Yes," he said thickly, reaching for her arm.

But as her weight came in by him she said in a practical voice, "I have to start knotting a small hammock, first thing. Child-size."

It broke his mood.

"Look. I'm sorry, but I've changed my mind. You go on back to yours, we should get sleep now."

"All right." The weight lifted away.

With a peculiar mix of sadness and satisfaction he heard her light footsteps leaving him alone. That night he dreamed strange sensory crescendos, a tumescent earth and air; a woman who lay with her smiling lips in pale-green water, awaiting him, while thin black birds of sunrise stalked to the edge of the sea.

Next morning they ate by candles, and set out as the eastern sky was just turning rose-gray. The ancient white coral roadway was good walking. Peachthief swung right along beside him, her backpack riding smooth. The moondogs pattered soberly behind.

Jakko found himself absorbed in gazing at the brightening landscape. Jungle-covered hills rose away on their right, the sea lay below on their left, sheened and glittering with the coming sunrise. When a diamond chip of sun broke out of the horizon he almost shouted aloud for the brilliance of it; the palm trees beyond the road lit up like golden torches, the edges of every frond and stone were startlingly clear and jewel-like. For a moment he wondered if he could have taken some hallucinogen.

They paced on steadily in a dream of growing light and heat. The day wind came up, and torn white clouds began to blow over them, bringing momentary coolnesses. Their walking fell into the rhythm Jakko loved, broken only occasionally by crumbled places in the road. At such spots they would often be surprised to find the moondogs sitting waiting for them, having quietly left the road and circled ahead through the scrub on business of their own. Peachthief kept up sturdily, only once stopping to look back at the far white spark of Station Juliet, almost melted in the shimmering horizon.

"This is as far as I've gone south," she told him.

He drank some water and made her drink too, and they went on. The road began to wind, rising and falling gently. When he next glanced back the station was gone. The extraordinary luminous clarity of the world was still delighting him.

When noon came he judged they were well over halfway to the landing. They sat down on some rubble under the palms to eat and drink, and Peachthief fed the moondogs. Then she took out the fertility-pill box. They each took theirs in silence, oddly solemn. Then she grinned.

"I'll give you something for dessert."

She unhitched a crooked knife from her belt and went searching around in the rocks, to come back with a big yellow-brown palm nut. Jakko watched her attack it with rather alarming vigor; she husked it and then used a rock to drive the point home.

"Here." She handed it to him. "Drink out of that hole." He felt a sloshing inside; when he lifted it and drank, it tasted hairy and gritty and nothing in particular. But sharp too, like the day. Peachthief was methodically striking the thing around and around its middle. Suddenly it fell apart, revealing vividly white meat. She pried out a piece.

"Eat this. It's full of protein."

The nutmeat was sweet and sharply organic.

"This is a coconut!" he suddenly remembered.

"Yes. I won't starve, coming back."

He refused to argue, but only got up to go on. Peachthief holstered her knife and followed, munching on a coconut piece. They went on so in silence a long time, letting the rhythm carry them. Once when a lizard waddled across the road Peachthief said to the moondog at her heels, "Tycho, you'll have to learn to catch and eat those one day soon." The moondogs all looked dubiously at the lizard but said nothing. Jakko felt shocked and pushed the thought away.

They were now walking with the sun westering slowly to their right. A flight of big orange birds with blue beaks flapped squawking out of a roadside tree, where they were apparently building some structure. Cloud shadows fled across the world, making blue-and-bronze reflections in the sea. Jakko still felt his sensory impressions almost painfully keen; a sunray made the surf line into a chain of diamonds, and the translucent green of the near shallows below them seemed to enchant his eyes. Every vista ached with light, as if to utter some silent meaning.

He was walking in a trance, only aware that the road had been sound and level for some time, when Peachthief uttered a sharp cry.

"My bicycle! There's my bicycle!" She began to run; Jakko saw shiny metal sticking out of a narrow gulch in the roadway. When he came up to her she was pulling a machine out from beside the roadwall.

"The front wheel—Oh, he bent it! He must have been going too fast and wrecked it here. That Ferrocil! But I'll fix it, I'm sure I can fix it at the station. I'll push it back with me on the way home."

While she was mourning her machine Jakko looked around and over the low coping of the roadwall. Sheer cliff down there, with the sun just touching a rocky beach below. Something was stuck among the rocks—a tangle of whitish sticks, cloth, a round thing. Feeling his stomach knot, Jakko stared down at it, unwillingly discovering that the round thing had eyeholes, a U-shaped open mouth, blowing strands of hair. He had never seen a dead body before (nobody had), but he had seen pictures of human bones. Shakenly he realized what this had to be: Ferrocil. He must have been thrown over the coping when he hit that crack. Now he was dead, long dead. He would never go on the River. All that had been in that head was perished, gone forever.

Scarcely knowing what he was doing, Jakko grabbed Peachthief by the shoulders, saying roughly, "Come on! Come on!" When she resisted confusedly, he took her by the arm and began forcibly pulling her away from where she might look down. Her flesh felt burning hot and vibrant, the whole world was blasting colors and sounds and smells at him. Images of dead Ferrocil mingled with the piercing scent of some flowers on the roadway. Suddenly an idea struck him; he stopped.

"Listen. Are you sure those pills aren't hallucinaids? I've only had two and everything feels crazy."

"Three," Peachthief said abstractedly. She took his hand and pressed it on her back. "Do that again, run your hand down my back."

Bewildered, he obeyed. As his hand passed her silk shirt onto her thin shorts he felt her body move under it in a way that made him jerk away.

"Feel? Did you feel it? The lordotic reflex," she said proudly. "Female sexuality. It's starting."

"What do you mean, three?"

"You had three pills. I gave you one the first night, in the honey."

"*What?* But—but—" He struggled to voice the enormity of her violation, pure fury welling up in him. Choking, he lifted his hand and struck her buttocks the hardest blow he could, sending her staggering. It was the first time he had ever struck a person. A moondog growled, but he didn't care.

"Don't you ever—never—play a trick like—" He yanked at her shoulders, meaning to slap her face. His hand clutched a breast instead; he saw her hair blowing like dead Ferrocil's. A frightening sense of mortality combined with pride surged through him, lighting a fire in his loins. The deadness of Ferrocil suddenly seemed violently exciting. He, Jakko, was alive! Ignoring all sanity he flung himself on Peachthief, bearing her down on the road among the flowers. As he struggled to tear open their shorts he was dimly aware that she was helping him. His engorged penis was all reality; he fought past obstructions and then was suddenly, crookedly, *in* her, fierce pleasure building. It exploded through him and then had burst out into her vitals, leaving him spent.

Blinking, fighting for clarity, he raised himself up and off her body. She lay wide-legged and disheveled, sobbing or gasping in a strange way, but smiling, too. Revulsion sent a sick taste in his throat.

"There's your baby," he said roughly. He found his canteen and drank. The three moondogs had retreated and were sitting in a row, staring solemnly.

"May I have some, please?" Her voice was very low; she sat up, began fixing her clothes. He passed her the water and they got up.

"It's sundown," she said. "Should we camp here?"

"No!" Savagely he started on, not caring that she had to run to catch up. Was this the way the ancients lived? Whirled by violent passions, indecent, uncaring? His doing sex so close to the poor dead person seemed unbelievable. And the world was still assaulting all his senses; when she stumbled against him he could feel again the thrilling pull of her flesh, and shuddered. They walked in silence awhile; he sensed that she was more tired than he, but he wanted only to get as far away as possible.

"I'm not taking any more of those pills," he broke silence at last.

"But you have to! It takes a month to be sure."

"I don't care."

"But, ohhh—"

He said nothing more. They were walking across a twilit headland now. Suddenly the road turned, and they came out above a great bay.

The waters below were crowded with boats of all kinds, bobbing emptily where they had been abandoned. Some still had lights that made faint jewels in the opalescent air. Somewhere among them must be *Gojack*. The last light from the west gleamed on the rails of a moveway running down to the landing.

"Look, there's the seatrain." Peachthief pointed. "I hope the dog or whatever got ashore. . . . I can find a sailboat down there, there's lots."

Jakko shrugged. Then he noticed movement among the shadows of the landing station and forgot his anger long enough to say, "See there! Is that a live man?"

They peered hard. Presently the figure crossed a light place, and they could see it was a person going slowly among the stalled waycars. He would stop with one awhile and then waver on.

"There's something wrong with him," Peachthief, said.

Presently the stranger's shadow merged with a car, and they saw it begin to move. It went slowly at first, and then accelerated out to the center lanes, slid up the gleaming rails and passed beyond them to disappear into the western hills.

"The way's working!" Jakko exclaimed. "We'll camp up here and go over to the way station in the morning, it's closer."

He was feeling so pleased with the moveway that he talked easily with Peachthief over their foodbar dinner, telling her about the cities and asking her what places her tribe had seen. But when she wanted to put their blankets down together he said no, and took his away to a ledge farther up. The three moondogs lay down by her with their noses on their paws, facing him.

His mood turned to self-disgust again; remorse mingled with queasy surges of half-enjoyable animality. He put his arm over his head to shut out the brilliant moonlight and longed to forget everything, wishing the sky held only cold quiet stars. When he finally slept he didn't dream at all, but woke with ominous tollings in his inner ear. *The Horse is hungry,* deep voices chanted. *The Woman is bad!*

He roused Peachthief before sunrise. They ate and set off overland to the hill station; it was rough going until they stumbled onto an old limerock path. The moondogs ranged wide around them, appearing pleased. When they came out at the station shunt they found it crowded with cars.

The power pack of the first one was dead. So was the next, and the next. Jakko understood what the stranger at the landing had been doing; looking for a live car. The dead cars here stretched away out of sight up the siding; a miserable sight.

"We should go back to the landing," Peachthief said. "He found a good one there."

Jakko privately agreed, but irrationality smoldered in him. He squinted into the hazy distance.

"I'm going up to the switch end."

"But it's so far, we'll have to come all the way back—"

He only strode off; she followed. It was a long way, round a curve and over a rise, dead cars beside them all the way. They were almost at the main tracks when Jakko saw what he had been hoping for: a slight jolting motion in the line. New cars were still coming in ahead, butting the dead ones.

"Oh, fine!"

They went on down to the newest-arrived car and all climbed in, the moondogs taking up position on the opposite seat. When Jakko began to work the controls that would take them out to the main line, the car bleated an automatic alarm. A voder voice threatened to report him to Central. Despite its protests, Jakko swerved the car across the switches, where it fell silent and began to accelerate smoothly onto the outbound express lane.

"You really do know how to work these things," Peachthief said admiringly.

"You should learn."

"Why? They'll all be dead soon. I know how to bicycle."

He clamped his lips, thinking of Ferrocil's white bones. They fled on silently into the hills, passing a few more station jams. Jakko's perceptions still seemed too sharp, the sensory world too meaning-filled.

Presently they felt hungry, and found that the car's automatics were all working well. They had a protein drink and a pleasantly fruity bar, and Peachthief found bars for the dogs. The track was rising into mountains now; the car whirled smoothly through tunnels and came out in passes, offering wonderful views. Now and then they had glimpses of a great plain far ahead. The familiar knot of sadness gathered inside Jakko, stronger than usual. To think that all this wonderful system would run down and die in a jumble of rust. . . . He had a fantasy of himself somehow maintaining it, but the memory of Peachthief's pathetic woven cloth mocked at him. Everything was a mistake, a terrible mistake. He wanted only to leave, to escape to rationality and peace. If she had drugged him he wasn't responsible for what he'd promised. He wasn't bound. Yet the sadness redoubled, wouldn't let him go.

When she got out the pillbox and offered it he shook his head violently. "No!"

"But you *promised*—"

"No. I hate what it does."

She stared at him in silence, swallowing hers defiantly.

"Maybe there'll be some other men by the River," she said after a while. "We saw one."

He shrugged and pretended to fall asleep.

Just as he was really drowsing, the car's warning alarm trilled and they braked smoothly to a halt.

"Oh, look ahead—the way's gone! What is it?"

"A rockslide. An avalanche from the mountains, I think."

They got out among other empty cars that were waiting their prescribed pause before returning. Beyond the last one the way ended in an endless tumble of rocks and shale. Jakko made out a faint footpath leading on.

"Well, we walk. Let's get the packs, and some food and water."

While they were back in the car working the synthesizer, Peachthief looked out the window and frowned. After Jakko finished she punched a different code and some brownish lumps rolled into her hand.

"What's that?"

"You'll see." She winked at him.

As they started on the trail a small herd of horses appeared, coming toward them. The two humans politely scrambled up out of their way. The lead horse was a large yellow male. When he came to Peachthief he stopped and thrust his big head up at her.

"Zhu-gar, zhu-gar," he said sloppily. At this all the other horses crowded up and began saying "zhu-ga, zu-cah," in varying degrees of clarity.

"This I know," said Peachthief to Jakko. She turned to the yellow stallion. "Take us on your backs around these rocks. Then we'll give you sugar."

"Zhu-gar," insisted the horse, looking mean.

"Yes, sugar. *After* you take us around the rocks to the rails." The horse rolled his eyes unpleasantly, but he turned back down. There was some commotion, and two mares were pushed forward.

"Riding horseback is done by means of a saddle and bridle," protested Jakko.

"Also this way. Come on." Peachthief vaulted nimbly onto the back of the smaller mare.

Jakko reluctantly struggled onto the fat round back of the other mare. To his horror, as he got himself astride she put up her head and screamed shrilly.

"You'll get sugar, too," Peachthief told her. The animal subsided, and they started off along the rocky trail, single file. Jakko had to admit it was much faster than afoot, but he kept sliding backward.

"Hang on to her mane, that hairy place there," Peachthief called back to him, laughing. "I know how to run a few things too, see?"

When the path widened the yellow stallion trotted up alongside Peachthief.

"I thinking," he said importantly.

"Yes, what?"

"I push you down and eat zhugar now."

"All horses think that," Peachthief told him. "No good. It doesn't work."

The yellow horse dropped back, and Jakko heard him making horse-talk with an old gray-roan animal at the rear. Then he shouldered by to Peachthief again and said, "Why no good I push you down?"

"Two reasons," said Peachthief. "First, if you knock me down you'll never get any more sugar. All the humans will know you're bad and they won't ride on you anymore. So no more sugar, never again."

"No more hoomans," the big yellow horse said scornfully. "Hoomans finish."

"You're wrong there, too. There'll be a lot more humans. I am making them, see?" She patted her stomach.

The trail narrowed again, and the yellow horse dropped back. When he could come alongside he sidled by Jakko's mare.

"I think I push you down now."

Peachthief turned around.

"You didn't hear my other reason," she called to him.

The horse grunted evilly.

"The other reason is that my three friends there will bite your stomach open if you try." She pointed up to where the three moondogs had appeared on a rock as if by magic, grinning toothily.

Jakko's mare screamed again even louder, and the gray roan in back made a haw-haw sound. The yellow horse lifted his tail and trotted forward to the head of the line, extruding manure as he passed Peachthief.

They went on around the great rockslide without further talk. Jakko was becoming increasingly uncomfortable; he would gladly have got off and gone slower on his own two legs. Now and then they broke into a jog-trot, which was so painful he longed to yell to Peachthief to make them stop. But he kept silent. As they rounded some huge boulders he was rewarded by a distant view of the unmistakable towers of an airpark, to their left on the plain below.

At long last the rockslide ended, quite near a station. They stopped among a line of stalled cars. Jakko slid off gratefully, remembering to say "Thank you" to the mare. Walking proved to be uncomfortable, too.

"See if there's a good car before I get off!" Peachthief yelled.

The second one he came to was live. He shouted at her.

Next moment he saw trouble among the horses. The big yellow beast charged in, neighing and kicking. Peachthief came darting out of the melée with the moondogs, and fell into the car beside him, laughing.

"I gave our mares all the sugar," she chuckled. Then she sobered. "I think mares *are* good for milk. I told them to come to the station with me when I come back. If that big bully will let them."

"How will they get in a car?" he asked stupidly.

"Why, I'll be walking, I can't run these things."

"But I'll be with you." He didn't feel convinced.

"What for, if you don't want to make babies? You won't be here."

"Well then, why are you coming with me?"

"I'm looking for a cow," she said scornfully. "Or a goat. Or a man."

They said no more until the car turned into the airpark station. Jakko counted over twenty apparently live ships floating at their towers. Many more hung sagging, and some towers had toppled. The field moveways were obviously dead.

"I think we have to find hats," he told Peachthief.

"Why?"

"So the service alarms won't go off when we walk around. Most places are like that."

"Oh."

In the office by the gates they found a pile of crew hats laid out, a thoughtful action by the last of the airpark people. A big hand-lettered sign said, ALL SHIPS ON STANDBY, MANUAL OVERRIDE. READ DIRECTIONS. Under it was a stack of dusty leaflets. They took one, put on their hats, and began to walk toward a pylon base with several ships floating at its tower. They had to duck under and around the web of dead moveways, and when they reached the station base there seemed to be no way in from the ground.

"We'll have to climb onto that moveway."

They found a narrow ladder and went up, helping the moondogs. The moveway portal was open, and they were soon in the normal passenger lounge. It was still lighted.

"Now if the lift only works."

Just as they were making for the lift shaft they were startled by a voice ringing out.

"Ho! Ho, Roland!"

"That's no voder," Peachthief whispered. "There's a live human here."

They turned back and saw that a strange person was lying half on and half off one of the lounges. As they came close their eyes opened wide: he looked frightful. His thin dirty white hair hung around a horribly creased caved-in face, and what they could see of his neck and arms was all mottled and decayed-looking. His jerkin and pants were frayed and stained and sagged in where flesh should be. Jakko thought of the cloth shreds around dead Ferrocil and shuddered.

The stranger was staring haggardly at them. In a faint voice he said, "When the chevalier Roland died he predicted that his body would be found a spear's throw ahead of all others and facing the enemy. . . . If you happen to be real, could you perhaps give me some water?"

"Of course." Jakko unhooked his canteen and tried to hand it over, but the man's hands shook and fumbled so that Jakko had to hold it to his mouth, noticing a foul odor. The stranger sucked thirstily, spilling some. Beyond him the moondogs inched closer, sniffing gingerly.

"What's *wrong* with him?" Peachthief whispered as Jakko stood back.

Jakko had been remembering his lessons. "He's just very, very old, I think."

"That's right." The stranger's voice was stronger. He stared at them with curious avidity. "I waited too long. Fibrillation." He put one feeble hand to his chest. "Fibrillating . . . rather a beautiful word, don't you think? My medicine ran out or I lost it. . . . A small hot animal desynchronizing in my ribs."

"We'll help you get to the River right away!" Peachthief told him.

"Too late, my lords, too late. Besides, I can't walk and you can't possibly carry me."

"You can sit up, can't you?" Jakko asked. "There have to be some roll chairs around here, they had them for injured people." He went off to search the lounge office and found one almost at once.

When he brought it back the stranger was staring up at Peachthief, mumbling to himself in an archaic tongue of which Jakko only understood: ". . . *The breast of a grave girl makes a hill against sunrise.*" He tried to heave himself up to the chair but fell back, gasping. They had to lift and drag him in, Peachthief wrinkling her nose.

"Now if the lift only works."

It did. They were soon on the high departure deck, and the fourth portal-berth held a waiting ship. It was a small local ferry. They went through into the windowed main cabin, wheeling the old man, who had collapsed upon himself and was breathing very badly. The moondogs trooped from window to window, looking down. Jakko seated himself in the pilot chair.

"Read me out the instructions," he told Peachthief.

"One, place ship on internal guidance," she read. "Whatever that means. Oh, look, here's a diagram."

"Good."

It proved simple. They went together down the list, sealing the port, disengaging umbilicals, checking vane function, reading off the standby pressures in the gasbags above them, setting the reactor to warm up the drive motor and provide hot air for operational buoyancy.

While they were waiting, Peachthief asked the old man if he would like to be moved onto a window couch. He nodded urgently. When they got him to it he whispered, "See out!" They propped him up with chair pillows.

The ready-light was flashing. Jakko moved the controls, and the ship glided smoothly out and up. The computer was showing him wind speed, altitude, climb, and someone had marked all the verniers with the words COURSE SET—RIVER. Jakko lined everything up.

"Now it says, put it on automatic," Peachthief read. He did so.

The takeoff had excited the old man. He was straining to look down, muttering incomprehensibly. Jakko caught, *"The cool green hills of Earth . . . Crap!"* Suddenly he sang out loudly, *"There's a hell of a good universe next door—let's go!"* And fell back exhausted.

Peachthief stood over him worriedly. "I wish I could at least clean him up, but he's so weak."

The old man's eyes opened.

"Nothing shall be whole and sound that has not been rent; for love hath built his mansion in the place of excrement." He began to sing crackedly, "Take me to the River, the bee-yew-tiful River, and wash all my sins a-away! . . . You think I'm crazy, girl, don't you?" he went on conversationally. "Never heard of William Yeats. Very high bit-rate, Yeats."

"I think I understand a little," Jakko told him. "One of my aunts did English literature."

"Did literature, eh?" The stranger wheezed, snorted. "And you two—going on the River to spend eternity together as energy matrices or something equally impressive and sexless. . . . *Forever wilt thou love and she be fair."* He grunted. "Always mistrusted Keats. No balls. He'd be right at home."

"We're not going on the River," Peachthief said. "At least, I'm not. I'm going to stay and make children."

The old man's ruined mouth fell open; he gazed up at her wildly.

"No!" he breathed. "Is it true? Have I stumbled on the lover and mother of man, the last?"

Peachthief nodded solemnly.

"What is your name, O Queen?"

"Peachthief."

"My god. Somebody still knows of Blake." He smiled tremulously, and his eyelids suddenly slid downward; he was asleep.

"He's breathing better. Let's explore."

The small ship held little but cargo space at the rear. When they came to the food-synthesizer cubby Jakko saw Peachthief pocket something.

"What's that?"

"A little spoon. It'll be just right for a child." She didn't look at him.

Back in the main cabin the sunset was flooding the Earth below with level roseate light. They were crossing huge, oddly pockmarked meadows, the airship whispering along in silence except when a jet whistled briefly now and then for a course correction.

"Look—cows! Those must be cows," Peachthief exclaimed. "See the shadows."

Jakko made out small tan specks that were animals, with grotesque horned shadows stretching away.

"I'll have to find them when I come back. What is this place?"

"A big deathyard, I think. Where they put dead bodies. I never saw one this size. In some cities they had buildings just for dead people. Won't all that poison the cows?"

"Oh, no, it makes good grass, I believe. The dogs will help me find them. Won't you, Tycho?" she asked the biggest moondog, who was looking down beside them.

On the eastern side of the cabin the full moon was rising into view. The old man's eyes opened, looking at it.

"More water, if you please," he croaked.

Peachthief gave him some, and then got him to swallow broth from the synthesizer. He seemed stronger, smiling at her with his mouthful of rotted teeth.

"Tell me, girl. If you're going to stay and make children, why are you going to the River?"

"He's going because he promised to talk to his father, and I'm going along to see he comes back. And make the baby. Only now he won't take any more pills, I have to try to find another man."

"Ah yes, the pills. We used to call them Wake-ups. . . . They were necessary, after the population chemicals got around. Maybe they still are, for women. But I think it's mostly in the head. Why won't you take any more, boy? What's wrong with the old Adam?"

Peachthief started to answer, but Jakko cut her off. "I can speak for myself. They upset me. They made me do bad, uncontrolled things, and feel, agh—" He broke off with a grimace.

"You seem curiously feisty, for one who values his calm above the continuance of the race."

"It's the pills, I tell you. They're—they're dehumanizing."

"Dee-humanizing," the old man mocked. "And what do you know of humanity, young one? . . . That's what I went to find, that's why I stayed so long among the old, old things from before the River came. I wanted to bring the knowledge of what humanity really was . . . I wanted to bring it all. It's simple, boy. *They died."* He drew a rasping breath. "Every one of them died. They lived knowing that nothing but loss and suffering and extinction lay ahead. And they cared, terribly. . . . Oh, they made myths, but not many really believed them. *Death* was behind everything, waiting everywhere. Aging and death. No escape . . . Some of them went crazy, they fought and killed and enslaved each other by the millions, as if they could gain more life. Some of them gave up their precious lives for each other. They loved—and had to watch the ones they loved age and die. And in their pain and despair they built, they struggled, some of them sang. But above all, boy, they copulated! Fornicated, fucked, made love!"

He fell back, coughing, glaring at Jakko. Then, seeing that they scarcely understood his antique words, he went on more clearly. "Did sex, do you understand? Made children. It was their only weapon, you see. To send something of themselves into the future beyond their own deaths. Death was the engine of their lives, death fueled their sexuality. Death drove them at each other's throats and into each other's arms. Dying, they triumphed. . . . *That* was human life. And now that mighty engine is long stilled, and you call this polite parade of immortal lemmings *humanity?* . . . Even the faintest warmth of that immemorial holocaust makes you flinch away?"

He collapsed, gasping horribly; spittle ran down his chin. One slit of eye still raked them.

Jakko stood silent, shaken by resonances from the old man's words, remembering dead Ferrocil, feeling some deep conduit of reality reaching for him out of the long-gone past. Peachthief's hand fell on his shoulder, sending a shudder through him. Slowly his own hand seemed to lift by itself and cover hers, holding her to him. They watched the old man so for a long moment. His face slowly composed, he spoke in a soft dry tone.

"I don't trust that River, you know. . . . You think you're going to remain yourselves, don't you? Communicate with each other and with the essences of beings from other stars? . . . The latest news from Betelgeuse." He chuckled raspingly.

"That's the last thing people say when they're going," Jakko replied. "Everyone learns that. You float out, able to talk with real other beings. Free to move."

"What could better match our dreams?" He chuckled again. "I wonder . . . could that be the lure, just the input end of some cosmic sausage machine. . . ?"

"What's that?" asked Peachthief.

"An old machine that ground different meats together until they came out as one substance. . . . Maybe you'll find yourselves gradually mixed and minced and blended into some-some energic plasma . . . and then maybe squirted out again to impose the terrible gift of consciousness on some innocent race of crocodiles, or poached eggs. . . . And so it begins all over again. Another random engine of the universe, giving and taking obliviously. . . ." He coughed, no longer looking at them, and began to murmur in the archaic tongue, *"Ah, when the ghost begins to quicken, confusion of the deathbed over, is it sent . . . out naked on the roads as the books say, and stricken with the injustice of the stars for punishment?* The injustice of the stars . . ." He fell silent, and then whispered faintly, "Yet I too long to go."

"You will," Peachthief told him strongly.

"How . . . much longer?"

"We'll be there by dawn," Jakko said. "We'll carry you. I swear."

"A great gift," he said weakly. "But I fear . . . I shall give you a better." He mumbled on, a word Jakko didn't know; it sounded like "afrodisiack."

He seemed to lapse into sleep then. Peachthief went and got a damp, fragrant cloth from the cleanup and wiped his face gently. He opened one eye and grinned up at her.

"Madame Tasselass," he rasped. "Madame Tasselass, are you really going to save us?"

She smiled down, nodding her head determinedly, yes. He closed his eyes, looking more peaceful.

The ship was now fleeing through full moonlight, the cabin was so lit with azure and silver that they didn't think to turn on lights. Now and again the luminous mists of a low cloud veiled the windows and vanished again. Just as Jakko was about to propose eating, the old man took several gulping breaths and opened his eyes. His intestines made a bubbling sound.

Peachthief looked at him sharply and picked up one of his wrists. Then she frowned and bent over him, opening his filthy jerkin. She laid her ear to his chest, staring up at Jakko.

"He's not breathing, there's no heartbeat!" She groped inside his jerkin as if she could locate life, two tears rolling down her cheeks.

"He's dead—ohhh!" She groped deeper, then suddenly straightened up and gingerly clutched the cloth at the old man's crotch.

"What?"

"He's a woman!" She gave a sob and wheeled around to clutch Jakko, putting her forehead in his neck. "We n-never even knew her name. . . ."

Jakko held her, looking at the dead man-woman, thinking, She never knew mine, either. At that moment the airship jolted, and gave a noise like a cable grinding or slipping before it flew smoothly on again.

Jakko had never in his life distrusted machinery, but now a sudden terror contracted his guts. This thing could fall! They could be made dead like Ferrocil, like this stranger, like the myriads in the deathyards below. Echoes of the old voice ranting about death boomed in his head, he had a sudden vision of Peachthief grown old and dying like that. After the Rivers went, dying alone. His eyes filled, and a deep turmoil erupted under his mind. He hugged Peachthief tighter. Suddenly he knew in a dreamlike way exactly what was about to happen. Only this time there was no frenzy; his body felt like warm living rock.

He stroked Peachthief to quiet her sobs, and led her over to the moonlit couch on the far side of the cabin. She was still sniffling, hugging him hard. He ran his hands firmly down her back, caressing her buttocks, feeling her body respond.

"Give me that pill," he said to her. "Now."

Looking at him huge-eyed in the blue moonlight, she pulled out the little box. He took out his and swallowed it deliberately, willing her to understand.

"Take off your clothes." He began stripping off his jerkin, proud of the hot, steady power in his sex. When she stripped and he saw again the glistening black bush at the base of her slim belly, and the silver-edged curves of her body, urgency took him, but still in a magical calm.

"Lie down."

"Wait a minute—" She was out of his hands like a fish, running across the cabin to where the dead body lay in darkness. Jakko saw she was trying to close the dead eyes that still gleamed from the shadows. He could wait; he had never imagined his body could feel like this. She laid the cloth over the stranger's face and came back to him, half shyly holding out her arms, sinking down spread-legged on the shining couch before him. The moonlight was so brilliant he could see the pink color of her sexual parts.

He came onto her gently, controlledly, breathing in an exciting animal odor from her flesh. This time his penis entered easily, an intense feeling of all-rightness.

But a moment later the fires of terror, pity, and defiance deep within him burst up into a flame of passionate brilliance in his coupled groin. The small body under his seemed no longer vulnerable but appetitive. He clutched, mouthed, drove deep into her, exulting. Death didn't die alone, he thought obscurely as the ancient patterns lurking in his vitals awoke. Death flew with them and flowed by beneath, but he asserted life upon the body of the woman, caught up in a great crescendo of unknown sensation, until a culminant spasm of almost painful pleasure rolled through him into her, relieving him from head to feet.

When he could talk, he thought to ask her, "Did you—" he didn't know the word. "Did it sort of explode you, like me?"

"Well, no." Her lips were by his ear. "Female sexuality is a little different. Maybe I'll show you, later. . . . But I think it was good, for the baby."

He felt only a tiny irritation at her words, and let himself drift into sleep with his face in her warm-smelling hair. Dimly the understanding came to him that the great beast of his dreams, the race itself maybe, had roused and used them. So be it.

A cold thing pushing into his ear awakened him, and a hoarse voice said, "Ffoo-ood!" It was the moondogs.

"Oh, my, I forgot to feed them!" Peachthief struggled nimbly out from under him.

Jakko found he was ravenous, too. The cabin was dark now, as the moon rose overhead. Peachthief located the switches, and made a soft light on their side of the cabin. They ate and drank heartily, looking down at the moonlit world. The deathyards were gone from below them now, they were flying over dark wooded foothills. When they lay down to sleep again they could feel the cabin angle upward slightly as the ship rose higher.

He was roused in the night by her body moving against him. She seemed to be rubbing her crotch.

"Give me your hand," she whispered in a panting voice. She began to make his hands do things to her, sometimes touching him too, her body arching and writhing, sleek with sweat. He found himself abruptly tumescent again, excited again, excited and pleased in a confused way. "Now, now!" she commanded, and he entered her, finding her interior violently alive. She seemed to be half-fighting him, half-devouring him. Pleasure built all through him, this time without the terror. He pressed in against her shuddering convulsions. "Yes—oh, yes!" she gasped, and a series of paroxysms swept through her, carrying him with her to explosive peace.

He held himself on and in her until her body and breathing calmed to relaxation, and they slipped naturally apart. It came to him that this sex activity seemed to have more possibilities, as a thing to do, than he had realized. His family had imparted to him nothing of all this. Perhaps they didn't know it. Or perhaps it was too alien to their calm philosophy.

"How do you know about all this?" he asked Peachthief sleepily.

"One of my aunts did literature, too." She chuckled in the darkness. "Different literature, I guess."

They slept almost as movelessly as the body flying with them on the other couch a world away.

A series of noisy bumpings wakened them. The windows were filled with pink mist flying by. The airship seemed to be sliding into a berth. Jakko looked down and saw shrubs and grass close below; it was a ground-berth on a hillside.

The computer panel lit up: RESET PROGRAM FOR BASE.

"No," said Jakko. "We'll need it going back." Peachthief looked at him in a new, companionable way; he sensed that she believed him now. He turned all the drive controls to standby while she worked the food synthesizer. Presently he heard the hiss of the deflating lift bags, and went to where she was standing by the dead stranger.

"We'll take her, her body, out before we go back," Peachthief said. "Maybe the River will touch her somehow."

Jakko doubted it, but ate and drank his breakfast protein in silence.

When they went to use the wash-and-waste cubby he found he didn't want to clean all the residues of their contact off himself. Peachthief seemed to feel the same way; she washed only her face and hands. He looked at her slender silk-clad belly. Was a child, his child, starting there? Desire flicked him again, but he remembered he had work to do. His promise to his father; get on with it. Sooner done, sooner back here.

"I love you," he said experimentally, and found the strange words had a startling trueness.

She smiled brilliantly at him, not just off-on. "I love you too, I think."

The floor-portal light was on. They pulled it up and uncovered a stepway leading to the ground. The moondogs poured down. They followed, coming out into a blowing world of rosy mists. Clouds were streaming around them, the air was all in motion up the hillside toward the crest some distance ahead of the ship berth. The ground here was uneven and covered with short soft grass, as though animals had cropped it.

"All winds blow to the River," Jakko quoted.

They set off up the hill, followed by the moondogs, who stalked uneasily with pricked ears. Probably they didn't like not being able to smell what was ahead, Jakko thought. Peachthief was holding his hand very firmly as they went, as if determined to keep him out of any danger.

As they walked up onto the flat crest of the hilltop the mists suddenly cleared, and they found themselves looking down into a great shallow glittering sunlit valley. They both halted to stare.

Before them lay a huge midden heap, kilometers of things upon things upon things, almost filling the valley floor. Objects of every description lay heaped there; Jakko could make out clothing, books, toys, jewelry, myriad artifacts and implements abandoned. These must be, he realized, the last things people had taken with them when they went on the River. In an outer ring not too far below them were tents, ground- and aircars, even wagons. Everything shone clean and gleaming as if the influence of the River had kept off decay.

He noticed that the nearest ring of encampments intersected other, apparently older and larger, rings. There seemed to be no center to the pile.

"The River has moved, or shrunk," he said.

"Both, I think." Peachthief pointed to the right. "Look, there's an old war-place."

A big grass-covered mound dominated the hillcrest beside them. Jakko saw it had metal-rimmed slits in its sides. He remembered history: how there were still rulers of people when the River's tendrils first touched Earth. Some of the rulers had tried to keep their subjects from the going-out places, posting guards around them and even putting killing devices in the ground. But the guards had gone themselves out on the River, or the River had swelled and taken them. And the people had driven beasts across the mined ground and surged after them into the stream of immortal life. In the end the rulers had gone too, or died out. Looking more carefully, Jakko could see that the green hillslopes were torn and pocked, as though ancient explosions had made craters everywhere.

Suddenly he remembered that he had to find his father in all this vast confusion.

"Where's the River now? My father's mind should reach there still, if I'm not too late."

"See that glittery slick look in the air down there? I'm sure that's a danger-place."

Down to their right, fairly close to the rim, was a strangely bright place. As he stared it became clearer: a great column of slightly golden or shining air. He scanned about, but saw nothing else like it all across the valley.

"If that's the only focus left, it's going away fast."

She nodded and then swallowed, her small face suddenly grim. She meant to live on here and die without the River, Jakko could see that. But he would be with her; he resolved it with all his heart. He squeezed her hand hard.

"If you have to talk to your father, we better walk around up here on the rim where it's safe," Peachthief said.

"No-oo," spoke up a moondog from behind them. The two humans turned and saw the three sitting in a row on the crest, staring slit-eyed at the valley.

"All right," Peachthief said. "You wait here. We'll be back soon."

She gripped Jakko's hand even tighter, and they started walking past the old war-mound, past the remains of ancient vehicles, past an antique pylon that leaned crazily. There were faint little trails in the short grass. Another war-mound loomed ahead; when they passed around it they found themselves suddenly among a small herd of white animals with long necks and no horns. The animals went on grazing quietly as the humans walked by. Jakko thought they might be mutated deer.

"Oh, look!" Peachthief let go his hand. "That's milk—see, her baby is sucking!"

Jakko saw that one of the animals had a knobby bag between its hind legs. A small one half-knelt down beside it, with its head up nuzzling the bag. A mother and her young.

Peachthief was walking cautiously toward them, making gentle greeting sounds. The mother animal looked at her calmly, evidently tame. The baby went on sucking, rolling its eyes. Peachthief reached them, petted the mother, and then bent down under to feel the bag. The animal sidestepped a pace, but stayed still. When Peachthief straightened up she was licking her hand.

"That's good milk! And they're just the right size, we can take them on the airship! On the waycars, even." She was beaming, glowing. Jakko felt an odd warm constriction in his chest. The intensity with which she furnished her little world, her future nest! *Their* nest . . .

"Come with us, come on," Peachthief was urging. She had her belt around the creature's neck to lead it. It came equably, the young one following in awkward galloping lunges.

"That baby is a male. Oh, this is *perfect*," Peachthief exclaimed. "Here, hold her a minute while I look at that one."

She handed Jakko the end of the belt and ran off. The beast eyed him levelly. Suddenly it drew its upper lip back and shot spittle at his face. He ducked, yelling for Peachthief to come back.

"I have to find my father first!"

"All right," she said, returning. "Oh, look at that!"

Downslope from them was an apparition—one of the white animals, but partly transparent, ghostly thin. It drifted vaguely, putting its head down now and then, but did not eat.

"It must have got partly caught in the River, it's half gone. Oh, Jakko, you can see how dangerous it is! I'm afraid, I'm afraid it'll catch you."

"It won't. I'll be very careful."

"I'm afraid so." But she let him lead her on, towing the animal alongside. As they passed the ghost-creature Peachthief called to it, "You can't live like that. You better go on out. Shoo, shoo!"

It turned and moved slowly out across the piles of litter, toward the shining place in the air.

They were coming closer to it now, stepping over more and more abandoned things. Peachthief looked sharply at everything; once she stooped to pick up a beautiful fleecy white square and stuff it in her pack. The hillcrest was merging with a long grassy slope, comparatively free of debris, that ran out toward the airy glittering column. They turned down it.

The River-focus became more and more awesome as they approached. They could trace it towering up and up now, twisting gently as it passed beyond the sky. A tendril of the immaterial stream of sidereal sentience that had embraced Earth, a pathway to immortal life. The air inside looked no longer golden, but pale silver-gilt, like a great shaft of moonlight coming down through the morning sun. Objects at its base appeared very dear but shimmering, as if seen through crystal water.

Off to one side were tents. Jakko suddenly recognized one, and quickened his steps. Peachthief pulled back on his arm.

"Jakko, be careful!"

They slowed to a stop a hundred yards from the tenuous fringes of the River's effect. It was very still. Jakko peered intently. In the verges of the shimmer a staff was standing upright. From it hung a scarf of green-and-yellow silk.

"Look—that's my father's sign!"

"Oh, Jakko, you *can't* go in there."

At the familiar-colored sign all the memories of his life with his family had come flooding back on Jakko. The gentle rationality, the solemn sense of preparation for going out from Earth forever. Two different realities strove briefly within him. They had loved him, he realized that now. Especially his father . . . But not as he loved Peachthief, his awakened spirit shouted silently. I am of Earth! Let the stars take care of their own. His resolve took deeper hold and won.

Gently he released himself from her grip.

"You wait here. Don't worry, it takes a long while for the change, you know that. Hours, days. I'll only be a minute, I'll come right back."

"Ohhh, it's crazy."

But she let him go and stood holding to the milk-animal while he went down the ridge and picked his way out across the midden heap toward the staff. As he neared it he could feel the air change around him, becoming alive and yet more still.

"Father! Paul! It's Jakko, your son. Can you still hear me?"

Nothing answered him. He took a step or two past the staff, repeating his call.

A resonant susurrus came in his head, as if unearthly

reaches had opened to him. From infinity he heard without hearing his father's quiet voice.

You came.

A sense of calm welcome.

"The cities are all empty, Father. All the people have gone, everywhere."

Come.

"No!" He swallowed, fending off memory, fending off the lure of strangeness. "I think it's sad. It's wrong. I've found a woman. We're going to stay and make children."

The River is leaving, Jakko my son.

It was as if a star had called his name, but he said stubbornly, "I don't care. I'm staying with her. Good-bye, Father. Goodbye."

Grave regret touched him, and from beyond a host of silent voices murmured down the sky: *Come! Come away.*

"No!" he shouted, or tried to shout, but he could not still the rapt voices. And suddenly, gazing up, he felt the reality of the River, the overwhelming opening of the door to life everlasting among the stars. All his mortal fears, all his most secret dread of the waiting maw of death, all slid out of him and fell away, leaving him almost unbearably light and calmly joyful. He knew that he was being touched, that he could float out upon that immortal stream forever. But even as the longing took him, his human mind remembered that this was the start of the first stage, for which the River was called Beata. He thought of the ghost animal that had lingered too long. He must leave now, and quickly. With enormous effort he took one step backward, but could not turn.

"Jakko! Jakko! Come back!"

Someone was calling, screaming his name. He did turn then, and saw her on the little ridge. Nearby, yet so far. The ordinary sun of Earth was brilliant on her and the two white beasts.

"Jakko! Jakko!" Her arms were outstretched, she was running toward him.

It was as if the whole beautiful Earth was crying to him, calling to him to come back and take up the burden of life and death. He did not want it. But she must not come here, he knew that without remembering why. He began uncertainly to stumble toward her, seeing her now as his beloved woman, again as an unknown creature uttering strange cries.

Death," he muttered, not realizing he had ceased to
 ran faster, tripped, almost fell in the heaps of stuff.
ongness of her coming here roused him again; he took
a few more steps, feeling his head clear a little.

"*Jakko!*" She reached him, clutched him, dragging him
bodily forward from the verge.

At her touch the reality of his human life came back to him,
his heart pounded human blood, all stars fled away. He started
to run clumsily, half-carrying her with him up to the safety of
the ridge. Finally they sank down gasping beside the animals,
holding and kissing each other, their eyes wet.

"I thought you were lost, I thought I'd lost you," Peachthief
sobbed.

"You saved me."

"H-here," she said. "We b-better have some food." She
rummaged in her pack, nodding firmly as if the simple human
act could defend against unearthly powers. Jakko discovered
that he was quite hungry.

They ate and drank peacefully in the soft flower-studded
grass, while the white animals grazed around them. Peachthief
studied the huge strewn valley floor, frowning as she
munched.

"So many good useful things here. I'll come back someday,
when the River's gone, and look around."

"I thought you only wanted natural things," he teased her.

"Some of these things will last. Look." She picked up a small
implement. "It's an awl, for punching and sewing leather. You
could make children's sandals."

Many of the people who came here must have lived quite
simply, Jakko thought. It was true that there could be useful
tools. And metal. Books, too. Directions for making things. He
lay back dreamily, seeing a vision of himself in the far future,
an accomplished artisan, teaching his children skills. It seemed
deeply good.

"Oh, my milk-beast!" Peachthief broke in on his reverie.
"Oh, no! You mustn't!" She jumped up.

Jakko sat up and saw that the white mother animal had
strayed quite far down the grassy ridge. Peachthief trotted
down after her, calling, "Come here! Stop!"

Perversely, the animal moved away, snatching mouthfuls of
grass. Peachthief ran faster. The animal threw up its head and
paced down off the ridge, among the litter piles.

"No! Oh, my milk! Come back here, come."

She went down after it, trying to move quietly and call more calmly.

Jakko had gotten up, alarmed.

"Come back! Don't go down there!"

"The babies' milk," she wailed at him, and made a dash at the beast. But she missed and it drifted away just out of reach before her.

To his horror Jakko saw that the glittering column of the River had changed shape slightly, eddying out a veil of shimmering light close ahead of the beast.

"Turn back! Let it go!" he shouted, and began to run with all his might. "Peachthief—come back!"

But she would not turn, and his pounding legs could not catch up. The white beast was in the shimmer now; he saw it bound up onto a great sun- and moonlit heap of stuff. Peachthief's dark form went flying after it, uncaring, and the creature leaped away again. He saw her follow, and bitter fear grabbed at his heart. The very strength of her human life is betraying her to death, he thought; I have to get her physically, I will pull her out. He forced his legs faster, faster yet, not noticing that the air had changed around him, too.

She disappeared momentarily in a veil of glittering air, and then reappeared, still following the beast. Thankfully he saw her pause and stoop to pick something up. She was only walking now, he could catch her. But his own body was moving sluggishly, it took all his will to keep his legs thrusting him ahead.

"Peachthief! Love, come back!"

His voice seemed muffled in the silvery air. Dismayed, he realized that he too had slowed to a walk, and she was veiled again from his sight.

When he struggled through the radiance he saw her, moving very slowly after the wandering white beast. Her face was turned up, unearthly light was on her beauty. He knew she was feeling the rapture, the call of immortal life was on her. On him, too; he found he was barely stumbling forward, a terrible serenity flooding his heart. They must be passing into the very focus of the River, where it ran strongest.

"Love—" Mortal grief fought the invading transcendence. Ahead of him the girl faded slowly into the glimmering veils, still following her last earthly desire. He saw that humanity, all that he had loved of the glorious Earth, was disappearing forever from reality. Why had it awakened, only to be lost? Spectral voices were near him, but he did not want specters. An agonizing lament for human life welled up in him, a last pang that he would carry with him through eternity. But its urgency fell away. Life incorporeal, immortal, was on him now; it had him as it had her. His flesh, his body, was beginning to attenuate, to dematerialize out into the great current of sentience that flowed on its mysterious purposes among the stars.

Still the essence of his earthly self moved slowly after hers into the closing mists of infinity, carrying upon the River a configuration that had been a man striving forever after a loved dark girl, who followed a ghostly white milch deer.

AND SO ON, AND SO ON

In a nook of the ship's lounge the child had managed to activate a viewscreen.

"Rovy! They *asked* you not to play with the screen while we're Jumping. We've told you and told you there isn't anything there. It's just pretty lights, dear. Now come back and we'll all play—"

As the young clanwife coaxed him back to their cocoons something happened. It was a very slight something, just enough to make the drowsy passengers glance up. Immediately a calm voice spoke, accompanied by the blur of multiple translation.

"This is your captain. The momentary discontinuity we just experienced is quite normal in this mode of paraspace. We will encounter one or two more before reaching the Orion complex, which will be in about two units of ship's time."

The tiny episode stimulated talk.

"Declare I feel sorry for the youngers today." The large being in mercantile robes tapped his Galnews scanner, blew out his ear sacs comfortably. "We had all the fun. Why, when I first came out this was all wild frontier. Took courage to go beyond the Coalsack. They had you make your will. I can even remember the first cross-Gal Jump."

"How fast it has all changed!" admired his talking minor. Daringly it augmented: "The youngers are so apathetic. They accept all these marvels as natural, they mock the idea of heroism."

"Heroes!" the merchant snorted. "Not them!" He gazed challengingly around the luxe cabin, eliciting a few polite nods. Suddenly a cocoon swiveled around to face him, revealing an Earth-typer in Pathman gray.

"Heroism," said the Pathman softly, eyeing the merchant from under shadowed brows. "Heroism is essentially a spatial concept. No more free space, no more heroes." He turned away as if regretting having spoken, like a man trying to sustain some personal pain.

"Ooh, what about Ser Orpheian?" asked a bright young reproducer. "Crossing the Arm alone in a single pod, I think that's heroic!" It giggled flirtatiously.

"Not really," drawled a cultivated GalFed voice. The lutroid who had been using the reference station removed his input leads and smiled distantly at the reproducer. "Such exploits are merely an expiring gasp, a gleaning after the harvest if you will. Was Orpheian launching into the unknown? Not so. He faced merely the problem of whether he himself could do it. Playing at frontiers. No," the lutroid's voice took on a practiced Recorder's clarity. "The primitive phase is finished. The true frontier is within now. Inner space." He adjusted his academic fourragère.

The merchant had returned to his scanner.

"Now here's a nice little offering," he grunted. "Ringsun for sale, Eridani sector. That sector's long overdue for development, somebody'll make a sweet thing. If some of these young malcontents would just blow out their gills and pitch in—!" He thumped his aquaminor on the snout, causing it to mew piteously.

"But that's too much like work," echoed his talker soothingly. The Pathman had been watching in haggard silence. Now he leaned over to the lutroid.

"Your remark about inner space. I take it you mean psychics? Purely subjective explorations?"

"Not at all," said the lutroid, gratified. "The psychic cults I regard as mere sensationalism. I refer to reality, to that simpler and deeper reality that lies beyond the reach of the trivial methodologies of science, the reality which we can only approach through what is called aesthetic or religious experience, god-immanent if you will—"

"I'd like to see art or religion get you to Orion," remarked a grizzled spacedog in the next cocoon. "If it wasn't for science you wouldn't be end-running the parsecs in an aleph jumpship."

"Perhaps we end-run too much," the lutroid smiled. "Perhaps our technological capabilities are end-running, as you call it, our—"

"What about the Arm wars?" cried the young reproducer. "Ooh, science is *horrible*. I cry every time I think of the poor Armers." Its large eyes steamed, and it hugged itself seductively.

"Well, now, you can't blame science for what some powerhounds do with it," the spacedog chuckled, hitching his cocoon over toward the reproducer's stay.

"That's right," said another voice, and the conversation group drifted away.

The Pathman's haunted eyes were still on the lutroid.

"If you are so certain of this deeper reality, this inner space," he said quietly, "why is your left hand almost without nails?"

The lutroid's left hand clenched and then uncurled slowly to reveal the gnawed nails; he was not undisciplined.

"I recognize the right of your order to unduly personal speech," he said stiffly. Then he sighed and smiled. "Ah, of course; I admit I am not immune to the universal *angst*, the failure of nerve. The haunting fear of stagnation and decline, now that life has reached to the limits of this galaxy. But I regard this as a challenge to transcendence, which we must, we will meet, through our inner resources. We will find our *true* frontier." He nodded. "Life has never failed the ultimate challenge."

"Life has never before met the ultimate challenge," the Pathman rejoined somberly. "In the history of every race, society, planet or system or federation or swarm, whenever they have expanded to their spatial limits they commence to decline. First stasis, then increasing entropy, degradation of structure, disorganization, death. In every case, the process was only halted by breaking out into new space, or by new peoples breaking in on them from outside. Crude, simple *outer* space. Inner space? Consider the Vegans—"

"Exactly!" interrupted the lutroid. "That refutes you. The Vegans were approaching the most fruitful concepts of transphysical reality, concepts we must certainly reopen. If only the Myrmidi invasion had not destroyed so much."

"It is not generally known," the Pathman's voice was very

low, "when the Myrmidi landed the Vegans were eating their own larvae and using the sacred dream-fabrics for ornaments. Very few could even sing."

"No!"

"By the Path."

The lutroid's nictitating membranes filmed his eyes. After a moment he said formally, "You carry despair as your gift."

The Pathman was whispering as if to himself. "Who will come to open our skies? For the first time all life is closed in a finite space. Who can rescue a galaxy? The Clouds are barren and the realms beyond we know cannot be crossed even by matter, let alone life. For the first time we have truly reached the end."

"But the young," said the lutroid in quiet anguish.

"The young sense this. They seek to invent pseudo-frontiers, subjective escapes. Perhaps your inner space can beguile some for a while. But the despair will grow. Life is not mocked. We have come to the end of infinity, the end of hope."

The lutroid stared into the Pathman's hooded eyes, his hand involuntarily raising his academic surplice like a shield.

"You believe that there is nothing, no way?"

"Ahead lies only the irreversible long decline. For the first time *we know there is nothing beyond ourselves.*"

After a moment the lutroid's gaze dropped and the two beings let silence enshroud them. Outside the galaxy was twisting by, unseen, enormous, glittering: a finite prison. No way out.

In the aisle behind them something moved.

The child Rovy was creeping stealthily toward the screens that looked on no-space, his eyes intent and bright.